The FURIOUS PHARISEE

A HISTORICAL NOVEL BASED ON THE LIFE AND TIMES OF SAUL OF TARSUS

BY AL DUBLANKO

(INSPIRED BY A TRUE STORY)
ACTS 2:1 TO ACTS 8:40

 FriesenPress

One Printers Way
Altona, MB R0G 0B0
Canada

www.friesenpress.com

Map Illustration by Paul Schultz

ISBN
978-1-03-916868-8 (Hardcover)
978-1-03-916867-1 (Paperback)
978-1-03-916869-5 (eBook)

1. FICTION, CHRISTIAN, BIBLICAL

Distributed to the trade by The Ingram Book Company

The FURIOUS PHARISEE

TABLE OF CONTENTS

CAST OF CHARACTERS

Antonius and Antoine—father and son, captains of the <u>Castor and Pollux</u>

Saul and Miriam—brother and sister who leave Tarsus for Jerusalem

Caleb—patriarch of the family business in Cyprus, father of Barnabas

Agabus—mysterious businessman in Caesarea

Gamaliel—President of the Great Sanhedrin, Pharisee and grandson of Hillel

Sarah—Gamaliel's stately wife

Shimon ben Gamaliel (Gammy)—son of Gamaliel, friend to Saul

Leah—younger sister of Gammy, daughter of Gamaliel, a Jerusalem beauty

Barnabas—son of Caleb of Cyprus, brother of Mary, and new follower of Jesus

Mary—Barnabas's widowed older sister, mother of John Mark

John Mark—son of Mary, nephew of Barnabas, very involved teenager

Caiaphas—High Priest, son-in-law of Annas, chubby and conniving

Annas—former High Priest, head of priestly family and the actual seat of power in Jerusalem

Malchus-head servant of Caiaphas, and a man with a very good ear for things

Samuel—Shammai-ite Pharisee, teacher in the Synagogue of the Freedmen

Rachel—youthful sister of Samuel, a devotee of her brother

And many more …

PROLOGUE

APRIL, AD 33

Our saga begins fifty-five nautical miles out to sea in an area directly south of the mouth of the Cydnus River which passes through the diverse and cosmopolitan city of Tarsus on its journey from the snow-capped mountains of Cilicia. Upon reaching the coast, the generous flow quietly empties into the Great Sea, later to be known as the Mediterranean.

From here, the ship's intended course is due south; a heading that will take it to the tip of the northeastern finger of the island of Cyprus which will be then followed by a back-and-forth dance with the currents as it plows its way down the east coast of that island to the pastoral port of Salamis.

Among its small collection of passengers are two extraordinary people.

Saul, who was born and raised in Tarsus but then sent away to be educated in Judaism, and his sister, Miriam. With each wind-driven lurch, the lumbering vessel plies its way further and further from their secure and familiar family home in Tarsus to a strange new world in far-off and exotic Jerusalem.

Tarsus is also the home of the well-traveled captain and his able crew.

The captain's young son, busily scurrying about the ship, easily fills the role of amiable ambassador to all those who sail on this industrious vessel.

PART ONE

CHAPTER ONE

The Great Sea

Off to the west of the rolling vessel, a plume of misty spray exploded like a small volcano from the waves, quickly followed by another and another. Shiny black backs discolored by patches of rough barnacles, rolled on top of the shimmering blue water and the crew erupted with unreserved excitement. The watchman was eagerly pointing and then began bellowing, "Whales!"

The varied collection of passengers rushed clumsily to the rails, most having only heard of these magnificent creatures in childhood stories and no one wanted to miss this spectacle. Squeals of delight and beaming smiles emerged as all understood that they were particularly fortunate to be seeing these gigantic creatures. That glee quickly changed to concern and then to a sprinkling of fear when the pod of fast-moving leviathans changed direction and veered directly toward the helpless ship. The most nervous of the gawkers began a hurried retreat for the safety of the middle of the vessel, quickly calculating that less-exposed space as a refuge from such unpredictable beasts and it was only the captain's confident stance that kept the other nervous passengers from panicking. The captain was obviously delighted and indeed, thankful to the sea gods for allowing his passengers to experience such a rare sight. He also knew that any actual clash with these shy giants was unlikely, almost unheard of, no matter what fantastic tales that their childhood storytellers had painted in their youthful imaginations.

After witnessing the boldness of their captain, the passengers slowly and hesitantly returned to the rails just as the majestic creatures surfaced nearby, a few slowly lifting their massive heads to expose huge inquiring eyes that seemed to examine the ship and its animated inhabitants with equal curiosity. Before long, the whales moved off with leaping schools of fish scattering in all directions in front of them, no doubt their attempt to escape the continual feeding of the monsters of the sea.

Other than the appearance of whales, these waters were a relatively peaceful and uneventful place these days-only a short half century after the end of the bitter civil wars between the ruling families of Rome. Gone were the epic sea battles and the political intrigues of fifty years ago, replaced with a strange harmony that ended the all-encompassing territorial conflicts that had dominated life and politics throughout this Great Sea.

That warring period had been a confusing time for all countries involved for each conquered region was eventually rewarded or punished based on which of the Roman combatants they had chosen to ally themselves with. Successfully choosing the eventual winner granted valuable rewards to the fortunate local political powers, and none had been given the luxury of remaining neutral. This had fomented tremendous stress and intrigue throughout the empire, often creating smaller wars between neighbors simply because of their choice of which Roman to support. Betting on the wrong emperor had proven very costly for many.

Currently, only the most-foolhardy of pirates would dare challenge the strict peace that the ever-expanding Roman navy had imposed upon the entire sea, and that was only for a quick foray of plundering with an equally fast retreat into some unknown harbor to quickly blend back into the population. These plucky bandits were aware that, as with most things in the Roman world, brutal penalties imposed by the navy were the inevitable consequences of breaking even the silliest law that masqueraded as good government policy. For them it seemed that defying Rome was an important and much enjoyed portion of any loot they managed to steal.

The lingering peace had also, although quite unintentionally, created a peculiar military problem. Presently, the only place that politically eager Roman upstarts could distinguish themselves was the inland frontiers of Germania or the dangerous cliffs of the Celtic islands. Ambitious and aspiring young generals, mostly the sons of wealthy senators and the kind with which Rome was teeming, desperately wanted to make a victory ride down the main street of the Forum in Rome and thereby launch another well-paid political career of their own. When out on the frontiers looking for a victory, these unknowns had to be very careful not to challenge too large a contingent of the fierce northern tribes when they went off to expand the borders of the empire. Although the wild and unpredictable hordes always provided a worthy foe, they were erratic and unpredictable, relentlessly and without mercy attacking the disciplined and orderly Roman phalanxes in the dark forests. Any vestige of that victory, augmented with the proper garnishing, ensured these generals a triumphant return to Rome complete with a noisy parade of their own. Conversely, any defeat quickly ended their political ambitions.

It was curious to the army's foot-soldiers, those men who had actually braved the fighting and who had been wounded in these ferocious encounters, just how the battle reports changed between the solemn northern encampments and the cheering streets of Rome. Sound defeats were somehow transformed into great victories on the long ride home, restated as marvelous successes which always resulted in great monetary reward for all returning and compliant warriors.

After thirty years of undistinguished rule, the current emperor, the docile and disengaged Tiberius, was in his waning years. He was a reluctant Roman tyrant whose early claims to fame were his own successful campaigns as a youthful general in the frontiers north of the Alps. Lately, he was almost entirely absent from Rome, retreating to the island of Capri where he lived quietly, often fearing that he would only be remembered for his wife's embarrassing domestic antics.

Tiberius had divorced his first wife at the command of his stepfather, the all-powerful Emperor Augustus, thus leaving the real love of his life and dutifully marrying the famously licentious Julia. He was now expending great effort to avoid her while, at the same time, enduring the ridicule that her unquenchable immoral behavior brought on him. Curiously, Rome could easily accommodate the moral scandal regarding Tiberius' wife and it also chose to ignore the persistent rumors of all types of perversity that took place on his island retreat where he now spent the majority of his time berating his underlings. This all made perfect sense to him for he knew that the only thing Rome could not abide was any show of compassion or weakness from its leaders.

Distracted with his other interests, Tiberius wisely left the day-to-day governing of the empire to a host of very eager and dangerous sycophants who vied openly with his devious and politically hungry sons, the entire assembly maneuvering for position in the event that the emperor suddenly left this life. He often mentioned, to any who cared to listen, that he lived under the constant feeling that the vultures were circling over his golden-garlanded head.

The great cities which lined the coasts of the Great Sea were enjoying the prosperity that this peaceful era brought and the sea lanes were awash with ships moving between Rome, Carthage, Alexandria, Tarsus and hundreds of other ports. It was undeniable that Rome, with all its blemishes and warts, and they were many, had accelerated a previously unknown movement of goods and travelers and this in turn sped along an unavoidable mixing of national ideas and customs. This was the inevitable result of the rush to do business and to exchange valuable products throughout the empire. Predictably, such cultural merging and national economic expansion brought a level of concern to the suspicious military commanders who were constantly on guard, always fearful of uprisings or boiling conspiracy among those whom they ruled but did not care to understand.

Faithfully resisting these disconcerting modernizing trends and always suspicious of the results of any cultural mixing that went with such changes were the religious leaders of the many regions, all bastions of their unique societies and men who were intent on preserving their ancient ways. Their dithering stance meant that they appeared to always be resisting Rome, a sort of underground and undeclared war with its influence, and most definitely, with its many gods. Despite their efforts, the economic and cultural effects of Roman domination were creeping across the waters, sped along with each ship that docked.

Indeed, this very ship was a perfect example.

After watching the leviathan pod cross the bow and disappear to the east, many of the excited passengers remained at the rails well into the evening. They were hoping to catch a glimpse of even more whales but were instead treated to leaping dolphins, flying fish and diving cormorants. The rich currents in this area fed incredible numbers of creatures and all around, rolling and swirling boils of all varieties of sea life were seen darting through the water and feasting on smaller prey. Fully entertained and noisily excited, the passengers slowly returned to their individual tents after many pleasant hours of scanning the waves.

The captain could not have ordered a better end to his first day out.

CHAPTER TWO

The Captain

An eerie groan coming from high in the overhead rigging attracted only a disinterested glance from the red-bearded captain of this wind-driven ship. Years of sailing these azure waters under the direct tutelage of his deceased father had taught him to pay attention to every creak and shudder and he had learned to listen vigilantly to every grunt and moan of this lumbering lady as if she were speaking directly to him. Sometimes she complained of small matters that were irritating her and sometimes she delivered him secretive whispers of future problems. Today, the captain clearly understood, she was just enjoying the swaying ride and singing along to the rhythm of the waves.

She was a unique ship, fitted with a high and majestic bow line and three large masts. She was loved and was meticulously maintained and protected, for this vessel was the important engine of his family's impressive wealth and was also an important purveyor of their ancient Phoenician heritage.

As a boy, on those occasions when his seafaring father would return home after long months away, the captain had, with a measure of amusement, watched the mock jealousy displayed by his mother as she teased his grinning father about this enchanting and mysterious woman who demanded so much of his attention. It was the family's private riddle.

When he became a teenager of fourteen years and it was his time to join the devoted and adventuresome crew, he witnessed for himself the special connection his father had with his ship. He soon learned that this bond was not unique to his father but was common among all other successful captains, something which crews and deckhands admired but also made all manner of crude jokes about. Rotting decks, wobbly rails and rocky shorelines strewn with the remains of similar vessels were the obvious evidence of less attentive skippers.

His father had wisely counseled him to ignore the guttural levity of the common men who populated the crews and to keep himself slightly apart from them, to learn from the wisdom that only experience and successfully completing each new adventure would bring.

The captain's name was Antonius and his red beard and wild, wind-blown mane of hair made him an awesome sight.

He was the third generation to command this ship, inheriting it from his father who had taken over from his father and it had been this grandfather who originally built and sailed it in the early and much more adventuresome days of the expanding Roman Empire. As a small boy, Antonius often sat at his grandfather's feet, totally mesmerized by the riveting stories of Cilician pirates boldly kidnapping Julius Caesar, or Antony and Cleopatra's politically-charged love story, or the massive sea and land battles such as the world-changing Actium, all personalized with intricate details provided by his much-travelled grandfather who, very truthfully, admitted that some of these he had personally witnessed, while others, he had happily avoided. The engrossing tales created a gallery of images that danced through his youthful imagination and at times, even many years later, made him yearn for those valiant and hero-making former days. The political calm of the last decades under Tiberius had made sailing these waters a much safer occupation, but often, it seemed a lot less stimulating and at certain times, even a boring endeavor.

Upon realizing that the present version of political tranquility would likely endure, his father and grandfather had decided to invest in this much larger, but admittedly slower and impossible to defend, merchant ship. For this reason, they also chose to sail under the protection of the daunting and unchallenged Roman navy and admittedly, this added security had come at a sobering price. The toll was a commitment by them, and most of the rest of the independently owned merchant fleet, to keep the Roman Empire with all its wants and needs, supplied. What that meant was that they were constantly ferrying an endless array of provisions and soldiers and armaments, along with diplomats and their entourages, all at the command of the military government of Rome. This was a never-ending assignment that kept them on the move, criss-crossing back and forth between the numerous ports in the Great Sea.

On the surface, this task appeared boring and repetitive and smelled of a humiliating subservience to Rome, but in reality, this arrangement had many other unanticipated rewards beyond just providing a very secure living.

To begin with, it allowed the captain and his twenty-year-old son Antoine, who had joined him just over two years ago, a colorful life of adventure and relative prosperity complete with safe travel and limitless exploration. Few other subjects of this empire had the luxury to freely experience the joy of unimpeded travel.

The father and son were of pure Phoenician ancestry and carried the heritage of those historic boat builders and adventurous seamen in their blood. They were very aware that it was they, the proud Phoenicians, who had dominated the Great Sea for the last thousand years or more. The prowess and seamanship of his sea-going forefathers had slowly converted these fearsome and unpredictable waters from the impassible barrier it had once been to landlocked populations, to a watery highway that unraveled the mysteries of the known world.

Over the centuries, while sailing to the recognized limits of known humanity, his Phoenician forefathers had been eye-witness to the rise and eventual fall of many of histories powerful but short-lived empires and all these dynasties had employed the skills of these ancient sailors to their advantage before disappearing into the unforgiving dustbin of antiquity. The hardy and enduring seafarers had faithfully served, quietly observed and successfully stayed out of the way of the Egyptian kingdoms, the Persian Empire, the Greeks, the Israelites and a few other less dominating empires, all the while making a tidy business profit.

Their unique boat designs, originally created using the massive cedars of Lebanon as their backbone, had been only slightly altered over the centuries and were now the staple of all current shipbuilders, including the present-day Romans.

With this in mind, the patient captain remained convinced that his family and their seagoing heritage would outlast these brutal and power-hungry Romans as well.

The compensation for the maritime services provided to Rome, although adequate, was not exceptionally lucrative and the rates for moving their cargo were absolutely non-negotiable. The clever captain had quickly learned that there was substantial income to be garnered along the way in the buying and selling of additional commodities, many of which bordered on the bizarre and merchandise which he had access to at the far-flung ports that he sailed to. His Roman masters seemed completely disinterested in any extra activities he involved himself in, thus leaving him at liberty to pursue his side business.

Over the years, Antonius had recognized the quirky tastes and fashions of the rich and vainglorious who resided in the different ports that he called on and this information provided intriguing opportunities that only a traveling merchant like he could take advantage of. Most often, the allotted Roman cargo did not require the entire ship and thus, there was always space for the captain's many "special" deliveries.

After Cyprus and a quick side trip to Caesarea in Judea, the captain was planning to sail south to exotic Alexandria in Egypt. In the past, when he sailed out of that immense and exotic harbor, his lower hold was bloated with outlandish bounty, almost all from deepest and darkest Africa. Most were treasures secretly brought up the Nile to the waiting warehouses of Alexandria by strange-looking men who plied the mysterious southern extents of the crocodile-infested river. These peculiar but cagey traders were always eager to deal with the cautious captain.

To the captain, the strikingly tall and midnight-black boatmen with their flashing white smiles and strange skin markings were as breathtaking as the caged creatures they brought to him. These were clever men, merchants who were very adept at introducing only a few of their latest prizes, holding others back so that there was always something which had never been seen before by the eager buyers of the Roman world. The thirst throughout the empire for strange, playful apes or dangerous snakes was unquenchable as was the constant need for lions and leopards, beasts that were either destined to become unique pets or the Forum's savage killing machines.

From his years of experience, the captain was well aware of the months of the year when the massive camel trains would begin arriving in the northern ports near Antioch of Syria, each bringing more of the rare and savory spices from the mysterious and exotic far east. On every yearly trip, the slow-moving caravans brought new and unknown flavors into his world, zesty seasonings which always enflamed the imaginations of the Great Sea's chefs. These trains of the desert were always loaded down with colorful and shimmering cloths as well, striking fabrics said to be magically created by worms, and the crafty captain spent many hours negotiating the purchase of large quantities of these, knowing that he could easily hawk them to vain and wealthy women in the distant ports. The wily caravan merchants, also careful not to flood the markets, shrewdly allotted their valuable merchandise, which in turn, kept their prices extremely high. The overland flotillas began arriving with the yearly spring equinox and the captain would always arrange his sailings to be in the harbor of Seleucia, just a few miles from inland Antioch, to greet them.

Equally profitable but a lot more secretive was the side venture of supplying rare metals. These were greatly sought after in every port for they guaranteed the very best materials for artisan figures, cooking items and more importantly, swords and other weaponry. These ores were mined in the mountains of the north country, near the dangerous frontiers of the Black Sea, and the captain, very discreetly, bought and delivered ingots of the most valuable metals to the persistent metal-workers situated around the Great Sea. Whenever his ship arrived at a major port he was quickly visited, usually under the cover of darkness, by local artisans and clandestine sword makers who were constantly in search of more and purer precious raw materials. His hold maintained a small but surprisingly adequate supply of these and he had also learned to allot these in small quantities.

It was an unspoken but clearly understood pact that the Romans need not know where and by whom the new and stronger weapons were being crafted. It was also to remain a closely-guarded secret from which Roman mine the best ingots had suspiciously disappeared. Obligingly, most ship captains were aware that no Roman had ever wanted to examine the deepest and dankest parts of their ships.

Humorously, the captain's wealthiest and most indulgent customers seemed uncontrollably stimulated by just the rumor of more exotic and rare treasures. There was endless and oddly competitive interest among such people for stranger animals, juicier fruits, tastier spices or sparkling and shiny trinkets not yet imagined. The lure of plundering the wealth of yet another unexplored region of the world was constantly enticing a few of the most adventuresome men and these explorers often returned with fantastic stories of adventure and unimaginable landscapes filled with strange creatures. Every foray into the unknown inevitably resulted in a renewed supply of extremely expensive and highly touted spiritual charms sent from the gods, followed with the promise of more treasure, coming shortly, from that region.

This competition assured the captain that there would always be customers rushing to meet his ship and he, with a theatrical and mysterious flair, loved to cultivate this trade with rousing and slightly exaggerated stories of his own. He enjoyed holding the affluent spellbound with flamboyant descriptions of the bizarre items he would be bringing to them: shortly.

What was always curious to the captain, was that the costlier the item, the more the self-indulgent desired it, as if the trinket itself distinguished them as successful, wealthy, and wise. Owning a rare article somehow made it seem that they possessed a secret connection to that mysterious, unexplored world and displaying treasures and relics of crippling cost seemed to immediately make one more envied within the curious hierarchy of the rich.

The captain's talkative and socially effusive young son was becoming a force among these people and he was able to make each customer feel they were exclusive in their pursuit of the world's newly discovered pillage. His salesmanship was truly a gift and he was expert at inflaming their desire to spend even more.

Such was the present state of the economy of the Empire. The rich were constantly increasing in their wealth and power, a station they unabashedly flaunted, while the overtaxed and burdened subjects of the conquered countries were continually mired in their Roman-created poverty.

This unpopular system required a large and brutal army just to maintain the precarious status quo and this in turn required more and more taxes. That in turn required more conquest and even more subjugated taxpayers. Observing that this was the ongoing reality and being very practical, this seagoing family had decided many years ago that, yes, the best way to remain protected and affluent was to remain a required and dependable supplier of services to this ever-expanding empire.

CHAPTER THREE

The Journey South

By late afternoon, the captain had assured all that the overhead creaking and groanings were indeed the ship's agreeable response to the gusts in the always reliable northeast wind as it blew down from the mountainous, northern plains of Cilicia into the east end of the Great Sea. His gnarled and bearded face scanned the horizons and he liked what he saw.

Gazing over his ship, he noticed Saul, the young Jewish man from his home town of Tarsus who was ritually swaying back and forth while standing at the rail, monotonously chanting the evening oblations to his strange, demanding God. He glanced about and noticed that others on the ship were observing him as well. Knowing that the Jews sometimes attracted a varied array of reactions, he sauntered to the middle of the ship and placed himself directly between frowning passengers and Saul while he stared the others back into their own worlds. Antonius understood the confrontational nature of the Jewish religion and knew that Saul would be quick to engage any who would make any derogatory comment.

Long ago the captain had decided that he would not allow any silly religious arguments on his ship and he was quick to squash any thoughts of confrontation.

Looking up, he saw that sea birds were soaring lazily overhead and there were no thunderheads or ominous clouds to be seen. The small swell of the waves also told him that it was safe to leave the big sails unfurled into the night. That was indeed fortunate, for they were pulling them at a steady pace in a southwest direction and he was making only a slight correction with the two side rudders and the triangular front sail hanging out over the bow. This setting gave them the due south they required.

It was the typical spring wind in the Great Sea, or as the Romans had renamed it, Mare Nostrum, or "peaceful sea," as if they alone now owned it and somehow had made it obey their command.

Just before darkness had set in and when the ship was peacefully quieted, the captain noticed a loose rigging and barked a loud "tighten up" to his son Antoine who looked up at the loosened and flopping tie. He half-smiled at the non-essential, dangling rope and repeated the command to the gaggle of sailors that made up the crew. They all looked up and the one they called "Spider" immediately pounced and quickly shimmied upward, his feet tightly pressing on the heavy main mast from where he slid out theatrically on the smaller crossbeam with only his bowed legs wrapped around it. While out there, he hung upside down and in this inverted position, he tied off the loose strapping. He then did an acrobatic and contorted lunge to the mast and within seconds was back on deck being rowdily applauded by the other crew members. The crew clearly understood that the loose rigging provided no threat but the captain loved to demonstrate the order of command and the skill level of his crew. His handsome son also understood the theatrical benefit of performing such a drill for the gawking passengers.

Spider, himself loving the attention, bowed to the applause he received from the amazed and well entertained passengers, his face lighting up with a gap-toothed and ear to ear smile.

CHAPTER FOUR

Tarsus

Leaving Tarsus was always a bittersweet departure for the captain but he always left immediately after the worst of the windy storms of winter had subsided. It was his home and had been his family's home for as long as anyone in his clan could remember. The large stone villa next to the beautiful waterfall in Tarsus was testament to the family's enduring financial success and the lively household was again expanding with the recent growth and prosperity of the sailing industry. He, his wife, his oldest son Antoine, now with him on the ship, four younger children and an array of in-laws, servants, and constantly visiting family had necessitated the latest expansion to the already sizable home. This project he happily left to his capable and demanding wife.

The wide waterfall in the center of Tarsus, picturesque as it was, marked the lower end of the turbulent and tumbling upper section of the Cydnus River which flowed down from the snowy mountainous peaks of Cilicia. That impressive ridge of mountains stood thirty miles back from the sea and this space allowed for a lush and fertile lower plain. As the river cut its way down through the mountains, it passed through a tight gorge called the Cilician Gates and this narrow corridor between towering mountain walls was the only pass between the northern highlands and the coastal flats.

Over the centuries, these gates had served as an appreciated and constricting protection from the many barbaric invasions from the north that other cities in Asia Minor had experienced. This canyon was easily defended and that fact had discouraged many marauding intruders and small looting bands, leaving the city a relatively peaceful oasis in warring times.

The city of Tarsus was fifteen miles inland from the shores of the Great Sea and starting from the bottom of the waterfall, was blessed with the wide and slow-moving river which became its most valued asset. After eight miles it flowed into a large, sufficiently deep and very useful lagoon. The river then exited this small lake and continued its slow journey, meandering peacefully to the sea.

The lake was the unique and outstanding feature that set Tarsus aside as a major port. The slow-moving last section of the river was deep enough to allow almost all seagoing ships to access the lagoon and use it as an inland harbor. For that reason, it had become a favored center of maritime commerce.

The lagoon's shores were lined with easily accessible loading docks, ship repair facilities, barracks for traveling soldiers and fenced and guarded compounds for the storage of goods waiting for transport. Nearby were well supplied markets with preserved meats, breads and produce for the fresh provision of ships and the farmers of the lower plain surrounding Tarsus were doing very well keeping this thriving maritime industry outfitted. Indeed, this lagoon was an important focal point of shipping on the entire northeastern limits of the Roman Empire.

Accessing the lagoon from the sea required the towing upstream of ships against the river's gentle current and thus a separate industry had grown to provide this service. A healthy supply of oxen was spread along each bank of the river and many years of their plodding had worn deep but solid tracks into the shoreline. There were both towing and steering teams of oxen, each expertly tugging on long ropes to keep the ships moving and centered as they crept upstream. The river was not overly deep but almost all ships could be dragged up to the lagoon, including the Roman galleons. The size of these required some of the chained oarsman to offload and, like the oxen, help pull the vessel against the weak flow.

The miserable scene of those pathetic prisoners, chained and whipped for their efforts while others inside constantly pulled on the oars, was something the captain had witnessed many times. This was a debasing spectacle of human misery he wanted to avoid but which did not seem to bother the affable Romans in the least.

His own ship was at times the carrier of such chained and condemned men, for this miserable bounty seemed to be the immediate and inescapable consequence of any Roman conquest, but for him, it was certainly not a favored cargo. When he had such prisoners aboard and personally witnessed the broken mass of humanity, it required a herculean effort for him to just withhold his normally generously supplied opinion.

Sailing back out of the lagoon was almost as tricky and required the oxen on each side to keep the boats centered and under control. If timed correctly, the mouth of the river would be at high tide and the ships could easily navigate and cross the small bar.

A few of the very largest ships, those equipped with rudders underneath, remained out at sea and were resupplied by a fleet of smaller, but expertly rowed, open-bowed boats. A handsome living was made shuttling the passengers and supplies to and from the newest and biggest of the Roman fleet and wise captains of such deep hulled vessels did not want to even think about getting grounded in the muddy silt of the river's bottom.

These local provisioning boats had also been the training grounds for many a young Tarsus sailor and over time became the school where they learned about tides and draughts, winds and sails, winches and ropes and the art of anchoring. This was often the beginning of the never-ending, lifelong education of the apprentice seaman whose recurring dream was to sail away as the first hand on one of the bigger vessels.

The captain's ship, the *Castor and Pollux,* was wisely outfitted with two small rudders which were mounted on each side of the rear portion of the ship and these were controlled by the swinging beam across the back of the ship. This beam was connected to the large pole on the pulley system above the captain's cabin and from which he could easily steer. The rudders protruding outward along the sides had allowed the ship to avoid damage from grounding in a few places when the captain had been surprised by shifting sands below. This also allowed her to access many shallower harbors that were still common around the Great Sea.

CHAPTER FIVE

Tarsus and Rome

The Romans had a curious regard for the city of Tarsus. They had punished and then rewarded this city many times in the previous hundred years as it had vacillated in its befuddled support for the changing leadership of the Roman Empire. Attempting to please the most recent conqueror, the city had sometimes foolishly, but always bravely and with hearty gusto, been a willing and active participant in the history of the Republic.

Tarsus had initially supported Julius Caesar in his quest, but later the city became a favorite of Mark Antony who rewarded it by giving it municipal freedoms and independence. He made it one of his military and economic centers and declared it a "free city" as a reward.

It was in Tarsus that Cleopatra came to meet and make an alliance with Mark Antony in 41 BC, towed up the river to the colorfully festooned lagoon in a ship covered in gold with silver oars and decorated like the house of the gods, much to the delight of the people of Tarsus. Cleopatra herself was adorned as Aphrodite and as expected, the two leaders started a torrid love affair that ended with the defeat of Mark Antony's army, the suicidal snake-bitten death of Cleopatra, the total conquest of the Egyptian navy and the tragic destruction of the most beautiful parts of the breath-taking city of Alexandria.

It was often agreed that of the many devastating incidents that these vindictive, internal Roman battles brought, the most appalling was the burning of the library of Alexandria which resulted in the tragic loss of over a million original and one-of-a-kind books, scrolls and ancient records. These had been collected over the centuries from all over the known world, the oldest rumored to have been on the ark that Noah built. Chronicles of cultures long ago extinct were lost to this senseless attack, some burned and many just disappearing in an orgy of wild-eyed theft as the structure smoldered. This infamous incident was still a source of ridicule and embarrassment for the Romans as irritated scholars throughout their empire derided them for such a barbaric and needless loss. Their response was to revise the original report to portray this as an accidental fire and a purely unintended consequence of war. In fact, the fire may have been started by disgruntled Egyptians, they claimed.

The end of the "civil wars" left Rome with one emperor in control and that outcome did bring about the present peace, albeit an armistice kept by forceful and brutal means. Under Augustus, Tarsus continued having the enviable status of "free city," and as all inhabitants of the Empire now recognized, this was no small thing. Among the benefits was a freedom from Roman taxes and the ability to keep their own local laws and this meant they could retain their customs and bylaws, appoint their own magistrates and make local laws as required. All that was invaluable, but the biggest advantage to the locals was that anyone born in Tarsus was automatically a Roman citizen.

Citizenship was easily the most cherished possession among the subjugated of the empire. The respect of Rome for those that bore this distinction was surprisingly non-negotiable and endowed the bearer with rights and privileges protected by Senate law. Therefore, to be a Roman citizen was very highly prized, especially in the far-off reaches of the empire, and even more so when compared with the unchecked brutality that Rome displayed in dealing with others not bearing this honor.

CHAPTER SIX

The Stoics of Tarsus

Tarsus, as well as being a maritime center, was noted as one of the most important seats of study for the Stoics. Stoicism was a curious belief, almost a religion to the ancient Greeks and it had remained a popular philosophy in the centuries since. The belief was based on the observations that man was born with a self-centered and flawed nature and Stoicism taught that through much effort and study, a person could change his nature and become a noble, altruistic citizen. This was an appealing theology to many cultures, including to many of the cosmopolitan Jews who were spread around the empire and who were quite willing to mix such thoughts with their ancient religious practices.

One of the passengers aboard this sailing, the young man named Saul, had been purposely sent away to Jerusalem in an attempt to protect at least one son of a prosperous Jewish family from being infested by such seducing notions.

Curiously, the Romans regarded the Greek culture with both envy and distaste. They envied the civility and the outwardly intellectual demeanor that the fading Grecian society had developed into after their early military and barbaric beginnings. They also envied the constant pursuit of knowledge and rational thought, plus the struggle for sound government which the Greeks had almost developed. Although they were not very good at it, the Romans also copied the practice of public debate rather than force to settle or to air grievances, and they were captivated with the Greeks' love of athletics and sports extravagances.

Conversely, their distaste and impatience for the Greeks was based on their tendency to get paralyzed by useless debate and discussion, completely forgetting that it took forceful action and strength of will to implement new ideas. The saying of the day was, "the Greeks are the mind, but the Romans are the muscle."

Tarsus, in its isolation, was perfect for the practice of Stoicism in that it was affluent, peaceful and still deeply immersed in Greek tradition. For those reasons, it was full of rich, eager students sent by wealthy families, all hoping their son would be amongst the most brilliant of the esoteric scholars. Beyond the obviously contradictory and self-centered appeal of striving for great public recognition, there was a disarming truthfulness that made Stoicism popular. It seemed to be imprinted into most men to want to be a better person, an internal striving to be more moral, more noble and at peace with one's self, or as some cynics commented, to at least escape man's paralyzing internal guilt.

As comical as the site of enraptured students sitting at the feet of some teacher in the large Greek temple of Tarsus was, or as unproductive as the wide-eyed youths arguing this ethereal philosophy at the waterfall appeared to be to the very practical captain, he had nevertheless chosen to send his son to the Stoics at an early age as well. That act was his personal acknowledgement that the aspirations of becoming an honorable and virtuous person were indeed worthy of some effort.

In his travels, the captain had seen past the theoretical definitions of good and bad. He had seen pure evil expressed physically in the actions of men who had no regard for others and worse, men who made no attempt to be in any way virtuous. These were men who had long ago abandoned the pursuit of any personal morality but rather lived in a beastlike state, dedicated to indulging themselves to the fullest and fixated on feeding their animalistic natures. These brutes were capable of unspeakable actions and he knew that without some inner direction, his son could become enthralled and influenced with these men who by sheer force and unchecked brutality had often become the rich and powerful elites. The captain had learned that such men were inwardly, desperately wicked. He did not want this to become a life-altering attraction for his son.

Beyond Stoicism, it was also expected that if you were from Tarsus, you possessed a clear and clever mind to go along with your inherited Roman citizenship. The captain's son, quite obviously, possessed both of those qualities.

Although the captain believed in the ultimate goal of stoicism, he was also wise enough to recognize the stage of his son's education when the arrogance of intellectualism, a trait which so easily had crept in amongst the Stoics, became the bludgeoning tool of their particular brand of self-promotion. Before that irreversible malady had completely overtaken the lad, he enticed his son to join him on the ship.

Antoine had flourished greatly in his two years on the ship, a burgeoning curiosity and a brilliant intellect now loosed from the constraining bonds and limits of dull educators and totally set free from the thought-killing parameters of Greek and Roman religious teachings. Within months, Antoine had ceased repeating the tired and meaningless Stoic slogans and the unproven theoretical proclamations and had begun another sphere of education. This one demanded much more depth of learning and intense application for the teacher was "experience" and the method was "open-minded observation."

CHAPTER SEVEN

The Ship's Passengers

From the rear of his vessel, the captain thoughtfully gazed over the three distinct levels making up the top deck of his ship and locked in on the raised deck at the very front. This area housed a makeshift shelter that took up half of that upper space which was the private quarters of eight Roman soldiers that he was transporting to Caesarea on the west coast of Judea. The battle-hardened warriors freely roamed this upper space when they were not in their shelter sleeping off the numbness which came courtesy of two full barrels of cheap wine they had brought on board. One day out and most of them had managed to stay drunk for the better part of that day.

The soldiers had also lugged generous quantities of food on board, including fragrant breads, bulging bundles of fruits, figs, dates, along with copious amounts of highly odorous meat. At first glance the sheer volume of supplies seemed excessive and indeed would be if meant to feed less gluttonous men.

Among the supplies were large slabs of salted pork which were devoured with a noisy festiveness, followed by the eviscerated bones being thrown overboard in a curious arm-flinging ceremony that seemed to give them great delight.

This small troop was a curious mixture of races and personalities and this was a calculated and deliberate practice of their military commanders. The fact that there was such diversity was the result of the curious battlefield decision practised by the Roman army to either conscript their foes or kill them on sight.

The captain had often transported such soldiers on previous journeys, almost always in similar mixed and varied collections of nationalities, fulfilling the custom to isolate and send the defeated and conscripted soldiers far from their homeland to a posting where no prior allegiances would interfere with their service. The promise of a career in the army, along with a quiet retirement in some faraway paradise, was the only option given to dying by a Roman sword and although this was rationally chosen by many, it was surprising that just as often a good number of fanatical adversaries rejected this choice as cowardice, asking instead for, and quickly receiving the more "honorable" fatal stabbing in the battlefield.

In this group of eight, three men spoke a broken Latin with a swinging rhythm which the captain recognized as from the far-off land of Spain. These three sat together on the deck, obviously enjoying the wine and the journey while laughing and telling loud stories. They were of a pleasant appearance and swarthy coloring and each man had an easy smile.

Three others sat slightly apart and it was instantly obvious to the well-travelled captain that they were less trustworthy. They reminded him of the opportunistic dregs who hung around the ports of the Great Sea and he concluded that if they were not in the army, they would probably be thieves. They were sullen and secretive, constantly scanning the ship and its passengers while downing cup after cup from the large barrel. He appreciated that they were under the army's control but he mentally marked them as possible trouble.

The legionnaire in charge of this small group was a professional looking soldier who spoke in the precise Latin of a native Roman. He was not particularly big but was muscular and had the obvious respect of the other men. There was a hard, almost bored look to this man and he seemed to drift into his own thoughts often, appearing as one who had long ago and after many battles, lost the eagerness and outward formality of an army newcomer. This man would do his duty without mercy, the captain surmised, guessing correctly that this was also not a soldier you wanted to have as an adversary.

The last man of the eight was very different and from the very first, became the focus of the captain's curiosity. He was gigantic, fully head and shoulders above any of his companions, but he moved easily and quickly like a graceful athlete. He was youthful looking, was powerfully built with massive shoulders and huge arms and stayed separate from the rest of the heavily-drinking group. He had a distinctive, almost glowing, thick yellow mane of hair that reached to his wide shoulders, but most striking of all were his large, light blue and deeply piercing eyes.

The captain had first seen such men when he sailed with his father into the Black Sea to the mouth of the Danube River, a little over seven years previous, on an emergency resupply of the Roman army. The army was battling an expansionary war in the north of Germania and had fought these local giants to a standstill. The troops were in desperate need of being resupplied for the upcoming cold winter and food and fresh soldiers were desperately required. Smaller river boats met his large ship there to shuttle these supplies to the legions as they frantically attempted to hold the line of the hard-fought advances of the summer campaigns.

It was a commonly known fact that these tribes fought any and every foe viciously, even slaughtering each other before the Romans arrived and that such killing took place with a chilling brutality. Thankfully for the Roman armies, they were now a greatly depleted and weakened force and their numbers had dwindled severely over the centuries, a fact that allowed the Romans to withstand the ferocious and almost diabolical onslaughts by simply outnumbering them.

In that Black Sea port, the captain had also heard bizarre reports of even larger and more beastlike men, if they could indeed be called men, who lived in the Caucasus mountains along the north and east side of the Black Sea. The captain's opinion was that Rome should have known in advance of the dangers of engaging such creatures from the historical disasters they had suffered from starting fights with the Senone Giants, but it was the lure of riches and tax money and continual expansion which seemed to make all previous failures forgotten. These creatures were undoubtably descendants of the famous giants that had dominated the ancient histories and they had the well-earned reputation as fierce, warlike, and even cannibalistic. Thankfully, the captain had not been ordered into these regions since.

Recently captured and conscripted, this big soldier appeared very bright and observant, quietly watching the crew as he moved about the ship unhindered. He was closely observing the passengers, noticing their apparel and their actions but he spoke only to the leader of his own group. When he did speak, it was in a bellowing, deep voice, twice as loud as a normal man and he had a strange and heavy guttural accent when he attempted to use the little Latin he knew.

The more the captain observed this huge captive, the more it became apparent that he was an intelligent being who endeavored to learn all that he could from the new world around him. At the port of Tarsus, the captain had noticed him lift and carry the large amphorae of wine easily and he appreciated that those casks normally required two strong men to just roll them about.

Antonius had heard the Roman commander call him Julian and whatever name he had in his previous life, it was now to be forgotten. He was to regard himself as a Roman military asset and as property of their army. The huge man seemed strangely at peace with his new existence and appeared comfortable in that role, an easy smile painting his face when he saw something interesting or something new.

Five steps below the upper deck of the ship was the lower, middle level which made up the large center portion of the ship. Prominent in this area were two raised hatchways that could be covered and sealed so that any waves lapping over the sides would not leak into the lower cargo deck. These were situated centrally between the large masts and had a long wooden beam above them which was connected to the masts. This was the attachment point for the smaller sliding rails with their pulleys used to lift the heavy cargo from the lower decks and which then allowed the loads to be slid to the side of the ship for easy loading and offloading. When the ship was being constructed, his grandfather had devised this method and it had certainly repaid any costs because of the speed and ease of unloading and loading heavy bundles.

Once the cargo was stored below the main deck and the hatches sealed, the passengers could be placed on this large deck, encircling the raised hatchways. The captain provided any travelers with small tents that protected against rain, wind, or the hot sun.

Antonius thought it rather interesting that he had bought these sturdy tents from a Jewish tent-making family in Tarsus and coincidentally, a couple of members of that family were on board for this trip. One was that youthful and showy Pharisee who was, once again, praying at the rail.

Over the years, this Jewish family had become very affluent making their unique shelters from the thicker longhaired hides of goats that were native to the cold mountains above Tarsus. In those years, the captain had come to know the patriarch of this family very well and a neighborly and businesslike relationship had developed. It was a relationship which had remained until the tent-maker's recent death.

The demand for these well-made, water-repelling and excellently insulating tents had remained steady, being a favorite of the Roman army, and the tent maker constantly required the services of this ship to deliver them abroad. The older sons of the deceased patriarch were now dutifully carrying on the tent-making business, and from all reports, the family business was still flourishing.

Originally an outgoing and aggressive businessman in the strongly secular city of Tarsus, the father of this Jewish family had drastically changed his personal focus some ten years ago and had become a follower of the strictest Jewish religious sect called Pharisees. Knowing a little of the Jewish teachings involved for any claiming to be a Pharisee, the captain thought it best if he put the young rabbi and his accompanying sister just below his cabin which was on the raised rear deck. This would wisely keep them as far away from the Roman contingent as possible. Not only was he aware that the young girl was pretty and would attract the attention of the soldiers, especially the three dregs he had identified in his mind as trouble, but beyond that, the general animosity between the Jews and the Romans was well known. He wanted his first voyage of the year to be an uneventful and peaceful trip and he was not interested in settling any political or religious squabbles aboard his vessel.

The young rabbi was well known by the captain and had been a boyhood acquaintance of his own son for many years in Tarsus. In fact, he had this youth on board at other times as he traveled back and forth from his schooling in Jerusalem to visit his family in Tarsus. Saul was his name and the captain was acutely aware that he had grown to be loud and outspoken and more than a little bit proud and defiant. Any physical distance between the Romans and him would be helpful.

The captain also understood that the aroma of the salted pig that the Romans were gorging themselves on would be repulsive to Saul. It was his hope that the smell would mostly be dissipated into the winds, especially if the pig-eating remained at the front.

The remainder of the passengers were situated in the middle area, slightly closer to the soldiers. They were a family of ten who required all three of the remaining tents. They were going to Salamis on the island of Cyprus and they were treating this journey as a sacred pilgrimage to their ancestral home. It was quickly learned by all on board that this type of journey required a certain level of music, loud singing, continual feasting and the uninterrupted enjoyment of wine. Their music was lively and the robust choruses brought a festive atmosphere to the ship as they cut through the low swell to Cyprus. When the music and drinking started, the captain was again pleased that he had situated their tents midship, a useful and entertaining buffer between the Pharisee and the Romans.

It became immediately obvious that Saul and the captain's young son, Antoine, were enjoying each other's company once again. Anytime that his ship duties slowed, Antoine would drift over to where Saul was sitting or join him at the rail, scanning the waves while reminiscing about their former days.

The captain also noticed that Saul's attractive sister was usually within hearing distance, watching her brother attentively and scrutinizing both men as the two bantered back and forth. At other times, she joined in laughter with them as they recalled some childhood prank that she had either heard about or had personally witnessed as the annoying little sister who had escaped the house to follow her older brother in his adventures.

This easygoing and adventurous child's life had ceased when their father chose to follow the teachings of the Pharisees because fraternizing with a Gentile was forcefully discouraged as dangerous to the purity required by their new version of Jewishness. The boyhood friends saw little of each other after that.

The demanding and peculiar restrictions brought by the Jerusalem version of the Pharisee sect, as constraining as they seemed initially, had steadily intensified over the years as the spotlessly robed and very pious visiting missionaries became more and more rabid in their demands for separation from all impurity. With each new, fresh-faced and zealous Pharisaical proselytizer, came another and increased call for a more restrictive lifestyle and it seemed that "impurity" was being redefined constantly. The more confining rules were presented as recently discovered revelations or as forgotten but very holy insights which were just now being demanded by God.

The ultimate effect of this "demanding," was almost complete isolation and separation from any who did not agree, even to the point of estrangement from other Jews and in the most severe teachings, separation from close family members as well.

Inevitably, a galling haughtiness among the Pharisees and their followers developed, a product of believing that they were superior and had a special calling within Judaism itself. The two boys, previously partners in exciting boyhood adventures in Tarsus, had grown far apart as a result.

CHAPTER EIGHT

Saul's Father, Gideon

Saul's father, thoughtfully named after the Jewish hero Gideon, had over the years of indoctrination become a precise practicing Pharisee, personally convinced that the salvation of the nation of Israel and all Judaism was only possible by the strictest fulfillment of every aspect of Moses's Law with special attention to the placement of every period and exclamation mark. Obedience, more obedience and even stricter obedience was the message the visiting Pharisees preached, constantly repeating their tedious doctrine, altering their message only when they would find a more remote or obscure regulation of the Law to lay upon the congregations. In fact, finding or interpreting some additional tenet gave them intense pleasure, convincing many that such inspiration was coming directly from Hashem, the Jewish appellation for their God's unspoken name.

It was a curious fact that in the city of Jerusalem, the very heart of the Jewish faith, there was three separate sects of Pharisees, each division proclaiming that their particular version of Moses' Law was the correct and perfect one. In turn, each had sent their dutiful missionaries out to the dispersed Jews and their contradictory and fractioning messages often caused confusion in the remote Jewish congregations. Eventually they all agreed on one point and that was that God had allowed the Jews to be conquered throughout history as a punishment for their departure from the strict obedience to the Mosaic laws and this was the very reason that Jews were dispersed to the remote locations like Tarsus rather than possessing a glorious and unchallenged kingdom in Judea and Samaria. It was undeniable that their message was intense and demanding, but it had a mystical appeal to many devout Jews who were longing for the promise of a restored and powerful Israel and more importantly, the coming of the future Messiah. The very thought of that champion inflamed the imaginations of all Jews.

Gideon, an ambitious and fiery man, accepted and acknowledged these teachings wholeheartedly and decided to send his youngest son to the very seat of the Pharisees, the Holy City of Jerusalem, and to the most celebrated of all the pharisaical teachers, Gamaliel, the grandson of the famous and revered Hillel.

Saul, young though he was, would take on the duty of representing the family and expressing their devotion to the Law while his father and brothers tended to their lucrative and growing tent-making business. The exceptional intellect of Saul had convinced Gideon that it was possible for this son to become a great teacher, or at least a better one than the questionable and easily flummoxed Pharisees that continually traveled through Tarsus. He may possibly even become the family's celebrated representative in Judaism.

Saul's three older brothers were important parts of the family business and had married young and started families and Gideon knew that in order to provide a different route for Saul, he must take drastic action while he was yet very young.

It was with this very purpose in mind that Gideon and a youthful Saul had twice braved the long and arduous journey to Jerusalem for Passover, partially convinced by these traveling teachers that Temple worship was their lawful duty, but equally spurred on by Gideon's other and more secretive objective.

Upon arriving in Jerusalem, Gideon was immediately impressed with the respect and almost reverential fear that the common Jews showed to the Pharisees as they paraded the streets. In their overt displays, they were always being careful not to dirty their beautifully flowing, blue-fringed robes which were adorned with colorful sashes and other dangling decorations. Each item of their garb had some mystical ancient meaning attached to it and each bobble outwardly declared the devotion to some minute definition of the Law for the wearer.

The majesty of the golden-roofed Temple with all its ritual ceremonies, culminating in the emotional and moving blood sacrifices, all mixed with the enticing and exotic oriental atmosphere of Jerusalem, created an unmatched passion in the city's people for their religion and this experience deeply moved a wide-eyed Gideon. Tarsus Jews certainly did not take their religion nearly as seriously, he readily admitted.

Quite early, Gideon noticed that Jerusalem was a place of extremes. In it were the most spiritual people he had ever met and, surprisingly, the angriest. He was shocked by the intensity of the hatred toward the Roman occupation in the holy city. In Tarsus, being a Jew did not automatically mean you had to possess the festering animus toward all things Roman that he was witnessing here.

Taken in its entirety, the beautiful and unique city of Jerusalem, bedecked with an ancient and profound spirituality, was overpowering, and Gideon and his son thirstily drank it all in.

On their second trip, a year after the first, Gideon approached the famous Gamaliel with the proposition of Saul becoming his student. At first, the teacher was hesitant to take on such a young scholar but decided to interview the lad before rejecting him. He was very impressed at the boy's command of Hebrew, common Greek, some Aramaic, and a sprinkling of other languages that he himself could not identify and which no doubt had been learned on the docks of Tarsus.

This was obviously a brilliant mind, Gamaliel surmised, a boy who already had a fundamental understanding of Moses's Law at ten years old and who had a very strong will, but he needed direction in his education. As his own son, only a few months older, was being raised and taught in the Pharisaical tradition, Gamaliel decided that the two would be good companions in learning. So it was that Saul became not only his youngest student, but also a member of his household and a close friend, boyhood companion and sometime competitor of young Shimon ben Gamaliel II, affectionately known as Gammy.

The fee that Gideon paid for this education was substantial, but he was proud to pay it and had willingly submitted it for the last ten years.

It was a much more mature Saul who now traveled with his sister. The young man had spent ten dedicated years at the feet of his mentor and it was obvious that Gamaliel's influence on him was immense. He was a different person.

Saul truly was a Pharisee of the Pharisees.

CHAPTER NINE

The Captain's Son

From his perch at the rear, the captain noticed that Saul was bedecked in a fine ceremonial robe at prayer times and it was clear that he was totally convinced of his own significance, taking very seriously his place in the unfolding future of the Jewish world. That world obviously included this ship, far removed from Jerusalem. The captain also noted that Saul was being very preachy and dogmatic while conversing with Antoine, his robust, athletic and Stoically-trained son at the side rail of the ship.

What a contrast, he thought.

In Tarsus, these two had been close boyhood friends, running and playing at the waterfall, always discovering something new in the markets and thoroughly enjoying their youth. Like men everywhere who had been apart for some time and had come into their own, there were now great differences and, undoubtably, there would be a competition of wills starting with a "statement" of their personal viewpoints.

The captain was confident that his gregarious son, although dressed in the garbs of a seafarer and not appearing at all an intellectual, would fare well in any conversation with the Pharisee for he had honed his fervent Stoicism with deep and diverse conversations with many traveling intellectuals and learned men. Indeed, Antoine regularly and quite eagerly searched out such intellectu-als, craving robust conversation and finding great pleasure in deep discussions.

Even though he was yet an apprentice to his father, Antoine was already wise in the world of business and could judge the character of most people upon sight, learning early to gauge the inherent truthfulness and honesty of people. He did this, not so much by their words but also by their eyes and their demeanor. His youthful, almost cherublike looks, together with his wild black and curly locks, disguised the maturity and wisdom possessed by this polite young sailor and his disarming, wide smile and dark eyes also gave him a handsome and trustworthy charm which made all want to befriend him.

Although immersed in the academia and intellectualism of the Stoics for eight years, Antoine now had a practical teacher in his father and in the few years since coming aboard, he had been scrutinizing and shadowing his father closely. It was here that he learned the minute details in both sailing technique and business acumen. It was also from his father that he had learned to read the faces and discern the trustworthiness of those he met, understanding that there were men to be embraced and men to be avoided. He had discovered how to politely refrain from any involvement with those of dubious character while leaving no insult or animosity. Most importantly, he had refined an inherited strength of character from his father and was beginning to understand when and where to use the power that his position offered.

This developing wisdom had allowed his father to give over the directing of the day-to-day duties of the eight-man sailing crew to Antoine very early into his apprenticeship. Early on, his son had accurately identified the strengths and weaknesses of the crew and had gained their respect and compliance with compliments rather than force. This had them competently completing their tasks with minimal orders. More importantly, the crew responded to this young man without the usual resentment of the older, more experienced sailors to a young upstart.

CHAPTER TEN

Saul's Sister Miriam

Saul's sister Miriam, younger by one year, remained close to the small shelter provided to the and she busied herself around that sanctuary with meal preparation and maintaining the strictest of cleanliness rules, as per their Jewish traditions. Miriam was raven-haired and pretty, a girl who flashed a quick and easy smile that lit up her tanned face almost continuously. She moved about her world with an unpretentious confidence and natural grace that always attracted approving glances. In preparation for their voyage, she had carefully packed their approved foods and whatever else was required for their cleansing needs, for Miriam knew that Saul was determined to keep the letter of the Mosaic laws at all times, even amid the inconvenience of travel. She would do her best to assist her brother in his pious fastidiousness, but she was also very inquisitive and was excited with this opportunity to see a world that she had never-before witnessed. This was her first time venturing away from the contented family home in Tarsus, the place where she had lived a privileged and sheltered life and her unbridled curiosity was being awakened and stirred with each new segment of this voyage.

Like the captain, Miriam was entertained with the conversation of the two young men at the nearby rail, listening intently as the exchange between her

Pharisee brother and his Stoic friend left the initial amusing recollections of their childhood pranks and then passed the level of explaining their present situation. Not long after, their exchanges turned to their deeply held beliefs and convictions. This was, of course, unavoidable and entirely expected, for such is the way when highly principled and devoutly religious men meet.

Antoine, as is the manner of a Stoic, forcefully explained that it was his belief that man could reach a state of higher integrity by the intense study of the nature of the noble virtues and then, in a work-like manner, implementing and living by them. There was a high and exalted state of morality to be achieved as the reward for one's intense efforts, he professed. Anticipating Saul's response, he questioned any motive for pursuing such virtue other than the reward of possessing a virtuous character itself, explaining that he doubted that the pursuit of morality simply to achieve an after-death reward was itself moral, contrary to what most religions taught.

Was not the promise of such future reward just a disguise for delayed self-indulgence? Was this not a hedonistic pursuit of yet-to-come pleasure and reward to be heaped upon oneself in the future, he reasoned, somewhat logically.

Godliness should be it own reward, should it not, he asked.

Saul, rising to the challenge, partially agreed with this explanation but stated that there was a higher, supreme essence who demanded that man rise above his now reduced nature and therefore it was not just a self-designed and therefore indulgent calling. He confidently stated that this Being had chosen the Jewish people to be the ones who could accomplish this transformation and then could be a light unto the other nations. This perfect and heavenly Being had given them the laws that would accomplish such a change of attitude through Moses and obedience to these laws would make a man acceptable to this God, as well as to himself and to mankind in general.

Saul spoke with a burst of pride when describing the sect of Pharisees, of which he had recently become a teacher, labelling this one group as those who had dedicated themselves to this heavenly objective through obedience to every command. He pointed out that this made them the spearhead for the promised restoration of his nation, an event which was prophesied and therefore inevitable, but which first required a difficult cleansing of the citizens of Israel and then of the whole world.

Saul passionately explained that this "cleansing" had a further purpose. That was so that God's promised interaction with the Jews, in the form of the

Messiah, could appear. Until Israel became worthy of this through contrition and strict obedience, there would remain no national freedom, no restoration of honorable Jewish leadership and most importantly, no Messiah. The fate of the entire world remained in jeopardy, totally dependent on the success of the Pharisees, he declared.

Saul had a comical strut, a little like a rooster, which emerged when he imagined he was making an irrefutable and earth-altering point. Miriam knew it well. The rest of the passengers, although not hearing the conversation, were secretly entertained at the strange back-and-forth, two-stepping gait that inevitably would appear when Saul and Antoine met.

Antoine, on the other hand, remained almost motionless, politely listening without interrupting.

CHAPTER ELEVEN

Saul, the Pharisee

Although they were mainly focused on their own obedience to the letter of the law, Pharisees also saw themselves as protectors of the purity of the "under-standing" of Moses's Law for the whole nation of Israel, and because of this, they eagerly challenged any and all who deviated from their particular version. This meant that they constantly demanded that Israel follow the Law in the exact ways they had decided were accurate and any divergence was quickly met with a zealous and often aggressive challenge. Added to that, if they decided that the divergence was a heretical or dangerous deviation, punishment was loudly and forcefully endorsed and, when possible, meted out. Although advocated and witnessed by them, the punishments were always carried out by others so that their pure pharisaical hands remained untarnished. Lately, it was the Romans who decided who should be punished and how severely, a fact that irritated all Judea but particularly enraged the Pharisees. "That duty is ours," they loudly professed for they alone could determine how severe the beating or how many stripes to lay on their brethren.

As part of the obligation of Pharisaical devotion, exposing sinful acts in others was not to be considered an annoying duty, or worse, a betrayal of a fellow Jew, but exposing a failing became a holy endeavor and implementing the scriptural punishments was labelled virtuous and sacred. As a result, the Pharisees were constantly on the lookout for adulteries, sabbath violations or desecrations of the Temple and this in turn created the curious occupation of religious espionage, an occupation that flourished in just one place-Jerusalem.

In Jerusalem, there had, over the years, developed quite a gaggle of shady spies who made their paltry living dragging violators to the Pharisees for monetary reward.

Although not extremely lucrative, it remained holy work, did it not, was their reasoning.

Saul's glowing description of the Pharisees to Antoine had purposely left out this side of their activities for he knew that Gentiles could not possibly understand such pure devotion.

Miriam also noticed this curious omission but said nothing.

Truthfully, Antoine did not completely understand all of Saul's religious explanations for such personality-altering intensity left Antoine more than a little confused. What he did notice was that the easy-going youth he had known as a child had been replaced by a stern and intolerant man who smiled little. This caused Antoine to wonder if this sour persona was a demand of his religious teaching as well or if Saul had become secretly depressed and irreversibly unhappy.

Saul's sister, Miriam. had also noticed the gradual change in her brother with every yearly visit and within herself, she blamed the intolerant religious teachings for creating a hardness in her formerly inquisitive and bright sibling. She did not like the transformation and, if truth were told, she feared this dark side of him slightly.

Secretly, Miriam possessed an unspoken personal reservation of leaving laid-back Tarsus for the inflexible zealotry of Jerusalem and this fear was based on the possibility of herself somehow being overcome with this distasteful version of the faith she loved so dearly. She had never made these feelings known to Saul but on occasion would ask a contrary and penetrating question about his teachings that would surprise him and even cause him to wonder. Some of these questions he could not immediately answer he admitted and he knew better than to spin vague epithets to his sister, but those times of uncertainty did not diminish his eagerness for the Law. As with committed zealots, he dared not question his own stance, even when he could not find a logical or reasonable response to questions. A sharp pang of guilt emerged for even entertaining the possibility of self-doubt and that guilt quickly drove any additional questions out of his thinking.

CHAPTER TWELVE

Miriam Enters the Discussions

During their conversations aboard the ship, Saul and Antoine had come to a general and somewhat amiable agreement that, yes, it was the responsibility of man to obey, to strive and to work to please either God or man and thus be accepted by either the deity or oneself. Miriam had quietly listened to this convenient yet compromising treaty and was bursting with thoughts of her own.

The years of quietly listening from her upper perch in the women's section of the synagogue, and then studying on her own, had led to quite a different notion in the mind of Miriam. Although most women paid little attention to those rabbinical readings, she had listened, and listened intently. She had grasped and embraced the beautiful concepts in the ancient writings, words about the love and graciousness of the creator Hashem and she understood Him as a Being who dearly loved His creation. Hers seemed a God that neither her brother or Antoine spoke of.

Miriam was deeply influenced in her view by rich concepts that she held and admired personally, even though such concepts were not currently being emphasized or expanded on by Jewish teachers. Very early in her life, she had noticed that the profound concepts she was embracing were often lost in the pettiness of religious postering and in the excessive burden of minute detail that was laid upon sincere Jews, all in the name of Moses and she had decided that she did not want to waste time and energy debating such unimportant ramblings. She did not want to interrupt or disagree with her brother or Antoine but her obvious discomfort betrayed her as she recognized the familiar tactic of contrived opinion masquerading as religious or philosophical truth.

"Your sister seems to be bothered by our harmony," Antoine finally commented to Saul, misreading what was making Miriam squirm. Her normally relaxed expression had become clouded and her brow furrowed.

Saul recognized the look on his sister's pretty face and knew that she, out of respect for him and his friend and following the prevailing custom, was remaining silent. One of his sister's great qualities was her humility and politeness and often she would silently allow someone an unchallenged opinion or even a ludicrous conclusion when she could easily dispute or even embarrass them. Saul also knew that this kindness that came so easily to her was not because of weakness or any lack on her part but exactly the opposite. It was rather a manifestation of the strength and confidence that she possessed. She did not require any person's admiration.

Her superior intelligence, bathed in pure unpretentiousness, allowed her this benevolence to others, plus she was totally devoid of any need to promote herself. That this approach to others was even possible confused Saul immensely for at this point in his life, he was utterly driven to be noticed for his great wisdom.

Antoine seemed very interested in what Miriam thought and although hesitant, Saul warmed to the thought as well. He suspected she would have some disagreement and therefore he was admittedly less eager than Antoine to hear it.

"Well, Saul, are you going to ask her to speak, or do we remain ignorant of her views on this matter?" announced Antoine, poking Saul playfully.

Reluctantly, Saul nodded at his sister and asked, "What is it, Miriam?"

Slowly and deliberately, Miriam began to speak.

"I agree with you both that on a lower, more self-indulgent level, a man's life is ordered by that man's choice of actions alone. He eats, sleeps, plants, harvests, and seems to be the master of his destiny. But like an animal, everything he does, he does for himself, for his own existence, satisfying his immediate needs, for that is the nature he is born with and that is his natural state. He will even be generous and kind when it benefits him to be. This is a dangerous existence for mankind, for on that basis he can also excuse any excess or any act, good or evil, that betters his plight or satiates his wants. On a higher level, the level which you two are speaking about, there is a higher calling that transcends the base nature of men. Where I differ is that, by my observations, it seems that it requires the interjection of something like a God to even make a man realize that there is a higher nature to be striven for. Without that realization, men remain in a beastlike state their entire lives, never aware there is a higher calling. Even when enlightened of our low state and made aware of the dangers of our shortcomings, all we can do is struggle mightily just to control that base nature. Mostly, we are overcome with selfish endeavors and then we rationalize our actions with religious or self-serving platitudes. Hashem made this struggle a lot easier. He took the confusion out of our hands when he gave the Ten Commandments, rules given to curtail the selfish nature. He gave them for people individually and for our nation so that we could live together without killing each other. Sadly, if you know our history, the rules did not change our national natures or do anything to change our individual character. Likewise, obedience and self-deprivation are laudable and help societies in general, but I suspect will not give the ultimate results you two speak of."

She could see Saul thinking hard and before he could answer, she continued.

Turning to Antoine, she said, "In our writings, our father Abraham was called by Hashem while he was still a pagan, when he had yet done nothing to please the Divine One. Therefore, I think that the nation of Israel exists because God interjected His thinking and His desires and involved Himself with one man. He chose Abraham and therefore, by coincidence, our nation. This had little to do with whether we are greatly successful in our obeying of His commandments, so I think there must exist another way to please God. Like Abraham, it may have more to do with being able to hear God or somehow being mysteriously linked to Him, which it seems was how our ancient father pleased Hashem."

She carried on, "Both of your arguments are the same, that men can do things that change their nature by themselves; it is only your pathways that differ. Only the names of your gods are different. This does not make sense to me, for it seems evident that without Divine intervention, whatever His name, every endeavor of man's mind is ultimately self-serving, even his so-called good intentions and his religious pursuits."

The two men looked at each other and knowingly nodded, acknowledging the soundness of her statement.

Miriam had not disappointed them. Her logical statement ended that day's debate, not allowing for, or inviting response. To silence them had not been her intent, but that was the inevitable result.

The Miriam they had known since childhood had entered the arena, a clear thinker since she was a very young girl, unimpeded by personal or previously held institutional dogma that had to be defended at the expense of obvious truth. Her words were always carefully and thoughtfully chosen and her forthrightness had often threatened other insecure Jews who were not aware that her insights and precise words were always given in a spirit of kindness and with the ultimate benefit of the receiver in mind. Miriam rarely offered a conflicting opinion in the spirit of argument, but when she did, she had usually precisely weighed the facts beforehand and decided that truth was worth the disagreement.

Her pleasant, smiling face gave the young woman a trusting demeanor and a quiet dignity but her overwhelming strengths were her inquisitive active mind and a trusting and open heart. Saul was aware that it was now his responsibility to protect that pure heart as his father had in her childhood years and that was a task that perplexed him totally. Most times she seemed far from needing any of his protection.

Miriam's intimidating intellect and piercing rationale had made many a Tarsus Jew shrivel in her presence and her wise father had successfully taught her to temper her responses, learning quickly that even the simplest and clear-est of points could not be understood by narrow or insulted men who had no ability or desire to learn.

Unlike many others her age, she had easily conquered and moved past her traditional upbringing, mastering the family and household duties by the age of eleven. She then graduated to understanding and co-managing all aspects of her family's business, easily earning the approval and gratitude of her loving father and older brothers, meanwhile learning many of the languages required for her father's business.

By sixteen years of age and while Saul was away in Jerusalem, Miriam had committed to precise memory the books of Moses and Joshua, plus the history of Israel in the Chronicles and the record of the Kings as well. She, with the covert help of her oldest brother Josiah, had managed to get her hands on the writings of King David, Solomon, Isaiah, Enoch, Josher, and most Greek scholars as well. Her gifted and blossoming mind was able to remember and understand exactly what she read and together with a talent for sound reasoning, could decipher traits and themes in scripture that were completely missed by less capable intellects. These understandings and interpretations spilled into the beloved family conversations and those around that table had learned quite early that what Miriam stated as fact, was likely correct. The local rabbi had also learned to be very cautious and exact when teaching Torah if Miriam was within earshot.

A turning point in her life came with Gideon's illness.

Two years ago, her father had suddenly started to lose weight. At her mother's desperate pleadings, he had visited one of the most respected Greek physicians of the city and the diagnosis was not good. It was an internal disease that the physician had seen many times before and it always led to a slow and painful death within months.

Miriam was devastated and could not imagine her privileged and tranquil Jewish life without her protective father. Although he was now a strict Pharisee and had his rules and overbearing traditions, he loved her to a fault and had not forbidden her the learning she craved as some other Jewish fathers had their daughters. Truthfully, Gideon greatly admired the incredible talents of Miriam.

The threat of his imminent death made Gideon want to put his affairs in order and one of the things he wanted to accomplish was to find a worthy husband for his only daughter. Miriam suspected this and knowing that few prospects for a husband of any intellect were in the Jewish community of Tarsus, she outlandishly proposed a deal to her father. If he agreed to not making a match for her in Tarsus, she would join Saul in Jerusalem and marry the most devout Pharisee she could find there, but only after Gideon's death. Her amused father agreed and then wrote and made Saul aware of this, making him a co-conspirator in this unusual agreement. Amid their sadness over the ordeal Gideon was going through, the three of them managed the occasional half-smile when thinking about this strange and unprecedented arrangement.

The pact began an intense and all-consuming campaign for Miriam.

Rather than passively waiting for her father to die, she decided to become wholly involved in her father's treatment. She convinced her older brother to borrow every scroll of medicine from the nearby university and, feverously, she poured over them. Soon she had consumed them and had learned all that was to be learned from these physicians and their medical writings. She visited the most trusted doctors and there learned of the latest techniques used by the army to operate on wounds and infections and then she scoured the markets for powders and medicines that were recommended. Miriam soon realized the clear limitations of the knowledge available and decided that she would have to go beyond the learning of the physicians to help her father. She decided that there was no reason to be hampered by ignorance, and she let her mind and imagination run loose, hoping that there was some cure that had been overlooked.

She knew that God had told Moses that the life of all things was in the blood so she quickly decided that the practice of bloodletting was not going to help as it took life away and only weakened her father. Reading the conclusions of the Grecian philosophers, it seemed that the essence of life itself was in extremely small particles that collectively made up the body, particles which they called "atom-os," elements not further divisible. Further thinking about the blood made her deduce that if the life was in the blood and if it was be made of particles so small that they were not visible, there may be other particles both beneficial and harmful that could be in the blood.

This rationale led her to look at any injury that occurred in her family with new questions, and she became convinced that the washings required in Moses's law were wisely given for their health benefits and not only as religious purification. This was an epiphany for Miriam and soon she was examining all the laws of eating and cleansing given to the Jews in Moses's Law in a different light, beginning to consider them as practical and actual health directives given by a more "practical" Divine mind. She became an enthusiastic promoter of the practice of the washing of the body, much to Saul's approval but for completely different reasons, insisting on the intense cleansing overall and the ongoing purifying of any injury.

In this way, Miriam discovered a mysterious principle in Moses's writings. She claimed that the scriptures contained varying depths of understanding, a multi-layered sequence of truths that were there to be mined and discovered but only if one was willing to move past the shallow and limiting religious aspects promoted as the only reality. This understanding propelled her to revisit each portion of the texts and delve more intensely into them for she suspected that hidden from the shallow human mind were deep insights of great benefit and beauty. She immediately found that these deeper discernments were endless and the deeper she dove, the more they opened to her. Almost immediately, she became aware that she could not plumb these depths in her lifetime and that she was insidiously hampered by holding on to former understandings or previous childish and shallow conclusions she had learned in the local synagogue. Achieving deeper understanding by loosing her mind from previously held shallowness became the daily mantra for her life.

She tried to explain to her father and to Saul that she considered her human nature, including her personality, a boundary or restriction to further understanding, admitting that it would take a great humbling to proceed past some of her preconceived notions. She explained that one must be able to admit that either their previous understandings were totally wrong, or that they were understood only partially, in order to move to a higher life with clearer understandings but neither was able to comprehend what she was talking about.

On a practical level, this search for her father's health meant she became convinced that the rushing waters of the Cydnus River were not only cleaner but healthier than the slow-moving and sometimes stale waters below the falls. She had insisted that, in the family house, only the upper water be used for washing and cooking. The ancient record of Alexander the Great getting a near deadly fever from bathing in the lower and sometimes stagnant Cydnus, only confirmed her suspicions.

Miriam also made it a habit to weekly visit the international markets at the lagoon, shopping for any new medicine or procedure that would help her father's illness and the result was that she was learning of many treatments for other maladies prevalent within the Jewish community, not just her father's. It was not long before word got out that a Jewess was becoming an expert on many medications and therapies and the community was soon calling on her for help, proud that one of their own women, young though she was, could treat sickness and injury or assist with almost all problems, including tricky baby deliveries.

Having Miriam among them was truly a blessing for the Jews of Tarsus, especially for the frightened women who purposely avoided the rough Greek physicians and word of her skills spread quickly. She had started this journey into the secrets of medicine to treat her father but very soon, she was being called to doctor many others. As her reputation grew, she became busier and busier, often occupied from dawn to dusk, often being called out throughout the night as well.

This did not surprise Gideon at all. He had become aware very early in her life of the amazing mental abilities of his daughter and he watched with wonder as she consumed all the books and scrolls that she could get her hands on. Her thirst and aptitude for knowledge was daunting and it steadily grew as she matured. His "deal" with her was in his thoughts daily as she attended to his every physical need, as was his admiration of her talents. He often wondered if there was any Pharisee in Jerusalem worthy of a wife of this caliber and that thought was quickly followed by a hearty chuckle at the humbling and precarious situation that some proud and unsuspecting Jew would find himself in should he end up the husband of Miriam.

Unexpectantly, but quite happily, under Miriam's care her father regained his appetite and soon carried on directing the family. Things stayed that way for well over a year.

After that, the throbbing and pressure he felt in his bowels began to slowly increase and the bouts of intense pain began to become more frequent. Miriam had found a powder ground from the seeds of a red flower of the Taurus mountains that took the sharpness off the pain but left him swooning and incoherent. Gideon, sensing his days were numbered, called his older sons together and expressed in detail his vision of the family's future business plans, giving his direction on the divisions of responsibilities and how to keep it profitable in his and Miriam's absence. With these things off his mind, Gideon spent his remaining days speaking individually and endearingly to each of his children, complimenting and encouraging each one and blessing each son and their families. He fussed lovingly over his young grandchildren, laughing and tickling and praying over each of them. He was indeed slipping away but his inevitable departure was being crowned with beauty and grace.

One Sabbath, he woke late and was having great trouble breathing, Miriam rushed to him and mixed the pain-killing powder but Gideon shook his head in a final refusal. As her burning tears flowed unabated, her precious father quietly slipped away, his hand in hers.

Her tender care had given them nearly two more years than the physicians had predicted, but that did not relieve the stinging loneliness she felt at his final departure.

Discouraged and depressed, Miriam stayed in her room for many days after Gideon's passing, feeling strangely deserted and guilty that she had not saved her beloved father. With his passing, a portion of her life seemed to pass away as well.

With her father gone and the tent-making business and the family home now under the direction of her brothers, Miriam soon felt divorced from any reason to remain in Tarsus. Within a month, she began to inquire about Jerusalem from Saul who had made the emergency journey home when he was informed of the worsening condition of his father. Although saddened with his father's demise, he spoke often to her of his own disconnect from all that his family was enduring. His heart was truly far away in Jerusalem and the prospect of leaving soon began to intrigue her.

Before long, there came an intense anxiousness to begin the next phase of her life and it showed in Miriam's preparations and in her diminishing interest in her previous life in Tarsus. Later that month, Saul made the arrangements for them to leave and they delayed only long enough to celebrate a last family Passover together.

CHAPTER THIRTEEN

Fighting the Currents

Leaving the coastline of Cilicia at high tide while still under the dull light of the morning's waning moon had given the big ship an immediate head start and the captain was delighted with the progress they had made on their first full day out at sea. At this speed, he knew that he could ride the north-easterly wind through the night and reach the most northernly point of Cyprus by early morning. He also knew that their progress would slow greatly after that as they would be fighting a slow but steady northern-bound sea current that flowed up the east coast of the island. They would need all the power of this northeastern wind to allow the zig zagging course needed all the way down that coast to Salamis. He had performed this dance with the sea many times in his life and was confident in both the ever-present winds and his ability to use the breezes, even when they did not blow out of the ideal direction.

As darkness fell, the passengers settled in and the ship became quiet. Only the methodical slapping of the swell against the wooden sides as the ship was heard as it plied its way forward. Occasionally, the guffaws and snickering of the contingent of soldiers broke the quiet as well. The soldiers seemed content slurping their wine and telling their stories of war and adventure well into the peaceful evening and Antonius was pleased to see them so relaxed. Experience told him that could change and he wanted no turmoil on his ship curtesy of angry or agitated Romans.

Antonius's heart jumped when he heard the unmistakable *poosh* repeated many times out to the west of the ship that night and in the dim moonlight he caught the spouting of more whales whose sleeping masses bobbed on the surface. The mammoths of the sea were quieted for the night and the captain took it to mean that good fortune would be his on this first leg of the journey.

This ship had two wooden images mounted at the exterior of the front bow. Each was placed on a side of the front protrusion sticking up slightly above the rail and these were purposely mounted near the soldier's quarters. Nightly, the superstitious Romans would lean over the side and rub their hands on the two carved figures, simply for luck. The captain's grandfather had these symbols of popular Roman demigods fashioned and attached there and he named his ship the *Castor and Pollux* after them. Their prominent placing was his father's attempt to alleviate any seagoing fears and to show a level of respect to the Roman legends.

The captain was foggily aware of the account in the Jewish Torah of the happenings in the Garden of Eden and when inevitably challenged by traveling Jewish Pharisees about the pagan images adorning his ship, he simply explained that these carvings were just a lowly infidel's interpretation of the Cain and Abel story. He very much enjoyed the befuddled and frustrated look of the ultra-religious at this reference and it did his merry heart good to see them stomp away with no retort, pulling on their beards, confusion in their eyes and muttering to themselves.

Throughout the Great Sea, the names of Castor and Pollux were used often and were touted as helping those who were in trouble when at sea. Antonius was very pleased that his well detailed figures impressed the onlookers in all ports and were admired for their artistry.

Antonius was not a superstitious man and he was more than a bit skeptical of such legends, but the important thing was that his passengers often mentioned the feeling of safety with the presence of these two, so he regularly had them cleaned and painted. If their mere presence on the front of the ship made his passengers more comfortable, then they were doing their job and he was satisfied with that. Beyond that, if they were involved or somehow did intercede in times of trouble, well then, that was a benefit he would eagerly accept and appreciate.

Throughout the night, the captain and his son alternated between checking the direction of the ship by the guiding stars and short periods of sleep. This was the routine that they had developed over the years and now he could only sleep in a succession of two-or-three-hour naps which gave him all the rest he needed.

When morning broke and because the winds had been strong and steady, easily maintaining the speed of the ship, the northern tip of the finger of Cyprus appeared to the south and they had only to make a slight correction to the east to give themselves a safe distance off the rocks. The ship began to slow noticeably even though the wind remained steady and Antoine looked over the side and recognized the seaweed and flotsam that clearly identified the expected counter-flow.

To overcome the opposing current, they began their curious dance of tacking by heading hard to the east under partial sails, making very little south-ward headway except to move away from the island. They held this course for three full hours, moving away until they were out of sight of the island. This was then followed by a barked order from Antoine and the crew exploding into motion. Almost immediately the ship was in full sail going directly down-wind, due southwesterly at a good steady pace. This tactic of slipping slowly away from the island followed by returning under full sail would be repeated many times over the next few days and repeating it meant that they would eventually claw their way south to put them in the bay outside Salamis.

The captain noticed that in the short breaks, his son still found time to seek out Saul and keep the animated conversations going. As before, the two men were under the watchful eye of the Saul's younger sister.

Miriam was thoroughly enjoying the fresh sea breezes and the warm sun and would only retire into the small tent if one of the Roman soldiers was wandering the ship or came close. She was a tallish girl, slender and slightly awkward which added to her appealing femininity and her curly black hair falling alongside her face accented her dark eyes which were constantly averted from the front of the ship. It was obvious that she and her brother did not want anything to do with these rough men.

What was also growing painfully obvious was that many of the soldiers were intent on drinking their way to the next port. Because they were entirely engaged in that endeavor, their intrusions to other parts of the ship were limited.

As the noise level of the drinking men increased, the large family situated between Saul and Miriam and the front of the ship were also being careful to keep a distance, no doubt aware of the reputation of military men. A petite teenage girl traveling with them was seldom seen outside the tent structure, a wise precaution by the husky mother who did not mind staring down any soldier.

The middle-aged and well-muscled matriarch of this household was obviously the one in charge of the family group and the captain's evaluation of her was that she was very capable of using her heavy pots and strong arms on these soldiers if the need ever arose.

To this point, all had remained calm with the soldiers and the observant captain felt indebted to the quiet commander and his huge, blond enforcer. It helped that the massive soldier did not join in the wine drinking revelry, remaining completely sober while observing all the activities on the ship. He wandered from the upper deck only to watch closely as the crew took up or unleashed the massive sails. He occasionally asked a question of Antoine in his heavily-accented and broken Latin and seemed to be truly engrossed in the new adventure that was now his life.

Antoine had stopped and chatted with the leader of the soldiers a few times and at those times, the large, blond man stayed close and listened intently as the centurion relaxed and his tongue loosened. Both the huge man and Antoine became enthralled with the riveting stories of military conquest that the commander told, many of which the giant had never heard before. It came as a complete surprise to him that his captain had fought the wild Celts on the islands of Britannia for the giant's ancestors had also fought off the ferocious raids of these savage hordes from the North Sea.

Antoine learned that the centurion was most recently a captain in the Germania wars and it was there that his large battalion had surrounded a small group of the colossus-like men with their vastly superior numbers. His Roman general had made the risky choice of offering the giants the opportunity of life rather than death and this time the depleted enemies surprised them. Shockingly, they chose to surrender rather than employing their usual tactic of running wildly to their own slaughter for the sake of some sort of honor that apparently only death bestows.

This centurion had subsequently been rewarded for his bravery in those wars with this young man as his personal charge. He had given him his Roman name of Julian and then proceeded to enjoy the novelty, companionship and unchallenged protection that Julian provided. Theirs had grown into a mutually satisfying relationship and the commander had come to recognize an intelligence and complexity in his compatriot that far exceeded the other men under his command. Along with cleverness, this mammoth man possessed an unquenchable curiosity of the new world he was now traveling. He seemed at peace with his new life as a Roman soldier, even though he was technically a captive, and he was genuinely excited when he was told that he would be accompanying his commander, "his new friend" to far off parts of the empire.

Dawn broke on the third morning to the scurrying of the crew as they flew about tying lines and gingerly wrapping and then unwrapping the sails, all under the hand motions and soft-spoken directions of Antoine. The ship responded obediently and they zig-zagged away from the coast and then hurried back, each time gaining many miles southward. Antonius recognized the familiar landmarks each time they came close to Cyprus and knew that they had yet many more miles to go that day.

This monotonous corkscrew rhythm had been slightly interrupted in the early morning hours when one of the three soldiers that Antonius had earlier identified as trouble, began wandering the ship in a drunken stupor. It was apparent that he and his two likeminded cohorts had spent the entire night draining the keg and when the other two had finally collapsed into an inebriated coma, this character decided that his reveling was not yet complete.

Just before dawn, he began calling on the large family to come out and play their music and dance and he was getting frustrated at the lack of response. It was dawn when the mother finally emerged from her tent with a large vase in her hand and began yelling in a broken tongue at the drunken soldier. The tent door of the Roman commander swung open at the disturbance and the irritated commander barked out quickly and forcefully to the inebriated soldier. The wobbly soldier completely ignored him.

The drunk continued to make his swaying advances toward the well-prepared woman and in response, she had thrown back her wrapping robe and her muscular arm drew back menacingly, holding the metal pot high.

Another quick military command sent the massive Julian bounding down the steps to the site of the disturbance. The staggering soldier, deciding that he was now invincible, foolishly took a mighty swing at Julian, missing wildly and almost falling. He then thought it would be better to take a run at him.

Julian niftily stepped aside, grabbed his shoulder and yanked, spinning the surprised soldier around and facing directly away. Julian then reached down, wrapping a large arm around the waist of the soldier and picked him up and set him on his hip like a toddler. The waving of arms and kicking of legs of this brawler riding on the big man's hip made a truly comical picture which started the big lady laughing loudly. She then began taunting the captive mercilessly with all manner of threats and insults.

"You child of a dung beetle, come back here and I will rearrange you," she yelled.

Soon the rest of the ship was howling in laughter as well, much to the embarrassment of the captured and totally helpless soldier. Julian turned and easily toted the limp soldier up the stairs where the captive, finally realizing the absurdity of the picture he presented, also began to laugh loudly at himself. The unamused commander had a rusty iron shackle ready and Julian held his captive tight as he was chained to the ship's railing by his foot. A day in the hot sun, along with the waning effects of the wine, would be punishment enough for this performance.

Antonius nodded his thanks to the legionnaire and big Julian and received agreeing nods back.

The captain was very impressed with the ease of the action and made a quick mental note of this scenario, contemplating the possibility of finding himself a giant enforcer like this. Such a creature would be priceless both for the heavy chores on the ship and the added benefit of security in times like he had just witnessed.

CHAPTER FOURTEEN

Cyprus

Because of its position in the eastern end of the Great Sea, the large and ancient island of Cyprus, encircled with cities and ports on all sides, was the natural stopping off place for almost all nearby maritime travel, regardless of the direction. Paradoxically, and no doubt because of this convenient location, it had been a repeating chapter in almost every conquering nation's history, each considering it as belonging to them until such time as the next vanquisher arrived.

The Cypriots had a curious semi-subservient relationship with their many conquerors. Over the centuries, they had seen their coastal cities dominated by the Phoenicians, Assyrians, Persians, Greeks, and now the Romans. The much-celebrated arriving and then abrupt and much more humble exiting of foreign governors was not that unusual to them, nor in the long run unexpected, and generally the profitable business of the island was not seriously interrupted simply by chiseling a new name above the ruling regime's headquarters.

Within the last one hundred years, Cyprus had come under Roman domination and therefore had been claimed as a Roman province in 58 BC, only to be given away immediately to Egypt as a gift to Cleopatra and her sister, by Mark Antony. It returned to Rome with the climatic defeat of Mark Antony at the Battle of Actium in 30 BC in the latest episode of its convoluted history and now was prospering quite well under its present situation. Wisely, most citizens had no wish to break the peace they now enjoyed with any reckless notions of freedom or rebellion.

Although they were thankful for their continuing affluence, there was a slight measure of embarrassment among Cypriots over the ease with which they were repeatedly conquered but, as expected, that discomfort passed quickly.

The city of Salamis was situated on the mouth of the slow moving Pedieos River which flowed through flat agricultural land on the east edge of the island. Originally, Salamis was only important as one of the ten Greek city states on the island but the construction of a large sea wall extending into the deeper water had made it the most attractive harbor for larger ships looking to resupply and obtain cargo. For this reason, two centuries before, the Greeks had chosen Salamis as their seat of government on the island and in those times, it had slowly grown and prospered. With the emergence of the Roman fleet and their preference of the more accessible southern shoreline, the capital of government was moved to Paphos on that side of the island, leaving Salamis much more sedate and colonial. Some would even call it backward.

Although this meant that a large amount of the commerce that followed the Roman ships went elsewhere, Salamis remained a major port for connecting all the northeastern countries along the shores of the Great Sea. This partial isolation meant that it retained its Hellenistic atmosphere rather than succumbing to the less amiable Roman environment and therefore the city maintained a charming and at times, a warm and turbulent mix of the flavors of the exotic eastern countries of Syria, Cilicia, Persia and Judea. Because of this multi-cultural freedom, its population was dominated by citizens of these countries who had taken up permanent residence in the peaceful and protective city. It was a spread-out metropolis and extended for over a mile along the shoreline, giving it a rambling, unorganized feel.

The same current that the *Castor and Pollux* was fighting, the slow continual movement of water which flowed northward along Salamis, proved a great blessing for the residents of the city for it provided a rich and reliable supply of fresh fish caught just offshore and, thankfully, this bounty was there no matter the season. Whenever there was a war or famine that forced desperate and fleeing people to move out of their ancestral homelands, Cyprus became a favored haven. As a result, the city of Salamis was populated with large enclaves of citizens of other countries and nationalities with many of the immigrating families having been in Cyprus for many hundreds of years now. Of these, many had married locally and had disappeared into the well-mixed population, long ago abandoning their practice of separation into racial or national districts. A few, because of their more intense religions and traditions, had maintained an area of the city as their own and rarely intermingled outside those self-imposed boundaries.

Such was the Jewish district.

The Jews had first appeared in Salamis as early as 500 BC when a few families had escaped the onslaught and captivity of Nebuchadnezzar of Babylon that had descended on Israel. Rather than staying there and eventually being carried away to Babylon, they heeded the prophetic warnings, preserved their wealth, and prudently slipped away to Cyprus.

By the time the Medes and Persians had convinced a few thousand Jews to return to their homeland, rebuild Jerusalem and restore their once grand Temple, these Cypriot Jewish families were firmly entrenched in a very comfortable, peaceful life of their own. In fact, they had established their own version of Jewish culture in Salamis and as a result, they were not open to leaving such a peaceful and prosperous setting to return to the precarious mountaintops of Judea, no matter what they dutifully chanted every Sabbath in the synagogue. Their wisdom was vindicated when only a hundred years later, Judea was once again overtaken by swarms of Greeks. Two centuries after that, the Cypriot Jews were once again proven correct upon the arrival of the dominating Romans.

Similar Jewish communities were to be found in almost every city along the Great Sea now, with the largest in Alexandria and each community had expanded over the years by natural family growth and a fresh and constant supply of emigrants leaving the ongoing and often dangerous wars in their homeland. The destruction of the original Temple, followed by the rebuilding of another of lesser quality than Solomon's gleaming edifice had produced only a feigned attraction to their ancient homeland for most and past a few pilgrimages to that holy mount, Jews tended to remain fully entrenched in their newly adopted countries.

What kept them separated as Jews in the foreign lands was the never-ending demands and varying degrees of dedication to keeping their old traditions, albeit with many convenient accommodations and various local alterations.

They were reminded weekly in synagogue that theirs was a higher calling, a voluntary severance from all others to be a national representation of the One true God and as such to hold themselves above the debaucheries of the world. This special calling was inescapable and that was plain from the teachings of Moses which were continually punctuated by the grand tales and miraculous heavenly deliverances told in their homes and repeated in their schools. To most, their strict but comforting religious lifestyle did not demand them to be physically present in Jerusalem.

For the present time, to maintain this separation in foreign lands and to have a place to develop their devotion to that God, they developed the phenomena of the synagogue. These were local meeting places where Torah was taught, Jewish traditions were rehearsed and encouraged and where the community gathered for all its socializing. This successful footprint was repeated throughout the empire wherever Jewish communities existed. Besides allowing Jews to practice their religion without having to constantly travel to the Temple in Israel, synagogues soon began to be the center of all aspects of Jewish life in the dispersion, even containing local Jewish courts set up to settle the community's disputes and apply Jewish religious laws to its congregants. This was an incredibly important service that kept many Jews out of the local and much more brutal jails. These local courts were the lower "Sanhedrin," and each community had its own copy of the original one in Jerusalem.

The importance of the synagogue to Judaism had developed in the time when the Greeks, with their modern Hellenistic ideas and culturally seducing practices, had permeated the nation of Israel to the point that they had almost replaced all the ancient Hebrew ways and traditions, starting with the growing ascendency of the exact and precise Greek language over Hebrew. Soon Greek-speaking Jews were bandying about such ideas as fairness, equality, and even democracy: alluring ideas no doubt and thoughts that severely challenged the Jewish reality. Their flashy and appealing "civilized" culture aggressively targeted the ancient beliefs and traditions, even influencing the Temple priests, some who shockingly began bathing in the public baths and participating in Greek-style gymnasiums. Many priests began wearing foreign fashions and modern Greek tunics around the Temple in a show of modern and enlightened thinking which confused many other Jews who thought that they were not faithfully protecting the sanctity of the Temple.

This Hellenistic encroachment became rampant in Jerusalem and the leading priestly families of that city, men who were expected to be keepers of Jewish tradition, were soon being appointed for political reasons by the ruling Greeks who, wisely and sneakily, were much more interested in dealing with compliant and modern-thinking holy men. It soon was evident that these chosen families were extremely grateful to hold this lucrative and influential position and before long, the sanctity of the office of High Priest itself became a laughingstock to both the Greeks and the Jews. Rumors of the most despicable violations of the purity of the Temple by the irreverent Greeks were spreading throughout the country, followed closely by questions of why this was being tolerated. Most vexing to pious Jews was that the priests themselves were not only not incensed, but even involved in the desecrations.

After one particularly vile abomination, a single outraged and pious family from the hills of Samaria reacted violently, slaying the Greek violator and starting the Maccabean revolt. A religious uprising was not anticipated by the governing Greeks or their urban Jewish cronies and it spread quickly and violently through the towns and villages outside of Jerusalem. The sweeping outrage of the common Jews caught the militarily-declining Greeks in a weakened condition and the defiant family organized and led a successful rebellion. It was a Jewish revival of sorts which resulted in many slain and headless Jewish priests and rapidly retreating Greek military men. The rebellion also established nearly one hundred years of Judean independence and expansion which had not been seen since the kingdom of Solomon. This was between the years of 150 BC to 50 BC.

This ended, as many other prosperous times did for Israel, in disastrous internal strife which once again allowed easy domination of the divided Jews. This time, that domination was curtesy of the expanding Romans.

The local ruler that the Romans appointed was Herod, a half-Jewish, half-Idumean building genius installed as a reward for his support of Augustus and for serving as his general in this region. The promotion from general to royalty gave Herod access to incredible amounts of taxation money and he craftily used his new-found wealth to win favor with his Jewish population, mainly by remodeling the Temple to close to its former glory.

By the time the Temple was restored to a place of Jewish pride, the synagogues had already been established as the local place of worship and had become the most important and everyday part of the Jewish religious scene both in Jerusalem and around the world. The Romans understood that the Temple was a special place to the Jews but in a nonthreatening, festive and ceremonial religious context and they saw no danger in its restoration and expansion. Its presence actually helped keep the peace.

As talented students of revolt and conspiracy, the Romans knew instinctively that it was in the synagogues that the political intrigue and call to action would take place for that is where the sermons that were full of defiance, religious fervor and stubborn devotion to their ancient writings would be heard. They also knew that these sermons always stirred strong feelings of national liberation under a powerful king the Jews called the Messiah. This prophetic rumor had been a constant fear of their client king Herod who was always on the lookout for the One who would displace him. Nowadays, the Romans shrewdly employed a few willing and well-paid informers to keep them abreast of any developing mutiny stirring in the synagogues. This was a familiar ploy which they used whether the insurrection was taking place in Jerusalem or in the various synagogues throughout the breadth of the empire.

Generally, the Romans regarded their Jews as an industrious and peaceful lot, occasionally infiltrated with a few proponents of national liberty. These radical men were easy to identify for they simply could not keep their intentions quiet.

CHAPTER FIFTEEN

Caleb ben Israel and the
Family Business

One of the Jewish businesses that had been in Salamis for over 120 years belonged to the family of Caleb ben Israel. This was a tight-knit family of well-to-do trading merchants, importing and exporting goods between their home port of Salamis and the major cities of Israel, Syria and Egypt. What had made them consistently successful was the presence of intimate family members, three sons in fact, in the major cities of these countries.

The youngest son, Barnabas, lived in Caesarea and operated in that city and in Jerusalem. A second son, Joshua, lived and worked in Alexandria, Egypt and had become an important part of the half million Jews living in that exotic city. He had recently been appointed to an important post in the Sanhedrin of Alexandria. A third son, Moshe, lived in Antioch of Syria and at times seemed more Persian than Jewish to his siblings. A younger sister was destined to a life at home and she was doted on by her father who deeply loved his devoted but mentally-deprived child.

There was another sister. She was the oldest and was a widowed sister of Barnabas and his brothers. Her name was Mary and she lived in Jerusalem.

All family members were becoming independently wealthy by importing goods from their original home in Cyprus. Their father Caleb had remained there and become the focal point of the extensive trading and importing. This family had learned to only import goods that would sell at large profits and they continually varied their merchandise, their futures not tied to just one product, as were many other importers. As a family, they had discussed specializing in a copper mining business, olive oil shipping, and a few others when these products seemed to be hugely profitable and in large demand, but their wise father suggested that they not do this. He had taught his sons to read the future needs of their customers carefully and then supply that need by buying the excess supplies at a bargain from other ports where each other brother was located. The key to this plan was the constant communication in the form of letters sent weekly on ships and these communiques alerted each family member of upcoming business opportunities. The energetic father oversaw this approach to their business and so he was at the harbor daily in anticipation of one or the other of his sons' pouches. Early in his life he had recognized that communication was becoming very easy as ships were constantly sailing these waters and were almost always successful in their journeys. Some ships had even started a regularly scheduled sailing and that was changing the import/export business completely. Wisely, he encouraged his sons to invest their profits in land and other business opportunities in the countries they were in.

Caleb could not hide his pride in the acumen of each of his sons and watched happily as their abilities to gauge future needs and desired products grew into almost prophetic realms.

Barnabas, his youngest son at twenty-four years, had been sent to Israel to assume the family business there because of the untimely death of the husband of Mary. Her husband had been the family's trusted representative in Jerusalem and in all of Judea and he had been extremely successful, leaving his wife and his sole son, John Mark, independently wealthy.

In the five short years since his brother-in-law's death, Barnabas had himself prospered greatly, purchasing land, expanding the list of reliable customers between Jerusalem and Caesarea, and most importantly, being the great help that his sister Mary had needed. Even though he was young himself, he was especially helpful in being a mentor and friend of her teenage son, John Mark.

Barnabas had widened and solidified his business connections by expanding to other cities in Judea, such as Lydda and Hebron, and there he quickly was becoming a versatile and trusted supplier to many other merchants requiring goods that were not available locally. His weekly letters to his father and brothers contained a steadily growing list of goods that he could import and resell and Caleb was impressed with the eagerness and strong work ethic of his youngest son. From all the feedback he was getting, he understood that the growing success was really a statement to the trust and confidence that the new customers had in this young man. Unlike a great many businessmen, Barnabas had also proven to be a kind and compassionate person, one who could be completely depended upon.

One of the valuable products that Caleb Ben Israel could rely on selling at a profit were the military tents made by Gideon, his old friend from Tarsus. He had recently learned of Gideon's passing when he had ordered more tents for the Roman garrison in Caesarea and he realized that he would dearly miss not only a reliable business cohort, but a kind man who had grown into a friend, even though they had seen each other only sporadically.

Today, he was eager to have Gideon's scholarly son, Saul, arrive in Salamis and to refresh pleasant memories of days gone by with Gideon. Saul was arriving with a shipment of twenty large tents destined for the mobile units of the Roman army in Judea, unique and specialized heavy-duty winter tents, shelters which Caleb had purchased from Gideon's family.

What Saul did not know was that the tents stashed in the ship's hold were to be forwarded on to Barnabas in Caesarea. A simple monetary payment would take place when Saul arrived, the tents would remain aboard the ship and they would be on their way to Caesarea to be received and delivered by Barnabas. A handsome profit was to be made by both families and the army's purchaser would be happy with the efficient delivery of such a needed and hard to procure product.

This was a prime example of another lucrative transaction of the kind that Caleb ben Israel and his family had been conducting for many years. Barnabas would offload the tents and deliver them that same day to the garrison at Caesarea and receive immediate payment.

On his end, Barnabas was to arrange delivery to the *Castor and Pollux* of a bundle of recently acquired and precisely transcribed scrolls, ceremoniously blessed in the inner court of the Temple, each having been lovingly copied by the quill of the most respected scribe of Jerusalem. Scrolls such as these were extremely valuable and much coveted and had been requested by the largest synagogue in the Jewish community of Alexandria, all as per the last letter of his brother Joshua.

Moshe, in Antioch of Syria, had also sent a letter to his father, just as he had to his two brothers, asking them to search out a source for fish netting. There had been a fire and the local net-maker was getting older and was not sure if he would bother rebuilding his small factory. From that, Moshe was expecting a shortage of netting and calculated that the price would increase greatly in the Antioch area until a new manufacturer was in place.

At least, all that had been the plan. Since his last letter ordering the twenty tents, almost two months ago now, Barnabas's family had not heard a word from him.

It was understandable that Barnabas could have been busy over Passover as he was a devout and dedicated worshiper and he would undoubtably have been at his sister's home in Jerusalem for that feast, possibly even staying there for quite a time, but it was unlike him to not send a letter pouch with at least a greeting in all this time. That was extremely unsettling for his father.

Generally, almost every ship leaving Caesarea for Cyprus had something from Barnabas for his beloved father and he had never gone this long without a business deal or inquiry dispatched to at least one of the members of his family.

To date, five ships had arrived in Salamis from Caesarea and each brought not a word for Caleb. He generously reasoned that, as in the past, Barnabas may have taken a trip to Hebron or even as far as Damascus to scout out new business opportunities, but he had always informed his father in advance when he would be away. Barnabas had always planned these trips when no pressing shipments were due as well. This break from normalcy was completely out of character for his courteous and respectful son and Caleb was greatly bothered.

There were other, more disturbing rumors that added to Caleb's anxiety concerning Barnabas.

First, there was news circulating of increasing activity by the Roman-hating zealots in the north of Israel and it was well-known that there was a small cluster of these Jewish rebels operating within Jerusalem itself. These were dangerously religious men, zealously patriotic and totally focused on driving out their Roman subjugators, most convinced that this was their life's calling. Such men were aggressive, forceful and often thoroughly disgusted by the lack of passion of their fellow Jews for their cause. They were also constantly attempting to solicit wealthy supporters, financiers such as Barnabas, to their side. A few months previously, Caleb had been approached in Salamis by a supporter of the zealots who was trying to find an offshore supplier of easily hidden weapons, specifically the favored curved scoriae. Caleb had politely and wisely refused to get involved, much to the consternation of the devoted rebel.

He suspected, quite rightly, that such passionate and underground rebels would target one such as his son.

There was also a rumor that another large taxation was coming from the cash-strapped Romans and Caleb wanted to make sure that his sons were not sitting on easily detected bags of money but were only taking payment in hard goods or future orders of other merchandise. These were much harder for the lazy tax collectors to find and levy. This evasive tactic had been successful over the years and generally worked because of his family's ability to acquire and relocate goods without touching the actual products. It had worked well, even though the Romans had graduated to using aggressive locals to collect their taxes., the presumption being that these collaborators would know the particulars of the population and could ferret out the hiding places of taxable goods and coins. The Romans wisely paid these hated collectors a percentage and as expected, the collectors became quite effective, often overly zealous, at squeezing every penny they could out of their beleaguered but elusive Jewish brethren.

By finalizing their deals with "promised" future goods and only taking delivery when needed and reselling those goods as quickly as possible, Caleb and his sons had avoided having on hand large amounts of taxable goods or cash, a strategy that had worked well for them in the past. Of course, they were wise enough to always pay a mediocre portion of tax and this only after much protestation and lamenting. Caleb had written to Barnabas two separate times about this new coming levy and also had no response.

Most disturbing to Caleb was a curious report brought back by a few Jewish friends who had been recent visitors to Judea. These friends had returned excited and rejuvenated in their spirits and were eagerly talking of a new prophet who was causing quite a stir in Jerusalem. Apparently this one had risen in the Galilee and like all the other prophets Caleb had heard about, was declaring Himself to be sent from God. Reports were that He had surrounded Himself with the poor and other equally unremarkable followers, a gaggle of smelly fishermen and even a hated tax collector or two and that He was making a reputation among the disaffected poor of Israel by constantly condemning the respected leaders. This "prophet" was annoyingly elusive and would appear suddenly in Jerusalem at the feasts, lecture in the Temple, get in huge arguments with the leaders and then disappear back to the Galilee.

One of Caleb's trusted neighbors in Salamis had witnessed this so-called seer on a recent visit and was quite enthralled with Him, saying he had seen miraculous "healings" done, even claiming that this One raised a dead man in Bethany, a small town only a day's walk from Jerusalem.

"Impossible," cried an exasperated Caleb, but the neighbor declared it was true.

This report had both bothered and confused Caleb until he asked one of the traveling Pharisees from Jerusalem about it. The Pharisee had informed him and the whole congregation at the synagogue that, yes, there were some apparent miraculous events happening around the self-proclaimed prophet, but the wisest of the Pharisees, and even the High Priest himself, had explained these unusual phenomena. They had declared that this was the work of Beelzebub and that this prophet had a devil that allowed these things to happen. He gravely warned the congregation to keep their distance from such seducing teachers and trust only the Pharisees.

This explanation had started a heated discussion in the Salamis community as a couple of locally respected elders had asked the Pharisee to explain just how good things could be done by the evil one. The extremely zealous but youthful Pharisee had become flustered at this unexpected challenge and his rebuttal was short and simple: to challenge the wisdom of the elders and High Priest was dangerous and bordered on sacrilege, so he would not dignify that question with an answer. Had not the priests been appointed by God himself, he demanded. This quieted the questioners. The answer also satisfied Caleb's curiosity about the prophet but not the anxiousness about his son.

There was more.

The talkative neighbor had also informed Caleb that when he had been at the Temple at the Feast of Tabernacles and heard this prophet, he had seen Barnabas in the crowd and he was listening to Him as well. He had tried to get through the pressing horde to greet the young man, but Barnabas had left when the prophet left, following in the small contingent that seemed to be close to the prophet.

For all these reasons, it was a greatly bothered Caleb ben Israel who waited for the arrival of the *Castor and Pollux*, hopeful that Saul, who he knew had been a leading student in Jerusalem and who had often bragged about being close to the leaders, could help explain just what was happening and provide him some peace of mind. He also knew that Barnabas was scheduled to meet the shipment of tents at Caesarea and hopefully Saul could contact him and even carry the letter of slight rebuke he had written to his son for his puzzling actions.

CHAPTER SIXTEEN

The Ship Arrives in Salamis

It was early in the afternoon when the messenger knocked on Caleb's door and informed him that there was a large, three-masted cargo ship entering the harbor. The sails were down and the small boats were towing it into place along the recently remodeled and repaired sea wall. This rocky wharf provided welcomed shelter from the southern currents and allowed easy access to the ships on a top walkway which eliminated the need of labor-intensive skiffs ferrying cargo back and forth.

Caleb hurried to the docks, a quick fifteen-minute walk from his family home, and arrived just as the last of the lines were being secured to the familiar ship. As he had hoped, it was the *Castor and Pollux*, captained by his old acquaintance and business associate, Antonius. He knew that on board would be both his shipment of tents and Saul of Tarsus.

When the securing of the ship was completed, the mixture of passengers began their preparations to leave. First, the contingent of soldiers, noisily and without asking permission, scampered over the side, leaving all their gear aboard in a disorderly heap. They were obviously returning to the ship and their annoyed commander and big companion kicked their mess into a pile and covered it with a large blanket.

Next came the family. They scurried about, chattering non-stop while gathering up all their belongings and then they helped each other to the top of the sea wall where they lifted their parcels onto their backs and left the harbor and pointing this way and that, very happy to be "home."

Caleb spotted Saul from afar and immediately noticed that this lad had matured significantly in the three years since he had last seen him. He also noted the spotless and expensively fringed robe Saul had put on as he neared the harbor. This was the traditional garb of the Pharisees of Jerusalem and when worn was intended to exact a level of respect and awe from the Jews who recognized it. What Caleb was not expecting was the young lady who emerged from the tent behind Saul, carrying a small sack and who was obviously accompanying Saul.

He waved a warm, quick greeting to the young Pharisee but then went directly to speak to the captain to ensure that his ship was continuing to Caesarea. As far as the captain knew, the twenty large bundles that were below deck were for Caleb and were to be offloaded here in Salamis. He was surprised and pleased to be told that he would make an extra fee by leaving them on board and offloading them at Caesarea instead. Once this arrangement was completed and the fee paid, Caleb turned his attention to Saul.

Originally only business acquaintances, Saul's father and Caleb had grown to know and trust each other as friends. On their previous trips to Jerusalem, Saul or his father, Gideon, would seek out and visit this family anytime that their voyage went through Salamis. The two days it took to provision the ship with fresh water, preserved meats and fresh fruits, plus the time to exchange cargo, was always an enjoyable interlude and gave the opportunity to renew the friendship between the family patriarchs. The warm hospitality offered by Caleb's household was always appreciated and thoroughly enjoyed.

On their first voyage, when Saul was but ten years old, he had met Barnabas who had not yet left home for Jerusalem. Barnabas was five years older than Saul but treated the young boy with a pleasant kindness while showing him around Salamis.

Today, Caleb's first words to Saul were of comfort for the death of Gideon and he spoke tenderly and emotionally of the great friendship that had developed over the many years. As the pretty young lady grew closer, Caleb stopped speaking and looked intently at her.

"Is this Miriam," he blurted with genuine amazement in his voice. He was not expecting her and if asked, his first thought would have been that Saul had married without his knowledge. This was a genuine surprise and he was delighted to see her, at first forgetting that she would be by now grown up for he had met her only on his one visit to Tarsus some eight years prior when she was a mere eleven years old.

Because of his lingering anxieties, Caleb desperately wanted to speak to Saul in private, but Captain Antonius interrupted and called out, informing Saul that they must be ready to continue their voyage on the day after tomorrow-at high tide.

Just before the small group left the docks, Antonius again called out and stressed that would be the third hour of the day, then a third time he shouted to be here mid-morning, no later. The captain had obviously dealt with the problems of late passengers in the past. Everyone waved back and laughed at the good-natured persistence of the captain while making their way into the city.

Caleb's anxieties were not quickly relieved for when the new guests arrived at his home, they were greeted with a large and sumptuous afternoon meal that his wife and servants had prepared. Saul, as was the custom of the Pharisees, stood and recited a long and loud prayer that held the other diner's captive and waiting, after which he requested multiple bowls of fresh water and proceeded to wash his hands repeatedly. At that point, Caleb and the others, obviously having been through this extended performance before, waited no longer and began their feasting.

The Pharisees persisted in performing these obsessive rituals publicly, and as many suspected, they did so to cause conviction and some admiration from less devout Jews. Sometimes, as today, the ostentatious religious routine seemed to have just the opposite, slightly annoying effect.

When the delicious meal was over and Miriam and Caleb's wife retired to the deeper confines of the house, Caleb and Saul strolled to the portico at the back of the sprawling home where they could talk in private while listening to the waves break gently on the nearby rocky shore.

"Saul, you know my son Barnabas is now in Israel and carries on our business there."

Saul nodded knowingly.

"He and I keep in constant communication with every ship from Caesarea by letter pouch, and we have done this for many years now." Caleb waited for Saul's nod of understanding.

"It has been months and there have been five ships come and go and I have received no letters from Barnabas. I am growing very worried as this is very unusual for my son. I do not know what has happened."

Caleb paused, wringing his nervous hands slightly and Saul easily recognized that he was near desperation.

"He knows better than to get involved with the zealots and that seedy bunch, but he is naturally a generous man and as you well know, Judea can be a dangerous and demanding place for a youthful and well-to-do merchant. I think that I would have heard if he were injured or something serious had happened as all his business contacts know me, but I have received no word from them either."

Saul listened patiently to this upset father, scouring his memory for clues from the few times he had encountered Barnabas in Jerusalem. There was nothing he could remember that stood out from the short conversations they had when they met on the streets. He had always thought of Barnabas as a devout man, a successful and wealthy Jew who was enjoying his time in the heart of Judaism. His impressions of him were that he was intelligent and cautious and a man to be trusted, but truthfully, Barnabas was little more than just a passing acquaintance.

His host continued. "I am also very concerned about the upcoming Roman taxation and how we Jews will prepare for that, but nothing about that would account for his not writing."

Caleb paused and then continued in a quiet voice so no others in the house could hear. "One of my neighbors who went to Jerusalem for the Feast of Tabernacles said he saw Barnabas at the Temple but did not get a chance to speak to him. Apparently, Barnabas was listening to some self-made prophet and," Caleb looked around conspiratorially, "then he followed the prophet out of the Temple."

Caleb whispered to Saul, "Do you know anything about this prophet named Jesus?"

Saul had listened reservedly until the mention of the name Jesus. A deeply held contempt for the many deceivers of Israel began to rise within him and it was all he could do to maintain a dignified response.

"I have indeed heard of Jesus, although I have never met him myself," replied Saul.

In Jerusalem, Saul's daily study routine and his newly assigned task of teaching the younger students, along with his personal avoidance of the common markets and dirty streets where this prophet was said to frequent, had not allowed for even their casual meeting. Attending the Temple on festive occasions with the unsophisticated hordes of pilgrims was something he had also managed to avoid, simply by attending to the Temple rituals very early in the mornings and then, quickly leaving before most others had even arrived.

One of Saul's numerous frustrations with common untaught Jewry, quite possibly his most biting irritation, was how easily his Jewish countrymen accepted the unceasing array of false teachers as substitutes for what the Jews really needed. Saul knew that what they required was a deeper devotion to the Law-just as he and all fervent Pharisees had completely committed themselves to. That principle was not complicated, a truth he shouted at them constantly on the street corners.

Saul was aware that Jerusalem's leaders, both Sadducee and Pharisee, had confronted Jesus and quite uselessly debated and questioned Him on His doctrine and His strange and out of character actions. Getting nowhere, they had declared Him false and illegitimately born. All genuine scholars knew that there was nothing good that could come out of Nazareth.

It was evident that Jesus attracted only the most common of followers, mostly the poor and sickly, and the majority of those were naïve and easily confused. Anyone who fell under His spell was clearly not educated in the Law and were therefore easily deluded by the appeal of the unexplainable powers He possessed.

Caleb listened intently as Saul condemned this upstart "prophet" for His arrogant treatment of the High Priest and the leaders of Jerusalem, even rudely calling them "descendants of the wicked one." It was clear that Jesus was unaware, or willingly ignorant of the importance of these leaders and it was also plain that He did not understand the reverence Moses had demanded for these positions. Worse yet, it seemed He just did not care. He had spoken openly about the Temple being destroyed and, Saul admitted accusingly, and He seemed to enjoy that thought far too much.

Saul's words came in a forceful deluge and he kept talking until he felt sure that Caleb completely understood the dangers of these types of men. Just as importantly, Saul wanted Caleb to recognize that it was the Pharisees and their perfect keeping of the Law that would lead to the ultimate salvation and restoration of Israel, but he seemed to lose Caleb's attention when he kept repeating that well-worn and much echoed pronouncement.

Caleb, again bothered by the continual self-promotion of the Pharisees, interrupted Saul and said, "Promise me, as a family friend, that you will search out Barnabas and see what has happened to him. You may want to ask my daughter, Mary, if she knows anything for I have not heard from her recently either. She lives in Jerusalem close to your Rabbi Gamaliel's house."

Mary was his oldest child and she and her husband had gone to Judea over ten years ago as the first branch of the family business. After her husband had fallen ill and suddenly died, Mary chose to stay in her beautiful mansion in Jerusalem and raise her only son there.

With that solemn promise made to Caleb and all other business matters taken care of, Saul and Miriam relaxed and enjoyed the hospitality of the elderly couple, who easily and instantly became warm friends.

Miriam took an unexpected and deep interest in the youngest of their children, a girl of eleven. She was easily recognized as slow, struggling just to learn to speak and was totally dependent on her doting parents. When Miriam tenderly hugged the daughter and softly stroked her hair while softly singing a Psalm of Hashem's undying love, the young thing's eyes filled with tears at the unsolicited warmth she was receiving. The young girl clung to Miriam's arm devotedly throughout the rest of the visit.

When encountering such people, Saul felt no compassion for them at all, wondering just who's sin had caused such malformation.

He made a mental note to speak to the misplaced sympathy and devotion of Miriam when they were alone. Jerusalem society looked upon such unfortunates infinitely more harshly than his sister had just shown.

Early in the morning of their third day and just as they were preparing to leave the comfortable home, Caleb again cornered Saul and reminded him about their previous conversation and once more gained an assurance that Saul would indeed locate Barnabas immediately upon arrival in Caesarea. He would put him in touch with his father, he assured.

All seemed well, but when the two couples strolled toward the harbor, Saul noticed the restlessness behind the easy smiles of Caleb and his wife. He recognized the unease, remembering the loneliness in his own father's face each time he put his young son on a ship in Tarsus and his heart was moved at the memory of his father's great emotional upset and personal sacrifice each time he had left.

As the hand-rowed boats strained and tugged the large *Castor and Pollux* away from the seawall and into the northwestern current, Saul and Miriam waved their final goodbyes to Caleb and his wife, who watched until the big ship was out of sight.

The trust shown him by this couple made Saul proud to be a Pharisee for he had a feeling that such reliance was due to their confidence in his religious practices. Often, such thoughts permeated Saul's thinking and they always warmed him and filled him with pleasure. As he had done many times before, he inwardly rededicated himself to the task of meticulously following Moses and the Law for this was the very fountain of all the admiration he was receiving.

Of that, he was sure.

CHAPTER SEVENTEEN

The Eastern Voyage to Caesarea

A single sail of the main three was raised on the big ship and that was set at an awkward angle. The combination of a steady northeast current and a countering breeze pushing southwest required this setting and with the help of the straining rudders, this would give the ship a slow but certain southeastern progress.

With every hour and every hard-fought mile, the bobbing ship was not just leaving the modern but uninspiring island of Cyprus behind, it was nearing the shores of a historic land that was the birthplace of some of the earth's most ancient and hallowed cultures. It was approaching the home of archaic civilizations steeped in bygone histories, the source of legends and tales as old as time and replete with great accounts of both faithfulness and disobedience. The looming coastlines spoke of great kingdoms and historic rulers, giants and giant slayers, famous conquerors and the remnants of the conquered, all of which had taken place upon the mystical mountains and within the deep valleys just east of sandy coastlines which made up the farthest eastern reaches of the Great Sea.

The captain had set the course for many miles north of Caesarea, aiming where he knew the easily seen Mount Carmel would appear. He did this so that he could use the wind from the north to push him southward along the tame coastline into the peaceful and thickly walled harbor of that modern city. The spring winds were thankfully remaining constant and their progress, although slow, remained steady.

The captain called on his passengers individually and mentioned to all aboard that at this slow pace, their voyage would take five or six days. Although this was not totally unexpected, it was still annoying to the impatient Saul. That meant that both the upcoming Sabbath and the Feast of Pentecost would come and go while they were journeying at sea.

Saul had originally hoped that the time between his father's death and his returning to Jerusalem would not have taken as long as it had. Regrettably, he had already passed up two of the three holidays that Moses's Law commanded Jewish men to celebrate at the Temple and missing those celebrations was a major disappointment for one intent on observing these holidays exactly as commanded. This was a devotion to the traditions he had learned at the feet of Gamaliel and which he remained determined to fulfill in every aspect, proudly aware that his stance set him apart from many of his Jewish brethren. Sadly, most Jews were much less obedient, plus they did not seem too bothered by foregoing any prescribed feast day, whether their excuse be valid or flimsy. As one could predict, Saul did not hesitate to call out his Jewish brethren on this and other of their failures, often pointing to his own precise record. The Pharisee Saul found it extremely satisfying to know that Hashem could not possibly find any spot or blemish in him.

As the ship settled into a steady and rocking progress, the passengers on board also eased their way into the crossing and slowly began to appear outside their small tents. The eight Roman soldiers were back on board but were much more subdued, either because of strict orders or, most likely, needing rest and recuperation from their two days on shore complete with the resulting head-aches. The Cypriot family had been replaced by three different groups in three smaller tents and Saul and Miriam remained just below the captains' quarters, as before.

After the initial assignments of the crew and the rigging of the sails was completed, there was little to do but be vigilant. Antoine soon found his way over to the railing beside Saul's tent and from his impatient shuffling, it was obvious he had something on his mind. Saul looked up from reading his small scroll and greeted him, himself eager for more conversation to help deal with the monotony of sailing.

Antoine's surprising question came without any preamble. "Saul, what is the Messiah and why is He so special for the Jewish people?"

Saul was taken back, genuinely astounded at this query from Antione, a Gentile who had shown little previous interest in the details of the Jewish religion. Rather smugly, Saul considered himself an expert on this very question as hardly a day went by that Messiah was not discussed and investigated in the exhaustive teachings of the Pharisees. Indeed, the ultimate goal of all the dedication of the Pharisees was not just to please God, but to please Him to the point that He would send Messiah.

Saul began his ready and well-rehearsed reply to Antoine by speaking about the greatness of this future king who would be in the royal line of the famous King David and who would powerfully overthrow any conquerors and kingdoms that oppressed the Jews.

Noticing no reaction from Antoine except a blank, uncomprehending stare, Saul hesitated, then began again by emphasizing how Messiah would enhance and re-establish the importance of the Law and how He would judge and condemn all those that violated it, including the Romans, whose name he said in a whisper while looking askance toward the front of the ship.

Again, no visible response or any sign of understanding from Antoine.

Saul was growing a little louder with each sentence and Antoine could tell that his level of passion was growing: this was obviously a very important subject for Saul. The description he was giving was one of greatness, of strength and of power. Although the passionate words were directed at Antoine, the increased volume was now catching the attention of the ship and because of the lack of understanding in Antoine, Saul was getting a little frustrated and his rooster-strutting had returned.

Saul suddenly paused and looked at Antoine intently, curious about such a question. "Why do you ask about our Messiah," he asked abruptly.

Antoine looked around, almost like he was conspiring with Saul.

"Well, when I was helping those two men come aboard," and he pointed to two new travelers in the middle portion of the ship, "I asked them where they were going and they told me that they were going to Jerusalem because the Messiah had been crucified there and then resurrected. They said they had to get there because He was alive again and was appearing to those who followed Him."

The directness with which Antoine blurted out this news caught Saul off guard.

"I can understand the Romans wanting to kill anyone who would do the things you say the Messiah would do for He evidently would defeat the Romans easily, but these men said that it was the Jewish leaders and the elders in Jerusalem who wanted Him killed." Antoine's voice trailed off. "That I don't understand."

It suddenly dawned on Antoine that Saul's acquaintances in Jerusalem were the group being accused for Saul had often mentioned his closeness to the most important men of Jerusalem.

Now, Antoine was sincerely confused. His question had unintentionally included a probing of Saul's personal stance on these events, even sounding like a criticism, and an unintended tension had just erupted between them.

Saul was immediate in his defense of the much-learned and politically important brethren in the city of Jerusalem. Not questioning the possibility that something like a crucifixion had happened and that it probably was sanctioned by the High Priest and the elders, he replied, "If such a sacrilege as you speak would have been tried on the real Messiah, God would have immediately destroyed those opposed to Him. Our prophets say that the angels watch over Him lest He dash His foot. No harm can come to the true Messiah." Saul's hands and arms were waving about wildly to emphasize his statements. "If a crucifixion was accomplished, well, that proves that this was just another false prophet. The elders were absolutely correct in whatever judgment they sought fit to bring on Him."

The vehemence and intensity with which he had responded, not to mention the volume, surprised Antoine and caught the attention of Miriam who looked up quickly from her bowl of dates. This outburst was certainly a departure from the sedate Saul that only a few days ago had spoken so rationally with Antoine.

Upon observing this emotionally charged exchange, Miriam was again reminded of the differences she had been noticing between the calm and relaxed Saul of Tarsus and the fiery, passionate Saul of Jerusalem. The further they progressed from her quiet home town and its easygoing atmosphere, the more she realized that her brother's heart had long ago been captured by the religious excitement and fervency of the city she would soon call home.

Truth be told, Miriam was a little bothered and almost embarrassed by what she had just heard on the ship.

After a long and uncomfortable pause, Antoine again spoke.

"Well, those two travelers certainly seemed sincere, but they may be just confused. Maybe you could speak with them and help them out in their misunderstanding." He was pointing to two men in front of a midship tent who, curiously, were studying Saul and Antoine intently.

Antoine was becoming extremely curious, even a little excited to see how this would play out, but he also wanted to defuse the tension that his question had created. "Is that not the calling of your particular sect, enlightenment of the Jews," he chided with an attempt at humor.

Saul looked over at the two men disparagingly, inwardly disgusted that once again, ignorant and uncommitted Jews were so easily led astray by any prophet or self-proclaimed holy man. There seemed to be a never-ending supply of those who were easily duped by anyone desiring a following. After a few moments, his ire subsided somewhat and he finally decided to take Antoine's request as a compliment and not the challenge that his quick temper had reacted to.

Quite by coincidence, Saul recently had a great awakening of his own. He realized that it was becoming his duty as one of the rising and elite leaders in Jerusalem and one who, without any doubt in his mind, represented the best of the Jewish nation around the world, to protect the Law and the Mosaic traditions from self-important interlopers and false messiahs. Yes, he decided, he would accept this responsibility as a challenge and he would quickly correct the two travelers.

It was his life's calling. Again, of this, he was convinced.

CHAPTER EIGHTEEN

Dealing with Law Breakers

Secretly, not yet daring to speak to anyone else about it, Saul had been pondering a very radical concept. He had fleeting thoughts that Israel's success as a nation may depend on the eventual eradication of any weak or troublemaking Jews who would dare challenge the established leadership or who refused to follow the Law. He went so far in his thinking as to accept that if it meant using the help of the powerful but unsuspecting Romans, so be it. Saul was aware that many less intense Pharisees would not agree with that view and he suspected, no he was sure, that included his respected teacher, Gamaliel. For that reason, Saul had kept such extreme thoughts very private and deeply buried. The idea of such militant action, as much as it may be needed in the future, still frightened him slightly and just how this much-needed purification of Judaism would eventually happen was not yet perfectly clear to him, but he was convinced that Hashem only respected complete and blind dedication and would reward only those who were the most faithful and committed. Hashem, much like himself, did not respect anyone who did not live with anything short of that level of devotion, or as he had heard it called, "fanaticism" and of this, he was also sure. The fact that he and Hashem were in total agreement on that matter, also pleased him greatly.

In practice, the longstanding collaboration between the Roman Empire and the High Priest of Jerusalem had allowed the Jews a generous "freedom" to practice their religion with minimal interference. For this liberty, the elders were expected to keep their population controlled and peaceful for the Romans. As part of that control, they had forbidden the Jews to kill each other, whether for religious penalty or as capital punishment for criminal activities. The Romans reserved that unsavory right for themselves and, without question, they were very good at that task.

Many patriots in Israel saw this as a deal with the devil himself and the leadership had an ongoing struggle just to keep the various factions of zealots from rebelling against them as well as their Roman captors. Most Jews well knew that they kept their lofty positions only as a reward for their collaboration.

Added to all that convoluted political intrigue, the crafty Romans recognized that lingering just beneath the façade of feigned brotherhood, there existed a vicious loathing that the Jews had for other Jews who held opposing religious views. Knowing that, they had wisely forbidden them the right of punishing each other over what the Romans considered trivial religious superstitions. It was a fact that the ferocity of the verbal arguments about the proper way to wash one's hands even confounded many good and observant Jews, so the savage physical punishments purported for each other over similar details of their religion was completely beyond understanding for even the most curious Roman.

What the Romans did understand very well was that the fiery Jewish zealots, although quiet just now, were determined to rise up in revolt eventually and copying their heroic Maccabees, free the country from any oppression, whether that oppression be by Romans or by misguided and high-ranking Jews. These patriots believed that only their rebellious, sometime suicidal actions would hurry the coming of Messiah. They would be His soldiers and His strong arm.

This uneasy and persistent balancing act, constantly stoked with unceasing internal religious disagreements, kept the leaders in Jerusalem in a state of continual tension, deftly attempting to appease each offshoot, and with each faction being convinced that they were the only ones promoting the true intentions of God.

Miriam overheard the conversation between Saul and Antoine and because her rational mind was still unhindered by obsessive and blinded commitment to one dogma, she could easily predict the actions of her brother should he speak to the two men Antoine had mentioned. She grimaced at the thought.

Over the last months, Miriam had listened to Saul's jaundiced descriptions of the differing factions inhabiting Jerusalem's streets and synagogues and even as an uninvolved outsider, she had easily recognized that each sect was completely entrenched in the narrow thinking of their group with absolutely no ability to understand the other. Knowing this, she could see nothing but a very loud argument and trouble ahead for Saul and the two travelers.

Up to this point, all the notorious Jewish infighting had only been rumors in her peaceful faraway world, but she was afraid that she would now witness a major confrontation of unbending Jewish brethren and that thought made her just as queasy as did the rolling of the waves.

It was only a few short hours after that, following multiple hand washings to ensure his cleanliness, and after donning his most impressive Pharisee's robe, that Saul made his way to the other side of the deck and approached the men in question. Antoine watched from the upper perch of his father's cabin, busily tying and retying a certain knot in a totally unnecessary rope.

Miriam, whose gentle pleadings were unable to stop her brother, winced.

"Brethren," Saul started, noticing immediately that they were not in the least impressed with his intricate garb. As a matter of fact, they barely acknowledged him. Both men did not seem interested in a conversation and their quick look at each other seemed to be a guarded warning. The two simply responded to Saul with a silent, nodded greeting.

"I understand that you are traveling to Jerusalem, as I am," Saul started, again receiving only a faint glance of recognition from the two.

"It is a shame that we are missing the celebration of first fruits, would you not say, as this is such a blessed time in Jerusalem," Saul said in an obvious attempt to draw them into the conversation.

Again, no response other than another nodded acknowledgement.

"The captain's son tells me that you are going to see a great teacher." Once again, Saul's statement resulted only in a guarded glance between the two travelers.

"I am from Jerusalem and have been away for a while attending to the burial of my father and am not aware of the happenings there. Please tell me what has happened in my absence that concerns you so much about this teacher."

Saul had finally blurted it out, beginning to be annoyed with their lack of response and their wariness.

One of the men, a tall balding man, stood up from the bundle on which he was seated and inspected Saul and his sparkling garb intensely. He then turned and gazed out over the vast sea as if he were deciding whether to speak to him. Once more he refocused his attention back on Saul and his gleaming tunic for a much longer time, finally looking out to sea and slowly and very deliberately walking away. He followed the rail to the front of the ship and did not look back.

Saul felt the sting of this blatant rejection immediately and not being accustomed to an important Pharisee, one such as himself, being treated with insignificance, he had an immediate surge of anger. He turned his attention to the other man who had remained seated and who was also assessing Saul's costume. Saul realized from the scowl that this man's assessment was not one of admiration as well. It was painfully obvious that these men not only did not give any status to him, but they seemed to have a disgust of what he represented.

"Well, what do you have to say?" Saul finally barked, looking this one in the eye, almost expecting him to also refuse any conversation.

The man kept his gaze on Saul but was less dismissive, looking the blue and white garments up and down for a moment and then he gave a slow, knowing nod of recognition to Saul.

The Pharisee's mood seemed to mellow a little but his impatience was still growing. Saul then noticed the purple dye on the hands of the man, marking him as a tradesman who worked with the famous dye pits of Cyprus. Saul knew about this type of man, for occasionally his family had employed them when they received requests for coloring of the goat hides used on the tents they manufactured.

"How long have you been away from Jerusalem?" was the first words out this man's mouth, interrupting Saul's examination of his hands.

"Almost six months now," replied Saul quickly.

The tradesman paused and was calculating the time in his mind, then surprisingly asked, "If you are from Jerusalem, you must know about Jesus. The teacher from Galilee?"

Immediately, all Saul had heard about this Jesus, the latest in the string of never-ending Messiahs, came flooding back again. Gamaliel had explained about false prophets and their danger to Israel and Saul, feeling that he was well taught and expert on such matters, made an immediate judgment of the present encounter without having to hear any more.

Forcing himself to remain calm, he responded, "Yes, I have heard of Him. I recall that He would show up in Jerusalem for some of the feasts and gather quite a crowd of rabble in the Temple. I never met this one or saw Him, as you know the Temple is overrun by outsiders on feast days, so I feel it is best to stay clear of the unclean and barely faithful."

Realizing that this may have insulted the man, he quickly continued.

"What do you know about this one called Jesus?"

Saul saw the seated man's hesitance to answer and hoped that his belittling reference to the unclean would not end the conversation, although Saul thoroughly believed it accurate and warranted.

With his traveling partner remaining down the railing and showing no interest in this exchange, the tradesman cautiously continued the conversation on his own.

"My friend and I heard Jesus speak in the Temple for two years in a row and from His very first words, we have believed that He was sent from God. He had great power and was able to heal any sick and even raised the dead."

The tradesman rose from his seat and stood directly in front of Saul. He was large, muscular and when standing was even a little imposing.

"At Passover this year, because of their jealousy and hatred, the High Priest and the elders and even many Pharisees," he said, pointing to Saul's clothing, "conspired to kill him. They dragged him before Pilate, but the Roman found no wrong in Him, so they got a mob together and finally forced the Romans to crucify Him. They put Him in a tomb and guarded it, but the third day He came out of it. Resurrected."

The man had wasted no words and his accusation of Saul's entire world was unmistakable and fearfully direct.

While listening to him, Saul's countenance had taken on a scowl, which was easily recognized by the storyteller.

"You as a Pharisee believe in the resurrection of the dead, do you not?" queried the man, obviously knowing the answer.

Saul was not used to being challenged on his beliefs, especially by an uneducated and purple-handed tradesman. The conversation had taken on a direction that made Saul very uncomfortable but he was determined to remain rational, especially as he could now see the focused interest of Miriam and Antoine across the swaying deck. He felt he must answer the last comment.

"What proof do you have that he is resurrected," Saul responded, somewhat peaceably, attempting to not let his skepticism show or have this discussion immediately degrade into a full-blown argument.

"We received a letter in Salamis telling of all the times the Master showed Himself to His followers after His resurrection," replied the man, who seemed to slowly be warming to Saul's inquiries. "We are going there to see Him for ourselves."

The man was voicing an amazing and compelling belief and it rang with his sincerity and with increasing excitement in his voice.

"Can you imagine what is in store for Israel with a resurrected Messiah? This is that which was spoken of by the prophet Isaiah," he stated, totally expecting that this Pharisee would know the Messianic prophecies of that book.

The references to Isaiah that this commoner was using were complicated and hard to interpret for the best scholars and this man's manhandling of them was an immediate irritation to Saul. The lowly tradesman's understanding of such scriptures could not be any deeper than a simple reciting of these passages, exactly as they were read in the synagogue on any given Sabbath, followed possibly by a little discussion or a pittance of fundamental teaching. This unschooled buffoon with the weirdly stained hands did not have the years of intricate study that Saul had and therefore did not have the right to ascribe those scriptures to anyone, especially to Jesus. Calling him "Master" or teacher was also gnawing at Saul and now he was straining to keep his formidable temper in check.

Miriam, who was looking on from her tent but could not hear the conversation, recognized from his constant shifting and awkward stance that Saul was growing angry.

"You are making a grievous error by making a crucified Nazarene into Messiah. Making Jesus into Isaiah's predicted fulfilment simply based on second and third hand reports, and those probably fabricated by those who followed Him and who have an interest in reporting that He is alive, is complete foolishness and very close to sacrilege. Those telling you such things would not want to be seen as deceived or stupid, or just easily swayed, so naturally they would spread the rumor that He was resurrected," Saul replied, now adding some bite into the conversation. "Our true Messiah would not be crucified at the hands of pagan Romans in the first place," he added firmly and with a definite air of finality.

The man stopped and studied the Pharisee for a long couple of minutes and Saul was convinced that his wisdom was causing this man some serious thoughts. A tinge of pride crept back into Saul as he observed his own ability to withhold his anger and impart scriptural wisdom. This proved, once more, his special calling.

After a few quiet moments, the man raised a colorful hand and slowly pointed to his traveling partner, who was still gazing out over the sea toward Israel and was obviously lost in his own thoughts and out of earshot.

"He has a brother in Israel, a very noble man by the name of Cleopas, who with his wife were very close followers of Jesus. He just received a letter from Cleopas telling of a stranger who joined Cleopas and a friend as they were walking to Emmaus a few days after Jesus was crucified. They were talking among themselves about the crucifixion and what it meant and how they had thought and hoped that Jesus was the Messiah. Like you, they questioned how could this have happened and wondered if they were indeed mistaken about Jesus. The traveler, also walking the road, joined them, and Cleopas wrote that when the stranger heard what they were talking about, He began with Moses and for the next few hours showed in the scriptures how the Messiah was indeed to be crucified and abused. It was late in the day and they stopped at Emmaus at the little inn and the stranger was going to go on, but they compelled Him to join them for dinner and tell them more. At dinner, the stranger broke the bread in the same way Jesus broke it when He fed five thousand with a few loaves and Cleopas said that immediately their eyes were opened and they recognized that it was Jesus. Then He suddenly disappeared. Cleopas said that their hearts literally burned when the stranger was talking with them and the scriptures about Messiah became infinitely clearer, as never before. He immediately wrote his brother to come and see the Master for himself, so we are going to Jerusalem."

The tradesman waited for Saul's reaction.

Hearing nothing, he added, "Cleopas has no reason to deceive his brother."

Saul had heard enough and, yes, he finally erupted. "You are a fool on a fool's errand," he shouted. "You are deceived by a charlatan who got His just rewards for misleading Israel and now rather than admit your deception and let the matter die, you are being deceived again by others who would somehow profit by keeping you and your type from abandoning the cause."

Saul was yelling out his words now. Beads of spittle were flying everywhere.

"These stories of miracles and appearing and disappearing Messiahs are titillating and exciting to the unlearned, but to us who know better and have studied the scriptures diligently, they are just the latest tactic of the enemies of both God and Israel, tactics meant to blur the eyes to the real task of us Jews. You and your kind only delay the real coming of Messiah."

This vicious attack did not seem to surprise or upset the listener who at hearing it, merely returned a kind smile as one would to a young child just taking their first wobbly steps. This condescending expression angered Saul even more and he took it as a cutting insult. He began to stomp back and forth and he lifted his chin and began looking askance at one then the other of the two men. By then, the older of the two was turned and observing the once peaceful conversation. He could not possibly ignore it any longer as the volume of Saul's diatribe had increased and was heard by all on the ship. Even the Romans were watching with amused interest.

The tension was broken as the voice of Miriam was heard above the slap of the waves on the side of the ship. She had wisely and quickly prepared a meal for Saul, half expecting that either he would invite these travelers to his tent or that a meal would be the excuse to extricate him from an uncomfortable situation. Her logic had been proven correct.

Saul spun at the sound of her voice and without further comment, he retreated to his tent.

Antoine, while appearing very busy, had observed the total exchange and had heard large portions of it for he had inched himself closer and closer. The row had captured his interest and now he was extremely curious to find out more from Saul but realized that it might be best to let his friend cool down for a while.

Saul was not content to let his sister think he had in any way been bested and desperately wanting some retribution, discharged on her all the obvious errors of the traveler's argument.

After his rant, she innocently asked, "Was he arguing with you or was he simply relating to you what he knows or what he has come to believe? This is different from one of your Pharisaical debates that you enjoy so much, is it not?"

Saul shot her a disapproving look but then realized that she was not challenging him but accurately describing how the conversation had progressed.

"What difference does it make?" he answered, trying now to appear reasonable to his sister.

"Well, someone who has personal knowledge of an issue is not changeable in their stance no matter how loud you protest. They know what they know. Someone who merely debates theoretical concepts can either be convinced to hold a different position by logic or pressure, or will engage in a mental war to defend their previous concepts, sometimes even being overcome by the other side of the debate. When they feel the debate is a contest between intellects, the debaters easily get insulted and angry if their concepts do not dominate. Being bested is taken as a personal insult."

She is being very careful with her words, thought Saul.

He was thankful that she said no more but simply supplied him with a basin to wash in and followed that with salted fish and a flat bread.

CHAPTER NINETEEN

Approaching the Exotic East

Saul and the two travelers purposely avoided each other and dodged any further conversation for the remainder of the crossing, definitely a hard thing to do within the confines of a small ship. During those days, the Sabbath came and went, as did the Feast of Pentecost. Normally any Jews on board would have gathered to celebrate such times but both Saul and Miriam made no effort to engage the two men and it was obvious that they were also content to keep a safe distance.

Halfway to the coastline of Judea, the ship had come under a swirling and often changing wind and Antoine had been engaged hoisting and lowering sails in response. The captain was also busy, constantly resetting the rudders to contend with the billowing sails. The agile crew members seemed to relish this time to crawl the upper rigging, busily furling and unfurling sheets and generally showing off their daring to the appreciative passengers below.

Throughout those demanding days, Antoine remained curious to learn Saul's version of that tense and boisterous exchange but found no immediate opportunity to catch him alone at the railing on his side of the ship, the side conveniently away from the two Jews.

On the fifth day, the captain announced that land was in sight and he could see the heights of Mount Carmel. This was almost exactly where he had been aiming for and at this point the crew adjusted the rigging for a slow southward push of the last twenty-five miles along the now faintly-visible coastline to the city of Caesarea. If the sea remained as calm as it was presently, they could sail directly into the majestic stone-walled harbor, but if the waves came up at all, they would anchor offshore and wait for the swell to diminish before entering the narrow opening.

The captain was using only one of the larger forward sails to avoid any unwanted large gusts taking them off course and they were making steady but slow progress by hugging the coast where distant sand dunes dominated the shoreline. Beyond the dunes, the heavily forested hills of ancient Samaria loomed.

After a full day of irritatingly slow progress and when the sun began sinking in the west, they were still many miles away from the bulwarks that marked the entrance to the harbor of the city.

Because of a small swell, Antonius decided to drop anchor some five hundred yards offshore and wait for the safe light of morning. The groans of the disappointed passengers had no effect on his decision and being the courteous but cautious captain he was, he pretended he heard nothing. The four main anchors were dropped and the ship rode the gentle roll through the night.

When all was quiet, Antione sidled up to the railing, hoping for one last conversation with his boyhood friend. Saul saw him approaching and happily joined him there.

"Well, this may be our last time to talk to each other, Saul," he started. He knew that Saul would probably disappear into his religious life in Jerusalem and the chances of their meeting again were slim.

"Yes, my friend, and I have enjoyed our time together," replied Saul honestly, not imagining ever leaving the Jerusalem he loved and traveling like this again.

"May I ask how your conversation went with your two traveling countrymen and what did you learn about their Messiah?"

Saul had taken the days since his outburst to think about that confrontation and, above all, wanted now to present the case for Israel and the reasons for his stance.

"Antoine, our history is old but it is annoyingly consistent. Our God separated our ancestors from all other nations and promised us that if we would serve and obey Him, He would prosper us as a nation and a people. We have constantly failed to keep our part of that bargain and our record is one of golden calves, rebellion against Moses, listening to Balaam, intermarrying, rejecting a prophet's leadership for that of a king and a host of other disasters, thereby insulting our God. We have many more centuries of similar failings as well. These and other rebellious actions toward Hashem finally caused Him to punish us by sending the Babylonians upon us who were soon followed by the slightly gentler Persians, who also dominated us. We lost our kingdom and the beautiful Temple that Solomon built and most of our people were scattered and have never returned. Many of our tribes are now lost to the furthermost parts of the earth. Darius assisted us in returning to our land and serving our God, but again, we did not keep Hashem's commandments, so the Greeks came. Just like all other times, we allowed the Greeks and their pagan culture to pollute our house once more. The family of the Maccabees rose against those outsiders and for a short time God restored us to a glorious kingdom, then, sadly, we wandered yet again. Now we have the Romans filling the role as our 'allowed' punishers. We have always wanted a Messiah to come and rescue us from ourselves and I guess, this is the desperate hope of every Jew, so anyone who rises with any charisma ignites our longing for a supernatural deliverance. This is why the ignorant are so easily led astray. If any man can appear to do something magical or even use the evil one to do tricks, they immediately call him the Messiah."

Saul paused his story, hoping Antoine was understanding his passion.

"The Messiah will not come while Israel is not obeying the Law of Moses perfectly. The Pharisees, of which I am proudly one, are the only ones who understand this and thus have a solemn calling in Jewish history. It is our mission to fulfill the commandments and traditions that please God and make us worthy of the Messiah. These two are just more of the ignorant who desperately want their chosen hero to be the Messiah. One can hardly blame them, but so strong is the self-delusion that they are now imagining that they are seeing their dead leader alive again, walking the roads of Judea."

Antoine, listening closely, seemed satisfied with this logical and reasoned explanation from Saul. Miriam, who again was positioned to hear the conversation, showed no response.

Saul, not yet satisfied that Antoine realized the historical importance of such Jewish religious arguments and the importance of the Pharisees, continued. "Furthermore, there is the constant danger of these types of troublemakers upsetting the Romans and you are aware, I am sure, that this could bring more violence and repercussions upon our people. Our oppressors are allowed by God as our national punishment for disobedience and this we must grudgingly accept, but the immediate problem is that the Romans do not understand the difference between the rebellion preached by these so-called messiahs and our righteous insistence on following the ancient Law of Moses rather than their pagan Roman laws. They see both as treason and only the negotiations of our High Priests and elders keep the severe punishments of the Romans at bay. The result of every one of these false prophets is to bring more oppression on Israel, get more Jews killed and add grief and sadness for us. In Jerusalem, the leaders have concluded that it is their sacred duty to find and eliminate the trouble makers before the Romans get involved. This is for the safety and peace of Israel."

Saul's emphatic declaration should have ended the matter and with Antoine it did somewhat, but Miriam was disturbed with that answer.

"Saul, if you are always trying to mollify and appease the Romans and Messiah will by His power free Israel from their tyranny, is there not the chance that you could be found on the wrong side of that battle and be found fighting against the Messiah when He does appear, simply to keep the peace with Rome?" she asked logically from her perch at the tent.

Saul, hearing this surprising reasoning from his sister, replied pompously, "Well, we will have no trouble identifying the Messiah when He comes, for we have studied the scriptures and are experts on His characteristics. He will announce Himself to those who have kept the Law first. I have no doubt that it will be to us Pharisees that He will come. At that time, we will be found following Him, and yes, we will be found by His side opposing our Roman oppressors."

Saul's response generated another host of questions in Miriam's mind but she knew that these would only be seen as a challenge to Saul in front of Antoine, so, she held her peace. She was suddenly very determined to learn much more of the Messiah for what she had just heard had not satisfied her inquisitive mind at all.

Antoine also decided to leave the conversation there but was not entirely content with such an easy dismissal of the two earnest men on the other side of the deck or their deeply held beliefs. In his earlier conversation with the two, he had been captivated with the openness and honesty in their description of their journey and he was surprised at Saul's immediate antagonism to them and to their cause. In his gut, Antoine also felt the other two travelers had something authentic and genuine about them. They were common men with no axe to grind and seemed to have no ulterior motive other than finding out the truth.

PART TWO

CHAPTER TWENTY

Caesarea

The flickering lamplights of Caesarea began to shine brightly as the evening darkened, bathing the modern city in magical candlelight. The brightest glow was from Herod's immense palace, itself bathed in warm candlelight which lit up the sky at the far south end of the city. It was sparkling beautifully in the fading evening light, decorated with white marble columns outlining patios that were extending far into the sea. Feasting politicos could be seen wandering these distant terraces, dressed in their best and waited on by an army of servants.

This coastal metropolis was the largest and most impressive of the jewels in the many accomplishments of the mentally unstable, yet genius, King Herod. Although dead for over thirty years, his masterpieces of architecture were constant reminders of his incredible love of planning and creating and were still appreciated by those that had benefitted from his industrious era. Conversely, they were ever-present tokens of his tyranny and domination to the poor and unfortunates who did not participate in his wealth. His splendid edifices made those who knew of his erratic history almost forget that in fits of rage and paranoia, this crazed king had murdered his wife and sons simply on a rumor that they were plotting against him.

Early in Herod's life and as reward for his support in the Roman civil wars, Caesar Augustus had given him the Kingdom of Judea to rule, blindly overlooking the fact that he was only half Jewish. Roman leadership was not dependent on the purity of one's blood and Herod's ascension made complete sense to the appreciative Augustus. This led to the embarrassing situation where Herod's subjects constantly questioned if he was a legitimate Jew and therefore eligible to be their royal. While king, he went on a building and developing tirade like no other Jewish ruler had and as a result, his construction projects were numerous and legendary. These projects were liberally sprinkled throughout the land and this gave the country a period of unprecedented economic expansion and full employment.

The complete remodeling of the Temple Mount with its new and impressive walls had won over the hearts of most religious Jews and for them, this singular project had made Herod and his progeny almost tolerable. On the other hand, the creation of the volcano-shaped Herodian as a safe military retreat for himself, just eight miles south of Jerusalem and annoyingly visible from the Temple Mount, was viewed with great suspicion. Masada, Herod's winter retreat on a tabletop mountain overlooking the Dead Sea, was just an exotic rumor to most Jews, but it was another in the list of expensive projects whose complicated design and in-depth engineering added to the fame of this madman.

All of Herod's undertakings were beyond impressive but most agreed that Herod's pinnacle of achievement was to construct a complete city at the site of a nondescript village on a flat, sandy beach of the Great Sea and then equip it with a deep-water harbor that rivalled the harbor of Alexandria. The beach location was less than ideal but it was surrounded by the extremely fertile plains of Sharon on which most crops in Judea were grown. The problem of no nearby fresh water was ingeniously solved by an aqueduct system twenty-five miles long that fed off the springs at the foot of Mount Carmel to the north. As the population grew in his new city and the need for water increased, he quickly twinned the aqueduct, promptly solving the problem with even more engineering.

The proximity of this large urban development to the ancient north-south coastal highway was also well planned, providing sanctuary and hospitality for travelers on that main inland route and making the movement of troops in and out of Caesarea easy. The ancient and much traveled road was rebuilt and was flat and stone-paved. It was now the preferred roadway, avoiding the meandering track through the high mountainous regions known as the Patriarch's Way.

A day's ride south of Caesarea, the revamped road passed through the prosperous town of Lydda, from which one could access the road to legendary Jerusalem, a hilly, upward trek to the east. Positioning Caesarea on the coast seemed to be the best solution to many problems, not the least of which was that the Romans did not favor the rural and unpredictable Jerusalem as their seat of power.

While he was alive, the Romans had allowed Herod to keep his capital in Jerusalem but shortly after his death twenty-seven years ago, they moved their governors to Caesarea with only scheduled official visits to Jerusalem. The result of this move was an immediate explosion of population to Herod's new city. Hundreds of thousands of people were soon living there, all of them glad to avoid the snows and cold of the Judean hills in winter. Caesarea quickly became a melting pot of Roman, Greek, and Egyptian cultures, with a sprinkling of other nations, and of course a large and dominant community of Jews.

Because of the number and immensity of his projects, the reputation of Herod throughout the Empire was unmatched. Knowing that being too popular in the Empire was a risky position, he was always careful to include a level of obeisance to his rulers in Rome by displaying statues of Roman gods and ancient heroes in appropriate places which always kept his dominators satisfied. He was always aware that the Romans required ongoing proof that he and his family were still humble subjects and they were not getting any ideas of revolt.

Wisely, Herod sent most of his sons and grandsons off to Rome to be educated. The old fox was not all that interested in their being able to quote philosophers in Latin, rather he was greatly interested in them being life-long friends and school acquaintances of all the important Romans.

CHAPTER TWENTY-ONE

The Famous Harbor - Sebaste

To make it a truly important marine stop, Herod knew that ships of all sizes must have easy and safe access to this city. His solution was to build an enclosed harbor with massive stone walls reaching three hundred yards into the sea with a narrow, well-buttressed opening, thus making it a completely protected and deep harbor. He wisely constructed massive stone towers around this opening that absorbed any heavy seas, thus making the entrance and exit sheltered and available at all times and under all conditions. He also provided a fleet of towing vessels to move the ships in and out without needing wind power. It was the perfect maritime haven.

The captain had seen many ports in his years of sailing and had experienced the many ways that docking was provided but he was always impressed by the engineering and ease of operation that this truly modern miracle provided.

It was outside and a few miles north of these high and impressive harbor walls that the *Castor and Pollux* rested, waiting for dawn.

Early the next morning, at the faintest hint of light over the muted mountains of Samaria, Antonius shot up two burning arrows, signifying that he would like to weigh anchors and begin his approach. He was not surprised to receive a quick response from the tall spire at the entrance, indicating that they would be ready for him when he neared. He ordered the anchors raised and set the small triangular front sail at an awkward angle. Using the gentle northern breeze, the big ship began a slow crawl toward the dark gap in the wall. By experience, he knew the entrance was right under the signal tower.

The morning sun began faintly outlining the walls, making the scene breathtaking, even to those that had seen it many times before.

Antonius had heard stories of brasher ships that had successfully made the entrance at night and it seemed that the helpful towing vessels were always available if problems occurred but he also knew of a few shipwrecks that over-eager captains had caused by being too anxious. His father had taught him to be patient and always take a safe and cautious route away from any possibility of trouble.

The crew's noisy scurrying about and energetic tugging on the riggings had wakened all those on board and as the morning light finally peeked over the inland mountains, the passengers moved to the portside rail, oohing and awing and enjoying the slow crawl to the harbor while slipping along this beautiful city. They drifted closer to the shore while slowly moving southward and were soon passing the large villas and columned houses of the northern part of the city. There, they started seeing the morning candles being lit on the beautiful seaside patios of Roman officials and other fabulously wealthy families. Soon they passed a complex of high, Roman-style buildings sitting prominently on a foundation that started in the water and continued deep into the city. Even in the early light, the presence of Roman soldiers and tunic-robed servants hurrying around declared that this was the hub of the Roman government. Just south of that, now bathed in bright dawn light, they saw the huge hippodrome which stretched out along the shore with seating on the inland side for ten thousand. As Herod loved sport, he thought it manda-tory to have this venue where one could watch races and bet on his favorite chariot while being soothed by the sight of the blue waters of the Great Sea. All that happened while being cooled by the ever-present afternoon breezes. It was easy to understand why this location had become the social center of the cosmopolitan city.

Creeping along, they soon approached the massive harbor buttresses and the captain dropped the small sail and steered what progress was left in the ship directly at the gap. Two open and highly maneuverable boats with six large rowers each were waiting for the ship. They approached, one on each side, and threw their lines at the *Castor and Pollux*. They then tightened their ropes and began a steady pull of the big vessel, past the buttresses and through the opening. Once inside the walls, they pulled the ship across the enclosed harbor to a spot on the northern dock where the inside boat reversed expertly, slowing the large ship and spinning it until its siderail was parallel to the dock. The ship's lines were thrown to the waiting dockhands who pulled the ship snugly to the dock with large windlasses and there they secured it. It was a safe and professional operation and Antonius, the appreciative captain, enjoyed every minute of this efficient exercise.

Before long, a heavy but jovial harbor master approached and happily collected the mandatory fee for these expert services. He spent the next few minutes going over cargo manifests and then he pointed out the different locations in the harbor that provided the assistance the ship would need for offloading its cargo. After the captain and this official had finished their business, Antonius turned and nodded at Antoine, who bolted into action. The first order was to get the passengers off. He pointed to the Roman centurion, gave a quick hand signal and received a knowing nod in response.

He then approached the other travelers to offer any assistance they needed. He left Saul and Miriam to quietly begin collecting their goods.

It was obvious that Julian, the blond giant of a soldier, had never been here before. He had stood almost motionless at the bow of the ship since dawn, drinking in the spectacle that was Caesarea. He had seen many harbor cities on his journey around the sea, but this one was exceptional. The inside of the harbor was as impressive as the beautiful city that had slipped by this morning. On top of the interior harbor docks were roofed, columnated porticos that housed businesses and services required by the many ships.

Marble columns lining a harbor's docks? The big man chuckled at the sight.

This was truly an amazing place, he surmised. His attentive eye and intense curiosity were inundated with strangely dressed men draped in long robes and other never-before seen sights as he scanned the complete enclosure. It was his first taste of the exotic and mysterious Far East and his massive arm would raise every few minutes and point at rarities he never saw before as if he were in discussion with someone, but in fact, he was alone, frozen in amazement, standing majestically at the bow of the ship. Three other ships were also berthed in the harbor and they were in the process of being loaded or unloaded in a bustle of activity that had continued through the night. This resulted in the docks being piled high with all types of bundled cargo. There were caged animals, roaring out their displeasure, and even a line of shackled and very tall black men who were destined to a life of slavery somewhere in the far reaches of the empire. It took a barked order from his commander to rouse the giant from his daydreaming and remind him to grab his gear and get off the ship.

The chubby harbormaster had let the Roman garrison know that the *Castor and Pollux* was anchored offshore during the night, so it was no surprise that a small troop of armed and regally uniformed soldiers, marching methodically, were making their way along the dock to meet their companions. The detail of soldiers was noticeably surprised to see the huge Julian among the detail, weirdly adorned as he was in a comically ill-fitting Roman uniform. It was probable that some of these warriors had previously fought such creatures to the death in far off lands.

Saul took one last look at the big man, again reminded of the curious history of the Israelites and their own encounters with such giants right here in these hills. He had a quick moment of regret that he had not found out more about this unusual and mysterious creature, but within minutes, the marching troop had disappeared into the streets of the city, the blond and comically helmeted head bobbing high above the rest of the detail.

Herod had built a magnificent palace for himself in Caesarea and positioned it so that it stood imposingly above the south harbor wall, equipping it with an impressive viewing balcony. He had also labelled this jewel as his so that all travelers were made aware that all this was his creation, wanting his name pre-eminent upon their arrival. Irritatingly, the locals had given the harbor Augustus's Greek name of Sebaste.

Out of view and below his stark white roof and eye-catching palace walls were beautiful porticos, blue pools and lavish residences, each with its own private flower garden. He had purposely decorated each with expensive imported white and red Italian marble, favorites of his Roman colleagues and which he also seemed totally fascinated with as well. Since his death, the palatial complex was used alternately by his grandsons who, although much weaker leaders than Herod, were diplomatically allowed to rule certain smaller areas of Herod's previous kingdom by the generosity of the agreeable Tiberius.

One of the local services pointed out by the harbor master was a shop on the east side of the harbor where a cluster of busy looking men were arranging all manner of transportation for travelers plus the hauling and distribution of much of the merchandise piled on the docks.

Saul noticed that the two Jewish travelers he had encountered on board went immediately to this area and found a familiar Jewish man, Agabus by name. This man, Saul had also used to make his travel plans on other trips. This merchant could always be trusted to make the exact arrangements required for he was an honest and industrious man and seemed to always know who was traveling and to where and when. After a few minutes, the two were satisfied and made their way off the docks, slipping onto the main avenue and disappearing from sight. Saul was relieved with that for he was in no mood for any more frustrating confrontations with those two deluded zealots.

As he and Miriam slowly bundled the goods they had in their little tent, Antoine came over and informed Saul that he would offload the larger stored bundles that were held below the main deck momentarily, before any of the ship's other cargo.

These bundles represented all that Saul and Miriam valued and cared to bring from their former life. For Saul, this included a few prized Torah scrolls that his father had collected over the years, a few family heirlooms, a small collection of clothes and some tent-making tools he had used in his youth when his father still believed he should have a skill other than just the study of Torah. He brought these tools because of a late burst of sentimentality and an emotional reluctance to forget his father and the Tarsus of his boyhood.

Miriam brought a much larger bundle, lovingly packed with selected gifts and tokens of gratitude from her patients in Tarsus, along with a few of her best gowns and decorated robes which she hoped would be acceptable in the traditionalism of Jerusalem. Along with the gifts and apparel, she had packed her own precious scrolls which contained carefully written aspects of the newest medical techniques used by both Roman and Greek physicians.

Evenly dispersed and cleverly disguised within these two bundles, was a small fortune in gold and silver coins, placed very carefully as to make no sound. This was the monetary portion of the generous inheritance that their father had provided to his two youngest children.

Another larger pouch, laden with gold coins of great value, was concealed deeper inside the bundle and this one was purely the substantial proceeds of Miriam's labors with the sick of Tarsus.

Saul and Miriam waited patiently until all the other passengers had departed and then they slowly and deliberately took their time walking off the ship. Brother and sister realized that one segment of their lives was fading with that step over the rail and a totally new chapter was beginning. For Saul, one who had made this journey often, the upcoming days were not worrisome, but for his sister, all was new. Right now, she seemed in no great rush for this to transpire, moving only a few steps from the ship and doing that only half-heartedly before stopping to look back at the familiar vessel.

Helpfully, the harbor was alive and buzzing with activity and before long Miriam's internal worries began fading and she was again looking around at this new world. She was totally enthralled with Caesarea, thinking that indeed, this city was living up to all she had expected when she had imagined it back in Tarsus. The harbor was amazingly vibrant, deafeningly noisy and happily chaotic to the point it was almost frightening, and each part was unfolding to her in a colorful and unrelenting succession. All around her, insults and orders were flying in more languages than she could possibly understand. She was totally enthralled.

Saul understood the wonderment of his sister and watched as her attention went from the ship, over to the palatial edifice of Herod, back to the cargo-covered docks, then over to the caged and roaring lions on the far side of the harbor. She was cataloging detail after detail and her perceptive mind took in both the immensity of this place and the smallest detail of its dazzling features. As Saul expected, her attention was soon centered on the varied and diverse people on the dock and Miriam was again caught up in her favorite hobby, observing people.

The loud shouts and cheerful bantering of the busy sailors and deckhands who were manhandling the large bundles and stacks of cargo created a friendly atmosphere in the middle of this chaos and soon Miriam relaxed and began smiling warmly, appreciating the charm of the organized bedlam. She seemed very satisfied with how reality was coloring in the scenes of her previously undetailed imagination.

After jumping off the boat, a somber Antoine joined them for a final stroll. He had again realized that this was probably the last goodbye and that his childhood acquaintances were now embarking on a life that did not include people like him. He wanted to inform them of how much he had enjoyed the journey, speeded along with their many penetrating discussions and that he would remember them fondly.

Captain Antonius was standing at the front rail of the moored ship and he suddenly and without warning called to them and with an almost prophetic-like declaration, announced, "You will meet again: your lives are forever intertwined."

Mysteriously and definitely full of emotion, he turned away and stumbled his way to his cabin without another word. All three young people were speechless, having no response to Antonius's out of character, yet powerful outburst.

When their heartfelt goodbyes were said and they finally parted, Saul headed for the busy shop of Agabus to arrange their travel. He was growing very anxious to get to Jerusalem, not wanting to spend any more time in Herod's artificial jewel than was necessary.

Although Saul appreciated all the grand architecture, he was not at all comfortable with the pagan atmosphere of this place. Also, he felt it was a place with no history, no character and absolutely no depth of soul.

Saul knew that two days of hard travel were ahead of them and by Thursday they could be home and that would allow them to prepare for the sweetness of their first Sabbath in Jerusalem. Saul's innermost being craved to be bathed in that experience yet again and he refused to delay any longer.

Agabus, a Jewish man ten years older than Saul, was very outgoing and instantly put his customers at ease with a smile and a nod. His favorite response was "of course we can do that."

Oddly, this day there was a coolness in his voice when Saul approached wearing his Pharisee's tunic and Miriam immediately noticed the change of demeanor in the merchant. This was strange, she thought, for Miriam had envisaged that once they landed in Judea, such garb would automatically draw a favorable response among fellow Jews. At least that was what she had been told to expect.

Upon learning that Saul wanted to go to Jerusalem at once and that he needed a cart for his sister and their bundles, Agabus hesitated, but for only a minute.

"Can you be ready within the hour then?" he suddenly asked, disregarding any other plans that this Pharisee may have.

"I can get a wagon to take you to the inn on the main road and there is a small caravan leaving at the third hour from there," he stated, not waiting for replies but taking Saul's nods as total agreement. "You can ride a horse today and tomorrow, I presume?" he further questioned.

"We can be ready, and, yes, I can ride a horse," was Saul's laughing and confident reply. His Pharisee predecessors had decided that riding a horse was quite acceptable on certain days, but only when immediately followed by the correct prayers and washings. To the common Jew, the intricate rules of the Pharisees seemed unnecessarily complicated and quite confusing, and truthfully, most had very little interest in learning them. Sensing no further need, Saul removed his spotless tunic.

A wagon was arranged quickly and after loading their bundles, Miriam and Saul climbed on. The wagon took off at a rapid pace for the outskirts of the city, pulled by two burly but quick-stepping oxen whose immense bulk easily cleared the roadway ahead of them.

The grandeur of the harbor was soon replaced by the busy avenues of the city and with every corner turned, the entourage was exposed to the ever-changing neighborhoods of the city.

Upon leaving the seaside area, they moved away from the columned and statue-decorated Roman neighborhoods to the plainer but equally well-built areas where the Jewish populations lived. Striking odors, thick with the spices of the Orient hovered in the air and Miriam's head was turned continually with passing scenes of a culture she had only been told of and only flittingly experienced in her vivid imagination. The smells, the strange clothes, the languages: all were wafting over her and she instinctively loved them, feeling that they had secretly beckoned to her all of her life.

The wagon's destination was a large stone inn with an adjoining stable which was strategically situated on the side of the tree-lined road on the very outskirts of Caesarea. It was the place where large caravans were organized daily and from which travelers arrived and departed, all using the comfortable inn as the jumping off spot. Inside the inn, they met with a group of nine other travelers, three of which were female. Space was being made on a large wagon amongst the bundles for all the women and a horse was saddled and quickly made ready for Saul.

The weathered, leather-girded leader of this caravan went about adjusting the bridles and saddles of the horses and was aided by a grumpy, ominous looking and battle-tested assistant. Although the Romans were constantly patrolling the roads, travelers were still occasionally attacked by well-hidden and opportunistic thieves, so protection was also a large part of the duties of this caravan business. For that reason, the two in charge carried both broad swords and curved knives. The well muscled horses were wisely picked for their calmness and their ability to withstand the inexperienced riders who may or not be familiar with guiding a more spirited mount.

When all was finally ready, the leader called out and the few remaining travelers emerged from the stabling area.

Much to Saul's surprise, the two Jews he had encountered on the ship appeared. They seemed startled to see Saul as well. The man with the dye-stained hands politely nodded to Saul and then went about the chore of clum-sily mounting his horse. The other man avoided any contact with Saul and purposely looked away with what looked like an intended show of repugnance.

In fact, Saul did take offense to this obvious slight and Miriam noticed her brother's stiffening posture immediately.

Within minutes the caravan was on its way, leaving modern Caesarea behind and beginning a hurried push to make the crossroads town of Lydda by that evening. The journey to Jerusalem would normally have been a four to five-day walking trip, but with the horses and pushing the oxen hard, they were expecting to make it in two, if all went well. The clacking hooves of the horses, added to the thumping wheels of the oxcart, sounded out a steady rhythm on the new stone-paved Roman road as they headed south, every mile taking them deeper into the bowels of Jewish history.

CHAPTER TWENTY-TWO

Lydda

On this first day, Saul stayed very close to the ox-drawn wagon with its lumbering and oversize wooden wheels. This was a recent design of the Roman army and had been developed for carrying the heavy armaments of war that the legions moved about to wherever their conquests led them. The multipiece wooden wheels worked well on both the smooth stone roads and the mud tracks of the back country.

Saul's intent was to carefully watch over Miriam who had not traveled in this fashion before, but it was soon obvious that she was enjoying this adventure immensely, happily involved in spirited conversation with the other women on the wagon. A lot of hand motions, gestures, laughing and exaggerated facial expressions made up for her lack of knowledge of the local Aramaic language but the women were indeed communicating, sometimes loudly and, it seemed, successfully.

"Saul, isn't this wonderful?" was her repeated response whenever he drew near and he finally began to relax, beginning to understand that his sister was doing very well in her new surroundings.

The new Roman road was a much-appreciated improvement over the well-worn and rutted ancient highway that had been in use for millennia.

For thousands of years, this had been the overland route between the nations of Egypt and Babylon and all countries beyond. It ran from the coastlines of Gaza, through the fertile plain of Sharon, northward through a small gap in the Mount Carmel ridge at Megiddo, across the Jezreel valley and then to Damascus and points beyond. The development of shipping on the Great Sea and the building of Herod's Caesarea had diminished its importance as a great trade route, but it was still the chosen highway for those who needed to move around quickly on the land. Its new hard surface was suited perfectly for the efficient movement of the heavily burdened military.

Saul had paid dearly for this transportation because of the speed he had requested and he was a little surprised that the two travelers also felt the need for expensive and immediate travel. The presence of the two men irritated him constantly, but he genuinely appreciated that they remained far to the rear. That was as far away from him as they could get and still be just ahead of the trailing and gruff-looking second in command.

After three hours of steady and uninterrupted progress, the winding caravan stopped at a barn just off the roadway. It was well hidden in the dense trees growing along a clear bubbling stream flowing down from the Judean hills to the east. For some reason known only to Saul, he decided not to mention to Miriam that this stream started at Shiloh and that this was the very valley where the Philistines carried the captured Ark of the Covenant away. It was an embarrassing time in Israel's past and it was one of the sourest of defeats recorded in their all-too-honest written histories. Now was not the time for negative disclosures, he determined.

The oxen were quickly changed out for a new pair and every rider dismounted to give their horse a break and a spring-fed drink of water. A refreshing plate of dates and bread also appeared and these were much appreciated and quickly consumed by all.

Saul, of course, refused them as he was not sure they had been properly washed and prepared. Within a few minutes, the impatient leader and his gruff partner mounted up and circling through the group, indicated for the rest of the caravan to do likewise. Soon the noisy convoy was off, hooves again clacking while traveling through the alternating well-treed and heavily cultivated Plains of Sharon. The spring rains had decorated the sides of the track with blooming fruit trees and beautiful flowers, including the breathtaking blood-red roses famous in this valley. Skirting the bottom of the ridges, the route followed the bases of the mountains of Samaria to the east with the highway crossing multiple stone bridges over streams that tumbled down between these low mountains. Some of these flows spread quietly into small lakes and ponds, others meandered all the way to the Great Sea.

The warm day wore on and it was late afternoon when the outskirts of Lydda finally came into view. This town had flourished for centuries as a center for many Jewish businesses which served the needs of travelers who used this road-some who came for the benefit the Israelites but many who came to subdue, conquer and then tax them. Closer to the town, the terrain became rockier, less favorable for agriculture and it was obvious that the travel business was the most important reason of Lydda's continued existence.

Most inhabitants of Lydda were Jewish and the town had remained true to its ancient Hebrew name, which meant Valley of the Craftsmen. It grew and prospered due to its location on the trade route and its ability to provide abundant food and shelter plus the specialty items that the constant flow of travelers required. The men of the town became renowned for their ability to provide the best in saddles, strapping, leather goods, wheels and wheel repair.

The inns also did a thriving business, as Lydda was an important intersection of the main north-south highway and the Jerusalem-to-Joppa Road.

The centuries-old and much less impressive seaport of Joppa lay only ten miles to the west, built on a rocky outcropping which stood alone on an otherwise flat, sandy stretch of the coast. This location made Lydda almost a day's journey from many important places and that, in turn, made it a convenient place to overnight. In reality, most non-Jewish travelers saw no allurement to this flat-land town to justify its existence other than a comfortable bed among a collection of unremarkable inns.

For Saul, Lydda possessed a much deeper measure of significance.

Although in the most recent centuries it had become partially populated by what he called "pagans," the town maintained an enduring soft spot in his heart because of its place in the scriptural and romantic chronicles of his countrymen. Most appealing to Saul was the fact that it was located within the boundaries given by Joshua to his own tribe, that of Benjamin. The town was proudly listed in the scriptures as having 725 faithful Jews who bravely returned from the Babylonian captivity some five hundred years prior. These were enthusiastic Jews, pioneers returning to fearlessly resettle the lost land. There was no doubt in Saul's mind that some of these heroes were part of his own ancestral tree and he promised himself that one day he would search the synagogues of the town for his family's written record.

Added to that, Lydda was located near the foot of the historic valley of Ajalon, the exact spot where Joshua routed five armies of the Amorites and stopped the sun when needing more time to defeat them entirely. It did not matter to Saul that this unremarkable town was insignificant to others for this truly was an important place in the historical and religious heart of many Jews, especially Benjamin-ites.

Saul's affinity for Lydda went beyond ancient history as well. A sizable group of Jews, expert craftsmen that they were, had recently emigrated to Judea from his home town of Tarsus and finding little need for their leather and tent-making skills in Jerusalem, they had settled in Lydda and were now thriving in the booming Roman economy. The first successful group had encouraged others from Tarsus to join them and soon a community within a community had grown and prospered. Of course, they had established what turned out to be a large synagogue, one which Saul had periodically traveled to in his life as a popular young Pharisee and where he was always received with respect and special attention, just as would be expected for a favorite son.

Saul's first visit to Lydda was made to visit his nephew Andronicus and his wife Junia, children of Saul's mother's side of the family, but as his reputation as a superior student and an excellent teacher grew, he was now being invited to read and teach in the synagogue based on his status alone. Gamaliel always encouraged him to travel to nearby synagogues and visit other communities to spread his love of the Law and thereby encourage Jews who were less zealous. The honor and accolades that were showered on a Pharisee of the learning that Saul possessed were rewards in themselves and Saul became increasingly sure that his wisdom and sharp wit were exactly what these Jews needed. As was the custom, he dutifully accepted the handsome cash honorarium provided to him from the synagogue, a blessing which further convinced him that others agreed with his high assessment of his own value.

Today, the large, red-tinged sun was settling on the Great Sea to the west when the travel-weary group finally arrived in Lydda. They were promptly provided for at a comfortable inn, included in Agabus's practiced arrangements and, after a hearty meal, the group retired for a much-needed rest. They knew that the morning was but a few hours away and the hardest part of the journey was yet ahead of them.

Saul's two irritants had thankfully kept their distance from him and Miriam and at dinner, he shot them a menacing glare, just to remind them that he had not changed in his regard for them.

The next morning saw a fresh group of horses, and yesterday's two-oxen team was replaced with four anxious and well-muscled beasts to help pull the loaded wagon up the upcoming mountainous climb to Jerusalem.

Within the first hour of travel, the caravan left the flat coastal plains and began the climb up the ancient Jerusalem Road which followed the deep crevices and creek beds that wound their way down from the famous city on the mountaintops. The two men leading the caravan were joined by an experienced driver for the wagon as the multiple-yoked team of oxen required more direction than the previous day's team which had passively followed the road. The entourage left early and just as the day before, kept a brisk, steady pace. Within three hours they were approaching the village of Emmaus, where a short rest and a quick watering for the oxen and horses was scheduled.

Saul noticed that the two Jews from the ship had dismounted their horses and had crossed the road and entered the lone roadside inn of the small village while he and the others were encouraged to stay close, lead their horses to water and be prepared to remount shortly.

When the caravan pulled out, the two lagged behind curiously. Saul glanced back one last time to see them emerge from the inn where they continued an animated conversation with the innkeeper. After an hour or so, they came trotting up and rejoined the group, remaining at the very rear while talking excitedly between themselves and the trailing, grumpy guardsman who now seemed energized with their conversation. Fleetingly, Saul remembered the comment of the Jew with the stained hands about Jesus appearing at an inn in Emmaus after His death, but he quickly laughed that ridiculous thought away.

Saul loved this mountainous area and as a teenager had made it a personal project to thoroughly explore the extent of the lands of the tribe of Benjamin and all its importance to the Jewish nation. On his previous journeys to Emmaus, a village only a morning's downhill ride from Jerusalem, he had enjoyed the natural hot springs that gave this town the ancient and original name of Ha-motsah, mentioned in Joshua's writings when he allotted it to the tribe of Benjamin. Saul was an avid believer in the soothing and healing help from these waters for the sick and invalid and that alone had made this a favored destination. He often pictured General Joshua dipping in the warm pools while on his patrols around the country so Saul trotted his horse close to the wagon and explained to Miriam the historic significance of this village to their tribe. He then added that their father had also loved to soak in the soothing baths.

Others in the caravan took notice that Saul and Miriam were using the popular "common" Greek that was spoken in Tarsus and which was also used among most of the Jews who had dispersed around the Great Sea. Because they were now peaceful places to return to, an enclave of Greek-speaking Jews had gathered in most towns of Judea, bringing that world-dominating language with them and that included a large contingent in Jerusalem. The local Jews mostly spoke Aramaic, a curious language made of many varying dialects, which over the centuries had slowly replaced the ancient Hebrew previously spoken and which was now relegated to ceremony and synagogue readings only. This competition of languages often made unavoidable divisions between Jewish brethren until one or the other bothered to learn the other's chosen tongue.

500 years earlier, ancient Hebrew proved to be the one central and steady anchor of the dispersed Jews taken away to Babylon and points further east, and unlike the Jews of Judea, they had held on to that language religiously. Language and tradition were possibly the most powerful forces in the ongoing battle to keep them Jewish while they and their families thrived in the alluring civilizations of those tantalizing foreign places. A biting class structure had emerged within Judaism over the ensuing centuries with the far eastern diaspora Jews considering themselves much more unpolluted and superior because of their faithfulness in preserving Moses' Hebrew. They saw both the Aramaic and Greek-speaking Jews of Judea as inferior and diluted, an irritating and condescending attitude that often spilled over into the holiday feasts at the Temple when Jews from these far-flung regions mingled with the local Jews that spoke only the lowly Aramaic. The accusation was that the locals were just lazy, not extending the required effort to preserve Hashem's tongue. The Greek speakers from all points west were worse. They were regarded as almost pagan by the "pure" worshippers from Persia.

Saul, equally at ease in all three languages, had not decided if the practice of speaking only Aramaic was local stubbornness or just a lack of any formal education.

Miriam seemed quite at ease with this new language, chatting with the other women aboard the wagon in her broken, second-day Aramaic. She was listening closely and then chuckling along with them about some silly comment or private women's joke, already able to understand most of what her fellow travelers said.

After mid-day, and with about ten miles left to go to Jerusalem, the gentle rise of the road changed to sharp inclines and steep descents. The caravan leaders pushed relentlessly up these, stopping to rest the oxen and horses for a few minutes only when the top of each particularly steep rise was reached.

On one particularly convoluted section, Saul sidled up beside the wagon, interrupting the chattering women and pointed out a hilltop village partially hidden in the trees to their left and only a short climb off the main road.

"That is Kiriath Jearim, the home of Abinadab, where the Ark of the Covenant spent thirty years until our great King David brought it home to Jerusalem," he stated with some pride to Miriam.

Miriam well knew that this was a very much shortened version of the story of the disjointed travel of the Ark, beginning when it was captured by their arch enemies, the Philistines, many years ago. The abbreviated report reminded her that most religious Jews did not like repeating the negative parts of that story, preferring the heartwarming account of the dancing and rejoicing King David bringing the Ark back to Jerusalem. Saul had, quite noticeably, avoided the distasteful parts as well.

Miriam appreciated seeing the actual physical location of the places mentioned in the scriptural stories and she looked about carefully, finally being able to place them. Once again, this added vivid color and dimension to her mental pictures which were only vague images of places conjured from her readings of the sacred scrolls.

Miriam's complete knowledge of the ark's travels filled in the embarrassing and unwanted blanks that her brother had left out, but she graciously kept all that to herself.

CHAPTER TWENTY-THREE

Jerusalem

The final push into Jerusalem was the steepest and most difficult. All travelers in the party, including the animals, were tiring from the day's hot travel but as they neared the city, the heavily forested hills began to come alive, lifting the drooping spirits of the caravan.

In the shade and under the canopy of those forests were hordes of happy pilgrims. This was a colorful collection of boisterous and excited visitors who were camping in all manner of temporary structures under the overhanging branches near the edges of the roadway. Mixed in with the celebrating squatters were a number of eager businesses positioned to service them making it seem like small villages. These tents were the accommodations of the Jewish faithful who had come for the celebration of Passover and Pentecost and were lingering in the area, continuing to enjoy the atmosphere of the Holy City. At this time of year, their numbers always greatly outpaced the capacity of the city to house them so there were numerous encampments surrounding Jerusalem proper.

The traveling caravan wound its way through and the camped pilgrims were waving and shouting out warm greetings to the newcomers. Festive music flowed from the happy groups and soon children were running alongside the wagon and chattering away. The women on the wagon began throwing fruity treats to them for this was a customary greeting and the children scampered all around to gather the last of the bounty. The exhausting trip had suddenly become magical.

As if on cue, the group crested a small rise and looking downward, were instantly rewarded with the unfolding and breathtaking view of the west-facing wall of the Holy City.

Instantly, Miriam was overwhelmed. Hardly another word was spoken among those in the caravan as the beautiful panorama spread before them.

Colorful flowering trees sprung from the base of the wall and creeping vines engulfed the high wooden and ornately carved Joppa gate which faced them. The towering stone walls stretching away to the north and south were draped with other vines in full bloom of crimson and violet flowers. The lowering sun at their backs glowed off the whitish rock of the ramparts, lighting them with a soft, golden hue. To all who saw it for the first time, it was truly stunning and all in today's party were mesmerized, including the seasoned caravan leaders who had seen this sight hundreds of times before. The scene was utterly overwhelming, both visually and emotionally, effectively testifying to the reputation of Jerusalem as the City of Gold. It was Hashem's city, one which rose majestically from the yellow stone of these very mountain tops.

The hush that had descended on the women on the wagon was soon replaced with whispered words of blessing and then congratulations to each other. Such was the custom when travelers saw the walls for the first time.

A few hundred yards from the gate of the city was a large animal compound and the convoy leaders pulled into the fenced area and alighted from their fatigued and lathered animals. They were at the end of their journey and had safely and quickly delivered their pilgrims, just as contracted.

As the rest of the passengers were clumsily dismounting and collecting their bundles, the two Cypriot Jews that Saul had avoided for the entire journey approached and quickly snatched their knapsacks off the wagon. After a curious and overly-warm embrace with the grizzled leader of the caravan, they shot Saul a last mistrustful glance and made their way over the last few steps of the Joppa Road and disappeared into the open and massive wooden gate, slipping without incident past a couple of bored Roman sentinels who were watching the crowd come and go.

The gateway was an obvious point of congestion with vendor's empty wagons maneuvering in and out and scampering people hurrying around them. Many were leaving the city for the night but just as many people were pushing the opposite way, returning to their homes within the city walls.

After busying himself hoisting down their heavy bundles, Saul stood up and noticed that Miriam had not moved a muscle but was standing motionless with her back to him. She was staring at the towering walls above her. He moved around her and saw a serene look on her face and a flow of tears rolling freely and unchecked down her cheeks. In an unexpected show of warmth, he put an arm around her trembling shoulders. Saul, usually one who avoided emotion, appreciated this show of passion and was immediately thankful that she felt about his Jerusalem as he did.

He became slightly moist-eyed himself.

A little embarrassed, he wiped his eyes quickly, but then also looked up to lovingly drink in the flower draped golden walls of the city he cherished. Miriam finally noticed him.

"Saul, you have lived here for many years and have seen this sight many times, I know. I have only dreamed of it, imagined it, prayed for it, but never imagined that I would be here. My heart is so full with thankfulness and I could not be happier than I am right now," she said, barely above a whisper. "Thank you, my brother."

Saul was deeply moved. He was thankful that his normally businesslike and extremely logical sister had broken through to show such deep feelings. At that moment, he believed that this could possibly be the beginning of the deeper religious life he desired for his Miriam. Over the years, he had become persuaded that no Jew could get an inspired understanding of their God without a personal connection to the Temple and to the Law and this could only happen, Saul remained convinced, within the walls of his adopted and beloved Jerusalem.

Brother and sister were finally roused from their thoughts, being accosted rather rudely by a cavalcade of noisy porters, each clamoring for a chance to carry the heavy burdens laying at the feet of these travelers. Saul quickly took advantage of two strong-looking men to cart their heaviest luggage.

He announced, much too loudly, the location of the house of Gamaliel as their destination and that caught the attention of those that knew the city well. He also sent a nearby nimble and youthful messenger running ahead to inform the household that he and his sister would be arriving shortly.

After this, he reached into his bundle and retrieved his blue-and-white-fringed robe, the identifying garb of a Jerusalem Pharisee and he donned it carefully and ceremoniously. Saul knew it would be much more appreciated in Jerusalem than it had been in many places he had just traveled through. He was finally in his familiar haunts and the world was beginning to feel properly ordered to him once more.

As he and Miriam walked through the towering gate, Saul acknowledged the respectful nods and the courteously opening path that his distinctive clothing provided to him. Miriam did not detect this display of reverence for her eyes were examining every facet and detail of the mysterious and much anticipated world that was Jerusalem, down to the large white stones in the walls and the heavy timbers in the gate. She did not want to miss a thing. The wide road outside the gate had quickly turned into a narrow crowded street, a busy affair, snugly lined on both sides with an array of tall stone houses with exterior stairways leading to even higher floors.

All about them, there were intriguing gateways that allowed only partial glimpses into well-kept and treed courtyards where busy families were moving about. Everything was constructed with the charming off-white stone and this made the old city appear new and clean, while the worn rocks of the roadway spoke of centuries of use.

The first intersection of streets was entirely congested. A few remaining local farmers, surrounded by their shrinking piles of produce, had created a temporary market at this corner and were very noisily hawking the last of it in the remaining hours left in this day. Women were bartering and clamoring for any excess that the merchant would be discounting and bright-eyed children were running about laughing at big eared and lazy-eyed donkeys who were reaching and pulling on any spilled food they could find before being led out of the gate. All knew the familiar routine well.

Saul and Miriam pushed straight through the throng of the first few busy blocks and then Saul turned right onto a quieter and more subdued residential street. Here they encountered only a few subdued merchants and the market atmosphere was soon replaced by ever-present gaggles of children playing while their mothers were gathered at the large communal ovens that served whole blocks. Many of the residents stopped to greet Saul individually and it was evident that these alleys had been the hangout of this young man for many years. He knew these people well and all were delighted to meet his little sister Miriam.

This section of Jerusalem was the top of the highest point of the city, the height of legendary Mount Zion and this was the taller of the two mountain-tops that Jerusalem was built upon.

Saul and Miriam turned east onto another avenue and began a slow descent from the heights, entering the easily recognizable, wealthiest area of Jerusalem. The streets here were lined with higher and more ornate walls and each house had a beautifully carved wooden gate tastefully framed with even more flower-ing vines.

Saul stopped in front of one of the most impressive, one that he obviously knew very well, and he knocked loudly.

CHAPTER TWENTY-FOUR

Home

Within moments the elaborate gate flung open and a tall, very handsome and lightly bearded young man of about Saul's age let go an excited cry of greeting. "Saul, you have finally come home! So good to see you, my brother."

Saul clutched him warmly and jokingly demanded, "You are now answering the door? Did you fire all the servants? Have we suddenly become poor?"

They both laughed heartily and after much embracing and back slapping, their attention turned to the young woman waiting beside Saul.

"Gammy, this is my little sister, Miriam, who has come to live here in Jerusalem with me," he announced with gusto and a tinge of pride.

"Miriam, this is Gammy, really Shimon ben Gamaliel the second, but no one has the patience for that long a name."

The two closest and dearest people in his life were now standing in front of him, warmly and sincerely greeting each other and for this, he was over-joyed. It was apparent to Saul, as he stood back and watched that greeting, that he was experiencing a significant and major milestone in his young life. Meaningful and weighty changes were in the wind for both him and his sister and today, he was anticipating nothing but good.

Rabbi Gamaliel's home was really a complex of three separate houses slightly joined and arranged around the three sides of a spacious and well-treed courtyard with an enveloping wall. It created an inviting compound but also served to keep all others out. At the rear of the courtyard, beneath the upper servant's quarters, was a patio containing a large dining table and many chairs. It was here that on special occasions, elaborate formal dinners were served and in previous years the teaching of the students had also taken place at this table with many intense and deep scholarly discussions encouraged and resounding through the courtyard. A good portion of Jerusalem's most secretive and high-level political negotiations had taken place around this finely crafted and polished olive wood slab as well.

Immediately upstairs, on the left of the main gate, was the apartment that Saul had called home for the last five years after it was decided that he should have some freedom and independence from the family of Gamaliel. It was a spacious four-room abode with a small and separated cooking area. Saul had shared it, off and on again, with a few other students who had come from afar to study at this prestigious school. It was now his alone, and he paid a modest rent to the family from money he earned as an assistant teacher for Gamaliel.

Over the last decade, the school had been so successful and popular that the classrooms had to be moved out of the family compound to two larger halls which were only blocks away from this residence. Saul and Gammy had each taken one classroom and under the guidance and direction of the sagely Gamaliel, were gaining reputations as elite teachers themselves, this even though they were mere fledglings in a city full of aged, heavily-bearded and immensely learned rabbis.

Saul found out quite early that he relished the responsibility of immersing the younger students in the intricacies of the Law and, under the watchful direction of the cautious Gamaliel, he expertly imparted the intriguing Mosaic teachings, secretly reliving the enjoyable days of his own discovery of the treasures hidden in the Torah. Through his teaching, he was watching the same excitement and dedication develop and that was repeated over and over with every new student. For a full year before he had returned to Tarsus, he and Gammy each had a class of twenty bright young students, boys eagerly presented to Gamaliel by hopeful parents willing to pay the substantial costs. For his part in this training, Saul received a portion of the fee charged. This payment allowed him to easily pay the rent on the apartment and all his personal needs, plus he could add a little to the expanding pouch of coins hidden in a vase in his room.

The highlight of his teaching days was when he, Gammy and a few of his brightest students could sit with Gamaliel in the portico of this home and delve deeply into the Law, discussing, bantering, debating and mentally solving the most intricate dilemmas of Moses's recorded instructions. Saul gazed with warmth at the table, eagerly looking forward to renewing the intense study he craved so deeply.

Before long, he led his sister up the wide stone stairway to their apartment. The heavy bundles had just arrived and the two porters packed them up the stairs and into their very comfortable and airy rooms. Miriam, a little in awe, stood aside and quietly watched as Saul jingled his purse mercilessly while digging out a few coins for payment. He sent the well-tipped men away very happy.

Truthfully, Miriam had not expected such comfort and she realized that Saul had purposely understated the bright and very spacious accommodations when he described them to her back in Tarsus. He was grateful to see the pleased smile of Miriam, now sure that she would also love their new home.

In comparison, Jerusalem was a crowded city and the houses were more compact than the sprawling edifices on the riverbanks of Tarsus, and this had made Saul a little worried. Miriam, it was becoming obvious, was not at all concerned about such matters.

Saul motioned to her to follow him down the steps to the lower courtyard area where he showed her the modern conveniences that separated this home from many others she had seen in her life. There was a supply of water, clear, fresh water, that, as with other wealthy homes in Jerusalem, was mysteriously piped into this house and which was available next to two large tables for food preparation. Two middle-aged, female servants looked up from their chores and offered a warm and respectful greeting to Saul, followed by smiling and gushing warmth for Miriam.

There were large, shuttered openings in the lower level of the house, each located strategically to allow breezes to move throughout and which could be closed when the winter's cold came to Jerusalem. That shut in area would then include the large stone and brick oven in the outside corner of the patio, thus heating the main house. Right now, it was giving off the sweet aroma of freshly baking loaves.

Saul took her to an area at the rear of the houses that possessed Jerusalem's pinnacle of luxury. A wide doorway opened to a smaller area from which downward stairs led to two separate dressing rooms. From each of these rooms, stairs led further down into chest-deep water. Miriam recognized them immediately as the Mizpah baths that she and every Jewish person was so familiar with, but she had never seen baths within a private residence before. She, like all Jews in Tarsus, used the common communal Mizpah baths that the Jewish community had built next door to the synagogue.

Miriam had heard of such personal luxuries but had not expected all this to come upon her within a few hours of entering Jerusalem. She chuckled to herself, almost in disbelief, and contemplated what other wonders she would discover as she delved further into this amazing place.

Saul led her back to the courtyard where the grinning Gammy had brought out his mother and his sister. The two women beamed with pleasure, finally able to meet Saul's sister whom they had heard surprisingly little of over the years.

Sarah, the wife of Gamaliel, was a tall, regal looking lady, dressed in a stunning red and blue dress with a thin sheer wrap over her shoulders. This woman was obviously comfortable in the trappings of wealth and she definitely looked the part of one who was very rich. Surprisingly, she was instantly sincere in her warm welcoming of Miriam. Her smile was genuine as was her embrace, and Miriam's nervousness was quieted immediately. It was Sarah's sincere and laughing eyes that stood out, accompanied by raven black hair. Her intense and unfeigned interest in all parts of the conversation immediately added to the charm of this strikingly attractive middle-aged woman.

Because of her genuineness, Sarah was noticeably at ease greeting strangers and her warm, confident manner fitted her role in this busy household effortlessly.

She said with a mocking annoyance, "Your brother has kept you a great secret, telling us almost nothing about you, Miriam, but we shall become great friends. Welcome to your new home."

Gammy's sister, Leah, was close to Miriam's age and possessed a strikingly pretty and expressive face which was highlighted with her flashing and dancing eyes. She was immediate in her sincere affection for Miriam, drowning her in a close and ardent hug. She had her mother's beautiful hair and a wide, mischievous smile. Miriam was instantly taken with the naturalness and warmth of Leah, obviously a wealthy but totally unpretentious girl and she suspected right then that they would easily become life-long friends. Plates of figs and cakes appeared, delivered by equally cheerful servants and they all sat down at the portico and visited unhurriedly for long hours as the late afternoon disappeared into evening. Saul and Miriam were surrounded and soon engulfed by the welcoming and intoxicating atmosphere of their comfortable home.

With much sincerity and disarming humility, Miriam told the agonizing details of their beloved father's death and her conflicting thoughts on leaving Tarsus, followed then by her description of all the amazing events of the journey. She avoided mentioning her agreement with her father to find a husband in Jerusalem, and Saul, of course, noticed this. He wisely did not add to that subject although his enduring silence took all the restraint he could muster.

Tired and drained, Saul and Miriam finally retired to their apartment which had mysteriously been transformed into a warm, comfortable home while they were visiting. There were small candles placed around which burned warmly and more delicious fruit was waiting in a bowl. The servants, without Saul or Miriam noticing, had slipped in and provided for their needs, including all the washing utensils a Pharisee had to have. To Miriam, that thoughtful act made this stony apartment, immediately into a welcoming retreat. Dream-filled sleep came to both very quickly.

As dawn broke, Saul was awakened from his deep rest by the faint and haunting trumpets announcing the burning of the morning incense at the Temple which was followed quickly by the loud clacking of the front gate slamming shut. After meticulously washing and finishing his rapidly recited morning prayers, he slipped out of the apartment and ran down to the portico with the eager expectation of a long-awaited reunion with his mentor, Gamaliel. For over a decade this exceptional man had been his teacher, his private advisor and a trusted confidant whom Saul had learned to love almost as a father. He had missed him greatly.

Instead, He once again found Gammy who was finishing his morning prayers alone at the portico and they broke into easy smiles as they greeted each other yet again. Saul's travel-weary spirits were immediately lifted, warmed by his closest friend, and for all intents, his brother.

He had been living with Gammy since he was ten years old and Gamaliel and Sarah had judiciously treated them equally as sons and brothers with both their discipline and their love. The two boys had spent those teenage years experiencing times of closeness, antagonism and competitiveness, just as brothers often do, but they had come to truly love each other.

"Gammy, where is your father?" asked Saul.

"Well, apparently there is quite a disturbance this week at the Temple and Caiaphas has asked him to be there early to help quiet the crowds," replied Gammy.

"Disturbance?" Saul was immediately intrigued.

"Well, I don't know much about it, but it has something to do with the disciples of that prophet Jesus from the Galilee region whom the Romans crucified at Passover."

"What about them," pressed Saul, his curiosity immediately aroused. He was surprised that he was hearing the name of Jesus yet again.

"Why don't you wait until father gets home and he can explain it thoroughly. I expect him back at noon to prepare for the Sabbath."

Gammy had, once more, respectfully deferred to his father. This was something he often chose to do, even though he was quite capable and quietly brilliant.

Within himself, Gammy was poised and confident and he easily excelled in both the teaching of the Law and the keeping and promoting of the resulting traditions so his father was wisely using Gammy's scholarly talents to teach others as he was with his prize student Saul. Gamaliel was content to let Gammy's quieter, undriven personality flourish in this role rather than pushing him into assuming any premature leadership role. That would come soon enough.

On more than one occasion, Gammy's thoughtful approach to scripture had outshone Saul's fiery and emotional attitude, but the wisdom of Gamaliel was able to grasp the benefit of both methods, so he wisely arbitrated and often implemented a friendly ceasefire between the strong-willed lads.

Gammy had the tall, regal build of his mother and he had developed into a pleasant, dark-haired young man who easily broke into a large smile which lit up his youthful and handsome face. He had purposely shunned the arrogance and aloofness that often accompanies attractive people and accepted his privileged lot with a genuine humbleness. He was kind and quick to recognize a need in both his friends or strangers and was always eager to help. This openly contrasted with the actions of many fellow Pharisees who saw aiding the common Jew as below their calling.

Saul had noticed that in the years before he had left for Tarsus, there had developed a growing and considerable buzz amongst the mothers and daughters of the upper strata of Jerusalem. Many had found very important reasons to visit Sarah or attend the synagogue when Gammy was expected to be present.

Gammy took the resulting ribbing that Saul and others heaped on him for this obvious husband-hunting with jovial charm and he countered by declaring his life-long commitment to a lonely bachelor's existence. Torah would be his one love, he claimed. No one believed him in the least and all figured that Gammy would make an outstanding father and head of a household when that time finally came.

Meanwhile, the reality was that the adjacent street was often inhabited with aimlessly wandering young women eager just to get a chance to greet Gammy. These were suffering the pathetic, starry-eyed fate of the love-struck.

Leah teased him mercilessly over this and Gammy had learned to look both ways and walk quickly when he opened the gate and went out to the street.

There was a serious side to Gamaliel's son that was often overlooked by any casual observer. The deferring to his father could have been seen as a lack of strength on Gammy's part, but only by those who misunderstood what motivated this young man. His proximity to the daily decisions and intrigues of the Great Sanhedrin, the high court which his father had been president for the last three years, had allowed him to observe both the religious and political leaders of Israel closely. He found it both fascinating and at times, utterly disgusting, to witness the convoluted and inexplicable motives of the different members. He despised that his father had to deal with their outright dishonesty and pettiness and at times he was even repulsed by the actions of these so-called servants of Hashem, shrewdly choosing to not be present when and where such dubious deeds were being discussed and performed. He did not want to become immune to the shock of their evil or to become accustomed to their duplicities.

Notwithstanding the hypocrisy, Gammy had clearly understood from an early age that at some point the mantle of leadership of the Sanhedrin would fall upon him directly. His good heart, molded and formed by observing the benevolent spirit of his father, had made him determined that when that day was upon him, he would do his duty with piety and purity. Much too often he had witnessed the damage, both personally and nationally, that leadership motivated by self-interest and personal gain had done to the Jews of Jerusalem. Because of this knowledge and at this young point in his life, there was no driving urgency to be involved with the political life he was destined to. He especially did not want to live under the exhausting stress which he observed his father constantly dealing with.

Saul understood and admired Gammy's depth of devotion to crafting an untainted Israel, himself often wondering if that was even possible, and he had often purposely emulated Gammy's purity as a youth. He had on a few occasions, although reluctantly and slowly, changed some of his strong opinions on issues because of a more reasoned stance by Gammy, but that was a difficult endeavor for the temperamental Saul.

Saul recognized he was less inclined to be as benevolent with others as his friend and this had resulted in long, personal discussions with Gamaliel, who constantly reminded Saul that the Law, when understood correctly, would result in a unfeigned caring of others rather than an exultation of oneself. As evidence, Gamaliel pointed to the humbleness of Moses and his timid attitude, plus his unwillingness to demand any recognition from the people, actions which were crowned by his willingness to sacrifice himself for even the rebellious congregation in the wilderness. Saul had a very hard time understanding or even contemplating that side of Moses for such forgiveness did not come naturally to him.

Gammy was totally different, and although reluctant, Saul knew and recognized that difference.

From his earliest years, Gammy could not escape the fact that he was the great grandson of the famous and much respected Rabbi Hillel.

This man had emigrated from Babylon at forty years of age and worked as a simple woodcutter while craving to study and know the Law. He was rejected by the schools of his day, being in their opinion, not worthy of handling such truths because of his lowly position in life. But he persevered, proving himself worthy and he continually studied the Law for another forty years until his wisdom exceeded the noted scholars. This humble man became one of the great leaders of this nation.

This should have been a practical lesson to any Jews bothering to pay attention for it proved that the character of a man was much more valuable than the position his family holds.

That profound precept was not wasted on Hillel's great-grandson, Gammy. There was a sincere humbleness in the lad that came without effort and many remarked that he was indeed like his revered ancestor, both in tenacity for personal integrity and in thoughtfulness and kindness.

CHAPTER TWENTY-FIVE

Familiar Sites in Jerusalem

Disappointed that he had missed Gamaliel this morning, Saul came up with a new plan.

"I have missed this city so much, Gammy. I want to go for a walk around and drink in the smells of Jerusalem and hear the chatter in the markets again. Would you go with me," asked Saul.

Gammy laughed out loud and quickly agreed. He knew that this adopted brother literally thrived on the bustle and chaotic atmosphere of the streets of Jerusalem, plus he was aware that Saul also had a huge appetite for the political intrigue that this city had an unending supply of. It was in these noisy markets where aggressive verbal battles took place and where all the whispering and plotting started, and it was while wandering those alleys that one could feel the ancient call of this nation in one's bones. If one was paying attention.

"Of course, I will. Give me an hour, but remember, we want to be back for noon."

Saul went to his room and worked on straightening his best robe with the enlarged blue borders. It was with unabashed pride that he wore these garments, probably too much pride he admitted, but they identified him as a man of devotion and being identified was very important to him. He noticed that Miriam was busy and was scurrying back and forth as well.

She saw Saul preparing and approached him, a little embarrassed.

"Saul, I am going to the markets with Leah and would like to know if there is anything you needed," she asked.

Saul was greatly pleased that his sister had so quickly adjusted to her new situation. Inwardly, he had worried since learning of Miriam's agreement with their father that she may not feel at home in Jerusalem and wondered if she could handle its constant turmoil, its overrun streets, plus the deluge of opinionated and outspoken Jews. It was a totally different atmosphere than her secluded and tranquil life in Tarsus for sure. Miriam's surprising eagerness to plunge into the fray and chaos that was the market was a welcome first step in the relieving of these worries and he immediately realized he was being too protective.

"Ahem." She cleared her throat theatrically. "There is a small matter concerning finances," she said with a wry smile, waking him from his thoughts.

They both burst into snorts of laughter and any remaining tensions from the last weeks of travel and relocation seemed to wash away with the chortling. The finances, of course, were the bulging purses Saul possessed which contained considerable amounts of gold and silver coins, a good portion of it belonging to Miriam.

Their inheritances were partially provided for in this cash, but they were also to be supplemented with valuable tents and merchandise previously sent and stockpiled. Gideon had sent these to trusted business acquaintances in Salamis and Jerusalem and these would provide handsomely for their future welfare as sales were being made. Saul had already received some for the tents provided to Salamis from Caleb and he knew an additional three names provided by his father for other men he could collect from in Jerusalem. One of these was an old acquaintance of Gamaliel's, a wealthy merchant of Arimathea, Joseph by name, who made quite a living renting the tents as temporary housing for the traveling pilgrims. Saul had only yesterday, recognized a few of these unique tents spread around the forest as they had approached Jerusalem.

Because of her medical abilities and the special attention to the ailing women of the Jewish community in Tarsus, Miriam had collected quite a hoard of cash donations and costly gifts as a thank you for her care. Despite her protests, these gifts had been accumulating and after her father passed, she converted most of them to gold coins and had Saul carry that bag as well.

Having the male traveller carry them was the accepted custom and she hesitantly heeded it, not convinced that the rich robes of a Pharisee would be any deterrence for anyone intent on robbery. A third and much more valuable fortune she had hid away in her bundle and this, she would not be disturb until needed.

"Ah, yes," replied Saul and immediately disappeared into his room. He had an olive wood chest in which he kept such valuables and he brought the two bags of coins out. It was always wisest to travel with your money spread out so that in the worst case, a robber would be satisfied with the one bag, supposing he had gotten it all. The trick was to keep the bag with the least as the more visible and easiest to access. He began emptying both bags with the intention of dividing up the inheritances but was interrupted by Miriam.

"Saul, not now, please," she said with a warm smile on her face. "I prefer you keep our money, but I just need some for the market," she remarked, almost apologizing. He meted out a few old shekel coins for her and she held them for a moment, staring and calculating.

"Oh, all right, maybe a little more, if I just happen to see something I must have," she said with a loving and mischievous smile.

Saul doled out more than enough coins, careful to avoid any silver or gold ones, as these would attract unwanted attention and he slipped these into a smaller pouch for her. Again, he was pleased to see that her level of comfort had arrived so quickly, but on second thought, he should have expected nothing less from her.

Since he had returned to Tarsus and spent the last months of his father's life around his sister, Saul had been astounded with the remarkable abilities and mental faculties of Miriam, faculties which he had only partially witnessed on his previous short visits home. He had regarded all the bragging about her as parents promoting their only daughter but he now understood that, if anything, they were understating Miriam's talents. When he thought about her future in the traditional restrictive atmosphere of Jerusalem, his gut tightened. Today, he would not let his mind go there.

Was Jerusalem ready for the questioning and piercing logical mind of Miriam, he wondered.

Together, brother and sister descended the steps to the portico, where Leah, upon seeing them, broke into her wide and sincere smile. An instant relationship had indeed developed and the two greeted each other like life-long sisters.

Leah and Saul had grown up together since Saul had come to live with Gamaliel's family and the two of them had a rocky, almost antagonistic, brother and sister type relationship. Over the years, she had not refrained from expressing her criticism of his fiery temper and what she called a "stubborn arrogance." She had a begrudging respect for him because of his intelligence, but mainly she had accepted Saul as a brother because of his unwavering devotion to her father. The two had agreed to a truce a few years ago and had settled into a peaceful life with only the occasional confrontation.

The girls seemed prepared to leave but were curiously delaying, stirring about the courtyard aimlessly and just as Saul was about to ask why, Gammy appeared and the eager shoppers smiled and moved to the gate.

Quite uncharacteristically, Gammy had made prior arrangements with his sister to accompany them to the markets. In all his time living here, Saul had never witnessed any interest for shopping the markets in Gammy.

After the first block, Saul was ready to leave the main route and explore the familiar side streets, but Gammy was intent on following the two young ladies, keeping a comfortable distance that allowed them to talk freely. This was not the direction Saul had wanted to wander around in, especially wearing his sparkling Pharisaical garments and all, but the Great Cardo market was an acceptable second choice and as good a place to be found on the eve of the Sabbath as any, he grudgingly decided.

This particular street was just another in the list of Herod's ambitious projects to renew the dated city, and within weeks of completion, the renovated Cardo had taken over as the principal shopping area of Jerusalem.

The market was a long, straight thoroughfare with hundreds of identical stalls lining it, all filled with their unique product. There was a roof over each stall that reached from the edge of the street to the back wall and this cover was held up with Roman-type columns at the front of each stall. Many stalls had further constructed rooms on the roof as a second story storehouse.

As the city was still crowded from all the pilgrims who had invaded it for the feast of Pentecost, today's market was more congested than normal, crammed full of shoppers who were busy preparing for the Sabbath. In the busiest parts of the long avenue, the shoppers were almost shoulder to shoulder.

Leah led the small entourage to the vegetable stalls first. Their, the goods were always fresh, some surprisingly provided by the fields in the faraway Plain of Sharon. At nighttime the mountainous road from Lydda was occupied with carts and wagons filled with produce destined for this great market. The wide gate at the north end of the Cardo opened at sunrise to accept the rush of fresh produce that had navigated the same route Saul and Miriam had ascended only yesterday. These "imported" foodstuffs successfully competed with the local farmers and the result was that every morning, fresh goods, picked only yesterday, was being bought by the most eager of shoppers at surprisingly fair prices.

The hillsides surrounding Jerusalem were less productive for ground crops, but were ideal for the raising of livestock and orchard fruits. Fresh lamb, goat and fowl were delivered daily to this market from nearby farms and the fresh meats were regularly sold out early in the day. Saul was amazed at the hard-working farmers who could keep a steady stream of food coming to the city on a regular basis, and then suddenly increase it four or five-fold when the High Holidays brought a huge influx of hungry travelers. It was said that the city exploded to over a million visitors at these times.

The massive Cardo market seemed to continue on and on and the many shops had every conceivable artifact allowable in this city. It even had one shop that counted Saul's family's tents in the products available for sale.

Closing his eyes for a moment, Saul drank in the clamor and the familiar sounds he had been missing. The loud sales pitches yelled in different languages were music to his ears, as was the bartering and back and forth bantering of the buyers. Along this street, it had become an enviable skill to good-naturedly insult each other while haggling over the price of every purchase, and for some, this was great entertainment. For the less talented, it was just Jews out-shouting their neighbors in as many dialects as one knew and a couple that they didn't. Saul understood some of these languages, and some, he did not. For him and for many other Jerusalemites, just being a spectator of all this was truly a delightful experience in bedlam.

As they pushed their way through the diverse crowd, Saul noticed many of the identifying synched robes of the Grecian Jews who were walking about with their haughty air of superiority, and these were mixed with a sprinkling of the expensive and ornately hemmed robes of the Jews from Alexandria. Other costumes were present and he was engrossed with the vast assortment of pilgrims pulsing through the streets of Jerusalem, some even bearing the decorated turbans of Persia. Some of the out-of-town shoppers took a curious second glance at the two young Pharisees who were sauntering slowly through the market with no purpose other than to observe and be observed. Saul was pleased.

Saul's attention was soon captured by another immaculately robed Pharisee who was dressed much like himself but with a slightly larger fringe on his robe. This man, he quickly recognized, was of the competing House of Shammai, who upon seeing Gammy and Saul, burst into a loud prayer only a few feet in front of them.

"Oh, Holy Father of all and giver of all the Law to our holy prophet Moses," he started in a well rehearsed voice, "it is with a thankful heart that I am able to be your servant, not like these common Jews who do not obey the Law as we Pharisees do."

Saul and Gammy recognized the familiar prayer and knew that such performances were encouraged and becoming increasingly promoted by all schools of the Pharisees. Although they sounded weirdly self-obsessed, these litanies served the purpose of letting the Jews know that they were not fulfilling the Law as it should be and that there were men among them who were proving that it was indeed possible. Saul stopped, raised his hands heavenward in a show of agreement while his praying colleague continued.

Loud displays such as this were intentionally designed to be practiced in public where they showered great spiritual benefits upon the common people who could not help but hear them. This way all Jews could also participate in Hashem's benevolence simply by the hearing-at least that was the accepted reasoning for such recitals.

A good many more skeptical Jews claimed that such performances were nothing more than an arrogant public shaming of the rest of Jewry, publicly presented with the obvious purpose of unabashed and childish self-promotion.

Saul had asked Gammy once why he had not seen or heard of him ever praying in public, but Gammy deftly avoided the question until pressed continuously. Saul even remarked that Gammy might not be fulfilling all areas of the Law with his lack of public prayer. Gammy's response was that the usefulness of such prayers were, at best, questionable in his mind and they probably served the ego of the particular performing Pharisee rather than serving God.

It was all Saul could do to not take that as a personal criticism for he was a frequent practitioner of such showy performances.

It was only because of Saul's regard for the purity of Gammy's heart that he let the matter die for it was not at all like Saul to not doggedly pursue such disagreements, regardless of anyone's sensitivities. He was gaining quite a reputation as a ferocious debater and anyone other than Gammy would undoubtably have been subject to a much more animated confrontation.

An elderly Jewish matron, slightly bent over from some malady and only a few steps from today's overt display, stopped her shopping and peered at this trio of Pharisees as though she wanted to engage them in conversation. All three quickly moved away, keeping the proscribed distance from this imperfect Jewess who must have fallen out of favor with Hashem. Her crooked back was the unmistakeable evidence of such heavenly disapproval.

The lady read the scornful inference on Saul's face correctly but only nodded and uttered a quick, 'Shabbat Shalom." Gammy responded with a heartfelt greeting, but Saul did not look at her or in any way recognize her for he was sure he had heard a tinge of poorly disguised sarcasm in her voice.

After an hour of trailing their sisters, Saul was getting more and more anxious to move on and was thankful when Leah and Miriam finally turned and waved a pleasant goodbye to them and disappeared up the stairway leading to the street that would take them back home. Again, curiously overfriendly, Gammy waved and smiled a warm goodbye and then turned his attention to Saul, ready to now focus on Saul's request to see the city.

A thought flashed through Saul's mind but he quickly dismissed it.

Gammy and Miriam? No. They were too much like brother and sister and they had only known each other a few hours. Gammy was only being the gracious host he was always known to be.

The two men continued down the length of the Cardo, crossing back and forth often to avoid unclean or unwanted situations like the wandering Roman soldiers, or some obviously sickly person. They then took a different street back toward the heights of Mount Zion.

Saul led the way, stopping to examine Caiaphas's house with the beautiful stone archways and historically carved wooden gate, then circling past King David's burial site, and then wandering slowly past Herod's Jerusalem home. Gammy patiently followed Saul's meandering path and watched with understanding as Saul touched the chiselled stones of the walls of the most ancient homes, all the time pausing and listening carefully as the haunting notes of the trumpets and shofars from the distant Temple would drift over them. When fully satisfied, Saul nodded to Gammy and they started for home without speaking.

Saul felt that his parched soul had just been revived and that he had received new strength from the heavens.

CHAPTER TWENTY-SIX

Gamaliel

When Saul and Gammy entered their quiet courtyard, Gammy's father, the famous Gamaliel, was home and having a hushed but intense conversation with his wife Sarah around the large table in the portico. He was still in the impressive white and blue robe, colorfully fringed with gold tassels, which he wore as the President of the Sanhedrin but today, the animated movement of his hands betrayed an anxiousness not common in the usual restrained demeanor of the most respected man in Jerusalem. Gamaliel's calm and guiding wisdom was legendary in this city and this wisdom was always dispensed with even-handedness and an unemotional approach. It was only when he became excited about an overlooked nuance in the Law or a new discovery in the writings of the prophets that he showed such emotion.

Gamaliel and Sarah were keeping their voices down and it was very clear that they did not want to be heard by the rest of the family or the servants.

Miriam and Leah were busy in the open kitchen, happily helping the servants to prepare for the approaching Sabbath and chatting away like old friends. Upon hearing Gammy and Saul closing the gate, Gamaliel rose and with a beaming smile opened his wide arms to embrace his prized student and part-time son. His heavy beard had greyed slightly in the year that Saul had been away and the stress of Jerusalem had added a few deep wrinkles into his grinning smile, but his smile was genuine.

"Ah, here you are, Saul my boy," he said affectionately. He also embraced Gammy and motioned for them all to sit with them. After a few pleasantries, Sarah demurely excused herself and disappeared into the culinary busyness at the back of the house.

"We missed you terribly around here, Saul, and certainly the school has suffered because of your absence, but in the end, we were happy that you got those extra months with your father, blessed be his memory," said the gentle and always considerate Gamaliel.

Upon hearing the rich voice of Gamaliel, Saul began feeling the sweetness of being at home again. He was so grateful to be a member of this warm household. He admired and revered Gamaliel as not only a teacher and mentor, but as a deep thinker possessing an unusually broad wisdom, and beyond that, a man with a generous and compassionate heart, almost to a fault. If there was any criticism of this sage, Saul thought that at times he was too generous, too eager to forgive and possibly, too hesitant to punish Law breakers.

"It was my sister Miriam who gave us that extra time. She turned out to be as good a physician as any of those that take your money and only make you worse," replied Saul, immediately regretting such a critical and cutting reply to the optimistic tone of Gamaliel. Gamaliel chose to ignore Saul's sharp words.

"I look forward to getting to know her, such a jewel of Israel, and my wife has certainly informed me of how much of a blessing she was for you and your family," he stated. "Now tell me more about your family and your voyage and what news is there from Cilicia. How are the Jews there faring?"

Saul spoke for over an hour about his father's illness and death, his family's grief, and then he quietly and humorously related the curious arrangement his father had made with Miriam. He described the long sea voyage, telling briefly of Caleb ben Israel from Cyprus and his concern for his son, Barnabas. He even described the giant of a soldier he had seen on the ship, knowing Gamaliel had an unusual and sometime consuming interest in such creatures since their disappearance from this area a few centuries before.

When he mentioned the two Jewish travelers and their voyage to Jerusalem to see Jesus, their apparent resurrected messiah, Gamaliel visibly straightened. Gammy did as well.

"Is that what the emergency meeting was about, Father," Gammy quickly asked his father, temporarily interrupting Saul's story.

Gamaliel quieted him with an uplifted hand and pronounced with firmness, "We will have a peaceful, blessed Sabbath, thankful to have old and new friends here and we will speak only of the many blessings that Hashem has provided us. We will talk about this after Sabbath and then I will let you know all happenings. I have a special request for you both and I need your wisdom and prudence in these matters. Also, I would appreciate not discussing these troubles in front of your sisters if that is possible."

The two young men easily agreed to that, but all knew that this was a family that had an almost impossible time keeping secrets from each other and they openly admitted that the men's best efforts at secrecy were laughingly futile against the wiles of the women. Saul was painfully aware that he was no match for the persuasiveness and good-natured connivance of his sister Miriam.

As the sun set over the hills of Judea and Samaria, the sweetness of the Sabbath rolled in, announced by ageless, bleating shofars blasting their haunting notes from the highest corners of the Temple walls. The ram's horns wailed their warnings up and down the rapidly emptying streets of Jerusalem.

Gamaliel's busy household settled into the blessed peace of the Sabbath.

Within moments, all were enjoying the traditional prayers and soothing songs of praise that accompany the Sabbath meal and soon they drifted into the deep spiritual rest that this much-anticipated day always provided. All agreed that they could not endure life without the regenerating powers of the Sabbath.

Gamaliel's Sanhedrin duties were also forgotten during the Sabbath. It was a sin to bring yesterday's problems into the day of rest, was it not, and every Jew labored to "keep" the Sabbath holy by not letting his mind return to yesterday's troubles, or for that matter, worry about the looming struggles ahead.

This day of rest was certainly a gift from Hashem.

CHAPTER TWENTY-SEVEN

The Sanhedrin, Politicians, and Other Religious Men

The Sanhedrin had two bodies: a lower court that ruled on the daily and more mundane problems that arose within Jerusalem and nearby communities, and a much larger and more important body that met to judge matters that could not be solved by the local lower court. The High Court also dealt with the continuous and more contentious appeals of rabbinical decisions, especially in matters that might affect the Jewish people throughout the worldwide dispersion. Letters of request from desperate synagogues around the world were delivered almost weekly to Gamaliel's door, all requiring immediate resolution of another Jewish conundrum.

The lower court was composed of twenty-three locally chosen men and almost comically, that number had been decided on because it was Jewish tradition that required a minyan of ten men in agreement to make any legal ruling. If for any reason a vote was tied by ten men on each side of an issue, making a total of twenty men voting, then an extra vote was required. Over the years, it was also decided that only one extra vote was not enough to negate and overrule ten opposing votes, so the number of the court had been

137

set first at twenty-two judges. This was then increased to twenty-three for the rare occasion that a tie would happen between twenty-two judges. It was a typically Jewish exercise in both linear and convoluted reasoning but it successfully served the purpose of deciding the less important issues that arose daily. Throughout the Jewish dispersion, almost every community had set up a similar court to deal with their local matters.

The Great Sanhedrin was much larger and diverse in its membership. It consisted of seventy-one men. These were chosen from among the High Priest and members of his close family, leading members of the Pharisees, some notable Sadducees, some Chief Priests of the Temple, a few important men of the Levites and a few select common Jews whose family lineage was impeccable. Since Hillel's dominating presence, the president of this body was appointed from his progeny.

The high court in Jerusalem was regarded as the "supreme" court for all things Jewish and dealt with matters that could not be resolved locally and these often included especially offensive local rulings that were being appealed. Many of the lower courts that had made decisions around the world were found to contradict each other, also causing much confusion. The Great Sanhedrin, with its final judgments, was considered the correct interpreters of scripture and, of course, the Mosaic Law. It seemed that the correct method of plucking a chicken was of equal interest to those in Babylon as it was to the Jews in faraway Spain and the perfect resolution of such matters was expected to be determined in Jerusalem's upper court.

The persistent demand of the Jerusalem Pharisees to be ultra-precise required not only the exact interpretation of written Jewish Law, but it also an accurate application of all traditions as well and it was the traditions that instructed every Jew on how to prepare a Sabbath fowl perfectly, along with thousands of other such seemingly trivial daily rituals. All dedicated Jews worried greatly about just how Moses had performed those everyday chores and faithful Jews wanted and demanded clarity. For these reasons, all looked to the great institution in Jerusalem for their answers.

As president, Gamaliel would rule on the most obvious questions alone but it was the more complicated ones that made it to the floor of the judgement hall. Divorce issues, tithing questions, Sabbath work allowed, punishments and many other serious disputes were the areas that the Great Sanhedrin dealt with continually. Because of this, its influence on daily life in Judaism was all-encompassing.

Over the last decade, Jerusalem's less important lower court had become dominated by men who favored the strictest interpretations when making their rulings. Predictably, these men demanded the harshest reparation or punishment that the Law or, alternatively, the Romans allowed for breaking such rules. Other Sanhedrin's, those of the Jewish communities around the world, were less inclined to the severity of the one in Jerusalem for the far-off Jewish enclaves were less influenced by the relentless political zealousness of the Judean Jews.

As President of the High Court, Gamaliel filled a position that had for the last fifty years been given to the revered Hillel and each of his direct descendants, meaning that he alone had the overseer's responsibility and that occupied much of his time. Complicating matters for him was the fact that it was commonly known that his teachings and his personal disposition did not agree with the tone and rulings of Jerusalem's lower court and it seemed that Judaism had to be dragged kicking and screaming into the world that his grandfather had introduced. Hillel described a world based on loving Hashem, a tenet easily accepted by all, but also a world where one would love his neighbor equally as much. It was in the second command that the great problems lay for Judaism.

Until three years ago, the head judge of the lower Sanhedrin had been the venerated Shammai, a Pharisee who led an opposing school to Gamaliel's more forgiving academy, and consequently his rigid interpretation of the Law had dominated that court's decisions. The record of beatings and floggings as daily occurrences bothered Gamaliel greatly and he often felt obliged to step into their sphere and move a lower court decision to the higher court, hoping for more reasoned verdicts. The lower court did not appreciate this interference and the resulting political tension spilled into the ongoing religious debate between the two major and increasingly competitive Houses of the Pharisees.

Today, Gamaliel was thankful that Saul had returned for he could now turn over the responsibility of teaching at his famous school to the two reliable young men whom he trusted entirely. With Saul and Gammy taking over that aspect, he could concentrate on trying to counter the influence of the harsher lower court with a more righteous and prudent application of the Law.

Beyond creating a silent but deepening religious rift over many of his judgments in the higher court, the more severe and militant verdicts were gaining deeper support from the dangerous political "zealots." These were men who were more than willing to interpret the severe judgments as an opening to demand the harshest of punishments and thereby introduce violence into the everyday life of Jews in their quest to incite their all-to-complacent brethren to revolt.

Complicating matters even more was the fact that if these men could not get lawful "license," in the form of a favorable Sanhedrin decision, they were quite willing to use force in the form of an unruly mob to achieve their political goals. A violent Jerusalem was an easy atmosphere in which to expand their influence.

Gamaliel understood that this was dangerous for all Jews. The ever-present and scrupulously observant Romans were relentless in their pursuit of any sign of rebellion or insurgence and he realized that they would quickly move against any increase in violence, simply interpreting it all as rebellion, even if that violence was one religious Jew upon another religious Jew.

What this all meant in practical terms for Gamaliel was that every morning he felt compelled to make his way to the Temple compound and observe from the spectator's seats the rulings that took place in the judgment hall where the lower Sanhedrin met. His formidable presence did not go unnoticed and many decisions were no doubt made by observing the reaction and posture of Gamaliel but he rarely spoke in the lower court and would only interject when an obvious or grievous error was being made.

Since the death three years previous of the rigid but extremely honest Shammai, the lower court was gaining the shameful reputation of being easily manipulated by money and reward. This put even more importance on Gamaliel's presence at any important trials and while there, he increasingly found himself at odds with the scandalous attempts of the lawyers to use the court for personal gain or retribution. Many of the rich and influential of Jerusalem had garnered large portions of their wealth and political influence with the help, whether intentional or unintentional, of this dubious chamber.

Before this lower court, the plight of widows and orphans was always disgustingly predictable. The decisions favored the lawyers and the wealthy, who consistently came away with any savings the poor had managed. Such decisions were explained and supported by confusing jargon regarding the exactitude of Moses's Law, the "righteousness" of impartial and cold-hearted application of that Law and the evilness of such concepts as "mercy" when applying that Law. The traditional, but extremely one-sided divorce laws guaranteed the nation many unsupported women as well, a fact the court said was regrettable but unavoidable if the Law was applied correctly. The death of a Jew without a male heir left his inheritance to his brothers and the result was a nation abounding with destitute widows. Only the most charitable of Jews made any provision for mourning wives or the children of their deceased brothers. Gamaliel often wondered how such cold-heartedness had crept into the day-to-day functioning of this nation, but he could not change it unless he chose to rise up and overrule the traditional interpretations of the Law.

Truthfully, he well knew the main well-spring of callousness.

Gamaliel cautiously refrained from telling Saul and Gammy all his fears and suspicions regarding the court and he intentionally avoided any mention of the highly questionable actions of the High Priest who lately had taken to arresting and condemning religious and political opponents in the dark of night. He, possibly too optimistically, hoped that his continued attendance and influence could somehow refocus Jerusalem and the court, plus he did not want to make irreversible skeptics out of his two charges by destroying their respect for Israel's most influential leaders.

The mention of Jesus and the troubling, even ludicrous events that had taken place with this man, had harshly reminded Gamaliel that his voice was suspiciously, and quite purposely, being excluded from some of the more questionable processes of judgment. He took that as a slight but also a symptom of larger problems.

Both courts of the Sanhedrin met in the majestic and convenient Hall of Hewn Stones, but at different times. This Hall was a large, high-ceilinged room built on the Temple Plaza directly adjacent to the north side of the Temple Building. It shared a common wall with the Women's court and part of the inner Men's court, and as its name implied, was built with stones formed without the use of a metal tool. This was done as an expression of the purity expected in all the actions of this chamber and this intention was decreed by Herod himself after much consultation with Gamaliel's grandfather, Hillel. The setting, that of sharing a wall with the altar of sacrifice, should have reminded all involved of the solemnity and purity of the judgments rendered. The location was also a constant reminder of how closely connected Jewish common law was with religious Law and that Israel was a nation meant to have no distance or conflict between heavenly or earthly concerns.

Its originators had envisioned this place as a hall of justice for all Jews, a place where fair rulings would protect rich and poor alike, much as Solomon's courts had, but lately it had become a place to avoid as it became the tool of those who could financially sway and manipulate. Gamaliel's inherited position also made him the only one with the authority to interfere with the brutality and rush to punishment that was recently meted out for the smallest of infractions.

Recently, the lower court had begun meeting daily as there seemed an unending list of complaints among the population, a precious few eager to forgive and forget and even fewer willing to suffer any loss for the sake of peace among the Jews. It gave way only when the larger Great Sanhedrin was meeting.

The larger, Great Sanhedrin usually met weekly, but as the political hostility and division between the factions of the Jews grew, especially in Judea, more and more questions were being submitted and the usual weekly meetings had turned into twice weekly. The growing tensions also led to long sessions with much loud and irrational debate, often with awkward and bad-tempered arguments erupting constantly. Elegantly robed and distinguished sage-like rabbis screaming insults through their spittle-coated beards was not the level of purity envisioned for the Hall of Hewn Stones and Gamaliel was often embarrassed as this austere body humiliated itself again and again with its pettiness and childish behavior.

Lately, it was apparent that the Jews were growing even more contentious, eagerly segregating into their rigidly defined and competing sects which resulted in a predictable descent into chaos in the court. It seemed no one had the ability to see or understand the full affect of their sectarian hatreds beyond their own myopic view.

Gamaliel had even a deeper fear haunting his late-night thoughts.

Was God somehow "allowing" this sharp and dark descent into incivility by withdrawing His influence on the minds of the Jews. How else could one explain such suicidal national insanity.

To give the lower Sanhedrin court some semblance of clout, it was given control of the "external" Temple guards as its enforcement arms and this was a problem.

Since the time of Moses, all the Levite guards of the Temple were chosen and organized with the task of being the protectors of the religious purity of the Temple. They possessed only the power to arrest and punish violators of the sacredness of the House of Hashem, having no authority outside the

Temple area. Over the years this had slowly been changed and now there were another squad of guards who operated much differently.

There were still the ever present and richly costumed Levite guards. These were men chosen from the monthly influx of priests who came from all over the country to do their once-a-year Levitical duties at the Temple and were generally a jovial lot who stood at the many gates, greeting newcomers and directing them around the complex. They watched for the occasional trespassing Gentile and generally made the Temple area run smoothly and peacefully. These were unarmed, harmless and often had to be awakened from an unscheduled afternoon nap by a slap from the Captain of the Guard, harshly reminded of the "seriousness" of their duties. Each new moon brought a new group of these guards from the surrounding villages of Judea.

Operating alongside the harmless Levites was the other type of Temple guard. These were permanent fixtures around the Temple and they were paid a handsome salary out of the Temple funds. This meant they considered Caiaphas, the High Priest and controller of the funds, as their boss and as one would expect, they took their direction from him. These fellows were employed to hunt down and arrest any that the court, under the direction of the High Priest, accused. They were given the authority to inflict punishments, and that included the various beatings and floggings, all of which they seemed all too anxious to carry out.

This troop was easily recognized in the streets for they chose to wear a military style uniform complete with sword and knife, and they seemed to want to emulate the vicious Romans. Certain members had become close confidants and life-long recipients of the largesse of the High Priest's family and could be counted on to fulfill every personal wish of Annas or Caiaphas. Their direction and commands came covertly through Malchus, the menacing personal servant of Caiaphas and this arrangement allowed the High Priest to retain his appearance as the kind and loving father of the Jewish nation, not as the one who maliciously targeted political opponents.

The haunts of these men were not the sunny courtyards of the Temple but rather the dank, raunchy rooms and jail cells in the bowels of the tall Temple walls-jail cells that Herod the Great had constructed for nefarious purposes of his own. Although these dungeons were hidden away from the starry-eyed and religious pilgrims who were mesmerized by the beauty of the great House above, the permanent residents of Jerusalem were all too aware of the dingy vaults, a constant reminder of the intimidating power of the most influential ones in the city.

The sad truth of Jerusalem was that it was segregated into many warring religious and political sects and the spiderweb of relationships between them was almost impossible to decipher, even to the most politically astute.

Easily the most recognized and influential religious movement of the entire Jewish nation was that of the Pharisees. To Gentile outsiders, these men appeared to be pompous, arrogant egomaniacs who had very little in common with the rest of the Jewish people and who were constantly criticizing and rebuking their brothers. To the Jewish population, those that understood their nation's checkered history of constantly angering their God, it was hard to refute the message that the Pharisees brought and somehow had appointed themselves the carriers of. That message was "obedience or punishment."

In a curious historical twist, the Pharisees had been successful in transferring a semblance of Moses's authority to themselves, at least in their own minds, and to a lesser degree in the minds of the general Jewish population. Comically, they also vigorously attacked any attempt by others to share that mantle of authority, thus making it their primary mission in life to confront and disavow any teachers or teachings that did not arise from their sect. Protecting Jewry at large often took second place to their main occupation, that of protecting the reputation of their individual teacher or their beloved synagogue.

This religious "gang-ism" often culminated in compelling street-corner brawls, mostly verbal arguments that started between richly gowned, immaculately groomed and piously devout men but which often ended in clumsy, unathletic fist fights. Curses were flung about with abandon; smears were often yelled through bloody and swollen lips, and obscenities were uttered which mentioned the lineage of the opponent and his curious relationship to some beast.

These comical events provided a level of theatrical entertainment to the most cynical of observers and were accompanied by guffaws, applause and great laughter. The serious Pharisees were adamant that amusing the crowds was not the purpose of their debates but they could not seem to stop their childish displays. To many, the only noticeable benefit of these spectacles was the increase in business for the few merchants who were expert at repairing the tears in the expensive robes and removing deep red blood stains from pure white tunics.

The Pharisaical movements propagated themselves with competing schools of learning made up of young Jews sent to learn at the feet of Jerusalem's respected and powerful rabbis. Recently, their reputations for religious purity had suffered greatly from these conflicts but they could not cease their battling, for each believed that their academy was teaching the true Word of Hashem and that their particular rabbi was the closest to God. Wide-eyed students often believed that their teacher was the only spigot a thirsty Jew could access to drink from the refreshing waters of heaven. Ego-stroked teachers did nothing to lessen that belief.

Their most respected teachers, appearing extremely wise, could not escape the mental trap of considering their individual popularity, their increasing wealth and their inflated self-importance as Hashem's heavenly commendation. Once such "irrefutable" proofs of divine favor were established in their own minds, it became easy for them to consider their own thoughts as private directives from Hashem and on par with His prophet, Moses. From this lofty perch, condemnation of any other thinking was straightforward and even highly profitable. Argument and debate were then considered a sign of dedication to the truth. Contention in the form of protecting one's esteemed rabbi was then valued as a holy endeavor. To suffer a punch or two, even to the point of sporting a black eye, was highly prized.

The modern version of Pharisee, the type that enamored Saul, had begun just a hundred years previous with the Maccabees. Under that influence, the nation dramatically recognized its disobedience and failures before Hashem and were reminded of the blessings available when they would obey the exactness of the Law. The movement grew quickly in Judea and the irrefutable evidence of its truthfulness was the miraculous re-established country of Israel under the demanding Maccabees. All were convinced that the short but glorious national interlude happened because of the revival of Jewish piety that had obviously pleased God.

The Maccabean movement was a rural one, away from the crumbling, unimpressive and morally suspect Temple atmosphere and its devotees turned their attention to the local synagogues which became the pulpits for these new and pious teachers. Armed with their passionate message, schools of learning were appearing all over Judea and each proclaimed their precise version of required strictness and separation as declared by the Torah.

Of these teachers, the humble Babylonian woodcutter by the name of Hillel had become the most famous and influential of all. After struggling against the elitism of Jerusalem, his wisdom was finally recognized in numerous outstanding and unique judgments, so much so, that the leader of the Sanhedrin was forced to step down and appoint him as the President of that body. This happened around his eightieth year and he remained the president of the Sanhedrin until his death at the age of 120 in the year CE 10. The remarkable similarity to Moses's life, being divided into three segments of forty years, created dizzying forays of speculation and declarations of the uniqueness of this virtuous man, some even calling him the recipient of the mantle of Moses. Others went as far as warning of a damnation of those who did not regard Hillel as Moses' foretold prophet, with many learning to distrust any who failed to regard him in the very highest esteem.

In the last forty years of his life, Hillel had established a school of learning of his own which his son Simeon and now his grandson Gamaliel, perpetuated. Mainly because of his efforts, the reputation of the Pharisees grew in both size and respectability. It was from the study of the Law, mellowed by the words of Israel's ancient prophets, that an uncommon understanding emerged that separated Hillel from other honored teachers and had raised the estimation of the Pharisee's in general.

As the glory of the Maccabean period faded and the leaders of that family became just as corrupt as their predecessors, Hillel began to understand and teach a much deeper theology than just a cold obedience to the Law. He realized that the Law and the prophets were given to affect a Jew at a personal level, in their minds and attitudes, and the effect of the sacred writings was not to be expressed in just a national calling. Soon, this belief became the underlying foundation of all his teachings.

The Romans, when they finally came to rule Judea, found a strangely peaceable people whose leaders quickly agreed to an unusual truce with them.

"Allow us to serve our God under our Law without interference and we will not rebel," they proposed.

As a result of the call to a personal purity rather than demanding national and individual separation, there emerged a new period of peaceful coexistence for most Jews, at least for a short time, and it received its greatest theological and spiritual impetus from the halls and yeshivas of Jerusalem.

Hillel's initial approach to all problems was that within the Law itself there had to be the answers. Although venerated and quoted continually for these twenty-three years since his death, Gamaliel was watching his nation slowly drift away from his grandfather's teachings in their daily practices. More troubling, he was witnessing a drifting away from the call to personal decency.

In a strange twist, Gamaliel had heard that Jesus had often quoted his grandfather and had been soundly reviled for repeating Hillel's insights.

During the later years that Hillel was influencing Jerusalem, another young and strong-willed teacher emerged. He was a locally-born Jew, raised on the raucous streets of Jerusalem and being local, he shared the overtaxed, Roman-despising, political grievances that constantly fomented in Jerusalem. Shammai was his name, and just as the House of Hillel had grown, so grew the fledgling House of Shammai where "Moses" was also taught. The emphasis of Shammai was a return to the strictest obedience to the Law and to him, that meant a more rigid set of rewards and punishments for Jewish behavior which had no allowance for variations. His unyielding approach to all aspects of life went even further than most as he taught that Jews should not buy or sell from a Gentile, a teaching that was not popular with those who made a living in international trade. He taught that a Jew must hold to every letter of the Law and added the practice of personal shunning of those who did not agree. In practice, this was an attempt to shame and embarrass opponents into compliance.

After Shammai's recent passing, his close followers, feeling they knew the real intentions of their beloved rabbi, mimicked the rigidity of their teacher and began thinking they should also become disagreeable. They soon prized this outward approach and taught that this argumentative and miserable attitude was highly favored by Hashem. The predictable result was that these followers became more and more unbending and confrontational, making excuse for themselves by claiming that these actions somehow honored their teacher.

Whereas the House of Hillel taught that one should study all sides of an issue, the House of Shammai had no regard for another's opinion and in the inevitable and noisy street corner debates that both these sects of Pharisees loved and participated in, the Hillel-ites usually won the public's acclamation for they knew the Shammai-ites' argument as well as their own and thus could easily prepare for and counter any points made. This made the students of Shammai even more miserable.

Gamaliel taught his students well and they usually did very well in such public forums, but he had also taught them not to gloat for that just took away from the usefulness of the exercise. Such benevolent behavior also added to the respect for the House of Hillel, being regarded as godlier by the small crowds who bothered to witness such vain and self-absorbed arguments.

Lately, as the arduous and contentious Roman rule in Judea continued and was spurred on by the Roman's penchant for foolishly solving all disputes with unmatched brutality, a deep hatred was developing in the general population of Jews for the captivity they were under. There was a growing willingness to speak of rebellion in the back alleys and in the dark side rooms of some synagogues. This willingness was inspired in the Jewish imagination by their warm-hearted recitals of the way the Maccabees had viciously overthrown both the Greeks and those Jews that had conspired with them. The militaristic, angry approach of the Shammai-ites had an appeal to those who had begun to conspire against both the Romans and the Herodian puppet kings and Gamaliel was becoming very aware of the dangers of such back-alley plotting.

Notwithstanding the artificial boundaries Rome had drawn when dividing Herod's kingdom into four separate tetrarchies and allowing the Jews their own ceremonial royalty, a zealousness for a free and united Jewish country was still fomenting around the dinner tables of Judaism. The harsh doctrines of the house of Shammai were the perfect fit for such "zealots," whereas the soft, forgiving vein that ran through Gamaliel's teachings did nothing to incite the population or feed the anger.

Because the patriarchs of the House of Hillel inherited the Presidency of the Sanhedrin, the influence of the House of Shammai was kept in check in that revered chamber and was curtailed in any long-term political decision making, at least for the moment. In the streets and synagogues, the differences in interpretation were growing very apparent and had recently morphed from merely theoretical and vocal squabbles into a sharp and disturbing personal animosity between the Pharisees houses' and that dislike was escalating dangerously.

To demonstrate their increasing dedication, the Shammai-ites had stopped any civil discussions with the House of Hillel, or for that matter, with any who disagreed with them. Believing their path to be the only road to the salvation of Israel and greatly annoyed that their public teachings seemed to be having little effect, they introduced, encouraged and at times financed a new phenomenon in Jerusalem called the "mob." This was a collection of easily convinced, emotionally controlled and politically useful men who were encouraged to see themselves as having some historic importance and novel political power previously denied men of their lower status. This group tolerated absolutely no disagreement and believed the Shammai-ite message without question. When logic, rational thinking, or even a Sanhedrin decision did not go the way of the Shammai disciples, a few coins could quickly gather these fellows and the screaming and fist-waving pack could suddenly get the results that more reasonable debating efforts could not.

Ominously, the peaceful message of Hillel that was accepted and embraced fifty years previous was slowly being eroded by the seductive teachings of this new brand of Pharisee, fiery men who had an almost hypnotic appeal to the action-starved youths of the synagogues. These young men were raised in a time of relative peace and predictably, were responding to the seducing calls of defeating their oppressors and establishing a glorious Jewish nation once more. The ugly side of any such war—the bloodied, the wounded and the deaths—were just far-removed stories and need not be emphasized.

The ultimate result was that the traveling Pharisees from the House of Hillel were beginning to be seen around the Empire as bringing a boring and burdensome teaching consisting of a continual, boring, life-long obedience to Moses's Law. This teaching conveyed a daily, depressing reminder of the failure of one's nature and an unreachable perfection that screamed of a life of onerous guilt and submission. That was a colorless comparison to the exciting vision of unrestricted liberty and purpose that a rebellion presented. It was not hard to understand that as the tally of Roman brutalities against their countrymen increased, the Jews began drifting to a more militant way of thinking, both in politics and religion.

The third group that made up the broad term of Pharisee was the more religiously intense but non-political Essenes. Their devoted followers were spread throughout Judea, but in much smaller groups because of the radical changes in lifestyle that their teachings required. Essenes believed in living in a communal cluster and upon joining, rich and poor willingly gave up all they had for the community of believers. Their teaching also demanded a high level of piety that even the strictness of the other two sects did not approach. Only men were allowed into the celibate and highly monastic communities, further limiting the appeal of these Pharisees.

The more exclusionary communities that existed among the diverse Essenes had developed extraordinary and unusual rules which most Jews saw as unnecessary and ridiculous. After receiving much public criticism, the non-combative devotees withdrew to isolated sanctuaries, mainly in desert or wilderness areas where they could practice their piety in peace. These isolated havens demanded a regimen of daily purifying with bathing, much praying, no expressions of anger, a life committed to benevolence and charity plus complete obedience to the dictates of the elected elder of the group. Only a very few chose to commit to such an existence.

Members of this sect were dedicated to the intense study and interpretation of the oldest and, if possible, original writings of the ancient elders of Israel and because of that, were constantly needing to make new copies of the scrolls that they wore out with their daily readings and minute scrutiny. To make sure of their authenticity, these men were continually searching out the oldest and most precise scrolls that were available and then copying them perfectly on the most durable skins they could find. So dedicated to exactness were they, that a slight slip of the quill would cause the rejection and burning of a scroll that had been labored on for weeks. Their growing libraries contained some of the oldest and, in a few cases, the last remaining records of ancient Israel, especially after the tragic fire in Alexandria had wiped out many such documents. The method of storing their precious skins and parchments in sealed clay pots in a dry desert atmosphere was considered ideal and there were rumors that the Essenes were burying multiple copies they had made in remote secret caves. Apparently there had been a warning, akin to a prophecy and given by supernatural inspiration, that tragedy was coming to the Jews and such scrolls would be needed in the future.

Their legendary founder, Manehim, a friend and an early student of Hillel, had been a contemporary of Herod the Great and upon seeing the young Herod as a student, had prophesied that he would be king one day. Herod remembered that as a miraculous prediction and when he indeed became king, sent for Manehim to assist him. He again prophesied, quite correctly, that Herod would be king for a period of thirty years. When Herod was dying, the aged Manehim, feeling his usefulness in Jerusalem was over, went out and established an isolated community near the Dead Sea which was the strictest and most communal of all the Essene communities. The self-imposed isolation was his unspoken protestation to the politicking that to him had become an odious and distasteful part of Pharisaical behavior in the city. This attitude was memorialized and imitated by all his Essene followers who also labored to avoid Jerusalem and its abhorrent conspiracies from that time forward.

Manehim had been a deeply spiritual man who did not see much to choose between the other two sects of Pharisees. He saw them as men who seemed to love to engage in wordy, grandiose expressions rather than actual religion, so he decided that he had to remove himself from the Jerusalem weights that eventually seemed to overtake the good men who had begun their public lives so virtuously.

Even though they were not physically in Jerusalem, the influence of the Essenes on the city and the seats of power was strong, although subtle. Their monastic lifestyles were legendary and were a constant, nagging reminder of a level of spirituality that was possible for the Jewish people. The Essenes deeply believed in an immortal soul and spoke often of the differing spiritual dimensions and realms where men's souls existed. They seemed to have the ability to predict the future, as Manehim had with Herod, but as it is with men, it was not long before they saw themselves as having a religiously superior calling not meant for the common Jew. For this reason, they preferred to keep their studies secret, not wanting to see their pearls of knowledge handled by vulgar, contentious and unpurified minds.

The Essene's indirect influence on the nation was manifest in that their ritual washings had evolved into a curious practice among Jewry, that of baptizing in water as a signal of a new spiritual and mental beginning, a washing away of old wrongdoings and ways of thinking. Certain of their disciples had taken this practice outside of the community and were baptizing any who professed such an awakening. Within their community, the Essenes performed this washing daily, even more often if required, representing the evolving and continued growth of the spirit and indicating the abandonment of yesterday's stale thinking.

Through their growing years, Saul and Gammy had witnessed the stealthy and unannounced visits of one fully bearded, sage-like man who was always clothed in a plain white garment peculiar to the commune of Qumran. This curious character would appear at their home at least once a year and he always arrived without notice, sometimes bent from bearing heavy scrolls in his large cloth sack slung over his shoulder, other times leading a mangy and dust covered donkey. He would stay many days, excitedly chattering with Gamaliel, lovingly opening each scroll and pointing out one passage or the other with a scrawny, ink-stained finger. He refused any sleeping comforts but rather spent the night outside on a tawdry mat, rising early to continue his discussions in the morning. He used the mitzvah bath religiously and seemed to not want conversation with anyone other than Gamaliel. Always, he demurely covered his eyes in the presence of the very attractive Sarah, who quickly learned to avoid him as a courtesy to the hermit-like man.

Gamaliel once told the boys the story of this peculiar man.

He had been an extremely bright student of Hillel in his youth but had suddenly left the clamor of Jerusalem, preferring the solitude and mystical life of the desert and the leadership of Manehim. For many years now, he had served the Essene community as the collector of the most authentic and oldest versions of the ancient Hebrew writings, often scouring the markets of Damascus or Beersheba if new documents were even rumored. He and his complaining donkey were frequently seen traveling afar to collect some precious find, not leaving the acquisition of such documents to chance but personally visiting synagogues and family collections throughout the country. His quest became known nationally among scholars and lately he had been inundated with many old family scrolls and tattered copies of writings hundreds of years old, given by those who felt there may be some unseen value to these discarded family heirlooms. It was said that he possessed the oldest versions of Josher and Enoch that remained on earth and among his prized documents were parts of the original writings of Joshua which had been taken to Babylon centuries before in the captivity. His ability to read and write in the ancient languages, including old Hebrew and forgotten Sumerian were legendary. His visits to Gamaliel occurred almost always after some significant discovery had been made by him while pouring over a recently acquired parchment.

In Gamaliel, this old scholar had found an ally in his intense belief that many crucial documents, along with the knowledge and understandings contained in them, had been lost to the Jews and to the world since the time of Moses. He further believed that there were spiritual truths and insights that Hashem wanted to share exclusively with those who were not mired in theology and politics. Like-wise-minded, Gamaliel relished the days spent with this exceptionally clear and unfettered mind and he always appreciated the break from the murky politics of Jerusalem that these visits created. The mystical man had never been formally introduced to Saul and Gammy, so the lads referred to him as the wrinkled hermit.

It was true that Gamaliel was a bit wary of a curious and controversial belief that this mysterious recluse held and which he expressed to only a few trusted souls, of which Gamaliel was counted as one. The old sage spoke of an experience within the mind of a man that could link him directly with Hashem, just as Moses and David had become linked. He convincingly pointed out that the writings and even the thoughts of those two men were now universally accepted as being those of Hashem himself. Beyond that, Moses had become a professed "friend" of God, plus David had a heart like Hashem's. This Essene spoke of a calling for the Jews that transcended the teaching of strict obedience as a path to Hashem and he spoke passionately of a blending of the characteristics of Hashem with the minds and lives of men. If this happened, he claimed, men would by nature fulfil all that the Law intended. He went even further and described the coming Messiah as a complete and perfect blending of a man's mind and body with the unmeasurable qualities of Jehovah.

The last time that this learned man had appeared was over a year ago now and at the time, he seemed especially frail, struggling to speak clearly, often gasping for breath. He brought a single large scroll of Isaiah with him and with tearful eyes began reading many strange references to Messiah, those which spoke of suffering and rejection. He was deeply disturbed and fearful of the actions of his political and maddeningly frivolous brethren for he was adamant that Messiah was imminent and it seemed none were prepared for His appearance. Gamaliel, who usually was an eager participant in these scriptural discoveries, had remained pensive and quiet at the latest rantings of this old man, not sure if this was senility speaking or a dire warning that must be listened to. Deep within, Gamaliel somehow knew he should not simply disregard the Essenes passion.

Added to his messianic fears, the old man had a deeply held apprehension of oncoming upheavals and judgments for the nation of Israel itself. As a result, this devoted scholar, and meticulous librarian, had begun sealing most of his irreplaceable collection into the clay preserving jars and then hiding the originals in the deepest of the hundreds of caves in the rugged rocky crags surrounding the small desert community. He could not bear the thought of the last of many old and precious documents disappearing in some senseless, meaningless skirmish brought on by another callous rebellion of his brethren. To further preserve truths contained in his treasures, the community made multiple copies and spread them throughout the many caves in the region.

CHAPTER TWENTY-EIGHT

John the Baptist

Over the years, the reputation of the Essenes had mainly attracted older Jews who wished to retreat from distasteful experiences they had endured in their religious lives, but quite unexpectedly, one young disciple was brought to them by his parents as a very young child. They were adamant that the lad had a special calling and must not be contaminated with religion as it was practiced in Jerusalem. He was an unusual child who, although not overtly pious, seemed to have an inborn and natural spirituality, easily understanding the deep concepts that sometimes befuddled the rest of the community. He was direct and blunt, avoided flattery and spoke often and passionately about the coming Messiah. He was continually challenging all around him, even his overly pious elders, to change their ways, tear down their uplifted self-importance and do things humbly to please God. He spoke often of the importance of meekness and repentance to his friends in the Essene community, stating that this was the very nature of Hashem himself.

The community could not withstand or refute any points in his heartfelt preaching but they soon decided that his continual criticisms were a disruption to the peace of their settlement and at the age of seventeen, this one named John was politely asked to leave. There had been others asked to leave for a variety of reasons, mainly moral failings, but John was not numbered with them. When confronted, it seemed he had almost expected this response and without remorse embraced a solitary and reclusive life in the surrounding deserts.

Holding no grudge, John would occasionally come back to the community to visit, but his conversation grew more and more judgmental and almost frantic, eventually claiming he had seen Messiah with his own eyes. This made his old mentors and friends increasingly uncomfortable. His reputation as a deranged wild man was growing, but for many his regard as a modern prophet also grew and his chosen isolation reminded many of the ancient prophet Elijah. John would spend extended periods of time wandering the wilderness on both sides of the Dead Sea and had exchanged the white garments of the Essenes for a long-haired camel skin. This primitive attire further added to his prophetic legend.

Herod Antipas, one of the unremarkable sons of Herod the Great, spent half of his year living in Mechaurus, his inherited castle retreat on the eastern hilltops overlooking the Dead Sea. On his frequent trips to Jerusalem, Antipas would have to cross the Jordan Valley just north of the Dead Sea where John wandered and preached and where the easy access to the waters of the lower Jordan were perfect for his practice of baptizing those who believed his message of change and renewal. Most times when Antipas would make this journey, this wild man would appear just where the roadway cut through the river and where the convoy had to slow their progress for the bumpy crossing. For Antipas, it was always an unpleasant confrontation.

With piercing eyes and a loud voice, the bizarre baptizer would call out to the royal travelers, demanding they change their ways and prepare for the coming of Messiah. This dressing down and disrespectful upbraiding was an insolence not at all appreciated by such a regal and self-satisfied caravan.

Jews had heard this ancient and oft-repeated prediction of Messiah many times over the years, but never had it been preached with this authority and passion, or with the immediateness that John was talking about. Travelers who left the King's Highway on the eastern heights and descended westward into the Jordan Valley, or conversely, those whose went down eastward from Jerusalem, were likely to see John the Baptist as he became known. The wild-haired fanatic was, without fail, seen preaching passionately on the banks or waist-deep in the river, baptizing a new believer. Like Antipas, many travelers tried to avoid him while others attempted to denigrate him as just another of the self-appointed prophets who had led many away into the desert before. Many judged him as mentally deranged and eccentric, but all were disturbed and affected one way or the other by this child of the desert.

John's message of repentance and paving the way for Messiah became more and more pointed and accusatory and he did not shy away from confronting those who hurried by or who had gathered to hear him. He was obviously not impressed with the beautiful robes and haughty attitudes of the Pharisees who would come all the way from Jerusalem to see for themselves what the latest tumult was about. He met their arrogance with a vehemence that surprised, then embarrassed and infuriated them. It was his whole-hearted acceptance amongst the common people that protected him from immediate reprisals from the pompous religious ones and they remained leery of condemning him even after suffering many scathing tongue lashings and being insulted with names such as "vipers" and "snakes."

John's fatal mistake was to unleash this type of attack on the morals of Herod Antipas, one of the three remaining sons of Herod the Great whom the Romans had installed as kings as a family favor to Herod the Great. These sons were not near the leadership quality of their father and they spent most of their time in pursuit of money and pleasure, but the cagey Romans, for reasons of their own, had divided the father's kingdom into roughly quarters, which they called tetrarchies, and obligingly gave one to Antipas.

Antipas's quarter was further split into two areas. One part included a portion of the Galilee, and because of his first marriage to the daughter of local king in Arabia, the second included the hilltops east of the Dead Sea, including the area of the ancient Moabites. This was a prime location on the King's Highway, the famous trading route from Arabia to Babylon, and it guaranteed Antipas generous tariffs on the goods moving north from the huge expanses of the exotic south. These tariffs, along with an annual stipend from the Romans, kept his divided and expensive kingdom financed.

Antipas had ambitiously rebuilt the town of Tiberius on the shores of the Sea of Galilee as his capital and fawningly renamed it to honor the Roman leader, but because it was foolishly erected on an ancient Jewish grave site, very few pious Jews would enter there. This was a fact that most Jews found outrageously amusing. Antipas traveled often between his split tetrarchy and Jerusalem, fully enjoying the smarmy esteem of a self-professed monarch and stylishly moving around in a pretentious royal caravan. In truth, he favored the southern section of his divided kingdom for in it was Petra, the mysterious and beautiful city carved out of the rock cliffs. This section also included his isolated castle, Mechaerus, where he could hide away from the constant criticisms of the snarky Jerusalem Jews.

Antipas was in a life-long competition with his half-brother Phillip, to whom the Romans had also given a tetrarchy. As was normal in this family, Antipas saw himself as the superior of the brothers and went about publicly proving this by seducing and then marrying the beautiful and ambitious Herodias, who happened to be Phillip's wife and, bizarrely, his own cousin. In a confused attempt at deference to the Jewish divorce laws, he then divorced his first wife, the daughter of the powerful King of Arabia. This impulsive tactic proved to be an ill-advised maneuver that began years of military and economic trouble with Arabia, plus it drew ridicule and continual condemnation from the pious Jews. Marrying a brother's wife while that brother was alive was an obvious breach of the Law and it became the one sin that John the Baptist continually screamed out against.

Strangely, it seemed John knew just when the king would travel the Jordan Valley and when the caravan of the king would slow to cross the river. Without fail, John would be there and would loudly, and very publicly, accuse and embarrass him. The insecure king tried his best to ignore the attacks, often slinking down in his carriage or even hiding beneath a blanket but his new wife would not be continually humiliated in this way and convinced the king to finally arrest him. This was followed by a debauched celebration wherein his new wife and her attractive and enticing daughter convinced Antipas to behead the annoying, bug-eating accuser.

The angry outcry by the people for this attack was not anticipated by the puppet king and the result was that after his death, John's reputation as a sage or prophet increased greatly. It was being spread around that John's voice had been a visitation of the spirit of Elijah, or, even more troubling, that Moses had come back with an important message for Israel. The puzzling but moving message of John did not subside with his death as Antipas had expected and his only consolation was that his friends in Jerusalem, Annas and Caiaphas, had also suffered humiliation from John and no doubt, they somehow valued his impetuous and deadly action.

Undeniably, the one person who most appreciated Antipas's beheading of John was his new wife, the politically astute and thoroughly ambitious Herodias.

All three divisions of the Pharisees, knowing the regard that most of Israel had for John and his watery rebirths, were careful to remain outwardly noncommittal on the subject of "the baptizer." Secretly, many were relieved that their vocal adversary was dead and gone.

Saul had never heard Gamaliel speak of John with anything but reverence even when told of John's many vehement accusations of the actions of the Pharisees. He expressed no opinion and refused any comment even when pressed.

Saul was much less accepting of John and though he agreed that Herod Antipas was wrong to have had him beheaded and that sinful people like Antipas needed to change or be punished, he absolutely disagreed with John's irreverent criticism of the behavior of the Pharisees. Most of all, Saul did not agree that each man personally repenting and being baptized held more importance to the coming of Messiah than the nation's impeccable and universal keeping of the Law.

To Saul, the sin that Israel needed to repent of was "any breach of the Laws or the traditions," as taught by their learned men. It was also a fact that any criticism or irreverence to those whom God had put in charge of the nation was a direct insult to God as well and that amounted to sacrilege. Although Saul could not find any fault with Gamaliel's kind spirit and attitude, he sometimes found himself wondering about the lack of tenacity in his judgments and his benevolence toward those who openly withstood him, the illustrious President of the Sanhedrin.

PART THREE

CHAPTER TWENTY-NINE

Intrigue in Jerusalem

Late the next afternoon, as the sun was setting and the calm and serene Sabbath was waning, Gamaliel called Gammy and Saul to the courtyard table.

They listened intently as he began an intricate and detailed explanation of what was bothering him.

Although they had tried their best not to, the younger men had been pondering all the possibilities and admittedly, they had been distracted the whole Sabbath, both enduring a barrage of speculations in the midst of the normally placid rest day.

"There have been some strange developments this week that have completely set the city on edge," Gamaliel started, "and as President of the Sanhedrin, I am having a difficult time keeping order among the members while maintaining my objectivity on this issue. This case has not been treated fairly from the start and, even now, no civilized discussion has been allowed by the hot heads of the city. The lower court wants to condemn everyone involved as usual, plus there is great disagreement in the Great Sanhedrin.

"Saul, let me give you some background, and Shimon, there are new developments you are not aware of either," stated the Rabban, who never called his son Gammy but used only his formal name of Shimon.

"Over the years, you have heard me discuss and warn of the negative effect that the parade of self-made prophets has had on our nation. Whether they were teaching falsely or not, their blatant attempts to gather a following and draw disciples after themselves has caused many divisions amongst us." Gammy and Saul nodded their wholehearted agreement.

"I need not tell you how divided our School of Learning is from the House of Shammai and that the Righteous Ones have now separated themselves completely and have gone to the desert," he said, referring to the Essenes.

"In the time of my grandfather, we could discuss our differences and we could disagree, but we could still feast together and work for the good of Israel."

Both students noticed the strained tone of their mentor and recognized that he was struggling greatly with this issue.

"I fear that as leaders we have failed miserably and I include myself in that. We have conveniently labeled anyone who does not arise from our schools or agree with our thinking as enemies. It sometimes seems we have indeed been united, but not in a good way, agreeing only in our mutual hatred, or our jealousy, or our suspicion of each other." Gamaliel blurted this out as one confessing a hidden sin and it seemed that just saying this brought him some relief.

"We only agree with each other when we desire an ally in some misguided attempt to destroy one of our brethren. This rowdy mob that runs around Jerusalem doing the bidding of the High Priest or his friends the Sadducees, does not care a wit for the truth and by their sheer noise and threat of violence, they are now determining our course by shouting down any reasonable argument. I realize how easily we excuse such ridiculous and lawless actions when it fits our purpose and by doing so, we have abandoned just and proper implementation of the Law and have given in to our selfish aspirations. This cannot continue or someday we will be found fighting God," said the agitated Gamaliel.

Both young men understood the responsibility Gamaliel felt for the direction of the nation and saw how heavily it was weighing on him. Gamaliel had spoken often of how these divisions flew in the face of the teachings of his famous grandfather, blaming such schisms as rising from the blatant rejection of his famous tenet of "love your neighbor as you love yourself." That was the pillar of all his teaching and had set the atmosphere of Jerusalem for many previous decades.

"If your understanding of the Law does not produce such an attitude, then you need a purer understanding," Gamaliel said, pounding a fist into his other hand.

Such a statement openly conflicted with Shammai's explanation that you can only love your neighbor if they are faithful to the Law and he allowed no exceptions. Shammai's further argument was that if your neighbor failed in some point of the Law, he must be punished in accordance with the Law, also no exceptions. He went even further to say that failing to apply the allotted punishment was also a breaking of the Law by the one who showed mercy, once again, no exceptions.

Since his death, Shammai's disciples had taken this strange logic even further, openly stating that righteous punishments, even stoning resulting in death, were in fact, the purest expression of Hashem's love.

Saul spoke, "Rabban, does not this mob of which you speak, by coincidence, achieve what we are trying to teach to the people? Do they not produce a fear of breaking the Law just because of their ability to punish law breakers immediately? Our brethren may be being coerced and frightened into lawfulness, but they keep the Law nevertheless."

The question from Saul was not so much a challenge as an observation of the effectiveness of the mob.

"You are correct in your assessment, Saul. Our brothers do obey the Law more minutely when being closely scrutinized and threatened, but is that what we want our relationship to Hashem to be? Do we serve Him out of fear of retribution, or should it be as the commandment says-to love Him, respect Him, serve Him with a glad and willing heart? There is an ugliness in fearful obedience that cannot be pleasing to Hashem."

This conversation seemed a surprising departure from the teachings that Saul had grown up with and had been passionately expounded on by this very man, at this very table.

"Rabban, I am confused. You have taught us faithfully that every jot and tittle must be followed to make us worthy of the Messiah and we have taken these teachings to all the Jews of the world. Has this somehow now changed in your teaching?"

"No, Saul, I certainly believe that we as Jews are called, separated, and kept Jews by the keeping of the Law. But," he continued, "I am becoming convinced that there is something infinitely deeper that we can also attain with God. I have read carefully about the warm friendship our father Abraham had with Hashem even before the Law existed and of how our great King David was called 'a man after God's heart,' even as flawed as he was. I wonder if we have not ignored the weightier things of God, maybe there are other callings that please God more than pure obedience."

Gammy and Saul sat in stunned silence.

A whole new viewpoint from the man they called their Rabbi was emerging and their theological world was swaying dangerously. *What was happening?*

Gamaliel was clearly doubting himself and both Gammy and Saul noticed this, but they also understood that such thoughts were rising from a great yearning in Gamaliel to be purer before his God. Saul's memory quickly went back to the *Castor and Pollux* and Miriam's statement to Antoine and him. She had spoken of a link to Hashem and that sounded eerily similar to what Gamaliel was now saying.

"Rabban Hillel simplified a Jew's relationship to Hashem to only a few heart-felt commitments, but our great learning seems to have complicated that and created a perceived breach where we should have a connection. I fear our nation is not getting closer to God, maybe even slipping further away, despite all of our intense religion."

This was said with the finality of a judge's pronouncement, and a deafening silence followed.

The pause was broken by the appearance of Miriam, who apologetically made her way to the steps leading to her room. Both Saul and Gamaliel noticed the beaming smile and the lingering gaze of Gammy following her all the way up the stairs. A quick glance between them confirmed what they were both thinking.

Thankfully, this interruption changed the focus of the conversation and Gamaliel returned to the details he had started with.

"Saul, while you were away, Jesus, the teacher from Nazareth, was crucified and those who followed Him were scattered and disappeared. We thought the matter was over with and that we would not hear of Him again. We had heard of His brash prediction that He would rise from the dead, so Caiaphas posted guards at His tomb, only to have the guards fall asleep and fail to secure it. Now we are dealing with the growing rumors that He miraculously arose from the dead but only His most trusted followers can see Him."

Saul interrupted, "Yes, Rabban, I ran into two men on the ship from Salamis. One was claiming that this Jesus appeared to his brother shortly after He was crucified and they were coming to see Him with their own eyes. They were completely deceived and were convinced that He was still alive."

"Jesus of Nazareth was His popular name and He was considered a prophet. He was the one who could perform all the healings," continued Gamaliel. "Originally, we thought that with a little direction, He would become a disciple of Hillel for He often quoted my grandfather's statements that all the Law and prophets can be fulfilled by following the commandment to love God and your neighbor, but then when we questioned Him about divorce and a few other teachings. He did not agree with us, or with Shammai, or with Moses, saying Moses only allowed us divorce because of our hardened hearts. To test Him, we brought an adulteress to Him, a well-known prostitute, but He would not condemn even her. He attacked our morality instead. He broke the Sabbath by picking corn and eating and then He taunted us by healing a man's hand on the Sabbath. When we would challenge Him, He would use our scriptures against us and He was very good at that."

Gamaliel paused, his detailed but unemotional harangue was complete and he drifted into deep thought. The lines on his face and the furrowed brow were becoming more and more apparent.

"It was like He had a deeper, personal knowledge of the Law and the prophets that we had not seen before."

Gamaliel's startling statement came in the form of a quiet mutter, even a personal question.

"What did He do that got Him crucified," asked Saul, noticing that Gammy was now very quiet and visibly downcast.

"Well, He would always teach in the Temple when He came to Jerusalem for the feast days, and when we questioned Him about His strange doctrines, He called us all evil. He called us snakes and vipers, much like John the Baptist did."

Gamaliel looked at his son, deciding if he should go deeper, but then continued. "Once when I met him at the Temple, He stared right at me and told me that I was like a sepulcher, clean on the outside from all my washings, but inside full of corruption and dead man's bones."

Gamaliel's voice betrayed his usual personal strength and it was apparent that he was deeply affected by these accusations.

"But you cannot crucify someone because he insults you. What did he do that got him crucified?" pressed Saul.

Gammy finally jumped in. "Well, it certainly wasn't anything that He did, for I heard He did nothing but good for the people."

He flashed his father an inquiring glance.

"That is correct, Shimon, but even His good deeds must be examined carefully. If all the helpful healings ended up inciting the people against the leaders of the Temple or the teachers of the Law and thereby undermining Israel itself, was not the final product of the good deed, evil?"

Saul vigorously nodded in agreement.

"Many of our less tolerant leaders believe that He used the powers of Beelzebub to accomplish the healings," continued Gamaliel.

Gammy, with some hesitancy, asked politely, "Do you believe that, Father?"

"I do not know what to believe about that. My close friend, Nicodemus, tells me that everywhere that Jesus went He healed the sick and did good things. Once He even challenged our accusations with logic, asking how could evil do good. If He had just stopped there and had not opposed and fomented rebellion against us who teach the Law, I would have been the first to protect Him," stated Gamaliel, giving further hints at being personally involved.

The quizzical looks on the two young men's faces demanded further explanation, and so Gamaliel continued.

"It was jealousy. Truthfully, we were all jealous of His popularity with the people. Also, we were afraid of the people and the growing favor he had with the crowds. The day before Passover, He rode into Jerusalem from Bethany on a donkey and it seemed everyone in the city was out there singing His praises. You well know how jealousy can twist a certain man's heart."

Gammy and Saul instinctively knew who Gamaliel was accusing. The lust for favor and power by the High Priest's family was very poorly concealed.

"At that point, any excuse to arrest Him was jumped at and Caiaphas, not wanting the Romans to accuse him of not being able to control the people and himself being full of envy, decided that Jesus must die. He justified his decision as needed for the sake of the peace of Jerusalem. Of course, they hired some of their reliable and well-paid accusers, but what finally gave the priests and lawyers the reason they needed to demand He die was when Caiaphas got Him to admit that He proceeded out of God. This blasphemy, as you know, is punishable by death."

Again, Saul was nodding in vigorous agreement.

"But He would have to come before the Sanhedrin, wouldn't he, Father?" asked Gammy.

Gamaliel dropped his head and after a few quiet moments went on. "Yes, they brought Him to us early the next morning, accusing Him of this blasphemy but He would not open His mouth to defend Himself. We could do nothing but assume He was guilty. The witnesses were in total agreement," stated Gamaliel, defensively.

"Many of the Sanhedrin were not notified and were not aware of what was happening, so many were not present and only a few protested the trial. Nicodemus was shouted down easily and they accused him of being this man's disciple also. They bullied him, saying maybe he should be punished as well and I had no choice but to send Jesus to Pilate for the penalty."

It was apparent that Gamaliel did not want to even mention the notorious Roman punishment, or mouth the word 'crucifixion.'"

It was also obvious to the two young listeners that Gamaliel wanted to purge his troubled mind, so they remained motionless while he continued. "I have thought long and hard since that day about some of the teachings of this man Jesus and I find no great offense in what He taught. I cannot find fault with His actions either."

Saul was astounded at the last statement of his cherished mentor and wanted immediately to reassure him that the correct judgment had been made.

"Not so, Rabban. You may doubt yourself now because of your soft and generous nature, but you have taught us well and I remind you that it is the national keeping of the Law that is more valuable than any one man's life. Remember that, all your doubts aside, this deceiver could not withstand the righteous questions of the High Priest and so admitted His blasphemy. These are the facts as I have heard them, and nothing changes this. This man deserved death, as any that teach anything else than total devotion to Moses's Law also deserve."

Gamaliel's eyes settled tenderly on Saul, but they were still full of deep insecurity and questioning.

Gammy remained unusually silent.

"What is it that you wanted from Shimon and I?" asked Saul, eager to move on from this uncomfortable discussion.

"Ah, yes," continued Gamaliel. "Well, the frightened followers of Jesus who scattered when He was arrested have recently started showing up again here in Jerusalem. They slipped into the city quietly at first and hid away so no one knew they were here, almost as if they were still afraid. On Pentecost, a large group of them suddenly appeared in the streets near the synagogue of the Freedmen, and they were singing, shouting, and preaching about this 'risen' Jesus. Their tactics had completely changed and now they were boldly proclaiming Him rather than hiding. Since then, they have been preaching in the Temple courtyards and more and more people are joining with them. They are baptizing many, like John did, and there is a constant line at the great pool of Siloam waiting to be baptized."

"They should not be allowed to preach anything but Moses in the Temple courtyards," declared Saul defiantly.

"This is indeed creating a problem, Saul, as now there are more than 3000 of them that meet there daily. The priestly guards are afraid of any confrontation because there are so many, and of course, no one wants a big uproar that would bring the Romans into the Temple. Truthfully, we are not exactly sure what they are teaching there. Many of their followers are from all over Israel and I suspect that they are spreading their teachings in their home synagogues as well. I need to know what is being taught and I would like you two to listen to their preaching and report to me."

"Spy on them?" gasped Gammy.

"Nothing so nefarious, son, just find out what they are teaching so we can help both them and Jerusalem avoid further trouble. Saul, you speak many languages so I thought that you could possibly find out how widespread this is. Maybe a visit to your favorite synagogue, the House of the Freedmen?"

Gamaliel seemed almost apologetic. "It seems there are a lot of them there."

"Of course, Rabban, I would love to serve you this way and I can assure you that I will help root out this disease." Saul was feeling important and trusted.

"Please, Saul, be patient and peaceful, for we may be able with sound teaching to restore those who have been led astray."

Saul hesitantly nodded in agreement, but he was sure within himself that the only thing that would correct this heresy was harsh punishment including a sound beating or two.

"Also, I would like to keep our little scheme a total secret, even from our womenfolk, if that is possible. This is a bit unsavory I fear, and hopefully all will be resolved soon, but this information is necessary for me and there are none that I trust as you two."

CHAPTER THIRTY

The Matriarch of the School

The following day dawned with Gamaliel again leaving the house early and hurrying to the Hall of Hewn Stones while Saul and Gammy met at the table in the portico to coordinate the lessons that would be taught on this first day of the new learning period. It was pre-determined that Gammy would oversee the learning for native sons of Judea who spoke Aramaic, and Saul would look after those students from distant shores. He was more fluent in Greek and a few of the other languages that many of the transplanted students were most familiar with themselves.

Gamaliel's school was very capably administered by his wife, the Damascus-born Sarah, who was legendary in her ability to organize the details required to make the famous school function perfectly. This made Saul and Gammy's teaching jobs much easier but both remained very diligent in their preparation for their classes for they knew that at any time there may be a visit or a probing question from Sarah.

Because of her strict direction, every student knew precisely what scriptures were to be read beforehand, what materials were required, where they would lodge and when to be at the halls provided. Should they forget anything, they were quickly reprimanded by the curt tongue of the regal administrator as she made her daily inspections of the classrooms. Washing vessels, meals, scrolls and any other daily needs appeared precisely on time at the places required and the scurrying servants dared not tarry or be late for she possessed a penetrating look of withering disapproval that they did all they could to avoid. Truthfully, the normally pleasant Sarah had to work hard to put forth such a harsh appearance.

Upon first experiencing Sarah, it was tempting to assume that she was a cold and demanding taskmaster, but many students, including Saul, had experienced the tender and caring side of the loving mother that she was when students began the inevitable slide into the loneliness that a boy felt when far from home. She was always the first to notice, first to react with comfort and inclusion and first in the cherished memories of the students as they matured into young men.

A curious product of her powerful but peaceful character was that all had been infused with an impossibly high standard when choosing a bride, and quite unfairly, had become annoyingly selective and overly demanding of any they considered for marriage, much to the chagrin of the young women of Jerusalem.

To make things run smoothly, Sarah had acquired two airy study halls which were within a quick walk of home so that the daily meal preparations could be done from her comfortable kitchen and then easily delivered by the servants.

Her daughter Leah was also very competent, but she was much less eager than her mother when it came to placating rooms full of shy and ogling scholars. A generous amount of charming self-confidence, along with a stunningly pretty face had made Leah captivating and it was apparent that she could easily slip into the role, like her mother, of governor of the family business. For now, Leah made only occasional visits to the classrooms as her presence had almost a hypnotizing impact on the students and it took hours to remedy the disorientation of the young men after one of her stopovers. Both Saul and Gammy teased her about the "Leah" affect and laughingly accused her of purposely fogging the brains of their students.

Happy for his role, Saul fit easily into this highly efficient and peaceful operation and he was very comfortable with the daily feeling of important achievement that this reliable routine always brought. The educational professionalism of the School of Hillel was respected throughout Judaism and greatly envied, even in the highly competitive and theologically charged atmosphere of Jerusalem.

Sarah was constantly adjusting and improving aspects of the school and her rapt attention to the details formed an expectation of excellence that she strove for continually. It was obvious that she was pleased with the envied status of the school and the elevated social standing of her husband and his legendary family. Consequently, she refused to accept anything that would put that status in question, and she was doubling her efforts now that Gamaliel's mornings were being consumed by his demanding duties at the Sanhedrin.

As they sat in the portico, the young men received the latest lists of returning and also new students who had survived the intense scrutiny of both Gamaliel and Sarah. Only a few exceptional boys were accepted each year into the school. The taste for higher learning was immense in the world of the Jews and little boys dreamed incessantly of becoming famous scholars just to please their mothers and fathers. This yearning assured Sarah that every year there would be a generous number of applicants eager to attend this famous institution. Those accepted were chosen for both their scholastic aptitude and their family's secure financial situation.

Between Gamaliel and Sarah, they had reasonably concluded that in a choice between competing applicants, the choice would always go with the student most likely to remain in the school for a long period of time and whose family had adequate wealth for this to happen. After all, the fees were substantial.

This morning, Sarah presented Gammy and Saul with a scroll from the family treasury of personal handwritten parchments of the famous Hillel. Each were carefully wrapped in a protective skin bag.

These scrolls not only provided the scriptural context for the upcoming class but their authenticity was sure to overwhelm the newest students who would, possibly for the first time in their lives, handle one of the famous sages' personal documents.

Being dedicated as she was to the wisdom of her husband, Sarah had educated herself with enough understanding of Jewish thought to demand strict adherence to his curriculum, and mysteriously, she always knew if there was any deviation from his directions. Both Saul and Gammy did all they could to remain in Sarah's good favor, veering off topic only when compelling and interesting debate demanded it.

Truthfully, Saul preferred the traditional question and answer, back and forth, argumentized and often confrontational atmosphere allowed and even promoted in Gamaliel's classrooms. This method fit his personality and he was flooded with pleasure when each class started and intense and deeply stimulating issues were argued straightaway. This term, he was delighted with the two newest students in his class, as both promised quick minds, thus assuring that the mornings would be the definite highlight of his day. He and Gammy had agreed to use the afternoons to go about the task that Gamaliel had given them and left the afternoon discussions to be supervised by visiting Rabbis or the most competent senior students in the school.

As planned, when the midday shofar blasts from the Temple had sounded, Saul and Gammy came together to enjoy the small lunch that Sarah sent them.

Both men were feeling a little excited and somewhat smug as they prepared to launch their newest task for both felt ready to take on Gamaliel's secretive and covert schemes. Saul was going off to visit the synagogue as Gamaliel had requested and Gammy was looking forward to wandering the courtyard of the Temple, the very spot where these followers of Jesus met every day.

CHAPTER THIRTY-ONE

The Synagogue of the Freedmen

After their lunch, Saul and Gammy wound their way down the labyrinth of streets that descended Mount Zion to the roadway that ran along the base of Mount Moriah on which the Temple sat. This narrow, congested road sat in the depression between the two mountaintops and ran north and south, directly along the bottom of the high western wall of Herod's recently expanded Temple complex. The north end of the road disappeared into a cluster of alleys and passageways but going south, the busy street became the larger and famous Pilgrim's Road. This was the roadway that led devoted visitors upward to the Temple from the lowest part of the entire city, the Pool of Siloam. The road climbed for almost half a mile from the spring that fed the palatial pools of Siloam to the always crowded markets at the base of the Temple wall. From this roadway, pilgrims who were intent on performing their sacrificial duties turned east, arriving at the bottom of the enormous staircase that led to the huge Huldah Gates in the furthest south wall of the Temple complex.

When they first neared the road, Saul caught sight of the massive walls and then a small portion of the highest roofs of the Temple itself. As always, he was both overwhelmed and inspired, as was every pilgrim, when catching their first glimpse of this magnificent gold-fringed edifice. Gammy paused, noticing that Saul was staring upward at the grandeur above him and politely waited, knowing it had been almost a year since Saul had last been here.

They walked a short distance south on the crowded roadway, pushing through crowds of shoppers and surrounded on both sides by the markets whose specialties were the items required for Temple worship. When they neared the south end of the western wall, they nodded to each other and parted.

Gammy climbed the grand stairway on the west, up to the bridge that then arched back over the roadway and disappeared into the top of the west wall near the southwest corner of the largest court of the Temple. This was the nonformal entrance used mainly by the priests, but any Jew not making a ceremonial approach through the traditional southern gates was allowed to use it.

Saul continued southward along the stone-paved Pilgrim's Road. Although it was busy and crowded, it was not nearly as jammed as during feast times. On those busier days it was almost impassable, teeming all day long with the multitudes of visitors from all over the world who would "go up" to the Temple after their ritual body washing in the freshwater pools around the springs of Siloam.

This ascending roadway was newly refashioned by Herod as part of his Temple renovation; the chaotic old dirt and clay bricks had been expertly replaced with large new stones that formed two short steps followed by a flat landing. This pattern was repeated for the road's entire length. Under the new stones, Herod built a very functional underground waste channel that drained almost all the lower city and which continued out of the lower gate and all the way to the bottom of the Kidron stream. This had caused the locals to jokingly rename the lowest gate from Pilgrim's Gate to Dung Gate. With these upgrades, the talented architect and builder had eliminated many of the sanitary problems that had plagued the lower city in the centuries past. When assisted with the hourly surge of the spring at Siloam, this new system mercifully pushed much of the city's waste into the porous desert canyons of the Judean desert, many miles away. In response, this nutrient-rich flow stimulated renewed vegetation and trees in those canyons, thereby inviting a return of many familiar creatures on the verge of eradication in the normally arid gorges.

As it descended from the Temple area, the east side of the Pilgrim's Road was framed by high walls constructed with older, weathered and blackened stones, the remains of the ancient walls of King David's regal palace. Behind those revered ramparts were housed large renovated rooms and towards the southern end was a very select group of them which were enthusiastically claimed to be King David's actual Chambers. Those ancient and echoey rooms had now become the home of the Synagogue of the Freedmen.

This was the lowest area of the city and it possessed the least expensive housing, and as a result, was the most heavily populated. Along with the synagogue on the east, the street was lined with two-and-three-story stone buildings towering over and crowding in on any open space left over on either side of the roadway. The maze of houses, connected by very narrow alleyways, provided much needed rental accommodations to the many visiting pilgrims and the owners of these properties enjoyed a steady income from housing travelers so close to the famous place of worship. Almost every house had an upper room for rent, with most having extra rooftop space that could further house overflow crowds. These rooftops were extremely popular and provided refreshing breezes and a stirring view of the impressive south walls of the Temple area which loomed majestically over the whole lower city. Part of the charm of King David's lower city was the long evenings spent chatting with the Jews on the adjacent rooftops, a place where life-long friendships were often started.

The Freedman's synagogue was easily the largest and liveliest in Jerusalem, seating over one thousand men with a generous upper balcony for any attending women. On any given Sabbath it was always crowded to overflowing.

The congregation of this meeting place was originally composed of a host of freed Jewish slaves from around the Roman Empire who had hurried to the Holy City immediately upon being set at liberty, thus, its name, Synagogue of the Freedmen. More recently it included many other transplanted Jews, not necessarily former slaves but those who came from cities around the Roman world and who had decided to move to Jerusalem because of the promise of a deeper spiritual encounter. Because they emigrated from outside of Judea and generally spoke the universal Greek language rather than the local Aramaic, they were considered slightly impure Hellenists by the arrogant and elitist local Jews. In response, these shunned brethren preferred to worship apart and to gather away from such haughty attitudes, feeling the unspoken yet very tangible prejudice emanating from the pompous Judeans. At times, these more worldly-wise Jews wore this disapproval as a badge and as a uniting force.

The members of this synagogue sarcastically countered the snobby faultfinding by pointing to the rich Jewish cultures of Babylon, Alexandria,

Carthage and other places which they were from. They reminded the locals that these were historically the more obedient places that had kept the Jewish nationality alive when it had twice virtually disappeared in the homeland because of the locals' misdeeds before Hashem. Such a biting reminder usually silenced the chastised locals, but only for a moment.

Each country represented in the synagogue had naturally imported their language and, often in corners of the cavernous building and locked in private conversations, men could be heard speaking strange languages from the far reaches of the known Roman world. In the main services and general assembly of the synagogue, Greek was exclusively the language used.

Because of the recent influx of many wealthy Jews to Jerusalem, this synagogue had also become the largest and most financially influential of all in the city and this shift in financial power was more than a bit annoying to the local leadership, especially Caiaphas the High Priest. This man was always suspicious of any that he did not completely control or who rivaled, or at least did not add to, his riches.

Allowing "independent" Greek-speaking rabbis along with their libertarian and uncontrolled synagogues within the walls of Jerusalem? Well, that was always a matter of heated conversation within the walls of the High Priest's house.

Because he was from Tarsus, Saul proudly called this his home synagogue and was well known by all who attended here, counting many as friends.

What Saul especially appreciated about this assembly was that although they had experienced Judaism in its dizzying variations in their home countries, most freedmen had come to Jerusalem with common and very specific objectives. Their mutual goals were a zealousness for the Law and a love of the ancient traditions that permeated their faith, in other words, they wanted to be fully Jewish.

What also made these people unique was that they all possessed the adventurous spirit required to make such a life-altering move. As one could expect among such opinionated and passionate people, many boisterous arguments had erupted within these echoey walls while the precise details of achieving these common goals were being hammered out.

The synagogue was the center of daily life for these newly-arrived people, most escaping their cramped homes and meeting in the cooler and inviting halls where the inevitable discussions became intense and colorful. Just two doors down from the gate of the synagogue was a wine merchant who had decided to import casks the sweet nectar from each of the arguer's home region. Predictably, all was blamed on that poor man when those discussions escalated and could be heard up and down the Pilgrims Road. All in all, though, it was an inviting, exciting and friendly place to be.

Saul certainly felt at home there. Like himself, many had left less zealous family members behind and were pleased to find a group that did not need to be prodded and embarrassed into godly obedience. In fact, stringent compliance and religious zeal were greatly admired within the stony walls of this gathering place.

As he approached the entrance, Saul noticed that the street outside the beautifully carved synagogue door was blocked by several small groups huddled together and engaged in noisy and somewhat contentious discussions. So intense were these spats that the familiar stream of pilgrims wending their way up to the Temple had to push their way through the unmoving bunches to continue their trek upward. Saul was about to enter the synagogue gate when he heard the name "Jesus" spoken in Cilician, his boyhood language from Tarsus, and he instantly stopped to listen. Within a few steps was another group speaking in heavily-accented Greek and, out of curiosity, he moved closer and focused on them.

"It was just as Jesus and as the prophet Joel prophesied. It was an outpouring of the Spirit of God," one man was saying with conviction and intensity, "and it first happened right there."

He pointed to the upper room of the large house immediately across the street from the door of the synagogue.

"Heresy, that is pure heresy," shouted a very familiar figure in a deep and commanding voice, causing all heads to turn to him.

CHAPTER THIRTY-TWO

Samuel the Shammai-ite

Saul recognized the deep voice immediately and spun around. The booming declaration belonged to a large, well-built and captivating young man who, like Saul, was adorned with the robes of a Pharisee.

It was Samuel, a House of Shammai Pharisee and a very energetic and outspoken adversary of the teachings of Hillel, but strangely, a long-time friend of Saul.

A huge smile of recognition spread across Saul's face and he was instantly delighted to witness such a raucous indictment instigated by his blunt friend. This was exactly the way he preferred to remember his beloved Jerusalem. The last year of passively waiting for the death of his father had sapped him and he now realized that such emotional and vigorous debate is exactly what he had missed so much. It was good to be home and to be experiencing the explosive streets once again.

Samuel peered through the milling group, looking over the faces of his opponents, when suddenly he noticed the grinning Saul. Beaming with joy, he quickly left the developing argument for another day and hurried to his friend, embracing him warmly.

"Saul, you poor Cilician refugee, are you lost, wandering down here with the second-class Jews?" he teased.

Samuel had what very few serious minded and argumentative Jerusalemites had, a great sense of humor. He loved to laugh and taunt but was able to laugh at himself as well, a trait Saul both appreciated and deeply envied for it made Samuel very likable to all.

The press of the street forced them to retreat into the synagogue doorway where their greetings continued with boyhood enthusiasm.

"Where have you been, my friend? You promised over a year ago to visit our family home and enjoy my sister's cooking. Have you been dodging that risky experience?" joked Samuel deviously.

Samuel had teased Saul of avoiding romantic interests for years and he constantly and playfully presented his younger sister as his only possibility. Saul, in his attempt to match Samuel's humor, often ended up sounding very confused and this just added fuel to Samuel's teasing.

"I insist that you come to our house immediately, no more delay, as there have been many less intelligent characters hanging around trying to get a glimpse of my sister. I demand a brother-in-law with whom I can hold a decent conversation," Samuel declared. He then threw his head back in unrestrained laughter.

Saul burst out laughing as well and countered with the information that he had also brought a bride all the way from Tarsus especially for Samuel, although he immediately felt he presented that proposal with far too much seriousness.

It was Samuel's good nature that had kept Saul a close friend over the years of debate, argument and religious competition. Other Pharisees of opposing sects had let their discussions turn into bitter animosity but Samuel had a natural talent for comradery which simply would not let that happen.

Just then a sudden wave of singing and shouting rose from the milling groups across the narrow street and it grew until it was a noisy crescendo with other pilgrims on the upward road happily joining in what seemed like an unruly religious gathering.

"What is going on?" Saul loudly asked his friend over the clamor.

"Seriously, you must come to my house and I will inform you, but I will not talk over this incessant racket," Samuel declared. "My mother is in Hebron with her family and I am at home with my little sister. Come, for I desperately need some manly companionship."

Saul followed Samuel to his small but comfortable home, just a few minutes' walk away from the Pilgrim's Road. When seated in a very familiar chair which had seen many long and passionate religious conversations, he blurted, "OK, Samuel, what is going on?"

Before Samuel could answer, both men looked up as a pretty girl of about eighteen years appeared with two cups of wine and a small plate of dates. Samuel grinned widely and Saul, with great effort, finally tore his eyes off her and looked away, not wanting to stare after being struck with the maturing beauty of Samuel's sister, Ruth. He had not seen her for a year and was taken with the unexpected change from a gangly youth to a beautiful young woman.

"Thank you, Ruth," acknowledged Samuel. "You remember Saul, the confused student of Gamaliel, don't you?" Confusion was the ongoing and humorous charge that Samuel loved to prod Saul with.

"Yes, I remember him well, Samuel. And how are you, Rabbi Saul? I have not seen you in a while," she said, using the complimentary formal title. Saul was suddenly rattled, unsure if she was teasing him in the fashion of her brother as she had often done in years gone by, or if the greeting was meant in respect. He smiled warmly at her regardless.

Saul explained his long absence to them, including the loss of his father and his subsequent total commitment to Jerusalem and Israel. He told of his sister's coming to Jerusalem, wisely leaving out the promise of marrying someone in Jerusalem that Miriam had made to their father, but Saul saw Ruth poke Samuel jokingly anyway. They chatted easily for a long time and Saul was warmed with how pleasing Ruth's company was.

After an hour, as Saul was getting anxious to talk seriously with Samuel, Ruth withdrew knowingly, leaving both men to conspire.

"Saul, how much do you know about that Galilean prophet called Jesus," asked Samuel.

"Jesus again. Why does the conversation always go there," said an exasperated Saul.

Saul took a deep sip of wine and searched his memory and finally said, "I know that He had been coming to Jerusalem for about three years; apparently the people thought He was a prophet, possibly Elijah or some other sage who had come back from other spiritual realms. He performed some healings and other so-called miracles which were done obviously by the power of Beelzebub, and then this last Passover, He declared himself to be the very offspring of Jehovah and was rightfully crucified for that blasphemy. I ran into some of His deluded followers on the ship from Cyprus who were rushing to get to Judea because, apparently, this Jesus was appearing to His followers. They were claiming He was resurrected from the dead."

Samuel drank in the brief summary, noticing the heavy sarcasm of Saul, and then he added, "Well, the delusion does not end there. His followers, the ones who disappeared like frightened sheep at His crucifixion, crept back into Jerusalem and were secretly meeting in that second-story room across from the door of the synagogue where we met today. We knew they were in there, but we felt sorry for them." Samuel sat back and chuckled, "For over a week they hid, afraid to show themselves. We were sure they were hiding out of embarrassment after being so completely deluded but we later found out that some of them were claiming, and even convincing others, that they had seen Jesus alive, fully resurrected, and that it was He that told them to return to Jerusalem. Now, their claim was that He had beforehand prophesied that He would die and then be resurrected, but we are sure that they stole His body out of the tomb so they could keep the movement alive."

Samuel straightened his large frame, "On the feast day of Pentecost, we were gathered in the synagogue, bundling our first fruits as usual for the ceremonies and quite suddenly there was this huge commotion across the street. Over a hundred of them were hiding up there on that day. They started singing and shouting and making a huge noise so we went out to see what was going on in that upper room. We stood listening from the street below and after a while they started coming down the stairs, staggering around like one would expect of lowlife, drunken Galileans. They were singing songs from David's psalms and then began repeating specific readings of Moses and then they began quoting the prophets."

Saul sat transfixed and leaned forward, listening intently to this firsthand account of such strange happenings.

"We were laughing at them at first, pretty sure they were inebriated, drunker than donkeys who got loose in the orchards and that would have been okay, even that early in the morning, but then they also started to quote Isaiah, Ezekiel and Joel. They were claiming that this crazy show they were putting on was the outpouring of the Spirit that was prophesied." Samuel knew that Saul would know exactly the prophetic writings he was referring to.

"Argh," Saul guffawed, "every one of these movements claim that the holy writings speak of them exclusively. That is nothing new."

"My thoughts exactly," replied Samuel, "and we would have just ignored them and kept laughing except for a few other things. There was a strange clearness and even a weird authority that they spoke with, like it wasn't their words and, for sure, it did not seem to be the words of uneducated or wine-soaked Galileans. It was bizarre and out of place, especially coming from terrified people who had just spent the week secretly hiding in that room like frightened birds."

He paused and looked directly into Saul's face and continued solemnly, "Then there was the odd fact that everyone in our synagogue was hearing them quoting the writings in their native tongues. You well know, Saul, that our synagogue has people from all over the world and we speak Greek here for convenience, but most have a separate native tongue. Well, many heard this preaching and quoting of the sacred writings in the language of the country they were from."

A long, thoughtful silence followed.

"Yes, if you were wondering, some of them were speaking your backwoods Cilician. If you were here, you would have heard Isaiah quoted perfectly in that peculiar tongue," stated Samuel, who, again, could not refrain from a jovial poke at his old friend. His face became serious once more.

"I followed this up carefully and some of them were using complicated words and phrases in those languages that are not commonly used and that is not normal of someone who would have just recently learned these languages. Where and when did they learn to do this, we do not know. When we tried talking to them in these foreign tongues over the next few days, they did not understand anything we said and they could not use any words of those languages at all."

"Are you absolutely sure they did not know the languages beforehand and were just trying to trick you?" probed Saul, obviously searching for a logical explanation.

"No, we tried all sorts of tricks and I am convinced that they could not speak those languages," replied Samuel. "They definitely were the dumb, uneducated Galileans we thought they were who did not understand any of the words they were speaking. They proved that to us over and over."

Both men paused, obviously in deep thought, before Samuel continued.

"As you can imagine, this has greatly upset our synagogue, some claiming this was a visitation of God directed at our congregation because we are the only synagogue that contains all these languages. Several of our people have begun declaring that they now believe that this Jesus was the promised Messiah and that He indeed resurrected. Quite a few have joined up with them and been baptized in His name, you know, like that Essene, John, taught."

Samuel hesitated for a long moment before continuing.

"My closest friend, Stephen has become one of them and I have tried repeatedly to reason with him but it is like a whole different mind has entered him. He regards my profoundest insights and most complicated teachings as unenlightened and shallow and he is convinced that he has now received the Holy Spirit of Hashem. That is how they have labeled this tumult, you know. He claims the Spirit he received is teaching him, inspiring him and interpreting scriptures to not only him, but to all those who join that new way. He has lost any interest in talking with me anymore, except to tell me about Jesus."

Rachel's engaging smile appeared again, along with more food and wine. Once he had wrestled back Saul's attention, Samuel continued.

"They meet daily at the Temple. Their leaders, mostly those cowardly disciples that scattered so quickly when the High Priest arrested Jesus, openly tell stories of Jesus right there in Solomon's Porch and they do it with no fear at all. They repeat His convoluted teachings and tell of His supernatural miracles. They continually refer to obscure writings by Moses and the prophets that talk about the Messiah as being about Jesus. I have now heard that there are about three thousand people who meet up there and follow these Galileans. All this within a few short weeks."

"What has the High Priest got to say about this?" questioned Saul, curious as to why such obvious error would be tolerated and not vigorously prosecuted. Simply upon hearing this report, Saul had absolutely no hesitation judging these people and their teachings as being completely false, possibly dangerous.

"Well, he may be the High Priest, but he seems confused about what to do," replied Samuel. "This group is not actually harming anyone, at least that is what the priests claim, and there does seem to be a genuine harmony and cooperativeness among them, so Caiaphas doesn't know what to condemn."

A large smirk appeared on Samuel's face and he muttered to Saul, "They have him completely bamboozled." Both men enjoyed that image for a short moment.

"Worse than that, all the visiting pilgrims who go the Temple and accidently hear them, speak so well of these people that the leaders are afraid to make any move against them. Other than claiming that Jesus was Messiah, there is not a lot that we can accuse them of."

"Let me get this straight," said Saul, slowly and precisely forming his question, "They claim to have a different but more inspired understanding of the Law and the prophets, and they say they received this by opening themselves to what they call a Spirit?"

"Well, that's a bit simplified, but what you say is true," said Samuel, nodding.

"And this Spirit caused them to act drunk and speak in previously unknown foreign languages, and then this 'Spirit' completely captures the minds of good Jews and turns them away from the importance of the traditions and teachings of the wisest of our teachers and rabbis," asked Saul, who while speaking, was clarifying the situation to both himself and Samuel. He left that question hanging in the air for a while and then changed his focus.

"So, tell me, what do you think, Samuel," Saul asked pointedly, hoping he had judged his friend correctly on this matter. "What do you think Caiaphas should do?"

"I want to keep that opinion to myself for a little while, Saul. You know that time often exposes the error," answered Samuel, and both men understood that it was politically and personally precarious to venture into criticizing the High Priest's office.

Even with all his faults and failures, was Caiaphas not appointed by Hashem?

Over the years, both young men had heeded the warnings to be careful and not to openly express any criticism of that office or the man occupying it. Their fear was not of needlessly offending the man but more importantly, of offending God.

"But you must have thoughts. What are they?" pressed Saul. "You were not a bit uncertain when you called out the heresy today."

"Yes, I heard one of them say that the Spirit in them also made them an offspring of God, like Jesus claimed for Himself. That had to be called out immediately for that is a dangerous seducing thought, for sure," replied Samuel.

Samuel paused for a moment more and then he continued. "My thoughts are even more complicated, for I think there are three directions this can go." He had been dealing with this problem for weeks now and had obviously come to some conclusions which were weighing heavily on him.

"The first possibility is that they are correct, we are dead wrong, we are to be condemned and we need to repent and be baptized." Both men chuckled loudly at such a ludicrous thought.

"Second, it will run its course and like all the other messiahs, Jesus will be forgotten in a short while."

Samuel paused after that, waiting while the anticipation in his friend built.

"Okay, what's the third option?" Saul knew that Samuel had paused for dramatic effect.

The look on Samuel's face changed and he became intense.

"There is a more ominous and dangerous scenario playing out here and this may well be the work of evil, demonic spirits bent on destroying our Jewish nation. There is something supernatural about these strange and spiritual possessions for sure and the force of the words and thoughts that these people exhibit do not seem naturally concocted to me. If this was of God, these people surely would acknowledge the High Priest and our leaders for we know that God instituted them for our nation and God would not condemn what He Himself has instituted. This arrogant Jesus showed the height of disrespect when He called our leaders, a den of snakes, proving He was opposed to what God has introduced and blessed. Furthermore, if what they say were to be somehow correct, all that now holds us together as a nation of Jews is worthless and should then be dismantled, all our teachings and traditions are a stench in God's nostrils, just as this Jesus suggested, and as He predicted, the Temple itself should be destroyed."

Samuel's words were growing louder and more emotional with each statement.

As he spoke, his big hands were waving about. "Saul, tell me, should I believe God's appointed High Priest and all those who faithfully serve the commandments of Moses, including us who live in all the wisdom of Hillel and Shammai, or should I believe the self-serving blathering of uneducated Galileans who cannot even write their own names?"

Saul was surprised and more than a little impressed at the eloquence and intensity of the normally even-tempered Samuel.

"If it is the third option, Saul, and I believe it is, then we are in the fight of our lives for the Jewish nation. It is a supernatural war. We must not entertain even the hint of civility with these people, lest we too become bewitched and possessed. For the sake of Israel, we must consider them our enemy and use the wisdom given us by our great teachers to counter any influence these people have. It is left to you and I and our generation to protect the purity of the Law now. Unfortunately, there seems to be a lack of willingness among our older leaders to do so."

It was obvious that Samuel had moved past the initial disappointment with the weak response and lack of decisiveness he had observed in the last weeks.

Saul was growing emotional just listening to Samuel, deeply affected by the profound statement of his friend. Although in previous years they had sparred bitterly over the smallest differences in interpretation of the written Law, today he was in total agreement with Samuel's declaration. This mindset differed greatly from Gamaliel's, he understood, but Saul was now an adult and a Pharisee, a respected teacher himself and he was able to make up his own mind.

Without any further hesitation, he readily agreed that this present Galilean phenomena was indeed a dangerous and demonic attack on Israel.

Truthfully, Saul was instantly captured with the other thing Samuel had suggested. He had stated that he and Samuel, and possibly Gammy, were the men that were placed in Israel to spearhead the defense of Judaism. His mind raced at the thought. One day, and there was now no doubt in Saul's mind, their names would be remembered in Jewish history for what would take place in the very near future.

This intense, almost dark conversation was interrupted once again by Ruth's cheerful appearance. She brought more wine and sweet fruit to the two and she uncovered a loaf of warm, golden bread which she had cut into generous servings. The aroma danced through Saul's hungry senses and he soon found that he was hopelessly rambling. For the next few minutes, he grinned and babbled. Admittedly, his perplexity was not the result of the sumptuous bread alone.

"Samuel, are you trying to make Saul into a zealot again," she asked light-heartedly and both men knew that she had overheard the whole of their conversation.

"Let him remain in the House of Hillel, for we need Pharisees that have a heart to forgive and forget, rabbis who teach us to love our neighbors and are not always looking for reasons to berate their brethren," she said coyly, to which her brother responded with a laughing and loud, "Never, I must inspire him to do battle."

Saul felt a tinge of embarrassment at this obvious teasing and, strangely, at Rachel's willingness to speak of love. Such words flowed sweetly off her full and transfixing lips and he had no reasonable defense other than to appear busy and nibble the food. His swirling mind remained intoxicated by Ruth's presence as long as she remained in the room.

Samuel and Saul's conversation continued for another hour, ending with an invitation for himself and his sister Miriam to dinner the following week to try Ruth's version of cooked lamb.

Saul mentioned to Samuel that he would be visiting the Freedmen's Synagogue regularly to see these developments with his own eyes and Samuel agreed enthusiastically with that. He also informed Saul, with a tinge of pride, that he was being asked to visit other synagogues in Jerusalem and in nearby villages to explain the latest developments and if Saul was available, he would love for him to join him on these journeys.

This initial visit had been a revelation for Saul. He now began to understand the breadth of this heresy firsthand and how it was affecting Jews at the street level, some falling under the spell of the Galileans, others remaining completely opposed. Not many were allowed the luxury of remaining on the fence.

Saul was lost in deep thought when he began his walk home in the late afternoon heat. He climbed the congested Pilgrim's Road and approached the side street leading to the wealthier upper city where Gamaliel lived as had his father and his famous grandfather.

So engrossed in the latest news was he that he did not notice being rudely jostled by the eager and excited crowd that was suddenly pressing to get to the gates of the Temple compound. That was strange for it was already getting late in the afternoon and normally, the worshippers would be leaving the holy place. These people carried no sacrifice or gift, so Saul surmised that they were not going as pilgrims. Soon he overheard their excited calls of "Simon Peter is speaking in Solomon's courts."

Some ran to the stairway leading off the Pilgrim's Road that arched back across, while others darted for the three large southern Huldah Gates. For a moment Saul contemplated following them but remembering that Gammy was to investigate at the Temple, he decided against that and continued his slow walk home.

CHAPTER THIRTY-THREE

Pontius Pilate

Upon arriving at his home, Saul quietly slipped up the stairs, wanting to avoid Gamaliel or Gammy just then. He knew he must make sense of all of Samuel's disturbing words by himself, especially the not-so-subtle leadership criticisms that he had heard, all which included Gamaliel. These were very harsh words spoken against his beloved mentor that only a few hours ago he had shockingly agreed with.

No, he decided, he definitely did not want to meet with Gamaliel just now.

Saul informed Miriam of their dinner invitation to the home of Samuel and Ruth and when seeing the slight aversion in her eyes which was followed by an equally quick acceptance, something suddenly dawned on him.

Was his sister able to go to the lengths of devotion that he saw coming for himself? Was there a disparity in the way she and he saw such things?

Not wanting to think about that, he busied himself with a scroll.

Over a quiet dinner, Miriam casually informed her brother that Gamaliel and his family were not at home tonight or tomorrow, and Saul was instantly relieved. She mentioned that the whole family had been summoned to an official two-day function at the Roman Governor's Jerusalem residence.

Apparently, it was mandatory for the President of the Sanhedrin and his family to attend this mysterious and hastily-called function.

Although a young man, Gammy, was already expected to attend formal events with his father and mother. It was a political thing. As the next in line for the chief judge's permanent position, Gammy was already treated with a level of deference as the inevitable successor to Gamaliel in the Sanhedrin. Leah, also as expected, accompanied her mother. This mother and daughter made a much-admired duo and also as expected, they were scrutinized closely by the women in attendance, every trinket and bobble that they were wearing being thoroughly examined and evaluated and as often happens, secretly criticized.

Pontius Pilate was leaving for his official residence in Caesarea in the following week and wanted to clarify his relationship with the Jewish religious court before returning to his seaside capital. At least that was the official line given for this impromptu session of banqueting.

Reliable rumors were circulating that Pilate was not at all pleased with being forced to get involved with and crucify a Jew on what he perceived to be purely petty religious grounds on his last visit to Jerusalem. This was not the mandate or the agreement Rome had with Herod originally and it was also rumored that his outspoken wife had vividly and loudly pointed this fact out to him. He had erred greatly by letting himself be drawn into such paltry religious affairs by the sly Caiaphas, she screeched at him daily, and now, Pilate wanted to put an end to her prattling.

His was a complicated and convoluted life. After Herod's death thirty years ago, the kingdom was divided into four tetrarchies with the three outlying parts given to be ruled by Herod's surviving but inept sons, The most important and heavily populated tetrarchy of Judea was retained to be ruled by Rome itself. What this meant was that Pilate controlled this province directly and he or his governors were involved in all decisions. Much to the annoyance of the three puppet kings, his was also the absolute and final word for anything of consequence for the other three kingdoms as well.

The Romans were willing to operate under the previous working understanding they had with Herod regarding the division of government responsibilities and somewhat surprisingly, many of the locals favored this arrangement as well. For others, this condescending arrangement was confusing and outright distasteful.

Most puzzling was that the connected and politically powerful ruling Jews would gleefully appear to use the threat of Roman force on their brothers for their political gain, making it look like there was an unholy collaboration between the two. Other times, all understood that the violent Roman punishments were simply the result of knee-jerk reactions to any suspicious Jewish action that the Romans did not like, be they done by rich or poor. Using much vigilance and restraint, Pilate wisely kept these irritants to a minimum and the Jews were grudgingly existing under this precarious arrangement and, as always, some were even flourishing.

On this particular evening, Pilate was irate and bothered from the very beginning. He had finally admitted to his barking wife that he had been manipulated in the recent case involving a harmless religious prophet whom he was told was fomenting rebellion against Rome. The man was accused of making the claim to be the King of the Jews, a ridiculous and easily seen-through charge.

These months later, Pilate remained angered over this and the result was that the shameless and ill-advised maneuvering by the Chief Priest and the Jewish Courts had finally pushed him too far. He, as governor, was determined to reassert the dominance of the Roman military and of his superior intellect.

Pilate had another underlying reason to be upset. He, along with the many other territorial rulers in the Roman Empire, had been summoned to Rome at the conclusion of Tiberius's expansionary wars, some eight years prior. All were abruptly informed that Rome now wanted peace in their territories and that only enough soldiers would be allotted to each governor to maintain the peace and collect the taxes. Three separate armies would be held back in Italy, Spain, and Syria under the command of experienced generals and these would only be moved to troubled or rebellious areas as needed and at great expense. The governors were given extensive latitude to reign under those directives, but implicit in that latitude was a warning of the repercussions of their failure to keep the peace or have a drop in tax revenue.

"Peace and taxes," simple enough, the naive Pilate thought at that conference. And then he met the Jews.

The first evening of this event was a night of pleasant entertainment and feasting and Pilate was careful to make all aspects of the gathering according to the Jewish religious rules of even the strictest of the Pharisees. He knew that violating any traditions would be taken as deliberate and thus, an intended insult.

In private, Pilate often muttered and complained about the tremendous effort required to keep the Jews placated and wondered if all this appeasement would be worth it in the end.

On this evening, the gleaming halls of his Jerusalem palace were filled with immaculately costumed priests, wealthy and bejeweled Jews and heavily bearded and important scholars, all suspicious of the motives of each other and of the crafty Roman.

Pilate was resplendent, dressed in flashing, white festive robes and his wife was adorned in a flowing, gold colored gown which was the envy of all the women attending. From the beginning, it was evident that everyone was on their very best behavior. The food served was extraordinary and the wine flowed generously. The merry guests dined and laughed late into the evening and everyone went home flirting with the idea that Rome had somehow been reborn and was now a friend of the Jews.

The second day began with an early morning feast followed by a quick separation of the ruling men from their families to a private meeting with Pilate. Suspicions and whispering abounded as Jewish leaders sipped the expensive wine, murmuring to their colleagues and waiting quietly until Pilate began speaking to them.

From the beginning Pilate spoke directly and candidly with no regard for yesterday's sociability.

Most immediately understood that his words were an omen for the future, and as his address proceeded, they knew the words were indeed meant as a final warning.

He began the day by openly stating that Rome was getting reports of increased efforts by zealots in the north of the Galilee to gather men and weapons and that there were large contingents now in the cities of Tiberius and Gamla. He rose and strolled around the room, stopping in front of two rabbis known for their brave but foolhardy outspokenness against Roman domination.

"Anyone suspected or convicted of rebellion will be dealt with immediately," he barked directly into their bearded faces. He spun around to face the rest of the room. "Anyone who conspires with the rebellious zealots, harbors them, or colludes with them will also face Roman justice."

He then screamed his warning at the top of his lungs, "No mercy!"

Quite unexpectantly, Pilate had used the old Hebrew word thrown around by Pharisees when speaking about the punishment of fellow Jews who broke the Law. That word sent the many scholars in the room into a chaotic but chilling frenzy.

This performance immediately changed the atmosphere of the great hall and was followed by long minutes of dead silence.

Every Jew in the room immediately feared this man who seemed to perceive their religiously-driven hearts so well.

Pilate then continued.

He demanded that any news of these terrorists or their activity be reported to him immediately. He well understood that this statement flew in the face of the Shammai-ites in the room, those whose congregations were generously sprinkled with actual zealots and he was now including all other Jews who were sympathetic to the cause. His ominous stare directed at those he already knew to be culpable was warning enough and with that stare, any sense of cordiality from the previous day's feasting quickly disappeared.

He allowed his warnings to fester for many minutes while he strolled the room, looking directly into the eyes of shaken and frightened Jews.

A fearsome foreboding descended on the room and Pilate, a truly brutal Roman at heart, relished the paralysing tension. He was enjoying this.

He then informed the rulers of a new tax he was levying of five denarii per resident of the entire four tetrarchies. This was to offset the cost of the Roman Army's protection and he added that it must be collected within a month. He further declared that the tax must be introduced and collected by the Jews themselves. It took a few moments for the implications of this to sink in.

Then the room erupted.

The hatred of incessant and punishing Roman taxation was universal. This declaration resulted in much shouting and complaining but Pilate was resolute and unyielding, waving away any attempt to reason with him.

Lastly, and he had waited till the end, he informed them that if they were to punish any Jew for a purely religious infraction, no Roman soldier would ever be involved again. This was how it was supposed to be under their original agreement with Herod and that agreement would not be changed going forward.

Pilate knew that his declarations would anger these men so he had strategically placed five stern-looking centurions throughout the room, each wearing their impressive scarlet-trimmed body armor and brandishing their broadswords. Their very presence kept the vocal but fearful Jewish elders in their place.

Today, Pilate was adorned with the military royal blues and scarlets of the Senate of Rome and this striking show of power was not lost on the most observant ones in the room.

Over the years, Pilate had successfully worked within the strange Jewish justice system and well knew the mechanisms of the Sanhedrin. He knew that a good many of the civil and religious offences that arose were handled through the Jewish religious courts and dealt with through their ancient complex application of rewards and punishments. This was as per the agreement with Herod the Great and this arrangement had always help assuage the despised Roman domination. The punishments allowed to the Jewish Sanhedrin were somewhat trivial in comparison to the Romans and this fact annoyed the aggressive Jews who lobbied for more severe sentences. They were not satisfied with the petty fines and reparations or the proscribed donations to the charities, they felt that the lack of actual physical penalties just allowed the guilty to feel free to repeat their offences.

Knowing that he had angered this group of men, and being a master politician, Pilate left his last announcement for the very last.

He arose and declared, "If your courts have decided that it was truly a religious matter, and only after there had been a proper Sanhedrin hearing with credible witnesses proving that a crime had actually been committed, I will then not interfere with your religious judgments or punishments in the future."

The gathered men looked around, hardly believing what they had just heard. This was definitely a compromising sop extended to the Jews by this devious Roman, but what a stunning one.

His final words were directed to the High Priest himself and his meddling father-in-law. He pointed his finger in the face of Annas and then looked directly at Caiaphas. The centurions rose, slapped their broadswords and faced the gathering with menacing and warning looks, freezing all in their seats.

"I will allow you this freedom. But I warn you, do not bring your trivial religious arguments to my seat of judgment ever again. Do you not have any among you who can judge righteously, or is every one of you motivated by hatred and political advantage. I do not know a race of people so dedicated to abusing each other as you Jews. I will not allow any Roman soldiers to ever be involved in your childish squabbles or your diabolical treatments of your own citizens again."

The piercing rebuke immediately silenced the flabbergasted and powerless High Priest. He and his red-faced and furious father-in-law, Annas, slowly bowed in seething deference to Pilate. Many others in the room shot irate stares at the nearest Romans, feeling this remark was also directed at them and meant only to embarrass them and they began puffing and guffawing and wagging their heads at this damning verbal attack. What right did this pagan have to judge us, they muttered.

Only a very few, one of which was a stunned and motionless Gamaliel, felt the stabbing but honest sting of the reproach, knowing exactly what Pilate was referring to. Inwardly, Gamaliel felt totally exposed, feeling that he was the main person to be blamed. He knew he had allowed questionable and even fraudulent charges to be heard when as President of the court he could have easily dismissed them as false.

This pagan and untaught Roman had spoken with a directness and wisdom that had been all but lost in Jerusalem and his words had revealed the lack of character of the self-important men in that room. Gamaliel felt personally uncovered as the main culprit involved in allowing the perverted justice that had crept into Jerusalem under his watch. He immediately hung his head in shame and tears of regret washed through his long beard unhindered and his shoulders heaved in heavy sobs. Deep guttural moans escaped his throat as if the deep guilt that the tortured man felt was forcing its way out of his chest. The incensed and angry Jews around him, could not understand what was happening to this holy and revered man.

In that instant, Gamaliel made a life-changing vow to himself. He would correct his actions from this day going forward and he would be a better man and a better Jew. He would become worthy of the respect that his position and family name had endowed him with.

He repented.

Loudly, with much emotion and with no regard to his lofty position, he repented.

He repeated to himself that Jews were to be a light to the nations but here, they were accurately being rebuked by a lawless foreigner for being unjust and merciless.

When he was finally quieted and while frozen to his chair as the rest of the room churned in confusion, Gamaliel realized that this had not descended on him suddenly or without warning. The condition he found himself in was the result of a multitude of little compromises and small decisions.

In his quiet times, Gamaliel was still haunted by the memory of the day he had come face to face with Jesus, he and his immaculately robed comrades staging a confrontational meeting with Him by casting a women caught in adultery at His feet in a theatrical attempt to embarrass Him. They wanted to publicly expose some fault in His judgment. A very composed Jesus did not take the bait, not even bothering to answer them aloud, but bent down and quietly wrote each accuser's name in the sand followed with a single word.

How did Jesus know those things about them and was he, Gamaliel, really the vengeful hypocrite that the one scribbled word accused him of being? Gamaliel had used every trick of reasoning to make himself believe that he was not, but the dramatic scene was etched deep into his memory and it bothered him in his dreams and in his intimate musings from that time on.

He had originally felt that the plan to trap this man in some sin was faulty and self-serving and probably should not have been agreed to but he had slowly but surely become a politician in his later days and eventually co-operated with his Pharisee brethren in their plan. The integrity of Gamaliel and other good men had been eroded by years of such compromise and appeasement, plus the wearing effect of the daily warring sects of Jerusalem had clouded his usually precise judgment. He had convinced himself that peace amongst his brothers could many times only be achieved with a bit of negotiating with one's own conscience and that any lasting peace had to be paid for with something of personal value.

In a deplorable act of cowardice, he remembered leaving that woman alone with Jesus and slinking away with the others. It was not his finest hour and one which he had unsuccessfully struggled to forget by never mentioning it to anyone again. Since that day, he had completely avoided that small sandy spot along the south stairs of the Temple, never passing that way again.

Today, he had been exposed as had all the leaders and he could hide no longer.

As he pondered this declaration by Pontius Pilate, he rightfully suspected that this rebuke of their character would be quickly forgotten by most as had many previous rebukes and only the portion where the governor gave them leave to deal with their religious enemies would be remembered. It did not take a lot of foresight to realize that the statement would unleash a wave of accusations, contentious and bitter arguments and increased numbers of Sanhedrin hearings. Sadly, that flood would end in many violent punishments meted out by his callous and opportunistic Jewish brothers. Gamaliel determined that he would do all he could to stem the coming tide and become more of the man his venerated grandfather would want him to be.

What started that night within Gamaliel was a struggle for purity and integrity that dominated his thinking and would change his theology for the rest of his days. In the weeks following, Gamaliel was the first Jew to suspect that incorrect understandings of written scripture were the root cause of the hatred and violence that he was witnessing and that correlation was absolutely revolutionary to him.

In the next room, his wife, his son and his daughter were not aware of what was taking place in the adjacent hall. They loved their father and regarded him as pure in heart and would defend him to the death but Gamaliel knew he must confess his shady actions to them, no matter the pain and embarrassment.

When Gamaliel and his family left the festivities, he remained quiet for many hours and Sarah, sensing he was terribly troubled, finally coaxed him to admit his internal dilemma to her. Wisely, she did not try to placate him with any soothing compliments. She had not seen him in such a state of intense turmoil before and knew it best to give him unquestioning, but truthful and unbiased support, followed with the personal privacy to find the answers he needed so badly.

This type of self-examination was a condition not usually experienced and definitely not encouraged by Pharisees as they were always taught that they were correct in their thinking and that their unquestioning self-assurance was a good thing. Such assurance was healthy for Judaism and it was a condition to be envied and emulated. The Pharisees all practiced this stance and believed it served a purpose and was for the benefit of Israel, even if it required blindly subjugating any internal doubts. Doubting oneself was therefore regarded as sinful.

Gammy noticed the drastic change in his father but because he had not been in the closed meeting with Pilate, he was not aware of what had affected him so. Believing completely in the honor and uprightness of his father and knowing the wearing and convoluted politics his father had endured recently, he had his suspicions. He could not put those thoughts into words yet, not even to himself, and it was painful for him to see his esteemed and beloved father so deeply troubled.

After two tortuous days, Gamaliel gathered his wife and children around the portico table and tearfully opened his hurting heart to them. With overwhelming emotion, he declared his failure to uphold the virtues he had faithfully taught and that his elevated position required. To his surprise and amid tears and hugs and forgiveness, his confession caused the whole family to rededicate itself and seek to achieve the honor and integrity that their lofty status was called and destined to.

Of course, it was Miriam who first noticed that this family seemed to walk with more serenity and grace from that day on. The reason for this she would only learn years later.

CHAPTER THIRTY-FOUR

The Stunning City of Jerusalem

On the days that Gamaliel's family was busy with Pilate, Saul took the opportunity to take Miriam on a personal tour of the city he loved so much. They wandered the well-kept and richly decorated streets near Herod's Palace first, being enamored by the intricate carving of stone archways and rich wooden doors which had the inhabitant's family histories proudly carved on them. Saul pointed out the homes of the High Priest and all their extended family who, from the wealth displayed by their houses, were obviously among the richest people in Jerusalem.

The flower-draped stone walls, heavy with berry and fruit blossoms, were not the only barriers between the wealthy leadership of Israel and the common people, thought Miriam.

Saul avoided taking her to the Pilgrim's Road or near the markets below the Temple, hoping to shield her from the mayhem that was always taking place in those areas for he desperately wanted her first impressions of the city to be favorable. Miriam proved to be the perfect tourist, listening and quietly observing.

At home later, a very inquisitive Miriam began asking probing and uncomfortable questions of her brother. Since arriving in Jerusalem, she had recognized that there were many things bothering Saul, Gamaliel, his family and indeed the whole city. She felt like she was being excluded and she did not like the feeling of being left out of some poorly disguised, city-wide secret.

Daily trips to the market with Leah, plus the animated conversations she had heard there, had inadvertently exposed her to Jerusalem's darker side, one filled with rumors and whispering, and as a result, she suspected that she was being shielded from controversy by Saul and the others. Her curious mind abhorred not knowing and the feeling of being purposely sheltered was making this usually gentle girl very irritated, even angry.

She finally blurted, "Okay, Saul, what is going on? And please do not treat me as if you must protect your weak sister."

Saul knew that he had to be truthful with her, aware of being face-to-face with a formidable and piercing mind that would know if he somehow tried to placate her. At times, her abilities almost frightened him even though she was always kind and understanding and never condescending. Today, she was determined and unrelenting.

Saul related the previous day's events with his friend Samuel and his sister Ruth and, prodded with a few pointed questions from Miriam, reluctantly told all he knew of the controversy that had started on the feast day of Pentecost down on the Pilgrim's Road. When he mentioned that those involved were now meeting daily at the Temple, she stopped him with a raised hand.

"When are we going to the Temple, Saul," was her question. "I know that to you it is familiar, but remember that I have never seen it or approached it." By this, she was referring to the entire formal ceremony of washing, going up, buying an offering and presenting it to the priests, all requirements for her to fulfill the proscribed Jewish traditions.

She was really asking her brother to assist her, oversee her visit and that favored position made Saul suddenly proud

"We can go tomorrow; you can do your mikveh washings here and then you don't have to go down to Siloam as it is all the way down at the bottom of the city," Saul stated.

"No, Saul," Miriam interrupted, "I want to be a pilgrim and I want to approach as any pilgrim would. I want to wash where the daughters of Israel wash, exactly as those who do not have advantage. I want to approach my God with the humbleness that many want to avoid, as our King David said, 'Who shall ascend up the hill of the Lord, and who shall stand in his Holy place? He that hath clean hands and a pure heart, who hath not lifted up his soul unto vanity, nor sworn deceitfully. He shall receive the blessing from the Lord, and righteousness from the God of his salvation'."

Saul was stunned.

First, although he knew the writings of David and this exact verse he could recite on demand, he had never seen it nor heard it described with the simplicity and unexpected depth as his little sister had just so clearly stated.

She had applied it perfectly. It was as if she wanted to become one with the scripture in her actions and this was a level of devotion that was uncommon, even among the most pious of women. This was not just obedience.

At that moment, she achieved a level of respect in Saul's estimation that he gave to very few. She was going to live out the scriptures rather than just obey them out of duty. What a refreshing and unusual concept, thought Saul, but then, he quickly reminded himself that this was the precise calling of the Pharisees.

Somehow, Miriam's version of personifying the ancient words seemed strangely purer.

PART FOUR

CHAPTER THIRTY-FIVE

The Temple

The very next morning, Saul and a very joyful Miriam, carrying a bundle of new clothes, made their way down the Mount Zion streets toward the high western wall of the Temple. There they turned south onto the descending Pilgrim's Road, passing under the priest's Temple stairway, and proceeded downward to the complex that housed the many pools at the Siloam spring. Saul pointed out the Freedmen's Synagogue as they passed by, but Miriam was on a mission and barely spoke or acknowledged it. As they reached the ornate and already crowded Pools of Siloam, they separated to the private men's and women's sides to immerse themselves in the ritual washing required to approach the inner courts of the Temple. After the multiple washings, they again met at the common pools and even though they were jostled and bumped about in a crowd of eager pilgrims, Miriam was smiling broadly, relishing this much anticipated experience.

There was a large and noisy group gathered at the other end this pool and they were singing and praising and engaged in the familiar baptizing promoted by the Essenes. A loud pronouncement was made as they were being buried in the water that this was being done in the name of Jesus.

Once again, Saul felt a shot of anger rising in himself but he looked away and did not react. He glanced at Miriam who appeared not to notice and together they began the half-mile upward trek on the bustling Pilgrim's Road toward the base of the massive Temple walls.

As they began, Miriam halted. With an earnest look at her brother, said, "Saul, would you please guide me through this whole day. I want to know every detail about the Temple and the people involved. I want to experience it in all its meaning and to understand what each person's role is and what my little part signifies."

The sincere, pleading look on her face warmed Saul's heart and he responded with pride. "I most certainly will, my sister. And always remember, Father would be so proud of you right now."

Miriam began her unhurried, upward journey, pausing and singing a psalm at every small landing in a beautiful, melodic voice that almost went unnoticed in the noisy, congested street. Brother and sister were soon completely enveloped by other excited and dedicated pilgrims on their upward trek. Upon reaching the southwest corner of the Temple plateau and standing directly beneath the towering walls which constituted the highest and most imposing point of the Temple structure, Saul pointed to the right and they walked reverently to the bottom of the massive staircase that led northward and up to the three wide Huldah Gates. Surrounding the lowest portion of the staircase were wooden enclosures where softly-bleating lambs and cages full of cooing doves were conveniently placed. This was where one could purchase the offering required to fulfill their worship. Following Saul's directions, Miriam purchased a single white dove as a sin offering, being an unmarried woman. Because this was not a feast time, Saul did not purchase a sacrifice.

The duo then climbed up the wide stairs and passed through the center gate.

Miriam, holding her dove's cage gently in hand, followed Saul inside, all the while studying the enormous blocks of stone around the entrances. They passed through the high wooden doors into the cavernous inner auditorium that lay below the upper surface of the Temple. There was a wide, echoey corridor ahead of them that stretched to a grand staircase leading up into the sunlight. On all sides of the hallway were the tables of the men whose responsibility it was to sell the pilgrims the Temple shekels, or more accurately, an ancient half-shekel. Their tables were stacked high with these unique coins, the only currency accepted as payment of tithes as per the instructions of Moses. Nowhere else on earth were these coins used but in the Temple of Jerusalem.

Standing to one side, Saul explained that each day, Temple coins were exchanged for whatever type of currency the pilgrim had brought from his country and then these special shekels were deposited into the tithing containers provided further up in the Temple. These containers were emptied nightly and then the coins were brought down to be sold again. The exchange rates offered for the different countries' currencies were set by the High Priest.

To everyone's embarrassment, these rates were constantly changing and were not at all near the rates offered by the simple money changers in the open markets. Saul, not wanting to muddy the waters on Miriam's special day, reluctantly explained that the loud arguments presently going on were about these rates and that there was a continual disagreement between the pilgrims and the outwardly uncaring men at these tables. They knew that they would get their price in the end.

With no explanation, the pure gold coins of the pilgrims were given a much lower value within these sacred halls than anywhere else in the Empire for these money exchangers were expert at devaluing the amount of the currencies presented by the pilgrims and they always seemed to require some type of extra service charge. These questionable fees were then secretly split with the High Priest's family. The last bit of information was just a persistent Jerusalem rumor, so Saul did not mention it to his untainted and still naive sister.

Miriam bought a host of Temple shekels to pay her accumulated tithe on the money paid to her in Tarsus for her much-appreciated medical services. She realized that she had paid far too much for the Temple shekels she acquired but was not in any mood to argue or let this chicanery upset the delight of her first Temple visit, a fact her eager and sneering money changer appreciated while ogling the remains of her bulging money pouch.

With growing anticipation, Miriam slowly followed Saul down the length of the huge hall, straining to read the ancient writings and prophetic utterances carved into the surrounding walls and then they climbed the grand staircase which rose the full height and spilled onto the center of a wide and completely stone-paved plateau on the south side of the looming Temple building. Squinting in the bright sun, her eyes were suddenly fixed on the tall and glowing white stone building that rose behind a ten-foot-high wall just before her. The gold-fringed top of the edifice was gleaming in the bright sun and it was breathtaking. Its glistening surfaces were crafted to split the sun's rays into shafts of golden light that shot their brilliance around the whole complex. Miriam knew that housed below the golden roof, just inside that pure white building, were the two most sacred rooms in Jewry.

They stopped at the top of the steps and Saul explained that they were in the Court of the Gentiles, an open plateau that surrounded the actual Temple complex. The smaller and restricted areas of the Temple were kept unpolluted and separate from this common area by the polished stone walls in front of them.

The staircase they had climbed had left them almost in the middle of the southern plateau, and this area was open for all, including visiting Gentiles.

As possibly his most important project, King Herod had renovated and greatly expanded this area by building the new and imposing west and south walls much further outside the original ones and then creating various structures under the new parts of the plaza. He completed it with a new flat stone surface. This had created a significantly larger gathering area to be enjoyed before entering the restricted holy places. The renovation had more than tripled this upper region and Herod adorned it with features that made it a favorite for many other types of gatherings as well as the solemn Temple practices. The effect was that the Temple Mount became a center for all ceremonial and social life for both Jews and curious Gentiles who frequented the beautiful city.

Set on the outer edges of this expansion, and surrounding the entire new plateau, was a Roman-style, roofed portico with supporting columns. This covering gave extensive areas of protection from the hot sun and winter rains and became known as Solomon's Porch. This practical area quickly became the haunts of scholars, preachers and teachers who along with their followers, could enjoy the almost festival-like Temple atmosphere, yet maintain the solomness of all that surrounded them. Saul explained that on most days, there were all types of gatherings in those porticos and one could stroll the outside of the large courtyard and hear musicians, or news of different countries or even the latest Pharisaical enlightenment. Well known to local Jews was that in the dark corners, and spoken in very hushed tones, one could also hear the seditious views of those who would like to see Rome driven out.

The pair had not moved from the top of the wide staircase and were observing all by simply turning about. Just then, one of the four turbaned and handsomely robed priests who stood on duty at the top of the staircase, approached them. He was a jovial older man and seeing the dove in Miriam's little cage, he pointed them to the eastern end of the complex where the main entrance to the interior courtyards was. His intention was to keep the constant influx of pilgrims moving and to keep the top of the stairway clear, but he was also quite accustomed to newcomers becoming glued to the top steps in amazement. His polite manner got them moving, but not far.

Not to be hurried, Saul led Miriam around the railing of the stairs and out of the way. He continued his description by turning around and pointing to the second story dormitory complex built on the top of the portico of the most southernly wall. This sat directly above the high Huldah Gates and was therefore visible from anywhere south of the city. He explained that this was built by Herod to house the Levite priests who came, by their stipulated courses, from all over Judea or Samaria with even a few from the Galilee-all coming to fulfil their duty to serve in the Temple. The majority of Levites who qualified to serve in the Temple lived outside of Jerusalem and came once a year to serve, just as their allotted times required. These times, or courses, as they were commonly called, followed the calendar as defined by the moons and were limited to one month a year so they could still support their families at home.

Miriam listened intently to Saul's detailed description of these men and their duties, amazed at how their original ancient and seasonal obligations had evolved into the smooth-running performance that was occurring before her eyes. The living quarters provided here made things much easier for these intermittent priests as previously they had to find rental accommodations in Jerusalem itself, and although they were serving the Temple, they were not protected from being fleeced by the notorious landlords of the city.

Miriam was intrigued, peppering Saul with questions

They had in the space of a half hour, barely moved onto the wide plateau.

Saul was busily explaining that these immaculately clothed priests were trained, supervised, and under the strict control of the actual managers of the Temple, the more colorfully adorned Chief Priests. These high-ranking men were also Levites but were permanent appointees, well paid and working at the behest of the High Priest. More than a little sarcastically, Saul admitted that many of the Chief Priests were some sort of cousin of the High Priest and his family.

Miriam could not help noticing an ongoing theme with respect to the High Priest.

Saul carefully identified and explained the significance of the extraordinarily intricate decorations on the priestly garments which labelled them as loftier than the ordinary priests. These finely bedecked men paraded around the Temple complex with a serious sense of purpose while looking quite distinguished, all the time nodding condescendingly to the adoring pilgrims.

Saul went into the details of their official duties, mainly to train and oversee the transient priests, and soon he was describing many other tasks that they performed, including collecting the substantial receipts from the tables where money was changed and allotting that money to all aspects of Temple operations and upkeep. They were the day-to-day managers of all things regarding the Temple.

Unknown to most, and again shrouded in whispered rumor, was that any profit garnered above the required amount stipulated for all the Temple operations was quietly split between these Chief Priests and the High Priest's bag. Also, behind closed doors, these Chief Priests emptied the various offering containers arranged so freely around the large outer court, each designated for a specific Jewish charity. For this service, the priests always kept a healthy stipend for themselves, justifying the skimming as their "fee." After this, and with much pomp and ceremony, they loudly directed the distribution of the remaining but pitifully shrunken Jewish benevolence. The worst kept secret of the Temple was that their families benefited greatly from the charitable hearts of the visitors of the Temple with only a sop making its way to the real needy widows and orphans.

Paid out of the Temple tithing half-shekel was the legitimate purchase of the costly incense, all the priests' garments, the musical instruments, all cleaning and repair services and all other costs incurred in the Temple.

Again, with a hint of practised cynicism, Saul mentioned that their generous salaries made up a large part of those costs and although they were well compensated, these characters often showed up at weddings and family gatherings throughout Israel, beseeching all in attendance for extra donations. They declared important and immediate need for unspecified Temple emergencies, much to the consternation of the hosts and guests who clearly understood the obvious ploy.

Saul did not mention that the High Priest also ensured that there was an over-representation of his most loyal Chief Priests on the judgment seats of both the smaller daily court of the Sanhedrin and the large Grand Sanhedrin. These allies could be trusted to be the loudest proponents of his wishes and without question would follow his personal directives.

As Saul was relating all this to his sister, he realized how exhausting it was to balance the respect Jews should have for the Temple and it's priesthood, and yet avoid being completely fleeced by their extensive operations.

Saul then led Miriam to the western area where an opening in the plateau led to a much smaller stairway which descended sharply downward. There they were halted by a rough military-looking guard who simply stated, "You don't want to enter here."

Under the floors of the expanded plateau, the paranoid Herod had made provision for a complex of dank jail cells which were the preferred hangouts of yet another type of Temple guard. These were heavily armed sentries who willingly showed themselves as a more menacing force while patrolling regularly throughout the Temple complex. They were also permanent employees of the Temple and did as the Chief Priests directed, mainly watching for violators of the rules and harassing any who could possibly be perceived as a threat. Almost on the hour, a pair of leather-clad men, looking more like Roman soldiers than guards at the Temple, would appear from this staircase and make their brooding and ominous parade around the grounds.

Miriam was confused. Saul explained.

The easy-going priestly guards were traditionally concerned only with the sacredness of the upper Temple and were composed of the transient Levites who served by lot, and for only their appointed month. These unarmed and mostly pleasant guards were there to ensure that impure people did not enter the restricted inner courts and they watched that Gentiles remained outside of the inner sanctums. They were completely occupied by assuring that there be order and proper decorum, including the correct dose of solemnity within the confines of the Temple. Their duties were specific and only composed of keeping the atmosphere of holiness within the Temple complex.

The other group, the armed and permanent guards, operated both inside and outside the Temple walls. They referred to themselves as protectors of the Temple, but over the years had in fact become the enforcers of the decrees of the High Priest and his family, a function for which they were handsomely paid and were totally dedicated to. Busy with the weightier political issues, these were not concerned with the minor religious infractions that occurred within the confines of the Temple but willingly left that mundane work to the others. Their services were rarely required on the plazas, employed only if the festivities got out of hand and too much wine was involved and easily solved with a few hours in their cold cells generally sobering up the miscreants. No, theirs was a political policing and they were rightfully feared. Their fierceness and brutality to their Jewish brethren was well known should they be directed to arrest some rebellious, outspoken or inebriated soul.

Adding to their crude reputation, these men also had a strange and unique ability to find questionable witnesses who appeared magically in any dubious court case, plus they could gather a mob within moments if needed. To enhance their military look, they proudly carried shiny broadswords, exactly like the Romans soldiers, and it seemed that they dearly loved this adornment for it served as a dire warning of their seriousness.

This news both surprised and disgusted Miriam. Noticing her reaction, Saul wondered if he were giving her too much detail or putting the Temple in a bad light for her. Her penetrating questions had kept him talking freely and openly.

Saul, continuing with a little less edge in his voice, further described these jobs as permanent and well paid which had over the years evolved into a personal protection squad for the High Priest and his family. Originally, theirs was a Temple service that should be under the Chief Priests' direction, but now they only took their orders directly from Malchus, Caiaphas' personal servant. Quite regularly, they had been sent out of Jerusalem to protect and watch over Caiaphas or Annas or any other members of their family who had managed to make enemies of the general Jewish public.

The small staircase that led down to their world of prison cells was within fifty feet of the most westernly wall of the interior Temple and that put it adjacent to the outer wall of the Holiest of Holies. Along this wall were well-used spaces that were the closest spots one could get to the very presence of Hashem without being inside the gleaming Temple structure itself. In a departure from their usual callousness, these rough guards supervised these coveted areas with a strange reverence. It was here that devotees could lean against the most proximate wall and pray, or quietly read scripture or humbly prostrate oneself and experience being as close as one could get to the "shekinah" of their God. The guards had even resisted the temptation to charge a fee for access to the closest spaces.

While standing directly outside the walls that encircled the high edifice, Saul described how the Temple itself was made up of three separated areas within that enclosing wall. The far east end contained a large open area that was called the women's court for it was the entry area that all purified Jews, including women were allowed to pray and worship in. All worshipers entered the complex through the eastern-most gate of that gallery and that place was a continual bustling expanse. Men who came to sacrifice, proceeded directly through the Women's Court and into the next area. The eastern gate of the Women's court was named Beautiful and all who came to sacrifice, entered there.

At the west end of that court was a dividing wall which separated it from the men's court, the place where all the sacrifices were offered. A large curved staircase on this dividing wall was where the beautifully festooned priests would suddenly appear, singing and playing the proscribed instruments and setting the stirring atmosphere with their music. Other priests appeared as well and received the sacrifices from the hands of the women worshipers at the top of these stairs. The large doors at this staircase were usually left wide open and the women were not only allowed but encouraged to watch from the steps as a priest took their dove or lamb inside and undertook the ritual offering. Curious women worshipers could easily see the large, bronze alter of sacrifice just inside where the slaying of a lamb took place twice daily for the sins of the nation.

Beyond that altar were the imposing doors to the sixty-foot-high Temple building which housed the two separated ceremonial rooms.

The first and larger room contained the small, gold-covered altar of incense, where the sweet-smelling offering burned at the beginning and end of the day, as commanded by Moses. The incense was made from a combination of four specific spices, as commanded by God, and eleven other spices and compounds, as allowed at the discretion of the original incense makers.

Saul recited the story of the ancient family of Avitnus who had been making the incense for centuries and how they had dearly guarded the secret of their mixture. God had commanded that no other incense of the exact proportions be burned by Jews anywhere so they jealously kept the recipe a secret. To their private formula, Salt of Sodom and Amber of Jordan were added, but most importantly, a secret compound that made the smoke of the incense rise straight upward in the shape of a pillar. It was a serious national crime to attempt to duplicate it.

An international branch of this family that now lived in the Jewish community of Alexandria were claiming to have a more precise original formula as opposed to the "flawed" Judean mixture. As yet, the Great Sanhedrin had not made a ruling on this, but the vocal Freedmen's Synagogue where many from Alexandria now attended, were pushing for a return to their disregarded version of incense purity. Notwithstanding this acrimonious debate, those attending the Temple, and even those watching from afar, were visibly moved at the break of dawn and again at twilight as the fragrant and swirling column of smoke rose and went skyward, returning to their Maker. It was as if a fragrant chord between heaven and earth was re-established daily.

With passion, Saul explained to his sister how, as a twelve-year-old lad, Gamaliel had brought him here one morning and together they watched the freshly-washed and perfectly-gowned singular priest enter the inner court with a measured amount of the precious incense in one hand and carrying a pan full of burning coals in the other. While they waited outside, Gamaliel reverently told of how all the daily sacrifices represented and fulfilled Israel's required service before their God but, he emphasized, the incense was different. As it rose to heaven, it was the sign that there was to be a spiritual connection between the earthbound Jews and their higher God and the rising column of smoke and incense was their daily reminder of this higher calling. Saul had seen the eyes of Gamaliel overflow with tears as he spoke such lofty truths in a voice barely above a whisper. That was the first time he witnessed this godly sage overcome with such deep heartfelt emotions. They had tarried close by until the last of the column of smoke had disappeared, individually experiencing the flood of pungent and sweet aromas that wafted through the entire courtyard and then spilled out of the open doors to the streets below.

Miriam was strangely moved by this story as well, never-before thinking of the experiences that her brother was having in faraway Jerusalem in those years and how they had shaped his young life. She wanted to know more, so Saul continued.

Offering of the incense was considered the highest of the services a priest could do. It was a coveted honor and all priests wanted that personal experience. After many early morning disputes and even two or three incidents of priests shoving and punching each other, a system of lots was instituted to choose the serving priest many days in advance. This technique also wisely limited the ritual to once in a priest's lifetime.

When a priest's special day was chosen, his family members would often gather in the men's and women's courts to witness the ceremony in the pre-dawn glow and huge cheers would erupt when the smoke arose heavenward from behind the closed doors of the inner court. A day-long celebration followed for the priest, complete with gifts and accolades. It was truly a highlight of the man's life.

Shrouded in mystery, some priests had even claimed to be visited by Gabriel while offering the incense and were so affected by the immensity of this act that they were struck mute for a season. At least, it was rumored, that exact thing had happened with one a few years ago. Saul affirmed this as so to his wide-eyed sister even though he knew no other details, or even that priest's name.

Saul further explained that there was a secondary purpose to the incense. It was an extremely powerful and pleasing perfume that drove out the smell of blood that gathered throughout the day. As refreshing as the twilight offering was, it was the pungent morning offering that greeted the Temple area's visitors with a pleasant and lingering fragrance as it flowed throughout the whole plateau and drifted about. Its sweet perfumes wafted down the main staircase to the adjacent streets and on still, windless days even reached to the Pools of Siloam.

A thick veil separated the inner court from the even smaller Holy of Holies, entered only by the High Priest and that, only once a year. It was here that an extra measure of rare incense was burned on the day of atonement, just as specified by the Lord. In earlier times, the coveted Ark of the Covenant had been housed in this smaller room and it contained the tablets that the Ten Commandments were chiseled on by Moses himself, among other items. The mysterious ark had disappeared just before the destruction of the first Temple and all Jews believed that it had been hidden by the protective and conspiratorial priests, the whereabouts not to be divulged until Messiah Himself was ruling. It was a conspiracy that all Jews could proudly feel part of.

This exhaustive description of the inner Temple had taken Saul nearly an hour and both he and Miriam had hardly moved, deeply absorbed in the significance of each item Saul had described.

The cooing of the dove in the little cage caught their attention, so Saul led the way back to the east end of the compound and then up the few steps into the Gate Beautiful. They had to carefully wend their way through a few lame and tattered beggars who gathered daily at this gate, optimistically hoping to find favor with soft-hearted and repentant Jews.

Saul slowly led his sister through the crowded hall of the women's court to the base of the large curved steps that led into the men's court. As instructed, Miriam approached and placed her dove in the hands of a smiling, white-robed priest who nodded to her and then recited the whole passage of Moses that pertained to her sacrifice. Miriam watched intently as this priest passed through the open doors and approached the large altar. With swift and efficient movements, the dove was quickly offered. The sight of the priest wringing the neck of the dove mixed with the loud trumpeting taking place on the broad steps was so emotional and dramatic that often the observing women would start dancing and singing ecstatically, realizing that they had been forgiven in the eyes of their God. The enthusiasm of the musical priests, along with others melodically singing the psalms, emphasized that the rituals were being done perfectly as directed and this very polished routine consistently awed all pilgrims.

Miriam stared motionless for over a half hour, carefully observing the many ancient rituals of sacrifice that Moses had instituted. She saw the rites that were meant for women but also witnessed the larger and bloodier ceremonies of the men. A thought entered her mind and it spoke loudly to her.

Would there ever be an end to these rituals? Would Hashem ever be satisfied?

Saul watched from a distance, hoping that the immensity of the scene she was witnessing would somehow quench the life-long thirst of the questioning mind of Miriam. Her intense gaze assured him that she was recalling not only the written law concerning what she saw but that she was pondering the meaning and intent of these traditions. She was a penetrating thinker for certain, but Saul was not sure if that type of analytical mind was, in the end, a blessing or a curse.

Finally satiated, Miriam turned and began looking around. She looked up and saw the second-story balcony surrounding the perimeter of the otherwise open women's court. She noticed many women seated along this upper gallery and she sent an inquiring look to Saul. He smiled and waved her to the side stairway leading up to those balconies where she quickly ascended and soon disappeared into the throng of women. Some of these came daily to pray, some worked on the priestly vestments on large tables and some labored on the massive curtains and decorative coverings hung throughout the whole of the Temple complex.

Totally absorbed with this enterprise, Miriam slowly made her way around the balcony, speaking here and there to workers and worshipers, stopping and speaking at length to a small group at the very rear area, directly above the Gate Beautiful. She discovered that these were a special congregation of widows, women who came every day and were dedicating the remainder of their lives to prayer and fasting, beseeching Hashem for the blessing and prosperity of Israel. The legendary stories surrounding these prophetess-like women had reached Tarsus and now finding them hidden away and kept apart from the path of the crowds of pilgrims seemed slightly strange to Miriam. Understandingly, these women were not the favorite group of the High Priest for they were often relating dreams or visions aimed at the failings of Annas and Caiaphas, so because of those contrary inspirations, it seemed that they must be banished to the back of the balcony and kept out of sight.

Saul waited patiently at the foot of the curved stairs, quietly observing as men with their sacrifices met with the continual flow of priests who emerged and took their offerings. Unlike the women, the men accompanied the priest and their offering inside the inner court to the altar where the men were obliged to keep their hands on the heads of their sacrifice as it was slain by the priest. This was an unpleasant and deprecating exercise for most and was done to identify with the death of the animal which was dying in their place. Saul watched as the allowed portions of the meats from the sacrifice were then removed and quickly whisked through a guarded gate and taken to the priests' nearby-lodgings by a porter. This was the allotted portion for the priests and their families, just as Moses had instructed.

Near the bottom curved stair were large metal containers strategically placed to receive the half shekels that the pilgrims had purchased at the money changers' tables below. The metal pots clanged noisily as each coin was dropped in, catching Saul's attention and causing a wry smile to appear. The High Priest had called for a change from the quiet earthen pots of previous times and the wealthy, with their large stack of coins and practiced hands, became very adept at hitting the noisiest part of the new metal rims with each coin, thereby creating a comical musical rivalry to the trumpets and horns a few steps above. The longer the racket lasted, the more important and wealthier was the contributor and the clattering rims made a brassy witness to that fact.

The women's court balconies had been added by Herod to make it easier for the temple guards to keep a physical separation between women worshipers and the men who passed through that area. The "official" reason for the addition of the balconies was to keep the levity and socializing that naturally arose between men and women at a minimum. The Temple was to be a very solemn place, a fact that all agreed to with devious smiles, and it was not meant as a meeting place for romantics. Problem was, many married couples told fond stories of their original meeting at the Temple for it was the place where young couples could discreetly and without any criticism encounter a suiter. Parents of marriage age children who foolishly hoped the increased interest in the Temple was a sign of deepening devotion, soon became aware that the excessive visiting probably indicated that a wedding was on the horizon. Regarding this, Saul's quiet chortle went unseen by his preoccupied sister.

Saul viewed the windowless north wall of the women's court knowing that right behind it was the chamber of Hewn Stones that housed the Sanhedrin. That room could be accessed by priests through a rarely opened door from the men's inner court, but for all others, the entrance was from the outer plateau's northern doors. This was to accommodate Gentiles, criminals and the impure who were being dragged in. The north door also successfully kept the flow of preoccupied, often angry, Sanhedrin attendees out of the sacred inner Temple court.

Saul's mind drifted past those buildings, to the furthest northern end of the large Temple plateau. The remaining flat area ended against a high building called the Fortress of Antonia and this reviled place definitely was the most hated edifice of all Herod's building campaigns. Its towering height rivalled the main Temple building as if in some sort of perverted competition and that guaranteed that it was a constant irritation to the Jewish population. Infinitely worse than its mere size, the fortress was the permanent garrison of the Roman Army in Jerusalem and it had been placed next to the Temple purposely. The high towers had windows that overlooked the northern plateau and those entering the Sanhedrin were constantly reminded that whatever they were deciding inside was being watched and scrutinized from those upper perches. If so desired, all their lawful decisions could be quickly and easily overruled by the paranoid and controlling Romans.

Also, through those windows, the noise of Roman soldiers marching about or raucously reveling could easily be heard on the Temple plateau-another distasteful irritant. The dominating heights of Antonia served as a constant reminder to all Jews that Israel was not in complete favor with their God, regardless of all the busy, religious fervor performed inside the courts of the Temple. Most galling was that the cells of this very Roman fortress were often the execution sites for any overzealous Jew who had irritated Rome for simply wanting to be Jewish.

Further north and completely outside the Temple area walls and only a few short steps east of Antonia, were the large pools of Bethsaida that provided an alternate ritual washing site for pilgrims. These pools were fed, not by a spring as with Siloam, but by rain water channeled from the north of Jerusalem which filled huge underground cisterns beneath and north of the Temple area. These massive cisterns fed the intricate washing system of the Temple complex, providing a steady stream of fresh water to the sacrificial area for the final cleansing of the sacrifices.

When Miriam descended the stairs from the women's court balconies, she was excited and alive and feeling slightly secretive, but smiling widely at Saul. She opened her money sack filled with her half shekels and dumped them into the pots. Her obligations and duties were now complete and she was genuinely happy and feeling strangely relieved.

Brother and sister exited the Gate Beautiful where Miriam paused and rewarded an older and persistently begging lame man and a ragged woman with a hand out. Once outside, they turned south, back into the large courtyard of the Gentiles.

Immediately, their attention was drawn to the growing crowds filling the Porches of Solomon, which surrounded the large plateau.

The booming voice of a man, speaking in the local Aramaic but with the heavy accent of a Galilean, rang out through the columns. A few steps from the Gate Beautiful and directly in front of them, he was speaking to a gathered group, perhaps hundreds of people, sitting either on bundles or on the ground and all listening intently to the burly and roughly-clad speaker. His back was to the outside eastern walls with the rapt crowd sitting directly in front of him.

Saul and Miriam stopped to hear what was being said.

CHAPTER THIRTY-SIX

Preaching at the Temple

"Isaiah told us that He would be wounded for our transgressions, bruised for our iniquities, and the chastisement of our peace was upon Him. Friends, our understanding of Messiah was totally wrong. He was to be the Lamb of God first. Every day, just in there," and the big man pointed to the Temple complex, "we Jews take a little innocent lamb and put our hands on it and put it to death for our sins, just as Moses taught, but Jehovah himself became our Lamb in the form of Jesus, whom you killed just as the prophets foretold would happen."

Frightened and mournful cries erupted from the crowd.

"Forgive us, O Lord," rang out through the weeping listeners. Some were holding their hands aloft, pleadingly, others held their heads as if in pain.

Floods of tears flowed down the big man's face as he spoke each word with conviction and emotion and it was apparent that he was not merely reciting a memorized scripture. "It is finished, over, completed. Our sacrifice has been offered and accepted," he declared.

These words froze Miriam and Saul momentarily with Saul immediately analyzing this ingenious personification of the obscure utterances of Isaiah that he had just heard. He was not agreeing with anything he was hearing but he was urgently scouring his memory, looking for the apparent errors. Miriam was mesmerized with what had just been said and was noticing the intense fervor of the speaker who seemed to believe what he was proclaiming with all his being. She scanned the listening crowd quickly and noticed men and women in all forms of dress, some local and others, obviously pilgrims, who were visiting the Temple from afar.

"You did this in ignorance and out of a hardened heart but now God calls all to repent of our sins, be baptized in Jesus's name and He will send the gift of the Holy Spirit to you. He will change your evil thinking and give you a mind that can receive the truths that God wants so much to give to Israel. We have been blinded by traditions and wrong teachings for far too long."

A murmur went through the crowd and they looked quizzically at two men in Pharisees' robes standing close by who were, surprisingly, nodding in agreement.

Saul motioned to Miriam to move on and she did although slowly and reluctantly, looking back every few steps. Further down the line of columns, another man who appeared somewhat younger, was speaking to another gathered group.

"Oh Israel, think of it. Jehovah, the giver of all life, came in the form of a man and we killed Him. The Temple rituals all speak of Him and of a ransom, showing us that His death would be the required and effective sacrifice for our sin, finally satisfying Hashem, rather than continually killing animals. As He was dying, He declared that 'it was finished.' We who should have recognized our Messiah, became blinded by our imaginations and traditions, for we are stubborn and would not believe that Jehovah would come in such a humble fashion."

The young man paused and smiled warmly, "But Hashem is willing to forgive us and give us the same Spirit and mind that was in Jesus. This is what you witnessed on Pentecost on the Pilgrim's Road. The same mind has come upon them that believe and that is the greatest gift of all."

Miriam was transfixed. She had not heard such concepts before. In the few short minutes that she had been listening to these two speakers, the mysterious concept of Messiah was suddenly becoming clearer and greatly expanded as these men were boldly declaring a competing version of what His initial purpose was to be.

Jehovah somehow interplaying, even uniting with the minds of men, she questioned of no one but herself. *Was that probable or even possible?*

She had never heard Saul, her father, or any other teachers in any synagogues explain it so clearly or refer to Messiah as anything else than a conquering king. She felt an excitement within herself and quickly turned to Saul but the look on his face kept her from speaking. There was a scowl and a look of total disgust and he was perusing the crowd as if to catch more of his acquaintances listening.

As Miriam looked up at Saul questioningly, he dogmatically replied, "This is the rabble that my friend Samuel was telling me about."

He recognized her bewilderment over his statement and felt forced to explain further.

"Like confused little children, these," and he flicked a pompous hand in the direction of the growing crowd, "are those that followed that blasphemous false prophet whom the High Priest had crucified and now they are preaching that He rose from the dead. This 'Spirit' they talk about is their invisible and unprovable evidence, a feeble justification, meant to perpetuate their false teachings, but they have no learning or education in the scriptures and most can not even read. They are dangerous and deluded and want to infect as many as they can with this blasphemy. You just heard them teaching to abandon the Temple, including our traditions and even Moses's Law itself. This they claim would please Jehovah."

"That's not what I heard," responded Miriam, who quickly lowered her head and wished that she had not challenged her brother here. She smiled up at him quickly. "Show me more of the Temple."

Saul led her away from the outer porches, back to the south wall of the women's court. Placed against the outside of the walls and interspersed around were large urns which received the traditional and obligatory charitable offerings for the poor, the widows, the orphaned and other special needs circumstances. These were placed in the open court areas where all could easily access them and where it was easy to notice that an offering, and the relative size of that offering, was being made.

Admittedly, it was impossible to be a humble man in Jerusalem these days, for even the metal vases at the Temple sang out the praises of your big heart.

Saul explained that these pots were a favorite teaching spot of the Pharisees who saw themselves as leading the charity of Israel by example. He could not help himself and ranted that true religion was displayed by this charity and not just elaborate words like those they had just heard.

As he spoke, an obviously wealthy Jewish man approached a vase and after looking around, dropped his handful of clanking coins from a measured height in a practiced and flamboyant ritual. He searched the crowd until he received a respectful nod from many, including the approving Saul. The scrutinizing Pharisees were mercilessly vocal in their criticism of anyone that they observed donating only a penny or a mite and such a person would be exposed immediately by an embarrassing lecture. Miriam remained silent during this explanation, watching while another showy and loud performance took place.

Brother and sister continued strolling around the Temple square, noticing families and pilgrims involved in the activities that made the exterior plateau such a favored place. Some were having celebrations for their children, some praying in somber family memorials, other pilgrims were simply walking and gawking about. All around, Jews were gathered in spontaneous prayer groups on Solomon's Porch.

Herod's expansion had certainly made the Temple both more accessible and functional which some say, was his hidden desire. Others, much more cynical, attributed all his work to his great need to be accepted as a memorable king by his Jewish subjects. Whatever his ultimate reasons, the plateau was a lively, joyous and invitingly busy place to be.

Early every morning and again at dusk, large groups of pilgrims gathered on the surrounding hills to watch as the sun rose and set over the glowing golden walls of Jerusalem and the gleaming Temple building, its roof fringed in gold and standing sixty feet high above the plateau. Many claimed this was the most beautiful sight on earth. The undulating gold eave that trimmed the roofline sent focused shafts of brilliant sunshine down onto the visitors below and onto other parts of the city where for a few glorious seconds, certain spots shone with the radiance of Hashem. As these brilliant locations danced about with the moving sun, a rush to new sites was created by those that wanted to bask, if only for a second, in the glow of such heavenly favor. Such darting about had become a lively game for youthful pilgrims.

Many believed, and many sages affirmed, that the exact mountaintop that the Temple sat on was where God had created Adam before sending him eastward. Without question, it was the place that Abraham almost sacrificed his son Isaac. Under inspiration, David had purchased it for the site of the house of God and so it was a certainty that history, and Hashem Himself, greatly favored this holy spot.

Saul and Miriam could not help but notice more groups gathering around a few other animated and excited speakers in the porticos and Saul did his best to keep his distance from these. The crowded plateau began to thin a little as the day wore on but the special atmosphere of this holy place persisted. The presence of the smiling priests scurrying back and forth, accompanied by the constant, inspiring music drifting from the steps in the women's court was both soothing and inviting plus the gatherings under the porch roofs would occasionally break out in singing and shouting. Together with the priest's trumpeting, each activity added to the important and holy feel of this unique place.

On this day, the unwanted mixture of the holy and the blasphemous only served to deeply irritate Saul, but he worked hard to keep his mood from his sister.

The serene mood of the Temple was also affected by the occasional appearance of the armed and aggressive guards, some of who found it necessary to assert their importance by roughly correcting some overexuberant children or demanding an awkward measure of respect for allowing a bar mitzvah or special prayer at that closest spot to the Holy of Holies. It always seemed strange to Saul that men of such low character would be selected to protect such a magnificent place. This disgusting type of extortion, that of forced esteem and elevated position which they demanded for themselves, could not have been Moses' original intent for having guards, he thought.

When brother and sister had exhausted every corner of the Temple and felt the day was complete, they left by the less conspicuous gate located high on the western wall, near the Antonia Fortress. This one was commonly referred to as the women's gate, as many of the women who came daily to work or pray here entered through it without an accompanying male. This was allowable, for they were not approaching from the south as a pilgrim or as one bringing supplication.

The roadway descended from the gate into the maze of streets and Saul led the way home from there. Their walk home was quiet and full of thoughts and colorful images and Miriam was smiling widely, almost skipping along. She had been totally immersed in her Jewishness this day and it had been riveting, something she had craved for a very long time.

Her thankful heart was full.

CHAPTER THIRTY-SEVEN

The Jerusalem Plot Thickens

The rest of that week continued unusually busy at Gamaliel's house with only a short meeting with Gammy and Gamaliel to cover the latest teaching curriculum being discussed. It seemed that all three men wanted to avoid the "Galilean" topic for now, so it was not mentioned at all. Obviously, personal opinions and judgments on this issue were still in the formation stage with each of them, none yet ready to be fully discussed.

While strolling together to their classes, Gammy took the opportunity to tell Saul about Pilate's latest decrees and his willingness to allow the Jews their own judgments and punishments on religious matters.

Upon hearing this, Saul stopped dead in his tracks, slapped Gammy happily on the back, and yelled, "Yes!"

He was overjoyed to hear of this new independence allowed in these convoluted religious times. Gammy, on the other hand, was more cautious and feared a wave of predictable abuses from the divided Jewish community. He, much like his father, did not trust his brethren with that much unsupervised liberty.

After years of observing the political gymnastics performed in Jerusalem, and then watching Gamaliel as he dealt with the divisive factions demanding that only their voices be heard, each regarding their opinions as most important, Gammy had been left with much suspicion and distrust. It was a confusing emotion in the heart of this young man who generally was very trusting. Gammy hated bearing this burden of cynicism and longed for a day when Jews would be unified.

For this purpose, he had eagerly rededicated himself to the pursuit of truth and honor, just as his father had, but he also understood that until Jerusalem could be radically changed, the upcoming days would be turbulent and very confrontational.

Another week flew by and Saul and Miriam ended it by attending Sabbath services at the Freedmen's Synagogue. It was a surprisingly peaceful time at the synagogue given the drama that surrounded the building and Miriam had for the first time since they arrived in Jerusalem, prepared them a Sabbath meal. She quickly admitted to not being a great cook but the brother and sister nevertheless spent the day joyfully reminiscing about Tarsus and their family, thoroughly enjoying the pleasant memories of their childhood home. It was a refreshing and settling time and Saul thoroughly appreciated the easy company of his sister.

Gamaliel's house was overflowing with other Sabbath visitors and although invited to join their celebrations in the porticos below, Saul and Miriam preferred the quiet that this day had brought in their comfortable and quiet apartment.

Gamaliel, Gammy, and Saul met immediately after Sabbath sundown for what was becoming the weekly planning meeting. Saul reported that the Freedmen's Synagogue and some of its members had been involved from the very beginning with the latest eruption from the Galileans and he told of how the congregation was being so negatively affected. He reported that there were now two completely opposing factions in that congregation and they were at loud verbal odds with each other. Worse than that, the controversy was dividing families and lifelong friendships.

He carefully repeated the events as Samuel had told them concerning the strange happenings in that upper room across the street, telling of all the disruption it had caused on Pentecost and he related to Gamaliel and Gammy the mysteriously acquired ability of certain members of that group to speak languages from around the known world. Finally, he related what he had heard about the strange new skill amongst these people of interpreting ambiguous scriptures with unusual ease and then applying these to Jesus and, in some cases, also to themselves. For scholars like themselves, men whose lives were committed to such in-depth practices, this was extremely intriguing. Gamaliel and his son listened intently, not interrupting but drinking in the information without comment.

When Saul was finished his report, Gammy proceeded to describe the scenes he had witnessed at the Temple compound and it was much as Saul and Miriam had personally witnessed. He went further and gave much more detail.

Gammy had spoken with these people directly, asking many questions and they openly told him about a new "mind" they had experienced which without any effort on their part, called them into a special brotherhood with a deep love for each other. They felt compelled to meet and eat together, spend their time together and even have their possessions pooled together for the common good. This had reminded Gammy of the Essenes who demanded a pooling of all possessions upon joining them, except that these people were doing this voluntarily and seemed to derive great happiness from this. They were also very generous with their food and their time, gaining much favor with all who visited the Temple, even those who did not follow their teachings. Underlining all this, there were many reports surfacing of sicknesses being healed at the hands of the disciples of Jesus. This latest item seemed to perplex all three men, albeit for differing reasons and, today, no answer or explanation was attempted.

These were exactly the issues that would have to be addressed and addressed very quickly, thought Saul to himself. *This was dangerous stuff.*

Uncharacteristically, Gamaliel made no comments or proclamations and asked that Saul and Gammy continue their stealthy missions.

The following week passed quickly for Saul, mostly a blur of teaching and lecturing interspersed with visiting a few other small but influential Jerusalem synagogues that, like the Freedmen's, were also the home of elderly Jews who had immigrated from other areas outside of Judea. These congregations were experiencing similar upsets caused by the events of the Day of First Fruits on the Pilgrim's Road and they also did not know what to do.

Up to this point, Saul had been successful at keeping out of any public debate and was simply collecting information as Gamaliel had asked, keeping his voice quiet. He was, however, developing definite opinions and making strong judgments. Keeping them isolated to himself and Samuel was now a gigantic strain. One thing Saul understood completely was that once he entered the public fray, he would not remain at all reserved and his would be a clear and a loud voice.

He had to keep reminding himself that this was not quite the time for that irreversible battle to begin.

CHAPTER THIRTY-EIGHT

Samuel ben Shammai

On Wednesday of that week, Saul and Miriam visited the small house of Samuel and his sister and enjoyed the delicious lamb dinner that Ruth had prepared. Their visit proved to be a fascinating time on many levels and Ruth had gone out of her way to make an especially impressive feast, fussing over every detail, including keeping the atmosphere light. All four laughed heartily at the humorous and entertaining stories that Samuel related about himself and throughout the evening, it seemed he was especially attentive to Miriam.

Ruth and Miriam seemed to enjoy each other's company, except for a tense moment when Ruth outwardly criticized the strange generosity of the new sect of Galileans, calling it foolish and short-sighted to give away one's money. Miriam, disturbed by the inherent praise of selfishness promoted by this statement, politely asked, "But is this not what we Jews should be striving for, a better character and loving our neighbor with deeds rather than just words?"

The Galilean subject was tactfully avoided for the rest of the evening but it seemed that such strong opinions hovered dangerously close to the surface for all involved. Samuel had remained quiet during that exchange, observing Miriam's conversation closely from that time on. Before leaving, he and Saul made plans to meet the next day at the synagogue.

When they convened the next day, Samuels first words to his friend Saul were about Miriam.

"Your sister is unlike most Jewish women I have ever met, Saul," he stated, and then he waited.

Saul could not tell if Samuel was wanting him to tell him more about her or just letting him know that he had noticed the uniqueness of his sister. After an unusually long silence, Saul woke to the fact that Samuel was indeed waiting to hear more about Miriam and he suddenly realized that something more complicated may be happening here. He could only muster a "Yes, she is a special person."

Samuel, not satisfied, again remained silent and waited stubbornly until Saul continued.

Saul finally explained, "Miriam is extremely gifted with a remarkable mind, very logical, always analyzing writings and statements, but she is extremely blunt and honest. Whoever ends up with Miriam will find her a challenging life-long project but will also find one of the nicest and most sincere persons ever."

This honest statement gave Samuel plenty to think about and he would replay these words in his mind often over the next few days. Their conversation then turned to the Galilean problem, a topic that the whole city of Jerusalem was in an ever-increasing tizzy over.

As the most noticeable and outspoken of the young Pharisees of the House of Shammai, Samuel was an oddity, even within his sect. The rigidity of their teaching typically created an unfriendly, almost antagonistic atmosphere, therefore, his sect mainly attracted argumentative and sour personalities. This greatly contrasted with Samuel's easygoing charm, his twinkling eyes and his room-warming laughter.

He, like Gammy, was also the grandson of a great teacher. His grandfather was the notable Shammai, himself.

Although highly respected, the House of Shammai was in a theological competition with the more popular and markedly less rigid Hillel-ites and because of this secondary position in the academic and political pecking order, Samuel had not automatically inherited the position and public acceptance that Gammy was destined for.

Since his father had passed away early in life and had not been recognized as a great scholar on the level of Gamaliel, Samuel's position as a teacher in the House of Shammai was hard-earned and he had to fight to distinguish himself among the older teachers who had been direct students of his famous grandfather. It was his warm and outgoing persona that opened synagogue doors to him and had also attracted a growing number of students to their once shrinking academies.

Samuel brought an unusual blend of rigid and serious obedience to the Law and open-armed comradery, and this mixture seemed very attractive to a growing portion of religious Jews. When the House of Shammai was mentioned, Samuel's name was easily the most prominent even though he was a relatively young man.

Over their teen-aged years, he and Saul had clashed in public debate a few times in the public squares, each enthusiastically defending their schools' doctrines to the delight of their observing students. Each time, Samuel had defused the heated emotions of the debates with joviality and a friendly embrace. The fiery Saul was surprised and sometimes frustrated at this unique ability for it seemed that even when he had gotten the upper hand in the details of the debate, he had always been bested by simple heartfelt gestures and the approving glances that Samuel attracted.

This day, the two men found a quiet corner at the front of the synagogue where they were surrounded by olive-wood cabinets housing precious and carefully stored scrolls. It was in this revered spot that Saul proceeded to relate his recent experiences at the Temple for he now understood he could speak openly with Samuel. This liberty was a welcomed feeling and something that he had not felt he could do at Gamaliel's house in recent weeks.

In return, Samuel told him of a recent trip he made to Hebron and that he had found that a few disciples of Jesus had already traveled there and were actively teaching this new heresy. Not only were the "Way's" risky doctrines spreading to synagogues in villages and towns where they were creating debate and controversy, but more dangerously, they were spreading person to person, through family contacts and individual testimony. The two men agreed that this must be confronted quickly, the stretching tentacles in Hebron were proof of the encroaching danger. Similar reports from Bethel in the north had come in and one, even further, all the way to Shechem. Although vigorously agreeing on the need for swift action, they realized they had a problem.

"How do we condemn this as a dangerous heresy to be avoided when its adherents are devoted to each other, feeding their poor and hungry and generally appearing to be good Jews? You know how people are bewitched with good deeds," they stated to each other. "Also, there are constant reports of what looks to be supernatural miracles happening among them," lamented Samuel.

This irksome dilemma launched the two men into a probing discussion of the nature of the other-worldly delusions and how easily the unlearned could be tricked into thinking that a "miracle" had occurred. Both agreed that they could probably convince, or coerce the confused observers that nothing extraordinary had occurred but it must be made clear that those "healed" had merely imagined such happenings or, somehow, mentally manufactured them. They settled on this tactic and boldly predicted that in the future they would not see any further claims of the miraculous outside the original deluded group, especially once good and faithful Jews rose up and challenged this error.

"I've told you about my friend Stephen and how he has become a follower of Jesus," Samuel began, changing the topic. "Well, now others from this congregation have begun following these disciples and I have heard that the total number of followers in Jerusalem has reached five thousand. This is dangerous and getting completely out of hand and I am sure the Romans are beginning to take notice because I see more soldiers patrolling daily on the Pilgrim's Road. They are not interfering yet, just observing at this point, but if it goes much further, this could instigate a backlash that will be dangerous, maybe even fatal, for all Jews."

Samuel paused and thought very deeply about this and then continued. "Whatever we do, we first must realize that we are compelled to do it for the purity of the Law, and secondly, for the safety of the nation. We must protect our blind brethren from any repercussions from the Romans. The speed at which this lie is spreading is frightening and if unchecked, it could anger Pilate even more than he is angered already. If he feels he must get involved, we will again lose control of our own religious decisions and that would be disastrous."

Samuel pondered that for a second, "And if that happens, it will be entirely the fault of a bunch of rebellious Galileans. You know that nothing good ever comes out of Galilee, don't you?" he added, almost as an afterthought.

"I know you and I have already agreed that all this is wrong and dangerous. It seems we also have convinced ourselves that some drastic action must be taken on our part. Coming to agreement on all that was the easy part," replied Saul.

Samuel nodded his agreement.

"But I think I missed the discussion on just what action we are talking about," joked Saul surprisingly.

The big smile returned to Samuel's face, realizing that his tactics had been easily detected and exposed. He had been leading Saul to a forgone conclusion.

Saul continued, "Samuel, I can see that you have thought deeply about this, so just what action are you contemplating."

"Well, first we must publicly confront these false teachers. They have had free run of the city streets since Pentecost and no one has the courage to challenge them. They have taken over the porches of the Temple so that all who go there must pass close by them and hear their distorted preaching. This confuses people, for it appears that they are somehow condoned by the Temple priests or even Caiaphas himself, simply because they are allowed to openly use the area. We must get the High Priest and the Sanhedrin to make a ruling in which they refuse them the use of the porches. The authorities have been altogether too quiet about this. Saul, you have Gamaliel's ear and could influence him to speak out as it is partially his indecision that is adding to the confusion."

Saul could not argue or disagree with Samuel on that observation or on his logic in general. The more he listened, the more he warmed to the fearless, but well-reasoned, call-to-arms proposals of Samuel.

Saul knew from their many personal encounters that both he and Samuel were men who did not shrink at all from confrontation, in fact, they usually led the way, and it was now becoming obvious that they should be the first ones to engage the Galileans and their outspoken followers in what was probably going to become loud and hostile battles. Both men had previously challenged each other in the synagogues and in the public arena, but it was now time to graduate from childish debates over jots or tittles and wholly engage in protecting and then implementing the Law and thereby protecting the nation.

Just as if he were being directed by Moses himself, Saul's eyes were awakening to this fact.

Samuel, sensing a lingering hesitation in Saul and knowing that any action of this sort might put him in conflict with his famous mentor, wisely offered a compromise for the time being.

"Let us agree to confronting only the new converts of these Galileans and to showing them their errors, keeping it on a personal, one-on-one level. Let us avoid debating their leaders and leave that to the High Priest and the

Sanhedrin so that we do not step overstep our places. To start with, I want to speak to my friend Stephen and show him how deeply into error he has fallen, but I suspect he is avoiding both me and the synagogue."

Saul thought these words over for a moment and then added, "You are right Samuel, we must make sure that we remain in agreement with our leaders for I can see that the occasion will soon rise that these people will have to be dealt with by the courts should they not recant. Right now, they are on the very edge of blasphemy and I expect that any clash with them will likely push a few of them over that edge and then serious legal consequences will occur. Our courts must be ready and Gamaliel must be willing to move at that time."

Samuel was a little surprised at Saul's aggressive response.

"I was hoping initially for restoring these deluded ones to the truth, rather than focusing on punishing them," he stated, "but it is true that there may have to be repercussions if they will not recant and continue to blaspheme and pervert the Law. By the way Saul, I as a Shammai-ite should be the one talking punishment, not you. You are a soft-hearted Hillel-ite. What about loving your neighbor even if he blasphemes?"

Suddenly, serious Saul realized that Samuel was poking fun at him once again.

The last exchange caused Saul to pause in his thinking.

It was indeed curious that Samuel went to restoration of these criminals rather than punishment. No doubt it was the fact that his close friend Stephen was among the blasphemers, plus Samuel had other acquaintance in the synagogue that influenced his attitude and made him entertain the idea of not following the harshest of the Torah instructions. Within himself Saul decided, quietly, but with renewed determination, that he would always follow Moses's Law to the letter and not show a soft heart.

The un-called-for clemency that he had just witnessed in Samuel had shockingly exposed the deceit and trickery laying at the heart of the upcoming battle to Saul. He was certain that this struggle was not being recognized for its seriousness among all the other leaders in Jerusalem as well and he was convinced that this would undoubtably have to be addressed very shortly, both with Samuel and the leaders.

Someone would have to spearhead that proclamation, he reasoned pensively to himself.

Samuel, in an amiable spirit of cooperation, asked Saul to help him by attending the Freedmen's Synagogue on the Sabbath and begin combating these teachings in their home synagogue. He admitted that he felt his voice was becoming tedious and tiresome and that the congregation needed to hear from someone other than himself. This was a rare request for help from a normally confident man and Saul quickly agreed to do this, now determined to bring a more aggressive approach to his home congregation.

He was ready and very willing to rebuke any that were wavering.

CHAPTER THIRTY-NINE

Into the Fray

With this precarious alliance, the two historic opponents formally consented to join forces and act in unison. They would begin their mutual assault on the heresy with fervency and they would begin it without delay, they fervently announced, but only to each other.

Alone, in his very private times, Saul had feared that he may be isolated in his opinions and he even admitted that it may even be possible that he could be reading the whole situation incorrectly, but it was Samuel's confident voice that had helped drive away any such doubts. He appreciated the comradery and the feeling of harmony that had finally emerged between them.

With that, he buried any doubts of Samuel's determination.

As he pondered this new course of action, Saul knew that he must first keep fulfilling Gamaliel's initial request to discover all he could on this group. In his mind, there was no conflict in what he was doing for Gamaliel and beginning to speak out against the "Way." He was somewhat concerned that Gamaliel would not appreciate his going further by formulating a separate pact to outright oppose them, a pact which did not include his mentor, so he decided it was best to leave this new alliance out of any report to his teacher.

As Saul started walking home that day, it suddenly occurred to him that in their enthusiasm to confront the heresy, he and Samuel had not discussed the details of just what the heresy was. Like emotional teenagers, the two men had succumbed to the excitement of the upcoming battle with little thought. This made Saul chuckle and shake his head at their lack of preparation for the inevitable encounters that were looming. Gamaliel had drilled into his students that if one was jumping into a debate, one must be intimately aware of the position of his opponent.

Idly strolling the streets, lost in his musings and attempting to engage his logical and unemotional mind, Saul began to mentally list the items of greatest disagreement between himself and these Galileans. As this cerebral chronicle swelled, he soon realized that the conflict must be taken to a deeper level than just two sides having different interpretations of the ancient writings, annoying as their scriptural perversions were. The three sects of the Pharisees also differed on just these types of issues and no one was accused of blasphemy simply because of a contrary belief.

No, the basis of any serious accusation and the essence of their real crimes lay in their dangerous challenge of the Jewish traditional expression of the sacred writings that had developed over the centuries, those precious foundational interpretations which kept the Jews pure and separate. These historical ways of doing things were the righteous expression of the accumulated wisdom and understanding of their sages, so obviously, those ways were Jehovah's truth.

Moses commanded the Jews to keep the Sabbath and every Jew agreed with that command. Was it not just as important and possibly even more so, that the rabbis and scholars had instructed the people in all the meticulous details of just how that was to be done. To error in one detail was to error totally.

Saul spoke out loud to himself. "One could almost forgive them for disagreeing over some of our minute and sometimes technical teachings, but their twisting of the entire purpose of Messiah, or misplacing all the prophets' references to the Spirit, well, that is where the blasphemy exists for in the end it cleverly undermines Moses and the Law without outright denying it."

This was indeed a cunning wickedness, mused Saul.

Returning from his internal contemplations, Saul noticed the smirking faces of a few people passing by who were amused with the scene of this young Pharisee energetically debating with himself. They had somehow surmised from his confident look that the young Pharisee was pleased with himself, somehow winning the internal debate.

Saul chose to ignore them.

Now that he understood the blasphemy, his mental list began anew. So intent was he that as he jostled his way up the crowded street that he smacked directly into a fully uniformed Roman centurion.

Menacingly, the armed and muscular man stood perfectly still, remaining within inches of and planted directly in front of him. Usually, a Jew gave these pagans plenty of walking space, especially a freshly washed and rinsed Pharisee, so this collision was a surprise for both men. The normally gruff response of the Roman was replaced by a courteous nod, and in perfect Aramaic, "Excuse me, Rabbi Saul."

The soldier then courteously stepped around Saul and continued on his way.

A little dazed, Saul slowly recovered and continued his walk, but his attention quickly returned to the Roman. Saul recognized that face from somewhere but could not recall where. Then he asked himself, *"And just how did he know my name?"*

A few passing Jews who had witnessed this encounter were staring at the young Pharisee curiously. He chose to ignore them as well and returned to his ponderings, his cataloging of blasphemies beginning once again.

First and foremost was the claim that Jesus was the Messiah. That claim, in itself, did not constitute blasphemy, just a grievous error and an error that was a result of their obvious delusion. Being pitifully duped did not achieve the status of a crime in Jewish tradition, but the crime was in spreading the delusion as fact and thereby changing the behavior of devout Jews and endangering the nation.

Suddenly Saul remembered.

He had seen the centurion on the ship, the *Castor and Pollux*, this one had been accompanied by his huge blond legionnaire.

"What was a veteran warrior of the Germania Wars doing wandering the streets of Jerusalem," he asked himself.

Immediately, Saul wondered if he would see his colossal assistant around Jerusalem as well and he questioned just what type of reaction this giant would generate in this city. Would it be curiosity, fear, or an immediate hatred of a descendent of the old and dangerous adversaries who was now freely walking the streets.

His imagination began to race. *How would Joshua handle a Nephilim strolling through the Jewish capital?* The questions literally exploded in his thoughts.

With great mental effort, he forced himself, yet again, back to his list.

The Galileans claimed that Jehovah had poured out his essence on mortal men in the form of the Holy Spirit. Again, this was not technically blasphemy, for the prophets had told that this would take place one day but it will occur not as these people claimed it had. The rightful outpouring would come first to the High Priest and then to the leaders of Israel and then eventually trickle down to the uneducated. This was the accepted process and it fit Hashem's own regard for the importance of the offices He originated. Under their blasphemous teachings, Hashem had to step outside His own proscribed authority, go against tradition and choose the lowest of the low to reveal Himself to. That thought was outrageous, touching on seditious.

Again, it was their personal delusions that were the big problem, possibly even leading them into what would become an insurrection among the Jewish common people against Hashem's chosen royalty and hierarchy. Besides that…

His thoughts were interrupted again.

Intrigued, Saul flashed back to the polite Roman centurion again.

"How and why did he know my name? Was the army's accumulation of intelligence so complete that they knew minor players in the political scene of this city? Who was feeding them this information?" Saul's imagination began picturing a myriad of possible nefarious and clandestine scenarios.

Rebuking himself for wandering, he once more forced his concentration back to the disciples of Jesus.

They could not be accused of greediness or mistreating their followers in any way as all reports were that they looked after each other unselfishly and with joy. That said, their most recent actions were bordering on lunacy. They were selling off their possessions and giving the proceeds to the disciples.

Once again, this was not blasphemy, Saul admitted, but such outrageous actions reaffirmed to him the falseness and the depth of their delusion.

Who would now look after them in time of need? Who would buy the food to feed them when the money ran out? Could they trust these disciples to invest their money wisely so it would be there for their old age?

This abandoning of any regard for their future stability and their possessions was indeed foolishness, but Saul had to grudgingly admit that it did not technically oppose the Law. He shook his head and asked himself, *"What type of madness had possessed their minds to completely put their future into the hands of God rather than relying on sound financial planning?"* This thinking was totally foreign to Saul.

All the wise leaders he respected were wealthy men, men committed to supplying their families with plenty and as such were very astute with their investments.

Hashem had blessed the rich men with this ability, had He not? The poor were poor because of their lack of wisdom and planning.

It was common knowledge amongst all Jews that the more a man possessed, the more blessed he was of God and his money was the obvious evidence of his highly favored status with Hashem. Only a few overly-spiritual scholars chose to debate that, and inevitably, they were poor men. The scriptures themselves eagerly pointed to the examples of the great wealth God had rained down on Abraham, David, and Solomon. Conversely, most believed that any financial misfortune was proof of wrongdoing and was the judgment of God upon that person.

Once more, Saul was talking aloud to himself. *"It is not by chance that the High Priest and his family are amongst the richest Jews in Jerusalem. The blessing of Hashem is upon them. True, they had access to the abundant and almost unlimited Temple funds and had often used those for their own advantage, but this was also one of the benefits of being the High Priest, and besides, such practices were not specifically forbidden or even mentioned by Moses."*

He pondered that question further. *"Should not those in the service of Hashem live handsomely off their efforts?*

Yes," answered Saul to himself. He thought that was only to be expected.

Saul's mind drifted to other areas of not specifically "forbidden" yet controversial subjects which many times had caused great division between the wealthy and powerful and the common and, many times, defrauded Jew. It was true that there seemed to be no end to the desires of the wealthy for more money, more power, more adulation and more obeisance from any less fortunate ones and Saul saw no particular problem with such actions. These were indeed the rewards Hashem bestowed upon the fortunate and to greatly crave more favor from Hashem in the form of craving these monetary rewards was completely understandable. Should not a man desire to be more blessed by his creator? If that meant to crave more wealth, well, so be it. It was a good thing.

Saul had again stopped walking. His thoughts were so entirely dominating him that he had moved to the side of the street to concentrate.

From there he noticed two men of the Sadducee belief passing by. Such men went even further in their financial dealings, denying that there was any existence after death and thus no reason to fear any future retribution for financial misdeeds in this life. Although they believed in Hashem, they also believed that the highest form of worship of this God was to live deeply in His financial blessing and enjoy this life to its maximum. Poor men were understandably not attracted by such teaching for they would have to believe that they were not living under any of Hashem's blessings, possibly even under His disfavor. The Sadducees had a curious credo that they repeated: to gain financially was so pleasing to Hashem that it overruled any displeasure He would have over their methods, or else He would not bless them so.

Despite their small number, the Sadducees held immense influence over Jewish leaders and in fact, most greatly envied their financial achievements. If truth were told, most were doing their best to emulate them. These leaders were likewise consumed with the task of gathering great wealth for themselves but were unhappily burdened under the yoke of someday justifying their questionable actions at a judgment in an afterlife. The Sadducees, not so encumbered, did not acknowledge the prophets or their ramblings of love, peace, charity, and justice, themselves living only by what was specifically demanded in Moses's Torah. The strictness of the Law served them well and the prospect of mercy being extended to a Jewish brother or dealing with other-worldly angelic beings beyond Hashem was soundly ridiculed by them.

One of the favorite entertainments of the Sadducees was to tease the Pharisees with hypothetical questions of complicated situations in their future invisible heaven, knowing that the wisest of the Pharisees could not answer them with any certainty, only with speculation. This "game" had created a bitter animosity that continually festered between the two groups. With their unceasing mocking, the wealthy Sadducees portrayed an irritating arrogance and they certainly loved to embarrass all of their religious opponents, but they especially loved to irritate the Pharisees. If ever questioned, their self-serving argument had become their main defense.

For years the Sadducees concluded that if some morally questionable activity was not mentioned or specifically forbidden by Moses, it was then allowable. Adding to that was to contradict Moses, they heartily accused. This served the gluttonous Sadducees well, but it did not sit right with either Rabbi Hillel or Shammai, even if they could not outright find any scripture to challenge them.

Looking up as the two passed, Saul realized that he had again strayed way off topic and that he was standing on the same street corner where he had started this latest conversation with himself. He also noticed more amused smiles.

Saul forced himself back to the issue at hand, realizing that the poor would always be poor and the uneducated would always be fleeced by nefarious individuals. With that in mind, the purported financial skullduggery taking place among the people of the Way did not surprise him at all.

Saul recognized that forcefully controlled and subjugated Jews, men such as these Galileans, were especially vulnerable to the glow of some new liberating Messiah and predictably, quite a few such characters had arisen and led away their own small groups in his lifetime. Successfully destroying the myths of today's messiah to His followers would quickly expose Him and the obvious foolishness of their latest actions with their finances, he reasoned, so he saw no other practical tactic than to attack Jesus directly. At this logical conclusion, Saul smiled once more.

Saul restarted his meandering up the crowded street, again drifting into his internal debate, all the while being jostled and manhandled by the hurried throngs. He stayed along the walls of the street to escape the worst of the traffic.

When he finally reached his turn off the busy Pilgrim's Road and veered onto the quieter residential avenue, he quickened his pace. A few seconds later, Saul was once more abruptly halted.

Immediately in front of him was an enormous form, one which he simply could not avoid and which was casting a large shadow over him. Looking up, he was staring into the face of the massive, blond soldier whom he had seen on the ship.

The centurion and now his giant? The big man looked down and nodded to Saul in recognition but moved on before Saul could offer any greeting. Now completely puzzled, Saul wondered what the centurion and his massive assistant were doing in Jerusalem. *Was there some secret military action going on?*

Looking down at his hands, Saul realized that he would now have to wash himself thoroughly as he had physically bumped into the unclean man, if indeed he was a "man."

It took many minutes before Saul could return to his musings.

Once again, he began formulating what exact charge he could bring against Jesus and, by proxy, the people of the Way. His analytical mind decided to start a new list because, so far, he had found much error and much delusion but no outright blasphemy.

The verbal attack on the High Priest's character that he had heard on the Temple Mount the other day was getting very close to blasphemy, for that was openly opposing God's chosen leadership, but the speaker had made allowance for ignorance and repentance on the part of the High Priest. For some unknown reason, this amused Saul greatly and he chuckled a little to himself at the adeptness of the speaker to not totally incriminate himself and yet thoroughly condemn Caiaphas. A great host of local Jews would eagerly join in that condemnation.

Their teaching of repentance and being baptized was not blasphemous as this simply copied the teaching of that small group of Pharisees called the Essenes from which John the Baptist had emerged. This current group of disciples had changed the general call to baptism of John and had insisted that this be done in Jesus's name now. This new twist was at first, just annoying, but over the last weeks it was completely changing the original intent of the baptism that the Essenes practiced. Apparently, no more immersions were taking place down in the Jordan but were replaced by the constant flow of people being baptized in the pools of Siloam in the name of this Jesus. It was also said that many of those being baptized at this pool had previously been baptized by John. Saul contemplated fostering an argument between these groups but then remembered that Samuel had mentioned that all of John's close disciples were now followers of Jesus and some were now the most outspoken advocates for the new Way. That tactic would not work.

Saul's thoughts suddenly locked on something. They were teaching that their sins were being forgiven by Jesus and all good Jews knew that only God could forgive sins. By teaching this, they were making this Jesus into God and this was indeed blasphemous for the very fact it reduced Hashem to the level of man.

God himself had commanded Moses to have no other gods so this was a violation of the first and most important commandment.

The foggy charge was slowly becoming clear to him. Soon all the ramifications of such a distorted belief and its blasphemous nature were established in his mind and Saul became settled in his reasoning. He felt secure in his opposition to everything they preached and everything they did for it all was the outgrowth of this one insidious and horrific untruth.

He was also convinced that with a little investigation and superior logic, many more such desecrations of the Law would come to light.

There and then, Saul decided that he would begin with the tried-and-true accusation that, "Jesus made Himself God."

CHAPTER FORTY

Miracles on the Cardo

Saul continued up his familiar street and arrived at the wide Cardo Market just as he did every day on his route home. Upon turning into the market street, he stopped abruptly for immediately ahead of him was the large Galilean he had heard speaking in the Temple, and today he was surrounded by a large and very noisy group. The crowd was gathered directly in the middle of the avenue, obstructing all traffic.

An elderly, severely twisted and almost completely bent-over woman had pushed her way directly in front of the big man and was addressing him. The surrounding throng quieted in anticipation, expecting something extraordinary.

The large man bent over to hear her words, then stood up and paused for a long moment as if praying. Gently, he took the two hands of the woman and slowly and deliberately lifted them up. As he did, her bent back shook and contorted and then straightened. Within seconds, she was standing tall and erect, staring directly into the eyes of the large man.

Weeping and shaking slightly, she continued to stand straight even after her hands were released.

A joyous outburst, even some screams of fright, echoed in the street from all those surrounding this spectacle and the commotion caught everyone's attention among the shops of the Cardo. The result was immediate shouts of praise to God and many thanking "Jesus."

The woman, elderly though she was, was immediately overcome with emotion and began sobbing and then moving in a smooth rhythm, swaying side to side, shouting melodic verses of thanksgiving. Before long she was spinning and dancing in ecstasy. In her delight, she began to sing the familiar version of Moses's sister Miriam's ancient song of praise. Her shawl spun around her, clearing a space for her to dance without hindrance and all the while she was chanting the song loudly and with great passion. The swarm that enveloped her began to sing along and the melody rang up and down the market, now catching everyone's attention. Before long, she was joined by other ecstatic women twirling and swaying in delightful ecstasy, their arms entangled with each other and tears of gratitude flowing over their cheeks.

The entire street stood agape and motionless, all who were not directly involved in the celebration were watching intently. Off to the side, some of the spectators were also weeping and others were shocked into complete stillness, while some, for reasons of their own, fled the scene in fearful panic.

Saul was dumbfounded with what he had just witnessed. He backed up against a wall and stood there, leaning against the cold stone for a full five minutes before he could regain his concentration.

Slowly, his mind began to process all the ramifications and the dangers of such incidents. If what happened was not just a ruse or a staged event and the woman was indeed healed of an infirmity, then it had to be the work of demons, possibly even the prince of demons, Beelzebub himself. Saul had been diligently taught and he now agreed with the logic that evil could do what looked like good deeds to deceive the Jews and hinder them from their ultimate goal of fulfilling the Law.

Was there ever a more convincing way to deceive?

The steadily growing crowd encircling the Galilean was moving slowly along the Cardo and before long, they were an immense throng, completely pressing the big man who was dwarfed in the middle of the press. Saul noticed that other sick people were fighting their way to the man, most approaching from behind as he was speaking. Many were shy, only wanting to touch his robe and even they too were coming away excited and yelling praises.

Hypnotized by what he was seeing, Saul followed from afar, keeping a distance, wanting to observe without being recognized. As he followed, he was pretending to be interested in a nearby merchant's produce but he could not take his eyes of the big disciple from the Galilee.

Saul suddenly recognized two familiar faces in the crowd. These were two men clad in the familiar blue and gold fringed tunics of the House of Hillel, garments marked with the symbols that he himself wore. They were very close to the big preacher and were nodding in agreement, with arms waving in praise and assisting the infirm get to him. He knew these men well for they were former students with him in Gamaliel's academy and who, by their outward dress, were still wanting to be known as advocates of the pharisaical life. To Saul, this was a complete paradox.

Saul then recognized an older and fully-bearded man standing immediately next to these two, his soft eyes weeping and tears of joy running down his weathered face. This man was very familiar to him as well, a man he loved and respected.

This was Nicodemus, Gamaliel's lifelong friend and his trusted confidant in the Sanhedrin all through the years that Saul had been in Jerusalem. Today he was not arrayed in the fine garb he usually wore but just a simple robe and coat and he was moving along with the group who were following the big man named Simon Peter.

When the crowd finally moved on a little, Saul was startled to see Miriam standing completely still on the edge of a small shop on the opposite side of the Cardo. She was directly beside the spot where the woman's back had been straightened. Her eyes remained glued to the tumultuous group and on the big leader, but now the healed women was dancing directly in front of her. Miriam moved to her, joyfully holding her hands and swaying with her happily. Saul watched as his sister stayed with the woman and spoke intensely to her for many minutes. The ecstatic and now perfectly erect woman then left Miriam and continued on her way, following the joyous crowd and still shouting praises to God.

Miriam remained behind and watched as many more people touched the hem of the big man's robe and claimed to be healed. To Miriam, Jerusalem was hypnotic.

Saul had followed the commotion from across the street, remaining on the outer fringes of the crowd, and he had remained unnoticed by the preoccupied Miriam. He then backed away completely and kept out of sight, hiding behind a column. He did not understand why he felt he had to hide his feelings on such events but something told him that he should, plus he did not like the conflicting emotions this "healing" had brought to him. He somehow felt dirty, not pure in his heart and he could not understand why he could not be completely outspoken in his condemnation of men like this Peter, demonic deceiver that he was.

Part of what Saul loved about Gamaliel and his schooling was that there was a purity in all that was taught. No part of his teaching could be exposed as devious or without pure motives and therefore, nothing had to be apologized for. Saul had grown up in that atmosphere of purity.

For this reason, Saul was boiling inside at his own two-facedness at not immediately calling out the big disciple in front of the whole crowd. He had failed to declare the whole episode as evil.

He had remained quiet, even accommodating, and he was now in hiding and he could not rationalize why, even to himself.

PART FIVE

CHAPTER FORTY-ONE

Barnabas and Mary

Before long, the jubilant gathering following Simon Peter turned into the next street and Miriam, whose focus had also been lost in the excitement, turned her attention to two older women who were patiently seated at tables in the shop where Saul had first noticed his sister. He thought it a little strange that Miriam would be alone at the Cardo after only a few days in Jerusalem but this was not completely out of character for his independent and fearless sister. The little store's walls were covered with small vases and bags of mysterious substances and it was obvious that this was a stall where medicines and potions were sold. To Saul, this was not totally unexpected as Miriam had become an expert in healing ointments and concoctions when she was in Tarsus and he knew such remedies interested her greatly. Seeing her in her familiar element caused him to quickly relax any worries he had for her.

Jerusalem was situated on the far eastern reaches of the vast Roman Empire and it was very close to the desert caravan routes to the exotic countries of the Far East. Because of this, it had easier access to potions and powders that were not readily available in Tarsus. Shops here boasted of many concoctions only known by reputation elsewhere and many of these formulas were the closely kept secrets of such shop owners. Saul was instantly glad, even relieved, that she was exploring such interests for this meant she was feeling comfortable in her new home and this would keep her active mind protected from boredom.

Saul decided not to disturb Miriam just then, himself wanting to trail the Galilean's group a little further. He followed the crowd around the corner and then drew closer, keeping his face turned downward in a pointless attempt to not be noticed, all the while listening closely for any new blasphemies being uttered.

He heard nothing other than uplifting conversation, and that disappointed him.

He followed them around another corner and then two more where the group stopped and milled about as it was announced loudly that they would meet again in Solomon's Porch in the morning for prayer. Slowly, and only after much affection was shown, the crowd dispersed and went in different directions. Joyous shouts could be heard from blocks away as they dissolved into the myriad of streets and avenues.

A small nucleus which included Simon Peter, remained together and after a few moments they turned right onto a narrow laneway that Saul knew well. This street was close to the market and was a desired location for homes of the many wealthy merchants who operated their businesses out of the Cardo. A good number of Gamaliel's students had come from the families that lived on that street and Saul had spent quite a few evenings enjoying many rich meals in the houses nearby.

Devout fathers who were deeply involved in business, wanted at least one son to be a scholar or a lawyer and were willing and able to pay the handsome fees of such an education. Many sons had ended up in the famous classrooms of Gamaliel.

Yes, he knew these homes well for such social visits were a large part of his years among classmates and then later as a teacher.

The group, now down to seven men, moved further into the street of the wealthy.

Meandering about aimlessly and yet keeping his distance, Saul was attempting to look like an uninterested passerby while in fact he was watching and listening intently. Suddenly, he thought he recognized the profile of one of the other remaining men. Upon second glance, he was convinced that he recognized Barnabas, son of Caleb ben Israel from Salamis, from the island of Cyprus.

He quickly remembered that he had promised the elderly Caleb that he would contact this son in Caesarea and deliver the private letter to him. Feeling a little guilty at his failure to fulfill his promise to the worried father, Saul was about to call out to Barnabas, but he strangely delayed, almost hoping that Barnabas would somehow separate from this group. He followed them a little further until the men opened the wooden gate of a large house and began entering. It was then that Saul recognized the gate and recalled that he knew this house as well. Barnabas stood aside as if inviting them in and as he did, his eyes met Saul's.

The two men's eyes locked in recognition from nearly a block away. A huge smile of surprise exploded on Barnabas's face and he came bounding down the road to embrace a surprised and confused and, a little embarrassed, Saul. Saul began to sputter an explanation of what he was doing there but his babbling was swallowed up by the smile and warm invitation to join them in the house.

Finding no credible excuse and not wanting to appear fearful or distrustful, he passed through the heavy and expensively hand-carved door into a familiar large courtyard which he had twice visited with his father. He remembered it as the home of Barnabas's older and widowed sister, Mary. The courtyard currently contained over twenty-five people at a collection of tables that surrounded a small, ornate pool situated in the middle of a beautifully mosaic-tiled patio. There was animated conversations and warm embraces taking place everywhere among the group.

This was a collection of very happy people, he grudgingly observed.

"Saul, it is so good to see you. It has been a few years now and we have missed seeing each other, even when we both lived right here in Jerusalem. Come, I want to introduce you to some people."

Barnabas led Saul to a table where three men were seated, including the big Galilean he had just watched so intently in the street.

"Saul, this is Simon Peter," and he pointed to the big man, "and this is James and his brother John." Saul nodded to each the customary greeting, and Barnabas continued. "Brothers, this is Saul, originally from Tarsus but now one of Gamaliel's prize students and a long-time friend of our family."

Saul enjoyed the status Barnabas had just bestowed on him but he noticed that the three men appeared not to be impressed, even diverting their eyes from his clothing. Barnabas then turned to a servant girl who was delivering refreshments to the tables and asked, "Rhoda, would you please ask my sister to join us here."

Barnabas and Saul stepped aside and continued in conversation with Barnabas eagerly explaining that these men were disciples of Jesus and were very close to him and to his sister.

Saul could not contain himself any further.

"Are these the same ones who scattered when Jesus was arrested, some even denouncing Him?" he asked, much too loudly and with a sharp and cutting edge.

The surrounding tables grew eerily silent. Barnabas was taken back and could not speak.

"Yes, we are those ones," came an answer from behind him. Big Peter rose and slowly approached him. "Judas, one of His trusted ones also betrayed Him to the High Priest for a filthy bag of money and, yes, I denied knowing Him at all three different times, just as He predicted I would. Only young John here and a few women stayed with Him. It is something that we will live with forever and something I will always be ashamed of."

Peter came closer. Saul remained silent but stood his ground.

"After following Jesus for three years and witnessing with our own eyes all the amazing things He did and said, and after seeing countless miracles and knowing He was supernatural, we still did not understand what God was actually doing."

Saul was shaken slightly but managed to ask boldly, "Well, you seem to be certain now of such things. What changed that?"

"Jesus told us to wait in Jerusalem and He would send us the Spirit, the same Spirit that was in Him and which possessed Him entirely. This was the Spirit that was promised by Joel and Isaiah and many other prophets. We waited, just as He said and on the day of the Feast of First Fruits, fifty days after his crucifixion, our veiled minds were finally opened to all the truth of what God had done and what He has in store for us and Israel. Only then did we remember all the things He had said. Now, our understanding grows deeper each day. The fear that made me deny Him three times at Caiaphas's house ... well, that has been swept away, and my thinking and my valuation of this life has been changed forever. I no longer care what others think of me."

Getting no response from the quieted young Pharisee, Peter continued. "All the things Jesus taught have started to become clear and we see nothing in the Law and prophets that somehow or other does not speak of Him. Every day, more and more scriptures are being opened to our understanding and becoming clearer to those who can humble themselves and be taught by the Spirit."

It was obvious that this statement would irritate one committed to the pursuit of religious knowledge by study and debate but that had not muzzled the big man. Peter's candid confession had startled and confused Saul as he was not accustomed to someone not defending themselves or not making excuses for their past failures. Although it was said in an honest and disarming manner, Saul still took it as a challenge and felt the surge of the need to argue.

Barnabas, sensing more anger in Saul, took the opportunity to change the tone and introduced his sister Mary to Saul. She was a handsome woman of about thirty-five years with long, black hair, warm eyes, whose easy smile portrayed a beautiful spirit. The inviting and peaceful atmosphere in this courtyard was testimony to the welcoming and comfortable home she had created.

"Welcome back to our home," she said compellingly, making Saul feel comfortable instantly.

"This is my son John Mark whom I think you met when he was a lot younger," she said, referring to the visit Saul and his father had made ten years previously which Saul remembered only faintly. John Mark was a tall lad for his fourteen years, much like his Uncle Barnabas, and he nodded politely to Saul before quickly returning to helping serve the small courtyard crowd.

"I recently talked with your father," Saul informed both, finally getting his voice back, "and he is very concerned that he has not received his usual letters. He had not heard from you from before Passover and he was very upset. He gave me a letter to deliver to you, Barnabas, which I have at home and which I expected to give to you at Caesarea when you were supposed to deal with the tent delivery. I promised him that I would find you and remind you to contact him again."

Barnabas and Mary glanced at each other without speaking and then Barnabas responded.

"Saul, Mary and I have been followers of Jesus for a while now, Mary for over a year, and me, a few short months. The events over Passover, the days when they crucified our Lord, were so devastating to us that our very lives were turned upside down. We were almost destroyed and could not believe such evil deeds were possible among us Jews. A few days after our Lord's crucifixion, there were those amongst us who began seeing Him, alive again, just as He had promised. He kept appearing for about forty days to different groups of disciples and other people, in different locations, and even here in our house."

Saul's eyes swept the courtyard unintentionally with that thought but quickly returned to the brother and sister. "Where is He now," demanded Saul.

"Gone back to the Father, He had to, to allow the Spirit within Himself to leave just Him and embrace all of us. We did not understand until we received It also."

Saul snorted, shaking his head at this answer, "That's a convenient answer," he said just a little under his breath. "He's still dead."

"I saw Him. Mary saw Him, and He told us beforehand that He must go to the Father to allow the Spirit in Him to come upon us. Many of us who followed Him were gathered in one place on the Day of Pentecost when His Spirit filled us and completely changed us."

Barnabas's attention wandered for a few seconds.

"I guess I have been negligent about my business, but it does not seem to have any importance in our new lives. It seems only a foolish necessity."

Saul was again stunned by such a preposterous retort and it threw him into a confused silence.

"I would very much like to see that letter from my father though, and I promise I will write him back," Barnabas said. Saul could only nod his head in agreement.

Mary, seeing that Saul was momentarily speechless, interrupted and invited him to stay for a dinner with all these people but Saul was quick to refuse, suddenly wanting only to escape this lunacy. He sputtered his goodbyes and bolted out the large door into the narrow street. He walked trancelike to the corner, attempting to collect his thoughts, but there he stopped and leaned his head up against the cool stone wall, completely rattled by the day's events.

After a few minutes, Saul forced his way back to the Cardo and found the nearest stall that provided food and drink. He found a table alone and sat with a cup of wine while he rehearsed the confusing day.

First there was the commitment to fight the heresy that he and Samuel had pledged to each other, which now, after all he had seen, he was even more determined to carry out.

Secondly and very strangely, he had encountered the centurion and his captive assistant in two different streets.

Thirdly, there were the crowds flocking around the man he now knew as Simon Peter where he had witnessed what appeared to be some unexplainable healings.

Lastly, all the day's craziness was followed by what had just taken place in the house of Barnabas and Mary.

His peaceful and predictable Jerusalem life was exploding.

Beginning to be drawn into the circle of influence and to understand the immense unsettling power and scope of this Galilean delusion himself, Saul was suddenly realizing how unlearned people could be caught up in the excitement.

As he continued assessing the events of the day, Saul was being inundated with the belief that it was his destiny to be a major player in the upcoming battle for the soul of Israel. He could think of no other reason to be made privy to all he had except that he was being supernaturally "called" of God to expose and oppose this dangerous cult, one that could somehow seize and hold so tightly the devotion of such good and successful Jews as Barnabas.

By Hashem's great benevolence, mixed with his own brilliance, Saul had grasped an exact understanding of what these people claimed. He now knew it was blasphemy disguised as humility, evil powers deceitfully performing miraculous events and, although the modesty of Peter was at the time disarming, he now decided it was the work of men ultimately wanting fame and fortune.

A second goblet of the refreshing wine was consumed by Saul when another thought hit him. *Why was Miriam dancing with that woman and why was she so happy with these events?*

She should have known better.

CHAPTER FORTY-TWO

The Surprising Miriam

As Saul meandered his way home, he found himself stopping every few minutes and standing very still, rehearsing the events of this strange day over and over in his mind. Finally, after his third stop, he began smiling wryly, and began laughing at himself. He was snickering that such thoughts would affect him so intensely that he had forgotten to keep walking yet again, and because of that, he now found himself face to face with a lazy-eyed donkey who was wending its way through the crowd. The smelly animal was obviously used to the clamor and was expecting that all would step aside to give it space. Neither the ass or Saul had made any attempt to avoid each other so the animal simply lowered its head and shoved the startled Pharisee out of the way. The few that noticed this, laughed loudly, and finally with resignation, Saul joined in with them. Smiling broadly, Saul uttered a silent vow to himself. Attempting to be humorous, he declared that he would, from that time on, guard himself against the unwanted influence of any such pace-altering thoughts or long-eared animals, never again allowing either of them to push him off his committed path.

Quite out of character and remembering the hardness of the donkey's head, Saul roared out in a huge laugh at his scrambled, yet very serious pledge.

Saul arrived at his home and quietly slipped up to the second-story apartment. He could easily hear Miriam, Leah and Gammy's friendly conversation in the courtyard below where they were dining pleasantly but he was in no state to be involved in any socializing and just wanted to be alone. He heard Miriam enter later but again, he avoided her, remaining in his room thinking and praying and attempting to further order his thoughts before speaking to her or to anyone else.

The next morning Saul woke early and after his washings and prayers, he busied himself away from Miriam, remaining in his room. She finally approached him and asked, "Saul, are you feeling all right? Are you well? You seem to be avoiding me and the others as well," she said, finally stating what had become painfully obvious.

After looking at the soft and sincere face of his sister, he decided to open his thoughts to her.

"There are many things consuming my mind right now, Miriam, most of which I do not want to bother you with. Many are of great importance to me and to Israel as a whole. I fear a great upheaval is coming and soon, I must become involved in matters beyond my comfortable life as a student or teacher."

Miriam knew instinctively that she had pried open a floodgate so now she simply waited and Saul could not stop himself.

"I have seen the results of the delusion that many are under regarding the false messiah Jesus and I have seen how deceitful and conniving it is. Even Barnabas and his sister Mary, the ones from Cyprus, are deeply involved for they are housing some of the worst perpetrators of this blasphemy."

The words virtually gushed out of Saul, but he gave no further explanation. Miriam was confused. She asked him innocently, "What is this about."

"I saw with my own eyes the dangerous healings that they claim and I noticed that you did also. I saw you watching them at the market yesterday," Saul stated accusingly and this tone further puzzled Miriam.

"Yes, I did see some amazing things take place," Miriam responded sweetly, her tone setting Saul back. "And I had an opportunity to talk to an old woman who had her back straightened. She was so thankful and told me she had been crippled for over twenty years and had the priests make all kinds of sacrifices and spent all kinds of money on physicians, none of which helped. Her healing was something beyond the slow physical recovery that even a good physician could assist with though. She said it was immediate and all the preacher said to her was to believe in Jesus. If a daughter of Israel is set free from infirmity, is it not a good thing, no matter from whom it comes," asked Miriam innocently.

"The High Priest and our leaders have declared that this Jesus could do miracles only with the power of Beelzebub. Now, His followers have learned how to use those evil powers," stated Saul with an air of authority. It was a lofty stance that he knew was wasted on his sister.

"Does Gamaliel agree with that?" questioned Miriam immediately.

"I would be surprised if he didn't," replied Saul evasively. He suddenly wished he had kept quiet.

Miriam was uncomfortable with the direction and vein of their slightly heated exchange and she took advantage of the pause to change things. She sat down directly in front of her brother.

"On another matter, Saul, I wanted to ask your advice about something I have been contemplating since we arrived in Jerusalem. You noticed, no doubt, that I was visiting a shop of medicines and ointments on the Cardo."

Saul nodded his acknowledgement but only now was sure just what the pouches and containers in that store held.

"I have visited almost all such businesses in Jerusalem over the last week. I also talked with a few physicians and I am convinced that there is a great need for better medicines and more medical knowledge in Jerusalem. Would you, as my brother, have a problem if I began a store for medicines and a place of treatment for women in Jerusalem. Possibly I could buy an existing shop on the Cardo. Beyond that, would you help me to start it up?"

Saul was stunned. He was immediately reminded of the extraordinary abilities of his sister and was pleased to see that her medical interests were so quickly being rejuvenated. He also knew that she was absolutely tenacious when on a mission. Silently and thankfully, he was relieved that her sudden interest in business affairs was far removed from any that he was opposing. The tension between Saul and Miriam had completely disappeared.

Saul blurted out, "Oh, that would be such a good thing for this city and I would be honored to help you." The Jewish community of Tarsus had benefited so much from her skills.

"Do you need money?" he quickly asked.

They both laughed aloud, knowing that she had inherited substantial wealth from her father, as had Saul, plus she had accumulated a sizable stash from her doctoring of well-to-do women in Tarsus. She already was moderately wealthy.

"Thank you, Saul. I will start planning immediately," smiled Miriam. She knew that she not only wanted his blessing, but she needed the signature of a man of her family to lawfully proceed. Indeed, hers was a heady ambition and it could be legally tricky to finalize any land ownership details in the male-dominated Jewish culture.

"Gammy and Leah also think it is a good idea," she stated, making Saul a little irritated to know they had heard about this first. He could not understand why he felt this tinge of jealousy and he laughed at himself for it. He instinctively knew he should not interfere with the closeness developing between this family and Miriam and he silently convinced himself that he had no desire to.

Saul mentioned nothing else about the previous day, purposely avoiding discussing yesterday's agreement with Samuel for he knew that the perceptive Miriam probably already noticed his recent and growing differences with Gamaliel and Gammy and he did not want to add fuel to that fire. He disliked the feeling of hiding something this important from the principal people in his life but he also felt that his actions could be easily misunderstood. Current events had made him unsure that Gamaliel, Gammy, or even Miriam shared his ability to foresee the inherent danger that this new sect could grow to be.

Admittedly, on the surface the Galileans looked harmless, even godly, bantering around miracles like they had some special access to other dimensions, but when they were confronted, they would show their colors and of that he was convinced. Whenever Saul's thoughts went to challenging them, he began to mentally rehearse his scriptural arguments and his confidence in his vaunted arguing abilities made him once again convinced that he had somehow been chosen by Hashem for just this purpose. Deep down he had always felt a special calling and he was now more than willing to accept this as his proscribed mission.

The very next morning, Miriam, Saul and Gammy walked together to the Cardo markets which were already teeming with noisy merchants and customers. Not altogether surprising, Miriam had already found the perfect shop to begin her new adventure and it was the exact one Saul had seen her in yesterday. It was near the busiest corner of the route where the two men walked to class every day and where they turned onto the main road leading to the Temple area.

She showed them the stall proudly. It had a staircase up to an enclosed second level where there was a comfortable room with a window to the street. The street level front, like most of the other shops, was defined by two large columns twenty feet apart, with stone walls behind each column that separated it from the neighboring shops. This stall was surrounded by a cluster of shops that sold dry goods and therefore did not have the pungent odors of the meat and live animal vendors further down and that would be a blessing on hot summer days. The kindly greeting of a gray-haired abd bright-eyed older man to Miriam told both Saul and Gammy that she had already done the groundwork on this project leaving both men amazed at her boldness and willingness to act so quickly on her intentions.

"How much is the rent?" blurted out Saul. He now understood that this was not just a future dream of his sister's but may become a reality much sooner than he had imagined. He felt compelled to jump in immediately with some wise brotherly advice.

"Well," responded Miriam slowly, "this lovely man owns the store and has offered it for sale. He wants one thousand denarii."

Gammy and Saul locked eyes and their male protective instincts were instantly activated. Miriam let their speechless surprise and confusion percolate for a few seconds and then laughed.

"I offered him eight hundred and we have an agreement, subject to my brother agreeing and signing."

The two men again looked at each other and burst out laughing, realizing how adept this little girl was and just how little they knew or could add to this pact. Both now understood how respectful Miriam had been just to involve them. They nodded their heads in amused agreement and Saul and Miriam made an appointment for the ninth hour of this day to complete the deal legally. All documents were to be readied by a scribe in accordance with all laws.

This sister of mine certainly moves fast, concluded Saul.

Gammy left for his teaching class, chuckling all the way and Saul remained behind as he and Miriam discussed the exchange of money that he, as the male overseer of the family, was expected to make.

"One other thing, Saul," Miriam hesitantly inquired. "You mentioned Barnabas. As we were told on Cyprus, he and his family can find almost any spice or medicine in the empire. Could you tell me where I could locate him as I will need some supplies that are nowhere to be found in Jerusalem. Believe me, I have looked."

Saul loved the innocence of his sister and although he was wary of Barnabas and Mary because of their affiliation with the followers of Jesus, he decided that Miriam's request was all business and that he should have confidence in her obvious superior mental talents. He had watched her in the last year in Tarsus and knew that she, although sometime appearing naive and pure of heart, was certainly not easily duped or taken advantage of.

Saul informed her that Barnabas had a merchant's stall very near the north end of the Cardo, number three or four he thought, very close to the Damascus gate. He knew that for he had visited it a few years previous to repair some of his family's tents that were damaged in shipment to Barnabas. Saul's tent-making training had come in handy and he had been surprisingly thankful for that small break from constant study. He described the location of this stall to Miriam as next to the intriguing Ethiopian ivory store but also mentioned that if Barnabas was not there, he might be found at his sister Mary's house, just three short blocks from her new shop.

Saul left his sister in the stall chatting intently with the aged man, bemused by what had transpired in just a few short hours. He chortled away as he recalled how Miriam had expertly guided the conversations and the attitudes, allowing all involved to believe that they were helping her in making decisions when, obviously, she had already made the final arrangements. Yes, she was tender and devoted but she was remarkably unafraid and Saul grinned once more at the thought of any husband who foolishly would want to control or underestimate this remarkable young lady.

From the stall, Miriam went directly to the north end of the market street and after locating the ivory shop, noticed the bare stall next door. Her inquiries of the neighboring shops informed her that, yes, this was Barnabas's stall, but they opened only when shipments came in and, no, Barnabas had not been around for weeks.

Her eyes focused on the large wooden gate at the north end of the Cardo, historically referred to as the Damascus Gate because it was the beginning of the northern road that led to far away cities such as Damascus and to Babylon itself. Visions of exotic locales mentioned in the scriptures instantly danced in her mind, mysterious places well beyond the gates of this city, but for now she simply looked and imagined, determining to someday see such places.

No, today, Miriam was possessed of another mission. It was still early in the day so she went home and counted out one thousand denarii from her stash, an amused smile developing on her face.

After Saul and Gammy had left her that morning, she had discovered that the old merchant also owned the five adjacent stalls. Learning this, she immediately negotiated an option on the other five for an extra two hundred denarii. Within a year, she could purchase all of them for the same eight hundred denarii each, if she so desired. The elderly shop owner had mentioned that the prosperous shops in these adjacent stalls had been there for many years and the owners were happy to pay the reasonable rent for such a desired location, therefore owning them seemed a reasonable and potentially profitable investment to the very logical Miriam.

From her inquiries, Miriam had learned that purchasing this prime real estate was a rare opportunity as almost all the Cardo was owned and greatly coveted by the High Priest's family. It was also well known that if any sites were for sale, they were expected to be made available to that family first. The old merchant had jumped at the opportunity to sidestep that practice and he did admit to Miriam that over the years there had been extensive pressure put on him to sell his holdings to Caiaphas. A barrage of lawyers and scribes who worked for the High Priest's family had regularly visited him, constantly reminding him of what was expected so to avoid them knowing what was transpiring today, he was arranging for a discreet and independent scribe to handle the legal transfer. There were too many stories of last-minute legal interference and questionable practices by the usual lawyer friends of the priest's family to not be extremely secretive about today's arrangements.

Curious about this unusual opportunity, Miriam inquired about his reason for selling and the old man responded, almost overcome emotionally, that he had no need for worldly possessions anymore and although she did not fully understand that unusual reply, she chose to not question him any further.

Too excited to stay at home and wanting to find Barnabas without delay, Miriam followed Saul's directions to the carved wooden gate of the house that he had described. Her knocking was answered by a young servant girl and Miriam asked if Barnabas was available. She was courteously invited into the courtyard and then the servant disappeared into the large house. In the courtyard she saw a group of five women preparing breads and two others working on a spit of meat. Miriam wondered if these were the "dangerous perpetrators of blasphemy" Saul had referred to, chuckling to herself at the ability of her brother to see enemies everywhere.

A tall, statuesque lady delivered a basket of supplies to the table of the bread makers and then glanced up at Miriam, who was waiting just inside the gate. Miriam was certain that this was Mary for she was simply a younger version of her mother whom Miriam had gotten to know in Cyprus. Mary nodded an acknowledgement to her and quickly made her way over and introduced herself. Upon learning that she was Saul's sister, she invited her to sit and soon Miriam was pouring out all she could remember of her recent visit to Salamis with Mary's parents. She would have continued with more information had not the tall, lightly-bearded and well-clad Barnabas suddenly appeared. Mary made the introductions and then excused herself, leaving a puzzled Barnabas with Miriam.

Surely, she had not come on the same mission from his father as did her brother Saul, mused Barnabas. Knowing the poorly concealed animosity in Saul, he did not think that he would have suggested his sister make a cordial visit, so her presence remained a momentary mystery to Barnabas.

Miriam, sensing his discomfort, started in her broken Aramaic.

"Sir, your father described your family's business dealings quite extensively and told me of your ability to find needed products from around the empire."

Miriam then saw Barnabas visibly relax. "I have need of many new medicines, some fresh ointments, plus any books of new and effective medical treatments that can be acquired. I have heard there are such items in Antioch of Syria, and also Alexandria and I know that you have brothers there who are very adept at finding rare things."

"Can I inquire why you need these products? Also, you seem hurried and there is an urgency in your voice," replied Barnabas kindly, now using perfect Greek and knowing that Miriam would be much more at home in that tongue.

Miriam was a little embarrassed at her somewhat demanding manner and his gentle smile eased the tension. She told him of her business plans and as he listened, he nodded approvingly.

"I will contact my father and my brothers and I know that they will flood you with useful products. It is probably best if you make a list of the various medicines that you will need immediately and the approximate quantities of each. Also, a note about the types of medical books would be helpful, plus some limits on what new and "exotic" medical practices and treatments to send to you. There are quite a lot of local remedies around the empire, some may be effective, some not. I will include your directions and lists in my next letters to them."

Miriam instantly noticed an agile and quick business mind at work and wondered to herself why his stall was not full of exotic and profitable products imported to Jerusalem by his family. She saw nothing but potential there.

"I will have that list by tomorrow," stated Miriam. "How much of a deposit do I need to provide for this service?"

Barnabas paused for a long moment and then said, "None. We work on a twenty percent fee on all purchases for our trusted customers, of which I most definitely count your family. It is payable only after we have delivered the products to you."

Miriam was astonished at this rare arrangement, so she quickly asked, "Do you think that I could retain a standing order with your family, into the future?"

She had instantly recognized that Barnabas's brothers would be an invaluable source of needed merchandise stretching into the years ahead.

Intuitively, Miriam also recognized that she was pressing Barnabas a little, but she had sensed a slight reluctance and a curious indifference in Barnabas which mystified her. She was eager to establish this mutually profitable business relationship, not for just this one shipment but for the future and was searching for some indication from Barnabas that he also wanted to do business.

"Little sister, I would be happy to serve you as long as I continue in this occupation" he finally stated convincingly, but Miriam noted the interfering caveat that he had attached. She decided to be content with that answer for now and mentioned that she would be delivering the letters and lists by noon tomorrow.

Before leaving, she ventured a question. "Barnabas, if I am allowed, why is your shop empty? I was told that you have done no business there for months. You know that your father and mother are beside themselves."

She waited as he pondered how to answer that question. "Does it have anything to do with the prophet Jesus," she quietly asked.

Being openly questioned, Barnabas paused, deep in thought and contemplating the depth of the answer he thought was appropriate for this pretty and wide-eyed young Jewess.

"Actually, it has everything to do with Jesus," was his answer. "When you bring your lists tomorrow, I will tell you my story if you are interested and you will see why the importing business is of little importance to me anymore."

Just then a group of six men in Galilean garb emerged from a second-story room, heartily singing a psalm and descending to the courtyard. Barnabas joined them as they exited the gate, leaving Miriam alone in the elegant courtyard. She nodded to the busy women and exited as well, her curiosity suddenly aflame and her mind racing with even more questions.

On her way back through the Cardo, she stopped in front of her nearly-acquired shop and imagined it freshly cleaned, full of an array of healthy products and with people flocking to her upper room for personal advice. She giggled at her internal excitement and eagerness, noticing that she was once more extremely energized. That happy feeling reminded her of her former successes in treating sick people in Tarsus, feelings which were combined with the pleasurable memories of times of great learning.

Miriam was thrilled about arranging the deal for the shop today, but strangely and quite suddenly, she now found herself equally enthusiastic to hear Barnabas's story tomorrow. She returned to her apartment and nervously counted the money for the third time, then she paced about the empty apartment, and finally searched out Leah to help pass the time away.

She arrived back at the Cardo at mid-afternoon, just in time to see a middle-aged man with a large pouch slung over his shoulder being covertly led to the upstairs private room by the elderly owner. Miriam waited reservedly at the street level until Saul arrived and together, they climbed the steps to the room above.

Saul was astounded and more than a little bewildered at the future sales option that his sister had negotiated since that morning and sensing that she was capable of almost anything, he reminded himself that the whole Cardo could probably be hers as well, if she so desired. Suddenly, Saul was hoping that this peculiar thought had only come to him in jest, for he was a firm believer that inspirations and thoughts were not random, they arose with cause out of one's own mind. He also held that every imagination had its seeds in some form of possible reality.

Out of the large sack appeared three hand printed copies of the sales contract, each written on the newest of parchment, along with the register of the title of lands form created years ago by Hillel himself. The next few minutes were a flurry of signatures and waxy seals and the merchant, appearing eager to go, prayed a sincere blessing on Miriam and then quietly departed, leaving her the carved wooden key to the private room door.

Remarkably, without much fanfare and within mere minutes, it all belonged to Miriam. Saul and Miriam just looked at each other, astonished at the speed with which their last night's conversation had transformed into a reality, and truthfully, they had a feeling that the day was not over yet. The two women who ran their version of this store also seemed very pleased. The deal meant that they could finally rest from the demands of a business they had started forty years previously and they could now be the meddling grandmothers that old age graciously bestows on such women. Miriam had purchased their entire but depleted stock as well.

Saul was about to congratulate his sister when a loud disturbance down on the street level caught their attention. They looked out of the window to see a crowd of excited people running around the corner and racing down the street in the direction of the Temple walls. Others were standing around, yelling loudly and questioning what was taking place.

"A miracle," one was shouting.

"He's healed," another voice announced.

"What. Where?" resounded another.

"At the Beautiful Gate," yelled another. The name of Simon Peter was heard over and over, yelled over the din.

"Jesus healed him," another shouted confidently.

Saul said quickly, "Miriam, I will meet you at home later and we will celebrate your new endeavor but I must go see what this is about."

"Go, brother, do your duty; run and save Israel," Miriam teased with absolutely no malice intended at all.

CHAPTER FORTY-THREE

The Leaping Beggar

Saul flew off to the Temple Mount, his curiosity aroused and his wide-bordered robe flapping wildly. Upon reaching the lesser known women's gate, he was immediately swallowed up in a larger crowd that was also pushing into the Court of the Gentiles. Their numbers had swollen with every corner he passed as the news had spread through the adjacent streets of Jerusalem and everyone was excited and wanted to see for themselves if such a thing as a healing had taken place.

He rudely elbowed his way through the buzzing throng but his impolite pushing and shoving had no effect on the joy that had infected the gathering swarm. Waves of praise followed with beautifully sung stanzas of King David's psalms were heard coming from within the porticos ahead and the jubilant songs rolled their way back through the crowd.

Saul noticed that the center of the commotion seemed to be under a portico of Solomon's Porch, at a place directly opposite the main gate of the women's area of the Temple courtyards. He pushed his way along the outer north wall of the Sanhedrin and then past the outer wall of the women's court until he could see under the portico.

Truthfully, Saul was not surprised to see the big man Simon Peter and his friend, the young John, standing there, completely encircled by a buzzing throng. Their attention was focused on a strangely familiar but very dirty and unkept man who was standing next to them in the middle of the crowd. This beggar, draped with tattered and worn wrappings, alternated between affectionately grabbing their hands and leaping and dancing around them to the screams and shouts of the surrounding crowd. Saul looked closer, examining the ragged man intently, half expecting him to be one of the Galileans' friends who was acting out a part, but he recognized him as the crippled scrounger who sat daily at the only entrance to the women's court, the gate everyone called Beautiful.

He remembered that Miriam had given this very man a generous donation on their Temple tour mere days ago and he vaguely remembered his generous father distributing coins to beggars when they had first visited the Temple. As a Pharisee, he purposely avoided such unfortunates, not wanting to soil his pure garments or dirty his hands by any incidental contact with one who just may be under Hashem's curse or condemnation.

The times he could not avoid the persistent panhandler, those days when the pressing crowd forced Saul to pass close to him, he had been utterly repulsed by his distorted and twisted ankles and preferred to look away. No compassion had been aroused in him and there was no empathy in Saul for him or his family members who daily carried the man to this spot. His constant cries for alms were an annoying irritant to Saul. He was abandoned by Hahem, and therefore, by any good Jew.

As he pushed his way to the front of the crowd, he spotted Gammy standing rigidly at the very front, a mere twenty feet from the leaping and ecstatic man. Gammy's eyes were focused for a time on the man's feet, then he would glance up to the faces of the two Galileans, then around to the loud, pressing crowd and then back to the beggar. Saul pushed and shoved his way close and stood next to Gammy who at first did not rouse from his deep thoughts.

"What's going on, Gammy?" Saul shouted over the racket.

Gammy, noticing Saul, said firmly, "The beggar has been healed," and again drifted into his own thoughts.

A second tumult, much angrier in tone was rising behind Saul and Gammy. Irate and dangerous comments from the gathered crowd rang out as a contingent of unarmed and very nervous priestly guards, accompanied by two immaculately garbed Chief Priests, pushed their way through the excited crowd. Cries of "this is surely a good deed" and "leave them be" followed by "this thing is of God" were being directed at this small group of official-looking but nervous Temple servants.

Before the guards could get near, the young man named John cried out, "This is a blessing sent from God," using the sacred word "Adonai," which was traditionally used only inside the Temple and only in times of deep and fervent prayer.

Peter picked up the thought and boomed, "Since Samuel, all our prophets spoke of these days, days of refreshing." He looked over the packed common area and the totally jammed porticos, and he raised his big hand. The crowd hushed.

"You," he said, turning and pointing directly at them, "are heirs of those prophecies, and even before that, heirs also of the covenant with Abraham. It is through our nation that all the nations and people of the world would be blessed." Peter scanned the crowd and noticed young Saul in the very front scowling and shaking his head in refusal.

The crowd loudly murmured their agreement, rejecting any hint of disbelief, and calls of "that is nothing but the truth" rang out and resounded around the whole perimeter.

"Is this that blessing of which the prophets spoke?" someone shouted.

"When is it to take place?" another shouted at Peter.

"Is that prophesied blessing just about the healing of a miserable cripple?" a critical voice yelled in response.

Peter held up a huge hand again and the chattering quieted.

"No, it is not just about this brother being healed, as amazing and good as that is for this man," he said, pointing out the lame man, who now was still and was listening intently.

"When God," he said, again using the holy name Adonai, which severely irritated the nearby Chief Priests, "raised up His servant," and all knew immediately that Peter meant Jesus, "He sent Him to you first, to bless and favor you, so that you could turn from your wicked ways. This good deed is Hashem's proof of that."

Saul noticed that a small group of well-dressed Sadducees, close friends of the High Priest, had appeared and they were accompanied by the armed and battle-ready leader of the more dangerous Temple guards. This group had slipped out of the confines of the Sanhedrin's Hall of Hewn Stones, no doubt after a day of sitting in judgement, and were now standing shoulder to shoulder with the placid guards and the flabbergasted ceremonial priests.

The Captain of the Guard, feeling he must do something to please his superiors, shouted at Peter, "Do not desecrate the name of God by using it vain. Moses commanded that we not do this for it is his third commandment written by the very hand of God and we must not trivialize the qualities of Elohim by making His name common in this affair." It was the only charge he could think of.

As he spoke, he was extremely careful to use one of the traditionally "allowed" names of God. The priests and the guards woke from their confusion and shouted a noisy agreement with the captain.

Others in the crowd took up the challenge and shouted their vigorous response, specifically that God had glorified Jesus's name by resurrecting Him.

Upon hearing of a resurrection, one of the Sadducees, in a great, bellowing voice and shouting above the noise, called out "Resurrection? What resurrection? There is no such thing. What religious deception are these men practicing upon you poor ignorant Jews? Listen to us, you are our brothers. This is dangerous and deceitful, and you must stop this sacrilege."

The outspoken Sadducee turned, now expecting some action by the Temple guards and looked directly at the captain.

This was followed by a loud hissing from the crowd, a definite warning to the confused Captain. An overt and almost humorous posturing on both sides followed, including defiant hands-on-hips and very threatening arm waving. Any rough stuff on the Temple Plaza was absolutely forbidden and the result was that awkward and exaggerated body language was the only other allowable retort.

Hearing the supportive roar of the multitude for the Galileans made the once lame man begin his dancing and leaping again. The effect was that the crowd began once again proclaiming the goodness of their God and His blessings to Israel so loudly that all other voices were drowned out.

Every jump and every swirl by the exuberant beggar made the crowd more joyful and dangerously, much louder. His ankles were gaining strength by the minute and it seemed that the man was attempting to spring higher with each enthusiastic leap.

That beggar is purposely putting on this show, thought Saul. *He should take his new ankles and go home and leave the religious explanations to us.*

CHAPTER FORTY-FOUR

Arrests

The captain and the Chief Priests conferred quickly and announced to the crowd that they would hold Peter and John so they could be investigated in the morning by the wise elders and the High Priest himself. He, as captain, declared that he would not let this serious incident be resolved here by a noisy and unruly crowd: all must be done properly and legally. It was loudly announced that the two disciples were to be held "for their own safety." The two disciples of Jesus, looking every bit the part of prisoners, were led away to the rear of the Temple where they quickly disappeared down the well-guarded stairway which led to the infamous subterranean jails. Saul was impressed by the swiftness of this move and it was over before any in the crowd could organize any opposition.

After the "arrest," the mood of the congregation remained one of rejoicing and worshiping for the lame man danced and pranced his way around the porticos, receiving a loud and joyous refrain each time he was stopped and asked to tell his amazing story.

"I asked for money and got new legs," he repeated time and time again.

Saul and Gammy had stood frozen, hardly moving throughout this whole episode, transfixed into inaction by what they had just witnessed. They watched as others, obviously pilgrims and newcomers to Jerusalem, began inquiring about this mysterious Jesus and before long, visitors were pressing anybody and everybody around the whole plateau for an answer.

An elderly man approached Saul and Gammy and asked, "Rabbis, who was this Jesus and why was He crucified? How could such a miracle happen in His name?"

The two Pharisees, void of any answer to these straight forward inquiries, stared silently at the out-of-town man until Saul gruffly rebuffed him and sent him away. They watched as he then approached a worshiper under the portico, who greeted him kindly, and a warm, animated conversation was started.

Many more pilgrims were streaming into the Temple Plaza and these immediately gravitated to the outer porticos. For a long while Saul and Gammy watched as people gathered and listened intently to the other Galileans who had walked with Jesus. They were speaking fervently of the One they had followed for three years and they spoke with great boldness and clarity to a very hungry crowd. Every few minutes, just to add emphasis to their words, the tattered man would pass by each group, bounding up and down, hopping and jumping, now leading an ecstatic group of young children who had joined him in his wild dancing.

A strange thing was happening all the while. Many of the witnesses of the beggars cavorting began crying out to become followers of Jesus also.

Soon a group of over thirty eager new believers gathered in front of Saul and Gammy and they were anxiously waiting to get to the Pool of Siloam to be baptized. This was being repeated in all areas of the Court of the Gentiles.

"Let's get out of here," growled an angry Saul to Gammy who had remained mute and immobile, intent on observing every aspect of the peculiar happenings. They threaded their way through the stirring mass of people already in the Court of the Gentiles and then pushed through even more curious crowds that were arriving even though it would shortly be sundown and the interior gates would soon be secured.

The nervous ceremonial priests had called for the armed and permanent troop from below in anticipation of possible violence but sensing only a peaceful atmosphere, they returned to their Temple duties. The more serious guards were watching the crowds carefully, still fearing any reaction from the people because of the arrest of their leaders. Surprisingly, the crowd had remained remarkably calm and unaffected.

Saul and Gammy left without any further conversation between them, preferring to walk home in silence.

Each young man had differing ideas on what had taken place that day at the Temple.

CHAPTER FORTY-FIVE

Business Conflicts

Nothing was said between the two men until they reached the Cardo market, their quick walk being accompanied only by the haunting, fading music from the Temple following them through the streets. They finally slowed their march directly in front of Miriam's newly acquired stall where both men stopped and visibly relaxed.

"How did the purchase go? Did everything get finalized?" Gammy suddenly asked, breaking his silence. He seemed more than a little thankful to disrupt his very confusing contemplations.

When Saul heard the calm sincerity in Gammy's question, he also snapped out of his angry state and ceased his theatrical stomping. He looked in Gammy's direction and began chuckling. Gammy was intrigued and looked at him quizzically.

"Oh, it went well," Saul exclaimed with a laugh, "and I got a bigger surprise when I met Miriam here. She had arranged the deal so that she not only bought this shop but she has the option to purchase the whole block, down to that corner over there, all within a year. That old merchant owns them all and wants to sell them as well and all for the same reduced price. Miriam could have bought them all but wanted to approach things a little slowly I suspect, but you know my sister. Once she is established in her stall, I am sure she will finish the deal."

"Oh my," exclaimed a captivated Gammy. Then he paused and stroked his stubbly beard for a long time. Finally, he spoke.

"There may be a little problem with this," he said very slowly and with a note of trepidation. Saul could see him pondering something that was obviously bothering him. He was thinking hard.

Gammy scanned the rest of the valuable real estate in the block, probably the most desirable location on the Cardo, and then said, "This will make Annas and Caiaphas very angry. They have informed the few remaining independent owners on the street that the properties must be sold to them. They have bought up all the properties that came up for sale in the past and rumors abound that their scribes constantly approach the owners of those that remain. They are known to threaten them with all types of retribution in their attempts to force them to sell only to them. Welcome to the nastier side of that 'holy' family. Your sister may have unknowingly poked a coiled serpent with her purchase."

Gammy scratched his head quizzically and went on. "I suspect that today she purchased a formidable and vengeful enemy, along with the valuable real estate."

Both men stood in silence and contemplated that scary prospect. Jerusalem was ripe with tales of strong families, led by determined and wealthy men who had made the mistake of opposing old Annas and Caiaphas and they had always paid a severe price.

Gammy slowly continued. "I thought one stall would not be that bad, but six? Well, that will get Caiaphas' attention for sure."

Suddenly realizing something else, Gammy burst out in a howl of laughter, a huge smile appeared on his face and then he turned to Saul and, almost shouting, said, "It is your name as male guarantor on all the documents, is it not? You may have gotten yourself into a sizeable predicament, my friend."

Gammy wagged his head in amusement and with more yowls of unsuppressed amusement, started off for their home.

Saul stood speechless. He woke from the stunning effects of this revelation just as a whooping Gammy was making the turn off the Cardo. He took off, quickly running after him. He caught up at the gateway to their house where

Gammy was standing and holding the gate open. As Gammy had anticipated, there was a look of pure horror on his face.

"Meet with me and Father after dinner, would you Saul and I will relate all that took place today at the Temple and," he paused for effect, "just how much trouble you are in." Gammy headed for his room across the courtyard from Saul and Miriam's apartment, not waiting for a reply. One last laugh was heard from Gammy as he looked back on the lonely, stoop-shouldered figure of Saul.

Saul slunk his way up his stairs where he immediately encountered the broad smile of Miriam who had prepared a sumptuous bowl of lamb and fresh bread. As they sat down, Saul related what Gammy had told him about the new stall on the Cardo. He was beside himself, upset and fidgeting nervously.

Miriam listened quietly to his upset ramblings, not interrupting him at all. When Saul was finished, she rose and silently collected the dishes they had used. Saul was expecting a response or a reaction from his normally talkative sister and waited in silence until he could not suppress his anxiousness any longer.

"You know that although you own the property, my name is tied to the deal as your male guarantor and that may put me in a very precarious position in Jerusalem, both today and into the future, especially among the important leaders."

He paused and waited for her response but she silently continued her chores with her back to her brother.

"I was thinking that it may be a wise thing to resell the property to them and just rent a space from the priest's family. You made such a good deal that you could probably make a handsome profit by reselling it."

Miriam continued in silence and finished her cleaning. Finally, turning to Saul, she came and sat down in front of her agitated brother.

"Saul, I am not selling the stall to the High Priest. The store owner told me all about the bullying and pressure he was receiving from that supposedly pious family and the constant harassment from their henchmen. I am well-aware of the dangers."

Saul's eyes widened. "You knew and still wanted to go ahead with the deal?"

"Yes," she stated firmly, "and the owner would not have sold it to them anyway as he called them thieves and ungodly hypocrites who misused their sacred position to enlarge their family's wealth."

Her brother had gone suddenly very quiet and she knew that she now had his undivided attention.

"He also told me that he had other potential buyers but that all of them had been threatened away from buying by ruffians employed by a cousin of the High Priest. I know it is your name as guarantor but I will make sure your name never comes up as only I and the old owner have copies of those documents. Do not fear, my brother, I will take care of it, I will protect you."

The last statement by his sister shocked and roused Saul from his moment of fearful cowardice. Immediately, but also a little unconvincingly, he began reassuring Miriam that he was not worried about himself but was concerned for her. She politely accepted Saul's latest protestations but Saul himself was left with the embarrassment of his original words.

"What are your plans, Miriam," Saul finally asked in a conciliatory tone.

She thought deeply for a moment and then slowly responded.

"I will go tomorrow and purchase all the stalls so that whatever trouble this brings, I will only have to deal with it once. I will speak to the renters in these stalls and solidify and extend the existing rental agreements that the sweet old man had with them and assure them that I will not sell their stalls out from under them. I am told that as soon as the priest's family buys a property, they straightaway increase the rents and I can only imagine that is what they would do to all the merchants if they had control over all the properties on that street. After that, I will open my business as quickly as I can."

This was a bold and determined side of Miriam that Saul had never had opportunity to see before. He was intrigued with the instant emergence of a woman willing to battle such powers. He also understood that she held the high moral ground and as such, was almost inviting a public confrontation.

"You will find yourself fighting the High Priest, Miriam and that is a dangerous position to be in around this city," Saul cautioned, not sure what other advice he could offer to his determined sister.

"No, with all due respect to you, my brother, I will not be fighting the High Priest. He will be attacking an innocent daughter of Israel who needs to eke out a living and he would be doing that while she was in her unfortunate state of being fatherless. I will be viewed as another victim of his greed."

She paused and spoke quietly but directly to Saul now.

"Although this is the appointed High Priest, there are many complaints about him and his family and their indefensible behavior." Miriam looked at

Saul almost condescendingly. "I think I can handle any arguments that they present and I am confident that the Torah and the prophets are with me."

Saul had to concede the powerful point made by his little sister who on the surface could easily be mistaken for just another shallow, youthful dreamer or a girl who would soon be consumed by the usual interests of girls, namely romance and marriage. He had to agree with her assessment of the actions of the High Priest also, as this was often considered the most embarrassing non-secret in Jerusalem.

Early on in his experience in this city, Saul had been exposed to the lack of wisdom and honesty in the leaders of Jerusalem, discovering that their lofty positions were not earned by character or ability but were usually the result of favored family appointments. In turn, important posts were secretly sold to the largest contributor for any gain that they could exact from those positions. The colossal greed of many in power was only thinly veiled causing many to juggle an obvious dichotomy: the High Priest was Hashem's appointed man, but was a man not to be trusted. No longer bothered by this duplicity, Saul had gotten accustomed to this arrangement and it took new eyes, clear eyes like Miriam's, to see Caiaphas and Annas correctly.

The absence of scruples had other outcomes as well.

Good men, like Gamaliel and a few others, stood out the more and were noticed for their honor and morality.

Realizing now that Miriam had so easily and quickly discerned Jerusalem and its hierarchy, he nodded his begrudged agreement to her dealings and sincerely hoped that the day would not come when there was a confrontation between the priestly family and his sister. As questionable as their actions were, they were still the legitimately appointed and highest office of the Temple.

"You do not need to be present tomorrow, as your original family guarantee will suffice for the other purchases," she stated. "I will not put you in any more danger amongst your friends."

Her words were spoken kindly, but it was as if he were stabbed. Saul felt the sharp but unintended sting of Miriam's comment and realized that he had unwittingly exposed an unsavory attitude within himself. Even worse, he had sacrificed some part of their closeness with his unthinking remarks and cowardly advice. He felt suddenly exposed, uncovered by her clarity and personal integrity and whether it was a conscious choice on her part to take on the bullies of Jerusalem and proceed the way she had, or simply a total inability to be fearful, it was clear that Miriam lived in her own pure world and it was a world where life was not ruled by the shifting levels of morality that permeated Jerusalem politics.

"Can I come and just be a witness to what I am sure is a historic day for the Cardo Street?" Saul asked, trying to lighten the mood that had developed and to also show his support for her. His words were also an unsaid apology and he knew that Miriam would understand his intention and not require any greater assault to his pride. For that he was thankful.

"Of course, you may and I would be honored. And brother," she continued, "please excuse my abruptness; it was not meant to hurt you. Also, do not hesitate to inform me if you think I am overstepping the customs and traditions of this city or putting this house in some jeopardy."

Their warm exchanged smiles were a soothing balm and a slightly rejuvenated Saul excused himself and left for the lower courtyard to meet with Gammy and the Rabbi Gamaliel.

The topic of Barnabas and her meeting with him had not come up in their conversation and Miriam chose to leave it that way.

CHAPTER FORTY-SIX

The Name

Saul descended the wide steps into the evening coolness of the courtyard and made his way to the common table where the men would meet. Gammy was already there and he called for his father, who appeared momentarily. It felt to Saul that it had been a very long time since their last meeting because so much had happened, plus Gamaliel had been absent from the home much of that time. The early morning departures and late-night returns were the only glimpses Saul had of his beloved mentor lately.

They sipped the deep red wine of Shiloh and munched on the sumptuous bread and lamb provided, making small talk, but it was apparent that all three were eager and ready to delve into the new information they each brought with them this day.

"Gammy, why don't you tell us about the happenings at the Temple this afternoon," Gamaliel asked. He had been present at the Sanhedrin until early afternoon but had left the Temple Mount before the major events had taken place. Gamaliel had only heard about the ruckus when a messenger had arrived at the house, requesting the Great Sanhedrin meet first thing in the morning to deal with a huge disturbance and a few jailed Galileans. Gamaliel, as was required, dutifully responded by sending out notices to the

Sanhedrin recording scribes, who in turn notified all the regular members to be in attendance.

Gamaliel knew very little of the actual details and was eager for Gammy to give a thorough accounting of the day's special events.

Gammy started. "As you requested, Father, I have been going to the Temple every day after my class is completed and have been observing the people of this 'way' very closely. They meet in the Temple courtyards every day and they congregate all around the outer porticos, almost filling them completely. They now number in the thousands, so they are spilling out onto the interior square also. I am told they start arriving early and some stay all day while others come and go, but they seem to all be there for the morning and evening prayers. They gather in many small groups around the porch and listen as the different disciples that followed Jesus tell the most amazing accounts of His deeds and His teachings." Gammy momentarily drifted off into a distracted thought, but then refocussed.

"The crowds remind me of little children in a classroom, sitting speechless and in awe, wanting to hear the same stories repeated over and over. Two days ago, a man from Bethany who claimed that he was brought back to life by Jesus was there and telling his story. Regrettably, someone recognized me and a few Temple guards watching him and they took him out of there quickly, before I could speak to him."

Gammy's attention seemed to wander at that thought, but then he returned. "It was as if they expected me to do some harm to him. Today, at afternoon prayers, the leader, the big one they call Simon Peter and that young man John, were entering the women's court to go to pray."

Gamaliel interrupted. "Tell me Shimon, do they observe all the Temple rules?"

"Oh yes, they are very careful about that and I could find no fault in that regard. They are respectful and even assist in cleaning the porticos after they gather. I followed the two leaders closely because I wanted to hear exactly what they prayed for. At the Gate Beautiful, that lame man named Benjamin who has been begging there since before I was born, called out to them for money just like he does to everyone. They stopped and talked to him a bit, saying things that I could not make out, but then I distinctively heard Simon Peter say, 'In the name of Jesus, the anointed one of Nazareth, rise up and walk.' Old Benjamin sat there for a few seconds looking at them but then Simon

Peter grabbed his hand and pulled him up. I expected him to fall over, but as I was watching, his crooked ankles and bent legs straightened, right there before my eyes, and somehow, they were just not withered or bent anymore. I saw it happen."

Gammy was animated and the emotion in his voice unnerved both his listeners.

"The bones immediately straightened. I saw them move around with my own eyes! You remember how twisted they were, don't you?" Gammy enquired of his father who answered with a slight nod. Gammy repeated his statement once again, "Straightened, right there, right before my eyes."

Saul and Gamaliel shifted forward in their chairs, now in rapt attention. Gammy was getting worked up just telling the story and his long arms were waving about.

"Old, twisted up Benjamin started leaping around, very wobbly at first, and then he started screaming and shouting, as did everyone else who saw his legs straighten. That went on for a long while and more and more people joined in the singing and the praising. The news spread through the Porches and some people ran outside the Temple to the streets around, spreading the news. Within minutes, hordes of curious people began swarming in from the streets below."

"Peter and John were instantly surrounded and Benjamin grabbed their hands and would not let them go, dragging them all around the courtyard while he would jump and bounce, showing and telling everyone that these men had healed him. Things got very peculiar then and the people who were crowding around got very reverent and one man got on his knees, getting ready to worship the two disciples. I saw that Peter was extremely uncomfortable with that. When someone bowed to him, he screamed out emphatically. He told them, "It was not my power that healed this man, but that Adonai," and Gammy repeated that word very respectfully, "had given His power and characteristics to His servant Jesus and through that name, everyone now had access to the healing power of God."

A long pause ensued as all three men sat back and wrestled with the unusual thought that the great Hashem would anoint a man with His supernatural essence. Also, Simon Peter's comment that such power could be accessed by using the name of Jesus was totally unexpected and unheard of in Jewish teaching. Both Gamaliel and Saul began searching their scriptural memory to find a previous example of this.

Saul interjected, "Rabbi, you have taught us that such an anointing is reserved for Messiah and Messiah alone."

"It is true that Messiah is the only one who receives it without measure, Saul, but we must remember that our sages and prophets were partially anointed at times, even Moses received the precious Torah under such inspiration," replied Gamaliel thoughtfully. "His physical body was so affected by the inspiration that his face shone. Our great King David was likened in his heart to have many qualities of Hashem as well."

This statement by Gamaliel surprised Saul, as it showed an unexpected accommodation of what he thought was an obvious error in the Galileans' teaching, but he kept silent.

Gamaliel then said something that shocked both Saul and Gammy. "How and why these common men get this anointing and why is it not on Annas or Caiaphas, well that is something that I don't understand at this point."

Was their father admitting by those words that these works were done with a heavenly anointing?

After a moment, Gammy picked up the story once again.

"The Chief Priests and the guards began to shove people away and tried to disperse them, but Peter pointed them out individually and accused them of being involved in the conspiracy to arrest Jesus and giving Him over to Pilate. Peter went further and accused us all when he said 'Pilate was determined to set this Jesus free, but we Jews insisted on his death'."

This was said in a question-like fashion and Gammy looked at his father.

Saul instantly remembered his personal encounter with Simon Peter and how quickly he had confessed to denying his Rabbi.

Did Peter now feel he was guiltless and could openly accuse other Jews?

Gamaliel realized that his previous knowledge of and participation in these events was what Gammy was puzzled about. With that, he felt he must explain himself to his son and his prize student. Quieting Gammy, he started his very personal account of recent events, hoping to finally make clear the snippets of information that these two had heard, plus possibly give his own actions some justification.

"It is true that for the last three years, all the leaders in Jerusalem had an ongoing battle with Jesus, and for various reasons. He came to the feasts as all good Jews do, but each time, He would teach the most controversial doctrines and openly criticize all of us, especially the High Priest. He always labelled us as hypocrites. Jesus was infuriated with that notorious scam at the money changers' tables at the Temple, as are many of us, and He did not have to dig very deep to find out that the High Priest's family were the main beneficiaries of that racket. Everyone is aware of that swindle and many of us appreciated that He had the courage to call them out but that was just one of disputes the priests had with Him. He always made the Sadducees look ridiculous when they would try to dupe Him with their tricky questions so, they also hated Him. The hardest thing for me was that He also accused us Pharisees of all forms of corruption. Besides calling us hypocrites, He said we were abusers of the people and men who put heavy loads on the poor and the uneducated, loads we ourselves were not willing to carry. Beside all of that, He accused us of being false teachers, purposely teaching error because we somehow profited from it and for doing this, He called us snakes and vipers. His accusations were very personal and also incendiary, often putting us in danger among the crowds. Sometimes, what He said had some truth and because of that, He even convinced some pious ones among us to become His followers."

"What was your involvement with his death, Father?" Gammy asked hesitantly but with directness, his pure heart wanting no more concealments.

Gamaliel lowered his eyes and continued. "Caiaphas had Jesus arrested on Passover evening and called as many of the Sanhedrin to his house as he could find. I was there."

With that Gamaliel dropped his head and stared at the ground for a moment. Finally, he regrouped and continued, "He had sent Malchus, his personal servant, along with the Captain of the Guard and some troops to Gethsemane, knowing from one of his spies that that was where Jesus usually slept. They dragged Jesus in and accused Him of blasphemies and heresies, of course using their usual paid mob of witnesses against Him. Every time I asked them to give their evidence, they contradicted each other." Gamaliel paused and quietly muttered, "I should have known better at that point. I should have been brave."

"A few accused Him of saying that He would destroy the Temple but others said that He also promised He would rebuild it in another three days. We could not get any agreement among the witnesses or even ourselves and Jesus never said a word, just watched us fumbling about. Caiaphas finally got frustrated and demanded of Him if He was the Anointed One, the Son of the Blessed and I heard Him say, 'I am and if I say different, I would be a liar like you'."

"When He said that, I was completely dumbfounded. He said that we would see him, the 'Son of Man,' in the realms where only Hashem exists. I could not excuse that statement but did not know just what to accuse Him of or how to proceed. Caiaphas tore his clothes at that, calling it blasphemy and demanded of each of us that were there, a proclamation of His guilt. We all had to agree with the Law that He was deserving of death because of His statements saying He was equal with Hashem. Some of our company became so incensed at Jesus that they spit on Him and the captain and the guards slapped Him openly. Early the next morning, we gathered at the Sanhedrin for more deliberation, but by then it was already concluded that He had to die. As you know, the Romans were the only ones who could put a man to death, so He was sent to Pilate."

"Is that what Peter was referring to about Pilate," asked Saul.

"Yes, Pilate examined Him but saw no crime that deserved death, thinking that this was another of our famous religious squabbles and he attempted to release Him. At that point, old Annas took no chances and arranged for his rented mob to put great pressure on Pilate. Eventually, 'we' succeeded in getting Him crucified, just as the big Galilean has charged."

Gamaliel almost spit out those last words. "I made no attempt to preserve Him or to protect Him, even if I thought He was only a deluded Jew. I should have stopped this crucifixion."

Gamaliel's words poured out, spoken like a guilty man confessing.

Saul bolted upright and rushed to his defense. "No, Rabbi, why do you think like that? He was guilty of blasphemy and got exactly what a blasphemer deserved. I am thankful that Pilate has now changed the policy that allows us to stone these types without having to get his approval."

It was obvious that Saul was defensive of his revered rabbi and deeply disturbed that Gamaliel would judge himself so harshly.

Looking at Saul with thankfulness for his love and loyalty, he countered, "Thank you for excusing me, Saul, but the events of the last couple of weeks and especially those of today are a warning that there may be many things about Jesus that we do not understand. I thought I was obeying the Law that night, but now I seriously wonder."

Saul was astonished that Gamaliel would speak in such a manner and he was getting a little annoyed with his wavering.

After a long pause, a subdued and almost tearful Gamaliel turned to Gammy. "Shimon, please continue with what happened today," he whispered to his son.

"Simon Peter continued accusing all who would listen of killing the Holy and Just One. He also called Jesus the Prince of Life and said it was Jehovah who raised him from the dead. He claimed it was 'belief' in Jesus's name that somehow generated the power that healed old Benjamin's ankles."

Gammy paused and looked at his father. "What did he mean by that, Father?" he asked.

Gamaliel stood up and paced a few troubled steps back and forth for a moment and then sat back down. Saul and Gammy remained quiet, their hearts burning to hear their revered teacher explain these strange happenings.

Finally, Gamaliel spoke. "There are many different issues about names that your report has raised, Gammy. First of all, you know that we Jews are forbidden to utter the sacred name of Hashem. We also know that when we pray in the name of Adonai, our Lord," and he whispered it respectfully, "we release important and much needed portions of the characteristics of our God upon ourselves simply by uttering that very precise description of Him. It is as close to using a name as we can come. All the other terms we use are not names but descriptions of the characteristics of the Holy One, but if we ever call on the 'name,' we are to expect that portion of the nature and blessings of our God to come upon us. I suspect that Peter was saying that using the name of Jesus releases such unique supernatural power upon the user."

"That most definitely is sacrilege," exclaimed Saul angrily.

Both Gamaliel and Gammy were surprised at the outburst and Gamaliel answered him quickly. "Not if he indeed was the Messiah."

Saul bolted again. This statement left him completely stunned. "What are you saying, Rabbi?" he finally asked.

"Saul, Moses taught us that Hashem appeared to Abraham and the patriarchs in many forms. Sometimes he appeared as angels, sometimes as heavenly priests, sometime as a pillar of fire, sometimes a cloud, but always to declare Himself as a friend and the supernatural Almighty. These different forms were the only way our patriarchs knew Him and encountered Him. Later, when we were called as a nation to serve Him, He entrenched Himself as our supernatural deity and now could be known and referred to as Adonai or Lord, our national leader, teacher, and of course, our God. We did not know Him that way before, and as Adonai, He led us, fed us, and delivered us. We cannot deny that Jehovah is continually revealing Himself in changing and more detailed ways as the centuries unfold."

Saul saw that this was true, but shook his head in disagreement. He was in no mood to give this Jesus any possible credence or legitimacy whatsoever.

Gamaliel noticed and paused, struggling to explain himself. "I am not saying that this Jesus was the expected Messiah, but when the Messiah does appear, He will greatly add to our understanding of Hashem's characteristics and our prophets say that in fact He will fully reveal Hashem's qualities in a human form. This would require a new and even more descriptive name that we currently do not know. Using it with the reverence it would deserve, as we do with the sacred name Adonai, for example, would then put us into a never-before known relationship with Hashem. I think that these disciples of Jesus may have accidently stumbled across the wellspring that Moses spoke of. I am astonished that such uneducated and ignorant fishermen could understand that complicated principle."

Saul interrupted. "So, are you saying that when these people use the name of Jesus, they actually believe that the qualities of Hashem are available and becoming united with them?"

"Yes, I believe that is what they are preaching," replied Gamaliel, looking into the eyes of Saul, "and that is different than just using the name of Jesus as a talisman, or a magical formula. I am not even sure they understand the full repercussions of what they teach."

"If it is the case that they truly believe this, then they are absolutely and totally deluded, and who knows where the powers are coming from that can do the otherworldly things they can. Do they even know?" asked Saul with a tinge of fear. "That makes them much more dangerous to our nation than we originally thought for they are using great truths to delude. We must withstand these forces and expose these disciples as wrong and deceived or they will lead many of our brothers into error thinking they are somehow displaying Elohim."

Gamaliel and Gammy remained silent after this last outburst of Saul's. Saul noticed this silence but was not going to be dismayed from his condemnations.

"Don't you agree, Rabbi?" he asked, almost as a challenge.

"You are correct to question me on this, as only a few years ago, I taught you both that the ability of this Jesus to do the miraculous things reported was because He was using demonic powers," Gamaliel admitted. "After today, I am not so convinced," he stated hesitantly.

He noticed the panicked look on Saul's face.

"A couple of years ago, when one of our teacher's accused Him of casting out demons by the power of Beelzebub, He made a simple statement that I cannot get out of my head. He said that a house divided against itself could not stand. Every time someone got healed or a demonic spirit was cast out by Jesus, it proved to be a good thing and a blessing to that person and their family and the person's life was always better for it in the end. It does not fit with our teaching that a demonic power would make someone's life better. We believe all good things and all blessings come from Hesham."

"But you also taught us that even the good things from Hashem can be used for bad purposes, as with the Ark being carried into battle, only to lose it," declared a shaken Saul.

"Ah, yes, Saul," answered Gamaliel, "but the Ark itself was not evil."

"I am not entirely sure where the power comes from, but these miraculous events only serve to delude the people further and to sidetrack Israel from our calling and that, in the end, is an evil thing," argued a defiant Saul.

Gammy tactfully jumped in, asking, "Father, they talked about faith in Jesus's name making them whole. What exactly would that mean?"

"I have heard that term 'faith' used to describe an overwhelming belief that goes beyond logically agreeing with a notion," started Gamaliel. "This belief is a spiritual understanding that does not originate from study, logic, debate or even any desire to believe something on the believer's part. This is akin to being possessed by an unprovable thought, so much so that your mind is completely convinced and no reasoning or debate shakes that. One who experiences this 'faith' is completely convinced of the truthfulness of it and it stems from sources well beyond human learning, from somewhere deep within, just as our 'faith' in Moses."

Gamaliel thought about that for a few seconds and then added, "Possibly like the difference between the state of mind of Joshua and Caleb and the ten other men sent to spy out the land. It is written that they had a different spirit about them. They saw everything totally different and they believed it differently. A different set of eyes leading to different conclusions. Possibly that is what they mean when they refer to faith."

The discussion continued with Saul and Gammy describing the rest of the events on the Temple Mount, including the detention of the two men, the reaction of the crowd to the healing and then, the actions of the priests and guards. Gamaliel listened intently, knowing that he would be dealing with this issue in the early morning and he wanted this unbiased report as his buffer from what he knew would be a contentious and potentially distorted trial.

When they had finished their report and each man was momentarily lost in his thoughts, Gamaliel turned to Saul and asked if he could speak with him privately.

Gammy rose and left quietly and quickly.

Gamaliel poured himself a little more wine and Saul also accepted some, sensing the intense religious discussions they had just had were over. He was curious as to what was on the rabbi's mind and he was a little apprehensive that Gamaliel was somehow aware of his secretive pact with Samuel.

"Saul, I must talk to you about your sister Miriam," Gamaliel started.

Saul gasped, almost choking on his wine, guessing that his sister had indeed upset the peaceful atmosphere of the house with her bold real estate adventures. The wrath of the High Priest's family would most certainly be directed toward Gamaliel when they realized who she was and where she lived.

"Rabbi, I must explain. I did not know the situation with the High Priest's family when I encouraged her to proceed with her plan to open a business on the Cardo. If I had known, I would not have agreed to this purchase, even though I have nothing but confidence that she can make a business succeed," Saul declared apologetically and much too quickly.

"Much has taken place in the last few days," he continued, "and I know that I have not been as diligent as I should have been. I should have watched over her better." He was babbling on, making no sense.

Gamaliel silenced Saul with an upraised hand and an amused chuckle.

"Saul, all is well. You have indeed been a busy man since you returned but in that time I and my family have had the pleasant opportunity to be around and spend time with your beautiful and accomplished sister. Miriam and I also had a long conversation about this adventure into business and I made her acutely aware of all the snares and hurdles she would face. I also asked that she clear it with you. She initially asked about the wisdom of taking on the High Priest's family when she found that the stall was for sale and I encouraged her to proceed but warned her that your name would be implicated. I personally would enjoy seeing someone as clever and judicious as Miriam sparring with the lacky scribes and lawyers of Caiaphas and Annas. I also suspect that many others in Jerusalem would appreciate that as well. In the short time we have known her, we have become convinced that she is both wise and extraordinarily calculating when she has to be, but always in a very pleasant way. I am sure she will make this endeavor succeed no matter how ambitious it seems or how much you watch over her," the smiling Rabbi said, lovingly poking Saul in the chest.

Gamaliel paused, thoroughly enjoying the look on the face of a stunned and now completely confused Saul.

"That is not the main reason I want to talk to you, Saul."

Saul could not imagine what was coming next.

"It seems that you may be the last to notice, but my son Shimon is completely stricken by your sister. Up until now, he has successfully avoided all the prancing and parading girls of Jerusalem and eluded all the marriage proposals that the mothers of this city have imagined for their precious daughters. All that being true, he has now become a lovestruck child around Miriam. He has asked me to approach you and ask for her hand in marriage."

Saul's mouth dropped.

"Even if he hadn't asked for her hand, my wife and daughter would have forced me to adopt Miriam and steal her away from you and make her part of our family as they have learned to love her deeply in these few short weeks."

Gamaliel stopped talking and sat back and watched Saul.

The unease and foreboding in Saul vanished and a relieved sag engulfed his tense shoulders. A large smile broke out on his face and he exclaimed to Gamaliel, "Indeed, I am the last one to know this thing."

He paused, laughing out loud, and then asked, "Has my sister any knowledge of this, ahh, attraction?"

Gamaliel laughed again. "Saul, I think you have a special gift for missing the obvious. She has no doubt noticed his giddiness and has understood there was an intense interest involved. Although you are the first to be outwardly approached, I am positive that she will not be surprised."

"Well, I am totally in favor but I must talk to Miriam about this. I would not want to agree without knowing that she wants this also," said Saul, almost joyfully.

He did not need any time to decide if Gammy was worthy of his sister for he knew the man intimately and could not want anything better for Miriam.

"Understood," said a rising Gamaliel, "and let me know when you and your sister have talked. Right now, Gammy is a very dreamy, preoccupied young man," he said laughingly. "You and I definitely need him more focused than he has been, don't we?"

CHAPTER FORTY-SEVEN

The Trial

It was late and Miriam had retired when Saul returned to their rooms. He pondered the day's events long into the night before drifting into a fitful sleep, waking a little later than he usually did. He hurried to his classroom, dropping off that day's prepared discussions and assigning the supervision to his surprised but most senior student. He and Gammy found each other outside their classrooms and they hurried to the Temple to find a good spot on the spectator's bench at the Hall of Hewn Stones. They were there to watch how Gamaliel and the whole Sanhedrin would deal with Simon Peter and his friend.

They were definitely not going to miss this.

During their quick walk through the wakening streets, Saul was stealing sideways looks at his possible brother-in-law, examining this man closely while vivid memories of their playful youth flooded his mind with every familiar street and well-known corner. They had scoured every part of this city as youthful partners and sometimes rambunctious boys and now Saul was getting a little glum. He was realizing that such days were almost over and things would now be forever changed with the approach of all things adult.

When they reached the Hall of Hewn Stones, they were not at all surprised that the large spectator's seating area, consisting of rows of ascending stone blocks directly across the room from the raised seating of the Sanhedrin members, was almost completely full. They squeezed themselves into a spot directly across from the large presidential chair of Gamaliel who was standing off to the side discussing things with a small but serious looking group of Sanhedrin judges.

Another immaculately gilded chair, immediately to Gamaliel's right, was occupied by Annas, the aged father-in-law of Caiaphas the High Priest, who himself sat a little further from the center of the dais. This was a curious arrangement and it was obvious to all that it was meant to show who actually wielded the power of the priestly family. Indeed, it was Annas who had appointed his son-in-law as the High Priest to begin with. Today, Caiaphas was strategically surrounded by other members of his direct family, a menacing group of men with wealth and influence in Jerusalem who sat very close to the seats of power both in life and in this courtroom.

All the members of that family were present today and were gathered in a tight gaggle, solemnly whispering to each other. It was unusual to see all the representatives of this wealthy family agreeing on anything for it was widely known that they did not particularly like each other. Gamaliel correctly anticipated that they had been directed to be here to vote as a block, a political move meant to reinforce the wishes of Annas and Caiaphas. To see them so interested in the plight of Jesus's disciples, a rural and politically powerless bunch, was indeed strange.

Next to them was a contingent of heavily-bearded, very solemn, and overt scholarly men, many who were life-long devotees of Pharisaical teachings and whose judgments usually ranged in degree from the gentler approach of the House of Hillel to the stringent attitude of the House of Shammai. How their vote would split on any matter was always in question. This morning they were all wearing their very best robes and all bore a very serious countenance while bobbing their heads to each other in rapt discussion.

Saul noticed Samuel, his Shammai-ite friend, enter with a contingent of five younger students and for a moment he wondered about the wisdom of bringing youthful minds to this divided court. Samuel noticed Saul and sauntered up and greeted him warmly as an old friend. He looked at Gammy and although they knew each other well, simply nodded their acknowledgements curtly. Samuel, unexpectantly and with a flair of joviality, wedged his way onto the stone bench beside Saul, leaving his students standing awkwardly at the back of the hall.

Looking around the richly decorated room, complete with stunning red and blue draperies covering the stone walls, Saul noticed Gamaliel's close friend Nicodemus standing with another small group, isolated unto themselves. These were peaceable and honorable men known for their wisdom who always added a quiet, serene influence to the larger Sanhedrin. Gamaliel, as President, attempted to ensure that there always was a good representation of this type of non-political and sensible discernment in this fractioned body.

Also present and a part of the Sanhedrin Council were seven men of the Sadducees. These were rich men, some of whom were lawyers, but all were reliable supporters of and close social contacts of the High Priest's family. Over the years, many of their children had intermarried with that powerful family making a spider's web of confusing relationships.

Most Sadducees conducted business and functioned in their private lives with the help and counsel of the priestly family and most had acquired large portions of their wealth through obscure and complicated technicalities in the law. Because they were constrained in their actions only if Moses openly declared something as absolutely wrong, they were not burdened by personal morality or the nebulous "godly" spirit of the Law that some men were. This left them in the profitable circumstance that some described as "having no conscience." This condition allowed them to prey upon widows' estates in their lawyerly capacity and they often ended up owning poor people's lands by using legal tricks endorsed by their friend, the High Priest. All who wished to be wealthy envied this beneficial relationship and Jerusalem was generously sprinkled with many men who comically contorted themselves, attempting to garner the aura of legitimacy that Caiaphas' friendship bestowed upon his "questionable" partners. These seven, dressed in their best, moved about together, smugly aware of the envious stares of most in the hall.

Saul's eyes were drawn to the wide-open northern doors where, just slightly outside, stood a man who had the rigid demeanor of a Roman centurion. He was not in military uniform but he was easily identified by all who passed him when entering the hall. His erect military bearing, his Roman-style closely cropped hair and a deep red scar from ear to jaw easily identified him and it was obvious that he was not the least concerned about disguising himself. He appeared to be merely observing the proceedings but as his cold stare landed on many in the room, a shiver would run down their spines. As the court was open to all, no one could be certain if this was an officially assigned duty or just an unusual personal interest. Today, this one did not enter the hall itself, preferring to remain a few feet outside in the Court of the Gentiles. It was a convenient place where he could still observe and hear all the proceedings through the open doors and yet look up at his colleagues.

Soon, the shofars sounded their morning blasts and next door, the haunting ceremonial music of the Temple started up.

Gamaliel promptly sat in his chair.

All members quickly took their places and of the seventy-one spots, all but three were taken on this morning. It was an unusually large turnout.

Gamaliel began the proceedings by calling them to order with a loud voice and then he began explaining as best he could the activities of the previous afternoon, not adding any hint of preconceived judgment. Every pause in his speech was followed by muttered conversations and barbs thrown back and forth between each group of the obviously divided court. His commands for silence would call them back to order quickly.

He dealt with the first charge against the disciples.

The Sadducees had accused them of speaking and teaching of a resurrection. This charge was constantly being brought before the Sanhedrin by the Sadducees and, just as expected, it was again today. It did not seem to matter who was being charged or for what because the Sadducees just loved embarrassing the rest of the Sanhedrin members into defending themselves and their religious beliefs in the afterlife. This belief, they piously announced, was not a recorded teaching of Moses and was therefore a punishable heresy.

"Brothers, we would be foolish to accuse these men of any wrongdoing regarding the resurrection, as we cannot come to any agreement on this matter among ourselves," Gamaliel stated as he had done many times before.

As he spoke, Gamaliel looked directly at the agitated Sadducee delegation, who did not like their specific charge trivialized and so easily dismissed. They all rose in a noisy but predictable protest, upset that their indictment was once again discounted by Gamaliel and this seemed to be a cue to another large group sitting together in the viewing seats who also rose and began yelling and waving their arms in protest.

Gamaliel sat calmly waiting, having seen this performance before and knowing that this minor storm would soon lose its momentum. When it finally quieted, he rose and spoke again.

"There are only two issues that I see as relevant among all the others that you brothers have brought to me this morning." He looked up and down the seated hall, judging the reactions of the various groups.

"The first is, by what power these otherwise ignorant men can do these undeniable supernatural happenings, and secondly and probably more serious, is the issue of the name they use."

The hall quieted and it became immediately obvious that most of the congregation had not thought this through to the extent that Gamaliel had. By these words, they were challenged by the wisdom of the President to act in a legal and judicial manner instead of an unruly emotional demonstration.

"I understand that we want to accuse these men of using a name of God in vain, as Moses commanded us not to do in his third commandment. To do so, we must show to this court and thereby to all Israel, that to use Jesus's name as Hashem's, blessed be He, is indeed sacrilege. Also, brethren, remember that these are uneducated and ignorant fishermen. To show sacrilege, we must prove that they are knowingly rebellious to Jehovah by suggesting that they can now use that name as a substitute for the unspoken Creator's name. We know that speaking the name of Hashem releases the great qualities of our creator and we must prove that such an event did not happen yesterday."

Gamaliel paused, thinking deeply and then continued. "Brothers, we must make good judgments today, as this "Way" is gathering many followers and we must make certain not to fracture our nation further. We also must attempt to reconcile any who are deceived or misled before condemning them."

This statement was followed by a chorus of muttering, some in agreement, but many dissenting.

"Let us bring in the two men and inquire of them. Then we will know how to approach this problem," Gamaliel said, nodding to the Captain of the Guard who was waiting at the northern doorway.

The captain had regaled himself with knife and sword for today's event and was standing across the doorway from the quiet Roman in an outward act of defiance. He and his men were the only men in Judea who dared brandish a sword around as part of their duty and he was not letting this opportunity to strut in the presence of a Roman centurion slip away. At Gamaliel's command, he spun around, gathered more men, and disappeared.

Saul turned to Gammy and commented, "Your father's wisdom certainly gives this place a much-needed atmosphere of legitimacy."

Gammy smiled proudly.

A few minutes later, the crowd quieted as the captain and three large and heavily-armed guards led the two detainees in. The two Galileans were simply dressed and a little disheveled with wild and unkept hair, but otherwise they walked in confidently and the whole congregation's eyes were locked on them. One guard led them to the middle of the chamber, immediately in front of Gamaliel and the High Priest.

Annas jumped up immediately, his hand was in the air and he wanted to speak. He wanted all to know that he took these proceedings seriously, so seriously that he was quite willing to step on the toes of Gamaliel if need be. He also wanted all to know that he and Caiaphas had personally been the objects of attack by many of these disciples of Jesus.

"It has been reported that you two fishermen," and a tittering of laughter arose in the chamber at Annas' excessive drawing out of the word fishermen with an accompanying derogatory Galilean accent, "healed the lame man who begged at Beautiful. By what strange power did you do this?" He again dragged out the word "power" sarcastically, hoping that all would recall that he and others had already labeled all miracles done by Jesus as demonic.

This was a melodramatic and exaggerated performance of the kind that Annas was famous for, easily assuming the role of prosecutor and comedian.

"And further, by what name did you do this," he added.

Annas was convinced that he could make the case that they were calling on a false deity by using the name of Jesus and with his performance, he did not want the seriousness of that charge to be lessened in any way by a show of civility by Gamaliel. From experience, he understood that many of the judges could be swayed by argument and he wanted to be the one in control of that.

Just then a commotion erupted at the south door of the Sanhedrin, that rarely-used door that led from the inner Men's Court of the Temple. Normally locked, today the door flung wide open and Benjamin the beggar, familiar to all who had passed him every time they entered the women's court, pushed his way past the surprised Levite priests in the inner court and with shouts of praise to Jehovah, came leaping and jumping into the middle of the Sanhedrin.

Shocking all, he began dancing about in his tattered and slightly rank garments, waving his completely unnecessary walking stick and pointing it at his two healthy and completely healed ankles. A roar went up around the room and all who had not been present yesterday were suddenly smitten with alarm at seeing the perfect ankles that had been so bent and twisted. Benjamin, upon seeing their amazed looks, purposely jumped higher and shouted louder and then he clutched the shoulders of Simon Peter and his young friend, John, in a loving embrace.

Caiaphas' secret command to bar Benjamin from the hall had been skirted by the cagey old cripple. He had risen early and was, as expected, first in line to present a sacrifice for his cleansing which allowed him into the inner men's court. None had suspected that he would use that forgotten door to enter the judgment hall, thereby leaving Caiaphas' two guards standing aimlessly at the curved steps of the Woman's court.

Two other well prepared sentries had waited at the north door of this very hall to block him and now they ran and grabbed Benjamin, attempting to hold him down and stop his incessant leaping. The absurd result was that they ended up with pieces of his putrid clothing in their hands and were not hindering the dancing man at all.

Caiaphas finally stepped in. He knew any further move against the healed man would now be regarded extremely poorly, so he grabbed the two sentries and after smacking them forcefully on their heads, sent them back out the main door. A roar of laughter echoed off the uncut stones at that ridiculous and exaggerated scene.

Saul and Gammy looked at each other with huge grins and Samuel jumped up and approached Benjamin. He was looking intently at his ankles and then closely studying his face. Many others rushed over and examined the exuberant man, who alternated between jumping, praising God and rubbing his new legs. The hall became a stirring mass, all wanting to inspect Benjamin, some even touching and feeling the perfect ankles and leg bones and nodding approvingly.

After many minutes, a very annoyed Annas yelled, "Silence!"

All slowly returned to their seats, still wagging their heads in amazement and Annas turned his attention back to the two smiling Galileans in front of him who were now accompanied by their new, very noisy, and continually bouncing friend.

"Well, what do you have to say," he demanded, looking away. All this time, Annas had purposely averted his eyes from those perfect and infuriating ankles.

Benjamin picked up on Annas' discomfort and danced over directly in front of the High Priest and his arrogant father-in-law. He propped one leg up on the raised dais and pointed at it, wagging his head and holding his hands in an exaggerated, hands-upturned, querying motion. Getting no response, he changed legs and pointed again. Only then did he get a grudging non-committal nod of approval from Annas, a very hesitant recognition that something had indeed happened.

The big man, the one called Simon Peter, said calmly, "Rulers and elders of the people"—he looked up and down the rows of gathered men of the Sanhedrin— "are we being judged this day for an act of kindness shown to a crippled man?"

He put his big arm around the beaming Benjamin, turning him about so all could see. "Or are we called to account of how he was healed?"

He waited, but no reply came.

"Well, what are we charged with? You arrested us."

Annas, reading the mood of the gathered crowd and how excited and pleased they were that the poor cripple could now walk, spouted a quick, "Just how did this happen? Explain yourself."

Impishly, Benjamin inched his way directly in front of Annas and began a quick-stepping dance which ended with him leaping ecstatically, causing another roar of uncontrollable laughter to roll through the spectators, which in turn, made the High Priest shake with rage.

Simon Peter continued. "Then know this, you and all men of Israel." He pointed a finger at Annas and then to the whole Sanhedrin before turning and including all the spectators. "It is by the name of Jesus of Nazareth."

Annas and many others on both sides of the floor jumped up and shouts of "blasphemy" and "no" rang out.

Peter waited a little for things to quiet and then in a loud, booming voice, shouted out while staring directly at the High Priest and his father-in-law, "Who you," and his arm started at the High Priest and continued around the hall once again, "crucified."

The tumult that arose was deafening and was heard all the way into the Temple courtyards. Peter, now completely in control of the gathering, waved his arms to silence them and continued. "But whom Adonai raised from the dead."

The arrogant and previously quiet Sadducees, men who had been diabolically enjoying the uncomfortable proceedings so far, jumped and screeched their disagreement at the mention of anyone rising from the dead.

Peter, ignoring them, continued. "It is by that name," and he paused to let that thought about a name and all its deep significance, sink into the minds of all the teachers and scribes who were listening intently, "that this man stands before you completely healed."

At that, Benjamin restarted his hilarious jumping and strutting about, pausing in front of the angriest of the chamber, adding twists and turns into his joyous dance, smiling intensely and beaming, even spinning about like a child would.

That Benjamin was completely whole was evident, this could not be denied and the whole crowd was stunned into a forced silence as Peter's accusations and the explanation of this event began to sink in. To emphasize it, Benjamin continued his antics and then began showing off the completely straightened leg bones by running back and forth for the whole length of the room. He ran right out the door to a great gathered crowd who screamed in praise and, strangely, he stopped at the door to show himself to the Roman, even pointing up to the towers of Antonia where many soldiers were watching, leaning out of the windows and waving back happily to this healed man. Curiously, the Roman soldiers seemed very happy for him.

The younger disciple spoke quietly to Simon Peter, who nodded and raised his hand again, calling for silence. "Jesus, the man, is the very cornerstone that you supposed builders have rejected and now He has become the chief cornerstone."

His quoting of the revered psalms of King David and applying them to Jesus, was disturbing to the teachers in the crowd as Peter's words totally disagreed with their doctrine when explaining this portion. This was one of many mysterious references to Messiah that could not be fully understood until He arrived, they taught in their classrooms.

Peter continued with this reference. "For as David said, blessed is he that comes in the name of the Lord." Then Peter loudly stated, "So now, this very day, there is no other name under Heaven given among men."

Peter heavily emphasized the word "name" so that there would be no misunderstanding of what he meant. The hall erupted once again for many long and tumultuous minutes, the crowd now knew without a doubt that he was claiming a new name for their Holy God and to them, that thought was totally unacceptable and unlawful. "Salvation is only in that name," Peter shouted at the first lull in the tumult.

Everyone in the hall recognized that there were serious and insidious ramifications to what this man was saying and to accept any part was to believe that Messiah had already appeared. This proclamation flew directly in the face of the highly-educated Jews, those who taught Messiah's coming would re-establish a glorious Jewish kingdom by defeating the enslaving Romans and bring an era of peace to the world.

Their Messiah could not be killed by any individual or gathered power, including the Romans or the Jews and they all were convinced that was impossible. No, they absolutely could not accept this. These claims were ridiculous. To accept the renaming of Hesham to Jesus was opening the door to grave error.

Saul's agile mind was among the first to understand the danger of what the big man was claiming. He was now absolutely convinced that the Sanhedrin had to act quickly against them and fortunately, Jehovah Himself had set the punishment for such blasphemies. This was without question a desecrating of His holy name for vain reasons and a serious breach of the third commandment of Moses.

Samuel leaned over and confided, "I told you they were much more devious than what appears on the surface."

Saul nodded an agreement. Gammy also heard this but showed no response.

The court, Annas, Caiaphas, and Gamaliel all seemed stunned into inaction with these statements and Saul stirred impatiently, anxious for immediate judgment. He was beginning to get annoyed at the delay and confusion of the council and he could not understand the hesitancy. This was an obvious violation of the Law but the court seemed paralyzed by the outward confidence and boldness of the two followers of Jesus. They had just spoken accusingly to the court's leaders and had showed the same low regard for the elders and priests that Jesus had shown on His visits to the Temple and no one had yet rebuked them.

These lowly, poorly-clad and antagonistic Galileans were clearly not the same men as when they scattered in fear at Jesus' arrest.

The men of Jerusalem who gathered in the Sanhedrin this morning loved rhetorical and doctrinal arguments and lived for the bantering around of ancient words and theories, but this time they were completely bewildered and stymied. What they and all in the chamber had a problem with was not so much the words being cited, but the dancing, prancing and very rowdy Benjamin and his perfect and for most, highly seditious ankles.

Gamaliel, sensing that any more questions or answers were not needed, asked the captain to take the two disciples of Jesus, along with the noisy Benjamin, outside the chamber and hold them there.

As soon as the door was closed, calls for their stoning rang out, followed quickly by other calls to let them go for they had done a good deed. The gathering was divided in many directions, and vehemently so. Arguments between the factions began and spread through the seated witnesses as well, with a shoving match erupting near the Sadducees and pleading peacemakers running around to restore order. At it noisiest time, a few awkward fists were thrown but only one landed on the skull of a nearby spectator.

Gamaliel jumped up and silenced them all and calmed the chamber. He then slowly recapped what was said.

Technically, he pronounced, they had not used a name of Hashem for their personal benefit or for vanity; it was Benjamin who had benefited, so they could not be condemned for using it to benefit themselves. A loud, disagreeing groan went through the crowd as Gamaliel reread the commandment and its directive to avoid using the Lord's name in "vain."

This was a legal technicality, no doubt, and cleverly used by Gamaliel. They had done a good thing for someone else, he stated, and none could deny that.

That they were trying to apply the name of Jesus to Messiah was troublesome he admitted, and if they had outrightly rejected the traditional names of Hesham or Adonai, it would definitely be blasphemy, Gamaliel allowed. But they had used the acceptable "Adonai," albeit a little more commonly than most Jews would dare, and thus they were not in total violation of the use of a name of God. This convoluted reasoning caught the court off guard and no one challenged Gamaliel on his statement. In fact, most were thoroughly confused by his explanation.

On promoting the name of Jesus, Gamaliel agreed that this must cease and they must be warned of possible punishment, an action to which much of the hall awkwardly agreed.

What had slipped by most in the chamber was that Gamaliel never challenged that the disciples had used the "goodness" of God to somehow deliver the cripple.

Peter and John were recalled and the grinning and irritating Benjamin followed immediately behind them, shifting about in a quiet, continual dance that every few seconds required a small leap left or right. Someone outside had draped him in a new blue robe but his brand-new feet and ankles were still very visible.

Annas rose, again taking the lead away from Gamaliel and spoke in a squeaky high-pitched monotone, "It is the judgment of this pious court, appointed by the traditions of our holy ancestors and made of the wisest and most trusted men in Israel, that we extend mercy and justice to you. We will not punish you for your arrogance to us for we are merciful men, but we demand that you no longer speak about Jesus or teach in His name or do any deeds in His name from this time forward."

He looked about the chamber to obtain the nod of consensus of each member.

Nicodemus and three others close to him rose and turned their backs to Annas as an outward sign of disagreement. These four were alone in this opinion. Annas flicked his immaculate robe at them as if tossing those objectors aside.

Peter and John looked at each other and smiled and then Peter approached the podium. When only a few feet away, he said directly to Annas, "If you are indeed true judges of Israel, then we ask you to decide this. Should we obey you, or should we obey God?"

The room went deadly silent. Peter spent a long minute looking at a stammering Annas and then he turned and scanned all the Sanhedrin while waiting for a reply. He received none, in fact, most of the judges completely avoiding his eyes. He walked the length of the room, hands outstretched, pleading for an answer, searching faces for the response that did not come.

He stopped directly in front of Gamaliel and Annas and said, "Then we cannot help speaking about the things we have heard and seen with our very eyes. These are not vague conclusions arrived at in a secret corner of some school of yours. This was done directly in front of your very eyes."

Annas jumped up again. "We are warning you, if you preach in that name again, you will be arrested and punished, or worse."

Meanwhile, Benjamin had drifted to the large open door, past the sharp-eyed but expressionless centurion and was again showing his new ankles to the exuberant and milling crowd that had gathered outside. Upon seeing him, another jubilant roar erupted and they began praising God and singing about His goodness to Benjamin once again.

The effect on the Sanhedrin was immediate and Annas, not knowing what to do next, turned his back on the two disciples.

A recognizable psalm of David rose in the courtyard in increasing waves of jubilant praise, the sheer volume bringing worried looks to those inside the chamber.

In the confusion, Gamaliel took the opportunity to hurriedly release the two and declare the session closed. The hall began emptying.

Saul remained seated, watching intently as Peter and John were swallowed up by the boisterous and joyful crowd. He was furious, feeling as if the Sanhedrin had made a horrible mistake allowing these men to continue deluding the easily influenced and uneducated among them. It was more of those very unlearned Jews who were making such a dangerous ruckus outside and that uproar was the undeniable proof of such delusion. Celebrating Romans were now also dangerously involved, a good number hanging out the window openings of their fortress, smiling and very happy for Benjamin. Even the centurion at the door was smiling.

How long would the Romans remain just spectators of this division, he asked himself angrily.

Saul remained in his stony seat long afterwards and he was deeply bothered, almost sick to his stomach with Gamaliel's lack of condemnation, indeed, almost a collusion with the blasphemous application of a name of Hashem. This case was ideal for that purpose and it cried out for the punishment that Gamaliel was so obviously avoiding. Saul's growing worry was that this tolerance of obvious sacrilege would spread like a disease throughout the Jews and eventually bring about another national punishment by God and he was appalled at that thought.

Did not Hashem punish Israel when they showed misguided mercy and refused to severely punish the law-breakers?

This was the unfortunate pattern of this nation which had historically suffered many national calamities for abandoning the strict principals of the Law and Saul wondered if he had just witnessed something that again was a stench to the nostrils of God.

He finally rose and walked slowly and solitarily out of the hall, purposely avoiding Gammy and the crowd. He was wandering about in deep thought when his Shammai-ite friend, Samuel sidled up beside him.

"Well, my friend, what do you think about that?"

Saul knew Samuel would not be happy with the leniency shown to the two men, but he still felt he must defend Gamaliel.

"I am not sure anything else could be done," he reluctantly replied.

Samuel snorted in derision. "I fear that Israel will pay a heavy price if we keep allowing such breeches of the Law. We must be strong and defend the Torah and not be afraid of doing what needs to be done, or who we must confront," he said, challenging Saul's answer. "A man getting his bones straightened is not a reason to accommodate sacrilege. In fact, what looks like a blessing becomes evil when it is used to deceive good Jews." Samuel turned and pointed back to the judgement hall and said, "That disgusting display of leadership just proved our point."

Saul could not counter Samuel's argument. It was Gamaliel who had previously taught the premise that unexplainable supernatural occurrences, including fleshly interventions like healings, could be done by evil forces. Saul was wondering if Gamaliel was now completely changing his stance on that.

Samuel gathered his young students and waved a curt goodbye to Saul and disappeared down the Pilgrim's Road. Saul made his way back to his classroom and, although preoccupied, continued the day's lesson. He could not get what Samuel had said off his mind.

CHAPTER FORTY-EIGHT

Miriam's Business

Just as she had told Saul, Miriam had used the morning to contact the former owner of her stall and make the purchase of his remaining five stalls. Between them, they wrote a small note of agreement, Miriam paid him all the money and the deal was finalized within minutes. The old merchant seemed over-joyed that the pact was completed quickly and it was obvious that he wanted this portion of his life to be behind him. His unease and anxiousness while the paperwork was being processed caused Miriam to question if he was regretting the sale or if he was not feeling well. He related to her that he was indeed upset but only because he was waiting to hear important news from the Sanhedrin. Two dear friends, as he called them, were on trial there and he wanted to join other friends in prayer for their release.

Miriam avoided mentioning her close relationship to Gamaliel, the President of the Sanhedrin and upon leaving, the kindly man prayed a devout blessing on her, on her house and on all her future endeavors.

The old merchant's home was very close to where she had met with Barnabas and only a few blocks from the bustling Cardo and within minutes, Miriam was back at her shop. She had left him and the peaceful atmosphere of his home, only to be surrounded by the noise and commotion of the markets and in that drastic transition, Miriam realized that today's dealings had also irreversibly launched her into a new era of her life. From this day on, the easy-going and sedate existence of her adolescence was a thing of the past.

Strolling amongst the bustle of the street, Miriam circled her shop, visualizing it from every angle and picturing just how she could set her merchandise displays up and imagining tables and shelving lining the now bare stone walls. As she pictured her new stall, thoughts of the products and treatments that she would introduce began to excite and energize her. She was not just an adventurous Jewish girl using the old and sometimes questionable medical remedies, she was now beginning a business that would be depended on by sick and dying people, people desperate for help. This new endeavor would be much more demanding than anything she had attempted in her short life and she was realizing that she needed to greatly expand her knowledge and become an expert on all treatments. Undaunted at that challenge, Miriam instead smiled and realized that she was looking forward to this, indeed, this is exactly why she was drawn to this endeavor.

In one way, she was a little concerned. She would be scrutinized very closely and no doubt be attacked and criticized by those whom she had affronted merely by purchasing the stalls, but she told herself that this was to be seen as a blessing for it would force her and her business to be above reproach in everything it did.

Enthused and wanting to address these hurdles immediately, Miriam became even more eager to speak with Barnabas and speed the purchase of the supplies that he and his brothers could find. She was more than a little curious to hear the personal story he had promised her.

When the long, drawn-out trumpet blast from the Temple Mount finally sounded indicating midday, she hurried to the house of Barnabas' sister Mary. As she approached and was about to knock on the outer gate, she was stopped by a crescendo of voices coming from inside that sounded like hundreds of people speaking loudly at the same time. She stood back from the door and listened, realizing that the people inside were praying out loud and in unison. Suddenly, one voice rose above the others, saying, "Why do the heathen rage, and the people plot in vain? The kings of the earth take their stand, and the rulers gather together against the Lord and against His Anointed One."

Miriam froze, hand raised but unable to knock, hearing many other voices rise. Some of the voices were muttering general prayers for help and some were speaking of events that seemed to be referring to Jesus and she was catching snippets of others as well. The united pleas reached a peak when the many voices joined in asking for boldness to speak about Jesus even the more. That was soon followed by another petition rising in volume which beseeched God to continue to do miracles and wondrous signs in the name of His Holy servant, Jesus. Such detailed and specific prayers were completely foreign to Miriam, none of them following the traditional memorized entreaties of traditional Jewish prayers.

A chorus of amens rained down and just then, the ground began vibrating and the gate itself started rattling back and forth. Miriam stepped back from the shaking gate suspecting a small earthquake was happening and she grabbed the opposite wall for stability. She looked around but saw no other gates moving and she quickly realized that the vibrations came only from this house. Miriam stood motionless, confused, and suddenly, quite frightened. The vibrating ground continued for many minutes.

Astonished and afraid, Miriam sensibly decided to not bother Barnabas today.

She began a very slow and deliberate walk home, completely astounded by what she had just experienced and equally troubled that her logical mind could not process these strange events. Normally, she could quickly make sense of everything in her world.

When she arrived home, she penned a note of regret to Barnabas, asking if they could meet the next day at noon instead and sent a young boy servant to his house. She waited in the courtyard until the lad returned with a confirmation of the next day's meeting and only then did her anxiousness ease slightly.

When she started up the stairs, Gammy's sister Leah appeared and waved at her from the courtyard below. She was smiling a strange, knowing grin and Miriam returned the smile and wave but was confused by the smirk and giggling of Leah.

Was she missing something? What had she overlooked and why was Leah smiling like she knew a deep secret, the kind that girls loved to share and of which Miriam knew nothing?

Miriam remained in her apartment the rest of that day, sifting through her scrolls with her many notes on various medicines, completely lost in lists and compilations while the afternoon wore on. Her thinking alternated between her new business venture and what had taken place at Mary's house and added to that, she kept getting interrupted by the image of the devious look on Leah's face.

Her list of required medicines took a lot longer to complete than she had first thought because of the persistent interruptions in her thoughts and soon, she was getting a little annoyed with herself. Something was up, she decided, but she would resist the temptation to ask. Stubbornly, she would wait for Leah to explain.

Today's inexplicable events at Mary's house had made her nervous about tomorrow's meeting with Barnabas and, even armed with her long lists, she had a feeling that their meeting would be less about the importing business than about other very unusual things. She also decided it would be best to keep her meetings with Barnabas, complete with the rattling doors, confidential. From all the hints and clues she was receiving, Miriam sensed the strain that just mentioning the name of Jesus or His followers created, not only for Saul, but for others of this household.

Saul arrived home later in the afternoon, momentarily interrupting her meditations and it was clear that he was also in a troubled state. They knew each other well enough to know they both needed a little space and time. Miriam fixed a plate of fresh dates and other fruits she had purchased that morning in her wanderings in the Cardo and then poured them both a small goblet of fine Shiloh wine she found two doors down from her stall at the wine and olive oil seller's. The food and the wine had its intended effect and both began to relax.

Saul's mind went to the conversation he had with Gamaliel just last night about his sister and he searched deeply for the words to begin the discussion he knew he must have with her.

"Miriam," he started, "Gamaliel approached me last night about you."

Her thoughts began racing ahead, immediately wondering why she was being spoken about. Was it the purchase she had made and had Annas and Caiaphas complained to Gamaliel already?

"I don't know how else to approach this," he sheepishly confessed, "but it seems our friend Gammy is completely taken with your illustrious presence."

Saul said this in a teasing tone, just as an embarrassed and uncomfortable brother would nervously do.

Miriam relaxed visibly. To be honest, this did not come as a complete surprise to her for she was aware of the daftness that accompanied young men who were "stricken" and she had seen many of those indications from Gammy lately. Truthfully, she was quite enjoying the attention he was showering on her.

Saul went on. "In accordance with our traditions, Gamaliel approached me about a match between you and Gammy," Saul was fumbling for the correct words to tell Miriam. He studied her expressionless face. She was keeping very still and seemed to be enjoying her brother's growing discomfort with this topic. Deviously, she continued in her silence, deliberately waiting for more from the flustered Saul, keeping a very concerned and wide-eyed look on her face.

"Gamaliel mentioned that you probably would not be surprised, but I informed him that I must talk to you before giving him an answer, quite contrary to our normal traditions." Then Saul added in a rare attempt at humor, "The wise older brother's verdict is normally all that is needed." He paused. "Most of the time," And he struggled again, spouting, "I think."

She rolled her eyes at this and chuckled easily and Saul, wisely, left it there.

Miriam rose and slowly wandered about the room. For the moment she was lost deep in her thoughts and Saul knew better than to interrupt her. After many long minutes, she returned and sat across from him, a settled and contented look on her face.

"Saul, this is exactly what I promised our father that I would do and that makes me very happy. You know that back in Tarsus we were approached with six different marriage proposals and thankfully, Father always invited me to examine each one with him. He was a wise and kind man and would not insist on any marriage that I was not happy with. I think my pact with him was his gracious way of letting me be the one to decide when and who I would marry."

She paused in thought, remembering. "Father was much less concerned about me marrying a rich man and he often told me that the qualities of a man were determined by his generosity, his kindness and his thoughtfulness of others. This certainly describes Gammy, does it not?"

Saul answered her with an agreeing nod.

"I know that at this point it is infatuation and youthful attraction for both of us, but I see in him a great leader and an extremely just man. It will be exciting to watch him grow in his father's shadow."

Saul was again astounded by the depth of thought that this extraordinary young woman possessed.

"I would be honored to be his wife," she stated finally with an air of certainty, "but I have a few conditions that may complicate this arrangement, possibly even making me be unacceptable to Gammy or Gamaliel."

Saul was expecting a more overwhelmed and joyous acceptance of such a marriage and was not prepared for any caveats or hesitations.

"What?" was all a stunned Saul could mumble. He sat in confused silence.

Miriam again arose and circled the room repeatedly; she was obviously thinking over her next words very carefully. She took a small bite of the date in her hand and chewed it absentmindedly while pacing slowly around the room. Finally, she stopped and returned to sit once more in front of her brother.

"I do accept his proposal but would like to delay the marriage for at least one year."

Again, a long pause followed, with Saul calmly waiting to hear her explanation.

"I am determined to make my business venture a success and I believe that my full attention will be required for that to happen. Also, my wise brother," she retorted, teasing him slightly, "I have just arrived in my Jewish homeland and have not had the chance to explore the land or any of its people, except for a few crowded streets in Jerusalem. If I were to marry immediately, it would be my duty to remain here with my husband and I feel I must experience Israel for myself first."

It was now Saul's turn to reflect on his sister's words. Knowing her determined nature and thinking about her powerful curiosity, these were totally understandable ambitions, even though they were unexpected.

He politely inquired, "Just how would you explore Israel, Miriam?"

A mischievous smile appeared on her face. "Well, I thought I would get a trustworthy guide to take me to the places mentioned in our sacred writings and explain where and when such things took place. I also want to meet the Jews who live in the shadows of the great stories."

A confused and unwitting Saul was hearing his sister's deep longing, but still could not ascertain just what she was proposing.

"Saul," she exclaimed, laughing and a little exasperated, "I am talking about you. I wonder if you would take me to see Hebron, Shiloh, Shechem, the tombs and the monuments, the places that I have only read about."

She laughed at the astonishment in his face. "I know you love these places, for there is a passion in your voice whenever you describe them and that has put a hunger in me to see and experience them also."

Miriam was speaking out with the same emotion and excitement that Saul felt when he connected to the places described in the holy writings. Just the thought of accompanying her and standing in the places that he loved so much, stimulated him immediately. He could not possibly refuse her. He was at her mercy and both he and she knew it.

"I would love to take you around Israel," Saul laughed. "But when could we go?"

"You have one week until your students are free for the summer, don't you?" She asked, and he realized that this was not a plan that had just entered her head in the last few minutes.

"What about your store?" asked Saul.

"I will know tomorrow just when I will receive enough supplies to bother opening, and until then, I am free to explore," she answered, still careful not to mention Barnabas.

Saul's imagination, fueled by his own pleasant memories of the historical locations, was provoked and he warmed quickly to the idea of such an adventure.

"Let's plan it," he said suddenly, "and as long as Gamaliel agrees with my absence, we will do this."

The next day, the usual early morning meeting between the three men started nervously, but after Saul related his sister's acceptance to the marriage, things relaxed greatly. As he related Miriam's request for a year's delay and her desire to experience the land of Israel, Gammy and his father exchanged knowing glances which Saul noticed and immediately asked about.

"Well, Saul, both my son and I expected something like this from your sister. We suspected she would not act like the eager girls of Jerusalem who make finding a husband their one and only challenge in life and then jumping at their first proposal. Miriam is a remarkable and complex woman," replied a perceptive Gamaliel. "This is certainly good news and will bring immense joy to our household."

Gammy addressed Saul with a soft and emotional voice.

"Thank you, Saul," was all he could muster.

Gamaliel instructed both of his teachers to avoid any debates in their classrooms about the latest happenings at the Temple and Sanhedrin, providing them with unrelated topics to focus on with their students for the last week of classes. He wanted no complications before they broke for the summer and returned to their families. More serious discussion would probably prove to be much too burdensome for the lovestruck Gammy anyway, he teased.

Both Saul and Gammy were quite willing to keep the classroom discussions purely theological and politically neutral in the current atmosphere of Jerusalem as well.

CHAPTER FORTY-NINE

Barnabas's Curious Story

After their meeting, Saul bounded up the stairs to inform Miriam that all she had asked for was not only agreed to, but was appreciated as wise by Gamaliel and Gammy. He left that morning with a relaxed and clear mind, as if a heavy burden had been lifted and he joyfully remained with his class throughout the entire day. His talent as a teacher had returned and he spent the day instructing, encouraging, cajoling and many times rudely challenging his students in the demanding manner that he was becoming known for.

Miriam had taken the news from her brother with a peaceful and thoughtful smile. She sincerely thanked him for his understanding of her wants for she knew that such requests, sometimes seen to be demands, could be easily ignored by the men of a family who arranged such unions. This often led to intolerable marriages, bitter divorces and abandoned and destitute women and Miriam was determined that would not be her fate.

After Saul and Gammy left for their classrooms, Miriam descended the stairs and was immediately enveloped by Leah whose overjoyed enthusiasm was matched only by her mother Sarah, who joined in the celebrations. For hours the excited women chattered on about wedding feasts, children, guests, and every aspect of marriage they could until Miriam had to excuse herself to prepare for her noon appointment with Barnabas.

Miriam had grown up surrounded by brothers and, admittedly, was unprepared for the absolute delight the women were showing at the mention of a wedding. Surprising herself, Miriam was beginning to get excited at the thought of being married as well, so she forced herself to put that event out of her mind almost completely and set about to thoroughly enjoy her remaining days of independence.

She left an hour early for her meeting and stopped at her stall, once again examining it and imagining how she could arrange her shop for a good first impression. She considered telling the adjacent shops that she was now their landlord but decided to leave that for another day when she had more time and was a little less distracted.

She continued the short walk to Barnabas's sister's house impatiently, then wandered around a little, purposely delaying while waiting for the midday Temple shofar to blow. Upon hearing the familiar wail, she approached and rapped heavily on the wooden gate. Rhoda, the familiar servant girl opened a small porthole and asked her purpose.

Upon hearing that Miriam was here to see Barnabas, she opened the door and invited her to sit at a small table in the corner of the large courtyard.

Across the yard but well within her hearing was a group of eight men gathered at another table and speaking in Aramaic. One of the men was telling an intriguing story of roaring waves on a sea and Miriam distinctively heard the name of Jesus mentioned and immediately, her curiosity was once again stoked.

She noticed that one of the eight wore the under-tunic of a Roman centurion and was sitting slightly apart and not eating with the others. She knew that the very presence of a Roman was highly unusual and Jews would not normally be seen eating with such a pagan. Strangely, this man seemed almost accepted as one of the group even though there remained a distance between them. He bore no outwardly visible weapon and was completely oblivious of her, his back turned and earnestly listening to the conversation. One of the other listeners stopped the speaker and asked a question of him, referring to him as Brother James.

Miriam's attention was interrupted as Barnabas entered the courtyard, greeting the Galilean men with a friendly embrace before moving on to Miriam.

"Good day, little sister," he said in a kindly voice as he sat across for her. The servant girl appeared quickly and delivered a generous plate of flat bread, figs, dates, and fruits and then returned with wine. Miriam felt flattered at the attention with which she was being showered and nervously reached into her small carrying bag and produced many pages of parchment and laid them on the table.

"These are the items I would like to purchase for medicinal use in my new shop. Also, I listed many more, some just to resell," she said, stumbling a little with nervousness. "I have made four copies of each list so that you can send them to your brothers and your father. I did not want to bother you with having to make copies."

Miriam, for some unexplainable reason, also felt she needed her venture to remain a secret until it opened. She did not want any of the talkative scribes of Jerusalem spreading the news should Barnabas hire them to make copies.

Barnabas scanned the parchments with an experienced eye for many minutes and nodded approvingly.

"Did you write these lists yourself," he asked, aware that he was reading complex Greek terms written with the care and handwriting of an experienced scribe.

Miriam nodded in response, causing Barnabas to ask himself, "*Just what couldn't this girl do?*" He marveled at the precise and detailed listings, complete with meticulous descriptions of each item and the exact quantities she would need.

He read it completely and carefully, asking for clarification a few times and then he replied, "Some of these medicines are very expensive, some very rare and some, I never heard of before. We will do our best to fulfill this order but it may take a few months before any of this gets to Jerusalem. You are aware of the time involved?"

Barnabas waited for her response, wanting to make sure Miriam understood the complexity of her requests.

"Yes, I am aware of that and I am delaying opening my business until at least some of them are delivered. A good many of these medicines I have used in Tarsus and I know their effectiveness but I cannot find them in any stalls here in Jerusalem," she stated, wanting Barnabas to also realize that she understood the difficult task she asked of him.

"Until then, I am planning to tour Judea and Samaria with my brother Saul, to see the historic places I read about in our scriptures," she volunteered, a little too freely.

This comment took Barnabas by surprise. It was unusual that a Jewess could read the scriptures and even more unusual that she had free access to handle and possess scrolls. Many rabbis had forbidden women even the touching of any scrolls, citing the ease of deception of women, as with Eve.

"You read the scrolls?" he asked in amazement, and again asked himself, *"why wouldn't she, everything about her is different."*

"What languages do you read," Barnabas asked, venturing.

"Greek, some Hebrew and, of course, Cilician," she replied, not at all boastfully. By the legibility of the parchments, it was plain that she was also proficient in writing in these languages as well as reading. "And of course, Latin," she added as an afterthought.

Barnabas was beginning to understand that he was in the presence of an unusual lady, one who was unpredictable and very talented, and yet so young. They spoke at length about the business that she was contemplating but soon Miriam changed the conversation and grilled Barnabas about specific sights in Israel that were special to him. That conversation was unhurried and easy. Barnabas was relaxing and opening up completely about the joy he experienced in his travels as well. They found that they were surprisingly comfortable in each other's company.

After an hour of pleasant talk, Miriam finally asked Barnabas about what he had meant the other day when she asked why his business seemed unimportant to him.

Barnabas sat back and searched for a place to start.

"It is true that my family's business was the consuming aspect for much of my life," he started. He paused as if searching for the right words. "But in the last year, I have become a very different man with completely different values. My sister Mary, whom you met the other day, told me about Jesus of Nazareth whom she had come to believe was the Messiah. I, like most other Jews of Jerusalem, did not believe a word of this, thinking her seriously deluded. So, because I was so skeptical, she told me to come and see for myself. We knew that He came to the Temple for almost every feast, so last year at Passover, I went to see Him for myself."

That Barnabas was speaking with an unguarded honesty and from deep within his heart was instantly obvious to Miriam. He spoke with personal conviction and not as a purveyor of religion, or as one trying to sway her.

"I went to see Jesus out of curiosity and, admittedly, also to see the miracles. Indeed, there were many blind and lame who came and He healed them all. It was all very supernatural. For many that went looking, the miracles remained what they were fascinated by and they became very excited about those powers, but what captivated me were His words. He said things I had never heard before and it was His thoughts that seemed most supernatural to me, not like other religious thoughts originating from this world. He spoke of Hashem being His Father, saying things like, 'I do nothing without the approval of Hashem.' As He spoke these words, my former thoughts and the things I valued, even my plans for my future, began changing. The old stuff, previously so valuable and so time consuming, seemed so small compared to what He was talking about."

Miriam was captivated by Barnabas's simple description of his life altering events.

"Exactly what things did He say that affected you so dramatically?" she blurted.

"Well, He spoke of being born again. Not a repeat of our physical birth but a spiritual one, followed by growing and learning heavenly things, just as a child would grow and mature. He spoke of learning the truths directly from a heavenly teacher and not by the traditional education of this earth. Jesus explained that His words themselves possessed spirit and life, that in the hearing, they would change me and I was experiencing that very thing happening in my mind. I was coming to life."

He paused and reflected. "I did notice that many said they heard the same things as I, but the words seemed to not have the same effect on them. Those people later turned on Him. Jesus told us that it was His words that had no place in those people. He even claimed that some of them were being kept from hearing His words because they were not children of God. Being Jews, this made them very angry and they hated Him for those statements. Many of the thousands who had gathered around Him because He healed or fed them, simply could not receive this teaching. When He declared that He was the prophesied offspring of Hashem, most left Him and many turned on Him. He had predicted that they would kill Him one day, thinking they were doing

Hashem a favor and sure enough, they ended up hating Him so much that they finally demanded Him crucified this last Passover."

Barnabas's eyes watered over as he remembered those troubled times. He remained quiet for a long time, lost in his heart-breaking memories.

Miriam, who had been leaning forward listening intently, straightened. "That's not the end of the story, is it?" she probed, wanting him to continue.

"No, it definitely is not. I had followed Him closely, even going to Galilee for a while and I must say, I saw things that amazed me. Healings, Jesus ordering around demons, but again it was the teachings and His words about Himself that captured me the most. He was constantly being challenged by the leaders of the synagogues or teachers of the law and He handled them with ease. He not only knew the scriptures better then they, but He possessed the spirit of the scriptures. He warned all who followed Him about the hypocrisy of the Pharisees and as you must have already noticed, they hated Him for it and sought all the more to silence Him. They could not contend with His words or any of His teachings so they decided to just get rid of Him, agreeing that it was for the benefit of Israel that they should kill Him."

Miriam again interrupted. "But He did die, and I am told that His most devout followers scattered in fear. How could such "powerful words" allow that to happen, and where did you go when he was crucified? What about now? What are you going to do going forward?"

"You are correct Miriam, we did scatter, just as He predicted we would. There seemed to be a fog over our eyes and His predictions were not just idle words but they unraveled into horrible actions and manifested everything that He spoke, even His prediction of His death. There was no stopping that from taking place, in fact He said it must take place for He was destined to be the lamb of sacrifice. On that day, I hid in this house, like a coward."

It was evident to Miriam that the events of the last months were heavy on Barnabas's mind and she waited quietly for him to continue as he was being very deliberate with his explanations.

"Little sister, I know that these things are mysterious and very hard to understand, but He did not stay in the tomb and within three days was resurrected." Barnabas noticed the lack of reaction in Miriam, not knowing if it was disbelief in his last statement or if she was simply overwhelmed with the claim of the dead rising.

"His closest disciples, chosen as they were, also could not believe He was alive," he said, chiding her a little for her incredulousness, "but He physically appeared to them and to many of the women who followed Him closely. Even after seeing Him, some still could not believe He was alive but considered Him a ghost or an imagination until He sat and ate with them, or walked and talked with them. He reminded them that He had told them this would happen to fulfill both the Law and prophets but I guess no one could or wanted to believe it. Even after all His stimulating words, we were still stuck thinking about Messiah in our old traditional ways. It was as if there were scales on our eyes preventing understanding."

"That is a remarkable claim," said Miriam, "but really, it is easy for His distractors to refute because only a few of His followers claim to have seen Him."

"True. Even though up to five hundred of us saw Him, all of these were previously His followers. All of this very household saw Him but did not recognize Him until He broke bread at this very table," he said, pointing.

Once more, Barnabas teared up as his voice trailed off in a very personal remembrance.

"He appeared here twice. Once my sister Mary sat and talked extensively to Him. If this were a delusion or sham, then we all were deluded completely, capable of imagining the most vivid flesh and blood encounters. But like you say, the story does not end there."

Miriam was hopelessly intrigued.

"Every time He appeared to His disciples or to any other followers, He opened our understanding of what was fulfilled by His death. He continued to show Himself for around forty days and it certainly was an exciting time, never knowing when or where our Lord would appear next. At the end of those forty days, He told us He must go away. We really had no idea what that meant for us, but He told us to remain in Jerusalem until we received the promise from Hashem of the Spirit. We did as He said, not exactly understanding what we were doing and with many other of His words still very mysterious to us. As directed, we hung around Jerusalem, a few times praying at the Temple together, staying in various houses, but meeting daily in a large room down near the Pools of Siloam. There were about 120 of us together on the morning of the Day of Pentecost, all crammed into that upper room meeting place, when something noisy, like a strong wind, swept into the room. We saw small flashes of colored fire floating around and then hang above our heads. We stared at each other, not knowing what was taking place but immediately our minds were inundated with understanding. Scriptures and truths came flooding into our minds, not only the exact remembrance of His spoken words, but the understanding of them. We understood immediately that every wrong attitude and questionable teaching we had was being exposed, and our human, distasteful, self-absorbed personalities were being recreated by the power of our new understandings. The very thoughts and words had a life of their own and each possessed a divine nature of its own."

Barnabas was now speaking quickly and forcefully, but then he awoke from his personal outburst and looked at Miriam sheepishly.

"I am a changed person, little sister. The appeal of money and wealth has virtually disappeared. I can survive on what blessings the Lord chooses to send me but I will not be ruled by ambitions or accumulating wealth anymore. I have learned that the nature of Hashem is exactly the opposite to that. It is one of generosity. He freely gives us health and our daily food and keeps on meeting all our needs. I am a thankful benefactor of His goodness and I want to express His generous nature in return."

Miriam was stunned. She was hearing his words but only partially understanding his speech. She knew that she had never experienced what Barnabas was describing and she could not get her logical mind to fathom how a mental, or was it a spiritual understanding, could alter one's nature or personality. This was completely different from the hard work involved in changing one's actions that the Stoics and the Pharisees taught, that was for sure.

"Every time we gather, some words spoken by Jesus are remembered and in the relating, a clear new understanding is opened and we are changed even more. Jesus once told His disciples to not concern themselves with food or drink for does not the Heavenly Father feed the sparrows? No one considered that could be a reality, a new way to live and not just a sweet saying. With the help of the Holy Spirit, I am beginning to think and feel like that and, as a result, the business and all my precious investments mean less and less."

Abruptly, Barnabas stopped speaking, almost as if he had no more to say.

Miriam's struggle to understand showed in the furrowed lines in her forehead as she absorbed every word of Barnabas's testimony.

"Jesus said that you must become like a child to enter this kingdom," he interjected, recognizing that she was laboring greatly under these concepts, but thankful that she showed no antagonism to anything he had said.

Barnabas then added, "And it is not a physical kingdom which He spoke of, but one of the mind and deeper that that, one of the heart."

Miriam sat quietly, suspecting that this conversation would dominate her thoughts for a long time into the future. For the first time in her young life, she was being presented with a diverse form of Judaism and she, inexplicitly, felt a strange internal pressure to choose. Not knowing quite why she felt this way certainly discomforted her but Miriam knew she must answer many questions and then reach conclusions of her own.

Their time together had reached an end and Miriam thanked Barnabas profusely, leaving the lists for him. He assured her that he would send her requests to his brothers that very day and that he would send word about any possible shipments when he knew more.

After the big door closed behind her, Miriam took an even slower and more meandering route home, needing time alone to deal with her thoughts. She was admittedly uneasy, confused and a little distressed for she had always relied on her mental prowess to easily analyze and establish her truths. Today, she had just come face to face with a man who, although very bright, claimed that his understandings came not from education or his own intellect or even some advanced logic, but from outside himself and they were attained as a gift from Hashem. True, this was slightly similar to the concept she had introduced to Saul and Antoine on the ship, but back then it was just a futuristic theory of hers. The more she contemplated this, the more she grasped that indeed, she did not understand it in the way Barnabas had spoken of. That was for certain.

The one thing she readily admitted was that good things were happening around those who claimed this belief. Understanding this, she surmised quickly that this new "Way" would end up being a significant challenge to the type of Judaism that Saul and Gamaliel taught.

There was trouble coming into the Pharisee's world, she quietly predicted to herself.

From listening to Barnabas, Miriam had learned that the "Way" did not challenge the authority of the Law or the prophets; they took issue with the present leadership's traditional interpretations and mundane applications of those ancient writings. Although it appeared that these people were in some ways revolutionary, Jewish traditions were still being held to, its followers being among the most ardent attendees of the Temple and its proscribed prayer times, plus they worshiped Hashem with a new vigor and a purity usually only seen in very desperate Jews.

The main theological difference that Miriam could ascertain was that these disciples of Jesus spoke of being full of the Holy Spirit, an experience that Barnabas had described as resulting in an internalizing of the qualities of Hashem himself.

That new theology flew in the face of what all three sects of Pharisees taught, teachings which emphasized and thrived on soothing and mollifying the "unbridgeable" gap between Hashem and His creation. Being linked in some way with Hashem was for prophets alone and that for only small bursts of time, they grudgingly allowed but the distance between God and men was far too great to actually disappear completely. That was sheer lunacy.

Believing with an unrelenting ardor that obedience alone pleases Hashem, none of the Pharisees recognized any such thing as an "anointing" of the Spirit for mere common Jews. When they were pressed hard, Miriam allowed that they would acknowledge some "special" relationships with Hashem for the most virtuous of their sages, like Moses, Samuel and even King David at times, but nothing like that was for the population in general.

Yes, she decided finally, there was big trouble coming.

As she shuffled homeward on her circuitous and zigzagging route, she recognized that she was dawdling, deliberately taking her time. It was as if by her slow pace, she could somehow delay this upcoming and inevitable battle.

At every turn, Miriam's mind began foreseeing the looming theological battles which were about to erupt. She saw the proud and stubborn Pharisees ridiculing the devout disciples of Jesus for trivializing Hashem and reducing the sacredness of His name, followed by them demanding punishments for such heresy. In response, she could predict that these common people, with their deep and personal spiritual experiences, would simply relegate the outwardly ostentatious, hypocritical and self-absorbed leaders of Israel to the category of the corrupt and the blinded.

Worst of all, these were only the most obvious battle lines.

It was all too obvious that there was profound devotion on both sides of this conflict and for each, there was certainly no lack of passion. This is what made things so dangerous. Each side was convinced of the purity of their belief.

It was then that a sickening thought overtook her.

Miriam's calculating mind understood immediately that due to the passiveness and non-violence of the Galileans, a dangerous imbalance was likely. When she added in the lack of personal integrity of the powerful leaders in Jerusalem, she quickly saw that any clashes between the two could escalate and become dangerous only to life and limb for the disciples of Jesus. Once that happened, well, Miriam refused to go any further with that mental picture for people she loved were deeply involved on both sides.

Finally, and thankfully, Miriam reached her new stall and soothed her mind by soaking up the refreshing sight, thereby clearing her disturbed thinking.

The previous tenants had cleared out all but the few supplies Miriam had purchased from them, storing them in the second-story room, and so the place now looked stark and empty. She entered and climbed the narrow stone stairs to the upper area where, sitting in silence by the window, she watched the busy, crowded street below, vicariously absorbing the energy of the Cardo. There and then, Miriam decided that this peaceful room with its spectacular view had become her favorite spot in Jerusalem.

She was soon lost in her favorite pastime of deep and consuming thought.

Her mind turned to Saul and their proposed tour. She pondered the sites, almost fearing that the places they would see would not live up to the dreamy fantasies she had pictured in her imagination when, from the women's balcony of the Tarsus synagogue, she absorbed the convoluted history of the Jews. Later in her young life, at the times she secretly got access to scrolls and had devoured the writings of the prophets and historians of Israel, every reading added depth and rich colors to the imagined pictures in her head.

Miriam loved that a factual and vibrant history of her people had been presented in the sacred documents and that many times it was offered with painful truthfulness and unflattering detail, unlike most other histories. These ancient records proved to be more than just a partisan, religious indoctrination for Jews for they described not only the victories of Israel but more importantly, they also told of the many crushing defeats. To Miriam, that is what made them ultimately trustworthy.

Thinking about the actual sites of victory and defeat, she suddenly began to yearn to add layers of fact and color to the half-finished, black and white pictures.

With that yearning tugging away at her, she headed home to prepare for the upcoming adventure.

CHAPTER FIFTY

Saul and the Freedmen

Following a couple of busy days of intense instruction at Gamaliel's academy, days which provided enough mental balm to have his shaken confidence restored, Saul was once more ready for a visit to Samuel and the Synagogue of the Freedmen. Outside of the Temple porticos, this famed synagogue was now the main battleground where devout Jews and followers of Jesus were clashing and Saul was convinced that his presence would help keep his synagogue strong in defying these Galilean falsifiers.

Upon arriving, he ran into Samuel at the synagogue's gate but was quickly waved on by his friend, motioning him to follow to the very bottom of the Pilgrim's Road where the Pools of Siloam were. As always, the pools were crowded. Today they were surrounded by throngs of milling spectators, which included a small contingent of annoyed-looking Temple guards. These men were not pleased with their assignment to such menial duties and were expressing that by very roughly clearing spaces in the crowd for pilgrims who simply wanted to do their ritual bathing before starting up the Pilgrim's Road to the Temple.

The problem Samuel wanted to show Saul was that the largest part of the crowd was there to witness and cheer on the baptisms of new converts of the disciples of Jesus. The guards were now involved because this rabble was interfering with the normal operation of Temple worship.

Saul looked at Samuel questioningly.

"This happens every day now," Samuel said, obviously exasperated. "They are taking over the pools, forcing everyone to walk around them and they sing psalms and shout and cheer with every new baptism. They claim that their form of baptism is even more meaningful than that of John the Baptist, who, by the way, we now find was the cousin of Jesus. Look, there is my friend Stephen right in the very middle of it."

He pointed to a pleasant looking man in his early twenties who was assisting the line of new converts and embracing each man who descended the steps. Stephen cheered each ceremony on with great emotion and joy, and with his immense smile.

Saul saw that a few of the men on the outside edges of this crowd had noticed him and Samuel, and had began watching them warily. It was apparent that Samuel was in a much-advanced state of agitation. His daily duties as an officer of the synagogue having put him in direct contact with this group today and almost every day and it was affecting him greatly.

"Saul, they meet continually in that upper room across the street, singing, praying very loudly and constantly making an annoying racket," Samuel stated in a complaining voice. "Huge crowds are always pushing to get in there and when they can not, they feel they can just come into the synagogue and use it. Without asking!"

Most other times, Samuel's good nature and jovial ways could easily diffuse such hostilities, but this easy-going approach was not working with the followers of the Way. These people were seriously devoted and were not entertaining any form of compromise or negotiating on any of their new beliefs, or on their use of the pools, or their crowding of the public roadway, or the use of the open-doored synagogue. Strangely, their child-like confidence assumed that all these places were completely available to them and this entitled attitude annoyed Samuel the more.

Samuel explained to Saul that if they would only be offensive or argumentative, he could then engage them, for he loved a fiery debate and was a formidable orator himself, easily outwitting most. In the past, most of his opponents weakly descended into shoddy insults as their retort and when he got this reaction, he was convinced that he had successfully destroyed their weak arguments. At those times, only his friendly nature kept him from toying mercilessly with his opponents.

But this group was not interested in any debate.

Their lack of guile, stubborn though they were about their beliefs, gave them the aura of humility and child-like innocence and this garnered favor with a majority of the less intense members of his synagogue. Samuel realized that any unsolicited verbal attack on them would be scorned by the congregation.

For now, he was caught in the middle.

The two men left the pools and marched defiantly up the road to the gateway of the synagogue. Across the narrow road and coming from the same upper room, there rang out another shower of singing, mixed with loud praying. Samuel looked up in that direction and shook his head in disgust and clenched his fists. He turned and entered the synagogue across the street.

"They meet there, they eat there, some even sleep there and when that place is too full, they use our prayer rooms, our scrolls, and our spaces like we were in total agreement with them."

Samuel kept repeating his frustration with this unwanted arrangement and it was apparent to Saul that he had just been waiting for someone to vent to.

"Let's go to my house and discuss this further, far away from this riffraff," Samuel said. Without waiting for any response, he led the way with plenty of exaggerated stomping just in case any nearby observers were unsure of his feelings.

Samuel's sister, Ruth, was sincerely glad to see Saul again and flashed him a warm and welcoming smile. Samuel's mother had since returned from Hebron and Saul was truly happy to get reacquainted with her also. It had been a few years since he had seen her and she greeted him hesitantly, wondering why a former opponent of her son was now being treated like a lifelong friend, but she was polite and asked for no further explanation. The mother and daughter were scurrying about, working over a long line of baskets into which they were distributing bread and fruits and a small portion of freshly cooked lamb.

Samuel offered, "My mother and Ruth take care of the charitable distributions at the synagogue. They make sure no child goes hungry, or any widows get forgotten."

Saul was stunned, for he did not know of this. The mundane matters of his religion, like the feeding the poor, often escaped him and that was mainly because of his lack of interest, he admitted. Today, he was surprisingly impressed with Ruth and watched the dedicated ladies go about their work, which they did with practiced efficiency. His eyes drifted back to Ruth every few minutes and now he looked upon her with deepening admiration.

Before long, his attention turned back to an impatient Samuel.

The two men talked for hours, agreeing on much, once again thankful to find a cohort and sympathetic ear on the subject of "followers of the Way." They discussed the events at the Sanhedrin, both mentioning that they were unhappy with the result, but they did express some thankfulness that in that meeting Gamaliel had proved the foolishness of the charge brought by the Sadducees. Both Pharisees were well taught and were in complete agreement regarding the subject of resurrections. They knew they were also the experts on the many existences available for Jews in other spiritual dimensions, places that the Sadducees so easily and laughingly dismissed.

The two grumbled a little, disappointed that the charge of misuse of the Name of Hashem, clearly in their minds a violation of the third commandment, was not pressed further or presented clearer and they discussed this for over an hour. They repeated, word for word, the convoluted reasoning of Gamaliel, trying hard, but ultimately failing to understand his logic.

Total agreement came to them when the type of punishment for this misuse of the name was discussed. Samuel, to make his case, referred to Moses' scriptural reference to the son of Shelamith, immediately recalling that this man had a disagreement with another Israelite and cursed his opponent. In cursing him, he involved and uttered the name of Hashem vainly, for his personal gain, wanting to add importance to his curse. They agreed that this was a definite example of trivializing the sacred name and the holiness of Hashem for selfish motives. Moses clearly directed the whole assembly that they must stone such blasphemers, whether they were born Jews or not. Shelamith's son, you see, was not a pure-blooded Hebrew but was held to account and received a stony death, none the less.

Soon the seriousness of their conversation began to become apparent to each man. They realized that they were getting very close to not only endorsing but demanding the severest of penalties that one Jew could legally be given. Without implementing these punishments, Messiah would not come and restore the nation so, like it or not, one of these demands was the stoning of any blasphemers.

Settling for any lesser punishment was simply another form of disobedience. This conclusion was as unavoidable as it was uncomfortable to their "modern" Jewish brethren who considered stoning as ancient and archaic.

Saul left the house reeling.

He was full of wine, stuffed with good food and agreeable company, and carrying a few dilemmas of his own. His route home again passed that noisy upper room across from the synagogue door and his thoughts of the popularity and the confusing demonic abilities of these people returned like a flood. Today, more than any other, such thoughts infuriated him and he looked up to that second floor and growled.

During that entire day, one disturbing issue had been gnawing away at both men as never before. Although unspoken, it was overarching and begged for an answer.

Why did it seem so effortless for men in leadership to tolerate breaches in obedience to the Law.

Although Saul would not speak it out loud, he knew much of his growing agitation was directed toward the High Priest and to his own revered mentor, Gamaliel. These were men who held their lofty positions at the direction and command of Hashem, did they not? Saul, with every pang of criticism that was creeping into his mind, was caught in a perilous and growing quandary.

The followers of Jesus, by calling Him the Messiah, were breaking the Law but the leaders were also sinning by tolerating this sin. This was today's inescapable conclusion after all the wranglings and discussions of the two men. Not surprisingly, neither man wanted to utter those dangerous words.

Both Saul and Samuel, although very sure of their mental logic, were still very reluctant to declare themselves the ultimate judges and therefore, the accusers of the leadership of Israel.

PART SIX

CHAPTER FIFTY-ONE

The Tour

Suppressing his darkening mood, Saul finished his last week of teaching while looking forward to getting away from the drama of Jerusalem with the expedition with his sister. He had decided to travel south of Jerusalem on the first portion of the trip, suggesting that they break a complete Judean tour into two segments with a stop at Jerusalem in between a southern and northern portion. Miriam agreed and prepared all that would be needed. Eager and excited, they were more than ready when the first day of the week arrived.

Saul had hired a sturdy horse for himself and a large donkey with a very comfortable side saddle for his sister and after early morning prayers, they hiked through the Jaffa gate and mounted the saddled and well-fed animals at the nearby stable. Both travelers were in an ecstatic mood, enjoying the sunny morning with its clear Judean skies and the warm summer breezes blowing over the mountaintops. After months of busyness in Jerusalem, both were craving a time to just travel about and slow the hectic pace of their lives.

Since the day his sister had mentioned this excursion, Saul had been both rehearsing and relishing the opportunity to show her the sites. Although he would openly admit it to no one, equal to his devotion to the Law was his own hidden desire to explore and travel the world. Unless forcibly suppressed, he knew his loosed imagination and inquisitiveness could easily interfere with the serious study of the Torah and he continually struggled with this, settling on considering it an ever-present and sinful weakness which he must control.

Over the years, Saul had identified conflicting desires and interests within himself, things which sometimes interfered with his strict concentration on the Law, things such as travelling and being independent and carefree, things which he forcibly subjugated with constant readings of the Torah. These desires would often rise to tempt him, especially when the Torah readings would mention Mount Sinai or Egypt or some other faraway place. It was a losing battle, so he had learned to laugh at himself at such times and after receiving some advice from Gamaliel, allowed himself some gracious latitude. He decided that the pictures in his imagination only added to the richness of the Torah and needed not to be considered as opposing it.

Saul recognized this interest in Miriam also, and frankly, he could not understand people with no curiosity about their own Jewish history or who did not feel the draw of exotic and far-flung destinations. Her intense curiosity was testimony to Miriam's adventurous spirit and that had been punctuated by the fact that not many other young women would have willingly left home and launched the completely unfamiliar lifelong adventure that his sister had embarked on. Surprising but maybe not that unexpected, she showed no regrets upon leaving her comfortable life in Tarsus, and had in a few short months, immersed herself completely into her new existence in Judea. Looking back over those months, Saul was impressed at how quickly she had adapted to Jerusalem and its curious and confusing ways.

From the Jaffa Gate area, the two travelers started south on the western ridge that put them on the main Hebron Road and within minutes, they were on a height where they could look back at the city walls which were built on top of Mount Zion. Between those walls and this opposing southern ridge was the deep and infamous Hinnon Valley, a place where the disappointing historical kings of Judah had once sacrificed their own children. Saul reined in his horse and pointed down into the reviled valley that stretched along the south side of the entire city to where it met the Kidron Valley, far below the Pools of Siloam. The Hinnon was a sharp, rock-walled crevise, forested with a sprinkling of wild trees growing on unkept ledges which were the home of a smattering of goats that kept the underbrush under control. Because of its reputation, no buildings had been erected there and the only evidence of any use past the pasturing of animals was the occasional rocky entrance to ancient and pagan burial sites.

"Jeremiah renamed it the Valley of Slaughter and many of our sages consider this canyon to be the entrance to the horrors of Gahanna itself. Only the worst amongst us was buried there," Saul said to his sister and then paused, contemplating his next words, and then deciding to tell what he had heard.

"One of the followers of Jesus, the one who had led the Temple guards to arrest his former rabbi, hanged himself down there. He had tried to return the money he charged for his information, throwing it at Caiaphas, but I was told they bought a field with those pieces of silver further down in the valley. It is to be the place to bury any future suicides."

Saul rattled off the information with as little emotion as he could in an attempt to not let his intolerance emerge and blemish the spirit of their new adventure.

Looking across the steep valley to the highest point of the walled city, Saul made the pronouncement that King David was buried in that area, the uppermost point of the city.

After drinking in the southern view of the golden city with its undulating and blossom-covered walls, Saul turned his horse southward and the couple soon disappeared over the top of the first ridge, leaving Jerusalem behind. All around them were fields with rows of colorfully flowering vegetables and orchard groves, and as always, budding olive trees. The fields were busy with hardworking farmhands scurrying about everywhere. These were the fertile farms that provided for the everyday demands of the nearby city.

The road, millenniums old, was congested with donkey-drawn carts loaded down with the daily yields of these fruitful hills, produce which was headed to the stalls of the Cardo and the Pilgrim's Road. Interspersed amongst the carts were hordes of happy and chatty pilgrims who were also headed for the sacred city, but were walking on foot into Jerusalem as was the custom of those on the first day of their pilgrimage. There was a joyful outlook to these people and they were calling out heartfelt blessings and friendly greetings to other travelers. With the rising sun, the road was coming alive with a magical and festive feel and the merry atmosphere created easy smiles on the faces of all, including Miriam and Saul.

Their animals gingerly picked their way along the worn and ancient road referred to as the Patriarch's Way, named so because it followed the earliest recorded meanderings of Abraham and Jacob. The route went from top to top of the Judean mountains and before long, the landscape below opened to a long, sloping hillside falling off to the east. This slope was attractively covered with age-old terraces, resulting in curving lines of fully blossoming trees filling every level and wrapping around every curve in the hillside. The swooping steps descended gradually into a far-away valley which disappeared into the eastern desert.

Lush green grass grew under the trees and large flocks of sheep were grazing under their spreading branches, each herd watched by shepherds who wiled away their days on these hills as King David had as a youth. As the animals settled down from their early morning grazing, soft music came drifting up from among the groves as each watcher calmed his grazing sheep with familiar melodies on their flutes. Some of the shepherds were softly singing centuries old harmonies to their charges with soothing and melodic voices. One older shepherd entertained passing travelers by playing an ageless lyre on the roadside and accepting small donations. It was truly magical to Miriam and cresting that ridge from the city seemed to have instantly taken them back many centuries.

Trees, some covered in flowering buds, some with the first formation of fruits, were everywhere. The familiar bleating of circling sheep and goats who were drowsily looking for a soft spot to lay down, created a concert that soothed and entertained Saul and Miriam along the winding roadway. Surely the serenity and mystical feel of this place had led to the deep spiritual life that the great King David had experienced in his youth. One could definitely talk to God here.

Farther along the hillside they began to see glimpses of the small town of Bethlehem perched on the southern end of the ridge, watching lazily over the pastoral scene below it. At the final turn in the road before Bethlehem, Saul halted and jumped down at a small, rectangular stone building. He held Miriam's donkey as she dismounted at Saul's direction.

Proving she knew the writings well, she stated, "Rachel's tomb, I am guessing."

"You know the story well, how she died in childbirth giving birth to our father Benjamin while the family was traveling south. It happened on this very road, right at this spot," declared Saul as they approached reverently.

Miriam was certainly enthralled with all the history and sites of Jerusalem, but this place went back a thousand years before that city was even Jewish and it captured her imagination immediately. In true amazement, she was standing on the spot where her direct ancestor died giving birth to the father of her own tribe.

How much closer could she be tied to the stones of this edifice or to the strength of the ancestral women she descended from? She had just stepped back into her own history.

She circled the entire monument, feeling a deep primal connection to her beginnings as a Jew. She laid her tender hands on the ancient stones and rested her head softly against the wall, closing her eyes in deep meditation and there she lingered, leaning against the wall for a long ten minutes or so. She remained motionless and seemed to be receiving strength from its ancient feel.

Saul knew that Jewish women often claimed strength from their connection to the women of the scriptures and so he, out of great respect, remained still and quiet, letting his sister immerse herself in the depths of that union.

She moved slowly away from the wall and circled the structure again, observing it from every possible angle. Saul watched her every move, very pleased that her first stop was proving so meaningful. Above all, he had wanted this upcoming tour to have a purpose beyond just being a pleasant diversion. On every side of the monument, Miriam closed her eyes and quietly sang the Song of Moses that Miriam of old had first sung. She swayed rhythmically as her soft voice called out to those that had gone before.

After Miriam was satisfied, they mounted their rides and proceeded the mile to the small town. They dismounted at the largest and busiest inn along the road.

Saul quickly confirmed two rooms for them and an elderly man led away the horse and donkey to one of the caves that served as stables. It was early in the afternoon, but Saul had a plan.

He and his sister went to their small sleeping rooms and washed the dust off and then returned and sat down for a late lunch at the exterior patio area where all travelers ate.

Saul had one more place he wanted to show Miriam this day, so after eating, they walked to the crest of the hill which served as the center of the town and where the vista opened to the east and south. To the south, the ridge they were on dropped off quickly and Saul pointed out the crevice below where huge freshwater pools were located, each feeding into the other in a cascading order. These were part of the earliest infrastructure for the city of Jerusalem just five miles to the north, and they were originally constructed by King Solomon.

Saul pointed out that much of the water supply of Jerusalem had come from these pools and they had been historically connected to the city by an aqueduct. More recently, a pipe system engineered by Herod the Great had been constructed.

Herod had also directed water from here to a lavish hilltop edifice further south which he had created as his summer retreat from the heat and over-crowding of Jerusalem. Mockingly, many Jews accused Herod of building it as a place to run and hide when the Jews finally had enough of him.

Saul and Miriam could see the top of this volcano-looking creation in the distance named Herodian, no doubt by Herod to honor himself, and as they stood there, Miriam asked Saul if they could visit that fortress.

"Sure, we can. Of course, the top is a residence of Agrippa, now that his father is dead, but the surrounding areas are amazingly beautiful. We can go tomorrow and return here again."

They spent the remaining afternoon hours wandering the quaint little town of Bethlehem and chatting with prattling merchants and their equally friendly customers. Easy going and helpful locals led them to the oldest area and then to a spot known to be the place of the house of Jesse, David's father. Nearby, they also showed them the traditional home of Ruth and Boaz and each site elicited from Saul a repeating of the stories they had learned as children. For Miriam, it was as if an emptiness was being filled. Finally, exhausted but looking forward to the next day, they retired to the comfortable inn just as the sun was touching the western hills.

Saul and Miriam set off for Herodian early in the morning and the ride took a full two hours through the nearby orchards, followed with some remaining dense forests native to the region. They approached from the north and were soon engulfed in a small, modern village that had grown up directly below Herodian. The village existed to house the servants of the royal family and their ever-present bodyguards. Even in the seclusion of this area, there always seemed to be the need for these rough-looking men hanging about menacingly. It was rumored that many had been required to make the paranoid king feel safe. Similarly, his cowardly descendants felt they also needed protection from their overtaxed citizens.

At the northern foot of the cone-shaped mountain was a complex of lavish, clearwater pools on ascending terraces, each pond situated higher upon the layers which made up the sides of the mock mountain and each surrounded by walkways expertly encompassed with vegetable gardens. These pools were further surrounded by orchards of local fruits and all this was encircled with a stone-paved road that eventually climbed the slope through the orchards to the singular vaulted entrance situated halfway to the top of Herodian.

Under this portico was an impressive doorway to an equally imposing lobby that formed the only exterior part of the whole castle. The lobby led to a narrow and easily defended hallway cut through the rock of the mountain and which opened to the very private and completely hollowed-out interior. Sprinkled liberally within the cauldron of this fake volcano was a small village with buildings, spas, banquet halls and Herod's personal and fully secure bedrooms. All the rooms were decorated with marble statues, stone carvings and colorful mosaics, reminding all visitors that much of what was seen here was meant to impress Herod's Roman friends.

The circular road leading up to the entrance continued past the portico and eventually descended on the opposite side of the slope to more fields and forests.

Saul and Miriam dismounted and strolled through the lush public area of pools while chatting with other visitors who were eagerly pointing out the many schools of fish of various species and sizes. These had survived here since Herod's time and served as a convenient source of fresh food as well as a place of interest and serenity. The gardens were neat and tidy, obviously well-tended. They were filled with a variety of herbs and plants and interspersed with colorful flowering hedges that separated the courtyards, some providing delicious berries in season.

A series of private residences were set among the lower fields of pomegranate and olive trees and these were originally built as separate accommodations for Herod's many guests who warranted only a day visit inside Herodian. Most visitors were not allowed to overnight in the same place as the paranoid king. These residences were now looking a bit shabby but were still in use by Agrippa's adoring and always close-by parasitical acquaintances.

The whole area had definitely lost much of its importance since the death of Herod the Great over thirty years previous and none of his sons could afford the extensive upkeep that this castle in the rock was entitled to, but at least it was not completely abandoned.

Currently, this was the secondary residence of Agrippa who received a generous portion of the local taxes to help keep up his pretense as important royalty. Pilate had to often listen as the self-engrossed Agrippa complained of having to spend all his income on maintenance of this outlandish structure. To this point, Pilate had diplomatically offered a solution. He simply asked Agrippa if he would like to donate Herodian to the army as a southern barracks. The puppet king did not bother to reply.

A few steps below the portico entrance was a huge, echoey mausoleum. It was built by Herod as his place of final rest, ingeniously carving it into and hiding it in the lower mountainside. It was said that he was buried in a beautiful and extremely costly, rose-colored marble sarcophagus, accompanied by one wife who ranked one of plainer white stone. Entrance to this elaborate tomb was permanently restricted, not that Saul was all that interested in honoring this half-Idumean despot with his presence and then enduring the many washings it would take to rid himself of the sullying effect of Herod's bones. The restriction had much more to do with the continual rumor of looting by the locals.

Miriam was entirely captivated with all aspects of this place and while walking about, she became more and more absorbed in the grandeur of the magnificent structure. Although she had heard of the wealth and ambition of Herod the Great and had seen his work at Caesarea and in the renovations at the Temple grounds, she had not fathomed the affluence of this monarch or the obsession he had for building difficult, somewhat outlandish and expertly engineered projects. Her concluding thought about Herod was simply that this man must have been brilliant and that his brilliance was matched only by his inflated opinion of himself.

Seeing the unlimited wealth and status of this king made a strange thought pop into Miriam's head and she asked Saul, "Does Hashem place differing values on the lives of people?" Miriam paused for effect, "for we Jews definitely do? Are some more important to Him than others?"

She pointed to this elaborate structure as her proof.

Saul stopped in his tracks at the question, but before he could give his memorized answer, he realized the pitfalls that his thinking would have to navigate, many which Miriam would not let him simply avoid. He tilted his head to her, chuckled a little, but kept on walking. That was not the simple and easily answered question that it appeared to be on the surface.

After strolling the peaceful grounds for a few more pleasant hours, including a visit up to the guarded entrance itself, they descended the hillside and mounted their rides for the return to Bethlehem. They made a quick stop at the pools of Solomon where they cheerfully washed their dusty feet in the cool water and soon after, arrived back at the comfortable Bethlehem inn. It was mid-afternoon.

Happy but tired, they agreed to rest a little and meet in a short time for their evening meal.

An hour later, brother and sister were comfortably seated on the inn's patio, under the canopy of the large oak, viewing the eye-pleasing orchard terraces below. Both were fully satiated with the fresh roasted lamb and a goblet of the best drink of the area and with big smiles they were rehearsing the wonderful events of the day when a group of ten noisy, very dusty and highly excited people arrived at the inn. This group had come from Jerusalem this afternoon and were greeted with much fanfare and a warm familiarity by the friendly innkeeper. The troop was immediately led to two adjacent tables on this outdoor patio and it was very apparent that a small, middle-aged Jewish woman was given a special place of honor amongst them.

Miriam's attention was captured by the hauntingly familiar face of a man with a Roman-style haircut and a large scar from his ear to his jaw and she immediately recalled that this was the same man she had seen at Barnabas's house. At that time, he had been wearing the easily recognized undergarment of a centurion. Once again, he respectfully seated himself at a slight distance from any Jews at the table.

The innkeeper was scurrying about addressing every need of these visitors, but he was focusing his respect on the small, special guest. Saul's back was to the group but Miriam was watching them so intently that he turned to see what captured his sister's attention and he too noticed the out-of-place and strangely familiar Roman. Scanning the two tables, he saw a total of four men and six women. He then returned his attention to the second sumptuous plate of lamb placed before him and being unconcerned, Saul left any future gawking to his always curious sister.

Miriam heard one of the women ask the honored lady, "Sister Mary, would you show us the stable where He was born?"

"Of course, I will," she answered, and the whole assembly rose and exited to the smiling approval of the innkeeper. They all slipped past the big oak to a nearby cave entrance.

Miriam caught the innkeeper's attention, called him over and asked, "Sir, who is that woman, and what is she showing to these people?"

The innkeeper warmed to this courteous young woman immediately and he eagerly responded, "That is Mary, the mother of Jesus, and she is showing them the stable where He was born over thirty years ago when I had no rooms left in the inn. They had traveled here for Augustus's census and there was no place else to put them," he stated almost apologetically.

"I heard he was from Nazareth," countered Miriam, surprising Saul. Her brother was not aware that his sister knew much about Jesus at all.

"He grew up in Nazareth but he was born here, while they were traveling for the decree said they had to register in their family's ancient homes. He is from the tribe of Judah, you know."

The innkeeper turned to her questioningly, "Do you not know about Jesus, how they crucified Him and how God resurrected Him?"

Miriam, slightly flustered because of her glaring brother, gave no response.

Unaffected by her silence, he said, "You must know about the night he was born, how angels appeared and announced Him? It all happened here." He pointed to the cave and the hillside below. Saul made the glaring point of looking the opposite way.

The inn-keeper continued, excitedly relating a story he had obviously witnessed.

"Mary was just a young girl then and she told me that she had not been with a man but was overshadowed by the Holy Spirit."

Hearing this, Saul slammed his fist down and stood erect, surprising the innkeeper and causing Miriam to jump in reaction.

"Fables, nothing but impossible fables, conjured up after the fact, all aimed at making that Jesus seem to have been something special."

"Not so, young man," countered the old innkeeper quickly and defiantly, "I am a witness, for it was I who put them in that stable," he said, pointing to the cave entrance. "And it was I and many others who heard angels singing in the heavens, and it was I whom He healed of a withered hand in the Temple two years ago, and furthermore, it was I who lost a young son when Herod heard of a king being born in Bethlehem, just as predicted by all our scriptures. Herod certainly believed the writings for he came here and murdered all our innocent babies."

Then the older man paused, took a much-needed breath and gathered himself. "These are not fables, sir, all these things happened."

The gentle but adamant innkeeper looked Saul up and down. "And I fear that Israel may have missed their day of visitation."

Saul looked at Miriam and curtly stated, "I am tired and am retiring to my room. Let us be ready to leave at the third hour in the morning."

He left quickly, not looking back.

Miriam was left alone with the innkeeper but she remained seated, not following her heated brother. She poured herself another cup of wine, indicating she was remaining and asked the sincere merchant, "Please tell me more, sir."

He sat down opposite her, ignoring his duties for a while and related many details of the young couple who had arrived at his door over thirty-three years previous and all the strange and miraculous events of that night. The innkeeper then spoke of being in the Temple two years ago and hearing this same Jesus, now a grown man, teach. He told her the details of his own healing, but most dramatic was his account of his friend Lazarus from Bethany who had been sick and had died and then had been called from the grave after three days by Jesus.

"How could one not believe this was the Messiah?" he asked her fervently, a question for which she had no answer. Again, Miriam slipped into deep and quiet thought.

The large group returned from the stable and sat down to eat and listen to more of Mary's words.

Miriam could not quite make out what was being said, so she rose and wandered close enough to hear and she stood motionless and spellbound as Mary told incident after incident in the seeming miraculous life of her son. The Roman centurion noticed and politely motioned for Miriam to take his chair at the nearest table, but at this she awoke from her ponderings and suddenly disappeared to her room.

The next morning brought a light breakfast and an awkward time of maintaining their distance from the other group. With very little delay, Saul and

Miriam mounted their rides and left Bethlehem, continuing their journey south. Both avoided any mention of the last day's encounters at the inn.

They rode slowly along the hilltops, again following the well-worn and winding Patriarch's Way, and as they did, Saul described every village with its scriptural importance, thus adding a complete visual portrait to the mental images of Miriam.

Her constant smile was clear evidence that Miriam was enjoying this to the utmost. By late morning, they passed by the village of Ephrata as the road wound its way downward from the heavily forested hills south of Bethlehem. Saul pointed to a small and rounded hilltop to the southeast.

"That is the very hill that Messiah will descend onto, as told by our prophets."

A little further south the roadway levelled and followed the eastern edge of an undulating plain which was sporadically covered by heavy forest and grazing pastures out to the west. The treed portions were interspersed olive and oak trees.

"These are the plains of Mamre," Saul stated almost reverently, "and this is the spot where our father Abraham dwelt in the last years of his life. I can just imagine the grazing flocks roaming among those green pastures and all the neighbors recognizing the special calling of Abraham. He lived here but also pastured his flocks all the way south to Beersheba."

Saul looked around at the vast plateau. "That means he used another thirty miles of grazing. He must have been the biggest supplier of mutton and cheese in the whole region."

Skirting the undulating edge of this plain took till late afternoon where-upon they reached the busy approaches to the ancient city of Hebron.

This famous town was spread out on terraces that climbed the southern flanks of a ridge that rose above a well-watered valley below. The ridge wrapped around the fields and orchards in a semi-circle facing south and it ended at a high point at the distant south-western end.

Saul stopped at a large inn along the highway at the northeastern boundary of the town and found rooms for the two travelers. Moments later, they were settled into their very comfortable rooms, and shortly after that they met at one of the wooden tables in the pleasant courtyard, lured there by the delicious aroma of roasting lamb. Their original intention was to simply plan their next day's explorations, but both were starving and devoured two plates each without a word about tomorrow.

CHAPTER FIFTY-TWO

The Hebron Guide

As Saul and Miriam were rehearsing the nearby sites and deciding what was best to explore, a pleasant looking man of approximate middle age with a neatly trimmed beard and swarthy complexion entered the courtyard and looked about. Seeing the couple, he headed directly to the table where Saul and Miriam were still finishing the last of their meal and enjoying some juicy local pomegranates.

"Excuse me," he said, interrupting their conversation, "I see you are strangers to Hebron."

"Well, yes," admitted a hesitant Saul, not sure if a ruse or scam was about to be attempted on unwitting strangers and feeling a little unkept because of the pomegranate seeds spread all around. Miriam reached across the table and with a laugh, flicked a seed out of his beard.

"Let me introduce myself. I am Caleb, and yes, I am an ancestor of that Caleb," he added quickly, anticipating Saul's thoughts. All three at the table knew very well that Hebron was the promised and final home of that revered scriptural hero.

"I see that you are a Pharisee," he said, surprising both Saul and Miriam, "and I would like to be of service to you while you are in Hebron."

"Is it that obvious," inquired Saul, surprised at being so easily recognized as a Pharisee but forgetting about the blue fringe that slightly escaped his outer garment.

"I have made a living observing people and knowing what they want and need," replied the polite man. "I can assist you in any business endeavors, or direct you to any locations, or take you around my town and show you the amazing history, which if I am correct, is the reason you have come here."

Saul and Miriam chuckled to each other at the thought that they were read so effortlessly.

"What is your fee for such services?" asked Saul, hesitantly.

"It is ten denarii per day," he answered and after a quick discussion, Saul and Miriam soon had made an agreement for the following day, realizing that without a guide they may just wander around not knowing what was under their feet.

"Before we start in the morning, could I impose on you to follow me for just a moment," asked Caleb.

Saul and Miriam rose and followed their new guide out the opening in the low stone wall of the courtyard. He took them a few hundred yards further down the road and stopped on a raised rock. Standing upon it, he pointed through a flat valley to a high ridge to the east. It was covered with beautiful terraced groves and was the highest of all the ridges.

"That whole ridge, stretching miles south and also north and all-around Hebron, including where we are standing, is the mountain of Caleb ben Jephunneh."

He slowly swung his upraised arm in a great circle.

"It was promised to him by Moses and here it was that Arba and his sons, the massive Anakims, were first seen. It was my courageous ancestor, Caleb," and he said that with great pride, "who returned to capture these very hills from those giants, the colossal and ferocious creatures that had so frightened the other spies sent by Moses." He paused for effect. "As I will show you tomorrow."

They gazed at the beautiful ridge which Caleb had called a mountain. It was covered with well-tended trees and interspersed with flowering gardens brightly blooming on the immaculately trimmed terraces which step by step descended into the farming areas in the flat valley. Within a few moments, the intoxicating colors magically changed their hue, seeming to come alive as the sun sank behind them.

This man certainly has a dramatic way to introduce us to Hebron, thought Miriam, who, quite suddenly, was greatly looking forward to the next day.

CHAPTER FIFTY-THREE

The Market

Early the next morning, Caleb appeared at the inn while Saul and Miriam were enjoying a light breakfast. He was dressed with a simple knee-length robe gathered and tied at his waist.

"When you are ready, I would like to show you our markets," he said eagerly.

Saul harrumphed quietly but noticeably, thinking that in a town this rich in history, why would they waste time in a crowded and stinking market.

"This is unlike any market you have visited before," Caleb said directly to Saul, who quickly nodded in acquiesce, feeling a little embarrassed that his grunt was overheard.

On foot, they wound their way along the ridge to a slightly undulating plateau that formed the center of Hebron. On the edge of the town was a flat area which often remained open and unused. Today, at the perimeter of the clearing, a collection of braying camels and donkeys were gathered and were being closely inspected by keen-eyed caravan leaders in preparation for the largest of the desert's weekly auctions. Just past the collection of camels was another even larger area completely covered by a sea of colorful tents which were filled with all manner of goods. Some of the bounty was spread directly on the ground and some was being displayed on makeshift tables under light canopies. There were so many booths that alleys and trails were formed, leaving customers to somehow navigate through this confusing forest of structures and stalls.

Caleb led his charges past the camels and into the vast collection of tents. As they entered the bustling commotion, they were immediately engulfed in the most sprawling and chaotic transient marketplace they had ever experienced.

Caleb whisked them through the outer lanes to a central square that was fringed on all sides with large and well-provisioned tents, each tended by the watchful eye of its insistent vendor. Each was loudly exclaiming the praises of his goods to every passerby, and each was trying their best to attract uninterested customers before they could disappear into the smaller aisles leading off from the square. It was early, but the market was already congested and it had an exciting and inviting atmosphere to it. The upbeat chattering was accompanied by pleasant notes being played by a family of talented musicians in the middle of the square who were entertaining all, hoping for a small donation.

"This market is the main supply and trading spot for all of southern Judea, all the way from Jerusalem to the wilderness of Zin," their guide told them as they scanned the shops. "People come from many miles, some all the way from Jerusalem and many, from the coast of the Great Sea as well."

Miriam was literally glowing, her face paralyzed with a continuous smile and that was a fact that was noticed and appreciated by their guide. Caleb seemed to thrive on the atmosphere as well. He gathered Saul and Miriam close so they could hear him and he began explaining his enchantment with such a riotous place, calling it a freewheeling adventure into merchandising by locals, augmented by peddlers of rare treasure who came from the kingdoms around. Beyond that, there were hawkers of every nationality and every sort of shopkeeper one could imagine from parts unknown. Every week, new merchants and their various wares appeared.

Good-natured shopkeepers were enthusiastically waving, beckoning the trio as one would dear friends to stop and examine their exceptional pile of merchandise but then they quickly turned to the next person, searching for potential customers among the crowds which were now starting to fill the aisles.

"You can find all the familiar items that are available at every market, including the same exact goods found at Jerusalem's famous Cardo," he stated, "but there are things for sale here that are found nowhere else in Israel and only visitors to Hebron have a chance to purchase them. Many of them speak of Hebron's rich history and unique position at the crossroads of the deserts, the mountains of Judea and the coastlines. Many cultures are well represented here."

Saul still felt a little annoyed at the commercially persuasive tone of this guide and strolled off alone to a nearby booth, sure in his mind that this was just another boring and irritating market. His attention was immediately caught by a medium-sized tent on display which was made with an extremely light fabric unlike his family's heavier but more stable creations. An intense conversation started and Saul learned that these were beginning to be popular with the caravans and the other travellers that moved about for they were light and easily erected. Upon asking the cost, he was surprised at the reasonable price. His discerning mind began calculating immediately.

Inside this vendor's display tent were other supplies that one would need for traveling, such as water bladders and large totes made to sling over the saddle of camels. Saul was intrigued by the creativity and usefulness of these products, many ideal for those who traveled the nearby and ever-encroaching deserts and he was soon engrossed in the full display and was almost enjoying being good-naturedly accosted by the eager merchant. His imagination was quickly aroused concerning expanded business possibilities for his family's manufacturing operation back in Tarsus. Suddenly, he began realizing how quickly his religious career was being put in jeopardy and he laughed heartily at himself and moved on.

Miriam had been sidetracked into an eye-catching and flamboyant tent that had shimmering cloths draped off all sides of the protecting roof. Each sample was glittering with bold, vivid colors rarely seen in these regions and which had been tinted with the very richest of dyes. She had to admit that she not seen such fabrics in the comparatively colorless and serene markets of the Cardo. Her little time in Jerusalem had already taught her that the sedate religious tone of the city did not outright forbid, but subtly discouraged this type of blandishments on their conservative wives and daughters.

As the rising sun fully lit the fabrics, they shimmered delightfully and while shifting about in the breeze, they magically changed hues and tints. Miriam was mesmerized and could hardly take her eyes off them. She slid close and felt the feather-light and smooth cloth over-and-over again.

Their guide lingered in the middle of the square patiently. Many times, he had seen the hypnotic effect of such exotic trappings on unsuspecting visitors and today, as on many other days, he was thoroughly entertained with the growing fascination of his charges.

When both Miriam and Saul emerged, Caleb called them close and explained, "I wanted you to see for yourselves that this is indeed a unique bazaar, filled with products unlike any you may have ever seen before and, I warn you, you have only just begun. I must ask that you please do not get offended at some of the things you will see for this place is the closest in flavor to the ancient existence of our father Abraham. We must always remember that he lived peaceably among the most pagan and deviant sons of Canaan. Our father knew who he was and he certainly kept himself and his family separate from their pagan ways, but he lived here among them, traded with them, did business with them, and most importantly, watched vigilantly as they contorted and distorted themselves so perversely."

These spellbinding words arrested Miriam's attention immediately and she determined there and then to have Caleb explain himself.

He was speaking of different forms of life, was he not? She must get more detailed answers about Caleb's puzzling statements, many which she also had her own thoughts about.

Only later. After more shopping.

Caleb uttered this gentle warning to Saul and Miriam for he had many times witnessed the sudden shock of naïvely religious Jews who knew the biblical accounts of the conquest of these lands only as written stories and long-ago sanitized legends but did not comprehend the forgotten and unusual world that Abraham had actually lived in. He considered it an essential part of his job as a guide to introduce the historical aura of his city to any interested traveler.

Caleb was growing pleased that in this brother-and-sister combination he had found such surprisingly willing students. When escorting many touring Pharisees in the past, he had found that although they were expert on the subtleties of the Law in a purely scholarly fashion, they lacked any knowledge of Israel's history in practical details simply because many of these details were not specifically mentioned in the sacred writings. Worse, most lacked any interest in learning any facts that might challenge their limited religious versions, regardless of their historic truthfulness. He privately regarded these so-called academics as un-teachable and truthfully, this bazaar was all about discovering and learning.

Caleb had long ago realized that there was an ancient and veiled history that was being forgotten, remembered only by the few who bothered to study it in centuries-old Jewish records. As well, there were other books, an array of non-Jewish records which provided a history to those who dared step outside of the limited views allowed by their teachers and rabbis. Further and along side of all the writings, there was a physical history in this area, an account witnessed by buried utensils and unearthed weapons. If one was attentive, there was yet another history much harder to identify, a lasting record of ancient times evidenced by the strange local traditions and practices that had lingered in distant corners of rural Israel for eons. It seemed that the modern political scholars in Jerusalem had little interest in the truths buried in the sands and rock piles of rural Judea and Caleb could not understand such willful ignorance.

The smiling guide was aware that there were other surprises coming for these two in this bazaar and he thought best to let these travelers discover some of these for themselves. He did not want to dampen the inquiring mood that had been kindled with too much description or warning.

Saul had made it to the very next stall where he was again captured. This time, it was by a display of old scrolls and intricately carved family historical sticks that chronicled many Jewish descendants of the area, some claiming to record ancestries back to Joshua's conquest. Indeed, a few of the oldest ones possessed the familiar names of men who were listed in the Book of Joshua. He examined these documents avidly and the opportunistic merchant kept uncovering more and more intriguing and valuable artifacts in his attempt at a sale, all under the watchful and analytical eye of Caleb, who periodically wandered close.

Caleb was also watching over Miriam who had sauntered a few stalls ahead and was now entrenched in conversation with a weathered but bright-eyed older woman who was surrounded by dozens of small satchels of curious powders. Miriam was conversing haltingly in her poor Aramaic so Caleb drew close to assist. The two women were laughingly pointing to a small bag of powder and each was calling out a different name.

Caleb, very fluent in Greek, listened and finally whispered to Miriam, "She claims that it is mandrake, Rachel's secret formula."

"And what do you say?" asked Miriam playfully.

"I say that it certainly does affect those who take it but that may be because the partakers want it to, more than what is in it. Who knows if it is the exact mandrake that Rueben found? I also think that we have sadly lost most of the important knowledge that our ancestors possessed and used routinely. Even if it is the same mandrake, who would know how to prepare it? Without doubt, we have lost that particular knowledge along with much more of the wisdom of the ancients."

Again, his curious statement surprised Miriam. She often thought she was alone in her belief that mankind's intelligence and wisdom was rapidly eroding over the years since the creation of Adam. She knew that pompous scholars vehemently disagreed, believing in their arrogance that they were personally delving into areas never before understood, but Miriam had observed that most of the spiritual subtleties recorded in Moses's writings, those which were easily understood at the time of the writing, escaped any present-day comprehension and were often the subject of years of mental wranglings, bitter arguments, and great disagreement.

She had decided this from her reading of other histories as well, all which showed that men no longer understood things that were open and obvious in previous times. Miriam had a curious sense of humor and she thought it hilarious when some famous scholar celebrated his shrinking intelligence with great fanfare over some tidbit that was rediscovered. So commonplace were these understandings in ancient times that extensive explanations were not needed and therefore no elaborate written explanation could now be found.

In her private musings, Miriam feared for the future of Judaism and of mankind in general if this trend were to continue. The spiritual genius and fullness of character that Hashem had endowed Adam with seemed to have degraded severely with each generation, only to be replaced by a mixed human race overcome with a shallow and dark selfishness, almost completely the opposite of the original pure and generous nature. To her, man's shrinking intelligence was very evident. Miriam understood that her own mental abilities were revered and she was considered extremely intelligent, but she wondered if she was just a throwback and that she possessed what historically would be only a normal level of intelligence in the previous ages.

Miriam had also deduced that when one was overcome with self-promotion as it seemed most modern scholars were, the ability to contemplate or understand the pureness of the creation or ponder great truths was stunted, veiled by the continual scouring of events for any indication of one's personal greatness. This, she concluded, was indeed a curious blindness.

For Miriam, the disastrous result of this reduced mental capacity was a descent into a "common" idiocy that was not immediately evident because all thought alike now and most regarded this greedy and self-indulgent way of existing as normal or even enviable and a trait to be desired. As a mere teenager, Miriam had understood this, rejecting the premise that such mental perversion was the original created state of man.

Often, she had heard the depraved excuse for someone's self-aggrandization, "Is it not righteous to strive to be loftier, more highly regarded and wealthier than your neighbor?"

In her mind, this was a debauched stance and such attitudes were far too often followed rather than observing the deeper but less "profitable" musings of people like Abraham who had the time to wait patiently until Elohim came to visit. How could He expound His secrets if everyone was consumed with becoming wealthy?

The casual comment by the deep-thinking Caleb had certainly intrigued her. She suspected that there was much more to this man than what first appeared.

"What is your interest in such concoctions?" asked Caleb, changing her concentration.

Miriam, feeling Caleb could be trusted, told him of her upcoming business venture and Caleb was instantly intrigued. Upon Miriam mentioning her compulsion to do things differently, to treat all aspects of her patients that were suffering, including their thoughts and their relationship to Hashem, he stirred visibly and became excited. His strange reaction to her statement and his astonished gaze convinced Miriam that her assessment of Caleb's hidden depth was correct.

"How does a young girl like you, such a protected daughter of Israel at that, come to this path?" he asked, adding, "one would not expect this of even a Greek or Roman girl."

He, like others, had just caught a glimpse of the uniqueness of this little woman.

"It is a long story that I can tell when we have more time," stated Miriam, looking around eagerly at other stalls.

"Let me take you to other booths with even more exotic imports, straight from the ends of the earth," he exclaimed with growing excitement.

He went back and spoke to Saul, making a meeting point at the far end of this aisle and then he led Miriam around the corner of a street dedicated to apothecaries and stalls of healing tinctures and medicines. Seeing she was at once enthralled, he excused himself, saying he would be back shortly and for her to enjoy her shopping. Then he slipped away.

Miriam felt safe and secure as she wandered the familiar shops, recognizing many of the medicines as ones she had used in her treatments in Tarsus, but in almost every shop there were one or two that were unknown to her and which promised amazing medicinal properties. She noted the names of each and their alluded-to powers but refrained from any quick purchases, cautiously doubting many of the claims as just too fantastic.

The kindly merchants were all eager to show her their goods, all claiming a variety of results with each new bag. There were dried herbs and fine powders from the coastlines of Arabia, curious leaves and thick ointments delivered by mysterious ships from the Far East, pain-killing seed pods from the high mountain plains of Persia and an endless host of other balms delivered by the traders who brought such goods along the camel train highways. Each merchant explained their miracle merchandise in detail and pressured her just a little, each wanting a sale, but also wanting to remain polite and respectful.

After nearly an hour, Caleb re-appeared in the company of a much older, taller and white-bearded man who was slightly bent with age and was walking slowly. He possessed an ancient and serene aura that immediately caught the attention of Miriam.

"This is my Uncle Moshe," said Caleb to Miriam, "and I believe that he may be of great service to you."

Miriam nodded demurely in deference to the age and demeanor of this man, then looked at Caleb for a further explanation.

"Come, let us go to a nice little shop where your brother will meet us and where we can have a sweet drink. Moshe can explain many things to you."

The small group found an empty table at a refreshment shop in the common area and after a small lunch was ordered, Caleb spoke.

"I took the liberty to explain your business plans to my uncle and he was very impressed. He wanted to talk with you personally and I am sure that you will find his unusual knowledge very helpful."

The old man began speaking in a mixture of Aramaic and Greek, with shards of other mysterious languages thrown in, and he proceeded in telling his amazing story. Caleb added a comment here or there and interpreted the odd word that Miriam seemed to not understand.

He told of traveling with the wandering camel trains from his early youth and of being present in dangerous cities in the early days of the Roman civil wars some seventy years previous, but mostly, he spoke of seeing incredible sites and visiting peculiar peoples of diverse lands and traditions. He told of an era of his life when he had his own camel train, two hundred head of camels in all and that he specialized in delivering the rare spices, the colorful cloths and the medicines so sought after by the indulgent wealthy.

Having Miriam's complete attention, Moshe spoke of the power and potency of many of the medicines he had witnessed in his travels, a good many which he had used and administered himself and which he claimed had almost miraculous results. He then spoke of the practice of blending and mixing of these products by greedy and unscrupulous traders and merchants until there was very little potency left.

Miriam began to understand the variations of reactions she had witnessed when she had proscribed certain locally purchased medicines in previous times.

When done his amazing story, Moshe finished his wine, gazed on Miriam and stated, "Caleb tells me of your interest in the health of people's minds and that you have an understanding and some experience with the healing aspects of one's thoughts and beliefs."

Miriam was taken back with this disarming statement, not at all expecting this type of conversation from someone she had until then understood to be only a camel train merchant for his entire life.

Catching herself, she was instantly embarrassed with the demeaning, albeit well disguised, lack of regard or importance she had ascribed to this well-spoken and gentle man. Internally, she castigated herself for doing what she abhorred so much when done by others. This was an extremely intelligent and well-traveled man who sat serenely in front of her now and he was comfortable speaking in great depth about things only hinted at by the most modern physicians in the Jewish or Greek world.

Miriam always prided herself in her outward humbleness and this encounter had mercilessly exposed that duplicity, but thankfully only to herself. She suspected that Moshe had easily seen through her, but all he allowed to be recognized was extreme graciousness and for that, she instantly loved him.

Pulling her thoughts together, she opened her heart to him and told of her observations of people getting well even when she would secretly give them quite useless medicines. Such recoveries required that she only hint that the medicine would be effective and that the patient have confidence in her assurances. She went on and explained that she had observed that most sicknesses were accompanied and often predicated by great anxieties and stresses, including harmful thinking.

Miriam confessed that these were just a young girl's observations but suspected that thoughts and sickness, attitudes and wellness were somehow connected.

These comments caused a knowing and approving glance between Caleb and Moshe and Miriam noticed this. She wondered if there were truths that were easily understood in other cultures that she was just now beginning to comprehend.

Had this traveler experienced such phenomena and just how many late-night stories of such happenings had been heard in his tents?

She continued her story and went even further.

"There has been a whole series of miraculous healings taking place in Jerusalem among a group of people who have a great belief in a prophet named Jesus. I have personally witnessed this. The recipients claim an outside power comes to them and heals them, but then some also say it is dependent on their own belief or thoughts, whether they have adequate faith or not. I am completely intrigued."

Old Moshe queried her further. "Did you learn this from your brother?"

"Oh no," she said with a laugh, "the leaders in Jerusalem attribute this to demons."

Seeing his raised eyebrow, Miriam felt to explain herself even more.

"I have read most of the Greek and Roman medical literature and only one Greek physician mentioned anything about the possibility of curing a disease with the help of one's mind. It is something that remains unexplained. If the sickness can be attributed to or blamed on exterior supernatural causes, then of course the easiest force to blame is demons. Likewise, curing it would be attributed to Hashem. I believe there is so much more to this that is yet to be explored."

Moshe nodded his head in admiration of this mere child and quietly said, "I totally agree, little daughter."

She then asked him if there were any pure and worthwhile medicines to be had in the local market and the old sage assured her that there were indeed many effective remedies. He then paused as if listening to a voice inside himself, and soon returned his attention to Miriam.

"Let me find these for you, little sister, and I will keep watch in the future also, for there is a constant supply arriving in Hebron. New products arrive with each camel train. If you like, I will send you supplies regularly and will only send the effective medicines."

Astonished at her great fortune, Miriam could not be more thankful that she had stumbled into such an arrangement. Caleb was beaming, thoroughly pleased with this agreement. He was obviously overjoyed with the growing closeness between this young girl and his uncle.

Caleb noticed Saul approaching through the crowded alleyway, heavily burdened with what looked like a new prayer shawl, a large ancient scroll and a new leather phylactery. Laughing heartily at this scene, he jumped up to assist the struggling shopper.

"You have had a good time I see," he teased warmly.

Saul nodded and laughed out loud himself, knowing that he certainly had succumbed to the charm of this market.

"I guess I make a good tourist," he said, sitting at the extra chair.

Saul was introduced to the elderly Moshe and the two spoke openly. The friendly conversation continued longer into the day as Saul was more and more intrigued with the descriptions of the exotic cities the man had visited and he peppered him with unending questions. He was thankful to learn that his sister was getting wise counsel and expertise of this caliber and he expressed his appreciation of this to both Caleb and Moshe.

Caleb ventured, "Saul, it is midweek and we have much to see around Hebron. It will take at least a few more days, then it is Sabbath. Would you and your sister spend Sabbath with our family? We always have our Uncle Moshe and a few others also."

Saul looked at his sister, who was quietly enjoying the enlightening conversation while drinking in the colorful atmosphere of the busy market, and she smiled widely at the invitation. Saul shrugged a good-natured shrug and said, "Thank you, we would be honored."

Now that they were not pressured by any pressing time schedule, the explorers and their guide left their parcels, and their new friend Moshe, in the care of the small shop and continued their slow exploration of the other sections of the lively market.

Before long they were passing a stall that was full of ivory adornments that were intricately carved from the tusks of the great elephants of Egypt and Ethiopia. Such carvings were getting much rarer, for sadly, these massive beasts were also getting rarer and rarer. The great herds were receding south into the dark lands beyond Ethiopia, following the food and water. The endless green grassy plains and great forests surrounding the huge lakes of the Sahara region were being slowly but certainly replaced by the dry, withering heat of an unending barren desert and this had been happening since the times of Noah. The richness of nature, the billions of birds and the huge grazers were slowly moving on from that once lush expanse. Sadly, some creatures were already gone, never to be seen again as there were now only small pockets of greenery left, existing precariously at only a few shrinking oasis' feeding off slowly depleting underground springs. Over the centuries, the great life-giving rainfalls had dwindled in intensity and had finally ceased. Tragically, the elusive and highly spiritual desert people, those who recorded and dutifully expounded the histories of the entire world were also becoming rarer and rarer. Their bountiful cities were being buried under mountains of blowing sand and their starving carcasses were becoming the fodder for roaming jackals. They stubbornly hung on, desperately waiting for the return of the rains, wanting to remain in the land of their ancestors while now existing only on insects and snakes. The vast Sahara was becoming almost entirely the home of scorpions and vipers.

Miriam was captivated with a hand-sized piece of ivory that was intricately carved, showing a mother and baby elephant and she could not possibly resist buying it. It took a full ten minutes of haggling, with Caleb's help of course, and with much good-natured lamenting and theatrics by the stall owner. It seemed that his whole family would starve if she did not pay at least one shekel more. In the end, both buyer and seller were pleased with the transaction and all had enjoyed the good-natured banter. Miriam held it in her hand and loved the delicate detail it was made with, but she could not help the dark feelings it also brought to her.

Did one of Hashem's great creatures die to provide this ivory?

That pedlar's tent was followed by nearby stalls displaying various, color-fully painted vases and drinking cups decorated with beautiful scenes from all over the known world with some of the largest of the vases embossed with strange and fierce animals, some being creatures not known to either Saul or Miriam. They looked at each other and laughed out loud, thinking of the comical scene of them lugging such exotic loot to Jerusalem.

The shopkeeper, very expert at his craft, anticipated their reluctance and offered, "We will deliver it to wherever you live in Judea, guaranteed to make it safely and with no charge until it arrives safely at your home."

This news, of course, started a new and more intense round of bargaining which was followed by intense scrutiny and much discussion which ended with the purchase of a pair of contrasting, waist-high vases with lions and tigers expertly painted on each and a variety of cups required for mixing medi-cines. All were picked as the perfect containers for Miriam's new shop, but both knew that was just her convenient excuse for such an exotic purchase. The promised shipment was arranged and the delighted tourists moved on happily, now the best of friends with the beaming merchant.

By early afternoon, it became evident that the whole day was going to be devoted to the market. Realizing this, Caleb asked them if he could show them some special shops of more historic interest located deeper into the huge market. They quickly agreed and followed him down an alley to a cluster of stalls that were blatantly displaying a disturbing collection of unusually large items of warfare.

Miriam and Saul examined a huge, rust-pitted sword laying on a table which was longer than the height of any of the men standing nearby. Behind the table and throughout the remainder of the shop were fragments of armor, shoes, helmets and other tools of warfare that were all immense and not at all practical for any normal-sized soldier.

Upon seeing their curiosity, the shopkeeper drew near the table and pointed proudly. "Anakim swords, this big one believed to belong to Anak himself. It was recently unearthed when we dug the foundations for the new synagogue."

They noticed the enormous size of what was left of a leathery and strangely elongated helmet and a massive breastplate.

Caleb interjected, "Moses sent the spies to search out the land and the first thing they mention is the size of the inhabitants. They were fearsome creatures as you can see."

A fleeting image of the huge soldier on the ship passed through Saul's mind but even he would not come close to filling out this armor.

Across the aisle was a shop that kept its merchandise slightly hidden under blankets. Miriam approached it and looked closely, quite sure that she recognized the shape of a tooth except it was much larger than any she had seen before, almost matching the size of her hand.

"Sir, is that a tooth?" she quietly asked the wily and smiling merchant.

"Exactly, and I have many more like that for sale." he said quietly, pointing. "Some still in the skull." He lifted a worn blanket to expose a monstrous skull.

Miriam was transfixed, her curiosity and medical interest instantly aroused. The back of the stall was littered with other bones of enormous size as well.

Saul approached and peered over her shoulder and immediately snorted in repulsion and moved away. Being a Pharisee meant not touching or defiling one's person with dead things. For the sake of her brother, Miriam moved on, but would have loved to examine the skull closer. Another day perhaps, she reasoned.

The next shop offered a mixture of large and normal weapons. These were more military armaments but that which dated to the period from Joshua to David and the eager merchant was positive that some of them, absolutely no doubt in his mind, belonged to Joshua or David themselves.

Saul, much more interested in relics of this era, began carefully examining all the items and while he was preoccupied, Miriam sauntered back to the stall with the skulls, asking if she could see the large one again. Fifteen minutes later, she returned and whispered quietly to Caleb, who nodded knowingly. The small band moved on, leaving the exuberant and chatty weapons salesman disappointed but quickly focusing on the next customer.

As they exited that street, Caleb halted and spoke. "I apologize if that offended you, but I think it is an important, if not essential, part of understanding and appreciating what actually took place in our area and in our history."

Saul remained silent, but Miriam thanked Caleb profusely for showing this astounding piece of the history of Hebron.

"The hills are strewn with these reminders and almost every time we dig a little, another token of our victories is exposed," he stated. "You will see these locations later."

Caleb hurried them through the pungent food market, still crowded with women shopping for today's supplies, only stopping when Miriam's newest craving forced her to purchase a handful of fresh dates. He then turned the group into a side alley where the flavor of the market changed noticeably. There was a line of four very distinct shops, each presenting a different type of item and it appeared that Caleb had led them there with a definite purpose.

The two men attending these stalls were tall, narrow-faced men, whose dark skin was deeply tanned by the hot sun. They were dressed in the brightly colored, loosely flowing and airy garb of the desert people. Their flashing and intense blue eyes were the first thing one noticed, followed by a white, toothy smile and a deep, respectful bow to all. Their movements were measured and unhurried, giving one the sense that they were expecting you and that they were your dear friends. Their steps were smooth and it seemed they somehow floated rather than walked.

Caleb explained, "These are the desert people and they come only one or two days a week to this market. Each camel train stays for only a short while and then moves on and what they bring to the market is totally different from week to week. They claim, and I believe it is so, that they are Esau's children."

Both Saul and Miriam were speechless. If indeed these were the offspring of Esau, then once more the very scriptures they had often read and relegated to historical and distant stories were now standing in front of them in human form, very much alive, and emanating an almost other-worldly presence.

What an adventure, thought Miriam.

Caleb spoke to the older of the two men in Aramaic, but the man answered in a tongue that, although foreign, had the familiar sing-song cadence of the oldest Hebrew used in the Temple and synagogue services.

"He and his family roam from Beersheba to Alexandria and then all over Arabia, sometimes even going north to Babylon. They only come to this area once every few years or so. They come here mainly to honor their father Abraham as well, just as we Jews do and to visit his tomb," Caleb explained as he interpreted for them.

After more conversation, Caleb continued his translating. "I told him that you are from Jerusalem and he says he has many questions. As is a custom with desert people, he has invited us to dine with him and his family, tonight in his tent. This is a great honor that is not extended to everyone."

Miriam could see the hesitancy in her brother so she swiftly and enthusiastically accepted, which both surprised and pleased Caleb.

He spoke again with the man as Miriam inspected his table of succulent fruits acquired from wandering the mountains and valleys of the massive Arabian Peninsula. Many of these, Miriam had never seen before for each area was renowned for its own and very distinct variety of luscious berry. The older man noticed her interest and was quick to give her a juicy sample.

Saul was browsing over a large display of coins that were laid out on another table which varied from gold, to silver, to brass and to iron. A few more were carved bone but, by far, most were ancient-fired clay coins. The younger and much taller man with a closely trimmed beard sidled closer and approached Saul, finally speaking. He began, in perfect Greek, to describe the origins of each coin.

Saul immediately wondered how this man knew Greek, and furthermore, how did he guess that Saul spoke it? *Why did this man not assume that a Pharisee from Jerusalem would be more comfortable in Aramaic?*

Furthermore, any assumption of his favored language begged the question, "*Did these wanderers know of and understand the convoluted divisions of the Babylonian and Western Jews of Judea. The recent ruptures in Judaism were centered on the different languages spoken, a problem which Saul himself would be considered to be an integral part of?*

Saul was totally mystified but also, absolutely intrigued.

The desert dweller continued, proudly showing Saul the intricate writing on a particular rectangular ingot of silver. He carefully explained the ancient markings that designated it as a silver shekel by weight, pointing to other symbols that also marked and dated it as being from this exact area. Obviously, he was an expert.

Saul knew well that Abraham would have used four hundred of this exact type of currency to purchase the field and famous cave from the local tribesman, Ephron the Hittite. Abraham had purchased it for his family's burial site.

"*Could this be?*" he pondered.

The tall man, seeming to read his thoughts, said, "It may well be one of the very ones used to buy Machpelah, for they would most likely have been put back into circulation, or cached with the family's wealth, or dropped into the sand only to be found centuries later. This one we took in payment only a little distance away in the Sinai as gold and silver is much more reliable and can always be traded, unlike metal coins that have no value after one has left the country where they were made. These symbols tell us the dates, plus such markings were only from this region, so we know it is from Abraham's time and from Hebron."

Both men clearly understood the historical and sentimental value of such a find and the astounding possibilities of this particular ingot.

Saul was completely drawn in by the easy candor and extensive knowledge of this man. His original thoughts of the desert wanderers had been of an uneducated and even unintelligent people who roamed the wildernesses, a people who were subject to the unyielding forces of what was perceived to be a hostile environment. This perception was being quickly altered, and, indeed, almost erased.

"I would be interested in this shekel, if it is for sale and if the price were right," he offered. The man bowed in agreement but delayed any further progress in the transaction, instead he unwrapped another batch of coins.

This puzzled Saul, so Caleb took him aside and explained quietly what had just taken place.

"The ancient custom of new 'friends' is that if you want anything of theirs, you are simply given it. That silver shekel now belongs to you. When we meet them tonight at their tent, you will honor them with your presence and possibly a non-monetary gift that approximates the value of this silver shekel."

Saul was again amazed and Caleb explained further. "Their lifestyle does not rely on money. Past having food and shelter, which they have in abundance, everything else has only the value of history, or shared friendship, or exposed truthfulness and integrity. Those are the things that have value for them. Your problem now is to figure out what you can honor him with."

After witnessing such transactions a few times, Caleb had come to appreciate the thoughtfulness and complexity required in such an unusual barter. It was the "integrity" of the purchaser that would now become exposed to all involved, simply by the way he rewarded the giver. Suddenly, this had become a subtle test, but it was recognized as that by only a few. The greedy, those only interested in their gain were quickly exposed, but the honorable were also easily recognized. It was a unique opportunity to prove oneself and it was given to only a few by these trusting wanderers. The offering of the purchaser was always graciously accepted by these people, whether it was fair or not, as only the memory and character of the purchaser had lasting value.

Caleb often wondered if this approach was the desert people's attempt to mimic the generous actions of their tent-dwelling ancestor, Abraham. Such valuations spoke of the lack of regard for the trinkets of wealth in this life, a lack which Abraham readily confessed to as he searched for the mystical city of Hashem.

Was it such subtle assessments that Hashem Himself employed when looking upon His creation? Was the result of such an evaluation why He considered Abraham as truly His friend?

The tall man continued explaining the origins of many of the other coins and each was a history lesson in itself, one which Saul willingly embraced and absorbed. Meanwhile, while displaying another rare coin, the merchant retrieved a skin pouch, and when Saul's attention was absorbed elsewhere, he dropped the shiny shekel in. After almost a half hour of inspecting the bounty and learning much about many countries' coins, the tall man handed the small sack to Saul.

"We look forward to your visit," he added earnestly.

As they walked away, Saul anxiously asked Caleb, "What can I possibly give him for this treasure?"

"Something that you also treasure," he answered thoughtfully, using Saul's own word of evaluation of the ingot.

Saul retreated deep into thought and Miriam, who had been watching all this covertly, was intrigued and a little entertained with her brother's dilemma with the coins. Above all, she was delighted to see her brother completely relaxing, far removed from the constant nervousness and stress that the religious culture of Jerusalem had created in him.

Miriam then asked Caleb to take them back to the shops with the fine cloths.

The men browsed nearby as Miriam lovingly stroked and then wrapped herself in the brightest and softest of the sheaths of shimmering fabric. She purchased a generous sample of each of the brightest and engaged Caleb in a busy arrangement for future orders. This was much to his delight and caused even bigger smiles for the enthusiastic merchant and his colorfully-draped wife.

Caleb led Miriam and Saul down a few more streets where they absent-mindedly browsed the merchandise. He then found an exit from the market and delivered the weary couple back to the inn. It was late afternoon and their thirst for shopping was now completely quenched.

Caleb made the arrangement to rejoin them after a small rest but before leaving said, "I hope that the day was acceptable," to which both Saul and Miriam nodded their vigorous approval.

"For many it is just shopping for goods that perish, but there is a richness and a profound wisdom that one can only get by being involved in authentic experience. I suspected that you two would benefit greatly by our one-day history and cultural lesson as taught by that marketplace. I myself learn so much every time I visit there."

Saul and Miriam now clearly understood that this man was more than just a guide for hire and their trust and respect for him was growing immensely.

Totally exhausted, brother and sister needed the late afternoon rest to prepare for the evening.

When the time came, Caleb appeared at the inn and led them to the eastern edge of the town where a collection of sprawling tents had been erected. In the field below them was a herd of over fifty camels. A few of the beasts slowly turned their bored, imperial gaze to the passing group while grinding their cud in a funny sideways and unhurried chomp. Only a few were still standing as the majority had already settled into the awkward, elbows out position for the night.

Caleb pointed out a pure white camel that stood out among the others. "A great prize and worth a fortune among the desert people," he explained.

CHAPTER FIFTY-FOUR

The Desert People

Upon entering the largest tent-a sprawling structure familiar as the home of the nomads of the desert-Caleb, Saul and Miriam were soon settled into a surprisingly comfortable visiting area which looked out on the southern valley through the wide-open flap. No doubt, this framed viewpoint had provided this family many stunning and spectacular vistas on its wandering journeys from the warm southern oceans to the snowy mountains of Persia.

Both men and an elderly lady welcomed them warmly into the middle of the spacious common area which was supported with only a few poles and with light cloths separating it into rooms.

The older man, the same merchant they had met earlier in the market, was dressed in a long, golden-colored robe which opened to show bright blue pantaloons. His white hair and beard were oiled and shining.

The elderly lady, introduced as his wife, was adorned in a bright red robe-like dress covered with a shimmering blue shawl, so fine that the red showed through easily.

The tall man, the son to this older couple, also wore bright pantaloons but was covered on top with a spotless and almost translucent white tunic. Both Saul and Miriam had never seen such exotic garments before.

Almost immediately, two more women appeared, equally beautifully adorned. One was the wife of the younger man and the other their teen-aged daughter.

Before long, a sumptuous meal was spread before them and all were relaxed, laid back and reclining on soft pillows. Gales of laughter erupted throughout the dinner as tales of events and humorous accounts of the mishaps of the desert were told. It was evident that this tent easily provided needed shelter, but mainly, it delivered a warm and vibrant atmosphere in which these hospitable travelers of the desert were completely at ease with any stranger.

Contrary to what he had expected of desert wanderers, Saul found that the men were extremely well read and knew much of world history, speaking of many events that he personally had never heard of. Even the women could chime in on most topics and it was apparent that the long evenings spent around succulent meals were a veritable factory of knowledge and learning.

The caravanners spoke of adventurous men they had hosted who had traveled to the farthest ends of the earth, fearless nomads who had seen mountains and rivers of stunning beauty and size, and curious explorers who had witnessed sights not even imagined before. Both Saul and Miriam were mesmerized. As they listened, they were witnessing the unfolding of a richness and breadth of experience that dwarfed the limited life that they had so far experienced.

Their hosts spoke with an unsuppressed laughter in their voices and their faces detailed each word with smiles, or forced frowns, or moving sadness, thereby adding to the enjoyment of their stories. Theirs was a harmony of thought and open-hearted expression rarely seen in adults anymore, a harmony one appreciates in the purity of children before they learn to hide their real character.

With unfeigned interest and a generous measure of politeness, the hosts managed to extract much of the life stories of the young visitors, who upon the telling, recognized that they had led a sheltered and uneventful existence in comparison. Miriam's dedication to her sick father moved them all emotionally and the older lady rose and embraced Miriam with loving arms, holding her tight and humming the desert's mourning chant as she told of his passing. The exotic notes of her dirge cut through the sorrow of Miriam's story of her father and left her with a calming warmth at his memory. It was an enduring tenderness that she would experience from that time forward whenever she remembered her beloved father.

What magic was that, she often asked herself when she tried to fathom the effects that a simple song could have on the grief that could invade one's mind.

After the dinner, both younger women joined Miriam and their older mother in a different area of the tent and they soon were engrossed in the topic of childbirth. There had been two deaths at birth by the wife of the tall man. Miriam listened intently as the women described every symptom and in response, she began a long and complicated description of a breech pregnancy and what had sometimes worked for her to alleviate the problem.

Saul, after being captured by the men's fantastic stories of adventure, told his own short version of his life as chief student of the famous Gamaliel. This did not seem to impress the men, but when it was mentioned that Gamaliel was the grandson of the famous Hillel, knowing nods and approving words were muttered. The "rabbi from Babylon" was how they knew him and the reverent regard shown produced an immediate impression on Saul.

After seeing the reaction to the mention of Hillel, Saul paused for a long moment and slowly opened the satchel at his side and pulled out an old and tattered prayer shawl. Each man looked at the other questioningly and Caleb wondered what was happening. Miriam also turned and from across the tent, she gasped, knowing the importance of this item to Saul. Gamaliel had presented this treasure to Saul at his Bar Mitzvah and it had not left his side since.

"I would like you to have this, to bless your paths and assist your prayers to Hashem," he said. "This was the Great Rabban Hillel's prayer shawl for a short season and I am told it was the one he was wearing when he uttered those famous words that the Law is fulfilled in two things: love Hashem, and love your neighbor."

The tall man jumped to his feet and his father was instantly moved to tears.

"Brother Saul, this has to be your most cherished possession," he exclaimed.

He was trembling as he very carefully and reverently took the tattered cloth into his hands and then draped it over his weeping father's shoulders.

"We by tradition cannot refuse it, but please know it will be treasured and honored in this tent as long as we live," said the younger man.

The sincerity of the statement brought a flood of tears to Saul's eyes which he wiped away quickly. He broke out in a huge relieved smile and the atmosphere warmed even more. Another round of their excellent date wine was poured and its sweetness was thoroughly enjoyed.

"I will also be honored to know that Rabbi Hillel's prayers will travel the deserts with you," said a slightly tipsy Saul. The small hand-copied scroll of Gamaliel's teachings that Saul had also brought was left wrapped in the skin and remained unopened in the satchel at his side.

"Tell us, Rabbi Saul, what is the relationship between my Jewish cousins and Hashem at this time," asked the tall man.

Saul understood that these people had been uninvolved spectators through the centuries and had no doubt watched from a distance as Israel had both pleased and angered their God. They would also have been interested witnesses as Israel had been blessed and punished accordingly.

The directness and innocence of the question, combined with the warmth of the atmosphere, enticed Saul to be unusually open and candid. He explained how difficult it was to get Israel to follow Moses's Laws to the letter and how he had dedicated his life to this cause, as had other men called the Pharisees.

The older man quietly uttered a few words that were meant only for his son in a strange, foreign tongue not understood by Saul but which Caleb knew described persons of extreme and pious religious appearance but severely lacking spirit or the purity of truth.

Nevertheless, Saul pressed on to describe the errors and foolishness of his brethren and how often they were led astray, as with this latest so-called Messiah, Jesus. The wine had its affect, loosening his tongue even more, so he continued his diatribe and was soon relating the latest infuriating encounter in Bethlehem and the small group that was now claiming Jesus's unusual birth there.

The mention of Bethlehem and Jesus instantly stirred the attention of the men who began asking when this birth was to have taken place. When they learned that it was claimed to have happened in the time of the Roman census by Augustus, the two men gazed questioningly at each other while Saul rambled on with an even more pointed condemnation of the group called the Way.

The desert men were remembering the three deeply spiritual and gifted holy men from the Far East areas of Persia that had joined their camel train over thirty years ago. Very learned men they were, men who could read the stars and the heavenly signs, men who wished to quickly and quietly, leave Israel. They were watchers of the stars who claimed they had met the infant Jewish Messiah which they had found with the help of ancient prophecies, constellations and supernatural visitations. They had joined and traveled with this caravan for a short time, camouflaged as traders amongst the camel train and then they dispersed into the far eastern kingdoms. Curiously, they had mentioned that the child was born in Bethlehem as well.

More wine and more stories went late into the night until a tired and slightly wobbly Saul and Miriam finally convinced their hosts that they must leave. Great shows of affection and genuine love were exchanged by both parties who well knew they may never see each other in this lifetime again.

The short walk to the inn was a quiet but merry journey with Miriam softly singing and Caleb and Saul fully enjoying the fresh night air which helped to clear their foggy brains.

"I may be arriving a little later tomorrow morning," stated Caleb with a knowing grin and a slight slur. Laughing, they all agreed to this much needed rescheduling.

The next day, Caleb did arrive a little later than normal, but only minutes after Saul and Miriam had eaten and finished preparing themselves for another day of adventure.

At mid-morning, they left the inn on foot and followed the busy lower road to the west, skirting the very bottom of the ridge and walking down streets that wound around the ridge, closely following the base contours of the hills. Their journey took them above the area where the desert wanderers' tents had been only last night and they were shocked to see the complete expanse totally abandoned.

Caleb shook his head and exclaimed, "They are an amazing people."

Before long they were on a plateau slightly above the lower valley but below the top of the encircling ridge. This elevated plain was completely covered with pomegranate and olive trees.

Caleb explained, "This is the field that our father Abraham bought from Ephron the Hittite and many of the trees you see have sprung from the very roots of the trees that were part of that transaction. Saul, you now have in your possession some silver that may have been involved in that purchase, as well," he said, speaking of the silver ingot that had been given to Saul in the market.

Saul and Miriam drew near to the newest versions of the ancient plantings, feeling the rough bark of an ageless olive tree and recognizing that its constant regeneration represented the enduring resilience of the nation of Israel.

Caleb led them slowly through the fragrant and lovingly-tended orchard and soon a large stone structure peeked through the overhanging branches of the trees. It was a very large building constructed at the foot of a very steep portion of the ridge that dominated Hebron.

As they emerged from the trees, they approached towering rock walls built of gleaming and newly carved stones. They stepped upon the huge rocky apron that spread before the edifice which was already crowded with milling pilgrims and local worshipers.

This was the site of the Cave of Machpelah which had arms and chambers going deep into the rocky rise that formed the ridge. It had been purchased by Abraham centuries ago, along with the field they had just walked through, for four hundred shekels of silver. The original cave was bought by Abraham to bury his wife, Sarah, but was soon chiseled out and expanded to become the entire family's sepulcher. Originally, this spot was only a concealed cave entrance but it was now covered by this huge building which had been erected by Herod the Great. He built the edifice with walls forty feet high in a befuddled attempt to honor the Jewish ancestor.

Some thought it was a good thing that Herod had erected this huge structure if only to protect such an important tomb from the weather and other unwanted desecrations. Others, less impressed by Herod's motivations, loathed the interference of this half-Jew in such a sacred place.

Predictably, Herod made sure the building stones were chiseled with the telltale band around the perimeter of the face, clearly identifying to all visitors that it was one of his personal projects.

The trio climbed the exterior stairs into the building and stepped into the upper room of Herod's building. Within the walls and upon a floor which was built above the actual caves was a small synagogue which had side rooms spreading over other caves. These were quiet places where pious Jews could be alone to pray and read in peace while imagining the bones of their ancestors were just a few feet below. Caleb described every corner of the new building in detail. He also rehearsed the shapes of the original cave entrances, explaining that over the years, gates and stony barriers had been installed to stop unwanted access by worshipers or desecrators. The building walls now prevented access to all that.

Caleb related the persistent, age-old legend that during the four hundred years of Jewish exile in Egypt, the centuries when Abraham's and others of his family's bones lay exposed in the unsealed cave, the strange looking and now non-existent Hittites camouflaged and protected the small cave entrances from any interference from the belligerent and hostile Anakim giants. Thankfully, the Hittites had respected and honored Abraham, an old ally and friend who had lived peaceably among them. He was a man whose God had brought them all a time of unequalled health and prosperity while they lived close to Hashem's special friend.

Saul and Miriam wandered around the upper rooms slowly, praying and generally drinking in the atmosphere, all the while delighting in the spirituality of the spot so revered by all Jews throughout their history. Directly beneath them and laying quietly inside the sealed sepulcher were the weathered and drying bones of the father of the Jews, the one to whom Hashem had promised this whole land. Both visitors were deeply humbled at the thought of being so close to the patriarch's remains.

When they came together again, Saul slowly repeated the list of venerable Hebrews buried below them: Abraham, Sarah, Isaac, Rebekah, Leah, and then, a little later, Jacob, whose bones were brought back to rest here by his sons when Joseph was a great ruler in Egypt. After the four-hundred-year hiatus, a few local Jews were entombed here as well but that was soon discouraged as an impertinence to the greatness of Abraham. With a show of conspiracy, Caleb indicated that one of the fortunate few that had achieved enough status to be included in this spot was, of course, his ancestor, the famed giant-slaying warrior, Caleb.

When he was Pharoah's second in command, Joseph had made a special trip to Hebron explicitly to bring his father Jacob's remains to this cave, thus fulfilling the demand his father had made to not to leave his bones in a foreign land. This blessing, Jacob had demanded because he had learned about the promise of this land at the feet of his grandfather. Saul could just imagine the site of that little boy drinking in the words of the "friend of Jehovah," as his grandfather related the amazing promises of Hashem given to his offspring.

What was clearly understood by most Jews was that this place was not only a tomb and a resting place for dead ancestral bones, but much more importantly, it was the historical marker of the initial choosing by Jehovah. The purpose of the "choosing" was hotly debated and often less clear and all that could often be agreed upon was that Abraham and his descendants were to fulfill a specific and essential duty upon the earth.

Descending the stairs, the small party retreated a little and looked back upon the monument. There was an agreement between the three that it would have been even more genuine if the caves had not been covered with Herod's colossal structure. That said, they understood the justification for such a fortification.

Although they had a deep emotional attachment to this ancestral shrine and could have easily remained in the touching atmosphere, Caleb gently led them further west to a well-traveled roadway along the bottom of the rocky ridge. He walked slowly, obviously in deference to Miriam and Saul as the trail started a steep ascent and began winding back and forth through stone houses built to the very edge of the road. After a long mile and nearing the top, the trail made a sharp left turn and then straightened, leaving the houses behind and climbing directly to what looked like the highest part of the entire Hebron ridge. Emerging from the surrounding homes, they climbed another one hundred yards among foot trails to what looked like abandoned building foundations on the now-abandoned top of the ridge.

Caleb walked to a pile of large stones which were weather-worn and obviously ancient. It was plain that they were hand-carved and once used for buildings. He scrambled to the top of the pile.

"These are the foundations of the palaces of King David's first seat of power," he said proudly. "The houses we came through are constructed from the rest of the stones from David's buildings which sat right here. The Philistines took the stones they could easily move to build their homes."

Off to one side he pointed to a large, wide stairway rising up the side of the mountain, beginning and ending at no particular place. "Giant steps," he stated emphatically, "telling us that this was once the place of the city of Arba. The lazy Philistines simply could not move these massive boulders," he laughed.

Caleb was referring to the fact that it was the lazy enemies of Israel who dismantled and rolled the stones down to make their houses in the town when they had dominated the area.

Both Saul and Miriam awkwardly climbed the oversize walkway, wide-eyed and having to take two steps between each large, rising stone as they climbed further to the top of this southern and highest ridge.

"It is fitting that the first throne of David was established on top of the foundations of the city of the creatures that the ten spies were so afraid of." stated Caleb. "King David knew how to conquer and deliver us from the giants."

Saul and Miriam nodded in quick agreement.

The Anakim's staircase left both visitors breathless in many ways. All their lives they had heard about the large inhabitants of the land but both had somehow downplayed it to the realm of unimportant fables or the exaggerated stories of history. The reality of what their forefathers had faced was now becoming very apparent and the size of the creatures that could easily walk these steps was slowly dawning on Saul and Miriam.

Caleb continued up to the very top of the ridge and led them to a small stone monument and announced, "Jesse, father of King David. This is his original burial marker."

He left Saul and Miriam standing before the stone, touching it softly and realizing that the famous King David had probably handled this very monument.

He then called them over to the largest stone on the hilltop. "This is the marker for Ruth and we are not sure which one is for Boaz."

Continuing his chronicle, Caleb rattled off a list of familiar names mentioned in the sacred histories, names which rolled off Jewish children's tongues easily, all while sweeping his arms and gazing about the hilltop.

"They are all buried here," he stated.

This truly was a hilltop of scriptural heroes. Caleb then sat on a nearby stone and waited contentedly as the pair wandered about the mountaintop, a stony memorial to a more uncomplicated time in Israel's history. That had been an era when both the faithful and their enemies were easily recognized as either friend or foe.

Caleb finally rose and proceeded to carefully lead them down a well-worn, slippery staircase on the distant south side of the ridge. After carefully picking their footholds and descending over three hundred feet, they emerged onto a street that wound its way through a crowded neighborhood nestled against the bottom of the high ridge. He continued along the roadway, following the southern tip of the ridge until they came to a natural indentation in the steep upper rock wall that was over one hundred feet wide. It was partially obscured by overhanging trees but it was evident that the surrounding cliffs rose unbroken and vertically to the ridge above. Protruding out of the stony cliffs were colorful flowering plants.

"This was our first choice for the newest synagogue, set back nicely in that protective cove and we started our construction by beginning to remove the loose rubble that had accumulated in this crevasse. Within days it became apparent that this was an ancient burial pile for the Anakim and what we thought was a few feet of loose earth was a huge pile that filled a much larger depression that went back into a sharp crevice in the ridge. After a little digging, we saw that the walls of the ridge fall straight down to this level. It looks as if they threw their dead over the edges of that ridge, fully dressed in their armor and with their weapons, and then covered them with loose dirt. We are now aware that the mound of rubble you are looking at is either a pile of dead giants' bones or a tremendous opportunity to examine our history, depending on how it is regarded."

Caleb was obviously aware of the repulsion of the Pharisees for anything dead and buried.

"Is this where the skull in the market was from?" asked Miriam.

"Exactly, and that sword is the biggest sword found so far, so all surmise that it was Anak's," he said with a tinge of unbelief. "But we know that over the centuries and with each generation, the size of these creatures diminished, for Goliath was much smaller than the bones found here."

Miriam was fascinated and Saul was also strangely interested but kept his distance from the rubble.

A few men were lazily sifting through the outward extents of the pile, looking for trinkets or small items they could easily peddle but the main mound had only been slightly disturbed. Miriam could only imagine what would be found in the future. If indeed the succeeding generations were shrinking in size, then the largest skeletons and swords were yet to be uncovered. They would have been buried first and therefore deeper into the pile.

"There is a great controversy in our town, whether it is defiling to uncover these remains or whether it is a blessing to show how great was the courage of Joshua," Caleb stated, not indicating where he stood on the issue. "For now, no more excavations are taking place until the Great Sanhedrin in Jerusalem makes a final judgment and a proclamation on this."

Caleb's words awakened Saul's memory of what seemed a menial and unimportant discussion bandied about in Jerusalem. He could now see that no one there understood the significance of what was being asked. To most in Jerusalem, this was another boring legal property rights issue taking place in a far-off location, not of much interest to Jews anywhere else. The Pharisees in the court would look on it only in the light of remaining pure and would surely vote against any further digging as they had for many other cemeteries.

Only after Miriam's intense curiosity was satisfied did the small troop begin to travel a different route back, slowly circling around the lower roads of Hebron and eventually arriving at the inn. Their exploring had taken most of the day and they were hot, hungry and weary. The return walk had led them through vineyards and past children happily playing among the lower orchards.

Miriam, whose attention had been focussed on the magnificent sights of the day, noticed that several of the people she passed needed some form of medical help and many children were sporting bent legs or arms which was the usual lifelong penalty for breaking a bone. This annoyed her and she filed it away in her memory.

Caleb left them at the inn for the evening and made further arrangements for their animals to be saddled early the next morning. Saul and his sister retired immediately after dinner, completely satiated with not only food, but with overpowering images and by the dominating spiritual presence which Machpelah had imparted in them.

A disturbing thought had persistently danced through Saul's mind that day, one which greatly disturbed him and one he struggled to keep out of his thinking, for just contemplating it made his curiously guilty.

Was the world that Hashem created, the one which He seemed to be intimately involved with, much bigger than he and other Pharisees had allowed for?

The latest version of Pharisaical teaching was that Hashem was only interested in the nation of the Jews and more pointedly, that He was focused only on the most obedient Jews, thus limiting His all-knowing attention to just the Pharisees. Beyond that, and because different sects did not agree, it was buried in Saul's thinking that only he and his close friends were the pinpoint of Hashem's love and interest. The events of this trip and meeting amazing people claiming various links to God stood in strange contrast to that exclusionary thinking.

Indeed, Saul was having an intense and very internal struggle.

How could he deny that good men like Moshe and Caleb and even the strange desert dwellers may have an important place in Hashem's world. Somehow.

CHAPTER FIFTY-FIVE

Mystical Mamre

The next day, beginning at the third hour, the refreshed party mounted their well-rested animals and rode north. Stopping just before crossing completely over the Hebron ridge and looking west from a high point on the crest, they gazed over the immense forested area that disappeared into the western horizon. Caleb dismounted his horse and gathered his two charges.

"The Plains of Mamre. Although he is buried on the other side of the ridge, our father Abraham lived here." he announced.

From the Torah, Saul and Miriam knew this to be the place where Hashem appeared to Abraham in human form and where He supped with him, calling him His friend and telling him of the upcoming catastrophe of nearby Sodom. Their minds tingled at such exciting thoughts.

Caleb led the way down the gentler north slope of the ridge and it was not long before they were encircled by well-tended almond and olive trees. Within a mile, that changed and they were riding among spreading oaks interspersed with elan trees. Caleb kept leading until they reached a huge dead stump hidden deep in the forest which stood a full six feet above the surrounding ground. It was all that remained of a tree that was easily five times the diameter of the biggest oak growing nearby and its sides were debarked and chipped and defaced.

He quickly dismounted and stood on a massive root spreading away from this stump and said, "As we all know, since Noah, the rains have been decreasing from generation to generation until now. The Sinai and the Negev have few forests left and are almost all desert. I am told that the area west of the Nile is becoming drier very quickly and soon will be a complete desert also. In King David's time, these hilltops were still lush and forested and had lions, bears, and great herds of migrating animals wandering back and forth from the forests of Ethiopia, through an equally lush Sinai, all on their migration to Babylon. These forests are almost all gone, dried up with the lowest and hottest areas becoming deserts in our country as well. None of those great animals wander here anymore. No one can remember seeing a gazelle a gazelle or lion."

This was an ingenious description by someone who had obviously tied legend, scripture, and observation together and made the most reasonable conclusions.

"In Abraham's time, centuries before David, there were trees," and he pointed to this stump, "that were of such enormous size and bulk that small villages lived under the canopy of a single plant. While living under such trees, Abraham's whole family and household were supplied with many types of fruits and it seems that all sorts of vines intermingled with the large branches and yielded a continuous bounty. Many types of small animals also lived in its branches, all flourishing under its wings, enjoying the protection where they could survive on its yield alone. All kinds of birds nested in its branches which formed a canopy that reached many hundreds of feet high and spread out even wider than it was tall. Creatures of all sorts made these trees their homes and survived on the seeds and nutritious leaves and mosses."

Caleb paused a very long moment and said quietly, almost mournfully, "These trees no longer exist, at least not in this region, for the rains no longer come as before. Our father Abraham flourished under trees of this stature in Shechem, at Bethel, and then here, just as the ancient scrolls describe. He must have loved them for he always pitched his tent among them and his flocks flourished in their shade and grazed in grasses under them. It was among these trees that the angels of Adonai," and Caleb whispered that name respectfully, "came to our father."

It was apparent that Caleb had a picture burned into his imagination of the ancient splendor of this region and both Saul and Miriam were drawn into his vision, listening to his deep and passionate descriptions.

On foot, he led them away from the stump to a small rock outcropping, where Caleb sprinkled a little water from a small vase he had brought specifically for this demonstration. As he splashed the eight-foot-tall rock, the outline of a huge leaf imprinted into the flat portion of the rock became visible. The leaf was wider than the length of a man's outspread arms and only partially shown in its height.

"Legends tell us that one of these leaves could provide nourishment for a family for many days by simply boiling it in water and that the generous tree shed them continually throughout the year, a few at a time, as if directed by the creator," Caleb stated. Turning to Miriam, he said, "Any injuries wrapped with these leaves seemed to heal quickly and completely and with no scars." He sprinkled more water on a crude diagram etched into the rock, depicting an arm wrapped in a large leaf.

"Our father Abraham lived an extra-long and healthy life among trees such as these, and I am sure that there must have been other benefits that have been lost and forgotten that we can only just imagine. The Anakims knew of the special powers of these trees as well but used them for their devious purposes. Brilliant as they were, they were constantly perverting Hashem's gifts and using them in evil ways, and that became their downfall. When they could no longer figure out how to milk their strength, they cut the trees down and used them for weapons."

Miriam was completely intrigued.

Was this how they managed to produce the huge clusters of grapes that Moses had described? Were there strange qualities in the sap of these amazing trees that were mysterious and miraculous?

These, and many other questions would have to wait for a private conversation with Caleb.

Obviously, there was much that their guide was leaving unsaid and Miriam's inquisitive mind was getting severely provoked by the sight of such magnificent remains. A sudden jolt of fear came over Miriam.

Just how much information would be lost at the passing of such knowledgeable people like old Moshe or the caravan master. She must speak to them and soon.

Returning to their mounts, Caleb led them even deeper into the dense forest. He dismounted again and invited them to walk with him, leading the way to another dry and worn stump that had been ground down to ground level but was well over thirty feet in diameter. The area that the canopy of such a tree could cover was beyond imagination. The surface of the stump had been polished smooth by the steps of centuries of inquiring visitors and Saul and Miriam walked back and forth on it while Caleb explained. "This is a different type of tree with incredibly hard black wood that resists most knives or saws. Some of the Anakim's spears that we have found have shafts made from this wood, and they are still perfectly sound with no sign of rot. Obviously, these trees were still around then and somehow, they managed to cut and whittle them as required."

A little further up the path, a wizened old man was sitting on a rock and whittling away on a small piece of dark wood. He quickly looked up and hurried to uncover his display of miniature swords he had painstakingly carved from this very wood which he retrieved from softer buried roots he had uncovered as needed. Around his work area were strewn a small stash of wood shavings which Miriam noticed and politely asked if she could possibly buy. Baffled by such a request, the old man gathered them up, wrapped them tightly in a small skin bag and graciously received a small payment while handing them to her. Miriam thanked him and then asked Caleb if a sample of the previous tree was available as if she had just thought of some exotic use for these shavings. Caleb discussed this with the old man and for a few denarii arranged a sample to be delivered to his house before Sabbath. Saul, Caleb, and the old man all wondered what possible use Miriam would have for discarded bits of wood.

Through all this, Miriam was riveted and entranced. Her memory of the Torah description of the Garden of Eden was of it being a place with majestic trees that were much more than mere plants, but were, in some inexplicable way, both physically and spiritually alive. They carried the promise of life and health within their very makeup. Moses's writings spoke of them as being given by God for just that, for food and healing.

Did the type of existence that Adam had, an existence where all forms of creation were interwoven and depended on each other with each ultimately drawing on Hashem as their source, simply disappear and with it, the need for such supernatural trees? Did the trees themselves respond to the needs of the creation. Was this what Adam was driven away from?

Miriam had never before been challenged to consider whether those trees were spoken of as only symbols or if they indeed possessed qualities long forgotten. It was hard to even imagine the things that Hashem had installed in His perfect trees.

Miriam shook her head as if shedding some overwhelming incursion. Her amazing mind was completely overloaded, for these were far too formidable questions.

Was man supposed to be completely interconnected to other parts of the creation, she wondered. She understood that she had just caught a glimpse of something enormous. If that was in any way true, just how far had the world she presently lived in, fallen from Hashem.

The trio wandered the area, telling and retelling the many stories of Abraham that took place here and before long it was time to return to the inn and begin the afternoon's preparations for the Sabbath. It was a very absorbed and lost-in-thought Miriam who rode that loud complaining donkey over the ridge, back to Hebron.

Once at the inn, Saul and Miriam not only prepared their clothes for the Sabbath but also their minds and spirits, struggling to quiet themselves from all the excitement brought on by the adventures of the last few days.

Just before sundown, Caleb, now elegantly dressed in a white over-robe, returned to the inn and led them to his spacious home where he warmly introduced Saul and Miriam, as one would old friends, to his pretty, cherub-faced wife and his four bright-eyed children. That was followed by warm introductions to his sister, her husband and many more offspring who were washed and scrubbed and freshly clothed for the coming Sabbath. The aged Moshe was also there and it was a loud and merry household that welcomed the brother and sister from Tarsus into their spacious home and into their warm Sabbath.

Sumptuous plates of food had been prepared and the beautiful incantations of peace and rest were melodically recited by the women. Bread was broken and the traditional wine was poured in abundance. Soon smiles broke out everywhere as the coming in of the day of rest flooded over them once again.

This was a beautiful evening spent in the warmth of this household, filled with the telling of their families' histories, reciting humorous misfortunes and laughing at mischievous children and their clumsy antics. It was very late when Saul and Miriam wandered back to the inn, well within the Sabbath Day walk parameters, where they enjoyed the most peaceful night's sleep of their journey so far. Miriam had presented the two bags of shavings she had collected to old Moshe, both for his contemplation and to be included in the delivery he was arranging.

Early the next morning, Saul made his way to the local synagogue, meeting Caleb and Moshe there and the early morning was passed in prayers, readings, family blessings and good conversation. After synagogue, he returned to the inn and then accompanied Miriam to Caleb's house for the afternoon with more food and good relaxed conversation.

As the Sabbath waned and the final Sabbath blessings were recited, Moshe retrieved a large satchel and seated himself beside Miriam. While the trio had been off exploring Mamre, he had been very busy. He took out multiple pouches and vases of unusual extracts and powders, describing each in detail to an attentive Miriam who drank in every detail, even making markings on each container to classify and label them exactly. He said these were but samples and he would gather larger quantities of the useful ones for delivery. Moshe also assured Miriam that he could get most of these local remedies delivered to her within a fortnight.

Once again, gracious Moshe would not take any reimbursement until final deliveries were completed and Miriam was once more confused but warmed with the manner that business was conducted in the trusting eastern culture. Hebron had thankfully retained this quality. It had remained a place where a person's word and commitment to an agreement were much more valuable than contracts or down payments. The loss of this trust was much more devastating to all parties than any loss of money.

Caleb and Saul were engrossed in a conversation of their own, discussing an alternate route back to Jerusalem for Saul and Miriam so that more new sights would be seen. They agreed on a route past the ancient stronghold of Lachish, then past the Valley of Elah where these beautiful oak trees hid Saul's frightened army while Goliath roared in the valley below and, from there, they could go on to Lydda. This route would be a very long day's ride, but Lydda would provide a resting place and a chance to get reacquainted with Saul and Miriam's cousins who lived there.

All the treasures that Saul and Miriam had purchased while in Hebron would be shipped by cart to their home at Gamaliel's house, Caleb heartily assured. He would personally see to that.

A noisy, good-natured argument erupted as Moshe again absolutely refused any attempt at payment for his personal time and services, stating that he had come to regard Miriam as a beloved daughter. Very thankful and overcome emotionally, Miriam finally relented and accepted the act of love that this old sage was presenting.

CHAPTER FIFTY-SIX

On to Lydda

Early the next day, after a touching parting from their new friends, Saul and Miriam set out on their return route by again passing through the historic plains of Mamre. Within a few hours they were approaching the hilltop ruins of the once great city of Lachish.

Not much remained of this ancient border stronghold. At one time, it had been an important frontier bastion of protection from the Philistines who dominated the lower western plains. The ferocious battles of this region were also a distant memory. A few contented farmers lived in the only habitable houses remaining on the hilltop while they grazed their herds of goats and sheep on the southern slopes where a refreshing spring provided copious amounts of water for thirsty plants. It was easy to see how this agricultural city had fed thousands and flourished in the time of General Joshua, but hundreds of years later, when Jerusalem became the capital and the Philistines were gone, Lachish had quickly lost its importance. The two travelers dismounted for a break and washed the dust from their faces and necks in the cool and clear spring. The flattened ruins of the thousand-year-old city with its massive but broken walls encircled them eerily.

They soon resumed their journey north and within the hour crested a hill on the southeast end of a long, low valley. Saul had been here before and he announced it as the Valley of Oaks, or Elah, in the ancient tongue.

Again, in the thousand years since David was a lad, the valley had dried significantly. Whereas all the hills were once covered by these massive trees eight feet thick in the trunk and whose branches spread over an acre, there were only a few scrubby ones left growing in the lowest and wettest areas. The remaining trees certainly did not have the girth of those told of in ancient records and their foliage certainly did not have the ability to hide anything like the encamped army of King Saul.

Relating the story of David and Goliath from the hilltop, both brother and sister could envision a glorious rout, with the Philistines running for their lives out the far western end of the valley.

Pushing their animals hard, Saul and Miriam arrived late in the day at the busy crossroads town of Lydda where they acquired rooms at the same inn as when they made their original journey from Caesarea to Jerusalem. As they dined, they enquired about where the tent makers' shops were and made their plans to find their cousins in the morning.

The next day, after a good rest and a leisurely breakfast, the eager twosome sauntered through the industrial street that for centuries was designated as the area where tradesmen had their factories. A few inquiries led them to a shop cheekily named Tents of Cydnus, obviously after the river in their home city of Tarsus, making Saul and Miriam chuckle to themselves. A youthful man, an apprentice no doubt, was working hard on a goatskin, diligently scraping the hide when he noticed the pair. He looked up to see the couple entering the working area and he asked if he could be of service.

"We are looking for our cousins, Andronicus and Junia, sir," Saul said, possibly a little brashly, as if annoyed at being questioned by a mere tradesman.

After scrutinizing Saul curiously for a long moment, the youth said while pointing, "You can find them at the synagogue, two streets over." The lad continued watching them closely as they left in the direction he had indicated.

Synagogue? On Monday? Possibly a friend had died, Saul thought.

Approaching the large building, they saw a milling crowd of over fifty people gathered in the large, stone-paved courtyard outside the main door and a bearded speaker standing in the middle of them. They sidled close enough to hear.

"I was His disciple and I saw Him alive many times after they crucified Him," the man declared with genuine urgency and conviction. Murmurs rippled through the crowd and the spirited orator continued his sincere declaration of his belief in Jesus as Messiah. He was clad in the rough cloth that now seemed to be the favored uniform of the Galileans and his heavily accented Aramaic speech was easily identified as that of the Galilee.

After a few moments, the man's attention drifted and then suddenly turned to a small, twisted child of about seven or eight years who was directly in front of him but was propped against her father's leg. He approached the man and talked to him quietly and then reached down and took both hands of the child.

He spoke to the child, "Little sister, in the name of Jesus, be made straight."

A wave of excited murmurs traveled through the small crowd and then an expectant pause as everyone watched the confused child closely. Suddenly, witnessed by those watching her, the legs of the child moved and then stretched out and her little bent and crooked back straightened in an instant. With wide and inquiring eyes, the startled child looked down at her strange new limbs. Realizing something had changed, she awkwardly pulled herself to her feet using her father's robe. She stood there, wobbling unsteadily like a newborn fawn, and staring at quivering legs that had never held her up before. Upon realizing she was standing tall, she looked up questioningly at her father whose bearded face was completely soaked in tears. The child was dangerously unbalanced and still swaying and that was obviously from never walking before, but her face was now beaming and she began moving her legs around tentatively.

The gathered throng started screaming and yelling and an ecstatic burst of praise to God was let go that filled the courtyard and was heard down the street. An older woman who was standing next to the child, fainted to the ground, causing yet more confusion and some panic.

Miriam and Saul stood at the back of the crowd, stunned into silence. Neither could deny what they had just seen.

Saul reacted immediately. *These disciples of Jesus were doing it again. Once more they were flaunting their ability to do these strange things,* he thought.

"*How did they do this anyway? Who was teaching them how to access the demonic power needed to heal someone,*" he demanded silently.

Furthermore, he asked of nobody but himself, *why was he, such a committed Pharisee, always bumping into this bunch and how come they showed up in his world so often.*

Standing on the edge of this joyful crowd, he wisely kept his contentious enquiries to himself. For once, not having any answers, Saul the Pharisee was speechless.

The crowd continued praising Hashem and joyfully milling about, both amazed and a little confused at what they had just seen.

It was then that Miriam recognized her older cousin Junia, directly in the middle of the swarm and standing close by was her husband, Andronicus. Both were locked in an intense conversation with a few others. Before long, they approached the Galilean and remained engaged him in a deep and animated exchange which lasted for many minutes. Saul and Miriam remained at the distance, still stunned into inaction and not knowing what to do next.

"Let's go," announced a visibly shaken Saul, finally. He turned and began to retrace his steps but noticed that Miriam was not following.

"I will meet you back at the inn," she stated. "I want to wait for Junia, for I have not seen her for years."

Saul left without another word, strutting away angrily and shaking his baffled head.

It was late afternoon before Miriam made it back to the inn and she never volunteered any explanation to Saul.

He curtly told her, "We will leave in the morning and should be home by early afternoon."

He had decided that he had entirely no interest in meeting with his cousins or hearing why they were so involved with these Galileans.

In the morning, Saul and Miriam left Lydda. They took the familiar Jerusalem Road past Emmaus, over the crest and, finally, through the Jaffa Gate. The day's journey had been uneasily quiet, with Saul pensive and moody. As he got closer to his home, his mood eased a little and he and Miriam began chatting, reminiscing about the spectacular sites they had seen.

Upon dismounting at the stable and as they walked in the gateway, Miriam turned to Saul and said earnestly, "Saul, my dear brother, I cannot imagine a more incredible adventure than what we have just experienced. I will cherish and remember this my whole life. The stories and sacred writings mean so much more today to me than when we began our journey."

After a few blocks, she asked coyly, "When can we go north?"

The dark cloud hanging over Saul left and they both laughed heartily. This levity erased the stifled anger building in Saul since Lydda and his contorted face relaxed.

"Give me a week to recover," was Saul's jovial retort.

When they arrived at their home, waiting for them was a tightly wrapped bundle, three bulging sacks full of smaller containers, another larger wrapped parcel with brightly colored cloths peeking out and two beautiful vases. They were completely astounded that these could have arrived so quickly from Hebron and everything looked to be in perfect condition.

Tied to the outside of the largest bundle was a small pouch with large but familiar seeds inside, with a small note.

It said, "*These seeds were found in the burial mounds of the Anakim and may be seeds of the enormous grapes grown here. Use them as you see fit. Your friend, Caleb.*"

Miriam was speechless and found a spot for them amongst her most treasured items. A large smile appeared on her pretty face.

Their quiet, comfortable apartment was a welcoming sight and much appreciated that night and the next few days were spent close to home resting up from their enjoyable but exhausting trip. During those first day's home, there were long and enthusiastic conversations with a very inquisitive Gamaliel and his family, all of whom marveled at the adventures that Saul and Miriam were describing. Being one of the most important families in Jerusalem had destined them to limited travel for it seemed Gamaliel's presence was constantly required in the city and, regrettably, it had been many years since he had personally led his students to any of these places. The famous rabbi sat enthralled at the description of the strange and oddly spiritual desert people and he had endless questions about the burial site of the giants, but he seemed most completely taken with Miriam's account of the almost other-worldly qualities of the oaks of Mamre. He listened intently as she described each part and he nodded in agreement at her developing theory about such supernaturally linked aspects of the creation.

Repeated over and over was the family's regret that they had never experienced such a trip and Gammy was particularly unsettled and a tinge envious that another expedition was being planned for the following week to the north of Israel. He had toured some sites around the countryside many years ago, but he had not enjoyed the depth of experience that he was hearing about from Miriam and Saul, plus he had not had someone like Caleb to point out all the details of the journey.

Gammy was, quite frankly, jealous, but his very good manners hid his annoyed sentiments well.

CHAPTER FIFTY-SEVEN

Demonic Powers

Now that Saul was home again, the three men gathered for one of their usual meetings and Saul was fully informed of the continuing growth and the increasing good favor among the population for the followers of the Way. Provoked by this report, he described the scene he had witnessed in Lydda.

"The effect of these deceiving incidents on the weak-minded is alarming," he declared. "I believe that a proclamation from the High Priest is needed immediately about where these strange powers originate or I can see that all of Israel will be swayed," he demanded, without any doubt in his position. He assumed that all three were agreed that the time for action had arrived.

Gamaliel answered hesitantly.

"The problem is that there is no way to claim it as demonic when it is only good and beneficial things that transpire. People are helped, plus no money or other profit is demanded by these men."

"That is the cunning and devious part," exclaimed an irritated Saul. "The people's attention and their devotion, is being craftily led away from the Law by a seducing power that is made to appear to come from Hashem. These sorcerers initially claim to agree with Moses, yet cleverly, they turn the nation's attention away from his truth. It is ingenious and crafty and satanic, all at the same time."

Saul had now declared in words what had been formulating in his mind for weeks and today, he felt confidently stimulated, almost anointed, because it all made great sense to him. Gamaliel and Gammy remained hesitant and unconvinced but said nothing in rebuttal of Saul's new-found certainty.

Not mentioned in this conversation was the fact that Gamaliel had faced this question two years earlier when a ruling by the Sanhedrin was demanded by other indignant Sadducees and Pharisees about the abilities of Jesus. At that time the court could not agree if such inexplicable incidents and spiritual powers were from Hashem or from wicked sources. It was Jesus Himself who made the simple but irrefutable statement of "a kingdom divided against itself cannot stand," a statement that further divided and confused the most ardent of His enemies.

At that time, the official ruling of the Sanhedrin was, "We cannot tell where the power comes from."

This uncertain conclusion had made Gamaliel ponder another scenario, and that was the possibility of the evil misuse of divine goodness, a concept he had kept to himself for the last few years. Could evil men misconstrue Hashem's great blessings for their own gain? He suspected he was getting closer to the truth for he had often seen good used in evil ways in Jerusalem. Actually, it was a daily occurrence.

With respect to the Galileans, he had a problem. He could not apply that principle to Jesus or His disciples no matter how hard he tried. In all other cases, such influence-peddling always resulted in the perpetrator becoming wealthier, or more powerful, but these lowly Galileans demanded no praise or money for their abilities, generously praying for and healing people not confessing their doctrines.

"What was their ultimate motive," he asked to no one in particular.

At this point, Gamaliel also saw no evil intent in the disciples of Jesus, only a desire to spread their particular version of godliness. Completely missing was the maliciousness that he uncovered daily when making judgements of guilt and innocence in his court.

In good conscience, he could not agree with any of Saul's statements.

CHAPTER FIFTY-EIGHT

The Birth of a Business

The following day, accompanied by girlish chatter and great excitement, Miriam and Leah began unwrapping and examining the treasures that had arrived from Hebron. It was a glorious time, full of surprise and amazement and many hours were consumed discussing the beauty and usefulness of each item. The pile of goods in front of them seemed to propel the two young women on a perplexing new mission. Soon they were hurrying back and forth to Miriam's new business location and while there, they began examining, measuring and discussing, all the while enjoying themselves thoroughly and visualizing every treasure's possibility.

They tenderly fondled the brilliant new fabrics, clutching them for a long while, then hanging the colorful samples here and there. They stood back and examined them from every possible angle. It was quickly decided that many more swathes of the brightest of the fabrics were badly needed. These were to be draped around the columns and thereby infuse the stall with much-need color, undoubtedly softening the atmosphere and generating peacefulness. They were having the time of their lives.

All the decorations proved very engaging, but more importantly, the arrival of the generous shipment of medical supplies had created an authenticity to

Miriam's future dreams. An equally unexpected result was that with each new bundle opened, Leah was also catching the vision.

Later that day, while the two young women were still deeply engrossed in lively conversation about organizing and decorating the stall, Barnabas appeared and waited quietly at the curb until Miriam noticed him.

"Could I speak with you in private, little sister," he asked politely and with a smile, using what was fast becoming his endearing pet name for Miriam.

Surprised and slightly apprehensive, she invited him to the small office room on the upper level, leaving Leah to more planning and scheming. Knowing that it was much too early to expect news or shipments from Barnabas, Miriam was instantly concerned that the meeting was going to be somehow unpleasant, but Barnabas put her at ease very quickly with a big smile and his calming and easy demeanor.

Without any small talk, Barnabas went directly to the purpose of his visit.

"Miriam, I own a piece of land, actually a farm, just a mile away on the road to Bethlehem, and I think it may be the best field anywhere near Jerusalem. It continuously produces bountiful crops of wheat and barley, or alternately, fresh vegetables, and the field is ringed by pomegranate and fig trees. I have supplied many of the stalls here on the Cardo for years now. Caiaphas's lawyers have approached me many times over the years, continually pressuring me to sell, but I have never wanted to sell to them as they would just increase the cost of such crops to the vendors if they got it. I now would like to sell that piece of land."

Miriam was wordless, a little bemused, and instantly interested.

"I thought of you," he stated frankly, "or more accurately, I was directed to you."

Miriam was listening intently, but the last statement caused her to straighten.

"By whom," was her quick question. She was suddenly concerned that her name was so easily mentioned in connection to real estate.

"Let me say that I was directed to you by a divine inspiration," he said quietly, then continued. "I would like very much for the new owner to be someone who loves and appreciates the land rather than plunders it. Also, there are dedicated men who work the land for me and I would like to see them remain employed and prosperous and see that their families prosper as well. The land is valuable and it is a good investment as it produces a handsome profit at every harvest. The proper rotation of crops means an almost continuous, year-round harvest as well."

Miriam sat in silence, her quick mind contemplating the pros and cons of such an undertaking.

What did she know about land and crops, she asked herself.

"Is there someone who oversees the land for you?" she finally asked of Barnabas.

"Yes," was his quick response. "There are reliable workers, but most importantly, there is a very competent overseer who lives on the land with his family. He knows the land and loves it as his own. He faithfully meets with me after every Sabbath to report the weekly happenings and to turn over the profits of the previous week. Although I am a merchant and not a farmer, it still has been a joyous endeavor for me and no hardship at all."

Miriam thought deeply for a moment and then inquired, "Then, why are you selling such a successful investment, if you don't mind me asking?"

Barnabas's gaze wandered, and he was searching for the proper words. "As I told you when we met a few weeks ago, my values have changed and my expectations of the future are completely different than when I first came to Jerusalem and invested. I am determined to lay up treasures in heaven rather than in this earthly existence."

He did not explain further.

Miriam countered, "But you will have quite a fortune from the land, won't you?"

"I want to give all that to my brothers and sisters of the Way. We have realized that we have none amongst us that are richer or poorer or more important or less important, all are equal under Hashem. It is our faithless and greedy natures that make us worried about hoarding for the future, and anyway, we are expecting the soon return of our Lord when all things will change."

Miriam replied, "But surely you will keep some money for unforeseen tragedies, won't you?"

Barnabas's face lit with a warm smile. "Then I would be trusting in hoarded money rather than my Lord, would I not?"

Miriam was astonished at that statement. She could not argue with his logic but had never heard of such all-encompassing reliance in the interjection of Hashem into one's life before. This was truly a different type of trust.

They discussed Barnabas's asking price and the amount seemed reasonable to Miriam but it would require every remaining shekel of her inheritance and possibly even a little more. She knew that she may possibly need a cache of money to keep her shop going until it became profitable, so she concluded that she would need to find a source of capital if she were to consider this proposal.

After a few minutes of quick mental analysis, she nodded her approval to him and proceeded with a tentative deal with Barnabas, subject to her being able to find more money and to her inspection of the land personally. She promised that she would not delay, needing two days to arrange the details and would apprise him if there were any obstacles.

Suddenly, Miriam was venturing into areas she had never experienced before and the thought of borrowing money made her unnerved and uncomfortable even though she had already calculated the initial purchase amount, the expected return, and the terms and length of any debt. If the costs and returns Barnabas had quoted her were correct, this was indeed a good investment, even allowing for the possibility of a few less productive years.

Barnabas rose. "Little sister" and he again used the endearing label, "there will be a tremendous blessing upon you in the future," This he whispered almost prophetically. "You have bountiful gifts given to you by Hashem which He trusts you with and which will also bless His kingdom."

Barnabas left completely settled, having already eased the burden of worldly possessions and money from his mind and spirit. Such was not the case for Miriam.

Barnabas had just spoken about things she had not consciously thought or verbally expressed before. She had always felt an irksome nagging that her life was fated for some purpose that, as yet, she did not understand.

Beyond her own deeply held premonitions, just what did Barnabas know about her that she did not?

That was a disturbing thought and was proving very unnerving to Miriam.

Miriam remained in her small upstairs room pondering Barnabas' words and quietly re-assessing her transaction until Leah appeared at the top of the steps and questioned if all was well. She decided to disclose to Leah all that had just transpired, but asked for a few days of secrecy for she had many complex details to work out to finalize the agreement.

Leah listened quietly, observing both the eagerness and the trepidation of Miriam, then finally remarked, "I have never met a woman like you before, Miriam."

Very seriously she said, "I am honored to just watch you. Gammy was supposed to be the great heir of the famous house of Hillel but I know you will surpass anything he will ever do."

Miriam was sincerely embarrassed at this comment for she, with all her mental abilities, great knowledge and capabilities, did not have the burning need to be recognized or admired. She was simply walking through life's doors that, very mysteriously, were opening to her.

After a few quiet moments, she began to realize that she needed a lot of help with all her plans for there would just not be enough hours in her days to complete all she was contemplating. Leah's smiling face and pure heart reminded her that she had already found someone who was more than willing and capable to be that helper.

CHAPTER FIFTY-NINE

Saul and Stephen Meet

Saul left early that morning for a visit to the Synagogue of Freedmen and before entering, he paused at the gateway and listened as the upper room across the road hummed with the irksome mixture of joyous song, fervent prayer and soft praise. There was a constant coming and going from this room, either to the Pools of Siloam for another baptism or to the Temple for the times of prayer and each person's joyful face seemed to grate on Saul's nerves and infuriate him more.

Finally, fully disgusted, he turned and entered the synagogue's courtyard and there he found an animated Samuel in full debate with his friend Stephen.

This man, very similar to Samuel and Saul in age, had immigrated with a younger brother from the large Jewish community in Egypt after his father had died a few years ago. His mother had passed before that, leaving him and his fourteen-year-old sibling free to come to the heart of Judaism to find a deeper meaning to all that had taken place in his life. Samuel had immediately counted him among his friends as he was a passionate student of all things Jewish and he deeply loved the Jerusalem synagogue and its people. It was a new, welcoming home to Stephen and his brother Justus.

When Saul approached the two, it was Stephen who was passionately quoting the prophets and doing most of the speaking. He seemed to have the normally composed and verbose Samuel confused and confounded into a rare silence.

Samuel turned and seeing his fellow Pharisee, introduced Saul. "Stephen, this is Saul of Tarsus, a teacher of the House of Hillel who agrees with me that all this talk of Jesus and the Spirit is dangerous and it deflects us from the real purpose of our calling as Jews—to obey and fulfill the Law. He also agrees that your teachings may be outright blasphemy."

Saul was a little taken back at this combative introduction but nodded in a guarded acknowledgement.

Stephen turned and bowed his head slightly in recognition of Saul's presence, but turned back to his old friend Samuel and replied in a gracious tone. "The Law, the prophets and all the patriarchs were all just a foreshadowing of the Holy One, Jesus, who was the fulfillment of the purpose of all these."

Without even hearing the words, Saul was at odds with this man who would so blatantly disregard him by turning his back toward him.

"Are you saying the Law is not required now?" Saul jumped in immediately.

"Well, Hashem did tell us He would pour out His Spirit and if His very essence dwells within us, isn't that more pleasing to Him than our pathetic attempts to please Him through coldly obeying the rituals of the Law?"

Stephen had turned his attention to Saul now, recognizing that Samuel was deferring to this new ally.

Saul was speechless for a moment, a little dazed by the wisdom and logic of the thought just presented by this unschooled commoner. He was also taken back by Stephen's assuredness and his refusal to be cowed by Saul's aggressive accusation. This man possessed an unusual boldness and his nearby younger brother nodded in quick agreement with his brother's words. That brotherly agreement increased Saul's annoyance immediately and he paused momentarily to collect himself.

Within moments, Saul's internal anger exploded. He realized that he had, although for just a short moment, been lured into contemplating this man's way of thinking and he instantly became aware of how he had almost allowed that deception to enter his mind.

A small group of synagogue visitors were stopped and were gathering around them, curious about where this noisy argument was going.

"What do you know about the Spirit of Adonai," Saul snarled menacingly to Stephen. "A little excitement, some deceiving tricks and you are deluded like all of these blasphemers," he spit out. "You prey on the ignorant and remove them from the wisdom and influence of the teachers of the Law where their salvation is and more importantly, where the salvation of our whole nation is. No doubt you and those like you will require their money soon, as is the goal of all like you."

Stephen turned back to Samuel and said, "The Lord Jesus said that hatred and murder was in the hearts of those who crucified Him and your friend is dangerously close to that level of thinking, I fear."

Stephen stopped speaking at that and motioned to his brother. They left quickly, rudely abandoning the two Pharisees and the small gathering to the echoey courtyard.

"That may be an old friend," Saul warned as Stephen disappeared, "but he has become a blasphemer as well as a deceiver and he is a definite enemy of the Law."

Saul waited for a response from Samuel, and hearing none, carried on. "There will come a day when we will have to deal with his type, for the sake of Israel."

"You are right, Saul, but until then, we try to convince them to see their error," replied Samuel, who motioned Saul to follow him to the room where the scrolls were kept, deeper inside the main synagogue.

Once inside the small room and with the door closed, he spoke quietly. "Saul, it may appear that these people are influencing everyone in Jerusalem but let me assure you that there is still a host of devout Jews who are passionate for the Law and a good number are right here in our synagogue. Many have secretly come to me and offered their support and expressed their own outrage as well but they do not know how to proceed. They have promised me that when the time is right, they will do their duty and move against these Galileans and their followers."

Saul was overjoyed to hear this. He had been frustrated and wondered often if the noncombative and peaceful approach of the disciples of the Way had seduced all Jerusalem. This latest revelation of secret support confirmed to him that the time was soon coming to speak out more forcefully and not just to correct the deceived, but also to seriously warn any others who would be considering such a blasphemous teaching. He was also relieved to see that Samuel was not influenced by his personal friendship with Stephen.

Later that day, when Saul left the synagogue and started for home up the Pilgrim's Road, he was engulfed by yet another boisterous and happy group of Galilean converts going up for prayers to the Temple. This bunch were embracing each other, chattering back and forth, singing loudly, and very rudely using the whole road while telling all around them of Jesus and His resurrection.

He remembered his earlier pledge to Samuel so he stopped in the center of the street, directly in the middle of the irritating group, and raised his arms to heaven. He cried out, "That is all a lie, purported by Jesus' pathetic followers who stole His body. Oh Israel, listen to Moses for your salvation."

The small crowd stopped, looked at Saul and listened for a moment. They then wagged their heads in a show of great pity.

Saul heard their muttered comment, "Blind leading the blind," they said.

He was incensed and out of a lack of words, simply growled at them.

Miriam was waiting for Saul when he returned and when he had washed and finished his afternoon oblations, she presented him with a plate of sumptuous fruit and fresh and fragrant breads and then hung around suspiciously.

Saul pretended to not notice her but then finally said, "OK, what is on your mind, sister?"

Being exposed so easily caused Miriam to laugh out loud at her inability to be in any way secretive or stealthy. She delicately told him about the opportunity to purchase more prime Jerusalem real estate and yes, she confessed, it was land that was also desired by the High Priest's family. She carefully explained the financial benefits, finishing with the substantial cost.

Saul listened, albeit a little confused that she would be looking for more investment when her initial one had not even gotten started and so his furrowed brow betrayed him.

Miriam admitted to Saul that she had just enough of her inheritance money left to pay for this land after her previous purchases, but that would leave her with no money to finance her new medicine shop. She posed two questions to him.

First, what did Saul think of a transaction that would put her somewhat in debt? Secondly, and Miriam was very gentle with this request, would Saul mind lending her some of his substantial inheritance to finalize the deal? She purposely left out the identity of the seller for the final destination of the money as not important to the conversation, and, thankfully, Saul did not think to ask.

After a little contemplation, Saul decided that he was pleased and flattered to have his opinions held so high by his sister and after only a few easily answered questions on her part, he gave his endorsement for the deal. When he asked how much she needed to close the deal and yet have enough to operate, she shyly mentioned 500 shekels.

Saul was surprised. This was much less than he had expected and she explained that the weekly returns on the harvested produce would allow her substantial and immediate working capital from the land deal.

Not surprisingly, Miriam had a little parchment ready on which she had written the details of the promise of repayment of the shekels to Saul, all within one year. Saul was again amazed at her previously unknown but now very apparent business acumen, but he abruptly interrupted her.

"Miriam, I will not lend you the money," he announced in a serious voice.

A look of shock followed by a look of resignation and acceptance crossed her face, all in an instant.

"I will make a wedding present of it," he emphatically declared.

Over her tearful protestations followed by her declarations of thankfulness, the parchment outlining her indebtedness was ceremoniously destroyed, going up in a small flame.

"Will you go with me tomorrow, just a mile up the Bethlehem Road, to examine this land?" she asked of him. It was a task to which Saul agreed happily.

Brother and sister visited late into the night in their apartment that evening, growing more and more pleased with the proposed transaction but even more contented with their closeness and oneness of mind about things that were so quickly invading their previously small world. Saul even found time to tease his sister that her delicate hands would now be dirtied by digging in the dirt of Judea. Quite suddenly, she was an important farmer, feeding the hungry hoards of Jerusalem and both found that quite amusing.

Neither Saul nor Miriam could have predicted that leaving Tarsus would change their lives so dramatically and so quickly, but both, for their own particular reasons, were becoming increasingly mindful that their immediate futures would change them even more.

The next morning, they left the Jaffa Gate and proceeded up the road to the south and over the first ridge, following along other lush fields to a marked stone that designated the beginning of the land they were looking for. The entire property was surrounded on three sides by rows of fruit and pomegranate trees, many already laden with ripening crops. The large, interior field that was enclosed by the trees had rows of rotating crops, each growing in differing stages and it was plain to see that it was precisely planned and tended immaculately. Interspersed among the plants this day were bent-over field hands tending the plants. Along the roadside and midway through the property was a well-kept stone house with a small low barn behind which was surrounded with the customary flock of chickens busily pecking away in the grass. It was a beautifully serene setting. Outside the house was a robust-looking youth working on a new harness and fitting it to a bored, half-asleep donkey.

Saul and Miriam inquired about the overseer and the youth called out to his father who was working, unnoticed, in the barn.

Brother and sister spent a full and eventful morning in long conversation with this well-muscled and obviously hard-working man while strolling the entirety of the land. He had not been surprised at the visit, for he had earlier been made aware that Miriam would be examining the farm.

This man spoke only a little Greek so Saul's interpretations from Aramaic for his sister were much welcomed. Miriam was getting much better at the local language but still required help with the many words she had never used or heard before. The farmer, with endearing terms, explained each crop, complete with the work required to bring it to harvest and then the return he was getting by selling it to the vendors on the Cardo. It was evident that he was one with his position, a man who had found his calling in life. Miriam immediately realized that his continuing presence was the key to making this venture successful.

At noon they left the farm, assured by the overseer that he would stay on, secure in the knowing that the enterprise was in excellent hands and that any investment here would have minimal risk. When they reached home, Miriam penned a quick message to Barnabas to meet with her the next day and bring a trusted lawyer. She knew Barnabas would understand the curt message.

Again, Miriam avoided revealing to Saul that he knew the seller and again, Saul had not thought to ask.

That evening, Saul counted out his gift of 500 shekels for her and she added them to the hidden gold coins and other shekels stored away in her containers. She knew the Judean law stated that Saul would have to be present to fulfill the requirement of a male family member signing off, thus making the transaction legal, and she was a little nervous for she had not yet informed him that the land belonged to Barnabas. Miriam finally decided that tomorrow would take care of its own problems and she drifted off into a dream-filled sleep.

The next morning, when all parties involved met at her new store at the Cardo, Saul was indeed surprised and slightly agitated that Barnabas and Miriam were the two participants in the transaction, but mostly, he was a little embarrassed that Miriam would, by an intended omission, keep this from him. After a little thought, he realized that she had just wanted to avoid his predictable disapproval so he quelled his feelings and any mention of the disciples or people of the Way was avoided while the deeds and title papers were completed and signed.

An enthusiastic Leah, seeming to know all, soon arrived with food and refreshments and the solemn business transaction became a festive affair. Even Gammy had surprisingly appeared, much to the bewilderment of Miriam and Saul. Barnabas blessed and thanked Miriam when all was done and laden with his small fortune, headed for the Temple.

In a rare moment of second thought, Miriam sighed deeply and became unusually quiet and removed. Her brother and friends noticed this but chose to keep the mood jovial and light-hearted and soon Miriam joined in and was again stimulated by the thought of the enormous undertaking ahead of her. Miriam's private concern had little to do with any fear of the upcoming tasks, only that her unquenchable and free roaming curiosity would pay a withering price.

Would she have any time left to pursue life's deeper questions and, hopefully, find some answers?

"Well, brother, we must get that northern tour done quickly as my future looks very busy," she confessed, and all four people agreed with this obvious understatement.

That week's Sabbath was spent at their home with a protracted evening meal with Gammy and Leah. It was during that meal that Gammy casually informed Saul and Miriam of what he had learned.

"That fellow Barnabas seems to be one of the most influential men in the group of followers of Jesus. He and his sister provide food and shelter for many of them, including the leaders so I suppose he can use the money in his charitable endeavors. I have heard rumors of others selling their property and houses but I am not sure why. It seems to be the latest thing that this group is doing. Also, I have heard that many have given the money from such sales directly to the leaders."

Saul shook his head disapprovingly and with an air of presumed insight said, "It was just a matter of time until the disciples began demanding money of their followers."

Miriam dropped her gaze and held her peace.

CHAPTER SIXTY

The Northern Tour

Miriam and Saul started their northern adventure the very next day, riding the same comfortable mounts they had on their southern journey and, once again, leaving from the Joppa Gate. This time they turned to the north and followed the main roadway as it climbed the long, easy slope to the heights north of the city. From the crest two miles away, one could look back down on the stony walls of Jerusalem.

At the very top of that ridge, Saul dismounted and helped Miriam down.

Surprised that they were stopping after so little progress, she noticed the eager expression on her brother's face and knew to anticipate something extraordinary. He led her to a rocky ledge above the surrounding trees, a short walk up from the road and from which they had an unobstructed view in all directions. He instructed her to sit down as he would one of his students. Miriam chuckled to herself, after all her years of wanting so much to learn, she had finally made it into a yeshiva, albeit a private one and one led by her own brother.

He pointed down to the hectic roadway they had left their mounts on and began.

"This highway is the one our father Abraham traveled almost two thousand years ago when the Canaanites were in the land and as you can see," he steered her attention along the well-worn hilltop highway, "it follows the mountaintops north through Samaria, just as we followed it along the heights in the south. To the west of here, these mountains slope away gently and when the rains come, the streams and rivers flow gently, allowing the watering of the valleys which open to the Plains of Sharon along the Great Sea. There the rivers become smooth and useful before they empty into the Great Sea."

Saul pointed through the western valley to the distant blue of the Great Sea, which could just be seen as a blue haze.

"That way is made of fertile land, easy to cultivate and over the years has been coveted by all our enemies. This was the valuable battleground where we fought the Philistines and the Greeks and now it is the Romans who take their turn."

Saul turned away from the well-treed and flourishing view and pointed east.

"But to the east, there are great crevices and canyons as the mountains fall quickly and steeply into the deep valley below. When it rains, the streams become torrents and raging waterfalls that tear away at the cliffs, depositing the earth on the valley floor, before they reach the Jordan River."

It was as if he were describing much more than just a physical landscape. Saul paused, scouring the scene, losing himself in deep deliberation.

Miriam waited patiently.

"In between those two extremes, at the tops of these hills and mountains, right here on the heights where daily life depends entirely on the blessings of Hashem, is where you find us Jews. We survive only by His provision, we prosper when He brings the rain, we suffer when He is displeased with us. He has set us on the mountaintops to be a light to the nations but also to be dependent on Him."

Miriam nodded in agreement at this very truthful insight.

Saul looked back at a small ridge jutting just northeast of the distant walls of Jerusalem and followed the ridge with his sweeping arm.

"That is the place where Jeremiah lamented over Jerusalem and that is his small village on the crest." Turning to the west, he said, "That high hill over there is where the prophet Samuel is buried, watching over the holy city from afar, from the hill of the Gibeonites. At our feet is the steep climb from the Jordan that thirty thousand of Joshua's men used to surround Ai by night."

Saul pointed to the high, rounded hilltop to the north.

"Joshua and his small army attacked directly from the east and lured the overconfident men out of the city, only to have these hidden soldiers burn their city behind them. You can see why they could march up this ravine undetected."

Miriam looked and saw a deep canyon below themselves whose bottom was not visible.

"Also, the whole army marched upward in that hidden valley to help the deceiving and cowardly Gibeonites who lived on those hills," and he pointed off to the northwest "when they were attacked by five kings, including the one from Jerusalem."

Miriam was quickly gaining an appreciation of the value of this raised viewpoint as Saul continued with a colorful and detailed portrayal of other historical battle sites and important characters who were mentioned in the record of the prophets and kings of Israel.

After an hour, Saul was done, happily having completed a remarkably passionate account of the conquests and battles with their wins and losses that had taken place within eyesight of Jerusalem. He proudly announced that all this had taken place here, within the borders of their tribe of Benjamin.

Miriam was truly enthralled, all the while asking a host of probing questions and being a true student of the lecture. Once more, she was visualizing the layout of great historical events that previously she had only pictured in her imagination.

Back on their mounts, they continued north along the high ridge for just a few miles until Saul stopped a local youth and asked about the cave. After a quick exchange, Saul and Miriam turned off the road and followed a descending pathway a few hundred yards to a rocky, forested outcropping facing to the northeast, well above the valley floor. They again dismounted and Saul cautiously picked his way through the surrounding underbrush, clearing a path until they reached the entrance to a cave. The stirring undergrowth caused a snake to scurry away from them and the slithering viper disappeared into the rocks surrounding the dark opening.

Saul froze and went no further. He simply pointed.

"King Saul and his men hid in here once while waiting until Johnathon routed the Philistines across the valley," he announced pointing north. After recapping that incident, they returned to the ridge and rode on.

Miriam was fascinated.

It was dawning on her that for the Jews of this northern area, their religion and their history, their victories and their tragic defeats, even their everyday survival was completely intertwined with the demanding hills and canyons they were riding through. She saw that one could not explain the history of the Jews without understanding the interaction of the land and its dramatic physical and spiritual undulations.

This was definitely not the same place where the peaceful pastoral life that Abraham lived, was experienced. The history of this area was one of war and constant struggle with the land, with pagan enemies and tragically, with fatal dissensions among the tribes.

They followed the winding ridge further north and Saul pointed out the sites of Migron and Micmash, finally stopping within view of a larger town slightly to the west of the dusty highway.

"That is Bethel," he said as he pointed west. Turning around, he said, "and that is the ruins of Ai to the east. You will remember that Abraham pitched his tent on the mountain between Bethel and Ai and built an altar to Hashem right around here." He looked about and then said with disgust, "It probably would still be here if the Canaanites had not had control for four hundred years until we routed them. Our faithful father lived his first years in this country on this very spot." He then added proudly. "Possibly right where we are walking."

That firm declaration made them feel like they somehow owned that hill and their willing imaginations were stirred with more colorful ancient scenes. Saul explained further. "This is also where Lot and Abraham were finally forced to separate, Lot chose the beautiful plain that was like the Garden of Eden when the Jordan flowed undisturbed and quietly, all the way to the Red Sea."

Pointing east, no such plain was visible, only the deep crevice that was now the dry and desolate Jordan Valley.

Miriam chuckled at the satire of Saul.

"Of course, that was before the great judgment of Sodom and Gomorrah, when the earth swallowed up the plain, sinking it to the depths it is now." He pointed toward the dry red mountains to the east which were surrounded by the encroaching desert. "Those burnt and bare hill are all you can see now."

Saul again commented. "Hesham always kept Abraham separate from the city-dwelling Canaanites, wanting him in the hills and mountains." After a few minutes to contemplate the meaning of that, he stated, "Near Bethel is also where Jacob met the Lord in a dream and saw the stairway to His presence."

With sudden emotion, Saul whispered, "This truly is a very special place."

Miriam was happily feasting on the wealth of information that her brother was giving and she privately scolded herself for underestimating him at certain times, or questioning his intentions. His Pharisaical demeanor and lifestyle tended to hide a mind that was curious and detailed and very diverse, and today, she was enjoying witnessing it at work.

Very privately, and only to herself, Miriam had concluded that constricting religious dogma was one of the most confining of all forces and most often was the source of stubborn ignorance, itself not allowing minds to explore the depths of God. She saw hints of this in her brother's constant pharisaical proclamations.

They continued along the wide road, imaginations aflame and always aware that this very track had historically been traveled by important patriarchs, dangerous enemies, very strange Canaanites and most of the mysterious and spiritual prophets of Israel. Such exciting characters would be a welcome change from the predictable Romans.

Soon they were passing the flowing wheat fields surrounding Ofrah, the birthplace of the reluctant warrior, Gideon. This area was the center of the major battles of Judah Maccabee, a time only 150 years ago when this amazing family began the campaign to rid Israel of the Greeks and their dominating and pagan influence.

After passing five more miles of rolling, neatly terraced and well-tended hill tops, the two travelers dropped into a wide and fertile valley with a small town sitting on the opposite ridge rising from the lush vineyards that covered the valley floor.

This was Shiloh, once the very heart and religious center of the entire Jewish nation and General Joshua's chosen capital. Back then, it was a thriving city, now it was reduced to insignificance. It was here that the shameful end came after over two hundred years of great blessing because of the presence of the Ark of the Covenant and the tabernacle set up by Joshua.

The declaration that it was considered Ichabod, or "Hashem has abandoned it," had left this a scorned and reviled spot.

Saul and Miriam pulled up at the single small inn perched on the crest of the ridge, which overlooked the dust-covered ruins of the once important city. At the foot of those ruins was the flat plateau where the tabernacle had been erected.

They unpacked for the night and refreshed themselves before Saul suggested a late afternoon walk. He led the way to the flat area and together they circled that deserted location, clearly seeing the dimensions of the tabernacle worn into the dry earth below their feet.

Saul pointed back across the valley they had ridden through to get to Shiloh, explaining that since Joshua's time, it had remained lush and well watered, covered with the bright greenery of enormous vineyards and surrounding orchards.

"That is the valley where the last remaining men of our tribe of Benjamin were allowed to kidnap wives from. The girls came and danced in the vineyards, just over there, and were willingly taken as wives by those poorly hidden men. At least that was the plan, it was a way for our tribe to survive, and you and I are alive because of this," said Saul, laughing.

Brother and sister imagined the comical sight of the mock kidnapping of squealing but delighted girls being dragged off by smiling and very happy Benjamin-ites.

They soon returned to the inn where the gregarious innkeeper told them stories of the many small Jewish villages spread in the rolling hills around them. It was a fertile area blessed with beautiful orchards and vineyards and the villages were populated with fiercely independent brethren who by their simple presence had become a barrier to further southward encroachment by the Samaritans. Tomorrow, Saul and Miriam would be travelling the usually avoided area where the Samaritans lived and Saul questioned him about what to expect.

The merchant described the region in much detail and then continued with the intriguing story of the Samaritans themselves.

As a Jew, his version of the history of the local Samaritan people was no doubt colored a little. He told of the forced intermarriage of the few Jews who remained in this area with their conquerors during the Babylonian captivity, a reality which created the despised and racially impure Samaritans. Conversely, these residents believed that because they were never taken away into exile, they were the purer race and the rightful children of Abraham and therefore, the "children of the promise." They even had built their own Temple to worship Hashem properly, not like the vacillating Jews of Jerusalem who were continually disobeying and being punished, even having their beautiful Temple destroyed. Saul and Miriam listened carefully and without comment to this intriguing and somewhat plausible version of Jewish history while they enjoyed the simple dinner that was provided to them.

The next morning, brother and sister continued on the ancient roadway through a narrow winding valley below high and heavily-terraced hills. Their first stop was at the large stone marking the burial site of Eli, the last of the priests of the tabernacle, where Saul gave an impassioned account of the life of this controversial priest.

After riding a few miles more, the narrow and winding valley opened to a sprawling and slightly rolling plain where they rode along cultivated fields and goat pastures and before long, began a long, slow decent to a larger valley surrounded on the west by two high mountains and on the east by an even larger mountain spreading eastward toward the Jordan Valley. Saul had been here only once before and trying his best to remember, he began a rambling commentary.

"We are approaching Shechem in the valley ahead." Pointing to the mountain on the east, he said, "This mountain is where Itamar, son of Aaron and the greatest of our High Priests is buried."

A half a mile more and they were entering the outskirts of the town.

Shechem was located at the intersection of three productive valleys which made it a busy agricultural meeting place with a thriving market on either side of the main road. A few hundred yards past the end of the market and a little off the road itself stood a stone structure with all the trappings of a large town well.

Miriam quickly asked, "Jacob's well?"

"Exactly," replied a pleased Saul. There was a sprawling inn very near the well and they dismounted and quickly had their animals cared for.

Miriam's attention was instantly captured. She wandered over to the well and almost immediately, she was in a lively conversation with an outspoken local woman. The woman, dressed in the colorful and distinctive robes of a Samaritan, drew a vessel of water from the deep well which she had attached to a long rope and offered Miriam a drink.

This was something Miriam had for many years desired. This was one of the earliest and most controversial wells in the history of the Jews and this one linked Jacob to the land and to the blessings of Hashem. In their ongoing history, her ancestors were tied to their wells even more than they were to the magnificent trees that sheltered Abraham.

Saul stood gazing at the surrounding mountains, spellbound by the overpowering history of the area. He was not pleased with the fact that the Samaritans now dominated the town and claimed much of that history as theirs but, he decided that they were only taking advantage of opportunities presented because of the failings of his Jewish brethren.

He noticed his sister was now chatting easily with other local woman and wondered if she clearly understood the inferior position of these half-Jews in the eyes of Hashem. As much as he was in awe of Miriam's mental prowess, he sometime worried for her naivete and her reluctance to make the harsh judgments needed of those who were so far below her well-born status.

He strolled back to the market, warming a little to the town when he saw the nods of recognition he was receiving, no doubt because of his well-marked and immaculately-fringed prayer shawl which clearly identified him as an important Pharisee. He chose to ignore the others who regarded him with a suspicious and wary glance.

Saul took his time as he leisurely roamed the stalls, noticing Miriam had returned to the one-sided conversation with the initial woman at the well. When Miriam finally joined him in the market, he could tell she was unsettled and he wondered what had taken place and upon inquiring if all was well, all he could get out of her was a guarded, "I have just heard the most remarkable story."

The merchants of Shechem were wily and aggressive and obviously comfortable with actively accosting the various types of customers who wandered in. Shechem was an intersection of important routes both north and south and east and west and that brought them quite a diversity of impatient travelers. Jews from the Galilee sometimes chose this shorter route to Jerusalem, avoiding the extra miles and the intense heat of the dry Jordan Valley and travelers from Syria and the eastern reaches beyond the Jordan could avoid the hilltops of Samaria by using this route. These had come up the stream that ran down to the Jordan from the east, the very same valley that Abraham had traveled centuries before and they would pass westward through the cleft between the two famous mountains on the west side of Shechem. From there it was an easier and shorter journey to the coastal plains near Caesarea.

The market and the well were conveniently situated at the entrance to the narrow and almost gorge-like cut leading to the west which separated Mount Ebal on the north and Mount Gerizim on the south.

After a half-hearted and uninterested stroll through the market, the two returned to the inn near the well. Both were mentally comparing this bazaar to the exotic marketplace in Hebron and they agreed that it did not measure up.

Before entering the inn, Saul called out to Miriam to join him. He was standing in the open area near the well and facing to the west. Saul pointed to the mountain on the right.

"That is Ebal. Up near the top, on the northern slope, is the foundation of Joshua's altar of uncut stones where he sacrificed to the Lord upon first arriving back in the land, just as Moses directed."

He pointed to his left and declared, "Mount Gerizim. Half the people stood in front of each of these mountains as the blessings and curses of the Law were read by Joshua."

He continued quickly. "It is imperative that we remember that forgetting to obey the Law brings curses upon ourselves and Gerizim represents this cursing."

Miriam waited quietly for the rest of the familiar passage, the declaration of the reward of blessings and prosperity that Mount Ebal represented, but curiously, none came.

Saul pointed to an edifice-like building barely visible on top of Gerizim and said, "The Samaritan's Temple." His disapproval of even the thought of a temple outside of Jerusalem was evident in the tone of his statement. "They are confused and do not know just what they worship."

Eventually, Saul relaxed and remained pleasant to all while he and Miriam visited with other travelers well into the evening. He rehearsed the stories of this area while attempting to discern their importance to the listening Jews until all were weary.

Although it did not have the charm and appeal of Hebron, they were very thankful to have seen Shechem. This place screamed out the story of the initial arrival of Abraham and then the ancient and enduring promise to his children as they returned from Egypt, but truthfully, it now had a strange foreign feel for most Jews had chosen to abandon it. It was now in the hands of the Samaritans.

Miriam asked just one more question. "Brother, do you think the Great Tree of Moreh was just like those supernatural trees in Mamre? And where do you think was it located anyway?" She was referring to the site where Abraham pitched his tent when he first came into in the land.

Saul pondered this for a while and then answered. "I do not know, possibly near where the well is now located." He continued, "there was something supernatural about the trees that Abraham followed and lived under, as every time he moved, he went only to the next tree. Besides Shechem, we are told he found them in Bethel and then, Mamre. Probably the great flood knowingly dispersed seeds of those trees from Adam's original garden, gently leading our father. Once we were established in the land, we Jews had no need to be led anymore and the trees slowly disappeared. Of course, the changing conditions have not allowed any of them to survive to this day as well. It is conceivable that just for Abraham, a few specially places ones had retained some of their original miraculous qualities as well, qualities that Abraham no doubt learned directly from Shem who knew the history of the original garden very well. Our guide Caleb, in Hebron, showed us the remains of just a few. I understand now why Abraham always remained in certain areas. He surely told all his children and grandchildren about their benefits for there is something very curious about Jacob ridding his family of the influence of pagan gods by burying Rachel's wooden stolen idols under the roots of the oak here in Shechem."

After a long pause and much more thought, he affirmed, "Yes, I am sure there is so much more to the trees than we understand, else why are they such a big part of Abraham's life?"

Saul recognized a distant look in Miriam's eyes and knew that although she was listening to his every word, she was probably comparing them with Moses's account of the earliest days of creation. By her questions, he also knew she was already regarding them as much more than just plants, attributing to them, multiple levels of spirituality. *What a mind*, he thought.

"What do you think, Miriam? What are your thoughts on those trees," asked Saul, finally.

"It seems to me that Adam's very existence depended upon such trees. He was taken out of the ground they grew from. He and they were made of the same material. They were given for food, health and long life and when he disobeyed, he was separated from the ones in the garden, forcefully and physically torn away from them. The ground was cursed and would not produce for him then as well. Gone was the easy exchange of life between Hashem's different kinds of creations. Adam could only get limited benefits from the creation, and just as we must, he had to use much hard labor to do that. The trees our father Abraham thrived under must have been only faint shadows of the original supernatural ones, themselves having to struggle immensely to survive in this hostile, cursed world. Still, as we learned in Hebron, there were great blessings and all kinds of benefits from being under them, even in their reduced state. Also, as you said, they only grew in certain spots, places that Abraham went to, acting almost like a map for him, as if the seeds of the great trees knew instinctively where Hashem wanted them to grow, just for his friend, Abraham."

Saul was fascinated.

How does she come up with that? he asked himself. Before he could say anything, she continued.

"If all this is true, and I am becoming more and more convinced it is, Abraham was almost like Adam before his sin, a true friend of Hashem. He walked and talked with Him among the trees, as did Adam. Also, Hashem supplied everything he needed as is evidenced by the bounty of the trees. Abraham did not labor or work at his own existence and it seems he did not labor or work at having favor with Hashem either. It was a very natural thing. Why then must we Jews work so hard at pleasing Hashem, worrying about every little detail, living in great fear of Him and the consequences of any mistake," she mused, almost to herself.

At that point, Saul wisely chose to remain silent.

The next morning, brother and sister left Shechem behind and followed the hills northward where Saul rehearsed battle after battle of the various kings of Israel. These were mostly the ongoing northern battlegrounds of Israel's first king, Saul.

Upon turning east, they arrived in the mid-afternoon at the city of Beit Shean, sitting on a rise overlooking the Jordan River. It had been an educational but uneventful journey through fields and small villages and they had left the Judean mountains behind them as they approached the wide expanse of the valley of Jezreel. Beit Shean was on the eastern end of this rich valley and Saul pointed out that they were now on the south edge of the large region called the Galilee.

Most of the history in this area revolved around the time when Israel strayed from prophetic leadership to the guidance of the notable judges. This included Deborah, whose famous, rounded Mount Tabor they easily viewed in the distance. Saul's recitation of this time in Israel's history was a rambling list of names and events, all of which were remembered and elaborated on by Miriam. Saul had the curious feeling that she knew as much or more than he did of this time.

CHAPTER SIXTY-ONE

Beit Shean

Beit Shean was actually two cities. One part was a smaller and much older, Hebrew city with crumbling defensive walls, complete with a few hundred remaining Jewish inhabitants. The other was a large, modern city created by the earliest Greeks and now further modernized with new Roman-styled baths and column-lined avenues. It was one of the famous ten cities of the Decapolis that were strewn through this part of the country, each established by the Greeks and which served as destinations for officials and the armies that moved about the Galilee and into the interior of Syria.

The modern flavor of the new city provided the type of food and entertainment that was familiar to frequent international travelers, but it surely was not one of the most desirable places for a pious Pharisee such as Saul. He found an inn owned by a Jew on the outskirts, conveniently built next to the main road and near the walls of the older city, and soon they were settled in.

That evening, Saul and Miriam walked into the older Jewish town and were immediately taken back many centuries. The ancient stone houses were patched with clay, and many needed much repair. The population seemed to be made up of almost entirely elderly Jews and all seemed poorly clad in colorless rough clothing. The cooking was done outside on a few communal clay and brick ovens.

The shame of this town seemed to linger from the time when King Saul and his sons' headless and naked bodies were gaffed on hooks and hung on the exterior city walls by the Philistines. They had found Saul's fully-armored body on nearby Mount Gilboa after a self-inflicted mortal wound and then added to the infamy of the first king of Israel with this shameful act of disrespect.

His ultimate end came only after sympathetic nearby tribespeople slipped in and bravely removed the bodies and burned them, according to their local custom.

The modern and commercial new city gained its considerable wealth from the richness of the crops of the Jezreel and from traders and travelers traversing the Jordan from all directions, especially those on their westward journey past the stronghold of Megiddo to the natural harbor under Mount Carmel at the Great Sea. This location made Beit Shean a convenient and natural stopping spot.

Saul and Miriam spent the entire following day exploring the gleaming new city, starting with a meandering stroll on the main avenue. The busy metropolis was a peaceful mixture of Jews, Samaritans, Galileans, Greeks, Romans and small populations of other nearby cultures, all proudly promoting their wares and their way of life in a market that was considerably smaller, but which greatly resembled the Cardo in Jerusalem.

Fresh fish from the nearby Sea of Galilee were on sale everywhere and this was without question the chosen delicacy of the region. At lunchtime, Saul and Miriam found a table in a corner of the market where an enthusiastic and musical Jewish couple were cooking these small fish and entertaining customers with all kinds of songs. The joyous atmosphere, greatly enhanced by the free-flowing wine, was only interrupted when a contingent of Roman soldiers sat down next to them.

Saul and Miriam finished their meal quickly and went back to strolling the streets.

Miriam found a uniquely drawn scene depicting King Saul's tragic end on a scroll-like parchment. It was striking in its detail and remarkable coloring and the artist had exactly captured the shades of the walls and surrounding landscape as well as the slumping and decapitated bodies. He had even sprinkled the scene with shocked and frightened townspeople. Curiously and without comment, Saul hurriedly purchased it for her, rolling it up and placing it in a pouch without looking at it again as if to quickly be rid of this forgettable incident in Israel's history.

There seemed to be an endless supply of even stranger items and many that portrayed highly controversial subjects in this vibrant city. Beit Shean was a place which delighted in its cultural freedom to thoroughly mix many cultures, thus making it a departure from the dominating Jewishness of Jerusalem. Many merchants insisted, some quite forcefully, that the two must see the rare and valuable trinkets in their shops and indeed, there were many unique and strange items to be seen.

Truth be told, Saul and Miriam eventually relaxed and enjoyed the day immensely. That is, except for a wrong turn to a street leading to the hippodrome where all sorts of unsavory characters were hanging about. Lewd women were brazenly strutting about and one particularly aggressive lady, in a state of partial clothing, spotted Saul and quickly headed straight for him as if she knew something about those who wore the blue fringed tunics.

She called out in an alluring tone, "Hello mister Pharisee, let us be friends for a while."

Saul and Miriam, realizing their mistake, quickly retraced their steps and fled to more familiar and peaceful boulevards. Later, brother and sister laughed heartily at the slip-up in direction but mainly at their own prudish reactions.

Saul wondered momentarily about other strange and related details.

The next day, in the early morning sun, Saul and Miriam sat at an eastward-facing table at the inn while their animals were being prepared for the anticipated long journey south. Saul took the time to tell the history of the low mountains which they were viewing across the wide Jordan Valley, identifying each ridge of the large and the dry hills that meandered northward and southward and framed the edge of the great rift that was now the Jordan Valley. Directly across from them were the mountains of Gilead and south of that, in the direction they would go shortly, were the mountains of Moab which stretched south all the way to the Dead Sea. Far off to the north, Saul and Miriam could easily see the glistening peak of snow-capped Mount Hermon in the hazy distance. They knew that most of the refreshing water of the Jordan originated in the melting snows from this gigantic but controversial mountain.

Saul recapped the account of the initial two years of battles that took place on those opposite hills by the wandering Israelites under the direct leadership of Moses and his apprenticing general, Joshua. That successful campaign ended with the destruction of the kingdoms of the two giant Raphaite kings, Og and Sihom, plus the capture of all territory east of the Jordan. It also marked the only area of the promised land that Moses was personally involved in capturing. Og's kingdom extended from the Jabok River which was a few hours' ride south, back north to Mount Hermon. Sihom ruled south of the Jabok, down to the land of the Moabites, near the Dead Sea.

The more famous of the two, and definitely the most feared giant-king of the time, was Og. He had flourished in this fertile area, commanding sixty walled cities spread out on the vast upper plains beyond the ridges that the couple could see. These spats had started 500 years previous when Og's ancestors had fought five kings and their ally Abraham to a territorial standstill, before returning Lot to his uncle. Og was one of the last of the largest strain of the strange looking Rephaites and that made him a great curiosity. For that, he was left hobbled but alive as a witness to Moses's might. His territory was given to the tribe of Manasseh after that time but as the mixed Jewish population of Beit Shean was proof, no certain tribal heritage had survived to this day.

On their way to the northern campaign against Og, Moses had first destroyed the Kingdom of Sihom, also a Rephaite, and the one whom the Lord had purposely hardened so that any peaceful gesture from Moses would be rebuffed. Starting at the Arnon River, which spilled directly into the Dead Sea, they battled their way north to the Jabok, decimating Sihom's entire population. This portion of the land was given to half of the tribe of Rueben and to Dan.

Miriam remembered the crude maps of the tribal divisions that she had previously seen and they helped her now understand and visualize those borders.

After mounting their rides, Miriam's stream of questions and Saul's enthusiastic narrating made the hours fly by while they trekked southward on the main road which followed the descending Jordan river closely on its undulating trip to the Salt Sea.

The winding river course was surrounded by rich plantations of date palms interspersed with fields of peppers and garlic and long rows of pomegranate and almond trees that thrived when close to the river's banks. Saul and Miriam were happily sampling the produce as they rode.

None of the farms strayed far away from the river as the extreme temperatures in this low-lying valley dried out all other vegetation. The surrounding hillsides, only a few hundred yards away, were now parched and burned bare of any surviving growth and it was evident that watering this land was hard and laborious and could be achieved only by small diversions of the Jordan.

What a difference this area was from the well-watered plain Lot had originally chosen some 1,500 years previous. Since then, the life-giving river and the lush plain had sunken greatly and the wide canyon was now subject to the dry and withering heat that killed almost all plants except those whose roots could drink from the saturated soils near the river. These days, the heavy rains that had watered this area in Abraham's day, rains fed by the saturated clouds which rose from the Great Sea, rarely made it past the tops of the Judean mountains.

Shortly after midday, the small entourage passed a crumbling military fortress that David had built on a ridge overlooking the intersection of the Jordan Valley and the wide valley which ran down from Shechem. The fortress was strategically placed across the valley from the gorge of the Jabok River as it flowed from the eastern heights into the Jordan River Valley. As important as this spot was militarily, it was also the historical route their father Abraham would have traveled from Haran into the land of the Canaanites and David had understood that if Israel were attacked from the east, it would surely be through that gorge.

The couple pressed on in their hot journey and in the late afternoon, they finally arrived at exotic Jericho. On the same site as the original city that Joshua had destroyed, the rebuilt town lay at the eastern base of the Judean mountains which rose steeply up to Jerusalem to the west, some 5000 feet above. This popular oasis was situated at a major intersection of travel routes arriving from three directions and had many inns to accommodate its many travelers. It was a favorite place to visit by Jewish pilgrims as well, for it was within a day's travel of Jerusalem and was blessed with flourishing orchards and garden settings watered by many natural springs. For those less inhibited, it also had all the amenities of the best Roman spas.

For the Jews, Jericho conjured up images of the most endearing of all Israel's victories, even if it that great ancient conquest was really a very strange non-battle. It was a heart-warming place and reminded all of the heady days of Hashem's direct involvement in the fate of their nation. All visitor's heard at least one version of the crumbling walls and many were treated to showy blasts of trumpets and their resulting echoes.

Tomorrow's travel would be a hot, slow climb up steep hills to Jerusalem, so Saul and Miriam retired early but only after enjoying the freshest and most luscious dates and wine they had experienced in all their travels. Their dinner was followed by long soaks in very private pools of warm, crystal-clear water.

Early the next morning, they started their ascent of the mountainsides.

The steep and sometimes narrow road was busy with other travelers ascending and descending between Jerusalem and the Jordan Valley and the laborious climb made Saul wonder how Joshua's army could have moved up and down these mountains with the ease described in the ancient writings. The present trail had well-worn switch backs and much repair work had been done to make it passable. With all these improvements, it was still a difficult and withering climb.

CHAPTER SIXTY-TWO

Bethany

In the afternoon, after six strenuous hours of persistent uphill plodding inter-rupted only by small breaks to rest the animals, they arrived in Bethany, a sleepy village just over the crest of the Mount of Olives from Jerusalem. Saul informed his sister that, thankfully, their journey was almost over.

They had stopped to again rest and water the weary animals and were enjoying a refreshing lunch at a small roadside inn when an excited group of around twenty people arrived and surrounded the entrance to the house directly across the street from where they were seated.

"Lazarus's house" was what Saul heard amid the excited chatter of the group. He and Miriam strained to hear more.

Soon a middle-aged man came slowly and warily out of the door of the house, followed by two women. He was looking around carefully and his eyes rested for a moment on Saul's fringed tunic at the table across the street. It clearly marked him as a Pharisee.

"Tell us about how you were resurrected," cried one woman in the small crowd.

"Did you know Jesus personally?" another asked, jolting Saul to attention at the mention of that name.

The crowd was quickly shuttled off the main road and into the private courtyard of the house and after that, Saul and Miriam heard no more. Out of curiosity, Miriam called the owner of the inn over and asked what that was about.

The hesitant man finally said, "That is Lazarus, the man Jesus raised from the dead after he had been four days in the tomb. A steady stream of people from Jerusalem come almost every day to hear his story and just to see him. It is not every day that you see one who was raised from the dead."

Miriam remembered last week's conversation about this friend of the inn-keeper in Bethlehem, but she said nothing.

The peaceful, relaxing days of Saul's tour with his sister came to a sudden and furious end.

"That is complete foolishness, a trick, a ruse," shouted Saul to the very surprised and instantly wary merchant. He paused what he was doing and looked Saul and his Pharisee markings over and over.

"No, it is not, sir. I saw these things myself," the man responded firmly but calmly and he busied himself clearing the table, not wanting to argue with Saul anymore.

Saul indignantly threw down a shekel which bounced off the table and came to rest derisively in the dust. He then rose and occupied himself with the animals, tightening straps and watering the beasts one more time. Miriam sat thinking for a moment but then decided to subdue her curiosity and join her brother in the last leg of their journey.

It was only another mile over the Mount of Olives and within the hour they were rounding the north walls of the city, passing through the narrow cut in the rock and approaching the Damascus Gate. Opposite this gate and set in the rocky hill were two of the oldest and since the rock cut, broken cisterns from Hezekiah's days. The two large recesses made the hill look like a huge skull. The base of this cliff face, the flat area below the stony mask, was the favorite place of crucifixion for the brutal Romans as it was close to their barracks at Antonia and its proximity to the road made for a looming and grotesque display. This spectacle was a constant reminder to all Jews, and any other travelers along the busy road, that Rome was still very much in charge. Violent and loud suffering served as a prolific reminder to any Jew who would think to rebel or oppose them, so punishments were done publicly and with as much gruesome suffering as they could elicit.

Saul and Miriam moved quickly and quietly past this site, then past the sepulchers and family tombs carved into the exposed face of the rock cut, past a quiet garden, and then rounded the corner to the western wall and onto the familiar stable outside of the Joppa gate.

They were home.

CHAPTER SIXTY-THREE

Jerusalem in an Uproar

Upon entering their courtyard, Miriam was immediately swarmed by Leah who demanded then and there to know every detail of her trip, circling impatiently while Miriam washed her face and neck. Leah was relentless, asking questions and drinking in Miriam's descriptive answers, making comments and obviously wishing that she had been there also. Leah would have loved such a trip of her own but her sincere interest revealed not a hint of jealousy or envy.

During this conversation, what became apparent to Miriam was that she was extremely fortunate to be in a position to go exploring the regions as she had. She had experienced an unexplainable richness from these two short tours and she wondered just how much more there was for her to discover in this expanding and complicated world.

Saul had disappeared sullenly into their rooms and remained there for the evening, not emerging until the next day. He woke early, wanting to meet with Gammy and Gamaliel, but he found Gamaliel had already left for the Sanhedrin, once more taken away by yet another early morning intrigue. For some reason, that irritated Saul greatly on this particular day.

Gammy and Saul did meet and they spoke for a long while, Saul describing the northern expedition, followed by Gammy detailing the latest incidents at the Temple. He had kept up his intense observations of the people of the Way and related more about them to Saul.

"There are many sick in their group who are getting well, some slowly, but also numerous immediate healings," he detailed, "but the latest happening is this selling of their possessions and giving all to the disciples. This seems to have caught on, and many are doing it."

"What would possess someone to do this?" asked a puzzled Saul. "This is not according to any direction or precept of the Law. Are they being coerced?" he asked suspiciously, but Gammy admitted not knowing their motivation.

Saul eventually answered his own question. "I suspected that those Galileans would somehow profit from this scam," he mused, pointing out that he had previously predicted the final motives behind such nefarious happenings.

"I have not heard of any such demands by the leaders," replied Gammy. "The followers tell me that their values have been altered and they do not consider anything as theirs, but belonging to all." Gammy paused. "Many are selling everything, including your friend Barnabas, who gave a small fortune to these men."

At hearing this, Saul was instantly furious. So mad was he that he literally ground his teeth.

Miriam's purchase from Barnabas came immediately to mind and to be reminded that he had agreed, even helped finance something that ended up in these deceivers' hands, well, that set off his formidable temper in an instant.

"You may be a bit relieved to find that the money is being used to feed and provide for all the followers and not just for enriching the Galileans. I followed these leaders and they are purchasing food and supplies as needed. They do not seem to personally be benefitting," suggested Gammy, "at least with anything that I can discern." He hoped this information would quiet his highly agitated friend.

"There has also been a serious incident with regard to this and it may change things in the future," he continued, refocussing Saul's attention.

"Yesterday, an older couple who had sold some property, got into a dispute with Simon Peter and the man and his wife ended up dead. Of course, the rumor is that they were struck down by Hashem for not giving all the receipts of that sale but the result is that many who thought about joining the group are now keeping their distance. They still meet every day in Solomon's Colonnades, and Saul, there are now many priests of the Temple who have finished their month of serving in the Temple but are now remaining in Jerusalem and spending their days listening to the teachings of these men. They have not gone home to their families."

It was plain that this point bothered Gammy a great deal for it gave the appearance to all that the Temple staff were approving of this new teaching.

"There are still many being baptized and their fervor is not diminishing like we predicted it would."

After a few minutes, Saul began really listening, concentrating on Gammy's words intently. Finally, he asked Gammy, this man he grew up with and who was closer than a brother and with whom he wanted desperately to be in harmony, "Gammy, what do you expect your and my involvement to be in all this?"

Gammy was taken back with the strange question, but Saul was now stimulated to keep asking and pushing for an answer.

"You and I have been privileged. We have learned under the wisest teacher in Judaism. We are the next generation of teachers of the Law. Is it not time for us to embrace our calling? There is no excuse for us to be hesitant or undecided. We must challenge this attack on Moses and the Law for it is a devilish attack on Hashem as well, even though its proponents want it to appear to be godly."

It was Gammy who now listened closely and then responded. "There is some truth to what you say, Saul. I guess the next question is what is to be done and what do we challenge. Do we condemn the healing of sick and infirmed Jews, or do we challenge their teachings of scriptures, much of which we agree with, or do we refuse them freedom to worship in the Temple? How do we exclude Jews from the Temple? Just what do we fight?"

Gammy looked intently at Saul and went on, "Do we condemn the feeding of the poor, plus are we willing to take that responsibility on ourselves? Do we tell any sick that they should not be made well but remain in their sickness?"

Saul had thought a lot about this and quickly answered. "First of all, we must be convinced within ourselves of the deceitfulness of their deeds and how the evil one can use supposed blessings to entice Jews away from their commitment to Hashem. If we are not convinced of the evil of such deeds, if we see any good in what they are doing, we will ourselves be confused by such happenings."

Saul felt he was speaking to himself as well as to Gammy. "The people's attention is being captured by the deceptiveness of the healings and that is leading them away from the purity of the Law. That is not only dangerous and deceptive, but it is pure evil."

Saul could see that Gammy was rattled and he was bothered greatly by the growing throngs of disciples of Jesus, but he was still hesitant, still unconvinced, and Saul wondered if his friend had somehow been influenced by the lure and appeal of these supernatural happenings. That possibility made him realize then and there that the key to this argument was the understanding that any supernatural events by these deceivers was a lying spirit. If that was true, then no single part, not even one of their comforting stories of Jesus, all the way to their complicated scriptural teachings could be accepted as they were also part of the lie. The Galileans, their teachings and their healings must be rejected entirely. Everything about them was false.

Saul realized that he would have to have further conversations with Gammy to expose the treachery but he decided he also needed to visit the Synagogue of the Freedmen after being a week away, if only to reestablish his own appraisal of just how powerful the deceptions had become.

PART SEVEN

CHAPTER SIXTY-FOUR

Miriam the Business Woman

The next morning found Miriam and Leah scurrying around the courtyard, opening yet another shipment of parcels that had arrived from Hebron in Miriam's absence. This shipment was once again sent by the knowledgeable old sage, Moshe and in it were small sacks of intriguing concoctions, each labelled with an explanation carefully printed in precise Greek. Each parcel was lovingly unwrapped, examined carefully and then taken to the new stall and stored in the upper room.

One heavy, completely wrapped and suspiciously-marked parcel was left untouched by Miriam who had it delivered directly to her shop without opening it. She gave no comment or any explanation to a very curious Leah who grinned widely at the prospect of adding some deep mystery in their lives. Before long, they left the house and made their way to Miriam's new stall at the Cardo Street where the two very excited girls were caught up in a frenzy of sweeping the floors and cleaning the walls. With this shipment, the time had come to open the new business.

As it was the first day of the new month, the neighboring shopkeepers, renters of Miriam's newly purchased properties, began appearing and after warm and sincere greetings, each promptly handed Miriam a bag of money.

They were paying their rent.

Their previous landlord had visited each of these merchants and told them of the sale of his properties to Miriam and they became quite eager to pay the fair rent and, thereby, establish the ongoing rate.

All were happy, almost impatient, to re-establish the reasonable amount for the old man had kept their fees well below the rates that the High Priest's family was charging for neighboring stalls. Caiaphas seemed to use any excuse to keep increasing the rate on his properties, and all knew they were getting a bargain.

Miriam thanked them for their promptness and assured each merchant that her rates would not change for the foreseeable future, immediately making each stall-owner into a friend.

By noon, Miriam was slightly overwhelmed with the immediate return on her investment and was bemused by the stack of bags she received that morning. She poured all the coins into a larger bag and laughingly jingled it before tossing it to Leah who made a great show of not being able to lift such a heavy load.

Thankfulness and amazement, followed with a lot of nervous giggling, was the atmosphere of that little stall that morning, even in its mostly empty condition.

Miriam was wondering about the land she had bought off Barnabas and how she should manage that, when standing outside her stall appeared the overseer of her farm.

He greeted her with a warm smile and she invited him into her upper office.

He seemed a little uncomfortable to be alone with a young woman, so Miriam had Leah join them in their meeting. When seated, he reached inside his covering robe and extracted three good-sized money bags. The first was the largest and it was bulging with the payments for the produce he had delivered to the different markets in the weeks since Miriam had taken ownership. It was delightfully full of shekels, mingled generously with Roman denarii, and he spilled the contents onto the wooden table in an entertaining explosion of clattering coins. The other two bags were only slightly smaller and held only a little less money. These contained the receipts from chicken, sheep, and lamb sales, and those coins also sang out their melody when hitting the tabletop.

Miriam at first gasped and then began chortling loudly. Soon all three people were laughing out loud at this audacious display and each were grabbing at a few coins that were threatening to roll off the edge of the table.

The overseer then began dividing the money just as he had done when he worked for Barnabas. A substantial portion went for wages for the various farm workers and that he counted out then stuffed back into one bag. A smaller portion, he separated for supplies and tools that he would need in the following week. He put that into a second bag. The largest portion, he dropped into the third bag which he pushed across the table to Miriam with a proud and satisfied look. Miriam was taken back by this immediate and generous profit.

"What about your earnings?" she asked the man.

"My portion is included in the amount for wages," he replied, holding up the first bag. "Of course, a part of my wages is included in the free rent on the farmhouse which is greatly appreciated by both my family and I. We also eat freely from the bounty of your farm."

Miriam sat quietly thinking and calculating for a few very long minutes. The overseer and Leah remained very still, not sure of how Miriam would react to how the proceeds were divided. Would she be pleased or disappointed?

Quickly realizing that she did not need any of these returns for her own sustenance and just this morning seeing how the Cardo shop rentals would provide more than enough to start up her new business, she made an immediate decision.

"Sir, I have a proposal."

Miriam spoke slowly and haltingly to the curious and intrigued man for she was formulating her plan, little by little, while she spoke. Methodically and precisely, she was putting her thoughts into words. Leah was helping with the precise Aramaic words when Miriam would get stuck.

"I would like to accept only fifteen percent of the weekly profits. This is to be delivered to the Temple as my tithe and my charitable offerings."

She paused and looked upward, thinking deeply. "I want you to have ten percent of the profits as an increase in your wage."

The surprised overseer began to thank Miriam, but she interrupted him by saying, "This is because I require of you an additional task, added to your daily duties and it is an undertaking which will require more of your time and effort."

The overseer was suddenly quieted by this statement and Leah's interest was most definitely piqued.

"I want you to keep the remaining seventy-five percent of the profits in trust for me and accumulate as much as possible. I will require a weekly accounting of that total. The reason for this stash of money is that I want you to find other farmlands of the same high quality as the one you manage for me. I know you will recognize a good investment when it appears and I want us to have the resources to purchase it with no delays. I also would like to keep this plan as quiet as possible."

With that said, Miriam sat back and observed her new employee. She saw in him surprise, which was soon replaced by deep contemplation and then the beginnings of eager planning. Seeing his immediate interest and what she read as approval, she was assured that she had appraised him correctly from their first meeting over two weeks ago.

He asked, a little hesitantly, "What type of land would you be most interested in?"

Miriam was pleased that he had already moved on from initial surprise to contemplating the plan of action.

"I was very impressed by the rotation of crops that you instituted at the farm, as it gives continual streams of income as different crops mature. Quite possibly, we could look for something that allows us the same opportunity for flexibility."

"That principal was brought to me by Barnabas for he told me of how his family business is built on responding to what is needed rather than providing just one product. We incorporated that into the farming plan," replied the humble overseer. "Of course, farming requires a little more planning and lead time than other businesses," he offered, obviously proud of his vocation.

"I was also thinking of investing in land that can be used to produce items that are less conventional and have no competition," Miriam offered. "Possibly something of value to travelers, or the Romans, or those with exotic tastes. I will leave that to another time when we are closer to investing."

The overseer's mind was now racing.

The overseer repackaged the money into the three bags after quite deftly calculating Miriam's fifteen percent. Before leaving, he said to Miriam, "Thank you for the raise in wages, but more than that, thank you for your confidence in me. I will not let you down. I will provide a weekly report to you of all our dealings."

The man left deep in thought but strutting boldly and with a renewed purpose in life.

Miriam noticed the last words of this man—*our* dealings—and a satisfied smile broke on her face.

Leah and Miriam sat peacefully, not speaking for a very long time, thinking about what had just taken place. Leah broke the silence, finally rising and asking in almost a whisper, "Where do you get the courage to do such things, Miriam?"

Miriam laughed out loud.

"I am not sure it is courage as much as it is just the absence of fear. Truthfully Leah, I have always been in a wealthy family and we never worried for the day's bread as many others must. All the comforts of life came easy and possibly are less valued and therefore less concerning to me. That has given me the freedom of mind to experiment and spread my wings. Also, if I did not have a generous inheritance, I would not be able to purchase what I have," she said openly and honestly.

Leah thought about this response but countered, "I know many wealthy women who have never tried any of the things you have already done. Do not underestimate your abilities." She then added jokingly, "My future rich and famous sister-in-law."

Miriam smiled and agreed. "I do recognize that Hesham has blessed me with a quick mind and I think it would be dishonorable to not use it fully."

Miriam looked up suddenly and eyed Leah closely. "Leah, you are so talented at adorning things. Your clothing, your hair, your room at home are so beautifully decorated and functional. Would you do something for me? Would you please take over with presenting my stall in a fresh manner? I do not know how to do it at all for I have no eye for such things and just thinking about it gives me a headache. All I know is that I want it to stand out, be festooned and eye-catching, yet dignified."

Leah's beautiful face lit up with a glow and a confidence that was instantly evident to Miriam. That very day, the little medicine shop on the Cardo became infused with an atmosphere and an infectious spirit that all would feel upon entering. From that curious and rewarding day on, the stimulating mood did as much for the health of many customers who wandered in, as did any medicines that they were sold.

These happenings also changed the outlook of Leah. She would no longer be the irresponsible young girl of the family, for from that day forward, she took on a new character and she began regarding herself completely differently.

Within days, Leah was transformed into an energetic and very focused business person. Gamaliel noticed it immediately, her mother Sarah was confused as to what had happened to her daughter, and Gammy was amazed, even proud.

CHAPTER SIXTY-FIVE

Cardo Upgrades

Miriam had asked the perfect task of her friend and the invigorated Leah beamed with delight and purpose. She disappeared downstairs and began pacing back and forth across the front of the stall, sometimes on one side of the street, sometimes across on the other, peering at Miriam's stall from every possible angle. She went down the Cardo in each direction and examined the view from a distance, tilting her head this way and that. She was lost in deep thought and hardly noticed that she was surrounded and jostled by noisy and pushy market shoppers. After an hour, she reappeared in the upper office, where Miriam was busy sorting and packaging her new collection of medicines from Hebron.

"I have an idea," she stated awkwardly. "You may not like it, but let me tell you about it. You must come down and see for yourself." Leah led Miriam out into the street.

Impatient shoppers were a little annoyed as they had to work their way around these two chattering and excited women who were standing all over the roadway while they pointed this way and that, then sauntered about, generally filling the air with animated discussion. The next-door merchants wondered aloud and asked each other, *what were these characters up to now.*

A host of ideas flew about and it was suggested, somewhat tentatively, that a mural on the back wall depicting a peaceful and serene landscape could cover that plain area and make potential customers stop and gaze and then come in to get a closer look. Further, if done correctly, such a scene would give a restful, inviting atmosphere.

Yes. That was decided on and given final approval within minutes.

Wooden shelving, if made with elegance and the best carpentry, including a set of comfortable chairs and a table for consultations, would make the stall functional as well as getting the sacks of products off the floor. Again, this was approved within mere minutes for this was sorely needed for the shop to work.

But, and this was the most exciting part, they both agreed that a major part of the appeal would be the brightest of draperies festooning all sides of the space and a bright new coat of colorful dye on the side stone walls. Within minutes it was suggested that painted images of apothecary's bottles should be etched on the sides of the columns as well. All of this should be extremely colorful and eye-catching from every angle of the Cardo and would make this stall stand out. Admittedly, these were unusual ideas, but they were appealing notions that the artistic Leah was aching to introduce to the otherwise drab street and if done correctly, things which would catch the attention of the passing crowd immediately.

Miriam was astounded and intrigued. She was pleased with Leah's ambitious plans and it was almost all settled when Leah tentatively asked, "Is it too much? Will it make your other tenants angry or jealous at the attention your store will attract. Will it be out of taste or not allowed in the Cardo?"

Miriam heard Leah's comment, but an idea had struck her when Leah mentioned "attract." She looked at Leah and quietly asked, "What if all six of my stalls became an attraction?"

The two young women stared at each other and the daring concept began working its way into their minds and was exploding into their imaginations.

"The whole block?" asked Leah incredulously.

"Why not?" responded a deadly serious Miriam.

So was set in motion many days of supposed clandestine planning but which included loud and jovial discussions with her dubious renters, followed by city-scouring shopping for the brightest draperies and then meetings with incredulous painters and artists, all creating a growing excitement that neither woman was familiar with. They did not want to expose the totality of their plans until it was certain that their ideas could be made to work, so some parts remained secret.

The adjacent renters were a little reticent, almost afraid, but all agreed when informed that there would be no cost to them. Miriam would finance the upgrades. Excited notes were sent off to Moshe and Caleb in Hebron, for Miriam wanted to have the latest products that flowed into that marketplace available for Leah's creations.

Within a week, a wagon load of exotic shelving, storage chests, satins and much more arrived from Hebron and Leah attacked the load with purpose. Hidden under the load was another well wrapped and very bony parcel labelled "For Miriam's eyes only."

CHAPTER SIXTY-SIX

Shadowy Happenings

While Miriam and Leah were searching for some hard to locate red and blue-dyed drapery fabrics at the lower market street, traditionally the fabric area located just below the towering western walls of the Temple, a strange thing occurred on the adjacent Pilgrim's Road.

A line of very sick people began quietly appearing on the street, a few being carried in on homemade stretchers, and it was announced that some of these had come from towns and villages outside of Jerusalem. All were being laid along the exterior walls of the houses that lined the west side of the pilgrim's street and strangely, they were being put directly in the hot morning sun. Some others limped and struggled their own way to the busy thoroughfare and likewise, took up a large portion of roadway along that same side of street.

When Leah asked what was happening, a talkative shopkeeper told them that the leaders of the followers of Jesus walked this road each morning when going up to the Temple and it was believed that their shadows would heal the sick as they passed by. Apparently, this had happened once before and that is why the people came so early in the morning for this was the time when the shadows were the longest.

Admittedly skeptical of such a tale, Miriam remained in the area, wanting to see such an episode for herself. Leah, consumed by bargaining and fabric hunting in the labyrinth of side streets, wandered ahead.

Within minutes, an excited racket was heard coming up the road, led by loud voices and even some shouting. Miriam began moving toward it but in front of her, she noticed a girl of about twelve years lying on and being restrained to a small bed with ropes holding her fast to the carrying rods. Sadly, but very evidently, she was not in her right mind. The pathetic child was drooling and grunting while pulling on the ropes and was an immediate target of sympathy from all that saw her. She was just one of many wretched cases strewn along the western side of the road.

As the noise grew, Miriam noticed the familiar Galilean man, Peter, as he was now known everywhere in the city, making his way quite deliberately up the stone street with a large, noisy crowd following him. From a mere twenty feet away, she watched as his shadow fell directly on the infirm girl.

The crowd quieted quickly as in anticipation.

The big man paused and looked down on the deathly thin and grotesquely grimacing child. He lingered there for a long while, his large silhouette falling directly on her. The young girl's severely contorted face began relaxing imme-diately and Peter's weathered and bearded visage broke into a look of soft thankfulness and his intense eyes moistened. His chin dropped to his chest.

While the shadow remained, the young girl's face softened even more and her previously wild and unfocused eyes now searched the gathered crowd for familiar faces.

Her parents began screaming praises to God, as did many others along the roadway. It was truly miraculous.

Miriam, astonished but not entirely convinced, kept watching the girl and her parents closely, waiting for some logical explanation to arise. Thankfulness and heartfelt emotion was their only response to the strange episode she had just witnessed.

The newly awakened girl was untied from her mat, released with the ten-derness of a small bird finally being freed. After much prodding and question-ing by many in the crowd, it became evident that she was perfectly whole and normal. The child was consumed with embracing her parents for her twisted mind had never before allowed her such a show of love. It was a love that had obviously been hidden somewhere deep within her.

Miriam waited many long minutes till the crowd passed and she approached the ecstatic family cautiously. When the young girl turned her face to Miriam, the most beautiful, serene aura surrounded her and there was a deep peace in the moist olive eyes. Miriam literally fell back a step, overcome with what she looking upon.

Miriam gulped.

Not only could these people heal physical sickness, but they could restore broken minds?

Miriam quickly admitted to herself that she did not understand what was going on here.

Her logical reasoning immediately asked a question of herself. What was healed first? It certainly looked like the mind of the girl was released and then the contortions that held her limbs so rigid, relaxed as a result. Were the healings that the people of the "Way" were able to perform the result of some ability to align minds or the 'soul' as some rabbis taught, with Hashem? Just how could that take place without the involvement of the little girl? She had been totally helpless, not participating in her deliverance at all.

In that moment, Miriam realized that she understood very little about the great working of Hashem, no matter how much she was applauded for her great intellect.

CHAPTER SIXTY-SEVEN

Finally, Arrests

Saul spent the following two days in the company of his old rival Pharisee, Samuel, and the two were in much more agreement than the Pharisees of the House of Hillel ever were with the more aggressive House of Shammai throughout their recent and rocky history.

They too had witnessed the crowds bringing their sick to Jerusalem to fall under the shadow of the disciples of Jesus and both men agreed that this was dangerous, deceptive and somehow blasphemous and if the Jews continued down this path, Hesham would be obligated to again punish them, just as He had done before.

They understood that this was a difficult position to take in this city that was aflame with all manner of astounding healings. More menacingly, both men knew that they would have to keep reminding themselves of why they were opposed to these seemingly miraculous happenings, so devious was the deception.

Any benefits that a few sick Jews received were not worth the penalties that a disobedient nation would face at the hands of Jehovah, they repeated to themselves, over and over.

On this subject, both men were unwavering.

It was suggested by a few that the leaders of the city were beginning to feel this way also, for already the disagreeable Temple guards had begun regularly patrolling through these streets and were taking note of the treacherous actions of the Galilean deceivers. They were watching everything with a new diligence. All occurrences were closely observed and reported on, and that included the insidiousness actions of each of the original disciples and their seditious and tricky shadows.

Well beyond the danger and confusion caused when these men's silhouettes fell on some deceived Jew, and infinitely more worrisome, were the increased patrols of the Romans who were also taking note of such strange activities and this Roman scrutiny was happening even though Pilate had promised not to interfere with Jerusalem's religious matters. Almost on the hour, small squads of Romans could be seen on the Cardo or on the Pilgrim's Road and even a few on the back streets, nonchalantly strolling about. On the surface, this did not appear all that alarming, but soldiers were also showing up in the Courts of the Gentiles on the Temple Platform, admittedly remaining unthreatening, but nevertheless looking daunting in their military array. The tension in the city was rising slightly every day.

Saul and Samuel had both noticed that the scarred Roman centurion, the one who had successfully infiltrated the gatherings of the people of the Way, appeared to be accepted and trusted into their inner circle. Because he was easily recognized, they were certain that he had been at the door of the Sanhedrin, at the inn in Bethlehem, and at other places where the Galileans were meeting, but alone.

Something was changing. Recently, this centurion was accompanied by three or four armed and equally intimidating soldiers who meandered about with him, eyes observing all, appearing very tense and ready to do his command.

Within this anxious environment, the numbers of disciples of Jesus had continued to grow and their noisy activities now filled the entire Pilgrim's Road and spilled into the side streets. The outside colonnades at the Temple had been almost completely taken over by the newest converts of the Way as well, all eager to hear the stories of Jesus repeated over and over. It seemed they could not get enough of them.

In all this, the growing acceptance of the followers of Jesus by the locals made the leadership increasingly nervous, but only for security reasons they assured. Those with any perception were certain that they detected the odor of jealousy.

Very officially, they warned others that the controversy and tumult made the Romans wary and unpredictable, thus making their criticism and opposition to this group a very righteous concern and they constantly assured all that their condemnation was not based on pure envy. They were not that small.

On his second day back at the synagogue, just as Saul and Samuel were teaching a small group gathered there, a young man flew into the room and ran to Samuel.

"They have been arrested, Samuel," he said excitedly.

"Which ones?" Samuel asked quickly, seeming to know immediately what this was about.

"There were nine or ten taken, all that were teaching in the porches," was the messenger's quick answer. "I think they were all His Galilean disciples."

Saul followed the disappearing Samuel out the door and raced through the crowd to the Temple Mount where a great commotion, fueled with yelling and complete confusion was rumbling through the colonnades. Angry shouts and heated accusations rang out and many of the agitated crowd were now swarming the meek and unarmed Temple priests. These poor souls were instantly regretting that they had been assigned this normally tranquil guard duty.

"Why are they being arrested," the crowd demanded.

"They have done nothing but good deeds for Israel," they insisted, some face to face and nose to nose with the frightened priests.

The pointed questions were getting louder and were changing into yelled demands from the stirring masses.

"We don't know," pleaded the terrified priests, who sincerely were not aware of why their armed colleagues from the jails below had suddenly instigated such a risky move.

The crowd was milling about the Gentile's plateau menacingly. Fearing violence, the High Priest sent an immediate order to completely clear the Temple and the surrounding courts. His chief priests walked through the crowd pleading for calm and assuring all that the disciples would appear before a very fair Sanhedrin hearing in the morning.

With much murmuring and complaining, the whole Temple area was eventually evacuated and the contingent of detained disciples were taken down the small staircase and noisily locked in the subterranean Temple jails.

Rough looking guards were then set at every jailhouse door and their number was doubled at the spots where the loudest of the Galilean's many friends refused to leave. The followers of the disciples were heartbroken to see these men disappearing into the dark recesses and many stood about calling out encouragement to the disciples as they were taken down the murky steps.

To any who remained around the dungeon's entrances, it seemed that these guards took great delight in the loud slamming of doors and clanging of locks. In reality, all of that was a part of their attempt at intimidation—the banging bars, the rattling of foot irons—and it was easy to see that these dregs certainly enjoyed making quite a show of it.

Samuel and Saul arrived just in time to see the very last of the arrests and soon they joined the disgruntled crowd as they were herded out of the Temple area. The massive doors of the southern Hulda entrance were quickly slammed and then barred when the Temple was finally empty.

The two Pharisees smiled broadly at each other. Both were pleased that the leaders were finally doing something about these false teachers. Caiaphas, it seemed, had finally stepped up and done his duty. They assured each other that they would be in the Sanhedrin early to finally witness the swift justice of the court.

On his way home, Saul noticed that he was being stared at and unceremoniously bumped and pushed around in the milling crowds. The expelled Temple crowd was still in the streets, stirring about and many of that bunch were not ready to slink away just yet. Any previous regard given to Saul as a Pharisee seemed to have disappeared as well. Twice he was surrounded by the upset and grumbling throng, but he escaped easily with no physical force landing on him. The crowd, although rowdy, showed their disgust and anger with his type by the surprisingly peaceful act of simply turning their back on him or calling him an asp and hissing at him.

As was his custom, and also an expression of his antagonistic personality, Saul defiantly displayed his shawl, today opening his Pharisee's robe even wider as if to taunt the crowd. After a few tense exchanges, he prudently, quickened his step.

Saul turned the familiar corner onto the street of the Cardo and was immediately faced with Miriam's new stall location. He paused and watched from a distance as his sister and Leah were engaged in a lively conversation, moving the heavy furniture and colorful vases about and then strangely, moving them right back to their original locations.

Saul decided not to stop and he slipped unnoticed by the preoccupied Miriam, completely enveloped in the buzzing crowd, many now diverting their normally approving gaze away from him. He was mindful that the events at the Temple were most likely the source of their disapproval, but again his response was a strutting defiance and a proud, self-important look on his face.

Caiaphas's move was for the ultimate betterment of these ignorant Jews, Saul said to himself convincingly, even though they were too stubborn or too unlearned to see it. The leaders had finally taken action and he was once again grateful to be aligned with the elite of Jerusalem, those who were not so easily deluded as the common Jews one meets on the streets, and those that he had just yesterday doubted Although Saul was eager that all should recognize his position, he also looked forward to getting home and congratulating Gamaliel on finally arresting these men. How he loved Gamaliel and Jewish justice.

Two stalls past Miriam's shop, Saul's jovial mood disappeared when a very upset elderly woman, obviously a follower of Jesus, stood directly in front of Saul and began calling him a snake and a child of the devil. Publicly, Saul had worked hard to look calm and arrogant and very pleased with himself and today, under this attack, he did his best to maintain this outward appearance, but internally, he was seething. She grabbed his best tunic by the border and proceeded to shake him, while yelling out his glaring defects. The disapproving harangue that he had endured and which far too many had agreed with, was direct proof that the cunning Galileans were not just taking the Jews' love and attention away from the Law but now they were influencing the uneducated in an outright uprising, a mutiny against the very ones who had dedicated their lives to preserving Israel. The poorly camouflaged revulsion and loathing he was experiencing made him all the more determined to rid Jerusalem of the danger of such people and their teachings.

"*How dare they!*" he finally exclaimed out loud to no one but himself as he raised his hand to shove her roughly away. Although he had never expressed his very private thoughts in such exact words, today Saul became convinced that to oppose him, a carrier of the wisdom of the Torah, was to oppose Hashem Himself and the events on the street were now making that very clear. He and possibly a few other chosen Pharisees were the embodiment of the mind of the Law. This he believed, and therefore, they were the doorway to the perfection commanded of the Jews by their God. Strange heavenly circumstances had made these few Pharisees the only pathway to God, he reasoned, and Saul was now ready to be used by Hashem in that way and any other way He required. A kindly old Jew quickly rescued the lady, pulling her away before Saul could strike.

His anger subsiding, Saul entered the courtyard at Gamaliel's home, looking forward to the tranquility that always enveloped this household.

Straightaway he saw Malchus, the scary personal servant of the High Priest, speaking intently to both Gammy and Gamaliel.

Saul drew near and the servant noticed him and fell silent but Gamaliel nodded for him to continue and motioned for Saul to come close.

"The High Priest has been pressured for the whole of last week and especially today. Their counsel is mainly about the financial aspect. His family, along with many Sadducees are adamant that he must do something. They are very bothered that every day, large amounts of money are given to these disciples by their followers. Also, with all the miracles happening in the Temple and on the streets, Annas is overcome with jealousy. He somehow feels that the office of High Priest is denigrated with each healing and I fear that tomorrow there may be grievous and irreversible errors made if wise counsel is not used."

Saul was astounded at the candid and conspiratorial words of this hugely influential servant. He thought of reprimanding him immediately.

Gamaliel, on the other hand, spoke to this man with a gentle understanding and Saul thought that very strange, almost as if he was colluding with the servant.

"We will contact all we can tonight for I want all the elders and wise men of Jerusalem involved tomorrow. Thank you for your warning," he said, and Malchus swiftly turned and left with only a slight, sideways glance at Saul.

Gamaliel sent his house servant to find the trusted messengers of the Sanhedrin, those whose official duty it was to inform all members of any quickly called court dealings. Throughout the evening these messengers called on the homes of the men of the Sanhedrin as directed, thus assuring their presence in the morning.

"Master," Saul asked Gamaliel, "why is the High Priest's servant working at cross purposes to the High Priest?"

Saul was clearly bothered by what he had just witnessed.

"His purpose is only to assure that the arrested men, and one must always remember that they are Jews and our brethren, are handled justly and with wisdom. He does not want his master to make a major mistake. Part of his duties are to protect not only the integrity of this High Priest but also the integrity of the office. Malchus recognizes that Caiaphas may be unduly influenced by the misguided intentions of those who have his ear." Gamaliel paused and then added, "His is a noble purpose."

Saul was not satisfied with this answer and pressed further. "He has overstepped his authority. What would possess him to want to defend these Galilean men?" These last words were only muttered and no answer was offered.

Gamaliel retreated into his house and left a confused Saul in the courtyard. Gammy invited Saul to sit, and he began speaking.

"Malchus led the group of Temple guards that Caiaphas sent to arrest Jesus in Gethsemane the night before He was crucified. I hear he got into a physical scuffle with the big disciple Simon Peter who happened to have a sword. Malchus was badly injured and had his ear cut completely off. Apparently, Jesus stopped the fighting and it is reported that he found the ear, washed it and placed it back on Malchus. You probably did not notice because there are no scars around that ear. It was instantly healed."

"One of the Galileans arrested today is that same Simon Peter, so you would think Malchus would like to see him arrested and punished, but apparently the healing of his ear changed his outlook somewhat, it softened him," Gammy stated.

Saul peered at the face and demeanor of Gammy for a long while before speaking.

"Gammy, that just proves that even the most influential Jews are being swayed by these supposed miracles. Whatever the source of this power, the Galileans are captivating and deceiving us and have turned us away from our focus—total obedience to the Law. They are very subtle and they have sneakily introduced a name that is now on everybody's lips, a name that has risen in defiance of the commandments. Added to that, they teach that the sacred Spirit of Jehovah is a common thing available to every Jew, even to those who do not honor the Torah completely, as we do. We were commanded by Moses to stone those who do these things. There is no other wisdom that we should be listening to. There is nothing in the Law that makes any excuse, not even a new ear."

Almost expecting such a reaction from his friend, Gammy thought only a few moments about what had just been said and then responded.

"Saul, my dear brother, I fear that you are like a man possessed who cannot think past his immediate emotions but is driven to the same conclusions continually. Surely, Hashem can do things in ways we do not understand so the first thing we should do is to ensure our motives are pure. These people of the Way have done you no harm, why do you need to punish them so badly."

Saul was losing his ferocious temper and was now at a loss for words, managing to only mutter, "I hate them. I hate them with a pure hatred. I hate what they are doing to our nation. I hate that they have bewitched our wisest leaders and I especially hate that they have so influenced you and your father."

With that he jumped up and bounded up the stairs to his apartment, leaving a perplexed Gammy sitting alone. At the top of the stairs, Saul turned to the quieted Gammy and yelled across the courtyard, "My hatred is righteous, it is holy, it is exactly what Hashem would want."

Gammy was stunned and his eyes followed the man whom he considered his brother and whom he loved deeply, but no words would come.

CHAPTER SIXTY-EIGHT

Another Trial

Saul awoke the next morning after a fitful sleep and he was still angry and upset. He avoided his sister and the rest of the household and slipped out unnoticed. As planned, he arrived at the Temple courtyards shortly after daybreak where a few small groups were already gathering in anticipation of the day's events.

Saul was intentionally wearing his best tunic that loudly and proudly identified him, and yes, he had rubbed it twelve times with the purified cloth washed thrice in purified rainwater to remove the invisible but deeply defiling stains left by the old woman's hands. Today he walked boldly through the groups that were milling on street corners. The crowd was stirring and anxious while waiting for the main gates to open, possibly unaware of the smaller gates above that rarely closed.

Saul avoided them and entered through the upper women's entrance. Expecting the courtyard to be empty, he was surprised to see the porches surrounding the plateau already filled with hundreds of people sitting around very quietly. He noticed that they were not just sitting, but were listening intently to different speakers all around the colonnades.

Wanting to know what was being said, Saul wandered to the closest speaker.

He immediately recognized him as the younger man who was usually with Simon Peter, the one they called John.

Saul was confused.

Was this one not arrested with the rest? Had he somehow escaped capture? The messenger had told Samuel and him that all the leaders had been arrested.

How had this one avoided arrest? Many questions erupted immediately in his mind.

Further down the west porch, he thought he saw Simon Peter himself!

Saul stumbled his way to where Peter was, now completely baffled.

He was looking about trying to locate a chief priest or a guar, hoping for some answers, all the while wondering if he actually saw them get arrested and jailed, or did he imagine that. No, he was sure of what he had seen and even Gamaliel and Malchus had confirmed their arrest.

He stopped questioning himself and began wondering when and why someone had released these men.

What had happened to Caiaphas in the hours since yesterday's arrest of these men to change his mind.

He came close and listened for a minute, not caring anymore that he was easily identified in his best garment and well aware that the crowd was watching him closely. Today, he was not at all concerned what they thought of him and he stuck his chin out defiantly, even staring down anyone who looked at length at him.

"We were all released by the Angel of the Lord," Peter said to a gasping and amazed group. "And we were commanded to come back here and keep preaching in His name."

"Angels indeed," snapped Saul in a low mutter, mainly to himself, but catching the attention of a few around him. He prudently slipped behind a pillar. "More theatrics and more deceiving," he declared aloud from his spot behind the column, causing more in the crowd to turn to him, suddenly looking for the hidden speaker.

Saul waited a moment until the crowd turned back to the speaker and then he quickly left, making his way around to the north side of the Temple building to the doorway of the Hall of Hewn Stones. He was looking desperately for someone who could explain why these men had been released.

Inside the Sanhedrin, his friend Samuel and a few of his most ardent followers were already seated and within minutes the rest of the elders of the

Sanhedrin entered and had taken their seats. Pushing past them, the High Priest and his family members arrived with the Sadducees, who also held seats in the Sanhedrin, following closely. It was evident that they had planned their group arrival to present a united front. Gamaliel was already in his gilded presidential seat.

All of these men had arrived through the small women's gate, avoiding the unpredictable crowds in the plaza and the porticos. Saul hurried to an open spot.

"Brethren," Caiaphas immediately called in a loud voice, once again usurping the traditional procedure whereby Gamaliel would normally chair the proceedings.

"We meet once again on this matter of the disciples of Jesus and their continual preaching of some sort of alternate 'salvation for the Jews' in His name. This is a persistent violation of the Law and we have warned them before. They chose to ignore our commands and therefore are in an act of rebellion to the wisdom of the offices appointed by Hashem. As Korah and Dathan were in rebellion to Moses, these are also in rebellion. Their actions will bring about the anger of Hashem upon all of us if we do not act decisively and without delay. With that in mind, we are holding them in the jails and they are now under our control. They cannot impress the crowds with any more of their supposed miraculous tricks."

Saul was confused. *They are in our jails? What did he mean by that?*

Caiaphas continued, "All must realize that it is legal, righteous and within our power to deal with their rebellion. Proper order and respect will be restored only if we act as a unified body here today."

The High Priest scanned the elders and leaders for reaction to his diatribe and he also peeked quickly at his father-in-law, old Annas, for some show of approval. He wanted to quell any attempt at disagreement within the Sanhedrin.

Satisfied that there were no objectors, he called out to the Captain of the Guard, "Go get them from the jails and bring them to us."

Saul was now tugging on his short beard, even more confused. He looked across the floor at Gamaliel for some clarity but saw nothing that could explain this.

If the High Priest did not know that these men were already teaching in the Temple courtyards, then who had taken it upon himself to free them? Was the court this disjointed?

A frightening thought occurred to Saul.

Would Gamaliel dare to set these men free without the agreement of the Sanhedrin first?

Totally bewildered, Saul sat quiet and completely still, wondering just what was going to take place. He scanned the other Sanhedrin judges and then the spectators, desperately looking for some explanation. He saw some observers snickering in their seats and was about to openly reproach these men when the door opened. The captain entered and he was visibly upset and leading a troop of very nervous guards who were quick-stepping behind him.

"I went to get them but they were not in the cells. These are the guards who were in charge of them last night but they swear that the doors were not opened at all. The doors are still locked but nobody is in there. I checked the locks myself."

Great guffaws, hooting and loud laughter erupted at this bizarre confession. In general, there was a very low regard for this squad of brutal enforcers and many seated in this hall were enjoying the embarrassment and the look of dread and fear on their faces.

A young man, a spectator who was arriving a little late, came in the doors just then and hearing the last of the conversation, yelled out, "Go look outside, over in the Gentile's Plaza, the men you put in jail are out there in the Temple courtyards and they are still teaching about Jesus."

The Captain of the Guard's head snapped around and he was absolutely stunned and surprised. Fear appeared on his face as he looked at the seething High Priest who said nothing but stroked his long white beard rapidly. A fit of rage was creeping up in him.

"Get them," he spit out at the captain.

The captain quickly gathered even more armed officers and raced out to the south porticos where each guard headed for a separate speaker. Reaching the outer edges of the ten or so individual gatherings, they were forcibly blocked by a wall of very solemn and determined people who were listening intently and who simply refused to move.

The rebuffed captain wisely retreated and chose to gather his troops into the middle of the Court of the Gentiles where he conferred with them quickly.

He then decided to politely "ask" the former prisoners to come with him to the Sanhedrin.

In the last few minutes, he had gained a grudging respect for these determined people and possibly a little fear because of the abundance of walking staffs sprinkled throughout the crowd. True, any such unintended weapons were in the hands of old people, but he wanted to avoid any possible incidents with either the elderly or the young and strong.

The captain was visibly relieved when the men he had jailed just the night before nodded their agreement and followed him slowly and voluntarily into the middle of the hall and then calmly stood together before the High Priest. Many of their gathered congregations also followed, surrounding the Sanhedrin room in an ominous encirclement. A few entered, filling any possible spectator place and many more were pressing up to the wide-open doorway. An ominous buzz from outside spilled through the yawning door.

The disciples showed no fear at all but looked about the chamber with almost condescending expressions, some even walking over and greeting familiar onlookers with a warm embrace.

Nicodemus left his seat on the judgment side of the Sanhedrin and came down and stood among them with each disciple extended an enveloping and earnest embrace to him. The old man remained standing with them, very markedly not returning to his deserted seat of judgement.

Caiaphas began his usual performance of strutting back and forth and attempting to appear in control but the whole congregation could not help noticing his nervous habit of pulling on the decorated sleeves of his priestly outer robe. Those who knew him well feared that his crimson-faced appearance and his heavy-breathing condition would not be able to withstand the pressure of today's proceedings.

While marching the disciples into the Sanhedrin, the observant Captain of the Guard suddenly became very concerned about another and possibly much more serious problem.

Watching his every move were four heavily armed Roman soldiers who were led by a serious looking centurion who seemed strangely concerned about what was happening to these Galilean people. He and his men had followed at a distance when the Temple captain, suddenly very politely, led the Galileans to the common door on the north side. This door was clearly in view of the windows of the Antonia Fortress, making it visible to all the remaining soldiers of the Roman garrison. Many battle-scarred faces were now appearing in these windows.

Leaving his armed soldiers standing just a few feet inside the door, the centurion walked in brazenly and found a seat on the long stone bench directly across from the most important judges of the Sanhedrin. He removed his helmet, exposing the long, now almost famous, scar that started near his ear and ran down along his jaw. He stared coldly at those in front of him.

Saul recognized him as the man he had seen in the group in Bethlehem, among other places, and this set his mind racing.

What interest would this political Roman have in a religious hearing? The centurion's presence sobered the raucous atmosphere of the hall immediately.

A rumor rippled through the chamber and passed from wagging head to wagging head. It was whispered that these disciples had been freed in the night by an angel and when this report made its way to where the Sadducees sat, they made a great display of their contempt for such tales by hooting and spitting vulgarly on the floor. Some laughed loudly and others mocked, but a few were genuinely frightened. A good number of judges did not react at all, remaining in deep thought until the hall quieted and the High Priest rose again.

Standing directly in front of Simon Peter, he twisted his clothing and fussed about even more, making quite a performance of straightening his gleaming and spotless robes.

Starting over, Caiaphas began parading his substantial girth back and forth, swaggering in a smug theatrical fashion while continually checking the faces of the crowd for looks of approval. Finally, he stopped a few feet in front of Peter's face and in his loudest voice, bellowed piously, "We commanded you not to teach in this name."

Peter seemed slightly amused but remained silent, simply shrugging a nonchalant shoulder.

Caiaphas again strutted away across the raised dais and then quickly returned. It was evident to all that he was now over his initial nervousness and was quite enjoying his own performance. He turned to his supporters and as if on cue they all began to call out the third commandment while some shouted other accusations, much to the approval of the nodding High Priest. Shortly, he raised his arm to call for silence.

"You well know that Moses called for the stoning of those who misuse the name of Hesham, yet you do this daily. Furthermore, you have encouraged every Jew in Jerusalem to do likewise."

He swaggered about again and then he moved into a beam of sunlight which shone into the chamber from the windows high above as if on cue. He was aware that his luminous robes were shining impressively and he waited in that glow for a further reaction from his crowd. The usual suspects dutifully howled and called out, allowing him to again search the faces of the crowd to gauge how his words and his translucent form were being received by his supporters in the court. He stole a furtive glance at Annas, his father-in-law and former High Priest, and thankfully, received an approving nod.

Caiaphas then looked at the collection of accused before him, for he was interested in gauging the reaction of these lowly Galileans to his priestly accusations.

Worryingly, he saw no panic in them at all, not even a look of concern but rather a detached disregard for the words he had just spoken. A few were even smiling back and forth to each other.

He swung around, his long robe twirling and shining, and again stuck his bearded face directly in front of Simon Peter's and stared angrily into the big disciple's eyes. After a moment he shouted again, ensuring that everyone in the hall could clearly hear and spraying the big Galilean with his spittle.

"You are determined to make this austere and respected body appear guilty of illicit acts with regard to Jesus, whom Pilate crucified."

He stole a quick glance at the centurion, now concerned that he had made an unwise and out of place accusation of the Roman governor. The soldier remained deathly still.

Collecting his thoughts, the High Priest again paced back and forth, giving his remarks time to penetrate the audience. "You want to make us guilty of His blood," he declared.

He strutted about some more and then surprisingly, without saying another word, Caiaphas flopped down on his gilded throne in a great show of weariness for having to deal with such rabble.

A hush came over the big hall.

The big disciple looked around, wondering if such charges required an answer. After a minute of nervous silence, Peter stepped up on the first step of the raised platform where the High Priest was now sitting next to a visibly uncomfortable Gamaliel. The president of this court had, so far, said nothing and had hardly moved a muscle.

Peter took his time. He was looking around the room and hesitating as if deciding whether to speak or not. The chamber remained hushed and waiting. It was now apparent that the futile attempt of the High Priest to control the proceedings had failed.

"Brethren, I will address your first point," Peter finally said. "But let me set the record straight. Last night you had us arrested and locked up beneath these very sacred floors in filthy dungeons that should never be used against your Jewish brethren. You put chains on us and threw us in with the rats."

Peter let that comment fester with the crowd, quite aware that most Jews would readily agree with him about the hideous condition of the dungeons, but then he continued.

"During the night, the Angel of the Lord appeared and opened the gates and commanded us to return to the Temple and keep telling all about Jesus. How your guards slept through this is indeed a mystery. It seems the polite angel locked the doors behind us as well," Peter said with a huge grin.

The tittering of the crowd exploded into laughter. The cluster of disciples poked each other and laughed aloud, also appreciating the humor of the situation.

The confused guards, those who had been responsible for the night watch of the prisoners, looked at each other with a growing level of fear. Peter smiled at them, enjoying his little joke and he walked over and put his arm around the nearest one.

"I wonder what Hesham thinks of your putrid jails now," a spectator who was seated near the door shouted.

The chief of the Temple guard, immediately enraged at the unflattering accusation, swung around and moved slightly in the vocal man's direction but he caught the almost imperceptible movement of the Roman centurion's hand telling him to remain where he was. He stopped dead in his tracks and then meekly retraced his steps. Things were suddenly getting very serious.

"So, I have a question for you and this assembly, and I do not think it is hard to answer. Should we obey you," asked Peter, looking directly into the eyes of the High Priest and then turning to Gamaliel with the same look, "or should we obey God?"

Simon Peter stretched out his upturned palms in a questioning motion.

Not a sound was heard in the hall, a deathly quiet falling in the room.

Completely flustered, Caiaphas stood up and with a faltering attempt at ceremony and without comment, turned his back on Simon Peter. No other answer came from the seventy-one members of the Sanhedrin, except for Nicodemus, who was standing shoulder to shoulder with Peter and approvingly patting the big man's back. Caiaphas sat back down quickly.

"Secondly," Simon Peter continued, knowing he had their complete attention and that he had a more important point he wanted to make, "it was Adonai, the God of our fathers, who raised Jesus from the dead, totally approving of Him. It wasn't us, or you, or any scholars."

He let that point resonate through the room and got some grudging nods of agreement, but there was also a swelling chorus of guffaws and calls of "liar" echoing off the walls in response.

Simon Peter obviously knew the core issues and was not going to allow this opportunity slip without declaring them. He turned slowly, taking in the whole assembly and pointing to all. After listening to the howls of derision, he replied with, "Whom all of you killed and are guilty of murder, for you hanged Him on a tree." Peter was now walking around freely between the judges and the spectators and he was looking directly into the faces of all.

The reactions in the room were varied. Violent and deafening retorts came from some and stunned silence from others. The noise of discord in the room was heard on the outer plateau by the assembled crowd and in the inner Temple court by the adorned priests who were already busy with their sacrifices. Most importantly, it was also heard by the Roman centurions who were now leaning out of the windows of their next-door fortress.

The clamor continued until Simon Peter, now in total control, silenced them all with a wave of his big hand and continued.

"Your confused opinions have no weight in this matter. What you think of Jesus does not matter at all, for God Himself exalted Jesus as Messiah and made Him the Prince and Savior. He did it so that He could bring repentance and forgiveness of sins to Israel. Your judgments have no weight, for Hashem has not only spoken, but He has also made these things come to pass."

All in the room felt the sting of his declaration and if there was any doubt, one of Peter's colleagues said loudly, "I'm sure Jehovah is also not all that impressed with your staged ceremony and your elaborate costumes either."

This upstart proclamation started a renewed barrage of insults flying about in the entire hall, Saul himself leaping up and calling out the sacrilege of saying such things. The noise went on for many minutes before Gamaliel finally stood and quieted the room.

Simon Peter took the opportunity to continue. "We," and he pointed to the others standing with him, "are witnesses of these things and so is the Holy Spirit, the same Spirit which God has given freely to all those who obey Him, just as you see happening daily in the Temple."

Cries of blasphemy, sedition and heresy rang out in a furious chorus as men who seemed unable to control themselves ran at the group of disciples in a simulated show of anger only to be turned back, far too easily, by the Temple guards who now formed a protective wall around the Galileans.

They were suddenly taking their guardsman duties very seriously.

The Roman soldiers tensed visibly but waited obediently at the door for a signal from their captain.

"They must die," was a chant that arose, starting from the area of the conspiring Sadducees and gaining volume throughout the hall. The High Priest nodded slowly in what was easily taken as approval to this chant and it seemed as if the decision had somehow been made.

Just then the centurion stood up and with a steely gaze made a calculated and overt show of scrutinizing every member of the Sanhedrin, spending a few extra moments staring at the most vocal of the Sadducees. This was unexpected and was an action that immediately quieted most of the squawking assembly.

This personal stare down of the loudest ones ended with the most royally adorned among them meekly looking at their sandals. The chant also diminished into a quieter but more menacing steady stream of mutterings for their stoning.

There was only a very small contingent of judges, those not easily influenced by either the High Priest or the wealth and power of the Sadducees, who had remained quiet and deeply troubled at the silliness of the charges. These took the opportunity to call out among themselves, shouting, "Release them."

Once again Gamaliel stood and for a whole five minutes attempted to silence the room completely. He also tried to settle the many side arguments taking place in the corners of the hall.

"Men of Israel," he shouted continually until the insulting and offensive comments directed at the Galileans ceased. "Men of Israel," he repeated, "consider carefully what your intentions are concerning these men."

Gamaliel's reputation for honest judgments and wisdom had its affect and finally silenced the room. He purposely began a calming discourse by reminding them of two other such religious movements that had risen in the recent past and had come to naught simply by letting them run their course. His words were received with relieved agreement by most when he said, "Leave them alone, for if their work is from human efforts, it will fail like the others."

Heads nodded in contemplative agreement throughout the chamber. That is, except for the most militant of the Pharisees, the most irritated Sadducees and the entire family of the High Priest.

It was Gamaliel's next statement that shook Saul and a host of others in the room when it was finally realized what Gamaliel was really saying.

Loudly and unmistakably, he said, "But if this movement is from Hashem, you will not be able to stop these men and you will find yourself fighting God."

In saying this, he purposely excluded himself from any further blame while issuing the dire warning. Not only that, Gamaliel was confessing the possibility that this upstart movement was of God. This was a total departure from the stance of all the other Pharisees in the room. Saul was totally stunned.

Gamaliel slowly pointed to the whole assembly to emphasize the responsibility they were taking upon themselves. At hearing this warning, some of the Sanhedrin members nodded solemnly in agreement but just as many screamed out, red faces contorted with anger and each demanding that some punishment was needed and must be applied.

Gamaliel's words of wisdom and warning slowly began changing the atmosphere in the hall and soon had deflated the intense anger. Of course, the militant contingent was still not satisfied. Those close to Caiaphas felt that the High Priest, his office, and the whole assembly had been falsely accused and even demonized by these unlearned Galileans and so much muttering and complaining followed. Noticing this, Gamaliel suggested a way out of the feeling of surrender and disappointment that he knew some felt.

The chamber had a historical tradition for such instances and it was called a flogging. It was a less severe punishment in which the accusers would remove their cloak or outer garment and lightly swat the accused in a symbolic show of shaming. Nicodemus and a small contingent around him disagreed loudly with this and refused to be involved; in fact, they stood with their arms outward, desperately trying to provide some protection to the bemused disciples.

The unresisting disciples were lined up and many of the Sanhedrin walked by and lightly swung their outer garments at the disheveled men. Annas, Caiaphas, many chief priests of the Temple and, as expected, all the Sadducees took a full swing with their heavy vestments, but it was soon apparent that the followers of Jesus did not feel the disgrace that this performance was meant to bestow. They stood tall, ready to receive each blow, even appearing to invite each swipe.

Caiaphas, not satisfied with the effect of this almost comical undertaking, jumped up and attempted another showy performance, warning of more drastic consequences if these disciples were to speak in this name again, but it was an empty sounding warning, and the disciples left the hall rejoicing and happy.

Within the hour, they were back in Solomon's Porch teaching and preaching, much to the annoyance of the completely disregarded High Priest. Not knowing what else to do, Caiaphas disappeared into his house and gorged himself on a whole lamb, two platters full of breads and a whole vase of wine, as was his custom.

Saul left the hall alone.

He was confused and dazed and greatly disappointed in Gamaliel. He craved solitude, needing to sort out his thoughts. The hands-off policy he had just witnessed did not fit the lawful demands of swift and decisive punishment, demands which he had been taught were the only way to please God.

True, Gamaliel had over the years tempered his teachings by emphasizing the premise of "loving one's neighbor" as his grandfather Hillel had taught, but Saul could not agree that any mercy should be extended to this obvious heresy.

Such misguided mercy was in fact sinful.

The more he thought about it, the more convinced he became that this was not in any way a complicated case. It should have been dealt with easily and decisively by the Sanhedrin and it was simply a refusal on Gamaliel's part to apply the tenets of the Law that allowed the Galilean rabble to walk free. That should have been obvious to anyone who observed the infuriating and perplexing trial.

For hours, Saul wandered the streets of Jerusalem that morning, confused and upset, wanting to be alone and wanting to be lost in the crowd. He did not want to face Gamaliel right now for he did not know just how to approach him.

Finally, after many tortuous hours, he made his decision and headed to the Synagogue of the Freedmen to locate Samuel.

Samuel saw him coming through the synagogue gate and in his warm, gregarious manner welcomed him, rightfully suspecting that the events of the morning would have had a devastating effect on his friend.

As expected, Saul's agitation was plainly evident to any that knew him. He was pacing back and forth but seemed wordless and he was pounding his fist at the internal argument taking place within, almost oblivious to the presence of his friend Samuel.

"What do you need, my brother," was Samuel's quiet and heartfelt question to Saul, knowing his proud friend loathed any show of weakness.

Without a pause, Saul answered, "A new place to live."

CHAPTER SIXTY-NINE

Saul Leaves Home

In the next few weeks, his first days away from the warm home of his adolescence, Saul not only grew more assured of his opinions but he also grew
angrier and more determined. He was becoming certain that the danger to
Israel from the heresy and sacrilege was greatly misjudged and even drastically
downplayed by those in charge. Living away from Gamaliel's relaxed house
with someone as forceful and disciplined as Samuel was concerning the smallest directions of the Law, reaffirmed to Saul that relentless adherence to every
jot and tittle was not only the correct path for the nation but was character
building and personally strengthening for each Jew as well.

"How could any Jew have personal integrity if he were not completely sub-
servient to the Law," was now his favorite question to any that would listen.
"Obedience is everyone's salvation," he preached relentlessly.

Although missing the penetrating insights of Gamaliel and the peaceful and
easy aura of his sister terribly, Saul was feeling a new independence and even a
sudden maturity. He was convinced that he was finally coming into his own
as an important part of the religious life of Jerusalem and he liked what he saw
in himself.

He was Saul, the brilliant Pharisee, and was no longer known as just "Saul the student of Gamaliel." Truth be known, he relished the sound of those words.

He was speaking often in other synagogues in Jerusalem and was becoming very well known to many. His influence and indeed his whole world, was growing.

At the same time, other parts of his life were expanding as well.

Saul was becoming more and more impressed with Samuel's sister, Rachel. He noticed the endless hours she and her mother spent caring for the poor and the widowed of the synagogue, a task which went mainly unnoticed and unrewarded. He appreciated her direct and precise speech when discussing anything regarding the Law and he was a personal witness to the immaculate and traditional house she kept. Whenever her image would come to mind, he would experience feelings that were warm and strange, emotions never before known to him.

It was true that Rachel was different from Miriam or Leah. She was less sophisticated than the way they were, missing the refinement and elegance which a life with wealth and privilege generates. Her sometimes blunt, outspoken way had offended some, but Saul easily overlooked that, saying he preferred such honesty. He saw in her a truly charitable heart, but above all, he was most impressed with her devotion to keeping all aspects of the Law exactly as her older brother had taught her.

Seeing her daily was also having a strange effect on him. He found himself looking forward to seeing her warm smile and was truly disappointed if she was not around when he returned to the house. Conversation was easy with Rachel for she saw issues in much the same way as he did and truth be told, she felt that even more should be done to curb the influence of the new sect. It was genuinely comical to hear Samuel and Saul call for restraint by Rachel when she would demand the two men be more forceful when dealing with people around the synagogue, suggesting with some seriousness that they carry a cane or stick with them to inflict some form of righteous and speedy correction for less serious crimes.

Out of a previously unknown loneliness, Saul was making a point of stopping by Miriam's new stall every second or third day, sometimes for only a few minutes, sometimes just to look and sometimes just to wave at her. He missed his sister dearly.

Leah would often find an excuse to leave the shop when Saul arrived and when left alone, brother and sister completely enjoyed each other's company. During those visits. Miriam was open, telling Saul about the joys and complications of being a business person and detailing what was taking place in her life.

Any reference to the great rift between Saul and Gamaliel was avoided by both of them.

CHAPTER SEVENTY

Miriam's Attraction

Each time that Saul went to see his sister, he was more and more impressed with the gradual transformation of the stalls that Miriam owned along the west side of the Cardo. Each shop was being festooned with bright trimmings and glimmering draperies and each was now cleaned and painted. What stood out and made them completely distinct from other redecorated stalls were the storied murals on the back wall of each, detailed scenes representing some of the favorite locations Saul and Miriam had visited on their tours. She had hired the best artists she could find and the results were truly amazing. Saul instantly loved the easily identifiable pictures and he appreciated that Miriam had chosen familiar scenes from their favorite places.

The detail of the artwork was striking and Saul was amazed at the ability of the untethered artists. He was seen staring for long periods at the intricate and meaningful details that each painter had hidden in his work.

One scene was of Rachel's tomb. The monument was lovingly enhanced with a ghostly ancestral figure which after much loud street-level debate was decided to be the spirit of the ancient mother of Benjamin. Another scene displayed the original cave entrance of Machpelah in Hebron, surrounded by the original grieving family. Jacob's well, with the surrounding landscape of Shechem was also painted, but Saul's favorite was the spreading tree that looked like no other with half-hidden inhabitants woven into its branches that one had to stand very close to decipher. Miriam's personal visions of Jewish history were being intricately included in the portrayals and Saul loved it.

Enthralled shoppers would stop and gaze at the depictions and the small details would eventually draw them deep inside the shops where the merchants could entice them with their wares, often successfully making a sale. The side walls of each stall were in the process of being adorned with other scenes as well. The familiar landscapes of Judea and Samaria had quickly become of compelling interest and a focus of the pride of the Jews in Jerusalem, with each new portrait attracting a fresh gaggle of visitors and potential customers. Shoppers flocked to the shops to see them, many returning over-and-over again, excitedly pointing out familiar places to others whom they had brought along. The result was that before long, jealous and grumbling complaints from the undecorated shops were heard, most complaining about the long lines and crowded streets in front of their competitors.

Miriam was continuously surprised at the enthusiasm created for the next unveiling of each new landscape, which for dramatic effect, Leah would keep hidden until it was completely finished. She would make a large sign announcing the exact date of the next uncovering and the nearby merchants quickly learned that they must prepare for large crowds on those days. Wisely, Leah had learned to give each individual depiction its own special day, many times tying them to a special day of the Jewish calendar if possible. Scribes and historians in the city were enthralled and were approaching Leah with ideas and opinions of what should be her next project.

This was a curious and growing phenomenon in Jerusalem, much talked about, and soon the talented artists were being approached by other shops wanting to draw in customers as well.

As Miriam had predicted to the hesitant merchants, this was fast becoming a favorite spot to gather and the profit-making benefits were being felt and enjoyed by the most hesitant of her renters. Yeshivas and academies began bringing their young students to see the historic scenes that were only read about in their classes.

Being the main attraction of the street, the area had drained some business from stalls further away on the Cardo and many merchants were getting frustrated that the only thing they received were rent increases from their landlord, the High Priest. He was continually accosted with waves of muttering and grumbling by his renters, so finally, totally annoyed by the never-ending complaints, Caiaphas went to the Cardo, accompanied by his finely adorned entourage, to see for himself just what the fuss was about.

At first, he was openly critical of such brazen decorating, muttering something about graven images, but that soon disappeared when he stood dumbfounded for over half an hour directly in front of the beautiful portrait of Hebron and the scene of the original cave entrances of Machpelah. The scene was lovingly created as described to the artist by older Jews who remembered it that way from over eighty years previous and every rock and crevice had some religious significance. Caiaphas walked away without comment or further complaint but still stubbornly refused to help his merchants in any way.

The milling crowds needed refreshment and the quick-thinking merchant across the street set out more chairs and tables and was making quite a profit selling a variety of fruit plates and goblets of wine to gawkers. All around Miriam's stalls, other merchants began making their own improvements to their stalls, which added to the general attractiveness of this unique region of the Cardo.

Saul was immensely proud of his sister, plus he truly appreciated that she benefited from the safety and protection of the house of Gamaliel, even though his personal disagreement had grown into an unsurmountable barrier between them. Gammy and he were not speaking anymore and they only saw each other from a distance and avoided any contact. His position as a teacher in Gamaliel's academy was taken by another after a final, disagreeable exchange with Gamaliel and he had not seen his former mentor since that day.

This was a price he was willing to pay, and anyway, thought Saul, what would he have in common or have to say to one he saw now as weak and in error.

It was in that weakness that Saul continued to see nothing but a great, growing danger to Israel.

After that disappointing trial of the disciples, Jerusalem had settled into both a curious acceptance of the daily miracles performed among the people of the Way and the corresponding barrage of accusations and calls of blasphemy by the religious zealots such as Saul. Jerusalem was truly a divided city over this issue and any resolution seemed impossible, especially when the causes of the dispute, the pesky and non-repentant Galileans, were walking free as birds in the streets of Jerusalem and making a continual clamor in that unruly upper room.

It was true that in the past the city always had an abundance of debate and religious acrimony, even over-heated arguments between Pharisaical groups or the Sadducees and the zealots, but it seemed that there was now a peculiar truce between these traditional foes as they focused on their common enemy, the followers of Jesus.

CHAPTER SEVENTY-ONE

The Brother and Sister Spat

A few weeks later, on a day when Saul was approaching Miriam's shop for a visit with his sister, he noticed Barnabas and his youthful nephew offloading heavy bundles from a narrow two-wheeled cart that had been pulled by a scruffy donkey to her stall. Wrapped inside the heavy bundles was a collection of large sacks, a few smaller skin bags, and many carefully wrapped, small earthen vases that Miriam was making room for and was spreading around the stall, placing them on her exquisite olivewood shelving.

Saul remained at a distance, waiting for Barnabas to leave, wanting only to speak with his sister, but Barnabas remained in a long and animated conversation with Miriam. Saul was suddenly impatient and finally, he left to return the next day.

Early the next morning, as he rounded the familiar corner onto the Cardo, he purposely slowed his stride and gazed again over the dazzling array of art and decoration that his sister had created on the street. The early sun hit the shimmering cloths decorating the columns, literally lighting them up.

As he approached, he saw Miriam in a quiet discussion with a richly clothed and very important woman while two other women quietly waited in line for their turn to speak with her.

Leah was also busy in the stall, chatting to other customers while adeptly filling small vases, marking them with instructions and then bundling them. With a pleasant and thankful gesture, she received payment from these customers and then quickly moved on to the next. The two women were running a profitable and efficient business thought Saul, and a strange tinge of envy crept into his thinking. Somewhere deep inside he begrudged them the success and happy freedom they had.

Saul decided to observe Jerusalem's new attraction at work for a while longer, so he sat across the street and watched the action while enjoying a serving of well roasted meat. The merchant, seeing him observing things so keenly, said, "That is quite a business those ladies have. They helped a few very sick women, the word got out and the flow of customers started. Now they are getting busier every day."

Saul turned to see Miriam smiling at him from her shop and then excusing herself from her customer for a minute. She rushed over and greeted her brother with a big smile.

"Saul, I miss seeing you so much, I miss our talks and I miss watching you gulp your food," she teased, and they both laughed easily. "Possibly we could spend Sabbath together?" she questioned. She looked back at the impatient lineup in her stall but would not leave until her brother had finally agreed.

Saul had not wanted to commit to returning to Gamaliel's compound, even for Sabbath, but he missed his sister terribly and yearned for her company. He was convinced that remaining apart from his old teacher and from Gammy was reinforcing and confirming the public statement that he wanted to convey and he was adamant about maintaining this distance, but the weeks apart from his sister were hard. Miriam's successful business was changing her into an outgoing, confident woman and Saul felt that he was in danger of losing the little sister he had watched grow up, so, he finally agreed to that special day with her.

On the afternoon before the Sabbath, Saul arranged his arrival at his old apartment just before sundown and entered without anyone noticing, just as he had when he would sneak in and out as a young lad. The beautiful Sabbath evening was spent alone with Miriam, and Saul even enjoyed staying the night in his familiar old room.

The next morning, the effortless conversation between the brother and sister changed and the uncomfortable and avoided subject of the falling out with Gamaliel and Gammy, her future husband, was confronted. Miriam sweetly asked Saul, "Why do you now disagree with Gamaliel after years of devotion to your mentor."

"It is not I that has changed, but them," was Saul's rather curt answer.

"No, Saul, my precious brother, you have changed. I always knew you to have a scriptural reason or logical answer for everything you did. That was your strength. It was also Gamaliel's way. Now I have seen you having irrational, emotional reactions, mostly out of anger or insult and this has happened since we have arrived here in Jerusalem. When we went on our tour, you were again my precious brother, at least until someone would mention these people of the Way or mention Jesus. You would immediately change into an angry, irrational zealot. Can you not disagree with them and let them be?" she asked.

Miriam was not prepared for or expecting the force of the answer she received.

"Not punishing them severely is contravening God's command given through Moses, Miriam. I, as a Pharisee, have dedicated my life to completely obeying his commands. It is the only hope for Israel and even listening to those who would sympathize or show mercy to these people is wrong and may itself be sacrilege. I will not be friendly to any who mistake weakness for mercy, or any that take evil as good and I now regard those who do not have such a love of the Law as my enemy and enemies of Hashem."

Saul's jaw was set. "To even debate with them gives them the appearance of credibility, so I will not hear their arguments or their teachings; they are evil and dangerous."

He had resolutely ended the conversation, clearly not wanting to further discuss the issue with his sister, but he desperately wanted her to understand that it was he who was on the correct path.

The rest of the day was tense and at sundown he left the apartment and slipped out without encountering anyone from Gamaliel's family. Miriam was stunned at the coolness of his departing.

Saul was a little surprised at the anticipation he felt as he approached his new home at Samuel's house. The dedication of this family to the Law and to maintaining the purity of their synagogue and to its charities was a comfort and reassurance for Saul. In sharp contrast, he had left Gamaliel's home upset that his former mentor's fluctuating ways had caused such division between he and his sister.

Alone in his bed that night, Saul once more took stock of his life.

That there was now a division with Miriam was a reality and Saul, painfully but finally, decided that he was glad of it, feeling that he had needed to cut off his close relationship with her to please Hashem. It seemed so strange to be at odds with her, such a completely foreign feeling and finally, he had to force himself to not dwell on his unyielding demand for separation for it depressed him terribly. As much as he thought he must live apart from her, he still was heartsick whenever her laughing image would appear in his mind.

At one point that night, admittedly in a moment of weakness and fatigue, Saul even questioned himself and his determined stance.

His mind wandered to the point of asking if shunning Miriam was truly a demand of Hashem or was it a self-imposed religious exercise which he had put upon himself to demonstrate his dedication. A quick jolt of fear told him to abandon that line of thinking for if he even entertained the thought that parts of his devotion were simply made up and were there only to promote his image, well that would destroy his whole concept of the permanence and steadfastness of the Law.

No, that was obviously a demonic thought attempting to seduce him and he abandoned it immediately.

CHAPTER SEVENTY-TWO

Who Will Feed the Widows?

The day after returning from the Sabbath with his sister, Samuel, Saul, and Rachel remained at their home and conferred well into the afternoon. They had a serious problem at the synagogue and Rachel was visibly upset because of it. There were a number of destitute widows who had received only a small basket of food over this Sabbath and the reason was that the usual weekly donations had dwindled severely. The members of their synagogue who now followed the disciples of Jesus, and this was a sizable and growing number, had bestowed all their charitable giving on these Galilean disciples, some giving their entire fortunes, and as a result, the usual adequate funds the synagogue had to assist the needy were severely restricted and this week had fallen far short.

Realizing that the Galileans' interference into the synagogue's charity had caused the problem had created a day-long fit of anger in both Saul and Samuel. All the money given to these Galilean fishermen would have easily fed and cared for the fifty or so truly needy widows at this synagogue, plus it would have added to the meager food-stores of many other struggling families. Even more maddening was that members of their own following, after giving their savings to the disciples of Jesus, were now depending on this synagogue for all their daily needs.

Samuel, Saul, and even Rachel had anticipated this and each had predicted this type of problem may happen when the new converts, in ill-advised fits of devotion, had given away their money. The crisis created on this last Sabbath had proven their suspicions correct.

Privately, the two men suspected that the problem may be even more devious.

In their secluded conversations, they had convinced themselves that the disciples were deceitful, skimming money and benefitting their own families in a pre-planned scheme and this Sabbath only confirmed their thinking. Having no prior evidence, they had kept these conclusions among themselves.

What was indisputable was the fact that the Galileans were neglecting some of their newest followers, especially those who were from this Greek-speaking Synagogue and were generously and greedily supplying the needs of those who were close to themselves. This left Rachel and Samuel and a few other kind-hearted people with the burden of making sure that the widows of their synagogue were adequately fed, and yes, that included those who were eager followers of these Galileans. Their compassion, unlike the Galileans' self-centered actions, was not limited to those who agreed with them but was pure-hearted charity. This they announced with a high degree of true humbleness to any who would listen.

Surprisingly, they received some hesitant agreement from a few of the widows of the Way who spoke Greek and themselves felt ignored by the others.

Rachel loudly commented that it was curious that after giving all their wealth to the disciples, there was not enough for the disciples to feed them. Where did all that money disappear to? It was all very suspicious, she announced accusingly in the lobby of the synagogue.

The fact was, Samuel's family was not rich like many other Pharisees' families were and they were now bearing a portion of the burden of the neglected widows both financially and with the time and energy required for food distribution. Added to that was the irritating knowledge that although the hungry readily accepted their gift of food, most rejected the providers as being a band of religious hypocrites, at least that was what their leaders continually called Samuel and other Pharisees in their daily sermons at the Temple.

This grated sharply on Rachel for after all her work, she expected more of an appreciative heart in these people.

It was decided that Samuel should confront Stephen and see if anything could be done to leave some financial resources in the local synagogue and not have it bled away by the questionable Galileans. He knew he had to be civil with his friend, but that would be difficult for Samuel was greatly upset.

While discussing this problem, Saul and Samuel had recognized that there appeared an internal division in the new sect and in their opinion, discord was now beginning to show. With a little ingenuity, that discord could be very useful.

They concluded that the root of the problem was the lack of concern by the original Aramaic speaking members from the Galilee for the newly baptized Greek-speaking ones. The Synagogue of the Freedmen was intimately involved in that struggle whether they wanted to be or not, for the Greeks were almost entirely attenders of this congregation. As with most problems between people, money was also a large factor. Samuel would start there.

The very next day, he cornered his friend Stephen and forcefully explained the synagogue's problem.

"There are widows from your group who were now a financial burden to the synagogue because of the questionable, if not immoral practice of demanding all their money be given to the disciples. None of this disappearing bounty was making its way back to help the needy," he accused, "and if not for the love and care of the synagogue, many would have been starving this Sabbath."

"Just where is all the money going," he demanded, hoping to embarrass Stephen into reconsidering his devotion to this group.

Stephen was speechless, his gaze dropping to his feet.

Seeing he had gained some moral high ground over Stephen, Samuel continued with even greater gusto. He alleged that the disciples were favoring their own families and their closest friends, conveniently forgetting the Greek-speaking Jews. These Galileans did not speak Greek and therefore felt no allegiance to them at all, he accused, possibly considering them spiritually deficient.

Then Samuel asked Stephen very pointedly, "Do you not see this division?"

Was his new form of religion so calloused that it could not recognize this problem? Past taking their money, did they not feel any compulsion to help them?

Samuel was being purposely abrasive with his questions, hoping to stir up some resentment in his old friend for the Galileans.

Stephen listened intently, not uttering a word but becoming uncomfortable and more visibly upset with each accusing fact. When Samuel was finished, Stephen began apologizing profusely for the problems this had caused. Without further explanation, he left for Mary's house where he knew he would find many of the disciples.

Shaken and heartbroken, he arrived at Mary's house and within minutes was sobbing and pouring his heart out to the three disciples that were there. He repeated the accusations he had just endured to Simon Peter, along with James, the son of the wealthy Capernaum fisherman Zebedee, and to Jesus's brother, also named James.

They were speechless.

Peter fell to his knees, holding his head and groaning at each accusing word. James could not move, as if the accusations had nailed him to the chair. When finished, Stephen stood apart, observing the humiliated men who, it was claimed among the believers, were divinely chosen for leadership. He watched the great sadness that swept over them and the nervous fear each man showed.

Had they failed their Lord yet again?

The suggestion of favoring one part of their group over the other bothered them the most and they kept repeating over and over that this was never their intention. All three agreed that, yes, they were indeed the ones to blamed, for they had somehow not been sensitive to their followers or had somehow unconsciously ignored this. This must be corrected immediately they declared.

Stephen, while waiting in the courtyard, was struck with a question of his own. *Why was there no one in the original group of disciples that could speak Greek?*

The sermons of the disciples at the Temple porticos had to be interpreted to those who spoke only Greek, so there was indeed an undeniable physical separation into two segments at these gatherings.

Had no one foreseen that a problem would ensue?

Within a few hours, a great meeting was called in the largest area of the Gentile Court at the Temple. Simon Peter, his voice quivering and with an open heart, described the problem to the gathering, quickly confessing his personal inadequacies and then directing the gathered crowd to choose seven trusted men more able to handle the collecting and allotting of money and the delivering of food that, he readily professed, was being so adequately provided for.

Tearfully, the big fisherman readily admitted all the mistakes made and begged the forgiveness of the believers who sat in a stunned silence. The gathered group of disciples of Jesus stepped aside and conferred for a moment and then Peter raised his hand to speak again.

Peter mentioned that he and the other disciples were called to minister the teachings of Jesus, not to wait on tables.

Those last words struck Stephen as strange and confusing, leaving him wondering if he had heard them correctly. From what he had been told, Jesus often insisted that He serve His followers Himself, explaining that He was a servant of the people. Stephen chose to ignore the complexities of Peter's strange statement and to think about it another day. The strange feeling of that statement would not leave.

The new arrangement was received with great favor by the crowd who after some prayer and conversation, chose seven men from among themselves. Curiously, and probably the result of personal guilt, all but one of the chosen men were Greek-speaking and Stephen was their first and easiest choice.

Closely watching this large gathering was Gammy who, out of his deep interest, remained glued to the fringes of the crowd while attempting to keep partially hidden under a nearby portico.

Gammy was confused and divided in his opinion of what he was seeing. All his life the Jewish religious experience was presented as Jews dutifully following decrees from those in authority, albeit the decrees were presented and believed as coming from Hashem Himself which then flowed through weighty and impressive individuals. What he had witnessed today was the leaders of this group trusting the wisdom of the followers, elevating the communal wisdom above their own. They had shown confidence in the integrity and wisdom of their converts and this was a concept completely foreign to his pharisaical upbringing. Somehow, this act of trust had converted the group into participants rather than just those who obey.

With this, Gammy was reminded of the relationship that Hashem had with his old friend Abraham, a relationship built on love and trust. He was also reminded that by Moses' time, 400 years later, that trust had been replaced with commands requiring obedience and punishment, hence the Law.

Stephen immediately shouldered his new responsibilities and made his way to the Synagogue of the Freedmen and searched out Samuel. With sincere humbleness he informed Samuel that the problem was being rectified, that he personally would be addressing the needs of the widows of this synagogue that followed the Way and even others if it was needed. He then handed Samuel a bag with two hundred shekels to give to his sister Rachel, more than enough to replenish the shrunken resources of the synagogue's own charity fund.

"If more is needed, please approach me first," Stephen begged of his old friend.

Later, when Samuel reported all this to Saul, Saul's first response was a fresh barrage of criticism. He outwardly wondered why these people had to be embarrassed and forced to do the right thing.

Rachel, a little more subdued, was just thankful to have the money she needed to keep her charity work going. She immediately went to the meat vendor and ordered six roasted lambs for next Sabbath eve.

Remaining angry, Saul was not willing to find anything commendable in the Way's actions and questioned why they wanted to start additional organizations anyway. The Temple and the synagogues were the places that charitable giving took place and it had been that way for centuries. If these people were so moved by the plight of the poor and so intent on relieving themselves of the burden of worldly possessions, their leaders should have instructed them to give away their proceeds directly to the poor and not through them. Saul saw nothing but questionable motives in all this and in his mind, he began wondering if even accepting help or charity from these blasphemers might itself be a grave error, possibly even a sin.

There was also the wider problem that was being created, one which Saul and Samuel easily identified but thought might be strangely helpful. This new charitable method removed sizable amounts of money from other local synagogues as well as theirs, and thereby cut deeply into the livelihood of the rabbis of these synagogues.

Hopefully, this sizable reduction in their incomes might finally get the passive rabbis to react, reasoned Saul and Samuel. Where once they were less critical of the Galileans, these wizened old teachers would now be jolted by their shrinking money bags into finally condemning the upstarts.

The chief priests had also noticed a sharp decrease in the amounts donated in the big vases strewn around the Temple Plaza where the charity of Jews was usually collected. For the first time in years, their secret percentage of the benevolent giving shrank and this was extremely disturbing. Most infuriating was the realization that the missing money was under the control of the Galilean leaders.

Over those days, Saul was infected with a new and very disturbing thought. Was this really what the current upheaval in the city was all about? Was it once again about money? Is that when the High Priest and the rabbis would begin taking this grave threat seriously?

New sermons and loud discussions condemning the manner that the money was being handled resonated with many Jews and this led to invitations for Saul and Samuel to attend other synagogues where they sharply criticized the act of separating these converts from their life-long and very caring rabbis, men who had dedicated their lives to their congregations and who married the children and buried the dead. Very loudly they exclaimed that the Galileans tore people from the familiar gatherings and bound them to themselves. Did these uneducated disciples see themselves as superior to other leaders and rabbis, they asked those congregations. How dare they?

It was one thing to have rabbinical disputes and debates over the soundness of one's theological position, these were not uncommon among Jews, but to regard themselves as spiritually superior or even "chosen" of God was the height of arrogance and pride. The Galileans went further, continually disparaging any teachings but their own, not unlike what Jesus had done, and this had convinced Saul that they were intent on doing nothing but dividing Israel.

He mentioned this observation in a synagogue harangue the very next weekend only to have an argumentative old Jew comment, "Just as all the Pharisees do."

It was all Saul could do to keep himself from thumping the man with the large scroll in his hands.

CHAPTER SEVENTY-THREE

Temple Priests and Wandering Pharisees

Over the next few months, Saul and Samuel exhausted themselves with debating and taunting and withstanding the teachings of the Way at every opportunity. They traveled outside of Jerusalem to dispute them in Emmaus, Bethlehem and other villages. They spent many Sabbaths visiting and warning Jews everywhere of the subtle yet demonic dangers of this new doctrine.

The depressing result of all their efforts was that they were frustrated, tired and were losing the battle. Their influence was waning while that of this group was growing steadily. Not only that, the unexplainable and seemingly supernatural events such as healings and strange demonic deliverances were continuing even outside of Jerusalem and these were having a cunning and seducing effect on many.

Extremely vexing to Saul was that every time he walked through the Temple courts, a larger and larger number of the traditionally garbed priests were listening to these disciples in Solomon's Porches with one ear while performing their prescribed duties. Some of the permanent chief priests were also being baptized and becoming part of this Way, often praying and worshiping with them while still clothed in the beautiful priest's garments.

How confusing to pilgrims was that, Saul asked often of anyone who would listen.

Frustrated, Saul and Samuel arranged an immediate meeting with the Captain of the Temple Guards to complain about these matters.

The non-committal captain readily agreed that this was an embarrassing problem and advised them that he had met with Caiaphas and discussed this very issue. The High Priest was likewise upset but informed the captain that he could not discipline or dismiss these priests as long as they performed their priestly duties. The problem was further muddled because the people of the Way encouraged priestly service and after joining the Way, their duties were usually being done with much more vigor and responsibility. All this was putting the High Priest in an increasingly awkward position.

At every turn, it seemed Saul and Samuel were becoming isolated in fighting the expanding group of heretics. The absolute worst and most troubling aspect of this battle was that many of their close Pharisee brethren were now becoming followers of these disciples, and …well, that was the final straw.

When Saul or Samuel would search out and confront these newly converted Pharisees, they condescendingly attempted to show how Jesus was the Messiah and, as such, was the fulfillment of the Law in human form. Older and supposedly wiser Pharisees and a generous sprinkling of younger ones, even a few former students of Saul, were being deceived and seduced and this made Saul angry, bitter and implacable.

When his former students came to him in public and tried to convince him of Jesus, he just screamed at them, calling them stupid and dangerous. Trails of spittle would run down his beard while he yelled and flailed and he often noticed the whole street staring at him with a guarded gaze. He despised that pitying look for it reeked of an all to familiar Jewish indifference.

Why were these Jews not as angry as he?

It was apparent to any politically observant person, but especially to Samuel and Saul, that the vaunted and normally confident leaders of Jerusalem, who by their very position were also the leaders of world-wide Jewry, were numbed into an embarrassing and frustrating inaction. Their paralysis seemed to be the result of fears on many fronts.

Firstly, the High Priest and his large but fragile family, greatly feared any sort of insurrection by the people, be that religious or political. They were constantly aware that they had received this lucrative office by the connivance of King Herod and his collusion with the Romans. That meant they did all they could to avoid even the perception of rebellion, whether real or imagined, and so they depended heavily on the respect that the common Jew had for their godly office. After all, they reminded everyone, their lofty position was established by Moses and Aaron at Sinai.

Prudently, they realized that there was an undercurrent of disgust for their particular family, so they worried about an internal rebellion among pious Jews to their many poorly-concealed indiscretions. To any logical Jew, it seemed remarkable that the priestly family's cure for this perception problem did not simply include discontinuing their greedy practices and questionable morals.

Secondly, there was the unpredictable Romans. Any sign of insurrection, local or national, would bring the harsh hand of the Roman Army down in Jerusalem and then on the nation. Although Caiaphas and Annas worked constantly on placating Pilate, they did fear that one day the present tenuous balance would be no more. If Pilate ever removed his protection of his new friend Caiaphas, who knew how the unpredictable Jews would treat them and their families?

Recently, the people of the Way had brought a third element for Caiaphas to worry about. This bunch had oft quoted Jesus's pointed words to Annas about the perversion of the office by his family and their cohorts, but now their preaching and teaching in the porticos carried much more serious accusations, openly citing them as the "murderers" of their Messiah. This was a huge problem.

Caiaphas had decided he could endure the name-calling for the sake of remaining in the seat of power and wisely realized that fomenting any deeper argument with them may be perceived as a civil uprising by the Romans which they readily would do, but only if and when they needed any reason to crack down.

The local Roman commander had long ago recognized the corruption of the Priest and his family, often joking about it directly to Caiaphas' face, so starting a fresh, ongoing argument based on defending his pure character seemed silly and not very practicable to the High Priest.

In the back of any politically observant Jerusalemite's mind was the real question, *'How long before the Romans decided on their own that enough was enough and they no longer tolerated this slippery priestly family?'* What would happen then?

Another question bounced around the heads of the "Holy" family.

Would there ever come a time when the people of the Way would rise in rebellion to the High Priest and his family. Would they include the Pharisees in such an insurgence, and would they want retribution for the death of Jesus?

These were complicated questions for Caiaphas and Annas who had not foreseen the growth of such a powerful religious movement in Judaism, at least one that did not include them.

CHAPTER SEVENTY-FOUR

Warnings from Above

Notwithstanding their disdain and strident vocal battles, Saul and Samuel had learned by simple observation that political rebellion was not to be feared from these Galileans. They openly preached passiveness, plus they demonstrated a strange enjoyment of persecution. The Romans seemed to understand this and the scarred centurion who moved so freely among the disciples would have reported their docile ways as well. It was almost as if they considered themselves fortunate to suffer for their cause.

The two Pharisees agreed that since there would be no violent response, there was no reason for allowing this Galilean rabble to take over the Temple and dominate the atmosphere of the city. They concluded that only a small amount of physical rough stuff by the Temple guards should be needed to remove them permanently from the Temple porticos, but nothing so violent as to catch the Roman's attention. Just enough to make the disciples want to leave town in fear.

Unknown to Saul and Samuel and to almost the whole city, was a previous, menacing discussion that had taken place at a clandestine meeting with the burly Roman commander. As he did when he wanted to make a serious statement, he was accompanied by two chosen and intimidating centurions at the secret meeting he called with the hand-picked delegation of the Jewish leadership. This committee consisted of Annas, Caiaphas, Gamaliel as President of the Sanhedrin and the very nervous and visibly shaking, Captain of the Temple guards.

Separately, these participants entered a secret chamber that Annas' family used, a room which was hidden under the Temple plateau and one which the Romans could access through a tunnel without being seen.

In that meeting, Pilate's recently announced terms were emphatically restated, that being that Rome would not interfere in Jewish religious matters. What the Romans wanted clearly understood was that any further persecution of this new group's leaders, namely Jesus's hand-picked disciples, would not be tolerated. All the Galilean leaders were to be left alone from this point on.

The latest occurrence of arresting the disciples proved to the Romans that childish religious squabbles had the potential to cause further turmoil and disorder in the streets and that was no longer a religious matter. The large, worked-up crowd just outside the Sanhedrin at the latest trial convinced them of that. When this happened, it suddenly became a Roman problem.

Caiaphas and Annas, were pointedly reminded that their family held their positions at the dictate of the Roman governor and they could be easily replaced. Following this reminder, they quickly agreed to all the terms, ultimately having no other choice.

The Captain of the Temple Guards, who seemed to always be caught between the two sides in this battle was genuinely relieved at not having to arrest the popular Galileans.

To these Roman declarationss, Gamaliel showed no perceivable reaction at all.

Also at this meeting, Caiaphas barely took his eyes off of Gamaliel, desperately wanting to see his reaction to this command. Since he had warned the Sanhedrin against punishing the disciples, no one was quite sure where this man stood.

Over the next week, word of the new Roman demand leaked out slowly and when finally hearing it, Saul and Samuel were furious to the point that items were being thrown about their house and nasty words were screamed at stone walls.

Admittedly, this secret declaration took much of the focus of their irritation away from their own weak Jewish leadership and put it on the despised

Romans and adding to the list of why Messiah was so needed to deliver them from these pagans, but they could not comprehend Rome's willingness to protect those who openly accused and challenged Jerusalem's leaders. These same weak leaders were the ones whom Rome had chosen and aligned themselves with and there was a certain degree of Roman protection extended to them as well. It was very confusing.

Saul was deeply suspicious and became determined to root out the motivations behind such a strange policy.

Was there something else going on here with the Romans that he did not know? Was it possible that the vast amount of money dropped at the Galileans' feet was buying this Roman protection? Could that explain why Roman centurions kept showing up at places where these disciples were gathering, sometimes in uniform, sometimes out?

Saul's skeptical and leery mind was buzzing, and a plan was hatching.

Before long, Saul made his move. He went for a walk.

The Captain of the Temple Guards was a chatty fellow who responded to compliments with exuberance and warmth and Saul was well known to this man even though they had never spoken beyond a few casual greetings in the Temple area. The captain was a competent and able person and made it his business to know the details of important and politically active people, especially those who he gauged as future leaders.

With all this in mind, Saul purposely sought him out, engineering what appeared to be an accidental meeting in the hectic street below the Western Wall. A warm and courteous conversation was struck and Saul praised him for his handling of all things around the Temple, kind words which caused a warm smile to appear on the captain's face.

Saul asked if he would have some lunch and a cup of wine with him and the captain eagerly accepted, aware that Saul was a respected teacher in the famous school of Hillel and an upcoming future political force in Jerusalem.

The two sought out a quiet place in the upper market where they found a hidden table, away from prying eyes. After a few cups of wine and a few more well-placed compliments, the captain quickly took Saul into his confidence. When asked about this secret meeting, he spoke freely, telling all the details. Saul listened carefully to the captain's every word and found that he was describing a disgusting show of subservience by the Jewish leaders, just as had been previously rumored and suspected. When Saul had his fill of this embarrassing report and was about to leave, he asked, "And who did the Roman captain bring with him?"

The quick, nonchalant answer caught Saul's immediate attention.

"Two centurions. You have seen them both around. The one with the big scar, you know, the one who oversaw Jesus's crucifixion and the bald one, the one who loves to beat Jews."

Saul went away from this meeting much more informed but no less chagrined about the High Priest's all too quick agreement with the Roman command. The captain's description of the quiet and subdued manner of his old mentor, Gamaliel, added to the disappointment he felt and he could not reconcile this with the usual decisiveness Gamaliel had shown over the years he had sat under him.

What would only be discovered years later by Saul was that there had been a previous meeting with the Commander of the Roman Army and a well disguised Gamaliel, who at the request of a certain centurion, appeared at the dreaded fortress Antonia under the cover of darkness. Details of that late-night conversation would remain Gamaliel's secret until nearly the day of his death.

Other thoughts niggled away at Saul. The strange appearance of the Roman centurion with the facial scar at almost every main event was much more than coincidence, decided Saul, but at this point he still could not unravel that mystery. He had just been told that this centurion had been in charge of the execution of Jesus so he could not possibly be a defender of these people. But why was he so often and so closely involved?

Somehow, with no explanation given to anybody, the Roman governor had been convinced to put a ring of Roman protection around the Galilean disciples of Jesus, but it did not make sense that this battle-scarred centurion would be put in charge of such a thing. One would expect that this soldier would be hated beyond measure by the disciples for executing their precious Jesus.

CHAPTER SEVENTY-FIVE

Miriam's Talents

In those busy months, Miriam's rejuvenated block on the Cardo had become the most alluring spot in Jerusalem to visit and a steady stream of free-spending customers were the reward for both her and her nearby tenants.

Within days of opening, and as Saul had witnessed from his table across the street, she had been visited by a very wealthy but frantic lady who was searching desperately for medication for her young daughter who was in the middle of delivering her first child. The delivery was not going well and Miriam quickly volunteered to come to their house and assist. The woman was at first hesitant but then led Miriam to the large house adjacent and connected to Herod's Jerusalem palace.

Within minutes, Miriam had determined that it was another partially breeched baby and if nothing was done, both mother and child would be lost. The old male physician who had been called was baffled and confused as to how to proceed, expecting the young woman to die the excruciating death of such a delivery and he did not want to be blamed. While he was occupied elsewhere explaining his dilemma, Miriam mixed a small concoction of medicines for the terrified young woman to drink. These relaxed her totally and Miriam proceeded to intrude and turn the unborn baby. Within minutes a healthy baby was born and the mother and child were fine.

This one event, when declared everywhere by the amazed servants of the household, was to open the floodgates of the city's sick to Miriam. The "report" was of the gifted female doctor who had saved the life of a descendant of Herod the Great, possibly a future king, and Miriam's name was soon on everyone's lips.

The predictable result was that Miriam became the first choice of all ailing or pregnant women, plus her reputation as a purveyor of truly effective medicines exploded. The immediate outcome was that her days were filled with a constant stream of needy people, many who were very wealthy.

Needing every minute of the day for her patients, she convinced Leah to completely manage all other aspects of the business. This was easily done, for Leah thrived on the new life she was experiencing and she blossomed with the opportunity, proving her worth from the very start. Their days and even many nights were hectic and productive and Miriam imparted much of what she knew and understood to her new partner who absorbed the information with eagerness and surprising ease.

Being regarded as an equal of Miriam had greatly altered the demeanor of Leah as well. She emerged within that relationship as a driven and unrelenting master, but only to herself. She had, in fact, become exactly like her mother.

Before long and out of sheer necessity, Leah had surrounded herself with smiling and productive employees who loved working with the very optimistic and incredibly beautiful woman.

CHAPTER SEVENTY-SIX

A New Hire

As the reputation of the effectiveness of the medicines of this new shop went out, Leah became inundated with impatient customers and soon realized that she desperately needed even space and that she had to expand. The small shop could not hold the shipments of medicines, ointments, exotic brews and other supplies that were arriving almost daily now. The upper office was much too small for Miriam to do anything but speak with her ever-growing line of patients as well.

Between Barnabas's shipments and constant deliveries from old Moshe in Hebron, a small warehouse was needed. Leah found this across the road, at the back of a less busy shop that had closed its olive pressing operation, buying oil from other suppliers. Abir, the friendly merchant was delighted with the extra income.

Miriam was pleased to find out that the negotiations, the contract, the organizing of the storage room and the hiring of Barnabas's nephew to ease their physical burden were all completed by Leah. She had performed all this efficiently and on her own initiative.

Both women had noticed young John Mark's value when he would deliver and then meticulously unpack the heavily bundled packages that his uncles sent to their brother Barnabas. At those times, Leah had inquired if he would be available to also help whenever the oxcarts from Hebron arrived. Young John Mark readily agreed.

Mark proved invaluable in sorting and organizing all the medicines and soon he was helping to meticulously measure out portions, a painstaking job that he proved he was very accurate at. He also showed a remarkable ability to absorb spoken detail, keeping it well categorized in his quick mind, and then he skillfully wrote a precise catalogue of all the products and their uses. This was a talent Miriam had not seen in very many Jews, save older and much more experienced scribes. She could only imagine what the future held for this lad with the special writing abilities.

John Mark was a trusting young man who interacted daily with the disciples who used his mother's house as their place of refuge when in Jerusalem. He had also intermingled with Jesus in His last year, a year when his mother had been a dedicated follower. This made him a fountain of knowledge and experience and He accurately recalled the details of the days he spent with Jesus when Leah and Miriam would ask anything. Strangely, he did not volunteer any information past what he was asked about. It was obvious that he was a bit conflicted in his growing friendship with the two sisters of prominent Pharisees, but he managed to always remain friendly and relaxed with them.

In passing, John Mark did mention that the big fisherman, Simon Peter, spent many hours relating his experiences with Jesus to him and Miriam looked forward to a day when she could just sit and listen to John Mark's telling of those interesting stories. A fleeting notion came to Miriam, almost a foreboding or curious premonition and she thought it might be very useful if Mark put that collection of stories in scroll form for others to read as well. Possibly she could even hire him to do that. Right now, she held her peace, for the time was not right and he was needed elsewhere.

It was during these warm fall months, months when Miriam's growing success was pleasantly complicating her life and creating exciting new opportunities and major challenges, that she realized she must settle her future with Gammy. The abundant harvest of her farms combined with the unforeseen financial returns, plus the satisfying busyness of her own shop which daily generated bags of valuable coins, had endued her with a strange and ever-growing purpose but that purpose went far beyond the making of such lavish amounts of money.

It was obvious to all that Miriam totally enjoyed her life. It provided her the ability and freedom to plan new ventures and let her imagination run wild with opportunities. Her dilemma was what would Gammy think of having a wife who thought daily of new businesses and who saw opportunity in every problem she faced? This was beginning to be a nagging and persistent worry to her. Would he want her to stop what she was doing, or to change? And what should she do with the fees and sizable profits that were accumulating?

Another, less serious problem was also developing. An overly-confident, young, and good-looking Pharisee had been finding every opportunity to visit the stall recently and he often kept young Leah embroiled in conversations that lasted much too long and interfered with the flow of business at times. Miriam wondered about where that was going and how quickly it would affect her business and she knew she must pay attention to that situation.

For her part, Leah adored her work in the shop and beamed with every sale and every pleased customer, so Miriam was willing to let any future developments remain Leah's concern and pretend she did not notice. Both women knew better, though, and the occasional knowing smile and raised eyebrow between them confirmed what they both suspected.

As this was happening, Miriam would happily meet with Barnabas at least once a week, each time with a varying and growing list of needed supplies. He was a delight to deal with, always courteous and helpful, but she could not seem to get him to open up when she asked anything about his friends, the followers of Jesus of Nazareth. She was sincerely puzzled at his reluctance for most of Miriam's other encounters with people of the Way could be described as them eagerly and almost urgently preaching immediate repentance to all who would listen. They seemed driven to accost anybody they met with their new beliefs, including her.

Barnabas's quiet, calm demeanor was just the opposite and somewhat out of character. He avoided any mention of his new faith unless she pressed him and over the time that she dealt with him, Barnabas remained resolute in this. It was evident that he had also counseled John Mark to be discreet and only answer pointed questions. This had made situations awkward a few times, but the amiable and unguarded Miriam took only slight offence to the thought that she may not be fully trusted.

One thing was for sure, the presence of the people of the Way in Jerusalem could not be ignored. Twice over the recent weeks, and in the street near the front of her stall, sick people were again healed. Once it had been by the shadow of the big disciple and once when other followers, strangely new converts, put their hands on a fevered child and uttered a prayer.

For this help for the infirmed, Miriam was truly thankful, but she struggled to comprehend the dynamics of such healings and desperately wanted to understand how such simple looking actions could make people better. The healings had occurred without the assistance of medicines and she suspected that they were facilitated by the sick persons own mental efforts, whether those efforts be overtly religious thoughts or just based on a sincere desire to be well.

This, of course, immediately led to another question. Some said it was believing on Jesus that facilitated the healing, but if a healing was dependent upon believing on Jesus, whose believing was it dependent upon, the sick person's or the one who prayed? What about sick babies, or that mentally deprived girl on the Pilgrims Way, whose faith was that? Her questions had put her into many a cerebral dilemma, but Miriam, being the amazing intellect she was, loved to find her way out of such puzzles.

A few years ago in Tarsus, Miriam had recognized and understood that the body had the capacity to heal itself if the source or cause of the disease was removed. She had decided that was a great gift given at man's creation. Given time, health was eventually restored and because of that, removing the cause of disease had become her main focus, followed by then simply assisting the natural work of one's body.

This "self-repair over time" was proven when a cut or bruise healed on its own, but Miriam, even with her vaunted mind, could not logically explain what could produce an immediate cure. Many of her evening hours were given to contemplating this mystery. She came to the inevitable conclusion that Hashem had to be involved and that led to an even more complicated dilemma.

What then was the power behind fatal sicknesses of which all of mankind would sooner or later succumb, was man ultimately at the mercy of demonic forces that would eventually destroy him, and furthermore, what was aging anyway?

Miriam constantly wished she had someone to ask these questions of and became angry at the silliness of Saul's self-imposed isolation from her.

Other questions haunted her mind.

Why did these people emphasize that believing, that elusive mental concept they called faith, was integral to their healings? Could the body react that quickly to its own thoughts and repair itself immediately? At those times, were one's thoughts assisted by some heavenly force? Furthermore, what about those whose minds were completely gone and then their sanity was instantly restored? When did Hashem assist one's thoughts of healing, and when did He completely intervene and deliver the weak-minded. And if that were possible, why did not Hashem simply heal all who called on His name, immediately.

One question always led to another, but again, she did not mind that at all.

Miriam was just waiting for the right day to delve into that with Barnabas who she was beginning to believe knew infinitely more than just the mundane complexities of business.

CHAPTER SEVENTY-SEVEN

Romance

The following week, on one warm Jerusalem evening, Miriam arranged a sumptuous meal for Gamaliel, Sarah, and Gammy, and while sitting around their family table, she opened her troubled heart to them. According to tradition, she did not want to speak of marriage and such related topics directly with the man destined to be her future husband and with Saul and her becoming completely estranged, she wanted Gamaliel to be her advisor on these matters. She had grown to love and respect this venerable man and now regarded him as God's replacement for the father she had recently lost.

In the quiet of the courtyard, Miriam served them the unhurried meal.

After dinner, she began in her usual direct manner.

"Gammy, I am deeply concerned that my actions have become a stumbling block for you and that I will not make the type of wife you expected, or require, in your position in life."

Miriam paused and peeked up to see the effect of her words on the handsome Gammy. She continued, "You are destined to become a ruler in Israel who needs a quiet, supportive wife, but I have come to realize and I am certain you have seen, that I am not that type of person. I do not want to hold you to an arrangement that is not going to be what you originally thought."

Gammy sat in silence looking directly into her face and Gamaliel wisely refrained from any comment, himself curious to see his son's reaction to Miriam's emotional confession. The hint of a smile broke on Sarah's stoic face.

The table went complete quiet and stayed that way until Gammy finally spoke.

"Miriam," Gammy whispered, "I have watched you from the day you arrived here. You are the most amazing and accomplished woman in Jerusalem and it is your unpolluted nature, your enthusiasm for life, and this effortless truthfulness that allows that. I am sitting here fearing that you have become disenchanted with me or a future with me."

"Oh no," gasped Miriam.

Gammy went on, "I never have been interested in a Jerusalem wife who is consumed by her clothing, or her jewelry, or the curl of her hair and has no serious depth to her. You are exactly what I want in a wife and I would be terribly disappointed if you ever became anything like the other women."

Tears were flowing from Miriam's eyes and she was fussing about, nervously wiping them away. Emotions that this talented but logical girl had never experienced before were suddenly flooding her, deep sensations that went beyond the devotion and love of her family that she had bathed in all of her days.

Is this what love for a man felt like? she silently wondered.

They smiled warmly at each other and Miriam knew he would indeed make a great husband and would be extremely easy to love and grow old with.

After a minute, Miriam collected herself and spoke again.

"But there is another problem. As you know, the business has grown so much that I have no time for anything else and more and more women are asking for help. I feel that I can be of some service to them but must expand my stall even more. I do not know where that will lead or what conflicts it will produce. Already I have made enemies of the High Priest and his family and I, no doubt, have put this family in precarious situations."

Gamaliel looked at his son and they both began to laugh out loud.

Now it was Miriam who was totally confused and as they continued laughing, she finally demanded, "What? What is it?"

Gamaliel slowly explained. "Miriam, you saved the life of Salome, daughter of Herodias, the fearsome wife of Antipas: you know, that wealthy woman who came to see you. You, my dear, quite innocently have made friends and debtors out of the strongest families and protectors in Israel. Those enemies that you speak of are now the ones who must beware how they treat you. Herodias is formidable."

He paused to let that thought percolate in the unsuspecting Miriam.

"Furthermore, she was completely taken with you and your remarkable abilities. She wants to provide a large house that the royal family owns, not far from here and only a block off the Cardo, as a place for women to go for help from you. It could be a place of treatment and care, with beds and a cooking area, as she saw how crowded your place is and how you struggled with the crammed space."

"But I am too busy already," countered Miriam. "I couldn't possibly do an adequate job of caring for many more."

"Herodias and I had a long discussion and we envision you training young women to care and treat other women. You would not have to do more, just teach others to do so. Look what you have done for Leah. In a few short months, she has gained more skill and knowledge than most physicians."

Gamaliel waited quietly for her reaction. It took a few minutes while a pensive Miriam processed all aspects of this. "I don't know if I have the finances to support such an endeavor and it will take a while to accumulate enough," she said thoughtfully.

Again, Gamaliel chuckled. "Miriam, you really do not understand. Jerusalem itself would support this. This would become the paramount charity of the city. Herodias would certainly see to that. Those young women who would work with you would be paid by gifts and donations and we will make certain it will not lack for financial support. It is important that the poor can get your help as well as those who can pay."

This appealed to Miriam immediately. Her mind jumped to Hebron and those unfortunate children with twisted arms and legs she had seen. If she could only train other women…, and her imagination, once more, exploded with the possibilities.

On the outside, she was speechless, but Gamaliel noticed that already her remarkable intellect had begun working; a detailed and complicated plan was being formulated in that extraordinary mind.

"The details I leave to you," he said, smiling warmly, and then added "if you agree" as an afterthought.

Gammy sat, beaming with pride from across the table.

"Only one thing," chimed in Gammy. "Herodias would like her name on this endeavor."

They all laughed and rolled their eyes, recognizing the ridiculousness of such ego.

PART EIGHT

CHAPTER SEVENTY-EIGHT

Saul, the Called

Saul's frustration, more and more being expressed as outright belligerence and anger, was increasing daily. Everywhere he went, he was continually confronted and provoked by the hated heresy. Especially annoying was that it was cloaked in and accompanied by what he had determined was a feigned godliness and pretend innocence. This was further complicated by the charade of condescending decency and deluded dignity in those he had now grown to despise. Any hint of acceptance or growing popularity of the sect was like pouring salt into an open wound for him.

In recent days, he was appearing everywhere and he was being very loud. Every street corner challenge convinced Saul that he was fighting for the spiritual future of Israel against a satanic attack which was using uneducated and simple people who were possessed and manipulated by evil forces.

At those times, he recognized that his diatribe was boring people, constantly repeating the same accusations, but he screamed them out regardless.

After many such confrontations, Saul's outward demeanor was also changing and it was plain that he allowed it to. When provoked on the streets in recent days, he refused to curtail his anger. When teaching other Jews, he was noted for his scathing and verbally abusive assaults. To any that wanted to appear even-handed, his wit and extensive learning seemed buried under offensive comments. When encountering any followers of Jesus, he ranted at them loudly while their response was a quiet and peaceful rehearsing of messianic scripture which he would immediately and mercilessly mock. He challenged their right to handle or even mention the sacred writings, never bothering to acknowledge their words and outright ignoring any truth in their statements.

Again and again in these confrontations, Saul arrogantly declared that he was properly educated. He waved a small scroll given to all Gamaliel's graduated students which declared him an expert and that he followed the Law without blame, challenging any and all to find any fault in him.

His outbursts in the streets were gaining notoriety with others who also despised the people of the Way and he was acquiring a small but dedicated following of his own. These admirers would watch silently from the fringes, experiencing a certain pleasure while Saul went from street corner to street corner looking for a fight. This dizzying practice soon earned him the reputation of being Jerusalem's greatest defender of Moses.

It did not take long before he received an unexpected and secretive summons to Caiaphas's house and at first, he was puzzled with that, even a little nervous.

Why he was being invited to the High Priest's home was unclear.

Samuel, himself a little surprised at the energy Saul had lately brought into their battle, encouraged him to take the opportunity to provoke the High Priest into more action against their enemies, if that were possible. Caiaphas and his whole family's unusual silence on this issue was not helpful.

Saul had passed by the house of the High Priest hundreds of times over the years, but had never seen past the ornately carved gateway which was always guarded by a particularly surly looking sentinel. Upon entering this day, he was impressed with the size of the outer courtyard and a little taken with the wealth on display.

Saul felt greatly honored when he was greeted with a show of much warmth by Caiaphas, his wife and their two teenage daughters. After a delicious meal of freshly roasted lamb spread on soft bread and covered with dates, cooked and served expertly by a very competent woman servant, the well-trained ladies of the family knowingly retired, leaving the priest and Saul to themselves. Saul also noticed that Malchus, usually very near to the High Priest, had not been asked to be at this meeting.

Soon, Saul and Caiaphas were comfortably seated on the main balcony of his palatial house, looking eastward and gazing upon the nearby Temple, just as the golden hue of the stones was subsiding into the welcomed coolness of evening. The scene was emotional, serene and inspirational, all at the same time and the lingering aroma of the evening incense of the Temple was drifting over them and filling their senses. It was a truly magical moment and Saul suddenly felt he was very important in both Caiaphas's and Hashem's eyes.

"Saul," Caiaphas began, "I and my colleagues have noticed you and your perfect zealousness for the Law," he said warmly, "and lately we are very impressed."

He broodingly stroked his long greying beard which fell and lay upon his extremely large stomach.

Saul's questions and nervous apprehensions were instantly relieved and he felt a pleasing spurt of pride. It caused him to sit up straighter.

Caiaphas, dull as he was to some things, was quite an expert at reading people and noticed Saul's almost invisible reaction to his compliment before continuing.

"You may have heard, for it is probably Jerusalem's worst kept secret, that our hands have been tied by the Roman governor regarding any actions we want to take against the leaders of this ridiculous heresy of the Galileans."

Saul nodded in confirmation, still only partially aware of all the minute details of that strange meeting.

"They have warned us that they will not allow us to bring charges against Jesus's disciples for a host of political reasons, but," and Caiaphas paused for a very long moment, purposely leaving the "but" to linger in the religiously charged air, "they curiously avoided the subject of what could be done with their converts. To me, and to our many lawyers, it seems that these cagey Romans, simply by not mentioning them, may have been indicating that if less important members of that cult were to be found violating the Law, they would not interfere with our dealing with them. You will remember that Pilate himself said we could take care of that ourselves."

Caiaphas paused and waited once more, intently watching to see if Saul had begun to understand the depth of the strategy being introduced to him.

Saul's furrowed brow indicated to him that this young Pharisee had understood him perfectly.

"Of course, I as High Priest am reluctant and even forbidden to lead any such campaign as this is certainly not my calling by Hashem, blessed be His Name. That being said, I absolutely believe Israel is in need of someone who understands the imminent danger that these people represent, someone who has the strength and will to confront and lead a crusade against these blasphemers."

After a long pause, Caiaphas announced, "I believe that person is you."

Saul sat riveted to his chair. Not a muscle moved in his face, but to Caiaphas, he was an open book. His stomach was fluttering and his mind racing.

Caiaphas continued, "You, like Moses, are chosen by Hashem to be a solitary leader and it is at times like these that great men are shaped."

He paused again and watched Saul even more closely to detect and discern any further reaction to what he was saying.

Saul was all at once stunned, honored, thrilled and slightly confused and the crafty priest had recognized all of that in him. He was completely overwhelmed at the opportunity, but he also wanted to not appear too eager.

"What about my friend Samuel from the Synagogue of the Freedmen?" he asked hesitantly. "He has been involved in this battle from the beginning as well."

"A good man, a devoted Jew, and a very good ally, Saul, and he may be your Joshua, but he is too sociable and welcoming and he tends to be too forgiving, wanting to overlook the sacrilege that his former friends are practicing. No, Saul, you are the one. You are strong in the Law and you will not be dissuaded by emotions and friendships. Your act of divorcing yourself from the influence of Gamaliel is proof of your great strength. Can I count on you?"

"What is it that you need me to do?" asked a dazed Saul.

Caiaphas leaned closer.

"We need you to be the leader. We have men, some spies if you want to call them that, among these people of the Way and they claim that they have heard the most outrageous statements made and they are willing to testify at the Sanhedrin of such sayings. You understand that many of these charges go nowhere unless someone keeps the focus on the actual sacrilege and continually presses the issues all the way to the Sanhedrin. If not directed and presented properly, nothing will come of all our opposition. We need you to expose and explain just what the heresy is and then demand the punishment, just as Moses demanded. We must show all Israel that we will now, without fear, follow Moses's commandments. This is your life's calling, my young friend."

Saul's youthful world changed suddenly and irreversibly with those striking words.

Later that evening, when Saul arrived back at his new home, Samuel insisted on knowing what was said by Caiaphas.

"He wants us to confront, convict and then insist on the proper punishments of the people of the Way. But, as before, we are not allowed to touch the original disciples," Saul reported.

He watched Samuel's reaction, not wanting to judge his friend harshly but remembering the seed of doubt that Caiaphas had planted about Samuel.

"That may mean we begin with some of our friends from the synagogue," added Saul, almost as a warning to Samuel.

A quieted Samuel fell into deep thought.

"But if we can convince them of their errors and they recant their blasphemies, surely that is more acceptable to Hashem," he pleaded, and Saul became immediately aware of what the surprisingly perceptive Caiaphas had seen in Samuel.

CHAPTER SEVENTY-NINE

Saul, the Persecutor

Armed with a new-found confidence, Saul suddenly felt unleashed. Most importantly, knowing he had the force and favor of the High Priest behind him, instantly quelled any lingering fears of rebuttal by any higher powers of Jerusalem who might accuse him of overstepping his authority. Whatever Gamaliel's puny assessment of him or his actions was, it mattered little now.

The next few days were spent in the Synagogue of the Freedmen where the re-energized Saul found any occasion to confront and rebuke any of the Way who dared enter its doors. His sarcasm and constant railing about their former neglect of the widows of this synagogue became so ugly that most of these people ceased using that synagogue altogether. For militant attenders, this was a welcomed relief.

Although Saul had been told of the election of Stephen and others to remedy the problem regarding the widows, he had promptly disavowed it as a showy attempt by the disciples to appear concerned and labelled it all as a poorly-planned cover up. He then screeched it so on every street corner.

On a daily basis, he shouted out even more nasty accusations, continuing to taunt and ask the Greek speakers why they were less important in this new faith than the ones who spoke Aramaic and soon this cutting remark had its intended effect. There began to be uncomfortable questions asked between the two factions. It became so uncomfortable for the two groups that the Galileans began meeting separately, completely away from the Temple portico and that only added fuel to the fires of division. Saul could not have been more delighted.

Thinking more about that unsettling issue, Saul decided to focus on the group of seven deacons, the men chosen to ensure that food and supplies were delivered to the needy. It did not elude Saul's attention that they seemed to represent a segregated portion of the group as well. That may work in his favor.

If he was legally restrained from going after the original leaders of the Way, well then, he would definitely attack the next level of authority among them.

Carefully planning his moves and believing that he clearly understood the hints and coded directives of Caiaphas, Stephen now became his favored target. Rightly so, thought Saul, as he seemed to be the most highly esteemed by his group.

It was openly reported that Stephen was able to perform some of the annoy- ing signs, like healing, and this added to Saul's decision that this man must be confronted and his influence neutralized immediately. It would become a much more difficult battle to eliminate the group if such powers were seen to be now available to others, those outside the original disciples.

Saul secretly sent word to Caiaphas of his intent to first move on Stephen, followed then by the other elected deacons. This news pleased both Caiaphas and his scheming father-in-law, Annas, and shortly after this communique was sent, in what appeared to be a complete coincidence, a small group of Greek-speaking men from the Synagogue of Freedmen, men full of fervor for the Law and hatred for all others, searched out Stephen at the Pool of Siloam and took issue with him there. Their loud and heated arguments and accusations shifted to the front of the synagogue door and then moved within its courtyards.

Relentlessly, over the next few days and in a seemingly coordinated fashion, these men continued their attack on Stephen and his small entourage. Saul made sure he was always present and listening as these men challenged and harangued Stephen concerning the commands of the Torah.

Oddly, these loud confrontations usually ended when a beguiling and per- suasive Stephen stymied them time and time again with an alternate and more understandable explanation of that same Torah. Most Jews who witnessed such confrontations easily agreed with Stephen, as did the half dozen or so young men from the Way who seemed to follow him closely.

After listening to a few rounds of this, Saul decided it was some sort of ungodly and demonic inspiration that the delegation was fighting. The frustration of the men was rising and they wanted to physically attack Stephen, but they knew they could not move against this man without a lawful charge.

All must appear very legal.

Oddly, the very next day while at morning prayers, two previously uninvolved men mysteriously appeared at the synagogue, claiming they had heard Stephen blaspheme Moses, calling him and the Law a thing of the past. These two, further accused Stephen of saying that this Jesus was God and that was undeniably blasphemy. They claimed that Stephen also said God could only be known and seen as Jesus, thus eliminating the Jewish religion totally.

Saul quickly cornered the men and asked, "Are you willing to testify of these things before the Sanhedrin?" The confident and well-rehearsed men assured him that they would.

At that, Saul became satisfied with their testimony and decided that he could now bring a legal charge against Stephen. Only a little disconcerting was the fact that he had never seen either of these men before and he wondered just where they had witnessed Stephen's crimes, but, in his eagerness, Saul successfully buried these piddling and haunting warnings.

Realizing that he must act quickly, Saul sent out messengers to a few select elders and their likeminded cohorts to meet at the Hall of Judgement for an important matter. He did not send such a notice to Gamaliel.

It was early the next morning, inside the Hall of Hewn Stones and at the poorly attended and usually boring lower Sanhedrin, that they made their move. Gamaliel was not in charge of this lower court and with luck and a little secrecy, he would not be in attendance.

The men of the synagogue, knowing Stephen was across the street in the upper room, stormed the place and grabbed the unsuspecting deacon. They pushed him roughly up the Pilgrim's Road to the base of the Temple walls where they avoided the crowded southern gate and dragged him, arm in arm, through the less traveled upper Women's Gate. From there they led him into the hall and in front of the Lower Sanhedrin. The arrest had been done with very little fanfare and with planned speed, the result being that Stephen was delivered to the court with only a few of his closest friends and his young brother hurrying behind.

Stephen had offered little resistance, not struggling against his arresting party so all who saw them enter the Sanhedrin, including the Roman soldier peering out of Antonia, suspected nothing.

The boring lower court was usually sparsely attended and today it was limited to only those notified. The everyday judges speedily concluded their scheduled mundane business, sensing a much more exciting case to deal with. This type of religious ruling was normally taken out of their hands by Gamaliel or the High Priest and it seemed a little peculiar to this body that the High Priest himself had quietly shown up this morning and was allowing them to proceed. Strangely, Caiaphas was the only man of any great importance in the hall and, today, he chose to sit in a spectator's seat.

Once the hearing began, the two witnesses repeated their charges to the judges and even added further accusations, saying that Stephen had bragged how Jesus would destroy this Holy Temple and change all of Moses's declarations. Stephen, alert and highly aware although being a little ruffled, was standing directly in front of the judges throughout the accusations. Saul and others noted that the reciting of the charges had no visible effect on him. He was calm, quiet, almost in a state of ecstasy, with a slight smile on his face that Saul interpreted as a sneer.

Finally, greatly irritated by the lack of concern being shown by the prisoner, Caiaphas jumped up. He waddled his obese body into the spot in front of Stephen, and stood there for a while. He had enough of Stephen's quiet flouting and lack of regard for the proceedings.

He almost spit out the question, "Are these charges true?"

Stephen turned to face him and after studying the High Priest intently, irreverently turned his back on him and the judges and began addressing the few spectators and witnesses.

He began a long dissertation of the history of the Jews, focusing on the special calling of Abraham and his progeny by Hashem and reminding all of just how often they had disobeyed and rebelled.

He then departed the usual recitations, sensing nothing he was saying was penetrating the obtuse High Priest or his henchmen and took a moment to look around the Hall. He heard the blasts of the sacrificial trumpets next door and it was obvious that a different thought came into his head with those notes.

Stephen quickly quoted the prophet's statement that Hashem "does not abide in houses made by hand," pointing next door, an action which appeared a clear attack on the reputation of the Temple itself. This caused an angry chorus to ring out. The loudest voice in the uproar was that of Caiaphas himself.

Men seated in the chamber began running at Stephen and screaming "Blasphemy" into his ears at the top of their lungs. This he calmly received without a word of defense or any show of fear.

"How dare you denigrate the holy Temple," they screamed time and time again.

Many began delivering slaps and then fisted blows to Stephen's head which seemed to have little effect on him except to start a little trickle of blood that ran down slowly from a cut above his eye. The crowd's attention was suddenly focused on the bright and oozing fluid sliding down his face and dripping onto the stone floor. Stephen's young brother rushed forward, pushing back any that his small fifteen-year-old frame could.

The sight of Stephen's blood excited many and sadistic smiles began breaking out all over the room. The tumult continued with all manner of vicious names and accusations being directed at him until the energy in the room waned and a nervous quiet returned to the room.

Stephen turned about and defiantly exclaimed, "You are a stubborn people with not one bit of spiritual hearing or understanding among you. You, like your fathers, resist God, persecuting His prophets and it is no wonder you did not recognize the Messiah, for you are the children of the very ones who killed the prophets for just predicting Him."

The stunned crowd regrouped and then began screaming the more at Stephen, Saul himself jumped up and began leading the charge this time. He ran headlong into the youthful brother named Justus who stared directly and daringly into Saul's eyes. Out of respect for the youth and not wanting to be physical, Saul retreated, possibly being a little too respectful in the eyes of a few.

When the racket settled slightly, Stephen again spoke. "You who claim to have received the Law supernaturally from Moses have disobeyed it," and he looked directly at Saul and then Caiaphas, and continued, "and have betrayed and murdered the Messiah it spoke of."

The reaction in the chamber was instant. Quiet and pious men who had lived their entire lives following every statute of the Law had now been indicted by this blasphemous Greek-speaking Jew and they refused to hear any more of it. They shrieked at him and spit at him, with some swinging their robes at him in disgust. One of the robes had a sharp button which opened up a new and deeper cut and soon more blood was dropping on Stephen's clothing.

"Stone him," was shouted from the back areas of the hall. The refrain began to grow and soon others joined in.

"No," screamed Stephen's brother who was now getting frantic.

Suddenly, as more and more blood began oozing from his head, Stephen pointed and yelled, "Look my brothers, I see Jesus standing in the glory of Hashem."

This was the absolute final insult that the men in the chamber would endure.

They seized this blasphemer and dragged him out the door and completely off the Temple courtyard, being as quiet around the Roman garrison as they could. Within minutes they were rushing him through the Damascus Gate to the quarry where throughout history, stoning's had taken place. Two burly men lifted Stephen high over their heads and then threw him down onto the rocks violently. In their rage they picked up stones and readied themselves for something that had not been done for many years in Jerusalem. A few of the larger men had seized young Justus and were holding him down while he kicked and fought to get to his beloved older brother. Half a dozen men took off their outer coats and laid them in a pile, not wanting them to get stained by the bleeding blasphemer.

Pausing and for a moment slightly doubting themselves, they looked around for some final approval and there was the young and respected Pharisee, Saul. Their hesitation disappeared when this Pharisee nodded his smiling approval. This pharisee most certainly knew the demands and intricacies of the Law. They were approved.

Suddenly the rocks began descending on the quieted and oddly compliant Stephen. The first fist-sized boulder bounced off his shoulder with a thud. The next, bigger by half, caught him behind the ear and drove his head down to the ground. The cascade continued until Stephen was dazed and cut and bleeding profusely from many much deeper head wounds. A large heavy boulder had twisted his arm into a strange shape and a large and sharp rock had exposed the bone on his lower leg.

As his blood oozed out of the deep cuts and his strength ebbed away, the final words of Stephen confused those within the hearing and would haunt many in the crowd. After being so confrontational and accusing in the Hall of Hewn Stones, he now asked Hesham to forgive his out-of-control executioners. This request, called tenderly out of the mangled mouth of Stephen, paused the attack for only a moment but for some it infuriated them further, sending a new cascade upon the limp and sagging body.

Enraged and sweaty men, when they had finished their deed, turned away in disgust and left the lifeless, rock covered body of Stephen to the elements. Their anger and hatred seemed satiated, at least for the present.

Finally getting loose, Justus crawled to the mangled mess that was his brother who now lay perfectly still. He looked around to see his other two friends staying far back.

"Run, get Peter," he yelled, "Quick, he must pray for him, raise him up."

One of the boys disappeared into the city and the other came and comforted Justus who was whimpering and weeping while rolling the rocks off his brother's beaten and bleeding body. Within moments, the other boy returned with John Mark in tow. Mark and Justus were the same age and were very close friends.

"Peter is not coming," Mark said quietly, almost apologetically, putting an arm around Justus.

"No," Justus moaned, crying out again. He looked down on his brother and then it finally dawned upon him that his brother was gone. Stephen's young life was over.

Immediately, he was angry.

"Would Peter have come if we were Galileans, if we could speak his language," he screamed in a fit of rage that took the few surrounding believers by surprise.

"Peter did nothing to protect my brother." Justus repeated as he rocked back and forth while holding the head of Stephen, moaning pathetically.

After a few moments, John Mark spoke. "Peter said to bury him in the sepulcher where the Lord was put, it is just over there," and Mark pointed to the edge of the cliff a short distance away. "Come now Justus, we will help you."

The violence of this attack disorientated and stunned Saul for only a moment. Within minutes he began realizing the need for haste so he gathered the most ardent of the crowd and after many passionate words, sent them in search of the other six elected deacons. He also instructed them to seize any who would dare oppose their righteous work, including any who would harbor these criminals. He constantly reminded them that this was a very holy quest.

Saul then hurried back to the Temple jails and located his new cohort, the Captain of the Temple Guard and told him all that had happened. Astounded, but strangely excited, the captain agreed to send his armed and ready men along to assist in the arrests and to prepare the jails.

Many long hours later, as the sun set at the end of that terrifying day, Saul and the disappointed captain were frustrated that they had only managed to arrest one of the remaining six deacons. A multitude of blasphemous people, some suffering from serious wounds of their own, were thrown into the jails for daring to interfere with the arrests, though. It seemed that the city had instantly sent word out and had quickly emptied itself of all the other criminals. The five other deacons had somehow disappeared into the countryside as had most of the Greek-speaking believers of Jesus as Messiah. All that were left were of little interest to Saul.

During all this, the Roman protection provided the original disciples had kept all of them, and their close friends, completely safe.

John Mark tried desperately to lead the devastated Justus to his home that day, but when they got close, Justus refused to enter. He realized that Peter and other disciples were likely in there, safe, warm and well-fed and these were men whom he did not want to meet on this horrible day. He was angry.

He turned away and left John Mark standing at the gate.

Justus's confused and incensed wandering would become a fixture within the community over the upcoming days. His stony presence at any gatherings put a coolness into the congregation from that time forward and only the most compassionate would take him in and feed and comfort him. In a strange twist, he had become a shunned outsider to the group his brother had died for.

News of Stephen's stoning had spread quickly and many Jews, even those not aware of the charges, were shocked at the vehemence capable by the most educated and learned men of their city. These events shattered the comforting vision they had of their holy Jerusalem being a godly and peaceful place.

Any who dared speak out against the execution or the arrests were instantly challenged and cowed into silence by other angry Jews who had finally tasted the stimulation that righteous punishment and godly violence provided.

Over the next few days, the degrees of a Jew's devotion were, in a very curious departure from the normal, measured by the quantity of fresh blood stains on their otherwise sparkling robes. Their threatening looks easily stopped any criticism of the boulder-throwing mob and this freedom to punish, like an opened gateway, provided an unopposed path for the further work of Saul.

CHAPTER EIGHTY

Miriam's Great Sorrow

As the day of terror continued, many heart-breaking stories and reports of violence began arriving at Gamaliel's door. Discreetly, Gamaliel counseled the hunted to leave the city and find shelter elsewhere and to do it quickly. "Don't look back," he warned. It was devastating to Gamaliel and Gammy to learn that Saul, once a trusted brother and almost a son, was not only involved but was the principal instigator.

What had happened to him?

Sure, Saul possessed a temper, this they knew, but they had not seen the capacity for such unchecked violence before.

Both men knew and had experienced the deep emotional grip of the call for total obedience to the Law, for Gamaliel himself had installed this into every one of his students, but it was always tempered with a peaceable regard for one's neighbor. Realizing that today's action was in part a result of the seeds he had sown in Saul made Gamaliel severely depressed and he was overcome with a cloud of regret and remorse.

Was he now reaping a violence that he had sown in his students?

Gamaliel was aware that such violence as was perpetrated on Stephen could easily spread through the city and be twisted into a political weapon, the perfect excuse for political foes to attack each other. He was terrified at the thought.

That was politics and that was something to be afraid of for sure, but what had happened to Stephen was pure violence disguised as righteousness, vindictiveness masquerading as godly obedience and above all, an attempt to justify oneself before Hashem by committing the harshest of acts as a show of one's total dedication. Evil men could now target any of their personal enemies and label it as an act of holiness.

Gamaliel and Gammy talked late into that evening and the old teacher explained to his son that a warped understanding of truth that inevitably led to such hatred, was the twisted offspring of those who were constantly trying to justify themselves to Hashem, just as extreme forms of obedience were often the attempt to cover a guilty conscience. Men often distorted truth to cover their sinfulness, he explained. Gamaliel was finally beginning to understand his famous grand-father's obsession with believing Hashem properly, starting with understanding His "nature."

This was a statement that would guide Gammy for his entire life and anytime he found himself even contemplating retribution or condemnation, he started an inward search of his personal shortcomings. He understood that most religious acts were an attempt to justify oneself before God, at least the violent version of Hashem that now permeated most Jews' thinking.

That evening, when they broke the horrifying news of her brother's activities to Miriam, her legs wilted and she physically collapsed, weeping for hours and mourning as one who has lost a loved one. Sarah and Leah stayed with her, constantly embracing and mourning with her. She remained in her room for the entire next day.

Barnabas, without any prior notification, missed their normal weekly meeting and Miriam desperately hoped that he was safe. She so wanted their friendship to continue, whether it was strictly business or, as she hoped, because they were indeed friends.

It was in this time, all alone in her room, that Miriam experienced for the first time what she had heard the teachers in this famous house call "Kavod."

This was the Hebrew term that was used to explain a time when all religious arguments, all logical conclusions, all rationale, gave way to just "knowing." It happened to a person when something, finally, really mattered.

For her, this was a deeply spiritual episode and an unusual one for the normally analytical Miriam. She could not put it into words.

She felt led.

CHAPTER EIGHTY-ONE

Bold Interventions

Restored in her spirit, Miriam rebounded and became determined that something had to be done to help the harmless people her brother was now persecuting. She spoke with Gammy secretly, not wanting to put Gamaliel in any awkward political position and between them they devised a plan. They would help the people of the Way escape.

Early the next morning, Miriam, her head covered and scanning the tense streets carefully, made her way to Mary's house and knocked insistently. The small window was warily opened by Rhoda the servant girl. After a long while, she finally opened the large door, and Miriam entered the courtyard.

The familiar yard was crowded with an array of people, many with sacks laying before them holding their only possessions and it was evident that they were very suspicious of her. There she waited uneasily for Barnabas.

When he appeared and kindly greeted Miriam, the gathered group seemed to relax a little.

Barnabas was a little surprised at the audacity of the sister of their persecutor to appear here and said so with only a slight smile, but Miriam ignored the comment and hurriedly told him of her plan. She was in no mood to debate. Things must be done and be done now. He relaxed and listened carefully.

"Saul is like a man possessed," she said, "and until he comes to his senses, we must get these people out of the city. I have this large building where sick women come for treatment and where we can house people safely and then escort them out. My cousins in Lydda will help. They have become converts to your faith also."

"You mean Junius and Andronicus?" asked Barnabas.

"Yes. Do you know them?" she asked incredulously.

"Oh yes, they are well known for their devotion and care for the saints," answered Barnabas.

Barnabas looked at the yard full of frightened people and asked, "Can we start this escape today? There are many more hiding out within the walls of this city."

"Bring any that are injured to the big house for treatment," Miriam pleaded. Gammy will arrange for as many wagons and carts as he can find and will get them to the stables where your friends work out of." She spoke of Agabus' business.

Barnabas smiled and thought, *nothing gets past this girl.*

So, it was agreed, and over the next few days many of the recognizable followers of Jesus, mainly those that spoke Greek, had successfully been dispersed into the countryside after being fed and treated at Miriam's hand. The night time traffic on the Jerusalem Road had increased significantly, assisted by the "helpful" Roman guards at the Jaffa gate who, "very strangely" found many reasons for detaining any that would pursue those escaping. It seems that some sort of very hard to obtain permit was suddenly required and any Temple guard was held for hours until escaping caravans were safely well on their way.

Intensely frustrating for Saul and the High Priest, they only found out about the massive migration out of town after much time wasted on many unsuccessful raids on deserted houses. Adding to Saul's fury was that, within days, reports were arriving that these people were popping up outside of Jerusalem and they were boldly preaching about Jesus and more and more people were being baptized in the surrounding villages. It was as if a strong wind had blown the seeds of this movement all over Judea and Samaria.

The mushrooming effect of the forced dispersal was indeed creating a bigger problem for Saul and the High Priest. These people were spreading their teachings in synagogues that were much more independent of the influence of Caiaphas and of the political pressures of Jerusalem. Stories of Jesus were becoming common fare in the synagogues of places like Joppa, Caesarea, and as far away as Damascus. These fantastic stories were now being openly repeated, even in the Sabbath services of the local synagogues.

Saul met with the Captain of the Guard at the dank jails under the Temple plateau on the third day of his campaign and was surprised and then embarrassed when the captain discreetly cornered him, took him into a private room and told him of the recent happenings in the jails.

Some of the women arrested had injuries, some major and some just invisible bumps or bruises which had apparently occurred during the overly enthusiastic arrests and Saul's sister had been showing up at the cells almost hourly, accompanied by Gammy who was touting his father's authority like a badge. They were demanding that these women be released for medical treatment. Miriam also demanded that any men with more severe injuries also be released to her for medical care. She was removing them to her place of treatment and upon examination of each person, she managed to find some serious malady in almost everyone. Injuries that needed ongoing treatment.

So far, simply because of the inference of political pressure by Gamaliel, the President of the Sanhedrin, they had been releasing them into her custody. To date, not a one had been returned to the cells after she finished treating them. When the captain called on Miriam for an explanation, she had simply told him that she treated them and let them go, their whereabouts were not her concern, just their health. How was he to deal with this, for he could not let women remain in the jails bleeding, hurt, and untreated? Even the one deacon he had arrested had somehow disappeared in all the confusion. Saul grit his teeth in seething anger.

This peculiar push-back had put the captain in a terrible position and it was a problem which he was eager to make Saul's problem. It was becoming clear to the Captain that he was ending up between Gamaliel's influential family and Caiaphas's devious intentions and this was a very dangerous place to be.

For the time being, Saul and the captain agreed to keep this quiet for it would not be wise for the city's population to learn that the guards were mistreating women. Mostly, Saul did not have it in him to accuse or rebuke or arrest his sister.

He recoiled at the very thought.

CHAPTER EIGHTY-TWO

Secret Plans Prepared in Jerusalem

Within the week, Saul realized that the important leaders he was pursuing had escaped Jerusalem and all he was arresting now were meek and frightened followers whom he could easily cower into submission. They knew nothing of the whereabouts of the deacons.

In desperation, Saul realized that he had to expand his territory of authority. He must be able to hunt them down in the towns and villages surrounding Jerusalem where they had all run to.

He again met with Caiaphas, who had his father-in-law, Annas, quietly listening in. This time Saul begged for the authority to pursue these men outside the city.

The cagey Annas reminded him, "You know that the Romans are now involved. They will not let you go and arrest people in Caesarea, or even Lydda, or anywhere in Judea. That area is completely under their governor and Pilate will not tolerate what Phillip or Agrippa will. No, Saul, I have a better idea. The Jews of Damascus have sent us word that the blasphemers have shown up in their city. In Syria, we can get much more assistance from the synagogues, they will even help you arrest and bring them back to Jerusalem as criminals. My cousin is the head of the main synagogue of Damascus and he will help you with that. We will give you travel documents and write instructions to them giving you the authority to arrest our enemies there. Also, we will send a generous gift to ensure that the Syrian governor will not interfere."

Annas, cagey as he was, knew that it would not take a lot to convince the small Roman garrison in Damascus that any Jews who ran away from lawful authority in Jerusalem were dangerous spies or zealots and not to be trusted.

Caiaphas, watching Saul closely and silently up this point, leaned forward and took Saul by his hands. "Saul, my son," he was almost whispering, "you are the Phineas we have been looking for."

The crafty High Priest knew exactly what example the Pharisees always retreated to as a justification for the severest punishment, even the putting to death of any who broke the Law or could be seen as an enemy of Israel. Saul was overwhelmed to be regarded in the company of such an ancient and obvious hero.

"The documents are your weapons, your obedience is the strong arm and this Galilean sedition is the plague," the priest hissed, knowing Saul was intimately familiar with the ancient story. He rightfully suspected that Saul would be delighted and empowered with his comparison with such a pillar of Israel.

"Plunge the javelin into the hearts of these enemies," the High Priest whispered with great conviction and emotion in his voice.

So, it was agreed.

Saul would take a band of trusted Temple guards with him on this secret mission to Damascus and bring back any of the Way that he could find, especially the deacons. He was encouraged by Caiaphas to arrest their families also, even their children, as a way to spread the "holy" fear of God. Documents from the High Priest were written and signed and ceremoniously sealed with the large ring on the High Priest's pudgy finger, all proving Saul's mission was not only lawful and legitimate but endorsed by the highest representative of Hashem in Jerusalem. It was all extremely official.

Such officialdom, straight from the hand of the High Priest, would also help Annas' cousin in Damascus convince devout but sometime hesitant men to assist in tracking down and snatching any blasphemers who were now hiding in their city. Caiaphas then handed Saul a sack full of silver coins to use as incentive to anyone who could help him. It struck Saul as curious that Caiaphas mentioned that thirty pieces of the shiny metal was the usual payment for such services, as if he was very familiar with such arrangements.

Saul left Caiaphas' house feeling restored and especially confident.

Within hours, the new commission had completely rejuvenated him and returned to him the joy of his sacred purpose, some of which the recent events had robbed him of. His disturbing quarrel with Miriam and his estrangement from Gamaliel had left him deflated and at times doubting himself, but today, he saw himself as the most important emissary of Judaism in the world. Beyond that, he was also the personal and trusted messenger for the most important man in Jerusalem, the High Priest.

Later that evening, as he supped with Samuel and was telling him of his new mission, Rachel was hovering very close, politely serving and pouring wine while listening and commenting and showering the smiling and invigorated Saul with compliments.

This particular evening, Saul could hardly take his eyes off her and once, when she leaned close to remove a bowl, her sleek, rich red shawl slid slowly and purposefully over his arm. The young Pharisee literally trembled.

Possibly for the first time in his life, Saul was completely speechless, save for a few minutes of incoherent babble. Samuel immediately knew his friend was hopelessly entranced, captured, befuddled and completely infatuated with his sister.

When alone, Saul turned to Samuel and said, "When I return, we must speak of things concerning Rachel."

"Of course, my friend," nodded the grinning Samuel.

It took only a single day to organize the horses and supplies for the armed and determined troop. The next morning, Saul and five well-armed Temple guards left quietly through the Damascus gate, hidden in the hazy pre-dawn light, deliberately staying out of the prying eyes of the Romans and pushing north at a hurried pace. They first rode east, quickly dropping down the rugged gorges of the Judean mountains and following the switchback road in the bottom of the wadi that led through Jericho and then started the long, hot ride toward the Sea of Galilee.

After a dusty day's ride, they reached Beit Shean and stayed at the same inn that Saul and Miriam had used on their northern tour. Saul sat at the exact table he and his sister had only months before and he pondered the spiritual and mental distance he had come since those peaceful days not so long ago.

He wished with all his heart that his sister could understand the intensity and purity of devotion that led him here today. Her opinion of him was not the only one that mattered anymore, but he truly wished that she could just understand.

Miriam, even with all her impressive mental gifts and sweet and generous nature, could not comprehend the passionate warfare demanded by Hashem or the sacrifices required by brave men who were protecting their homes, their country and their faith. That was indeed the weakness of women in general, he surmised and Saul was convinced that the recent events reaffirmed Hashem's unique call on only the men of Israel.

Saul then laughed outright to himself. Such musings were not something he would dare debate with Miriam, he admitted, but he was sure that there was undeniable truth to his thoughts, regardless.

In the last few weeks, when preparing the tactics to use against the people of the Way and identifying the important people among them, Saul had noticed that a small group of adventurous women were a large part of the many stories surrounding Jesus. This had further confirmed to Saul the ongoing errors and false teaching of this group, and another subject that he would want to discuss with his sister.

The next day, the determined posse left Beit Shean early, speeding along on the road northward, following along the east coast of the Sea of Galilee where they passed the small town of Gadarene. There they took a break and enjoyed the view of the beautiful blue lake below them with the town of Tiberius directly across the shimmering water. They looked north across the lake at the little fishing town of Capernaum and from his investigations, Saul remembered that this was the home town of many of the dangerous and protected disciples. The story was that Jesus had also lived there for a while.

Saul wondered just how many blasphemers were hiding from him in this seaside town, but knowing he had no authority to arrest any in the Galilee, he turned his troop up the ravine to the east and began the slow climb to the dominating heights above.

They arrived in the late afternoon at the mysterious town of Gamla.

This town resembled a fortress and was constructed on a sharp spine that rose singularly out of the floor of a mile wide ravine cut deep into the high plain. The steep, south slope of the spine was the location of the town and the incline so severe that the roofs of one house were level with the floor of the one above, so from afar the town looked like one big cascading roof. It was the perfect protection from outside attack. Any approach to the town was sharply uphill and only from one congested direction with the single tall wall sufficient to repel climbers. The north and west side of the spine was so steep and rocky that no enemy could scale them. Occasionally an adventuresome townsperson would accidentally fall when attempting to walk the sharp crest and such falls were usually fatal.

There was only one gated entrance to the small city and that was in the single eastern wall. Because it was so easily defended, it had a reputation as a hiding place for many rebellious zealots and other miscreants of the Galilee, plus it had proudly remained Roman-free. Gamla was regarded by the Roman army as inconsequential and not worth wasting time and soldiers on. If there ever came a need, it could be easily sieged with a small force sitting on the rims of the canyon.

Saul's small company was sheltered and refreshed over the night and early in the morning they prepared for their final days ride to Damascus. After a small climb out of the ravine past a beautiful thirty-foot waterfall, they rode the high plain that spread for miles below the massive snow-covered Mount Hermon.

In Moses's time, this area was the final stand of Og and before long they were passing the circular, rocky cenotaph named Gilgal Rephaim. This was refuted to be the final burial place of this giant king but no one could quite remember the pagan significance of such a curious geometric tomb. The Pharisee Saul was certainly not interested in visiting it. The wide extent and exactness of the rocky layout did catch his attention for a moment though.

The six-man contingent continued east, cutting through the black lava hills that marked the highest of these heights and by noon they began the slightly descending ride into Damascus. The troop, growing weary from their hot travels, stopped at a local well set among a grove of blooming fruit trees for refreshing drinks. There, a few passing travelers informed them that it was only another hour to the gates of Damascus.

CHAPTER EIGHTY-THREE

Lightning from Above

Mounting up again, they rode out of the grove of trees onto the side trail that led back to the main road, when without warning, a flash as bright as lightning completely encircled them. Noiselessly, it began swirling around and around them, moving in and out and through them, then it began crackling in the dry air. It continued darting about, unlike any lightning any of the men had ever seen and it changed shape and color, from a bright flash to an all-encompassing cloud of strange amber coloring. Its brilliance was so penetrating that they shielded their tightly closed eyes from it and tried to look away but it was everywhere.

The sudden appearance made all the horses rear wildly and the men's strength alone could not hold themselves on their mounts with all being thrown wildly to the ground. The whining and frightened horses bolted off into the woods, crashing through branches in their escape and tearing saddles off their backs.

Six terrified men were left lying on the dusty ground, dazed and incoherent, some whimpering and some frozen with fear. One of them was shaking uncontrollably and hiding himself under a thick bush, another crawling behind a large rock.

Saul lay in the middle of the road with no place to hide. He was completely blinded by the intense brilliance for he had, for a few daring seconds, boldly kept his eyes open to witness the swirling light.

Moments later, while the intense beam swirled, another strange thing happened. The whole group heard a loud booming noise, like intense thunder, so loud that they now covered their ears to protect themselves. It made their chests vibrate.

Oddly, when the others dared to open their eyes, there was not a cloud around and the terrorized men wondered if they had entered some fast-moving thunderstorm or some unexplainable weather phenomena.

Saul lay flat out on the ground. He was paralyzed with fear, completely unable to see. He was hearing the booming thunder as well as the other men, but he was hearing it as a clear voice and he heard it speaking to him in the ancient Hebrew tongue of his countrymen.

"Saul," it said.

Without any hesitation, Saul became convinced that Hashem was now visiting him and that He had come to strengthen him in his upcoming task. A guarded surge of pride arose in him, pleased to be visited by his God, just as Moses had been on the heights of Mount Sinai.

In mid-thought and interrupting Saul's vain imaginings, the voice repeated itself.

"Saul, why are you persecuting me?"

What? What was that? It took Saul a moment to realize what had been said.

All the strength drained from his body and he immediately began convulsing and shaking in fear while lying on the ground. He was frightened beyond any speech and could not understand at all what was happening.

Persecuting Him? How was this possible? He was serving Him. Why was he being accused?

An overwhelming dread fell over him.

Saul was both instantly terrified and totally confused. He was certain he was in the presence of the same one who shook Mount Sinai but why was he was being blamed by Him? Saul could not make sense of this. His mind was darting around, trying to understand what was happening.

Again, what did He mean by persecuting Him, how was he doing that?

The voice spoke again, interrupting his mental ramblings once more.

"It is difficult for you to fight against your pricks of conscience."

Saul's mind immediately went blank.

Now he was just frightened beyond words and he did not know what to ask. Although he had originally thought that this must be the one Moses had met on Sinai, he was now desperately looking for some other explanation.

How could he be persecuting Him? He had obeyed Hashem perfectly.

Maybe this was something false, something sent to confuse him.

No!

This was something supernatural and he was certain this was Hashem, but incredibly, he was standing alone before Him, accused and totally reproached.

When he tried to look about, he could see nothing as his eyes were etched and seared by the bright light and now, they did not focus at all. A translucent, faint whiteness was all he could see.

Saul settled himself slightly, collecting his thoughts and once more he wondered if it indeed was Hashem speaking, so he blurted, "Who are you, Adonai?"

"I AM JESUS, whom you are persecuting."

"Aaaaghh," a primeval scream of fear rose from deep within Saul's chest.

Sickly moans escaped from the pathetic creature rolling around on the dusty road, his dread suddenly tearing at his most inner parts. Saul was way past any emotion except a deepening horror of being accused by his God and being inescapably guilty.

He was completely wrong.

He was standing alone before his God.

He was totally exposed.

He had no answer.

.....................to be continued..

Printed in the USA
CPSIA information can be obtained
at www.ICGtesting.com
LVHW041625041123
762611LV00007B/10